THE WAR

Part Two

ISTU AWAKENED

Also available from New English Library

THE WAR OF POWERS

THE WAR OF POWERS
Part Two

ISTU AWAKENED

Robert E. Vardeman and
Victor Milán

NEW ENGLISH LIBRARY

First published in three volumes in the USA in 1981 and 1982 by Playboy Paperbacks

First NEL Paperback Edition January 1985

NEL Books are published by
New English Library,
Mill Road, Dunton Green,
Sevenoaks, Kent.
Editorial office: 47 Bedford Square, London WC1B 3DP

Photoset by Rowland Phototypesetting Ltd
Bury St Edmunds, Suffolk
Made and printed in Great Britain by
Richard Clay (The Chaucer Press) Ltd
Bungay, Suffolk

British Library C.I.P.

Vardeman, Robert E.
  The war of powers.
  Pt. 2: Istu awakened
  I. Title   II. Milán, Victor
  813'.54[F]   PS3572.A714

  ISBN 0-450-05788-7

—20,000	The reptilian *Zr'gsz* settle the Southern Continent and begin construction of the City in the Sky.
—3,100	Istu sent by the Dark Ones to serve the *Zr'gsz* as a reward for their devotion.
—2,300	Human migration begins.
—2,100	Athalau founded by migrants from the Islands of the Sun.
—1,700	Explorers from the Northern Continent found High Medurim.
—1,000	Tension increases between the *Zr'gsz* and the human settlers.
—31	*Zr'gsz* begin active campaign to exterminate all humans.
—3	Martyrdom of the Five Holy Ones.
0	*The War of Powers*: Unable to wipe out the human invaders, the *Zr'gsz* begin to use the powers of Istu. Most of the Southern Continent is desolated. In Athalau, Felarod raises his Hundred and summons up the World-Spirit. Forces unleashed by the struggle sink continents, tip the world on its axis (bringing Athalau into the polar region), cause a star to fall from the heavens to create the Great Crater. The *Zr'gsz* and Istu are defeated; Istu is cast into a magical sleep and imprisoned in the Sky City's foundations. Conflict costs the life of Felarod and ninety of his Hundred. Survivors exile themselves from Athalau in horror of the destruction they've brought about.
	Human Era begins.
100	Trade between humans and *Zr'gsz* grows; increasing population of humans in the Sky City. Medurim begins its conquests.
979	Ensdak Aritku proclaimed first Emperor of High Medurim.
1171	Humans seize power in the Sky City. The *Zr'gsz* are expelled. Riomar shai-Gallri crowns herself queen.

2317	Series of wars between the Empire of Medurim and the City in the Sky.
2912–17	War between the Sky City and Athalau; Athalau victorious. Wars between the City and Athalau continue on and off over the next several centuries.
5143	Julanna Etuul wrests the Beryl Throne from Malva Kryn. She abolishes worship of the Dark Ones within the Sky City, concludes peace with the Empire.
5331	Invaders from the Northern Continent seize Medurim and the Sapphire Throne; barbarian accession signals fresh outbreak of civil wars.
5332	Newly-proclaimed Emperor Churdag declares war on the City in the Sky.
5340	Chafing under the oppression of the Barbarian Empire, the southern half of the Empire revolts. Athalau and the Sky City form an alliance.
5358	Tolviroth Acerte, the City of Bankers, is founded by merchants who fled the disorder in High Medurim.
5676	Collapse of the Barbarian Dynasty. The Sky City officiates over continent-wide peace.
5700	The Golden Age of the City in the Sky begins.
6900	General decline overtakes Southern Continent. The Sky City magic and influence wane. Agriculture breaks down in south and west. Glacier nears Athalau. Tolviroth Acerte rises through trade with Jorea.
7513	Battle of River Marchant, between Quincunx Federation and High Medurim, ends Imperial domination everywhere but in the northwest corner of the continent. The Southern Continent becomes the Sundered Realm.
8614	Erimenes the Ethical born. Population of Athalau in decline.
8722	Erimenes dies at 108.
8736	Birth of Ziore.
8823	Death of Ziore.
9940	Final abandonment of Athalau to encroaching glacier.

10,091	Prince Rann Etuul born to Ekrimsin the Ill-Favored, sister to Queen Derora V.
10,093	Synalon and Moriana born to Derora. As younger twin, Moriana becomes heir apparent.
10,095	Fost Longstrider born in The Teeming, slum district of High Medurim.
10,103	Teom the Decadent ascends the Sapphire Throne. Fost's parents killed in rioting over reduction in dole to cover Imperial festivities.
10,120	Jar containing the spirit of Erimenes the Ethical discovered in brothel in The Sjedd.
	Mount Omizantrim, "Throat of the Dark Ones", from whose lava the *Zr'gsz* mined the skystone for the Sky City foundations, has its worst eruption in millennia.
10,121	Fost Longstrider, now a courier of Tolviroth Acerte, is commissioned to deliver a parcel to the mage Kest-i-Mond.

BOOK ONE
The Fallen Ones

PROLOGUE

No light defiled the sacred darkness of the chamber cruelly gouged from the mountain's interior. With a sense that was not sight, the gathered worshippers knew the presence of their priest and leader, resplendent in his long robes of pallid, fine-textured leather and headdress of obsidian and iridescent green metal. They perceived not the colors of Light, which were a lie; they knew the subtle shades of blackness.

The priest raised a strong hand and spoke to heads bowed in dark communion.

'In the secret places of the Mountain,' he intoned, 'pent in the stone that flows like water, that burns without the foulness of Light, the mother fluid of our race, there beats . . .' Ritually, he paused.

At once came back the ringing answer: '*A Heart!*'

'Our Heart.' Another pause, then, 'And it is lost to us.'

'*Lost!*' The word scored the soul with a keening of pain honed fine by the grinding centuries.

'But when shall we forget?'

'*When the Great Dark ceases to fill the space between the stars.*'

He nodded gravely. The blackness he wore like a shroud about him brightened in the non-vision of the faithful as he built to the climax of the ancient ceremony.

'But know you it shall be returned to us, and its power will again pulse through the veins of our People.'

'*So shall it be!*'

'And when that time comes, what will be our destiny?'

'*To conquer!*' The intensity of the shout caused the cavern walls to tremble.

'And when,' he asked, growing in size and power as he spoke

the climactic words of liturgy, 'shall our time come?'

Eleven-score and ten mouths opened to give the final response. But no sound came. The subterranean chill of the chamber grew colder still, and an icy wind swept over the worshippers, a wind from nowhere, like the wind that blows between the stars.

His eyes widened in mingled fear and religious ecstasy, muscles cording in great knots on his neck and back, the leader-priest felt the nearness of a Presence his kind had not known for ten thousand years.

The Dark Ones' time came again.

Far to the southwest, the mountain Omizantrim trembled. Across long years it had built itself in fitful vomits of core-stuff from the planet until it stood thus, a black fang piercing the sky. Now it jetted a cloud of boiling hot ash and smoke, a roiling blackness shot through with flame and vivid lightning. A herdsman watching his flock of one-horned deer grazing the short grass that clung to the lower slopes of the mountain, was caught by surprise. He screamed as the awful heat enveloped him, boiling water from his tissues in an instant, mingling volcanic cloud and human body in the deadly stew.

The cloud rolled on, leaving the herdsman with his charges, now turned to gray ash statues scattered randomly on a lifeless hillside. The folk who dwelt lower on the slopes were luckier. They saw the cloud spew into the night like venom from a serpent's fang and retreated to special shelters dug in the cooled lava flows that jutted from the mountain like diseased roots.

Others, farther away, viewed the eruption with foreboding. Timid and wise alike made signs in the air and muttered fervent prayers to personal deities. But the wise were little comforted by their godly importunings. They knew that Those whose voice spoke through Omizantrim were mightier by far than the gods of Earth.

Farther south, all lights were extinguished at once in a City whose foundations rested on nothing more solid than the air itself. The Sky City's new queen, celebrating her fresh victory over her hated sister and rival to the throne, felt outrage welling within her breast. She sat in her great entertainment hall watching a subtle and sophisticated drama involving a half-dozen stalwart and naked young men, an assortment of implements of curious design and even more curious function, and a lovely young girl of a house which had dared oppose

12

the queen's succession. The girl's screams marking that part of the program which the queen awaited most eagerly had only begun to echo through the hall when darkness fell abruptly.

Her pleasure thwarted, the queen ordered a hundred of the stewards of the Palace of the Winds, whose job it was to keep the lamps trimmed and filled with oil, exiled from the City in the Sky. The Palace Guard herded the unfortunates down the ancient avenue paved with skulls of past rulers toward the center of the City. Wailing, weeping, pleading for forgiveness, the stewards huddled at the lip of the Skywell. Her nakedness wrapped only in a lush fur robe, the queen had made a quick inspection of her City. In spite of the great festival she had decreed celebrating the victory at Chanobit Creek, she saw no lights. It meant that greater powers were loosed.

But it would not suit the majesty of the new queen to be indecisive and revoke the punishment she had commanded. Besides, having been cheated of the climax to which her private diversion had been building, she felt the aching need for some other release. The mass exiling would serve; the short walk from the Palace had made her sleek body hum with anticipation. A single hand gesture sent a hundred men screaming to their deaths on the snowy prairie a thousand feet below.

Later, when the drugged wine she had imbibed as part of her evening's merriment wore off, she wondered again why the lights had gone out all over the City. No comforting answer came.

And in that dark womb far to the north, the air began to vibrate and formed a single word from nothingness. That one word was the answer, the promise, the exaltation, the vindication of millennial faith.

The word was: *Soon*.

CHAPTER ONE

'Your Highness, Your Highness,' called the dishevelled youth. The knight was young, his cheeks hardly touched with downy beard. Tears rolled unnoticed down his dirty face. It was not merely the unendurable anguish of defeat that made him weep. Only an hour or so ago he had seen the loveliest face he had ever known – snarling at him over the hilt of a Highgrass dog rider's saber. The tradition of chivalry dinned into him over a lifetime of training had almost stayed his hand, but loyalty to his princess and the ages-old urge to save his own life had acted with a will of their own. He had heard his own voice cry out in terror as his bright, straight blade hacked the woman's face into a ruin of blood, brains and gleaming bone.

He had passed the test he, like so many other warriors young and unblooded, dreaded above all: he had faced mortal danger and had not flinched. But he wondered if he had not failed another test in the same moment.

'We've brought you failure and disgrace,' the youth almost sobbed. 'How can we restore to you what our worthlessness has lost?'

Moriana Etuul brushed a strand of red-gold hair from her eyes and sadly shook her head. She gazed past the young knight at the man lying exhausted and in dubious safety beside the broad race of Chanobit Creek. The day had dawned as if especially tailored by this man. The sky had been filled with low clouds lying in a cool white blanket on the land to keep the bird riders grounded and out of the fray. Without their most deadly weapon, the Sky City soldiers would prove easy prey. Believing this, Darl Rhadaman, Count-Duke of Harmis, had taken the forefront with his sword held high, the eerily diffuse milky early light glinting from his sword's keen edge and the mirror-bright steel of his breastplate. Then, his face had been alive and almost boyish with the certainty that he fought for right and would triumph in its cause. Now his sword was nicked and blunted, his armor so hacked that the deep metallic cuts already scabbed red with rust in the damp air. Dull eyes stared out of a face as listless as a slab of meat on the butcher's block.

His brown eyes met her green ones, but no contact was made. Pity welled in her heart for him. It had meant far more than his life to him to bring victory for his Bright Princess, as he called her. Now, defeated, he faced her beneath budding branches ripe with the promise of spring and renewed life. The contrast tore at Moriana's emotions. If the battle had not been lost, Moriana would now be Queen of the Sky City, instead of her sister.

If only he had listened to me, we might have won. Unbidden, the words rang in her mind. Angry at herself, she tried to soften her thoughts. The lusterless brown eyes turned from hers, and she knew he had heard the reproach as clearly as if she'd shouted it. This knowledge added another fresh cut on her soul.

Shaking herself, Moriana returned to the reality of the moment. The young knight who had led the dazed Darl Rhadaman from the field still looked at her beseechingly. She recalled what he had asked.

'You cannot,' she said without thinking.

He recoiled as if she had slapped him. Once more she reproached herself. He was a child and had just discovered that war was no glorious game. She had to give him something to cling to, or destroy yet another life in her fruitless quest.

'The best way you can serve me now is to live,' she said.

He brightened.

'You will permit us to fight for you again some day?' A half-dozen eager young voices echoed the question.

'If you wish, perhaps you shall. Some day.' She held back her tears with effort. 'But that's not what I mean. I want you to survive. Live out this day and many more so that I'll not have your death on my conscience, too.'

Bewildered, the youth blinked. Moriana turned to Darl. He regarded her through strange, old eyes.

'I'm . . . sorry,' he whispered.

Emotion blocked her throat. She reached to take his hand and pressed it against her cheek.

'You tried.'

'What will you do now?' Darl spoke listlessly.

'I can do two things. I can quit – which I shall never do as long as I draw breath. Or I can go elsewhere for assistance.'

'Where will you go?' he asked distantly. 'I have used up my stock with the folk of the North. Where will you find the men for a second army?'

Her lips drew back in grimace.

'I will not use men. Or at least, not humans.'

'I don't understand.'

'The builders of the City – Zr'gsz, as they call themselves. They live at Thendrun in the Mystic Mountains.'

A gasp burst from her listeners.

Still possessed by the awful calm of shock, Darl asked, 'What can you offer the Fallen Ones? You can't offer them the City.'

'By the Five Holy Ones, no! It's a matter of personal interest to the rulers of the City in the Sky to know how things go with them. There are artifacts, sacred relics, which the Fallen Ones would be overjoyed to recover. Without human aid, they have no chance of regaining them. And I think those trinkets a small price to pay for my City.'

'But what of your soul?' asked another underaged knight with a bloody-bandaged arm. 'They are evil. They are the soul of evil! How can you bargain with them?'

'The Zr'gsz are not the *soul* of evil, friend. You know little of the Dark Ones if you think any earthly evil can surpass theirs.' The intensity of the feeling with which Moriana spoke caused her to shudder. 'I hate the Dark Ones and fear them far more than you know. More than you can know. But I would sell myself to them . . .' Her listeners gasped again and drew back. 'Yes, I would do that if it would free my City from my demented sister Synalon. She seeks to return the City in the Sky to the Dark Ones, then give them the entire world. Do you think my soul too great a price to save your wives and friends and children from that?'

The young knight looked away in confusion and dismay at what he'd just heard. Moriana swayed, suddenly weary to the point of collapse. Almost by instinct, a hand went to clutch the Amulet within her bodice.

She felt a fierce impulse to tear the Amulet off and throw it into the clear, cold waters of the creek. Its mystically changing mixture

17

of dark and light in the central stone had brought nothing but doom and death. Then she recalled the impossibly high price she had paid for the talisman bestowing eternal life. She took her hand away.

'We must go,' she said, casting an uneasy look at the sky. Leaden and sullen in the dusk, the clouds hung close overhead. But not close enough to keep the Sky City bird riders from quartering the countryside around the battlefield looking for survivors.

A knight gave her a spare riding dog he'd caught fleeing across the ridge. He had already fastened in place small bags containing provisions and the earthenware jug which housed the spirit of her long-dead companion Ziore. Moriana mounted the huge animal, hiking up the skirt of her gown. To please Darl, she had worn this finery rather than the tunic and breeches and boots that were her accustomed garb. Now the delicate lacebird silk was ruined, stained with mud and blood and sweat, and she had hacked it off at the knees so that it wouldn't bind her legs. The Northern knights blushed and looked away as she settled unchastely astride the black and white dog.

They didn't understand she was a Princess of the City in the Sky, a warrior of great skill, not like the pampered hothouse flowers that were the Northern ladies. Moriana had no time for their affronted mores. Defeat knew no dignity; nor did death.

The party had just set out following the creek as it curved gently northward toward its eventual rendezvous with the River Marchant when the bird rider squad swept over them like a glowing cloud from the guts of Omizantrim. The boy knight who had guided Darl to safety fell with an arrow in his back. Others cried in surprise and pain as feathered messengers of death winged downward from above. Only Darl and Moriana survived, saved by thickening twilight and the almost naked branches overhead that screened them from the eagle riders.

Moriana looked back. The Sky City troopers hadn't realized any escaped their new slaughters. They passed once more above the bodies of their victims looking for signs of life. One figure stirred, trying to raise himself from the mud of the riverbank. A sheaf of arrows drove him down facefirst.

Moriana clenched a fist and ground it against her forehead.

Oh, my daughter, my poor daughter, a voice sobbed in her mind. But the princess took no solace even from the comforting presence that rode in the jug at her hip.

Turning their backs to the slaughter, Moriana and Darl Rhadaman rode north. North to the Mystic Mountains and the last stronghold of the ancient enemies of mankind.

'We're too late.' Fost Longstrider slumped in the high pommelled saddle atop his riding bear. The beast grunted sympathy with his master's despair. 'The battle is already lost.'

His companion made a bitter sound. She was a tall woman, with a brush of cropped red hair, high cheekbones, slightly slanted eyes of brown. Her mail hauberk clanked as she raised one arm.

'No, 'tis won,' she said, pointing. 'For them.' Her outstretched finger indicated carrion crows gathering like mourners around the bodies. Larger birds stalked among them, naked heads bowed and aggressively pecking for a larger share of the fine meal. Fost smiled in grim appreciation of the rolling wheel of death and life. One side, the other side, human, dog, eagle – it was all the same to vultures. Whatever misfortune befell others, they fed. And prospered.

Fost and Jennas rested their tired bears in a copse beyond what had been the right flank of the Sky City army. The field lay deserted now, save for the dead – and the feeding vultures.

It had been a long, desperate journey from the south where his lovely and beloved Moriana had left him dead in a city swallowed by a glacier. It seemed half a hundred years since his sorcerous resurrection by the Amulet of Living Flame, since he and Jennas, hetwoman of the nomadic Ust'alaykits, had arrived in Tolviroth Acerte, the City of Bankers, to find that the Princess Moriana had departed days, hours even, before they appeared. Now they had missed her again.

Fost considered Moriana's possible fate. Fled? Killed? Captured? The thought of the latter possibility turned him cold. Capture meant return to the Sky City to face the vengeance of her sister Synalon – and of her cousin Rann, warrior, genius, sadist.

Death would be better by far.

They rode on through the eerie stillness of dusk. Fost couldn't rid himself of the sensation that the limp bodies strewn so recklessly about would rise up at any instant with a friendly greeting or outstretched hand. He was no stranger to death; he'd dealt it himself on occasion. But he had little experience with such wholesale slaughter. And no stomach for it at all.

He had been horrified at the carnage at the battles of the cliffs, when he'd helped the People of Ust defeat the Badger Clan and their foul shaman. That had been the mildest of diversions compared to this awful carnage. Together in a heap to Fost's right lay more men and women than lived in either Bear or Badger tribe. He shuddered. He wanted to throw up.

Though they kept careful watch they saw no eagles. The bird riders were off chivvying the defeated, butchering stragglers and the wounded. The wind babbled to itself of the sights it had witnessed that day, stirring fallen banners and mocking the dead. The wind even spoiled the clean and optimistic odors of early spring with the gassy rankness of corruption. Fost took hold of the strap slung over his shoulder, held a leather satchel high.

'See, old smoke,' he said to the bag. 'This is the reward for your passionate desire for bloodshed. Don't your non-existent nerves pulse with excitement at the sight?'

A sniff came from the satchel.

'What could I possibly find to excite me here?' a voice asked peevishly. 'This is rubbish.'

Furious at the spirit's callousness, Fost swung the satchel up to dash the jug it contained to pieces on the ground.

'No,' said Jennas. 'Let him be.'

Ashamed at his angry outburst, Fost pulled the strap back over his shoulder and let the satchel fall to its riding position. He knew he was only venting his ire at not finding Moriana on the genie in his jug.

Following the path the routed army and its pursuers had taken, they passed the hill with its crumpled pavilion and heard the murmur of running water.

'I'm thirsty,' said Fost, 'and there were too many corpses in that stream back there for even the bears to touch the water. Let's see if this one is less clogged with dead.'

Jennas nodded. They rode toward the sound, angling toward a stand of trees well beyond the hill. Though none of the bird riders had shown themselves so far, neither felt like taking chances.

They were almost to the water when they heard the moan.

Without thinking, Fost booted Grutz's sides. The big bear rolled over the bank and into the water, never breaking stride. The icy water numbed Fost's legs. He barely noticed in the urgency that gripped him.

Another sad knot of bodies lay at the treeline. Dogs and men in the distinctive armor of the City States had been struck down by the equally distinctive arrows of the Sky City. The missiles protruded at angles that told they had come from above.

Fost pulled Grutz to a stop beside a young man who stirred feebly. His fingers raked furrows in the mud. An arrow had penetrated his backplate and jutted horribly from the center of his back, as if that, in all the broad earth, was where it belonged.

The knight had been trying to reach the creek. His first words to Fost confirmed this.

'Water. Need . . . need water.'

His voice rattled like a handful of pebbles on a tile roof. Fost dismounted and squatted by his side, studying the extensive injuries. A trail of bloody spittle ran from the corner of the young man's mouth. Fost doubted the youth was twenty.

'You're in a bad way,' said Fost, trying to remember the rough but practical healing lore he'd learned in his career as a courier on the highroads of the Sundered Realm – literally a lifetime ago. 'I don't know if you should have water.'

'You don't honestly think it matters, do you, you dolt?' asked Erimenes acidly from his jug.

Fost shrugged. The shade was right, though it surprised Fost that Erimenes had responded in this fashion. Compassion was not a trait he normally associated with the long-dead philosopher whose ghost rode in the jug at his hip.

The youth drank greedily from Fost's water bottle, which had been taken and filled by Jennas and tossed back to the courier without comment. Fost held the blond head cradled in his lap as the dying boy drank. Jennas urged her mount out of the stream and slid off beside them. Her boots went deep into the cold mud. She was as tall as Fost and just as strongly built.

The boy coughed. The fit came so violently that he jerked himself free of Fost's arms. To Fost's horror, he fell backward onto the arrow still in him. His weight drove it deep and snapped it off. He stiffened, coughed up bloodshot phlegm, then sank back with a sigh, as though sliding into a warm and soothing bath.

Fost bit his lip. The boy's chest rose and fell raggedly within his armor.

'The princess,' Fost said, hating himself for troubling the dying man. 'Do you know who I mean? The Princess Moriana.'

21

'Princess?' The boy nodded, then frowned, his face a bloody mask. 'Failed her. Failed her . . .'

Fost felt a cold black hand clamp his throat.

'She didn't – she's alive, isn't she?' he demanded. To his relief the youth nodded. A grimace twisted the young features as if the slight motion had pained the boy. 'Where did she go?' The knight did not respond. By dint of great effort, Fost kept himself from shaking him. 'Where did she go?' he asked again.

'The . . . three of them.'

Fost frowned up at Jennas.

'Three?'

'Ah – aye. Princess, Lord Darl and . . . Great Ultimate, is it getting dark so soon? And the spirit . . . the woman in the jug . . .'

'Woman in a jug?' asked Jennas, as confused as Fost.

'It must be the other spirit that Guardian told us about,' said Fost, trying to remember more of what the speaking, sorcerously living glacier had said. 'The glacier's name is Guardian,' he told Jennas, seeing her baffled look. 'When we left Athalau, the glacier told us Moriana had a spirit jug with her. He said something about the genie inside, but other matters pressed me then. Guardian had mistaken the other spirit for Erimenes. It put him into a fine rage.' Fost glanced at the blue form wavering by his elbow. He did not remember having uncapped the jar to let him out. Erimenes's face acquired a faraway look.

'A woman,' the spirit said musingly. 'As I live and breathe, a woman! This has interesting aspects I had not considered. Imagine, another such as I!'

'By Ust's snout,' muttered Jennas, 'one of you is more than enough. And you do *not* live and breathe.'

'A woman!' cried the philosopher. 'I can at last vindicate my teachings! What the two of us might do together . . .' The misty body of the shade glittered with dancing blue motes of light, spark-bright in the darkness.

'Be quiet, you,' snapped Fost. 'This man is dying, and you rant about another genie.'

'Not just any genie, friend Fost,' crowed Erimenes. 'A female! I wonder if it might be possible that we . . .' His face glowed with a lechery so luminous it astonished even Fost, though the courier knew the shade's ways by now. Erimenes had preached stark abstinence throughout his life, and then had thirteen hundred years to think

22

better of it. The long, lonely centuries trapped in his ceramic jug had been devoted to developing a totally hedonistic philosophy; disembodied, Erimenes could only experience his newfound ideals as a voyeur. Until the promise of another – female – genie.

Jennas scowled.

'The boy, Fost, the boy is dying.'

Fost swallowed and turned back to the dying knight. Erimenes's crude enthusiasm shamed him. And he was no closer to finding out what had happened to Moriana. He leaned closer to the youth.

'Where did she go?' No response. Fost dribbled water across the parched lips and asked again, slowly, 'Where-did-she-go?'

The young knight tried. In his fading mind he was glad that with his dying breath he could help his princess, the Bright Princess whom he and his friends had let down so badly.

'She went to . . .' His blurred, fading mind struggled to concentrate. 'Went to . . .'

Another coughing spell wracked him. He sprayed bloody foam all over the front of Fost's tunic. Fost gripped the boy's shoulders, trying to steady him.

The boy tried to say, 'To see the ones who built the City in the Sky,' but the coughing hit him again.

'To . . . City . . . Sky,' was all Fost Longstrider heard in the instant before the boy's head lolled back on lifeless muscles.

Gently he lowered the boy. He rose and looked at Jennas.

'The fool,' he groaned. 'She went back to the damned City.'

'And you will follow her.'

'And I'll follow,' Fost said. 'I'll follow.'

CHAPTER TWO

The fugitives rode north following the course of Chanobit Creek as it flowed toward its meeting with the mighty River Marchant. Moriana intended to keep to that course until they could cut northeast to the Mystic Mountains and avoid passing through the lava flows surrounding Mount Omizantrim like a skirt. Those dead lands of tortuous folds and black stone tentacles were well avoided at the best of times. Fell creatures stalked human prey there. Besides, Moriana had no appetite for a meeting with the Watchers, descendants of the loyal few entrusted by Felarod after the War of Powers to guard the flows of skystone. The Fallen Ones had used that gray igneous rock to build their flying rafts of war and commerce, and huge chunks of the skystone formed the base of the City in the Sky itself. The Watchers had passed long ago into legend, keeping vigil over the lonely centuries against a return of the Fallen Ones. How could she look any of them in the eye knowing she went to enlist the aid of their ancient enemies?

Nor was this the best of times to approach Omizantrim. Sometime during the night after the Chanobit Creek debacle the volcano had belched into deadly life again. Lightning and choking poison vapors now ringed the jagged crest of the mountain, and a spume of black smoke grew from it like a bloated, ghastly phallus raping the sky. Such was the power of that single eruption, that from time to time Moriana and Darl passed through areas rendered gray and unreal by falls of ash from the crater two hundred miles to the east. Glancing uneasily at the vast smudge defiling the eastern sky, Moriana wondered what unholy message the mountain had uttered.

She had the gut feeling that it boded her no good.

In another year Moriana might have appreciated the soft beauty

24

of early spring. Leaves burgeoned on the trees, and fields and meadows exploded with a profusion of wildflowers, pink canthas, ovuei as gold as the sunset on placid waters, even the rare royal minsithen mimicking the colors of the Empire of High Medurim. In contrast to Moriana's grim mood, those minsithen shone cheerfully, each a bright yellow star inset in five rounded petals of blood-rich maroon, enriching the air with subtle scents. The trees were deciduous, mostly sturdy spreading anhak, their bark as brown and shaggy as a hornbull in winter coat. Interspersed with the anhak rose stands of Upland tai, straight, slim yellow boles as graceful as elf dancers against the great gnarled shapes of their neighbors. Birds molted to show rainbow colors to the new season and sang to the travellers.

But neither the Princess nor Darl had eyes or ears for the splendor all about them. The bulk of the Sky City army had hurried south the day after Chanobit, but that did not mean she and Darl were spared the horrors of pursuit. With breaking of the weather, the war eagles once more had the freedom of the sky. They could range north to harry the refugees and then wheel southward to catch up with the lumbering columns of dog riders and infantry in time for a hot supper and boots of mulled wine. Moriana's every sense concentrated upward, eyes scanning the sky for sight of wings outstretched in the distance, ears cocked for the cry of a death-giving war bird carried to them on the spring breeze already laden with the smell of spring flowers and moist fertile earth. She wished Darl would rouse from his stupor long enough to take some of the burden of the searching off her.

If anything, his depression grew worse with every mile. His thoughts turned inward and he seldom responded, even when directly spoken to. After two days, Moriana ceased trying to communicate with him. She decided it was best to let him work alone through his depression, if he could. She knew no magic to pull the man back to the world outside his skull. Darl seemed momentarily a lost cause to her, lost like the battle, lost like her precious City, lost, lost, lost.

On the third day, they approached the juncture of Chanobit Creek and the River Marchant. As they rode, Moriana had collected dazed stragglers, tatters of her once-proud army. Her battered army was now sadly composed of knights in dew-tarnished armor turned as gaunt as their quarrelsome, hungry dogs by fear and deprivation; of Great Nevrym foresters slipping on foot through woods flanking the

25

riders, graceful and lethal as panthers even in defeat; of peasant footmen stunned and stumble-footed; and of adventurers hard-eyed and angry at seeing their dreams of conquest and plunder evaporate with the morning mists at Chanobit. Some still hailed Darl as their commander, in spite of his temporary mental infirmities. Gratifyingly, others called out her name with fervent loyalty on encountering the party. She felt small and soiled at the satisfaction she took in knowing that some, at least, gave allegiance directly to her instead of to her through the charismatic wandering hero who had taken her cause at Tolviroth Acerte.

Tolviroth Acerte. So long ago. Lifetimes ago. And a lifetime of struggle lay in front of her.

Since that first day after their defeat, Moriana had said nothing more of her intention of journeying to the keep of the Fallen Ones. Part of her disliked being less than candid with men so loyal. The practical side pointed out that there would be plenty of time to leave for those who disapproved. But that had to be later, when they were beyond the joining of the rivers, and most likely beyond the vengeance of the City in the Sky. Besides, her cynical self observed, even among the survivors were many who followed whomever was in motion at a given moment, not caring where they headed. They were like Darl, who needed to be led. Others realized that their numbers and the princess's intimate knowledge of the bird riders who pursued them gave the best chance of survival. Moriana knew the callowness of attributing faith to all who followed her simply because they followed.

The woodlands rose gently to a ridge that dropped off steeply toward the northwest. Moriana rode point with a bow in her hands. She felt responsible for the fate of these groundlings who followed her.

Before she reached the crest of a rise, she slipped from the back of her war dog. She patted the beast's blunt muzzle and whispered encouraging words in one cropped ear. The animal was trained to stand stock still and to make no sound. She had no fear of it running off or betraying her presence with barking when she scouted the ridgeline on foot.

It's a sign of becoming human, child, a calm, gentle voice said in her mind. *This concern for those you once would have deemed beneath your notice.*

Moriana paused, still hunkered below the crest of the rise.

'Aye, perhaps I'm not fully human. Perhaps my people had lived in the splendid isolation of our City too long.' Her mouth twisted bitterly. 'Certainly I can send humans to their deaths as easily as if I were of some other race.'

Don't use that stick to beat yourself, the voice said. *That is the most human trait of all.*

Moriana smiled briefly. Ziore of Athalau had spent her entire long life cloistered in a convent devoted to the ascetic teachings of Erimenes the Ethical. Like Erimenes, the nun had survived the death of her body, living out long, dusty centuries as a cloud of mist contained within the enchanted red clay of an Athalar spirit jar. Moriana had found the genie while stumbling in a haze of exhaustion and self-hatred through the streets of the glacier-entombed Athalau. Though Ziore's existence had been remote from human experience, the spirit was wise with a wisdom as deep and placid as a sheltered pool. Her soothing presence and loving words had been all that enabled Moriana to keep her tenuous grip on sanity through the brutal trials and disappointments of the last few months.

'Thank you,' Moriana whispered, feeling an immediate answering caress in her mind.

Arrow nocked but undrawn, the Princess of the City in the Sky moved up the slope. She placed her feet carefully to avoid slipping and falling headlong on the slippery mulch of fallen leaves underfoot. The anhak trees grew right to the crest where the soft black earth fell steeply to a broad flood plain. Here and there she saw great raw gaps in the terrain where the spring flood had undercut the bank and toppled a hunchbacked anhak. None was recent. Winter had been too brief for the melting snowpack in the far-off Thail Mountains to engorge the Marchant till it overflowed its banks.

She dropped to her belly. Nothing in the act struck the princess as incongruous. In years past when an heir apparent to the Beryl Throne and not an outcast, she had trained as a bird rider of the elite Sky Guard, a course designed to break all but the fiercest, most determined and toughest in mind and body.

Moriana had passed without the slightest favor being accorded her due to her station. Under the command of the youthful leader of the Guard, her cousin Rann, she had led a flight of Sky Guardsmen into battle against the Northern Barbarians. Now Rann was head of all Sky City soldiery, and Moriana's sworn enemy. But Moriana had not forgotten the hard lessons she'd learned from him. Not the least among them was that survival never took second place to dignity in the field.

With bits of sodden leaf and rich black loam clinging to her belly, she snaked to the crest of the slope. Above her and to the left grew an oval-leafed urylla bush. The short shrub sported no flowers and would not blossom until the white sun of high summer glowered down from overhead, but it provided excellent cover. The princess knew not to silhouette her head against the sky.

Noiselessly she wriggled to the bush, raised her head to peer through the branches. To her left the Chanobit made its final dash to meet and merge with the Marchant. Man-high rushes marked the banks of the river. She scanned them carefully. If the Sky City forces wished to mount a final ambush on the ground, this would be an ideal place to do it.

For ten long minutes she lay staring intently from between the leaves of the bush, eyes scanning the river, the mile-broad plain, the sky. The surface of the river rippled strangely clear. This time of year it usually clogged with flotsam, branches, barrels, scraps of cloth. The decaying corpses of trees, animals and feckless men were often carried downstream on the spring torrent, too. As she completed her thorough reconnaissance, Moriana pondered the shortness of the winter. Though it lengthened the growing season for the groundling farmers, a magnificent boon in the cool Sundered Realm where the planet's three-hundred-day year rendered the fertile time between frosts precariously brief, she found only ominous portent in it. Powers were afoot that interfered with the very order of the universe.

'And I'm about to unleash still more powers,' she said to herself, 'and fell ones indeed, unless the legends lie.'

Nothing moved on the plain, and Moriana saw no movement among the reeds other than the restless scurrying of a southwesterly breeze. High piled clouds rolled across the sky, but Moriana's practiced eye placed them many miles away. If the fluffy cumulus contained the wheeling shapes of war eagles, the birds would be too distant for her to see. Finally, as satisfied as she could be with an inherently risky situation, she nodded to herself and slid back down from the crest-line.

She rolled onto her back to descend the hill and instantly froze. Reflex drew the bowstring halfway to her ear before Moriana recognized the tall, broad-shouldered form who had stolen up to stand a handful of yards behind her.

'Walk warily, Stormcloud,' she said throatily. 'I might have let fly without thinking had I not heard you approach.'

The man smiled. His face was that of a fallen angel surrounded by a nimbus of curly golden hair. There was a decidedly not cherubic light in the cat-green depths of his eyes, but he nodded and courteously refrained from pointing out that the princess hadn't heard him.

'I trust your capabilities, Bright Lady,' he said.

In spite of herself, Moriana smiled back and smoothed a wisp of sweat-lank hair from her eyes.

'I'm glad somebody in this party does.'

'Oh, but all admire you, Your Highness. The way you rallied us together after the slaughter at the creek is commendable. No man could have done better.'

Moriana frowned. Was this some implied criticism of Darl? She saw no sign of guile on that open face. But then she suspected that Iatic Stormcloud could plot foul murder and continue to beam like a seraph in a religious mural.

Still, she had no firm reason to mistrust him and many to be grateful. It was the young mercenary, Stormcloud, who had led the reserves in turning back a flank attack that by rights should have been the final desperate thrust of the Sky City army. Had a war dog not panicked at the smell and upset the brazier Moriana used for her weather magic, the princess would have been able to maintain the ground-hugging clouds that kept eagles from the sky, and handsome Iatic Stormcloud would have taken his place beside Darl Rhadaman as architect of a great victory.

In spite of a lingering unease about the young mercenary, Moriana had been happy when she and Darl had encountered Stormcloud and ten survivors in the woods a few miles from the battlefield. Alone of the Northblooded officers of her army, he had taken her military abilities seriously. He had proved invaluable in persuading the other survivors of the rout that she knew what she was doing and that her commands should be heeded. And with Darl lost in a fog of melancholy, unable to cope with this first shattering defeat of his career, Moriana had found herself relying more and more on Iatic Stormcloud's air of authority and calm counsel.

Moriana became aware of the way her truncated skirt had ridden up her hips, baring pale skin. She wore nothing beneath the soiled, faded garment. Moriana's fine silk undergarment had chafed her unbearably as she rode, so she had dispensed with it. Deliberately, she drew the ragged hem of her skirt down to cover herself better.

'As far as I can tell, the crossing is clear,' she said, relaxing the bow, clamping the broadhead arrow to the staff with her thumb while pushing herself to her feet with her other hand. 'There's no knowing whether bird riders wait above the woods for someone to venture out on the open flats.' She paused, considering. "I'll scout. Stay here and cover me.'

Iatic frowned.

'My lady, is it wise for you to risk your . . .'

'Down! Get down!'

The shrill warning sang from the satchel at Moriana's hip. Without hesitation, Moriana cast herself forward, rolling down the slope into a clump of tai near Stormcloud. The mercenary hesitated, looking dumbfounded by the sudden voice from nowhere, but quickly recovered and threw himself into the scrub.

An instant later a flight of eagles swept overhead in a thunder of wings. The bird riders barely cleared the treetops, and leaves rattled on branches from the wind of their passage. Gazing upward, Moriana counted a score of them in chevron formation, javelins and short-bows ready to slay the unwary.

Let me out, a voice urged in the back of her skull.

Knowing how slight a movement the great Sky City eagles could detect, Moriana reached down, groped in the satchel without taking her eyes from the deadly formation swinging out over the flood plain and painstakingly untwisted the basalt cap of Ziore's spirit jar. She sensed the genie flowing like mist from her jug. Moriana concentrated and sent a thought warning to Ziore not to assume her usual form. A pink apparition swaying among the trees would be certain to attract the attention of any eagle looking that way.

The compact cloud of the nun's vaporous being went swirling into the bushes that hid Moriana, lending an almost imperceptible rosy glow to branches, leaves and the bole of a tai by the princess's elbow.

Never fear, my child, came Ziore's familiar thought pattern. *I've learned a few things since meeting you.*

'What are you doing?' whispered Moriana.

Trying to control the leader's emotions, came the mental reply. *I* can read his intentions clearly enough. He means to hide his men in the reeds by the river and wait until you try to cross the open space.

'Can you control him at such a distance?'

My powers grow greater with use. I think I can. Now hush and let me concentrate.

Flashing the shadow of a wry smile at the thought of being reproved by the cloistered, innocent spirit, Moriana lapsed into silence. Straining her every sense, the princess detected small, furtive sounds of the forest, little creatures scurrying from cover to cover or digging holes against the coming of night and predators. She felt a definite kinship with the tiny, hunted woods beasts.

So acute was her hearing that she heard the slow rise and fall of Stormcloud's breath ten yards away. She heard the wind whispering above the murmur of the river, heard the mighty throb of distant wings, heard now and then a scrap of human voice as the riders called to each other. The squadron turned slowly above the south-eastern bank of the Marchant looking for a likely place to land and lie in ambush without the necessity of remaining airborne for long, tiring hours.

They've seen no sign of us since immediately after the battle, Ziore said in Moriana's mind. *I'll try to convince the leader that we've passed long since, or crossed by another route.*

Moriana nodded. She watched the flyers through several more of their aerial circuits. One dropped out of formation, his bird's claws stretching down to seize the earth. Another rapped a command at him so sharply that the sound came clearly to Moriana's ears, though she couldn't understand its sense. The meaning became clear soon enough: the landing bird hammered the air with its spread wings and soared again, tucking its talons up against its pale belly feathers.

A bird rider peeled from the formation and arrowed his bird straight at Moriana's hiding place. Moriana caught her breath. Had her sister protected these men with a spell that allowed them to sense magical tampering with their senses? Was it possible they detected Ziore's subtle compulsions and now homed in on the source? Synalon and the sorcerors of the Sky City were cunning and knowledgeable. Moriana alone knew of the long hours of arcane studies her sister had devoted to such matters. But the lead eagle rose quickly, the others rolling into a long line after it, climbing toward the heights of the southern sky. They were a thousand feet

31

up when they passed overhead and vanished from Moriana's view in the treetops.

A long sigh gusted from Moriana's lips. A branch tickled one cheek and she brushed it away. Still cautious, she rose from the bushes.

A moment later the foliage stirred off to her left and Iatic Storm-cloud rose from his own cover, as silently as she. His eyes widened as he looked past her. Stormcloud blinked at the sight. Moriana turned to see Ziore's form hovering at her side.

'I take it we owe your familiar thanks for the warning,' the mercenary captain said, jerking his head in the direction the departing bird riders had taken.

'Yes, but she's not my familiar. Ziore is my friend.'

Stormcloud nodded polite acknowledgement at her emphasis.

'I was able to control the emotions of their leader,' Ziore explained aloud.

Moriana looked sharply at her spirit friend. Was the flush of success rendering the shade too talkative? Then she relaxed. If she couldn't trust Stormcloud with the knowledge of the genie's power, there was no one left she could trust. Not unless Darl came out of his damned self-hating fog.

'That could prove handy,' said Stormcloud, eyeing the pink figure appraisingly.

'Yes,' Moriana agreed curtly. Tugging down the hem of her skirt, she walked past him into the woods, aware of the man's eyes on her all the while.

CHAPTER THREE

Preoccupied, Prince Rann Etuul walked along a back street of Bilsinx, his stride eating up a surprising length of ground for one so short. Bulbous towers loomed on either side of the cobblestoned street, and in the distance in front of him rose tall minarets. Pale, drawn faces peered out at him through glass rippled with age and purpled by the sun. He gave them no more attention than he gave his surroundings. All his thoughts centered on the great gray oval of the City in the Sky floating a thousand feet above his head, drifting to the east like an immense stone cloud.

He similarly paid little attention to his companions, the three armed men in black and purple swaggering in a loose wedge before him and the thin and pimply adolescent mage who trotted behind. Hard-pressed to keep up with his prince despite longer legs, the young wizard Maguerr half stumbled and half ran while managing to stroke a wisp of ginger-colored beard and cradle a geode the size of a human head against his hollow chest.

Rann hummed a wordless tune as he walked and thought. The events of the past few days amounted to nothing more than history for him now. Past glory faded with the promise of future triumphs. His destiny, the destiny of Queen Synalon, the destiny of the City in the Sky lay to the east.

East. The City in the Sky, by some process forgotten even before men wrested control of it from the reptilian Hissers who had built it, could have picked one of three directions to move after it floated into Bilsinx from the west. From the central city of the Great Quincunx, the pattern it had followed immutably over the center of the Realm since Felarod had confined it after the War of the Powers, the Sky City could have gone north to Wirix, south to Brev, or east

33

to Kara-Est. Brev was the smallest of the Quincunx cities and had already made proper obeisance to Synalon. Wirix raged defiant and strong in the midst of Lake Wir, almost as remote from the land as the City itself. There would be little profit in conquering Wirix immediately.

The city that Synalon must subdue next was Kara-Est, richest seaport of the Realm, most powerful of all the five Quincunx cities. And it was toward Kara-Est that the City now headed.

On its last transit of Bilsinx, the Sky City had dropped a deadly rain of stones on the ground city's defenders, as bird riders wheeled down unleashing a steel-shod storm of arrows. An attack by the Highgrass Broad mercenaries had completed the defeat of Bilsinx, along with a commando attack on the Mayor's Palace by Sky Guardsmen under Rann's command. The city had fallen quickly under his brilliantly waged campaign and fighting prowess.

And more important than the fighting, the prince's honeyed words had soothed the anxieties and resentments of the subject Bilsinxt. They had even sent a body of their light cavalry to fight Moriana's army beside the very bird riders and heavy dog-mounted lancers and bowmen who had stormed their city. His diplomatic ways had turned a defeated enemy into a wary ally.

Now giant shapes grew in the large central plaza of Bilsinx like arcane fungi, turning into vast bloated sausages and rising upward toward the City silently floating overhead. Eagles harnessed to long, stout tethers guided the cargo balloons with a precision otherwise impossible. Time weighed heavily. Preparations for further battle occupied all of Rann's waking thoughts and even haunted his dreams.

He nodded in silent pride. Below the elongated shapes swung gondolas fairly straining with their cargoes of arrows, foodstuffs and a hundred other necessities in preparation for the coming battle of Kara-Est. Alone of all the Quincunx cities, to say nothing of the cities of the Sundered Realm, Kara-Est had substantial defenses against attack from the air. As it was the greatest prize of the Quincunx, so it would be the dearest won.

Everything proceeded well ahead of schedule. He had been inspecting warehouses of goods assembled since the occupation began, among them bundles of rare and expensive herbs sent over the Thails from Thailot, westernmost Quincunx city. Rann smiled wickedly as he thought of the aromatic bundles. Perhaps the smug engineers gazing through the complex ring sights of the rooftop-mounted ballistae of Kara-Est would have a few surprises as they strove to bring down their swift-winging Sky City foe. And the men of the seaport's aerial defense force, riding in light platforms beneath the living gasbags called ludintip – Rann had plans for them as well.

A high wash of shirred white clouds drifted between the City and the sun. Rann's sensitive nose sensed the promise of rain sometime that afternoon. He must expedite the loading. The Sky City eagles hated to fly in the rain, and it was injurious to their health to do so. The specially bred, intelligent birds were mighty engines of destruction, but they had definite vulnerabilities. For the birds' lungs, strained from hard flying, to breathe in cold damp air could lay them low as readily as iron darts from Estil catapults.

Rann needed his eagles if the assault of Kara-Est were to succeed. And he would have them.

'Maguerr,' he barked, not bothering to look back at the weedy journeyman mage who trotted at his heels. He scarce could stand to look at Maguerr, with his lank hair that seemed stranger to comb and soap alike, his inadequate beard, his beaklike nose with nostrils that seemed to exert an unbreakable fascination for his fingertips, his watery eyes and spiderleg fingers and pimples without number. But the boy was a genius in that special branch of magic that enabled the Sky City's forces to communicate verbally over great distances, and hence, indispensable. There were times when he annoyed Rann so much that the prince began to itch uncontrollably with the need to tie the horrid youth to some handy fixture and flay the skin from his wretched and unsightly face. Yet because of Maguerr's undeniable ability, and in a perverse way as partial penance for his own failure to make an end of Moriana and her clever groundling, Rann had attached the wizardling to himself as his personal amanuensis.

Maguerr's slippers scuffled along the cobblestones.

'Yes, Your Highness,' he whined. A tic twitched beneath Rann's left eye.

'Pick up your feet when you walk,' he rapped, 'and for Istu's sake try to learn not to talk through that damned proboscis of yours.'

'Yes, milord.' Maguerr's tone was obsequious and unruffled by his master's brusqueness.

Rann bit back a curse. He saw the slight head motions of the three escorts who walked before him. The prince seldom had need to raise his voice, yet here he was on the verge of screaming at his own secretary. Rann knew quite well that his Guards made sport of him, and he promised silently they would pay for it. At the same time, he toted up yet another debit owing to Maguerr, a debt he planned to collect with the most usurious interest once the mage was no longer necessary to his plans.

It had been long since his taste for torture had been sated.

'Take a memorandum,' Rann said. 'To Her Excellency Gomi Ashentani, Governor of Bilsinx by grace of Synalon I Etuul, Mistress of the Clouds, First among the Skyborn, of the Dark Ones Most Favored, and all the other usual honorifics.' He chopped the air with one hand.

Behind him Maguerr murmured to himself, impressing the words on his spongelike mind. Among his other unbearable attributes was numbered an eidetic memory. Rann gritted his teeth and continued.

'Milady Governor: You are hereby instructed to dispatch the ground forces left at your disposal, holding back a suitable reserve, to Kara-Est by no later than nightfall —'

Although Bilsinx was not just a conquered city but a thoroughly subjugated one, the hands of Rann's three Guards rested on sword pommels, and their eyes were never still. Bowstring-taut alertness was the rule of the Sky Guard elite, and even though they expected no trouble they scanned the street and storefronts with eagle-sharp eyes. They made no idle chatter; Rann would not permit it. They allowed themselves a measure of relief that the prince, impatient with crowds clogging the main thoroughfares, had chosen this side-street where no assassin could sidle to dagger range of Rann in the anonymity of a mob.

But they allowed themselves no laxity.

Yet it was the prince's sharp eyes that caught the telltale gleam of sunlight on steel in a doorway ahead and to the left.

'Down!' he shouted, hurling himself to one side, tucking in his shoulder and rolling to the stoop of a shuttered bakery, closed by the Governor's Ashentani's rationing decrees. When Rann came to rest, his scimitar glistened in a wicked arc from his left fist.

The Guardsmen's honed reflexes snapped at Rann's command. But not quickly enough. Arrows whined, went home with deceptively soft sounds. Sword in hand, a Sky Guardsman sank to his knees, eyes fixed on the red fletched shaft sprouting between them. Beside him a comrade choked on the steel point embedded in his throat.

'Get the bastards!' a harsh voice cried.

A man and a woman broke from the cover of doorways on opposite sides of the street and cast aside shortbows. The man straightened his left arm, causing a hornbull hide buckler strapped to his forearm to slide into his hand. His other hand brought forth a broadsword. The woman drew forth forth a rapier and maingauche with identical fretwork hilts. Two more men materialized behind them, weapons in hand. A fifth figure stepped from a farther doorway as the remaining Sky Guardsmen ran to engage the killers.

Rann gained his feet. He started forward in a crouching glide, only to stop and clutch at his chest as agony shot through him.

'Dark Ones!' he gasped, 'I've torn something loose!'

He had undergone terrific punishment in recent months. Broken ribs had been his reward when he sought to interpose himself between a raging Vicar of Istu and his helpless queen. His chest barely wrapped with bandage before he was off in the saddle again, Synalon had ordered him to Athalau and a nearer brush with death. An immense block of ice had fallen from the vaulted roof of the living glacier in which Athalau lay, striking down Rann and the Sky Guardsmen who had trailed Moriana, Fost Longstrider, and their treacherous spirit companion, Erimenes. Only the wildest luck had prevented the prince from being mashed into red gruel by the ice fall. And only the fierce, driven vitality and determination of the man and his lineage had enabled him to survive, with a dozen bones shattered and a score of muscles torn loose.

He had the best healing sorcery of the Sky City; but not even the peerless mages of the Soaring World could make him altogether whole again in the short time alloted them.

Conquest for queen and City had repeatedly called him forth half mended, still hurt and hurting. Now his wounds betrayed him.

He fought for balance as blackness veiled his senses.

'Your Highness!' he heard Maguerr call in alarm.

Rann struggled against the darkness threatening to swallow him. He saw his remaining bodyguard surge forward to perform his duty. With a musical skirl, the Guardsman's curved blade met the straightsword assassin. The woman with the rapier circled, watching for an opening. The next two assassins went wide to bypass the

37

combatants, making for the prince with deadly intent shining on their faces.

'Come forward and meet your death, dog lover,' snarled the Guardsman, Ahue. 'At least you'll know a good death from City steel.'

The assassin was a good man, strong wristed and supple, but his foe was of the superbly trained Sky Guard. Ahue's scimitar beat the larger blade aside. The killer screamed shrilly as the caress of steel severed veins and tendons of his swordarm. His blade fell, ringing on the cobblestones as his cry drowned in blood bubbling from slashed throat. Before he fell, the Guardsman was lunging for the woman, launching a vicious hail of blows that she was hard-pressed to fend off despite her paired weapons.

'Your turn, bitch,' Ahue cried, recovering to slash out again.

'Bitch, am I?' she snarled. 'Better than you who defends a eunuch! Or are the two of you lovers? Do you share his bed?'

Ahue viciously attacked, angered by the slurs both on him and his prince. Rann was a eunuch, castrated by the Thailint barbarians. The Guardsman's pride prevented him from accepting this insult calmly, even though he knew it was intended to enrage him and thus force him into a deadly mistake.

He slashed fiercely, incoherently screaming out his anger.

The black-haired swordswoman gave way. Her two companions hesitated. The one on the right, a lean straw-blond man who kept a pair of rapiers twitching before him like the antennae of some giant insect, feinted a lunge. The Guardsman's scimitar shot sparks off the twinned blades and sent the man reeling backward.

Ahue spun and lunged, almost gutting the burly red-beard who tried to dart by on the left and give his friend time to bring up his dirk for a parry. The red-beard lashed out with his spiked ball mace. Holes tapped in its haft made it whine like a banshee, a high, unnerving sound. The Guardsman was not distracted. He ducked nimbly below its lethal sweep and returned a cut that opened a long red dripping slash in the olive-drab fabric stretched taut across the maceman's thigh.

The three killers retreated. The Guardsman faced them with a wild laugh. A killing frenzy was upon him, and even seasoned slayers such as these quailed before his madness.

'Stand back!' barked the same harsh voice that had ordered the assassins forward. A tall woman strode forward. Her pale blonde

38

hair was cut square across the brows, though it swung free behind, brushing broad shoulders. In her hands she held a curious implement, the like of which the Guardsman had never seen before. He continued to smile defiantly, but his eyes narrowed at the peculiar weapon.

Though exotic, the device was not unfamiliar to Rann. By titanic effort of will he forced himself away from the pilaster he used to prop himself upright.

'Ahue, *get back!*' he shouted desperately.

In his frenzy, Ahue did not hear. Or perhaps he heard and for the first time defied an order from his prince and commander. It was the first and last time. Ahue brought his scimitar up from guard, preparing to hurl himself upon his new antagonist. The blonde woman swung something around her scarred left hand. A black blur whined toward the Guardsman.

Ahue cursed as a chain wrapped itself around his throat. A fist-sized leaden ball smashed into the side of his head, staggering him. He caught the chain in his gauntleted left hand. The blonde woman jerked the chain with all the might of her beefy shoulders. Ahue plunged forward, swinging wildly with his scimitar. The blonde fouled it with her chain. Her right hand turned and swept upward. Breath and life gusted from Ahue's mouth as the upturned sickle blade tore through his light mail shirt into his guts, ripping upward. The tip of the sickle curved within his ribcage to cleave his heart. For a long moment Ahue stared past the woman's left shoulder, breast pressed to hers as though in comradely embrace, his gore gushing onto the front of her body as his wide brown eyes gaped in final surprise. Then he fell.

The killers sighed. They had stopped to watch the dance of death between their leader and the berserk Sky Guardsman. Now they started forward again, watching Rann with grim singlemindedness. The blonde drew her sickle blade free, disentangled the chain from the corpse with a musical tinkle and stepped forward.

With unnatural clarity Rann heard the sounds: Maguerr muttering in horror behind him; the many-throated murmur of crowds in Bilsinx's main street, oblivious to the deadly drama being enacted a few hundred feet away; the scuff of soft sole leather on stone; even the hissing of gasses venting from the cooling corpse of Ahue.

'I am Prince Rann Etuul and you shall not have me so easily,' he said, pushing the tip of his chin toward the dead Ahue. Rann hadn't

39

expected any of these killers to follow the direction of his gesture. They were too good for that. But he'd lost nothing by trying.

He collected himself, pushed pain aside, forced the darkness from his vision. Battle lust sang its adrenaline song in his veins. He knew that for the next crucial few moments he would be able to function at almost full capacity. His mind had the cold clearness it always did when he went into battle. The sickness and desperation he had felt just heartbeats ago had been transmuted into exultation and anticipation. Fall he might, but he would drink deep of blood and pain before yielding to the Hell Call.

'Die, eunuch,' said the man facing Rann. The straw-haired young man danced forward, grinning, rapiers questing. Rann glided to him. The soles of his calf-high moccasins never left the street. The rapier points darted in a quick one-two attack. Rann's scimitar dashed them aside with contemptuous ease.

The youth raised an eyebrow and began to circle. Rann knew what he attempted; the assassin wanted to get the prince to circle with him so that one of his fellows could slip a blade in from behind. Rann circled in a direction counter to the other's motion so that their left sides came close and the man's body stayed between Rann and the deadly sickle and chain.

That was the weapon Rann feared most: *aizant-eshk* it was called, the devil's claw. The name was appropriate.

The blond man stopped circling a few steps before his right arm would have begun crowding the gray-green stone of a facade. Rann faced him coolly, left arm half extended with his blade, right hand open and held by his hip in readiness for a grab at the other's weapon.

Rann sorely felt the lack of a parrying weapon. Normally he carried a spike dagger of his own design tucked into his right boot. But he was in Bilsinx today as a Sky Guardsman as well as Prince of the Sky City. Sky Guardsmen prided themselves that they never carried daggers, except for those rare occasions when they fought on foot. In flight they never came closer than sword's length from a foe.

'Are you going to fight or wait for me to die from old age?' demanded Rann as the man continued to circle.

Something in the words affected the blond man. Rann saw his eyes glaze slightly with rage. An opportunity. Now all he had to do was capitalize on it.

40

He waited until he saw the other tense for a lunge, then snapped the scimitar in a whining overhead wrist cut. With a clash, the rapiers met in a defensive cross and caught the descending blade. The triumphant grin on the blond man's face changed to a look of astonishment as Rann deftly turned his wrist and thrust the curved sword down inside the other's guard. The point went into the assassin's neck where it met the notch of his clavicle. Blood fountained, his knees buckled, and the confident light in his eyes faded in an instant.

Experience and coolness had aided the prince. He doubted the others would fall prey so easily.

Rann ripped his sword free and spun, whipping the scimitar in an eye-high cut parallel to the ground. The black-haired woman was almost upon him. Her rapier fended the stroke, but her comrade's blood spattered into her eyes. As she blinked frantically to clear her vision, Rann brought the scimitar in beneath her maingauche in a quick backhanded return. The woman howled and doubled over, dropping both weapons to clutch at the rope intestines spilling from her belly.

The whisper of steel on steel warned the prince. He flung himself headlong, jarring every bone in his body. The lead ball of the devil's claw clattered by inches above him, drawing its chain after like a comet's tail. The weight ricocheted off stone polished to a high gloss by innumerable feet. Rann rolled fast as the blonde woman reeled in the ball. As soon as he was clear he pulled himself to his feet. His head spun; the adrenaline rush was fading fast and when it went, so would his already slim chance of survival.

'Now it is time for you to die, little man,' the blonde told him. He cast a quick glance at the red-bearded man and dismissed him as a real danger. The woman was a different case.

Rann needed to know more about the blonde if he was to successfully defeat her. Gathering that information would prove difficult. She was good, too good. As she neared, twirling the ball on a half yard of chain, holding the sickle loosely, her hand protected by a brass strap fastened to the haft as a sort of knuckleduster, he clearly made out the indigo mark on her right cheek. It was a convolute squared mandala.

From his limited experience in the City's commerce, he knew it for the tattoo of the Dyers' Guild in High Medurim. That explained her deadly expertise. The hereditary guilds controlled that city's industry with an iron hand. Those born outside a guild were forced to live on the dole or by outlawry; those born into a craft for which they lacked aptitude or interest, unless they bought out of their birth guild and into another, were doomed to the same fate.

But the guilds needed enforcers to keep power over their members, and to prosecute their ever-changing rivalries and feuds. They kept large contingents of professional killers. Some imported masters from Jorea, the North Continent, or the Far Archipelago. Others trained native Medurimites, providing opportunity for lucrative employment even for those forced to live outside a guild. But whether imported or domestic, the Weapons Masters of High Medurim were among the most perfect murderers to be found anywhere in the world. The blonde-haired woman with the feral look to mouth and eyes was one of that kindred.

That knowledge didn't cheer Rann. If anything, it drained some of his determination. At his fighting best he knew he was more than a match for gutter killers like her. But now . . .

'Yes, little man,' she cooed, moving closer. 'Your death is at hand. Come. Don't fight it. Let me dispatch you without pain. I promise you won't feel even a twinge.'

Over his left shoulder Rann heard low incantation. Maguerr was trying to summon help on his geode. Rann grimaced; the mage had more nerve than he would have credited him with. Small good his unexpected steadiness would do. The only people who might receive his call were in the City overhead. Even the swift eagles were unlikely to arrive before the issue was settled. Rann sidestepped toward the center of the deserted street, need for room overriding the worry that one assailant might get in back of him. He felt the first twinges of pain in his chest and knew help would not arrive in time.

'It is you who will die,' he said. Rann fought down giddiness. His words rang hollow in his ears, and he knew she laughed at him, this blonde killer from High Medurim.

'Your pet wizardling's magic will avail him naught,' she said, moving closer. 'Your eagles will take too long to arrive. Your corpse will be stretched out on the street for an afternoon repast. Your eagles *do* eat human flesh?'

The adrenaline rush was past him. Rann fought on nothing more than dogged determination. It wouldn't be enough.

He had no warning of the attack. One instant he faced the relaxed blonde, the next her sickle came spinning through the air toward his face. He dodged, hacking at the weapon as it whined past. The tip raked his right shoulder and left a burning wound. He felt warm blood pour down his arm onto his tunic.

The blonde's face twisted in rage at her missed stroke as she yanked hard at the leaden weight in her hand. She deftly spun the sickle back to her hand. Rann's blurred eyes were too intent on her. The big red-bearded maceman came for him. The prince's sword darted past the spiked ball and sheathed itself an inch in the man's left eye, almost by accident. His sword felt as if it weighed a hundred pounds now.

Bawling, the redbeard fell back. The blonde's arm moved in a blur. The chain of her weapon whipped about Rann's ankles. She uttered a cry of fierce delight as she pulled it tight, jerking the prince's feet from under him.

But even as he fell, the prince's right hand shot out to seize the chain. The blonde leaned forward to close with her intended victim; he pulled with a supernatural might born of desperation. The tattooed assassin lost her balance, fell. Rann served her as she had served his Guardsman, face twisting in a wild grin as he felt his curved blade penetrate her flesh.

But his life was done. The huge-shouldered man with the red curly beard loomed over him, face now a horrid mask, a single blue eye glaring wildly. The mace went high. Rann snarled in futile defiance as the spiked ball was silhouetted against the clouds.

The red-bearded man's head exploded in a welter of blood.

He fell heavily beside his leader's body. Rann lay gasping like a beached fish. He was aware of the distant sound of screaming, and another sound less identifiable.

Regaining his breath, Rann struggled out from under the blonde woman's body. Maguerr knelt in the street, clutching his midsection and retching dryly. Unsteadily Rann went to him and laid a gory hand on his bony elbow.

'You have my gratitude, boy,' he said in a voice that hardly seemed to be his own. 'Don't feel shame at being sick. It happens often when first one slays a fellow man.'

Such tender words from the fearsome Prince Rann would have shocked any of his Sky Guard. Maguerr merely shook his head.

'N-not that, lord,' he choked. 'The geode communicator. Was – aggh, my stomach – was in tune with it. What happens to it . . . I feel.'

Numbed and slow to comprehend, Rann fell back a step. His bootheel crunched on a fragment of the geode which Maguerr had hurled to burst the skull of the red-bearded assassin. Maguerr screamed.

'Breaking! Gods, it's shattering me!'

Understanding the mage's plight at last, Rann leaped to one side, lost balance, reeled, and stepped on yet another fragment. The mage fell over with the wail of one damned.

When the bird riders arrived, they found Rann Etuul, Prince of the City in the Sky, Marshal of the Sky Guard and commander of all the City's forces, dyed dark red with drying blood and scrabbling on all fours on the Bilsinx backstreets, diligently searching for pieces of Maguerr's shattered geode.

CHAPTER FOUR

Boisterous merriment boiled and soared, filling the great audience hall of the Palace of Winds clear to the vaulted ceilings far overhead. The festive week proclaimed by Synalon in celebration of her victory over her sister had dragged into its sixth day, only to have its vigor renewed once more by fiat of the queen, in honor of the miraculous escape of Prince Rann from the High Medurim assassins.

Torches guttered in sconces, splashing orange light on walls and making the ancient figures carved into them seem to writhe in the grip of nameless, unsettling emotions. Captive fire sprites thrashed inside crystal bell jars as tall as men, their furious hissing and killing heat contained by the thick greenish enchanted glass. All that escaped from the bell jars and into the great hall was their hellish blue glare. Great tables of veined green stone stood everywhere, piled high with the finest food and drink. The revellers circulated, drinking, eating, sniffing vapors from bubbling bowls of potions, trying to adopt the appearance of being successfully and spontaneously amused. Some danced a stately pavane to the strains of an orchestra brought up from Bilsinx. Others stood around discussing what a marvel it was that the mercy of the Dark Ones had preserved Prince Rann from the treacherous attack while their eyes searched for likely partners for later assignations.

But the sound of merrymaking had a false note to it like a gilded pot-metal coin dropped on a table. There were those in the Sky City who were not altogether overjoyed at their queen's victory over her twin, who by right of inheritance should have sat on the Beryl Throne in Synalon's stead. And even those who supported Synalon for reasons of conviction or expedience found it difficult to work up much cheer over the prince's survival. His was not a personality to attract tender sentiment.

On the highbacked throne carved of a monstrous single green beryl crystal Synalon sat at her ease, idly scooping berries from a silver bowl and feeding them to the ravens who perched on either arm of the throne. She wore her glossy black hair curled into an intricate knot atop her head. A thick unbound strand fell to either side of her beautiful sculpture-perfect face, lending it a decidedly misleading air of innocence.

Of all the revellers in the vast, crowded audience hall, she was the freshest looking. She had changed into a new gown only moments before ascending her throne, a gown woven of shimmering green and blue and pearl and silver threads. Depending on light, the viewer's perspective and the motion of the lithe limbs and body to which the garment clung like skin, the colors subtly changed. Debauchery, particularly of the sort mandated by Synalon, was hard work. Watching courtiers and subjects move about in a low haze of fatigue, Synalon smiled, a wicked light touching her cobalt eyes. A life of determined dissipation, interspersed with the harsh disciplines of black sorcery, kept the queen as fit as the toughest of Rann's Sky Guard.

The dancers strutted through the complex patterns of the Virgins' Recessional, commemorating the coming of spring. Synalon covered a yawn with a slender hand. Her subjects proved most tedious. If left to their own devices for an instant they lapsed into supremely trivial activities. It was ever up to her to make sure their celebrations held at least some semblance of life.

For a time she contemplated calling for the hornbull she'd had ballooned up from the surface and giving a demonstration of what she considered properly vivid recreation. Certainly her subjects were abusing the dance area with their . . . tedious meanderings.

Then a better idea came to her. The smile returned to her lips. It was much like the expression of a great cat that comes upon a tender and helpless kid.

She set the silver berry bowl on a stand beside the throne. Sensing their mistress had some new diversion in mind, the ravens beat their wings and chuckled evilly. Propping her chin on her right hand, she held her left in the air before her eyes, forefinger extended. A glow appeared at the tip. Slowly the finger began to turn in a circle, leaving a silvery trail in midair. Instead of dissipating, the trails remained and began to form a ball shape, as a caterpillar would spin a cocoon.

Eyes turned toward the throne now. Motion ceased on the floor as couple by couple the dancers stopped to see what magics their monarch performed. Fear and anticipation mingled on the faces of the celebrants, giving Synalon a warm flush of pleasure. Like most of her favorite amusements, the one she concocted now would bring delight to some and stark anguish to others. The revellers, well aware of this, felt a thrill of expectation.

When she had woven a ball of light in midair, Synalon brought up her other hand. Both palms cupped the glowing globe, shaping it, massaging it, infusing it with pseudo-life. Like her gown, it shimmered with myriad opalescent colors.

'What do you dream?' she asked her subjects. Her voice was as smooth and as strong as silk. At the sound of it the musicians ceased their efforts, though the words were clearly audible above the melody. 'This is the Ball of Dreams, my child. In it you shall see your deepest, darkest thoughts, summoned forth for all to see.'

She gave the globe a push. It drifted away from her, seeming to test the air like a scenthound casting about for a trail. The revellers fell back from the ball, trying to be unobtrusive. No one was overeager to be the first to have thoughts, desires, deep secrets called forth for the cruel amusement of the rest.

The scintillant ball darted toward a knot of courtiers gaily caparisoned in silks and the furs of animals specially bred by the genetic sorcerors of Wirix for the color and quality of coat. It hovered above the head of a paunchy, black-haired youth. The young man studiously looked away from the ball as its surface began to shimmer, then swirl with colors like oil on a pond. An image within the ball snapped into sharp focus: the young man naked on a luxurious bed grappled ecstatically with a blowsy older woman.

'Why, that's Sunald's mother!' exclaimed a burly, bearded comrade. The women in the group tittered. Laughter was taken up by the hall as a whole, laughter too hearty, momentarily releasing tension of those who know they may yet feel the axe. Furiously red to his high-flounced collar, the youth stalked out, head drawn down between his shoulders like a bird seeking a worm's hole.

'And where does the Ball of Dreams cast next?' asked Synalon in velvety tones. 'Will it be you? Or you? Or even you?' Her fingers stabbed forth each time indicating revellers. As their expressions

47

turned from mirth to horror, Synalon laughed delightedly.

With a perversity like that of the sorceress who had summoned it into existence, the ball ignored all of Synalon's prospective victims and swung next to float above the blonde head of the burly man's escort, who had laughed first and loudest at the revelation of Sunald's secret lust. She gaped in mute horror as the ball seethed with color again to reveal her, as naked as Sunald had been, spreadeagled on her back across a furry hassock receiving the eager attentions of a great war dog. Bannered on the dream sphere's surface for all to see was the woman's face, a face showing every indication of almost religious ecstasy. She screamed and fell to her knees, hands tearing at her bodice as laughter rained on her like blows.

The burly man tried to comfort his lady but she pulled away. He turned angry eyes toward the throne. Synalon lounged back, amused.

'Is this not more interesting than your pathetic little dances?' asked the black-haired Synalon, idly playing with a strand of her hair. 'Now that you know Lady Emele's most secret desires, perhaps you will accommodate her.'

Laughter rolled through the great audience hall.

'Or,' Synalon said, 'was the large black canine image in the sphere yours? Are you then a shape-shifter?'

Again the resounding laughter, a bit too loud, a bit too long. Synalon waved a long-fingered hand in acknowledgement of the success of her sorcerous entertainment, then turned back to the sphere.

The ball moved on, pausing at random to blight the mirth of one or another who had been roaring with cruel laughter only moments before. A tall, lean banker was revealed adjusting his institution's accounts to bleed funds into his own pockets; a matronly woman noted for announcing frequently, loudly, and at inordinate length that a woman's sole duty was motherhood was shown strangling the latest of her dozen brats in its bassinet, a look of orgasmic glee transfiguring her plump features; a civil functionary loathed by the populace for over-punctilious enforcement of statutes regarding the conduct of small businesses appeared nude, wallowing in a great heap of his own excrement, smearing it over his body and cooing like a giant baby; a noted cavalry officer was seen spurring his famed red war dog to the rear against a backdrop several veterans recognized as the ridge by Chanobit Creek.

The laughter rose to a hysterical crescendo. The matron lay on the marble floor in a faint. The banker hurried off to slit his wrists. As the cavalryman backed away from the half-dozen comrades in arms moving in his direction with lethal purpose and the bureaucrat stood laving his pudgy hands against one another while tears cascaded down his cheeks and chins, Synalon only sat on her throne watching with an amused smile on her face, feeding bits of spiced meat to her ravens.

The ball stopped, rose, as if seeking fresh prey. It descended in a gentle slope toward a clump of older celebrants who stood near one of the buffets. It settled at a point a foot above the head of the tallest of the group, a woman whose short reddish hair was dusted with white streaks.

Gilinon dun Krit, a powerful member of the Council of Advisors to the Throne, snorted disdainfully as she glared up at the shimmering sphere. Her companions, other advisors and their hangers-on, backed away from her as if afraid to be marked as having stood by her side. For a long moment the woman gazed up at the particolored roil of the sphere, the muscles standing out on her neck as stark as pillars, a vein beating visibly in her broad forehead. Then with a shriek of fury and despair beyond words, she drew a long dagger from her sleeve and flung herself at Synalon.

Palace Guards and Monitors anonymous behind brown iron salles lunged from their waiting places by the walls, cursing and driving the illustrious assembly from their path like so many cattle. Synalon threw back her head and laughed, a sound unutterably pure and sweet.

Her face a red demon's mask unrecognizable in its hatred, the Councillor reached the foot of the royal dais and raised her arm to strike. The two ravens swept down upon her, striking with beaks and black-tipped claws. The woman reeled back, beating impotently at the bird sinking its claws in her scalp and stabbing at her eyes with its beak. Its fellow lit on her dagger arm and dug its nails deep.

The venom on the birds' talons took effect. With an anguished scream, dun Krit straightened so spasmodically that both large black birds were flung aside. She began to twitch, then hop, until she was spinning about the pattern inlaid in the floor's center with her arms flung wide, a ghastly parody of the calm dance that had occupied that place scant moments before. Her face turned bluish-black and her tongue protruded between bloated lips. With a last garbled

49

outcry she fell to her back. Her body arched, flopped, black foam gushed from her nostrils, and then she lay still.

The silence of ghastly death filled the great hall. All cheer was stilled – except for the pealing laughter of the beautiful young queen.

Four Monitors made their way through the crowd and gingerly bore the body off. The revellers turned away.

'Come, the gaiety has just begun,' cried Synalon, clapping her hands for the orchestra to start afresh.

The Bilsinxt musicians looked at the faceless men bearing out their limp burden, and fell into a light and happy air. At a nod from Synalon a small army of servants invaded the hall, bearing fresh platters of meats and pastry and great tureens of wine and essences. Slowly the tide of conversation began to flow once more.

High above the assemblage floated the pearly sphere. Synalon looked to it again, motioned with a finger. It dropped.

Conversation ebbed. Another clique of Councillors stood not far from where the ball had found dun Krit, and it was toward them the sphere now moved. Once more it seemed to single out the tallest person present, this time a portly man whose red face was fringed by a white beard that grew to meet the rim of equally white hair circling the base of his great skull. A shorter, stouter companion in a blue robe and black slippers with flaring gingery sidewhiskers and rough cheeks spoke urgently to him in a high-pitched voice that quieted as the sphere descended.

A commotion at the entrance brought heads around. Prince Rann strode in without so much as a glance at the heralds who bawled annunciation of his arrival. Moving without apparent haste he quickly came to the cleared space before Synalon's throne. The crowd melted to give him way.

At a finger wave from Synalon, the sphere veered from above the Councillors' bald heads and followed the prince. Hearing an intake of breath from the crowd, the prince turned to see the shimmering ball floating toward him. Instead of kneeling before his sovereign, he crossed his arms and stood waiting, watching the approaching object with neutral eyes. It came to a stop over his head. The swirling crossed its face again. The tantalizing hint of a picture had begun to appear when Synalon clapped her hands smartly and the ball vanished tracelessly. Her pale skin was flushed all the way down the revealing front of her bodice.

One eyebrow raised, Rann knelt to make the customary obeisance.

'Rise, cousin,' Synlon said throatily. 'Accept the plaudits of the crowd gathered to offer thanksgiving for the survival of our most valuable servant.'

He crossed his arms again as the hall rang with applause.

'I thank Your Majesty,' he said dryly when the clapping ebbed. 'But I cannot stay to partake of your amusements.' The leaden inflection of the last word told what he thought of her ideas of diversion. They had some tastes in common but fetes and grandiose display were not among them.

Synalon pursed her lips.

'And why not, honored cousin?'

'I have only come to inform you that the preparations of your mages are completed. The conjurations are done. Magically, we are as prepared for battle as ever we'll be.'

A murmur of whispered comment ran through the hall. It was rumored that Synalon herself would take part in the coming battle with Kara-Est. The Dark Ones had bestowed new and frightful powers on her. She wanted the world to behold them, and to know fear. Those in the great audience hall already knew that fear.

'But why must you rush away, then?' asked Synalon peevishly.

'The mystical preparations are but a part of making ready for the battle,' said Rann. 'I must see to our men and arms.'

Synalon waved a hand languidly. As usual no rings adorned her fingers. Any ring she might wear interfered with the dangerous spells she cast so casually.

'Your burden yourself overmuch, cousin. Is our victory over the wretched groundlings not assured?'

'By no means, Majesty.' The crowd gasped. They expected Synalon's face to distort in anger, for her slim hands to clap furiously to summon guards to haul Rann off to torture and death for his defeatism. Instead, she rested her chin on one hand and regarded him calmly. Above her shoulders the ravens carefully preened blood from their wings.

'And why not?'

'Kara-Est is the most powerful of all the Quincunx cities. They have their aerial defenses and they know quite well we mean to take them on our next transit. Further, our ground forces are still en route back from the north. We'll have to rely almost totally on our bird riders.' He took a deep breath. 'I think we shall win, O Queen. But assuming that our victory is assured can only weaken us.'

Synalon gave him a mocking smile.

'Our cousin instructs us with his customary wisdom,' she said. 'Very well, Prince. You have our permission to return to your chores.'

He bobbed his head and knelt again.

'Oh, and how fares the loyal young apprentice mage Maguerr, through whom the Dark Ones acted to effect your rescue?'

'He does well, Majesty. He should be able to return to full service by the time the prow of the Sky City crosses the Cholon Hills outside of Kara-Est.'

'You are a man indeed, Prince Rann, to inspire such loyalty in your followers', Synalon said with a razor-edged smile. Rann colored furiously. Synalon alone could torment him with that knowledge with impunity. He rose and stalked off, the heel taps of his boots clacking angrily on the marble flagging.

'Oh, and one more thing, cousin.' Synalon's voice halted him just before the great double doors of graven green jade. 'Might you be able to spare a flight or so of your most stalwart Sky Guards for the evening? They need not bring their mounts. They, ah, shall have a mount supplied them.' She licked her lips which gleamed as red as fresh blood in the light of torches and captive salamanders. 'I feel the need of some slight stimulation.'

Rann did not turn, but the whole hall marked how his neck went red. His own favored diversions notwithstanding, he was a notorious prude and disapproved vigorously of his cousin's extravagant public displays of her sexual prowess and libido. He nodded jerkily and went out. The great doors swung closed with a resounding thump.

Flushed with happy anticipation, Synalon settled back on the crystal of her throne and called for more wine. Servitors hastened to her bidding.

The tall, red-faced Councillor turned to his companion. The smaller man's hands were still shaking with reaction and dread.

'Well, here's a curiosity, Tromym,' said High Councillor Uriath, smoothing the fringes of his white beard. 'I never would have thought I'd be *glad* to see that devil Rann.'

Tromym did not answer. Instead he lifted his goblet to his lips for a hasty gulp. Though he used both hands, a torrent of the purple wine cascaded down the front of his blue robe.

Off in the dappled distance of the woods a bird sang. Moriana walked a cathedral-like path beneath mighty trees, seeking some rest for her weary, tortured soul.

In every direction she looked grew trees. Most were yellow tai but every now and then the graceful tai stood aside for a tree giant, a shunnak with red bark shining on boles twenty feet thick, lifting blue-green clad boughs five hundred feet off the forest floor.

It was a scene of primeval beauty. Birds with long, brightly hued tails flew between the trees, small animals scurried about on missions known only to themselves. In the midst of all this tranquility walked Moriana, troubled and upset.

Ziore rode in her jug at Moriana's hip, doing her best to caress the worries from Moriana with comforting thoughts and her special gift of empathy. It should have been impossible for Moriana to remain wrapped in gloom, tormented by thoughts of past and future.

But a few miles to the northeast, an invisible presence beyond the leafy treetops, the Mystic Mountains loomed like eidolons, ancient, enigmatic, evil. Within them slumbered Thendrun like some dormant beast, the sole remaining stronghold of the Fallen Ones. Their nearness banished peace from the fugitive princess.

'But you know full well you've no other choice,' the nun Ziore said. She spoke aloud, feeling that in her present mood Moriana needed sensory reaffirmation that she was not alone, though her mind was ever aware of the presence by her side. 'And what can the danger be? The Zr'gsz will have dwindled over the centuries and most of their magic is no doubt long forgotten. They could prove no great menace to the Realm, even if they harbored such designs — which I'm sure they no longer do.'

'The Zr'gsz are long-lived but their memories are longer still.' Moriana's voice hardened. 'I'm betting they haven't lost much of their power. I will need redoubtable allies to seize the Sky City by force of arms.'

Ziore held still a moment, mulling this.

'You are right. But still, you mustn't worry. It's been ten thousand years since the War of Powers and eight thousand since your ancestors drove the lizard folk from the City. Surely after all that time they cannot nurse futile hopes of regaining their power? Their time is passed. If they are so long-lived, surely they are wise enough to acknowledge that?'

Moriana shrugged. 'It's what I'm gambling on.'

'And you are thinking of your other recent gambles that haven't worked,' said Ziore.

'I . . . yes, you're right. Darl is no better, even after he and I went into that small village to purchase new clothing.'

'He accompanied you. That is a sign of some progress,' pointed out the genie. 'It is the first indication of interest in the world around him since his defeat.'

'Our defeat.' The words fell like bitter droplets from the princess's tongue. 'And he showed only passing interest in these.' She looked down at the new clothing. Moriana had selected a wardrobe of the kind she had come to fancy in her own years of faring through the Realm: rugged tunics that laced up the front with leather thongs, canvas breeches with dog leather linings sewn inside the thighs to cushion the chafing of long hours in the saddle. The colors were russet, muted orange, burnt umber, the earth tones she favored, that set off her golden hair and vivid green eyes so well.

'Darl still thinks of you as his fairy princess,' pointed out Ziore. 'Seeing you clad thusly might have shattered his illusions.'

'Damn him!' flared Moriana. 'I'm not a toy to be put on display. I'm a woman and a princess. Not a fairy princess but one with the need to regain my City. How dare he pretend I'm anything but what I am?'

'Not all have your drive, Moriana,' quietly pointed out Ziore. The genie paused. Moriana felt fleeting touches over the surface of her brain, feathery tickles, light samplings. 'And Darl reads your thoughts as surely as I. He realizes the burden you carry over Fost Longstrider.'

'I killed the man I loved. And all for this.' Her fingers went to the black and white Amulet hung around her neck: the Amulet of Living Flame, which legend said would bring the dead back to life. For the promise of eternal life she'd killed Fost, driven her knife firmly into his heart, as they fought for possession of it.

'Your reasons were noble. The Amulet will allow you to best Synalon. Without it, your powers can never be used. She knows so much more of the black arts than you. Even if she slays you, with that in your possession you will live on and succeed.'

54

'Darl reads more than guilty knowledge,' Moriana said bitterly. 'He knows I can never love another man as I loved Fost. Not even Darl Rhadaman.'

'You are wise, my child. What you say is true. Darl's depression is great because of the loss. He hoped to win your favor with victory. He knows no other way of gaining your heart. His most romantic gestures and words carom off the shell you've built around your heart.'

'I loved Fost,' she said simply, a tear welling at the corner of her eye. She brushed it away, then rubbed the wetness from her finger onto the black and white Amulet. Even as her fingers touched it, the colors swirled in slow motion, black battling white for supremacy.

'You can love Darl − if you try,' said Ziore.

'I have my duty to the Sky City before me. After Synalon is defeated and I've regained the throne, *then* will be the time to consider affairs of the heart. Darl's withdrawal, painful as it is to me, isn't the worst of my problems.'

Though she had not spoken of it again since the evening of the battle, word had filtered through her small party that she intended journeying to Thendrun to ally with its denizens. That word was not well received. Her fellow refugees had begun slipping away, in ones and twos, walking away from sentry duty in the midst of darkness or falling back on the march until turning off unobserved into the woods. Among those who stayed there was talk; Moriana heard − or thought she heard − terms such as 'witch' and 'traitor to her kind' hissed behind cupped hands around the campfires when they halted for the night.

'I don't understand.'

Moriana started at Ziore's words, though they rang softly in the quiet of the woods. When Moriana writhed in the grip of a mood like her present one, the nun's shade would read her thoughts carefully unless Moriana asked her not to. The princess had made no such request. But she had forgotten that her dark musings were shared by another.

'What don't you understand?' she asked stiffly.

'Why the terrific resentment among the others about your going to the Fallen Ones? I doubt more than a handful of humans have so much as seen one in the eighty centuries since Riomar Shai-Gallri seized the Sky City. Why the intensity of feeling?'

Moriana stopped, allowed the forest stillness to settle about her for a dozen heartbeats before answering.

'Have you heard of the Watchers?' she asked.

'Well . . . yes,' answered Ziore hesitantly. 'My knowledge is second-hand through what I've overheard from others.'

'Then your education contains gaps,' said Moriana, grateful for the chance to speak of things other than her feelings for Darl and Fost. 'When Felarod and his Hundred drew forth the wrath of the World Spirit and broke the might of the Zr'gsz, they imprisoned the demon Istu sent by the Dark Ones to aid the Hissers in the foundations of the Sky City. This was only one of the deeds he did before the World Spirit departed. Some of the lava that has flowed in centuries past from the Throat of the Old Ones – Omizantrim – is a stuff called skystone. Worked properly with spells known to Zr'gsz adepts, the skystone floats on air like chaff. The City itself is built on a huge raft of it. The much smaller war rafts the Hissers rode into battle were a source of their strength as important as Istu himself. So Felarod summoned up a creature from the belly of the earth called Ullapag, whose cry, though inaudible to humans, is death to the Zr'gsz. And to aid the Ullapag and insure that the Hissers should no longer have access to their skystone, Felarod set a band of heroes, men and women strong and keen-sighted and skilled with bow and spear, to watch over the skystone flows until the Fallen Ones should be no more. These are the Watchers of legend.

'After ten millennia,' Moriana added, 'the descendants of the original Watchers remain on their lonely vigil at the foot of Omizantrim. Can you imagine the dedication that implies?'

'Yes, it disturbs me greatly. For three hundred generations to circumscribe their lives willingly to keep an ancient faith – it makes my own deprivation trivial, doesn't it?'

Moriana felt Ziore's bitterness at her own life. She could sense the troubling of her friend's thoughts and wondered if some of Ziore's gift had worn off on her. Being a nun in life following Erimenes's self-denying teachings and missing the rich realms of human experience had stunted her in many ways.

'Each person's problems, no matter how trivial, are enough and more for that person,' said Moriana, smiling wanly at being able to quote one of the genie's aphorisms back at her.

'But it's more than just the Watchers,' the princess went on. 'I take it you're not acquainted with children's fairy tales.'

56

'No,' Ziore replied. 'I was sent to convent at an early age. We had no time for such mundane trivia.' Her words rang as harshly as any Moriana had heard her speak.

'The favorite of them, even now, concerns the bravery and dedication of the Watchers in standing off attempts by the Hissers to regain their precious skystone mine. Whether there's any truth in them, I don't know. And when children cry or balk at eating their greens, what do mothers tell them? "The Vridzish will get you if you don't behave!"'

'So the Hissers are the legendary embodiment of evil to the people of the Realm.'

'And the Watchers the embodiment of heroic dedication,' said Moriana.

'Now I see why your men fear your destination – and why you do, as well.'

Moriana bit her lip. 'And have I reason to fear my course of action?'

'Have you any other?' came the sharp reply. 'I –'

The nun's voice cut off, to resume in Moriana's mind: *Someone comes*.

The princess went into a fighting crouch, hands on hilt of sword and dagger. She heard whistling, a jaunty carefree tune, and the crunching of leaves under boots.

'Well met, Lord Stormcloud,' she said as the tall blond youth strode into view.

He smiled, as radiant as the sun shining above.

'You requested that I not sneak up on you again,' he said. 'I saw fit to follow your advice.'

Straightening, Moriana took hands from weapons and smiled.

'I . . . I wanted to tell you, Iatic, that I am most grateful for the assistance you've given me. It wouldn't have been possible to come this far.'

He stood arm's length from her, smiling.

'Then perhaps the time has come for you to tender payment,' he said, lunging as he spoke.

Caught off balance, Moriana fell back against the trunk of a tree. Strong fingers clawled at her belt. She felt the brass catch give, felt her swordbelt torn away bodily and flung into the brush. Her fingers struck at his eyes. Laughing, he easily caught her wrists and threw her down.

Moriana felt a pulse of energy surge from Ziore. The spirit was trying to quell the mercenary's passion. Iatic's face purpled in fury. He savagely kicked the satchel, parting the strap and sending Ziore's jug spinning after Moriana's swordbelt. Moriana heard the jug strike a tree with crushing force. She screamed.

The air exploded from her lungs as the mercenary flung himself atop her. Moriana wasted no time demanding what he was doing; she felt the hardness of him prodding into her thigh as his fingers tore at the fastening on her breeches. She brought a knee up. He twisted his hips expertly to block and grinned at her. The Amulet, torn free of her bodice, shone like obsidian.

'I've wanted this for so long,' he panted. 'Watching you flash your breasts and thighs in that flimsy gown . . . ah! You've wanted what I can offer you. There we go! Now, down with your trousers and in – you'll be begging for more, Bright Princess, by the time I'm done!'

He held both wrists pinioned in one powerful hand while the other tore open her breeches. His body had the power of a seasoned warrior. But so did hers, and she was coming out of the numbness of shock she'd first felt at his attack.

'No, no, you've got no right to hold back.' He groaned in her ear like an avid lover, but in words no lover would utter. 'You've made your pact with blackness, you've sold your soul. Now collect some of the wages!'

He thrust. Snarling like a war dog, she tore her hands free. His smile widened sardonically as she grabbed his throat. Then, as her thumbs began inexorably to press his head back, the smile disintegrated and a look of disbelief came into his eyes.

Stormcloud clutched at her wrists with both hands. Sweat poured down his face. Her eyes blazing with insane rage, Moriana gathered her strength and heaved.

When armed men ran up from the camp, led by Darl looking fully his old self with broadsword bared in his hand, they found her huddled half-naked against the slick trunk of a shunnak, cradling Ziore's jug in her lap. The Amulet, now the purest white, hung quiescent between bare breasts. The genie hovered by her side. A few feet away Iatic Stormcloud lay sprawled, as limp as a child's ragdoll, eyes touched with the lifeless cast of porcelain.

His neck was broken.

CHAPTER FIVE

'And what forecasts have you for me?' Duke Morn, ruler of Kara-Est, slumped on his throne, speaking into his beard and not looking at the stubby figure who stood before him. 'Are we ready to meet the onslaught of ah, the, ah, Sky City?'

Rising from her knees, Parel Tonsho, Chief Deputy of Kara-Est, wrinkled her nose in distaste. The wind was in from the north, blowing directly across the great fen called the Mire. Not even the Ducal Palace in the Hills of Cholon overlooking the city was exempt from the sour reek of decaying swamp. Heightened by unseasonable heat, the smell overpowered even the pomades carried by the deputy's half-dozen armed and painted retainers. One of the youths caught her expression and tittered, thinking it directed at the duke's vagueness. She shot him a glance that froze him to silence.

'As ready as we shall ever be to trade with them on the battlefield,' she said, 'unless our *brave* partners in Wirix see fit to send us some of their mages to help ward off the spells of that damned bitch-slut, Synalon.'

Bony fingers stroked gray-shot beard.

'Oh, but our, our trading friends the Wirixers, ah, they're cautious,' he murmured as if to himself. 'They wish us to deal with the Sky City, bleed them penniless, that they do, and at the same time they marshal strength in case we fail in the exchange. Clever . . . clever business, indeed.'

Tonsho moistened thin lips. She gave the boy who had snickered a meaningful glare. Though for the most part Duke Morn was the distracted, feckless dodderer he appeared, sometimes he gave evidence that the shrewd statesman he once had been had not wholly died with his wife and only son two years ago. The boy pouted and stroked a golden bangle depending from one ear. Tonsho made a mental note to get rid of him at the first opportunity. He was obdurately stupid, and she could not abide that, even in her kept pretty-boys.

In the drafty throne room atop the Palace's highest tower they made a curious contrast, the duke and the commoner who actually ruled the dukedom. Morn's once mighty frame had shrunk to a spindly, emaciated shadow of its former self. His leonine head, once long and fierce, was parchment-skinned and hollow at the temples. Despite the sticky noonday heat unrelieved by the rank breeze crawling through open windows, he wore a heavy robe of yellow velvet trimmed with the fur of the rare *gazinga* of the Dyla Wilderlands. He huddled within its confines as though afflicted with chill. Whether heat or senility caused it, Morn virtually ignored Tonsho and idly rustled fingers among the maps and charts that covered the tables set by the curving stone wall to his side.

She stood before him, as stubby and ugly as a tree trunk but equally unyielding. Her slit-eyed face resembled that of a pit-bred fighting dog, her eyes watery gray and hair an indeterminate color suggestive of mice. Her lumpy body was decked out in an outrageous robe of scarlet and electric blue, and her shoes were yellow, curling upward at the toes. Tonsho was the most senior and powerful member of the Chamber of Deputies which administered the wealthy port of Kara-Est. She had clawed her way to that lofty position from the lowest gutter of the city's slums.

'The artillerists manning our roof engines can hit an osprey on the wing,' she told him. 'And our ludintip can hoist aloft gondolas filled with archers. For the first time in generations we will carry the war to the enemy in his own element. Most of Synalon's ground forces are still straggling back from the north, and her bird riders are diminished by two hard-fought battles in the last several weeks. Only the dog cavalry the City held in reserve in Bilsinx, the greater part of which already has marched on us according to our spies, is reasonably fresh. And they can be discounted.'

The huge, narrow head slowly moved up and down in a nod. Tonsho had no idea whether he comprehended her words or not. His lucid moments were both infrequent and unpredictable.

'On the debit side: their bird riders, particularly the Sky Guard, are consummately skillful and have the morale to absorb huge losses without breaking. We will have to inflict frightful slaughter on them to turn them back. And as they have made all too clear in recent days, they are more than adept at wreaking slaughter themselves. They have Synalon, who has announced to all the world that the Dark Ones have given her Their favor, and traded her increased powers. This may be true. Lastly, they have Rann. I credit him a greater advantage to them than the favor of the Dark Ones, or of the Three and Twenty Wise Ones of Agift into the bargain.' She smiled grimly at the thought of such an unlikely alliance.

'Well . . .' Duke Morn stuttered at a loss for words. 'Do what you can. Yes. Let this be your watchword: do what you can.'

'We will,' the deputy rasped. A cold knot gathered in her belly at the prospect of battle, but she held her mind rigidly from her fear. 'We may not win, Your Grace. But we will cost the City in the Sky dearly in this armed negotiation. Perhaps enough to render moot their dreams of conquest.'

She made abasement and prepared to leave.

'Yes,' the duke said slowly. 'I know what my part must be. You may leave now, Chief Deputy Tonsho. I will consult the weather. Meteorological data will be of vital importance in the coming conflict. Vital.'

She hid her grimace with another inclination of her head. He had been a strong leader, wiser than many and perhaps less destructive of his subjects than most strong rulers. Then a freak storm had blasted up the sheltered Gulf of Veluz overturning the tiny skiff in which his adored wife and son were taking a pleasurable day's sailing. For a week the duke and his navy searched the waters of the Gulf. The bodies of his wife and sole heir were discovered washed against the first lock of the Dyla Canal. The duke had seemed to shrivel on beholding them.

Since that tragedy he had been obsessed with the study of weather. He had his throne room transferred up to his pinnacle, inconveniently far up flights of stairs for Tonsho's short legs, and the charts and brass meteorological instruments, telescopes and barometers and astrolabes cluttering the cramped chamber were the only things in life that held any interest for him. Tonsho had ambiguous feelings about his fixation. It was sad to see a basically able man so reduced, but at the same time his infirmity cleared her way to power in the richest city of the Realm. And when all was said, she knew she was a more capable ruler than any highborn.

'I'm sure your observations will be of great value,' she said, and left. Her boys trooped obediently behind her, trailing a hint of perfume and the tinkling of weapons harness and gilt finery.

Fost laughed at the wind in his face and followed Jennas at a gallop down the long, sloping plain. Evening came down blue and cool all around, and the vast fields of flowers closed petals of white and yellow and crimson against the coming dark. It felt good to be alive, better perhaps than at any time since the courier had died and been reborn in Athalau.

'Come on!' Jennas shouted back at him. 'Grutz will be as sluggish as a fattened boar if he doesn't exercise. Make him work!'

Fost thumped his heels against the bear's furry barrel of a body. Grutz shot him a reproachful look over one churning red shoulder and dutifully lengthened his stride.

Riding the enormous steppes bear was like riding an avalance in full slide. Fost no longer felt the horrible queazy gut-clutching of motion sickness, nor did the constant back-and-forth whipping of his body threaten to part him, head from neck. He had never been much of a rider, but months in the saddle of the unorthodox southern mount had given him far more skill than he would acknowledge to himself. And it had toned him up as well. There hadn't been much exercise in simply riding the runners of his wheeled dog sled, as he had for most of his career as courier on the highroads of the Realm. Wenching and fighting had kept him more trim than most men then. Now he was conscious of a strength in neck, loins and belly he'd never before known.

Jennas had been riding Chubchuk, her own brown war bear, since both were cubs, as she put it. Pound for pound – and she outweighed the courier by a healthy margin – she was stronger than Fost, or any man he'd known. It wasn't plumpness; the feminine layer of subcutaneous fat, helpful insulation against the vicious chill of antarctic winter, merely softened the outlines of her powerful muscles, making her appear sleek and as strong as some great aquatic creature. Her greatest strength resided in her thighs and solid stomach, thanks to a lifetime of riding. The first time her muscles had clenched in orgasm around him, Fost's eyes had nearly popped out of his head. Since then many were the times when in the heat of passion she'd clamped him so fervently with her legs that he literally cried for mercy.

Tall green grass whipped at his legs. He was a handsome man, another thing he would not admit to himself. His face was more rugged than his years accounted for, showing signs of having been well-buffeted about and occasionally hacked open. His shoulders were broad within a hauberk of mail, his carriage erect, black hair blown back wild and free. When angered Fost looked like death on the prowl, but there were laughter lines prominent about his mouth and ice-gray eyes. He made a splendid barbaric pair with Jennas.

She grinned and waved as Grutz puffed up alongside Chubchuk. Her own chain mail shirt was unlaced down the front displaying a single swatch of canvas tied about her ribcage to keep her large breasts from bouncing uncomfortably.

Fost looked at her and thought how beautiful she was. He had considered her merely handsome before, and wondered now at his former blindness.

But she's not Moriana, came the pursuing thought. Fost knew deep down that no one could ever compare to his Sky City princess. No one, not even Jennas.

The light went out of his eyes and he let Grutz fall behind. He owed his life to the hetwoman of the Bear Clan. Wise and clever, an incomparable companion in bed and battle, she even laughed at his jokes. But Fost loved the golden-haired, green-eyed heiress to the Beryl Throne, she who had killed him to possess the gem both thought at the time to be the Amulet of Living Flame.

However, the gaudy bauble Moriana had taken from Athalau was not the Amulet but the Destiny Stone. This fey device had the power to alter the luck of its wearer, swinging between extremes of good and bad according to its own mysterious whim. The undistinguished pendant Fost had seized in his dying reflex had been the Amulet they both sought.

The Amulet exhausted the last of its power bringing Fost back to life.

Fost had to reach Moriana and tell her of her mistake. If she wore the Destiny Stone into battle with Synalon, thinking it made her invincible, she could perish. That thought formed a cold lump in the pit of the courier's belly. No matter what she'd done to him, he loved her.

He and Jennas rode north of the lava flows around Omizantrim, coming down off the Central Massif of the continent through the dark foothills of the Mystic Mountains. Following the Black River which flowed from the Mystics to meet with the Joreal at Port Zorn, they planned to take passage there through the Karhon Channel around the headlands of the Wirin River delta, and through the Dyla Canal to Kara-Est. It would be much quicker than faring overland as long as the army of the Sky City was interposed between them and the seaport.

They stopped on a high bluff overlooking the Black River. It was Jennas's turn to cook the evening meal. Fost, weighed down by his thoughts, went off by himself in search of his earlier lightness of heart.

Though he'd become an experienced rider, Fost still felt the day's jostling most poignantly in the kidneys. He wandered downstream through twilight touched with the scent of wildflowers and dead fish. He whistled as he searched for a likely spot out of sight of the encampment.

'I do so wish you would leave off that noisemaking,' Erimenes said sourly from his pouch. 'You can't carry a tune in a sling.'

Fost laughed. It was true enough. 'Whatever you say, old spirit,' he said, opening his breeches.

'If you did anything I said, you'd be much better for it,' Erimenes said loftily. 'For instance, right now you'd march back to camp and put what you've got in your hand to *much* more pleasurable use trying out certain variations I've designed especially for you and Jennas.'

Reflexively, Fost thumped the jug with his free hand. He resumed whistling.

'Ouch! You're a townsman, Fost. No country-born lad would ever urinate in a running river.'

That was true, too. Though he'd spent most of his adult life under the stars, he had been born a child of High Medurim's slums, and such he would remain. He shrugged.

And almost died.

Erimenes squawked a warning. Fost froze. When first he'd met the genie, Erimenes's inclination was to let Fost discover approaching danger as it jumped out at him. Erimenes declared this was in the interests of a rousing battle. He often derided the courier for his lack of adventurous spirit, his 'cowardice' in the face of overwhelming odds. The change in Erimenes's habits had come slowly after his brief return to Athalau. Fost didn't yet trust the ghost's reformation.

Water parted in a surge. Fost had a glimpse of toothed jaws opening wider than his own weight. He backed, frantically trying

64

to cut off the stream of urine. A four-foot-long beak slammed shut inches from his stubbornly spraying wand.

'Great Ultimate!' he cried, still scrambling for footing. 'What is that?'

'Something you're best away from,' advised Erimenes. 'Far away from. It appears most hungry. I certainly don't cherish the idea of my jug ending up in that maw.'

Fost sat down clumsily in his attempt to escape. A black head reared above him. Eyes like slits of red fire hungrily appraised him. Fost beheld his attacker as a bird like a black cormorant, but gigantic beyond imagining. Its neck reared a dozen feet from a body of unguessable size. Its head and pointed beak protruded eight feet. Fost had a few more brief seconds to see that the dripping monster was dark above and light below, and then it struck.

The beak drove down with lightning speed. Fost rolled desperately. The lancelike beak buried itself three feet deep in the soft earth where he had lain an instant before. Then the courier was up and running, fumbling to stuff himself back in his trousers and bawling at the top of his voice.

'Down!'

This time Fost knew better than to doubt Erimenes. He dived forward, gasping at an impact that drew a searing line of pain along his back.

Tucking his shoulder, he rolled. As he twisted, he drew sword from scabbard. The beak cracked with a sound like the gates of Hell closing. Dying sunlight glinted from teeth like spikes. The bird voiced a triumphant, whistling scream. The awful jaws descended.

A furred, dark form struck them like a bolt shot from a catapult. The monster went down with Grutz snapping and clawing at its head. In an instant the bird had its webbed talons beneath an oily body and snaked its neck out of the bear's embrace. The head cocked itself back preparing for another strike, eyes burning with unnatural hatred.

Grutz scrambled nimbly away from a vengeful thrust of the beak. Though they weighed a ton each, the bears were as agile as dancers on their feet. But as immense as Grutz was, he was dwarfed by the nightmare black birdshape that stood over him poised to kill this new interloper.

Roaring, Chubchuk lumbered down the slope to aid his companion. The hellbird turned its head; instantly Grutz darted in and

65

swiped it on the side of the head. The head reared, shrilling agony. Streaming black ichor dripped from parallel slashes below a burning eye.

Fost regained his feet, breathing heavily, sword held double-handed with one hand gripping the outside of its silver basket. He heard Jennas's angry cry as she charged into battle waving her greatsword.

The head darted at Fost. He leaped away, barely keeping his footing on the wet grass. His hauberk swung freely at his sides, its fabric of interlocked iron rings rent as easily as paper by the deadly beak. He felt wetness drench his back and knew it was his blood.

'Fost!' cried Jennas. 'Are you still in one piece?'

'Mostly,' he gasped, feeling the first waves of pain from his wound. 'Watch yourself. This thing's strike range is phenomenal.' Even as he spoke, the creature unleashed itself like a steel spring straight for the courier.

The monster's strike at Fost gave the bears a chance to close in on it, ripping and biting and snarling up a storm. The monster retreated toward the bank in an ungainly waddle. But it was not defeated. Its head moved with blinding speed. Chubchuk bawled as the beakpoint pierced his shoulder.

Grutz grabbed a scaly leg and bit. The bird collapsed, an unearthly keening echoing out over the rush of the Black River. It was up again on one leg in an eyeblink, holding its wounded leg to its belly, but Grutz's sally had given Chubchuk a chance to scurry to safety. The bears worked well as a team, but Fost realized that even those ponderous, furry engines of destruction were outmatched by this avian menace.

Fost saw Jennas circling wide behind the monster, coming up on its blind side. He knew then what he had to do. Ignoring Erimenes's shrill cheering, interspersed with demands to be freed in order to get a better view, he took the stoutest grip he could on the sword and sucked in a huge breath.

The flaming gaze fixed on him. Strength left him in a flash. His soul was being sucked out through his eyes, drawn out to fall into a void, into fiery scarlet suns.

'You limp-peckered, frog-witted son of a catamite!' shrieked Erimenes in tones ill-suited to the Realm's most distinguished dead philosopher. '*Move!*'

Fost moved.

'Yaah!' he screamed, soul snapping back into his body in a blaze of fury. 'Come and get me, buzzard!'

He had fully intended to draw the hellbird into a strike at him, dodging aside at the last moment while Jennas attacked from the opposite side. But instead of leaping out of the way, he stood his ground as the needle-sharp point of the monster's beak arrowed at his chest. Time slowed as his whole being focused on the black blade of the bird's beak. When it was an arm's reach away, he swung his sword. Power flooded him now, adrenaline-backed power. His lips stretched back in a maniacal grin. The beast made a horrid flutelike sound of surprise and agony as Fost's sword smashed its beak in two.

The head jerked back. Air hissed like a venting fumarole in the night as Jennas chopped half through the long, snaky neck with a slash of her greatsword.

Stinking black fluid spattered over Fost. The shattered beak opened and closed in mute agony as the head flopped at random on the half-severed neck. The monster waddled back two steps and slid over the river bank. Fost ran forward to see it come to rest partly in the water. It kicked twice, trying futilely to make one last attack. Then the light went from its eyes and it lay still.

Fost turned and threw up.

After a time he felt Jennas's touch on his shoulder.

'Are you hurt?'

He felt as if the left side of his back had been splashed with liquid fire.

'Not seriously.' He gratefully accepted a sip of water from her canteen, rinsed the warm water around his mouth and spat.

'A new War of Powers is in the offing. My divinations are being proven correct,' Jennas said solemnly. 'Evil creatures go abroad on the planet again, as the Dark Ones make plans to reclaim their dominion.'

The world spun around Fost.

'No, no, no,' he repeated over and over in stubborn denial. He wouldn't live in a world where the gods took active part in the affairs of men and where powers beyond comprehension played and lost human beings – and monsters – like pawns.

'I've heard of such giant birds before,' he managed to choke out as bile rose in his throat.

'Nonsense.' The cap of Erimenes's jug had slipped off in the fracas. The genie's column of mist wavered by Fost's side. The shade eyed him disdainfully. 'The natural helldiver is appropriately named. They were too common in my day, though I gather they've died off.' He gestured at the Black River, murmuring unseen in the growing darkness. 'But that bird is strictly a salt water creature. Might I point out that the Black River is fresh this far up from the ocean?'

Still Fost shook his head, too tired for words, mutely denying that which he could not bear. With surprising gentleness Jennas took his hand and helped him rise.

Grutz and Chubchuk hunched like fat gargoyles at the edge of the bank. Fost heard an odd, low moaning, an uneasy despairing sound that he took first for a roaring within his head and then for the wind in the reeds. But as his head cleared he realized it came from the bears. The long hairs on their necks and shoulders stood up like spiked harnesses and their wicked yellow teeth were bared toward the water.

Clutching Jennas's shoulder, Fost staggered to the bank's edge and looked down at . . . nothing.

'See?' Jennas said. 'It's gone.'

Fost pulled away.

'That doesn't mean anything. It slid into the water and was carried away by the current. The river's swift here.'

'No, look at the grass, Longstrider. The monster fell flat. The grass is crushed in all directions. Had it slipped into the water the grass would lie in that direction.'

The courier squinted. The lesser moon peeked up from the horizon, Omizantrim piercing its side like a dagger. Its rosy light showed black smears on the grass with steam rising in wisps from it. As Jennas said, the grass had been mashed down straight.

His knees gave way beneath him.

'Gods!' he cried.

'Yes.' Jennas was as grim as an executioner. 'The gods. And we are bound to fight their battles for them.'

CHAPTER SIX

The path into the Mystic Mountains was little more than a haunting memory. When the low, humped foothills had started to grow into jagged mountains the party had hesitated for a moment among the stunted ugly bushes of the ravine where the trail had petered out. Moriana stared up into the heights while the others rested their dogs and sweated.

Finally she said, 'This way,' and rode on. The party that followed her was three less than that which had stopped.

So it had gone. Half the remaining contingent had deserted after the death of Iatic Stormcloud. Though what had happened was apparent enough to all, and though Darl argued in Moriana's favor with all his old skill and verve, more than twenty knights and footmen had turned their mounts to the northwest and ridden back for the River Marchant and the City States of the Empire that lay beyond. This journey lay under far too many ill omens for even the strong of heart.

Another factor entering into the dwindling of Moriana's force was the cultural background of the men. These were northern men unused to women who could slay warriors as strong as the young mercenary captain with their bare hands. By her own testimony Moriana was a sorceress. Stormcloud's death convinced a number of her followers she was a witch.

Others had lost battles with conscience or courage as they neared the ramparts of the Mystic Mountains, low and uninviting. Now besides herself and Darl, who remained in a state of watchful quiet that was less alarming than his earlier detachment, Moriana's retinue consisted of five dog riders and eight footmen. All left in her band now, for reasons of their own, were not afraid to penetrate the citadel of mankind's ancient enemy.

She questioned none of them as to their motives. The princess wasn't sure she wanted to know why they chose to accompany her. All her attention had to be directed forward – and up, up into the Mystic Mountains.

The path mounted quickly along crooked switchbacks up almost sheer granite faces, straightening out now and again to follow the spine of razor-thin ridge.

'The drop – it must be five hundred feet,' came a fearful voice from behind. Moriana didn't turn to see who spoke.

'No, not five hundred,' came still another voice. 'By the gods, it has to be closer to a thousand.' The second speaker laughed boisterously, an action not shared by the others in the party.

For Moriana, a mere thousand-foot drop was like home. In the Sky City she often peered out from the forward prow down at the terrain as it slowly slid beneath her. No one in the City in the Sky harbored any fear of heights, not when their everyday existence depended on separation of City and ground of at least a thousand feet. Her training aboard the war eagles had accustomed her to much loftier vantage points with even less substantial footing than that enjoyed by the dog she rode.

'Your men fear,' came Ziore's quiet voice from the pouch at Moriana's side. 'Is there nothing you can do to calm them?'

'You are the emphatic one,' pointed out the blonde-haired princess.

'I have tried. It is a wearying job. The fears of several of the men are acute.'

'Those from the forest of Nevrym?' hazarded Moriana.

'Yes. They are more accustomed to the closeness of their forests. The precipitous drops of these mountains work against their courage.'

'With luck, we won't have much longer on the trail.' Her fingers lightly touched the hidden black and white stone of the Amulet around her neck.

'Darl bears up well,' added Ziore, almost as an afterthought. 'He returns to his former self.'

'With a little help from your powers?' asked Moriana.

'With very little help from my powers,' corrected the genie. 'He heals himself. It is for the best.'

Moriana fell silent then, not wanting to speak further, even with Ziore. She no longer knew what was for the best. All she knew was

70

what she had to do. Right, wrong, it made no difference. It was what she had to do.

She fell into the slight rolling motion of the dog between her legs as the creature struggled to climb ever higher into the mountains.

The sharp igneous rock of the mountains cruelly punished the pads of the dogs' feet, causing them to become slippery with blood. On trails often no wider than a strong man's shoulders such poor footing could be fatal. Knowing something of the geology of the Mystic Mountains, Moriana had prepared for this.

'Halt!' cried Moriana after another hour of upward struggle. 'Rest a while in the clearing beyond.' She pointed ahead to what amounted to little more than a widening in the narrow trail. But the area proved a narrow canyon leading back into a sparse stand of trees. A small spring spurted from rocks and provided a much needed diversion from the sight of nothing but hard volcanic rocks.

'My Princess,' said Darl, moving to her side. 'Should we put on the leather boots now? Our dogs are beginning to suffer.'

'Aye, pull them out and see to it, Darl,' she said, pleased that the man had taken the initiative to approach her on the subject.

'And,' spoke up Ziore, 'you might boil some of the *olorum* root found in the crevices yonder and apply the resulting sediment to the dogs' feet before putting on the boots. It will soothe and heal their torn pads.'

'The *olorum* root?' asked Moriana. 'One I am unfamiliar with. Thank you, Ziore. It shall be done.' Darl bowed and silently turned to see to it. More and more he seemed his old self. Moriana hoped the change went deeper than his visible actions. It pained her greatly seeing the man suffer so – and all for her.

Several men brewed tea and others tried to ease their nerves with stinging draughts of Grassland brandy. Moriana accepted a cup of steaming tea – a pleasantly bracing Samazant strain, not the resinous amasinj of the steppes – and allowed a grinning Nevrym forester to lace it with colorless liqueur. She sat on a rock and stared back the way they'd come. The mountains fell away in toothlike peaks of gradually diminishing size, becoming foothills, spreading away to the south and west into an open plain. To her right yellow prairie gave way in the distance to the brown and pale green patchwork of cultivation; at the edge of vision the black line of the forests that had sheltered them for the vital first days of their flight swam in heat haze.

Ahead of the princess rose Omizantrim straight and stark from the plain. As always in the last weeks, a plume of smoke grew from its maw, steely gray today. By a fluke of the weather – or something more, a possibility Moriana studiously avoided thinking about – the wind blew from the Throat of the Old Ones straight into the Mystic Mountains. They had been tasting ash on their tongues all morning, and some of the dogs sported reddened, running eyes from it.

To her left, away and southward, the scrubby short-grass plain was abruptly interrupted as the land dropped a thousand feet to the Highgrass Broad below. Far-off smoke spires lifted above the tall grass prairie. The Grasslanders engaged again in their favorite sport, it seemed, which was massacring one another in internecine feuds that kept them honed for mercenary work.

Darl saw that the dogs watered and canteens were refilled from the tiny artesian spring, always making sure that no one got out of sight of the resting place without accompaniment. In more and more ways was Darl returning to his former self.

Moriana was relieved at the precaution. These mountains had a feel about them she disliked, and she knew it went far deeper than mere superstition engendered by cradle fables. The *leitmotif* of the Mystic Mountains was black: black soil, black-stemmed shrubs, black birds wheeling on spring thermals overhead. The anhak here grew black, more gnarled than in the woods below, and higher up grew black pine, whose very needles were as much black as green.

From the woods upslope came a screeching, a rising-falling unearthly sound. The dogs started and growled. One whined and tucked tail between its legs. The four archers with the party, three Nevrym foresters and an Imperial borderer from Samazant, looked to their bows. Moriana did likewise.

'I don't like this place.' Ziore's subdued voice came from the pouch. Neither she nor Moriana felt her misty presence would do other than aggravate the others' uneasiness over the princess's sorcery.

Moriana shrugged, finished her tea and stood.

'Nor do I,' she said simply. 'Let's ride.'

Hissing, the monster lurched from a hidden draw beside the trail. The lead dog reared and leaped back, almost unseating his rider. Moriana drew the nock of her arrow to her ear in a single fluid motion. Her dog growled deep in his chest. The others set up an excited barking as the vast green shape slid across their path.

It was a monstrous lizard, twenty feet long and more. A crest of yard-long spines, yellow and curving, grew down its back, diminishing in size as they approached the tail tip – still out of sight up the gulley. Moriana recognized it as a sprawler, its immense body suspended between its legs rather than supported atop them. It turned a bony triangular head toward them and regarded them dispassionately with a yellow eye the size of a man's head.

Horrific as the creature was, it wasn't the giant lizard that drew muffled exclamations from the travellers. Three iron-hard spines had been removed where the wattled neck flowed into its shoulders. Where they had been sat a rider.

Tall and manlike, the being stared at them from within an elaborate casque of green metal that shimmered in the sun. His helmet and breastplate revealed few details of head and body, except a pair of flat black eyes as emotionless as the lizard's yellow one. On the being's left arm rested a great spiked target shield, whose rough surface suggested construction from the scaled hide of a beast such as the alien warrior rode. The right hand's three black taloned fingers and thumb gripped a lance. The stranger wore no boots; the feet the startled humans saw sported three toes, also tipped with black claws. The largest was hooked in a ring serving as a stirrup.

With reptilian patience, rider and mount gazed upon the travellers. Behind her Moriana heard a low wail, rising into a shrill frightened yapping as a war dog panicked at the smell and nearness of the monstrous lizard – or perhaps of the being who rode it. Easing her bowstring forward, she clipped the arrow in the bowstaff with her thumb and snapped the fingers of her right hand.

'Enough,' she said, and the dog was still.

Her companions looked from the monsters blocking their path to the princess, sitting tall in her saddle, her golden hair thrown fearlessly back. A mixture of fear and confidence radiated from their gazes.

Before Moriana said another word, the lizard rider spoke.

'Men.' The word came out oddly protracted, with an almost tubercular wheeze. 'Expected. Come.' With that abbreviated greeting, the lizard man goaded his mount with one knee. The monster lifted its belly from the dirt, turned its head and began crawling laboriously upslope. Moriana paused for a few seconds, considered and then followed, her dog shouldering past the cringing mount of the knight who had taken the lead. She forced herself not to look back. Not a soul of her party might be following her, but at this of all moments she couldn't show fear.

Only the emotion-sampling Ziore knew the princess's true condition.

She concentrated on studying as much of their peculiar guide as possible from the rear. He wore a breastplate and back of the same unfamiliar metal as his casque, and a skirt set with strips of the same stuff. His arms and legs flashed bare. They were dark green, almost black, like the needles of the pines that grew to either side of the wash they followed up the mountainside. From where she sat, the musculature looked human enough and the skin flexed as supplely as any human's. Now and then sunlight broke on the curve of the high muscle in a metallic glint, and Moriana guessed the being – the *man*, though unlike any she'd ever seen before – was covered in fine scales. The only jarring overt sign of his alienness, aside from his complexion, was his feet and hands. Somehow, Moriana found those small divergencies more unsettling than more obvious ones would have been.

'What do you think?' she said softly, directing her question to Ziore.

She felt the genie's puzzlement before the mental answer came.

I cannot tell. I sense no emotion that I can read. Or none that makes sense. A dark inchoate churning, shot through with – yes, with longing. And a feeling of fulfillment.'

'Fulfillment? How so?'

Ziore paused long before answering.

I can tell no more, she thought. *The thoughts and passions of the creature are so . . . so other. The dog we ride is far more easily accessible than this Zr'gsz.*

Moriana slid a hand inside her tunic and pulled the Amulet up so that only she could see it. Its surface was evenly divided between black and white. She grimaced in both annoyance and relief. She saw only ambiguous omen in the odd stone.

Letting the Amulet drop back cool and hard between her breasts, she marvelled at the craft of the long dead Athalar savants who had created the Amulet. Not only did it return life to the bearer but in some way it monitored the state of her fortunes. It seemed a facility of limited application. After all, someone blessed with good luck or afflicted with bad as a general rule needed no portents to tell her so.

But not always. And so she had come to consult the gem in situations such as the present that might bode good or ill.

And like now her answer was no answer at all. Equilibrium of black and white mocked her.

They neared the top of the round-crowned mountain. The lizard hoisted itself over the top, tail sweeping from side to side in a swirl of black dust. Moriana leaned forward and goaded her balky dog after.

What she saw made it hard to breathe. A horn of black rock rose before her, separated from the round-topped peak by a chasm so deep its bottom was lost to view in mist and shadow. Hung about the peak was a wreath of what she first mistook for cloud. With a quickening of her pulse Moriana finally realized it was in fact gray smoke from Omizantrim.

Far beneath them she saw a thin line spanning the void. A bridge? She scanned the peak with her eyes but saw no sign of keep or tower, nothing raised by hands, human or otherwise.

The princess became aware of the black-jasper scrutiny of the lizard man. She peered at the smoky wreath, finally catching some anomaly within. Slowly she made out shapes – but nothing like the battlemented walls she had expected. Instead, clinging to the mountain's shoulder was a clump of dark geometric shapes, blocks and angles jutting in disorder that appeared almost organic. A single emerald green gleam shone through the smoke.

The *Zr'gsz* did not turn at the sound of the rest of the party scrabbling up onto the mountain top. Still gazing impassively at Moriana, he raised his lance and pointed it unerringly toward the outcrop on the distant peak.

'Thendrun,' he said.

'You are welcome, humans.' The words were spoken with flawless diction, vowels duly voiced, plosives and labials properly enunciated. 'You may take for granted that many years indeed have passed since those words were uttered here.' Khirshagk, Instrumentality of the People, raised his goblet and smiled.

Before the beaten gold rim of the cup covered his mouth Moriana glimpsed blue-white teeth. Like the rest of him, they were almost human, incisors to the front, flat and shovel-tipped, and blunt grinding molars in the back. But his eyeteeth protruded like sabers, with a hollow behind the upper pair into which the equally formidable lower ones could socket when he locked his jaws. Humans and Khirshagk's ancestors had shared a diet of both flesh and vegetation — but more of the former.

Otherwise, its owner was what Moriana could only honestly call handsome. His face, narrow and finely boned, sported high cheekbones and a lordly knife blade nose that she found oddly familiar. His skin was bluish green, darker still than the sentry who had guided them across the narrow bridge to the keep. His startling cat-green eyes shone with intelligence in the light of torches flickering in black wrought iron sconces on the walls of the chamber.

To her surprise the reptile man had hair, black and lustrous, combed back from his high, broad forehead. All in all, he had the appearance of a perfectly human male of more than average comeliness.

Except for the clawed hands and feet.

Moriana sipped bitter green wine. Behind her she heard a whisper. Her head snapped around. She saw nothing but the curved wall of the Instrumentality's audience chamber. The wall was unadorned, of a dark green crystal. There were no hangings for furtive listeners to hide behind, and her eyes made out no seams revealing secret doorways. Moriana puzzled over the source of the sound.

Nor do I know, came Ziore's soft thought mingling with her own.

She was conscious of cool eyes on her.

'I am grateful for your hospitality, Lord Khirshagk.'

He smiled.

'You pronounce my name quite well, Your Highness,' he said. 'But you need not name me lord. I am Instrumentality of the People; I am a tool in their hands. Not master over them.'

Moriana returned the smile, letting some of her skepticism show. Most human rulers claimed that it was the people who reigned, and that they themselves were merely servants of the popular will. The reality was inevitably the reverse. She doubted whether the Zr'gsz and humans differed much on that score.

Khirshagk had met them at the gate of Thendrun in a green-trimmed robe of what Moriana at first thought to be unadorned black. Now in the flickering light she made out faint hints of patterns and arcane figurations. To her eyes they appeared black on black; she assumed he saw the contrast more clearly.

'Lady Moriana,' he had said, 'and Lord Darl. In the name of the People, I bid you enter Thendrun.' After the inhuman accent of the lizard rider, the cultured perfection of Khirshagk's words was as startling as his knowledge of their names, and of the rest of the party as well, whom he named and greeted one by one as they filed between the great black gates into the keep.

All those who had started the ascent into the Mystic Mountains accompanied her into Thendrun. Perhaps her men felt that in this lair of ancient magic and evil the presence of a sorceress was more asset than liability. She didn't question this small bit of good luck on her part. It was about time things ran smoothly for her.

Lizard men whom Moriana took for servants, lighter of skin than the Instrumentality and the gate guards who stood by with two-handed maces and tall rectangular shields, stepped forward to lead the tired dogs to kennels. The beasts snapped at them so viciously that the riders had to lead their own mounts.

The retinue was led to a great table in an apartment carved out of one of the many jutting blocks of crystal that formed Thendrun. The block tilted at thirty degrees from the perpendicular, though the dining chamber was hewn out parallel to the ground. The princess's men cast dubious glances at the nothingness beyond the windows and surveyed the steaming joints served them on black jade platters with varying degrees of uneasiness; rumors abounded about the manner of meat the Hissers savored most. But it proved to be good, hearty dog, served with piles of boiled greens and potatoes – basic Northland fare. When Khirshagk led forth Moriana and Darl, smiling sardonically at the men's scrupulousness, they had fallen to with a will.

'Come, Lady Moriana, Lord Darl,' said the reptilian Instrumentality. 'Here is food that might be more pleasing to your palates.'

'What my men eat is good enough for me,' said Darl.

Moriana hastily cut in. Strange feelings worked inside her, feelings that had no easily definable name. Going along with Khirshagk seemed more important than sharing the table of her stalwart band.

'What Lord Darl says is true. But if you have prepared special dishes for us, we would be honored.' Moriana cast a look at Darl telling him not to argue. He bowed his head slightly in acquiescence.

'This way, then,' said Khirshagk, a tiny smile dancing on his all-too-human lips. He led them down a long corridor and into another part of the keep, a part obviously different from the spot where they left behind their human comrades.

More refined fare awaited the highborn pair: small birds baked

77

in leaves, served whole and smoking; brittle crusted black bread; mushrooms; and a bowl of savory sauce so spicy that Darl and Moriana clutched their throats and hastily swallowed wine at the first taste.

The Instrumentality's circular chamber was forty feet across and carved in the center of a pyramidlike extrusion of green stone. Moriana judged it to be one of the highest points within the keep. A waist-deep circular well was cut into the center of the room. It was here that Khirshagk had seen his guests served on low tables carved of black onyx, while they reclined gratefully on luxurious furs.

Lounging back, Moriana noticed that Khirshagk was drinking only wine. He hadn't joined them in their meal.

'Aren't you hungry, Instrumentality?' she asked warily. 'Surely, such a feast isn't commonplace in Thendrun?'

'It is specially prepared for you,' admitted Khirshagk with some amusement. 'But I have already supped. As you might know, the dining habits of we Zr'gsz differ from yours.'

By no means ignorant of the rumors concerning the Zr'gsz culinary preferences, Moriana forebore to comment.

She noted that Darl ate with an appetite he hadn't shown for some time. She caught his eye and smiled and was happy to see the corners of his mouth turn briefly upward in reply. She turned back to Khirshagk.

'Since you expected us,' she said, meeting Khirshagk's gaze and the challenge she read there, 'no doubt you already know our errand.'

Wine swirled as Khirshagk rotated the goblet in lazy circles.

'Our divinations told us much, and we deduced some, as well. We are not wholly unaware of what goes on in the world beyond the limits of our admittedly limited preserve.' He spoke without apparent bitterness.

'Then you know what we've come to ask.'

'We do.' The Instrumentality smiled. 'What remains to be seen is what you have to offer us.'

She nodded deliberately. Her wine cup was empty. She bent forward to set it on the table, aware that Khirshagk's eyes followed the sway of her breasts inside her tunic. She had loosened the lacing in front to allow herself to breathe; now she wondered if that had been politic.

A *Zr'gsz* woman, slightly built and pale of skin, came to refill her cup. Moriana wondered how she walked across the stony floor without her nails clicking. By human standards, the lizard woman was attractive. A bit blunt of feature, black-eyed and thin-lipped, her jet hair confined at the temples with a stone circlet carved to imitate plaited strands, she moved with inhuman cadence, limbs swishing softly inside a lead-colored smock.

'I assume that mere riches mean little to you,' said Moriana, retrieving her goblet.

'More than you might think. Not that we care for gold as such. Living stone means far more to us than rock killed by over-refinement, tainted by fire, sullied by movement from one hand to another. But we do have dealings with your kind, more than you probably expect. The yellow metal comes in quite handy at times.' He sipped. 'But your point is well taken. We wouldn't aid you for any wealth you could offer.'

'I haven't much to offer.' She grinned. 'Have your divinations told you that?' She shook her head; the wine made it feel light. 'No, what I have to offer you will value much more than a few gold klenors, I think.'

She leaned forward. This time his eyes held hers.

'When my . . . my ancestors drove yours from the City in the Sky, your folk were constrained to leave behind certain items of ritual significance.'

'At risk of being slaughtered should they have tarried to retrieve them, yes.' His manner was languid, but his eyes glittered with interest beneath half-lowered lids.

'If we win, you'll get them back.'

He drew a deep breath. Setting down his goblet with a clink, he leaned on furs and steepled his fingers before his face.

'Ah, the relics of my people,' he murmured. 'The Jade Mace, the Bell, the Scrolls of Eternity, the Idol of the Blessed Child.' Reverence rang in his words. 'Yes, we value them . . . much.'

'All are intact, awaiting only you to reclaim them.' She spoke before realizing that the 'Idol of the Blessed Child' referred to what her people called the Vicar of Istu, the ugly stone effigy that squatted in the Well of Winds. The Rite of Dark Assumption, banned since Julanna Etuul had seized the Beryl Throne almost five millennia before, made the idol live for a short period with the spirit of the Demon of the Dark Ones, whom Felarod had imprisoned in sorcerous sleep in the depths of the Sky City. Moriana's sister had revived the rite — with Moriana meant to be the Vicar's sacrifice and bride. Only the timely intervention of Fost Longstrider saved her life. Moriana's thoughts tumbled and swirled thinking of Fost and his valor in saving her from that vile fate.

Ziore's gentle touches on the perimeter of her mind soothed and steadied her.

Moriana licked her lips. Khirshagk watched impassively. How much had his divinations revealed? He had an aura of vast power; she almost tasted it.

'For such inducement we would aid even the get of those who stole the City from us,' said Khirshagk. 'But we can offer little aid if neither of us can reach the City, is it not so?'

'Yes.' She had to fight to say the next words. 'We will help you regain access to the skystone mines, as well.' Darl let out his breath in sharp exhalation, but said nothing.

'You know what that entails.'

'I do.' The words hurt her chest.

'And the Heart?' He curled his fingers down, save for forefingers tipped forward to aim at Moriana like a weapon. 'The Heart of the People, which damned Felarod cast into molten lava in the Throat of the Old Ones, where his monster could keep it ever beyond our grasp? You'll help us retrieve that as well?'

The Heart of the People!

She had thought the tale of the huge night-black diamond, which smoked like a heart plucked beating from a breast and laid on the sacrificial brazier, to be mere legend. Fear seized her. The Heart was reputedly one of the most powerful of all the Dark Ones' gifts to their chosen. Only Istu himself was a greater sign of favor of the Lords of the Elder Dark. She didn't wish to think what bringing the Heart back into the world might imply.

But she had to trust the lizard folk. Closing her eyes and forming a thought, she asked a single question of Ziore.

The nun responded.

I cannot read this being. His motives are hidden behind a veil of blackness.

The princess had to make the decision on her own; even knowing that decision would affect the entire continent — the world! — she had to make it.

'We will,' she whispered.

A soundless shout of exultation rang through Thendrun. Moriana started, looked around. Khirshagk showed no emotion. Darl sat holding his wine goblet negligently in one hand. He had obviously heard nothing. It had been her imagination and nothing more.

'Then let the bargain be sealed.' Khirshagk rose and offered his hand. It bore a ring on the index finger, a dark emerald set in graven obsidian. The gem was worked in likeness of something only barely discernible, a face or a mask. Moriana made herself take his hand with no display of the reluctance she felt.

He lifted her hand, kissed it. His lips were dry but surprisingly soft. He then turned and offered his taloned hand to Darl, who got to his feet and gripped forearms heartily with the Instrumentality. Moriana gulped her wine. The imprint of Khirshagk's kiss burned on the back of her right hand.

They passed the evening in inconsequential talk. Khirshagk spoke with animation and wit, and displayed a surprising knowledge of the affairs of the outside world. Moriana guessed that the Hissers had some intercourse with true men (this made her feel better somehow), though the latter took pains to keep this a secret.

Professing a love for human music, the Instrumentality prevailed on Darl to sing, which the Count-Duke then did in a lovely mellow baritone. It was the lay of a rootless wanderer who beholds a wondrous lady and consecrates his life to her. He cannot possess her, for she is pledged to another. In the end he gives his life for her and dies with a smile on his lips. It was a common enough theme, but phrased with a bittersweet poignancy that brought tears to her eyes. Her reaction was odd in its way; the princess had no ear for music and cared little for it as a rule.

'Your own composition, I believe,' said Khirshagk when the song was done.

Blushing slightly, Darl nodded.

Moriana bit her lip. At once she understood. He had written the song for her. Darl confirmed it by avoiding her eyes.

'Well,' Darl said, rising and stifling a yawn with the back of his fist. 'I'm worn down with travelling, I don't mind admitting. I think I'll retire. Your Highness?'

'I'll wait a while,' said Moriana before she could stop herself. She wondered why she'd said that. It wasn't just pique at him for performing such a song in front of the lizard man. Her motives went

81

deeper – and Moriana didn't wish to examine them too closely.

He looked at her for a long moment. Then with a wan smile, he nodded.

'I wish you a good rest, my Lady. Your, uh, Instrumentality, I thank you for your gracious hosting.'

'You've more than repaid me with your song, Lord Darl.' He hissed flat syllables to a *Zr'gsz* female, who wordlessly lifted a torch from its bracket. 'Rissuu will show you to your quarters.' The tall man bowed and departed.

Moriana lay back. Her lips were dry, but she had no desire for the wine. Nervously the princess ran her hand along the black and silver fur beneath her.

'It's the hide of the greater weasel of Nevrym,' said Khirshagk. 'A cunning, deadly beast. We trade for them with the foresters.'

Moriana nodded. The men of the Great Nevrym were known to be reckless, enamored of danger. Of all the folk of the Realm it was easiest for her to imagine the Nevrym foresters trading with the shunned and dreaded Hissers, not through any love of them or for the Dark, but because of the essential lawlessness of their natures. It occurred to her that most of the footmen who remained with her were Nevrym men. She had thought it because of the toughness of the breed. Perhaps it was also because the keep of the Fallen Ones was not such a mystery to them.

Khirshagk walked to the wall as gracefully as a hunting beast. He reached a hand to the single torch burning beside the curtained doorway and snuffed it as a human might snuff a candle flame between thumb and forefinger. Moriana winced in sympathy, but he displayed no sign of pain.

'What you are about to see,' he said quietly, 'has been seen before by only one of your kind. And she was of your *kind* indeed.'

Hsst! went another torch. The room descended another step toward utter darkness.

'She?' asked Moriana. The word came out huskier than she intended. She watched him move. In motion, Khirshagk had the stop-and-go rhythm of a lizard, she noted. It was exotic and not at all repellent to her. Deliberately, he doused the remaining torches in the same way. She gave a little gasp as the jaws of blackness closed.

'Wait,' he bade her.

She waited. Gradually, she became aware that the chamber did not lie in total night. As her pupils expanded she began to discern the details of the room's spare furnishings once more, this time illuminated by a suffused green glow that seemed to come from all around.

'Thirty thousand years ago my folk came to this continent. Of all the vastness of this land you call the Sundered Realm, this was the place they chose as their first home. And they grew themselves a keep, nurturing crystals by arcane means until they formed the vast blocks and protrusions that are the Thendrun you see all about you. Crystals of emerald, Princess, such as the giant single crystal that is your Beryl Throne.' She saw the white gleam of his smile. 'You can see why we don't value what the Pale Ones call riches.'

A suspicion formed in her mind.

'And the City in the Sky . . .?'

'You are perceptive. It is no more than to be expected.' Before she questioned the cryptic remark, he went on. 'Yes, we grew the Sky City in much the same way from a bed of skystone. It's of a different substance, of course. It grew vertically in spire and towers instead of the angular shapes of our keep. And you're aware that it's not made of emerald. Nor does it glow with its own light, as do the walls of our dwellings.'

'It's beautiful,' she said. It was the literal truth, but it was a soul-disturbing beauty, a beauty redolent of the Dark Ones.

He came toward her. She stood, arms limp at her sides. Moriana forced her mind into the calm necessary to form the thought to the nun: *Ziore, what does he intend?*

You need me to tell you that?

Khirshagk put out his hand till his forefinger touched the untied lacings of her tunic. Her breath came shallow and rapid as the finger pulled down, drawing forth the leather thong. His claws touched the place where the garment came together below her breasts, and continued downward. The leather parted as if he used a knife.

'You are not the first Moriana to visit Thendrun,' he said in a rich, low voice. 'Nor the first Etuul.'

She blinked.

'A Moriana Etuul aided shai-Gallri, it's true,' she said. Her voice was almost as breathy as a *Zr'gsz*'s now. 'I am descended from her. I'm the first of my clan to bear the name Moriana since . . .'

Her words trailed away as he lifted his finger to her breast. The finger stroked. Moriana stiffened, remembering the black talon had sliced her tunic. But the touch on her nipple was gentle. She shuddered with surprised pleasure as the nipple grew erect.

'Since that Moriana came to Thendrun to gain the secret of true magic,' he said. He took his hand from her breast, dropped it. Her swordbelt fell to the furs with a muffled clatter. A moment later her breeches joined it, pared from her like the peel from a fruit. The razor claw didn't so much as touch the skin beneath.

She started to reach for Khirshagk. She had early guessed how the evening would end and had been steeling herself for it. Now there was no need for her fortitude. She had not lain with Darl since before Chanobit. Desire was a keen edge in her loins.

Khirshagk stepped back.

'In those days the Pale Ones had little magic besides that of Athalau, which is no real magic at all, merely the exercise of mental powers.'

'And what is true magic?' She felt the coldness of the Amulet between her breasts but did not look down. A cool breeze fondled her nakedness.

His hands went to his robe.

'*Power*. The ability to manipulate the beings of this world and the Dark beyond. That gift was given to the People alone. The earlier Moriana came to purchase that gift, and so she did.'

'And how did she pay for it?' Moriana almost whispered.

He laughed.

'She found the paying no ordeal,' he said, and parted his robe.

Moriana stared. Not one but two great penises jutted from his groin, one above the other, each one swollen-headed and wrapped with veins like a vine-wrapped column.

'We are similar, your kindred and mine,' said Khirshagk. 'But my folk are the greater breed.'

She sank to the furs and lay back. Her eyes were wide with expectation. His double erection was impressive, but she was not altogether certain what he intended to do with it.

He knelt between her thighs, took a member in either hand and pushed forward with his hips. Moriana lifted her hips to meet him.

'That way,' she groaned. 'But I've never done that before . . .'

In a moment, pain and pleasure mingled and overlaid one another. He lowered himself until he loomed over her like an idol supporting himself on muscular arms. Even in the wan emerald light his eyes shone like windows into blackness. He began to move to and fro, slowly. The skin of his members had the slightest roughness. The friction thrilled her almost beyond toleration.

Light began dancing before her eyes. Breath came short. Hot and cold chased tails through her body, touched her with fire, with ice, and the pleasure moved within her, possessing her utterly.

When the icy explosion came within her, she screamed with the fury of her own release.

She drifted from consciousness, floating timeless in darkness and satiety. At length her eyes focused again. Khirshagk still hung over her, and she felt the twinned rhythm of his heart yet within her. She didn't know how long she lay in her daze. She sensed he could have kept that position for hours, days – and more.

He slipped from her. Even the withdrawal gave intense delight. She gritted her teeth as climax seized her lithe body again. Winded, she lay back looking up as he put on his robe. For some reason the black against black figures were clearer to her now. They seemed to move with a life of their own. Or was that only a trick of the emerald witchlight?

'That first Moriana,' she asked. 'How long did it take her to gain the true magic?'

He looked down at her, his expression totally unreadable.

'*She* never gained it at all,' he said, leaving the chamber with noiseless tread.

Moriana stared up at the ceiling. It was concave and faceted like a gem. It focused her mental energies and flooded her with both vitality and unease. She blinked several times and looked away from the disquieting ceiling.

'Ziore?' she asked softly. 'What do you make of it?'

'I know not what.' The voice came from somewhere amid the furs strewn in the pit.

Moriana put her hand to the Amulet, clenching it hard. She couldn't make herself look to see whether the stone shone white – or black.

CHAPTER SEVEN

On that day appointed for battle by forces none living could comprehend, it seemed as if Nature herself rejoiced at the prospect for slaughter. When dawn poured itself over the horizon like soured milk, the Sky City floated some ten miles west of Kara-Est, where it was spotted by pickets posted in gondolas held aloft by ludintip, huge airborne jellyfishlike creatures. As they reported, the City showed no sign of warlike intent. No war birds circled its tall towers or winged in arrowhead formation to meet the aerial guardians of the seaport. To the immense disgust of Parel Tonsho, and Hausan and Suema, Senior General and Sky Marshal of Kara-Est respectively, a number of Deputies immediately expressed relief and demanded that their city's military alert be called off.

The alert remained in force.

At ten in the morning, aerial reconnaissance reported ground troops massing on the plain west of the Hills of Cholon. Smiling grimly – largely for the benefit of the court sculptor come to immortalize what the general was sure would be an epic victory with a heroic bust in marble – General Hausan ordered two thousand cavalry and three thousand foot soldiers, including almost a thousand archers, to come forth from the Landgate to meet the foe. Sweating, itching and weak-kneed within her ornamental armor, Tonsho watched the couriers ride out from the Hall of Deputies with considerable misgiving. At her side her covey of youths strutted and made muscles, bragging about how *they* would deal with the enemy.

Tonsho knew victory would not be so easy. Battle never was, especially battle against the fearsome Sky City. She silenced her chirping boys with an impatient wave of her hand. On this of all days she didn't want their arrogant prattle distracting her from the serious business of worrying, something no one else in Kara-Est appeared capable of doing.

Standing on the skywall beside the huge mandibular jut of the City's forward dock, Rann and Synalon watched the tidal race of armies in collision. Synalon held a heavy white robe closely about her against the wind. Her hair blew like black stormwrack around her pale face. Rann wore the black and purple of the City with the gold brassard on his left arm identifying him as one of the elite Guard. He needed no badge of rank; the blazing crimson crest on the head of the black war eagle was device enough.

'We shall be victorious, cousin,' said Synalon smugly. 'I feel it. I *know* it!'

Rann glanced sidelong at his queen. 'Is this assured by the Dark Ones?' he asked in a monotone.

'The Dark Ones?' answered Synalon, wildly, almost insanely. '*I* assure this day's victory, cousin dear. *I* am the one with the power. *I* will crush those crawling insects, those larvae, those pathetic creatures daring to oppose my will!'

Rann said nothing of his own preparations, of the army, the eagle riders and the part they would play, the magics performed by scores of mages in the City. For all he knew, Synalon might be correct. This day might belong to her and her alone. Shaking his head at the prospect, he turned attention back to the slow jigsaw merging of armies below.

Ghostly with distance, the sounds drifted to their ears: barking, shouting, trumpets ringing, the beat of drums. The white and azure banners of Kara-Est snapped above orderly rectilinear arrays, heavy spearmen massed in the center with archers on the wings and squadrons of cavalry on the outermost flank. Against them the Sky City ground troops, twenty-two hundred dog riders from the City and her subjugated 'ally' Bilsinx. The attacking force travelled in a shapeless, fluid formation that the regimented commanders of the Estil army thought disorganized.

In advance swarmed the Bilsinxt light cavalry hurling darts and arrows to disorder the close-packed ranks of the Estil. The heavier City riders couched lances and charged through, the skirmishers parting easily to either side like a bow wave from a war galley's prow. The lines met, purple and black against blue and silver. Several seconds later the observers in the City heard the dull hammerblow followed by a many-throated shout as the hours and weeks of waiting were consummated in steel and blood and death.

Rann smiled grimly. His nostrils flared and he imagined the coppery smell of blood. Beside him Synalon stood as pale and stiff as a marble statue, her thoughts alien.

Inexorably, the City floated east. The striving mass of men and beasts passed beneath. Though outnumbered and less massively armored than their foe, the Sky City forces held their army in savage deadlock. The Bilsinxt streamed past the enemy's flanks like quicksilver, driving arrows into the unprotected flanks and rumps of the Estil knights' war dogs. Between the skirmishers surged an inchoate, writhing mass pushing now this way, now that.

Rann nodded. Turning to an aide who stood by, he said, 'Order the artillery to commence firing. It'll give our crews good practice for what's to come.' The aide nodded and rushed away. 'Besides,' Rann said, leaning forward to grip the windworn stone of the wall, 'the Estil must be encouraged to reinforce.'

Less than a minute later, a rain of rocks and ballista darts spattered among the Estil. Dogs screamed and men choked, dying as the two-yard-long shafts pinned men to mounts and mounts to sod. A few riders and footmen fleeing for the rear became a trickle, a stream – and threatened to turn into a torrential rout.

Ludintip-borne observers signalled news of impending disaster. Hausan barked orders and scattered demotions like seedcorn. Reinforcements began to flood in from the hills.

'Cease bombardment,' Rann ordered. Several of his aides remarked among themselves he had not smiled so since he had come up from a diverting evening torturing the virgin daughter of Mayor Irb, late of Bilsinx.

The prince walked to where the apprentice mage Maguerr sat in a bishop's chair peering into a new geode.

'Get me Dess.' The visage of the City's ground commander peered forth one-eyed from the geode communicator. Rann spoke briefly; the other nodded. He had been a colonel of the Guard until an arrow robbed him of one eye and the binocular vision essential to bird-back warfare. Rann trusted Dess to carry out his orders, no matter how distasteful.

Reinforcements joined the Estil battles, roaring lustily with eagerness to be at the foe. No sooner were fresh troops engaged than the black and purple lines began to waver. In a matter of heartbeats, the City forces had turned their dogs' tails toward their enemy in headlong flight.

Back in the Hall of Deputies Hausan crowed with delight at the news and restored the ranks he had been pruning mere moments before.

'But, sir, the ludintip report that many of our reserve forces are marching forth to join the pursuit.'

'Are they now? Spirited lads! I shall see a medal struck to commemorate this day.' He turned to Tonsho and the Marshal with an expansive wave of his hand. 'Did I not tell you the fight would be decided on the ground? Let them fly their pet gerfalcons against us now. The day is won!'

Tonsho and the roundcheeked Suema exchanged thoughtful looks. Without a word, the plump little Sky Marshal left to issue commands of his own. Ludintip rose from the city, titanic animated gasbags, some as large as a hundred feet across. The oblate spheroids of their hydrogen sacs glared orange-red in the sun. Shield-sized nuclei moved freely across the surface of the sacs avoiding only the tightly held sphincters the ludintip used to steer. The vast fernlike feeding fans were folded beneath the creatures. Tentacles as thick as a man's thigh clung to special brackets set in the gondolas; much slimmer tentacles studded with sting cells carrying an agonizing nerve poison waved in agitation. The gondolas swinging below the creatures bristled with spearpoints and engines of war.

Smiling oddly for a man who has just seen his army routed, Rann went to his war bird and accepted the reins from a cadet, who danced back with obvious relief. The eagle scowled at him.

'Easy, Terror,' Rann soothed. The bird spread its wings once with ineffable emotion as the diminutive prince swung into the saddle. Rann gripped the shaft of the implement that rode in the lance stirrup by his left leg. He hoisted it in salute to his queen. Synalon returned his salute with a small, haughty upward motion of her chin. It was all Rann could expect in way of acknowledgement now that the Power was on her. He kicked vigorously and Terror exploded into the air with a boom of wings. Seeing the red-crested war bird soar, the bird riders of the City took flight as one.

A score of gold brassarded riders formed on Terror. Each carried a shield in one hand and a lancelike object similar to Rann's in the other. The implements were wood shafts ten feet long, each tipped with an eighteen-inch cylinder of red fired clay, capped and sealed with a curious glyph. A wire ran back from the cap to a ring set on a lever at the point where each rider's hand gripped. Through vents in the bottom of each cylinder came a dazzle of flame.

Bolts arched gracefully from the cloud of ludintip. Prematurely loosed, they dropped harmlessly into the Hills of Cholon beyond the lordly palaces and great houses. Rann's grin widened, but he did not fail to note that more of the Estil artillerists had prudently held fire than loosed in panic.

A shaft went by to the left, its whine lost in the thunder of Terror's wings. Rann let his 'lance' drop level, pressing the butt to his ribs with his elbow.

From the clay vessel came an agitated chittering. Guiding the eagle with his knees, Rann swerved in full flight until the tip of the cylinder pointed at a gasbag so immense that a full two score men and two catapults rode the gondola beneath. The chittering increased to a frenzy of liquid syllables just the far side of coherent speech. Taking measured breaths, Rann waited until the sound reached a crescendo.

His forefinger tugged the ring.

The cap snapped open. A blue nimbus of flame sprouted from the end as the sealing glyph was broken. An instant later the fire cloud became an arrow-straight line of fire between lancetip and ludintip.

The ludintip exploded in a brilliant blue flash as the fire elemental buried itself lustily in the hydrogen inflating the gasbag. Screaming, the Estil aviators began their last journey home.

Lines surged on either side of Rann, one red, one green, to converge on a second ludintip. Terror fought the thunderclap buffeting from the first explosion with powerful wings as another blossomed, and another.

With the wind at his back, Rann distinctly heard the tunk! tunk! tunk! of the City's own artillery, even above the screams and blasts and the tremendous noise of Terror's passage. A black bundle soared by, trailing smoke, to fall among the pitched rooftops at the western fringe of the City.

Rann glanced back. His cheeks grew taut. Only ten bird riders still followed him, spread in a loose echelon. The aerial artillerists of Kara-Est were proving formidable foes indeed.

Explosions splashed all over the sky as bird riders launched fire salamanders against the ludintip. The Palace mages of the Sky City had spent weeks conjuring small fire sprites into specially enchanted containers that would trap the creatures and their killing heat inside until the lids were opened and the magic seals broken. No more efficient weapon for eliminating the animated airships of the Estil existed.

Rann let the staff with its special jar drop in a lazy spiral to the cobbled streets below. Other bird riders would circle back to munitions carriers for more staffs. He had other concerns. With the unconscious skill of great practice, he performed the acrobatic feat of reaching for the recurved Sky City bow slung across his back while taking in the situation around him.

The tight formations of eagles had scattered themselves all over the sky on their firing pass through the ludintip. Smoke trails grew like vines into the sky on all sides. A score and more of the gasbags had been set aflame by the salamanders. Rann's own forces were too spread out among the remaining enemy forces for him to appraise casualties. In planning, it was assumed they would be high. All he could do was hope they were not too high.

Two hundred feet ahead and to his left a dark brown eagle suddenly flashed into flame. The prince heard the mingled screams of bird and rider as they tumbled toward the earth. They burned like paper in the embrace of the salamander.

Rann cursed. Special vents were tapped in the rear of each fire sprite's jar so that its eager chittering would tell the bird rider when it was fixed on target. The fire elementals sensed the presence of inflammable substances and sped directly for the most volatile when released. Some fool of a eagle rider had pulled the trigger without being certain what his elemental was tracking. It had struck a comrade instead of a foe.

There was nothing Rann could do about that. Nocking an arrow, he put Terror into a circling dive toward a fat orange sphere rising from Kara-Est.

The black iron frame bucked like a wild beast as the bow of the ballista slammed to. Engineer First Class Juun held her breath as she watched the missile's flight with eyes scarcely less keen than a bird rider's. The eight-foot spear reached the top of its arc, tipped down and punched between the ribs of a war eagle as the creature's wings rose to gather wind. The bird convulsed in midair. Cheers rang from the tiles of the roof as the creature plummeted, its rider falling at its side in a helpless flailing of limbs.

Two burly assistant engineers, bare backs gleaming with sweat in the hot sun, spun the double windlass to recock the ballista. Making herself relax, Juun scanned the skies for another target. She had two kills that morning. The bounty would mean luxury for years.

She gestured with a gloved hand. The platform on which the engine was mounted began to revolve, turned by more assistants. As it turned she caught the eye of her friend Falla manning a ballista mounted on a turret at the other end of the building. Two more engines were mounted on the other corners but these lay out of sight behind the pitched roof. Falla grinned and touched the tip of her nose; she had seen Juun's kill. Juun laughed and waved back, then turned to peer through her sights.

She shut her ears to the shrieks as a ludintip fell like a meteor in the next block. The damned Sky Citizens had hellish magic on their side, but even that wouldn't bring them victory over the freedom fighters of Kara-Est. The elite rooftop artillery would exact a far heavier toll of the invaders than their limited population could afford.

She heard a thump, glanced reflexively to her left. A round lump the size of a bushel basket had dropped on the catwalk connecting the two emplacements. Near Falla's end thick greenish black smoke roiled from the ball. Juun turned her attention back to the skies as the rattle of bootheels on stone told her the fire-control crews were rushing to douse the smouldering projectile.

A buff-colored bird entered her field of vision, swooping in on a rising ludintip, its rider launching a stream of arrows at the gasbag's nucleus with breathtaking speed. Shouting broke out to her left, the sounds of struggle. She ignored it, gesturing to her crew to position the weapon. Juun had only a heartbeat before the bird was lost behind its quarry. She drew breath, pulled . . . the missile arced and fell past the bird's fanned tail. She groaned as the eagle went out of sight, its wings almost brushing the taut bladder of the ludintip.

She didn't hear the creaking of the windlass working against the mighty pull of the bow.

'Snap to it!' she shouted.

A gurgling scream answered her.

Juun spun in the saddle, snatching at her dagger. The man on her left was sitting down staring at the shaft of a ballista dart that jutted from his belly. Figures writhed together on the catwalk, some obviously fighting to the death, others naked or partly so, striving belly to belly. In the eyeblink she had to absorb the strange scene, Juun saw others dancing drunkenly around Falla's engine, laughing, singing. A ballista server tottered an instant on the stone railing before plunging to the street eight stories below in a flawless swan dive.

A swirl of smoke curled around her face. It was aromatic; without meaning to, she inhaled deeply.

Her surroundings began glowing with a light of their own. She perceived a world behind the world she had known before, and this was a world she could almost enter. But not quite. Frustration brought hot tears coursing down her cheeks.

When Falla came to her with knife in hand and laughing, she welcomed her friend as she would a lover.

Above the battle for a moment, Rann gulped in great lungfuls of air. Though the sun was well past the zenith, the air up at a thousand feet was stinging cold and cut down his throat like a knife. His whole body tingled with manic energy. His every sense thrummed to the surging strength and pungent smell of the bird beneath him, the stinks and sounds and sights of the battle raging around him and below, the wind in his face. Even the burning line across his back, where an Estil archer had almost punched through his light mail, filled him with fierce exhilaration. Torture and intrigue, battle and flight, these were his loves, his fulfillments, the only ones available to the eunuch prince.

He experienced the latter pair to the utmost now.

Pressure from one knee made Terror drop his left wingtip and go into a steep bank. He surveyed the grim situation below. But it differed little from what he had expected.

Things had gone well for the City in the Sky. The staged 'rout' of their ground forces had feinted a good portion of the defenders out of Kara-Est. The burning bundles of Golden Barbarian vision-weed had been shot from the City's walls with commendable accuracy. Hits and near misses had incapacitated a quarter of Kara-Est's rooftop artillery. Rann had learned about the drug when he had been a field marshal of a combined City-Quincunx army that had defeated an incursion of the Golden Barbarians into the Sjedd almost six years before. Whoever breathed its vapors forsook the real world to travel in a realm of visions and delusions — or perhaps in an alternate

93

realm, depending on which school of philosophy one heeded on the subject. What mattered to Rann was that the victims' minds went elsewhere while their bodies provided conveniently helpless targets. High as he was, high enough to drift over the skywall into the City itself, he caught the resinous tang of the vision vapors.

'I hope everyone remembered to take the antidote,' he muttered to himself, the words inaudible even to Terror due to the rush of wind past his lips. The antidote to the drug was more costly by weight than gold. Synalon had grumbled over the expense, but Rann had persevered and knew himself now to be correct.

The assault had gone according to plan. Even so, three quarters of the rooftop engines still spat death. The water battery of warships anchored in the harbor were virtually untouched and the Estil forces, as diminished as they were, still outnumbered his own three to one.

He raised his eyes from the conflict below and peered at his City. A black and silver clad figure stood alone on the prow of the vast stone raft, gesturing with slender arms.

Synalon.

He wheeled, keeping her in view. He again wondered if she had as much of the Dark Ones' favor as she believed. He knew his royal cousin, knew that she was the most powerful magician in the Realm and most likely in the entire world, knew also that she was capable of overestimating her power.

He watched the mystic gyration of the sorceress's arms. Briefly he felt the age-old pang, an impotence predating his emasculation. For magical power, like political power, passed along the female line of the Etuul clan. He had no innate magical ability, nor the aptitude to learn spellcraft, though he excelled in every other thing he attempted.

'I should be able to feel the power flow, to know if Synalon's magic works or not,' Rann mumbled. But that was as inaccessible to him as knowledge of his own destiny. He was utterly at the mercy of his demented cousin, the monarch he loved and hated and, always, served.

He reached for another arrow and set Terror into a long, steep dive. Battle still raged.

Sun-heated stone stung the soles of her feet. Cold wind caressed her bare limbs. Synalon Etuul, Queen of the City in the Sky, shut her eyes against the sun's intrusion and strove to put her soul in touch

94

with darkness. Her guards stood about her fingering their weapons and nervously watching their ruler poise herself on the tip of the skydock with nothing but sky an inch in front of her toes. She ignored them as she ignored the arhythmic thunk of catapults arrayed about the walls, and the tumult of noise that beat like surf against the floating City.

Black hair snapped in the wind like a million tiny whips. Synalon wore a harness of black leather, a web woven about her otherwise nude body, leaving bare her breasts and the dark, furry tuft of her loins. What seemed to distant Rann some silver garb was only her own skin, as pale as moonbeams.

A black dot appeared in the center of her being. It grew quickly, and with it grew pleasure. Soon it was a sun, a black sun, consuming her in ecstasy and darkness. Her Guards cried out in alarm seeing black flames begin to stream from their mistress's body. She threw back her head and shrieked like a soul in torment. With an oath, a Palace Guard leaped onto the dock and raced to her.

Naked bones clattered on stone as the black flame scoured flesh from his skeleton.

The queen did not notice. Unholy pleasure possessed her. Yet through the midnight fires of orgasm burned the cold hard light of Will.

Come to me, the Will commanded. *You are mine. Take form before me that my enemies shall be destroyed. By my Power, by the City in the Sky, by the Dark Ones who have chosen me for Their own, I bid thee – come!*

Out over the bay a swirling stirred the air.

CHAPTER EIGHT

'Behold,' said Erimenes. 'The City in the Sky, precisely as Jennas predicted. *Now* do you believe her visions, Fost? I've told you all along to heed them.'

Fost glanced at Erimenes. The genie leaned jauntily on the weatherworn railing of the ship, as though the splintery, faded wood actually propped up his insubstantial form.

'You did no such thing,' growled Fost.

'Don't quibble. I hadn't thought you so small-minded. I've held all along that Jennas truly was receiving inspiration from Ust the Red Bear. If I didn't say so, it was only because I deemed it so painfully apparent to any thinking being as to require no comment.'

Fost paid no attention. The courier stared into the sky and tried not to be sick.

In any kind of sea, the caravel Miscreate rolled like a pig in mud. Fost and Jennas had turned green the minute she warped out of Port Zorn and stayed that way until the walls of the easternmost lock of Dyla Canal shut behind the Miscreate's round stern. On the sheltered waters of Kara-Est harbor even a beast like Ortil Onsulomulo's slatternly ship rode as smooth as a dream. It was the commotion of the sky beyond the pastel buildings on the waterfront that made Fost's gorge yearn once more for wide-open spaces.

The Sky City was exactly where Jennas had predicted. And it floated in the middle of a battle of awesome proportions.

'Now you know why no one else was willing to haul your carcasses down the coast,' came a voice from behind Fost.

Fost turned to the Miscreate's captain. He was something to behold.

The foremost mariners of the day were the black-skinned Joreans of the continent lying northeast of the Sundered Realm. The fact

96

that Ortil Onsulomulo was half Jorean tended in Fost's mind to balance the disreputable appearance of both him and his vessel.

Joreans believed that each sex possessed its own peculiar essence and that these essences were best not intermingled. Thus, except for purposes of procreation, Joreans tended to eschew intercourse with members of the opposite sex, taking those of their own gender as lovers instead. However, like most folk, the Joreans were not insensible to the lure of a little perverse fun. Sailors being what they are, the Jorean mariners were inclined to go all-out when indulging their taste for the unconventional.

Thus Jama Onsulomulo, master of the cog Swift, begot a son with a sallow, blonde-moustached Dwarven woman of North Keep.

With a Jorean's strong moral sense, Onsulomulo had taken it upon himself to see to as much of the lad's upbringing and education as he could. As a result, young Ortil spent half his time on the decks of Swift and half sweltering in the warrens and foundries of North Keep. The boy became a mass of unresolved conflicts between the openness and intellectualism of the Jorean and the dour materialism of the Dwarves. Ortil Onsulomulo became a sailor of notable skill while at the same time flaunting the fact that his vessel was a ghastly ramshackle tub that only a landlubber could possibly mistake as seaworthy.

As Fost, Jennas and Erimenes looked on with expressions ranging from bewilderment to glee, winged shapes and bloated balloons battled across a smoky sky. Anchored off the bow of Miscreate, broad-beamed carracks of the Estil navy flung a hail of darts into the air. One bird rider tumbled from his saddle and another pinned a rider to his eagle for a long fall into the greasy water of the harbor. Farther away, a ludintip shot sideways, its tentacles spasming to drop gondola and crew into the central plaza.

'A nucleus hit,' Erimenes said sagely. 'Some bird rider got either lucky or smart.'

In a single prodigious bound, Onsulomulo leaped to the railing of his ship. He swayed this way and that on the precarious perch. The half-Dwarf kept his balance with almost contemptuous ease, as if hoping to be flung overboard to his doom.

He waved a stubby arm at the sky.

'Swine! Rogues! Devil worshippers!' he screamed. 'You'll go too far, mark my words. The land has rejected you, the sea won't have you, and soon the sky itself will cast you from its bosom!'

97

He looked strange and wonderful standing there with his bare feet splayed on the railing. He was the height of a short man, massive of torso and head, childlike of limb. His hair was a curly orange brush, his skin reddish gold, his eyes liquid amber. Finely chiseled Jorean features mingled grotesquely with the Dwarven lumpishness of his body. Watching him, Fost wondered if he was in one of the manic spells that had gripped him periodically during the journey — or if he, like Jennas, were touched by some higher power.

A sharp bronze beak lanced through the water toward them. Fost barely made out the low black hull of a galley, its gunwales almost swamped by its own bow wave as twenty pairs of oars rose and fell with the same easy unison as an eagle's wings.

The courier cried a warning. Onsulomulo capered on the rail and shouted crazy laughter. But the black ship was not trying to ram them. It swept by, as clean and quick as a shark, rocking the much heavier caravel with the power of its passing. Streaming out from the mainmast in the stiff breeze cracked a familiar ensign: a red field emblazoned with a tentacled black triangle, from which glared a single red eye.

'Cowards!' Erimenes shouted at the fleeing ship. 'Go about! How can you flee from a handful of overgrown sparrows?'

Onsulomulo cackled laughter, a surprisingly ancient sound from one who looked to be Fost's age.

'Never in my hearing has anyone ever called the sailors of the Tolviroth Maritime Guaranty cowards, smoke-man,' he said. 'They've completed their commission of guiding some fat merchant fleet to safety. No one's paying them to stick around and fight the flyers.'

A rock cast from the City landed on the waterfront and bounced like a bowling ball along the pier. It struck an anchored merchant ship, scattering spars and sailors like eightpins. Fost gulped, acutely aware that he was heading into a witch's cauldron of battle from which the redoubtable warriors of the TMG were fleeing.

He felt Jennas's eyes on him.

'What now, Longstrider?' she asked calmly.

'We get the captain to put us ashore,' he said with no great enthusiasm. 'Then we try to find a way into the City.'

'Then we try to stay *alive* long enough to find a way into the City,' corrected Erimenes. 'You must beware of imprecision in speech, friend Fost. I've told you before . . .'

98

An unearthly moan froze Fost's blood in his veins. It came again and he realized it issued from his war bear Grutz's capacious chest, who sat man-fashion on his rump on the deck not far away. The bear stared into the air beyond the Miscreate's aft rail and hunched his head down between his shoulders.

'Look!' Jennas's brawny arm shot out.

Fost squinted. He made out a disturbance in midair. Ghosts of color danced within as though the sun's light were being broken into component colors. As he watched in uncomprehending fear, the disturbance grew and a tail dipped toward the surface of the bay.

'Ust preserve us,' breathed Jennas. 'A sylph!'

The spinning tail of the air elemental touched water and a waterspout loomed above the vessel, a thousand feet tall.

Though he expected it, Rann's lips drew back in a grimace as the waterspout blossomed in Kara-Est's harbor.

'She *does* have the power!' he exclaimed in wonder.

No one had summoned an air elemental of that size in centuries, perhaps not since the War of Powers. The Sky City's magicians traditionally dealt with fire sprites. Though Air and Fire were by no means inimical principles, it was testimony to the growth of Synalon's power that she could summon an unfamiliar breed of elemental outside the confines of a laboratory. And one so huge!

As if gravity had been reversed, an Estil war galleon leaped abruptly into the air. The water tornado sucked up another vessel, and another. From several miles away, Rann heard the screams of the doomed seamen, even above the roaring of the elemental.

The menace of the water battery was broken. That still left most of the rooftop-mounted ballista intact. Synalon claimed she could deal with those, too. What she had in mind was even more ambitious than summoning a sylph tall enough to peer over the parapets of the Sky City itself. Though Rann still doubted, he had little choice but to turn Terror's head around and start the bird climbing toward the City to execute the next stage in the conquest of Kara-Est.

Drinking air that intoxicated like wine, Synalon knew the exaltation of pure power. She had summoned a giant sprite and bound it to her will, as docile as a pup. Her creature sported in the harbor, scattering Estil ships like so many broken toys. But there were still the defenders on the pitched roofs of Kara-Est to eliminate. The sylph might be able to deal with them but not without endangering Synalon's bird riders — and perhaps the City itself. The sorceress-queen had another conjuration in mind that would better eliminate the Estil artillery — and at the same time demonstrate her own power in a unmistakable way.

She staggered slightly and clutched arms around her body. Pain grew in her like a metastasizing cancer. She clamped her teeth to hold back a howl of agony. The black sun had turned to red, and there was no pleasure in the fire that ate at her belly and limbs. Battle raged, her body the battleground and her mind and soul the prize. But still her Will shone brighter than the fire. Gripped by distress that transcended mere physical pain, Synalon shouted a word of Command.

A ball of fire enveloped her. Her guards fell back, throwing up their hands to shield their faces against the dreadful searing heat. Something had gone wrong. Their queen was being reduced to ashes before their eyes.

Then the flame vanished, rushing away across the doomed seaport as the giant salamander Synalon had conjured within her own body was set to do her bidding. It etched a line of death through the air, leaving ludintip and eagles alike flaming in its wake.

It cast itself into the waterspout.

Windows exploded in the two cities as the salamander's scream of agony burst like a bomb above the harbor. Water was the foe of Fire; Synalon had brought forth the sprite only to hurl it to horrid death. But not immediate death. Tottering, going to her knees on the lip of the pier, Synalon forced the salamander to remain in being, denying it the surcease of death that was its only desire.

Steam hid waterspout and harbor. Naked now, her glorious black mane charred to a smouldering, crackling stubble, Synalon clung to the stone of the pier. Though her body was drained of strength, though her skin stung as to the touch of a hot iron, she continued to work her Will upon spirits of Air and Fire, while her servitors watched in horror from the skywall.

Misty tendrils began to billow from the swirling cloud. Though the wind had been blowing out toward the harbor, they crept into the streets of Kara-Est, swallowing the city like a vast white amoeba. The surviving artillerists shouted in dismay and disbelief as the cloud engulfed them, hiding the sky from their view.

With an eagle's cry of challenge and delight, Rann launched Terror once more from the rim of the City. Behind him flew a hundred of the elite Sky Guard. Huge protuberances grew from the docks, became the sausages of giant balloons, silks gleaming in the sun. Though salamander-heated air filled the gasbags almost to the bursting point, they could not successfully lift the freight of men and arms that swung below. Five balloons towed by a score of straining eagles carried five hundred men toward the Hills of Cholon and the Ducal Palace in the wake of Rann's attack.

The Palace garrison saw them coming and sent a frantic signal for reinforcements to watchers in a spire atop the Hall of Deputies, who were only just visible above the unnatural fog. Then the bird riders struck. An arrow storm swept engineers from their emplacements. Detachments veered to land at preassigned parts of the Palace, while Rann and a dozen men attacked the tower.

Duke Morn awaited them. Somehow he seemed to fill his suit of plate and chain as robustly as he had before the death of his beloved wife and his heir. He held his head high. When the Sky Guard came for him, he killed six with a greatsword that flickered featherlight from side to side. The seventh he faced was Rann, and the duke did not prevail.

Still convinced the day was his, General Hausan despatched most of his defenders to aid the duke. Neither Tonsho nor Marshal Suema shared his optimism.

'Yes, yes,' the general cackled like a hen sitting on an egg. 'This will be the finest hour for the city. The very finest. We triumph on all fronts! The bird lovers are being repelled on all fronts. Oh, yes, a fine day. Fine.'

Sky Marshal Suema drew Tonsho aside.

'The plan, Excellency,' Suema whispered in the Chief Deputy's ear. 'Shall we execute it?'

Tonsho nodded jerkily. Her teeth chattered too violently for her to speak.

Claws scrabbled on the stone as Grutz heaved his bulk out of the water. Fost let go of the animal's stubby tail to hoist himself onto the dock. He scrambled into the saddle and turned back. Chubchuk appeared, with Jennas still aboard his broad back.

A cloud covered the harbor like a fleecy white roof. Sounds

echoed eerily beneath: screams, shouts, the crack of splitting tim-
bers, the roaring of the sylph. From above came the hideous keening
that had sounded since the fireball from the City had plunged into
the depths of the waterspout.

'A fire elemental, I do believe,' said Erimenes from his jug. 'Quite
amazing. Synalon's position as foremost enchanter of the age is
assured now beyond all doubt.'

'How nice for her,' said Fost. 'Let's get the hell out of here.'

'I think getting the *Hell* out of this scene is quite beyond your
powers, friend Fost.' The spirit chortled eerily as the two bears broke
into a soggy, squishy run.

The waterspout had cut through the anchored naval vessels like
a scythe. Then it began to rampage at random across the harbor,
picking up ships and flinging them to the points of the compass.

Even the slovenly Miscreate did not escape its attention.

Fost saw Ortil Onsulomulo. The golden Dwarf had climbed up
the Miscreate's rigging and clung with one hand while he shook his
chubby fist at the elemental. Then the wind funnel caught the vessel.
Fost had a final glimpse of Onsulomulo hurling defiant curses at his
enemy before man and ship vanished.

Fost turned away. He was all too aware of moisture on his cheeks
that had a taste different from the rank water of the harbor.

Leading the way, Fost rode for the southern fringes of the seaport.
He had no particular reason for heading that way. All he knew was
that the center of town wasn't going to be a healthy place. Battle
raged furiously in the thickness of the fog.

They rounded a corner and steel hissed reflexively into his hand
before his brain had time to evaluate the situation. A brown eagle,
its chest a blaze of white, swooped straight at them. Grutz snarled
a challenge, and Jennas unslung her greatsword.

The bird paid them no heed. It set down lightly in the middle of
the block and stood gazing over its shoulder at the rider clinging to
its back. The dark-haired woman rider slumped over the bird wore
the armlet of the Guard.

As he and Jennas watched, the woman swayed and toppled to
the ground. Fost dismounted and approached, sword in hand. The
bird beat its wings and screamed at him. He jumped back, then
looked closer at the prostrate form of the Sky Guardswoman and
sheathed his sword.

The bird let him near the rider. The osprey-feathered shaft of an

Estil arrow jutted out just below her collarbone. A trail of blood ran from a corner of the full-lipped mouth.

'I tried,' she told Fost, gazing up at him from beneath sagging eyelids. 'I . . . tried.'

'You did well.' There seemed little else he could say.

She coughed pink foam, sighed raggedly, seemed to shrink. Fost thumbed her eyelids closed. The eagle raised its head and uttered a single, lonely cry.

Fost straightened, casting his eyes warily up and down the street. He heard the clamor of voices and arms off to his right, toward the center of town. But under the fog which formed a few feet above his head the streets of Kara-Est were deserted.

He drew a deep breath, a decision made.

'Jennas. We've found our way into the City.'

The hetwoman looked from him to the eagle, standing with its fierce head wreathed in mist. Fost took a step toward the bird. It opened its beak in challenge.

Jennas brandished her sword.

'Ho, bird, here!' she shouted. Grutz and Chubchuk growled and lumbered about menacingly. The bird turned its head to glower at them, allowing Fost to vault into the saddle.

The bird cried in fury.

'Settle down, bird, there's nothing to fear. I mean you no harm. Damn!' The last word popped out as the feathered head swiveled to slash at his leg with a black beak. Fost drew his sword and pressed the tip to the side of the bird's neck.

'I mean you no harm,' he said, enunciating each word carefully. The eagles were intelligent and understood manspeech even though they couldn't speak it. 'I must travel to the Sky City. If you try to hurt me, I'll defend myself.'

The head bobbed. Fost hoped that meant assent.

'Come on aboard,' he called out to Jennas.

The woman hesitated, took a step forward. The eagle hissed. She stopped.

'I can't.'

'Certainly you can!' Fost twisted in the uncomfortably small saddle, keeping a sharp watch for interlopers. It was unlikely that soldiers of either side would be friendly to armed strangers in the streets. Anyone in the street would be fair game. 'Get aboard.'

Her approach was again met by shrill whistling from the eagle. It

103

batted at her with its wings as it stepped backward, clumsy under the courier's weight.

'It fears her smell,' said Erimenes. 'I don't think it likes bears.'

'It accepted me. Jennas, for Ust's sake, hurry!'

'With all due respect to the lovely and capable Jennas, you're hardly as steeped in ursine essences as she.'

At the mention of the Bear God, Jennas's face had gone thoughtful. She stepped back and let her greatsword slump until its tip rested on the granite cobblestones. She had reached a decision of her own, no less painful than the one Fost made.

'I am not meant to go,' she said. 'This journey is yours alone, Fost.'

Wings thundered overhead and the voices of men floated down through the fog. Fost's bird screamed. It twisted about under him, its wings beginning to flutter nervously. The bird longed for the air. Fost cursed and jabbed its neck, expecting the Sky Guards to start dropping through the misty ceiling. None came.

'That's ridiculous. *Get aboard.*'

'I couldn't,' she said, her brown eyes gleaming wetly, 'even were it intended that I do so. Yon beast can't bear both our weights.'

'She's right, Fost. That dead girl's a foot shorter than you, and no doubt weighs half what you do.'

'Shut *up*, Erimenes.' A catch in his voice almost choked him. He tried to lie to himself that it was due to eagerness to see Moriana again. He knew better.

'Nor can I abandon our faithful bears in the streets of this strange city,' she went on remorselessly. 'You can manage on your own. Nor are you truly on your own, O Chosen of Ust.'

'Jennas . . .'

She turned and mounted Chubchuk, her soft, 'Goodbye,' coming back to haunt Fost.

'My sainted self, Fost, quit dithering!' Erimenes shouted.

Face a mask of anguish, Fost nudged the eagle's flanks with both knees hoping this was the proper signal. The bird understood. It stretched its wings, hopped, thumped the air vigorously in an effort to raise the unaccustomed weight. The courier's heart almost stopped as the bird dropped from beneath him, but the next instant the wings caught air and smoothly bore him upward into the mist.

'Good luck, Jennas ! . . . I hope we'll meet again!'

'We shall,' she called after him. 'But not in happy reunion. Fare thee well, Longstrider. I . . .' The words became garbled by distance. Fost thought she added 'I love you' but couldn't be sure.

A moment of flight both timeless and weightless through the veiling clouds and then Fost was blinking in hot sunlight. The roofs of the buildings were completely covered by the fog. Off to his right the salamander still died in agony within a thrashing spiral of steam. Hoping the bird had sense enough not to veer in that direction, he pressed himself against its neck and clung.

Off to his left where the blunt cliffs of the hills shouldered out of the cloud, he saw the distinctive shapes of the Sky City cargo balloons dropping down with bird riders circling protectively above. Just ahead, a great number of the sausage balloons dropped toward the Central Plaza. The gondolas beneath bulged with armed men in the livery of Bilsinx. Though he didn't know what was happening, he knew enough of both tactics and of Rann to make a fair guess. With the fog to cover the maneuver, the prince had launched a feint attack on the Ducal Palace; when the Estil commanders sent troops to relieve the Palace, the main attack fell against the reduced forces in the Hall of Deputies, the nerve center of the defense.

The sky was nearly clear of eagles, though more balloons hung near the City bearing loads of arrows and javelins for the riders to replenish their ammunition. Most of the birds Fost saw were spiralling down among the assault balloons. That confirmed his guess that he was witnessing the killing stroke.

But what of the score of balloons rising upward toward the City in the Sky?

'Easy, easy,' he told the eagle, mainly to quiet his own nerves. To his surprise, he was not reduced to jelly by the knowledge he was alone on the back of a potentially hostile bird half a thousand feet in the air. Since first encountering Erimenes and Moriana, he had been through any number of appalling adventures, including several of the aerial variety to rival this hellride to the City through the combat all around him. That and the emotional numbness remaining after his escape from the wrath of a captive elemental a hundred stories tall accounted for his seeming calm.

He couldn't bring himself to even think of Jennas left behind in the now defeated city so far under his feet.

'Erimenes,' he whispered, knowing it was lunatic since none could hear him. 'Erimenes, why are so many Sky City balloons climbing back to the City? The battle's at its climax.'

'Guardian was right. Your eyesight is weak, indeed.'

'What?' Why was that confounded genie prattling about the sentient glacier guarding Athalau?

'Don't you see those "balloons" are orange and round? They aren't balloons, they're ludintip.'

'Oh,' said Fost, 'and we're flying right up into the midst of them.'

'There's always the opposite direction.'

Fost swallowed hard.

Singlemindedly, the bird beat its way upward. None of the ludintip's passengers seemed to be looking their way, Fost noted with relief. Their attention was fixed upward. A few eagles flying combat patrol around the City's perimeter swooped down, only to be clawed from the air by whirring flights of arrows. Then the living gasbags were above the rimwall, pouring lethal arrows on the startled faces of the attackers turned defenders.

Fost's eagle climbed up into the midst of the beings in time to see a flight of small black birds billow upward like smoke.

The five hundred men and women riding beneath the ludintip had not the slightest expectation of living to feel solid earth beneath their bootsoles again. Their only aim was to sow as much death and devastation as possible in the City itself before they fell. Synalon and Rann might triumph, but nevermore could it be said that the City in the Sky was immune to reprisal from the ground.

Dropping with her squadron of bird riders and Sky Guards, Colonel Dashta Enn was astonished to see the ludintip sprouting from the mist like red-crowned mushrooms and go rushing upward so fast that she and her flyers only had time to loose a futile scattering of arrows.

The audacity of the attack took away her breath.

Trained by Rann, she did not hesitate. The colonel was committed to the attack on the Hall of Deputies. The assault might succeed. Then all that remained would be the mopping-up of scattered, disorganized and leaderless forces. If it failed, all Rann's genius and the sorceries of Synalon could not alter the fact that the Estil armies still outnumbered their foes hugely and would crush them like a giant swatting a fly if they regrouped.

The City had to fend for itself. She swooped down to battle. Her eagle's talons raked cotton, then fell on unsuspecting prey.

*

Synalon sat on the stone pier, head hanging listlessly with her chin on her breastbone. It took all her powers of concentration to keep the sylph and the dying, screeching fire sprite under control. She didn't know if they were still needed. She dominated them now simply to prove her power.

Something brushed her cheek. It whined like an insect. She slapped at her face when she felt the sting.

'Your Majesty, beware!' screamed one of her bodyguards from the skydock behind her. Additional words were lost in a bubbling, gurgling moan.

Her fingers touched wetness. She pulled her fingers away in dismay. It took a few seconds for her inwardly directed eyes to register smeared blood. Her own. Someone had dared to attack her, Queen of the Sky City! And within her own territory!

She flashed to her feet. Her concentration broke. The waterspout leaped upward, dissipating in air with a great shout of joy at the destruction it had accomplished, leaving nothing behind but a rain of muddy water and debris. The salamander hissed relief as oblivion swallowed its agony.

The sky was filled with gaseous ludintip.

'Maggots!' Synalon screamed. 'You dare attack my City!' The rage burned her brain as the salamander had seared her flesh.

All that saved her life was the amazement gripping the Estil archers after their first volley when they realized that the wild, scorched, nude figure was Synalon herself. Now came clouds of arrows.

Screeching in fury, she waved her hands before her, covering herself with a shield of fire in which the arrows flared and disappeared without reaching her body. The survivors of her bodyguard shot back, but they were vastly outnumbered. Even as the raging queen blasted a second volley of arrows, a ludintip gondola bumped down on the gray stone. Howling like fiends, armed men and women poured forth. For the first time since the human capture of the City in the Sky, its ramparts felt the tread of an invader's feet.

Even with the allies she had and the death spells she commanded, Synalon could never hope to withstand such a fanatical attack singlehandedly. So savagely drained of energy that she could barely stand, Synalon teetered on the brink of the skywall. Hidden reserves of power were fed by her anger.

'Up, my children, up!' she screamed, her voice wild and fierce and mad. She threw her scorched arms up over her head, then pointed to her intended victims. 'Rend and slay the invaders, the groundling maggots! Slay them!'

Obedient to their mistress's command, the ravens of the Sky City burst forth from their rookeries. A boiling black cloud of death, they swept over the invaders like a firestorm from the guts of Omizantrim. Beaks pecked at the vulnerable membranes of the ludintip, plucked eyes from warriors battling impotently with bows and spears. Their talons slashed at the Estil commandos and each contact of claw with skin meant inevitable death. As Synalon stood and laughed while balancing precariously on her spit of stone, daring gravity to claim her in the moment of her triumph, her ravens slew the intruders to the last man and woman. Though the Estil soldiers killed the black attackers by the hundred, each raven that fell was replaced by a dozen more.

At last the screaming died. Only the sound of the wind could be heard over the ripping of flesh by a thousand black beaks.

Somewhere in the City a war eagle left alone by the ravens who mistook it for part of the City's forces touched down bearing a rider whose senses reeled with horror at the sight he had just witnessed.

The battle was quickly finished. Convinced of his triumph to the end, General Hausan was shot by Colonel Enn while posing for ten artists dashing off sketches to mark the epochal event of Estil history. Pudgy Sky Marshal Suema led a gallant delaying action against the bird riders while Tonsho, her nerve broken by the nearness of physical danger, fled downstairs to her private apartments in the south wing of the Hall. Suema and his men fell quickly. Scimitar in hand, Enn led the pursuit of the real ruler of Kara-Est.

They found her cowering among cushions and fine tapestries pulled from the walls. Her pretty-boys fought bravely but futilely; after a brief exchange of swordcuts Enn called for archers. The Chief Deputy's lover-bodyguards were feathered to fall among the silks. The scent of blood mingled with a dozen rare perfumes.

Tonsho cowered in the midst of luxury.

'No, no, don't hurt me,' she moaned, her eyes screwed tightly shut. 'For the love of all gods, *don't let Rann have me!*'

'Do you yield the city of Kara-Est?' Enn demanded sternly.

'Y-yes,' sobbed Tonsho.

And the thing was done.

CHAPTER NINE

With the unfamiliar, harsh syllables of the Zr'gsz tongue hissing in her ears. Moriana lay on her belly and watched. The jagged black stone beneath her stung with heat even though her sturdy tunic. Whether the heat came from the sun hanging low in the western sky or the fires burning far below she couldn't tell.

She stiffened as she sensed a presence nearby.

'Anything?' asked Darl Rhadaman r'Harmis, lowering himself beside her on the crest of the undulating line of cooled lava.

Moriana pointed with her chin. The main camp of the Watchers lay below. It was a somber place, reflecting its purpose. Walls of dressed lava rock holed like cheese supported flat basalt roofs. The windows had been hewn from the same green-black stone as the roofing. Moriana knew why. Wood, sod or thatch, anything combustible, couldn't safely be used as building material here on the northeastern slope of Omizantrim where hot sparks or ash might descend from the Throat at any time. A fresh dusting of gray ash overlay the compound, a remnant of Omizantrim's eruption weeks before.

The princess set her mouth. The Watchers' architecture might be practical but it did nothing to alleviate the grimness of the task they performed throughout long generations.

She saw them going about their everyday tasks. Men and women ground wheat together turning the manhigh millstone in a granite bowl with the strength of their own backs. Some knelt to whet the edges of spears and shortswords. A sweating, straining, curiously silent crew manhandled casks of fresh water gathered at springs below from the bed of a wagon built to survive the brutal broken terrain of the badlands. Over by the long oblong mouth of one of the underground bunkers in which the Watchers weathered Omizantrim's outbursts, a sturdy woman with sunbleached hair drawn back in a bun slit the throat of a squealing deer and began to give a group of children a lesson in butchering and dressing meat.

'It's like a combination military camp and monastery,' remarked Darl in a low-pitched voice that carried only a few feet. Moriana glanced at him, nodded slowly.

Since their arrival in Thendrun, Darl had emerged from the cocoon of self-doubt and despair that had wrapped him since Chanobit. On their second night in the emerald keep they had once again become lovers. Whether Darl knew or not what had occurred between her and Khirshagk, he said nothing of it. Moriana felt tempted to ask Ziore if he suspected. She didn't. That would be an invasion of Darl's innermost privacy.

Still, there was something about him that disturbed Moriana. Was it fatalism, discouragement or simply feeling the onset of middle years, the slowing that comes inevitably to even those as robust as the legendary Count-Duke of Harmis? He had held up well on the rapid march from the keep of the Fallen Ones, though. When they had to leave their wardogs behind to advance silently through the badlands, he walked with a firmness and sureness of step that put Moriana, a decade and a half his junior, to shame.

'Where's the creature?' he asked.

'It generally stays in the vicinity of the camp. Sometimes it moves in the dead of night. No one ever sees it. In the morning, it's simply gone, only to turn up elsewhere.'

'Foraging?'

'Apparently not. The Ullapag doesn't eat. It seems to derive its sustenance from the mountain itself.'

'The same animal has survived for ten thousand years?' Darl shook his head in wonder. 'We deal with potent magic.'

Moriana said nothing.

Something scraped behind her. She turned her head slowly to see Khirshagk approaching gingerly over the sharp lava. The height of a tall man, the Zr'gsz leader moved with surprising grace. However, he and all his kin were less skillful at silent movement than the humans in the party.

After a council of war with the followers who had remained faithful into the depths of Thendrun, Moriana had decided to send one knight back across the Marchant into Samazant to muster men for a new attempt on the City. Darl had been afraid they'd used up their stock of sympathy among the men of the City States. But last night Moriana's crying spells had revealed the Sky City occupation of Kara-Est. News of the seaport's fall would have reached the Empire by the time Sir Thursz reached his home country. Those tidings would make men reconsider the princess's pleas for aid.

A Nevrym forester had gone north down the trail from Thendrun to his home woods to consult Grimpeace, the head of the woods runners. The foresters lacked the instinctive fear of the Hisser that most of the Realm harbored, but they were known also as redoubtable foes of the Dark. This reassured Moriana that her appraisal of the Zr'gsz was accurate. It also let her hope the Nevrymin might aid her, especially since she had promised a substantial gift of gold in return. Like their neighbors the Dwarves of North Keep, the foresters had a healthy regard for specie.

'Have you located the hellbeast yet?' asked Khirshagk, lowering himself beside the humans. His limbs sprawled in a way the princess found disconcerting. His dark hide blended with the black rock and evergreens around them as if he had been bred in such surroundings.

'Not yet,' said Darl.

A file of men and women appeared abruptly below and to the left. They wore drab clothes like the folk in camp, with the addition of mottled green and black cloaks. The Zr'gsz were not the only ones practicing camouflage. Not even the four keen-eyed foresters accompanying them had known of that patrol's nearness.

'This country works both for and against us. You can hide an army in these folds. Not even the Watchers have a way of overcoming that.' Darl rubbed the dark stubble on his jaw. 'We may be able to bring this off, after all.'

'I hope you are right,' said Khirshagk.

Moriana reappraised her companion. After his bullheadedness and refusal to take her advice had helped lose the battle at the creek, she had fallen into the error of dismissing his military judgment. Now she was reminded that he knew more of infantry-lore than she; her greatest experience lay in aerial warfare. When the Watcher patrol appeared she had experienced near panic. Her imagination had peopled the tortured black landscape with hordes of Watchers closing unseen on them. Darl had restored perspective. If the intruders moved warily, the Watchers would only discover them through a stroke of luck.

'Maybe their vigilance has flagged,' she said, thinking out loud.

'No,' said Khirshagk simply.

'But . . .'

'Khirshagk, get back! It's looking this way!' At the urgent whisper from Ziore's jug, the lizard man slithered back down the slope. Moriana flattened herself on the rock and looked around wildly.

'What is? I don't see anything.'

'The Ullapag,' said Ziore. 'It sensed Khirshagk.'

'Can it read thoughts?'

'Poorly. Enough to feel the alertness come into its mind. I deflected its attention, set it at ease. I think.'

'I wonder if it can communicate with the Watchers?' asked Moriana.

'Probably,' answered Darl. 'But I don't think it has.' The routine below dragged along calmly.

The two slipped away to join Khirshagk in a fold of the lava. A caprice of wind carried acrid smoke from a fumarole uphill to them. Moriana and Darl coughed and blinked back tears.

Khirshagk rocked on his haunches. His eyes had a faraway gaze.

'The Heart. I taste its nearness.' Unconsciously, his tongue flicked from his thin-lipped mouth. It was forked. Moriana felt a disquieting tingle in her loins.

Moriana opened the lid of Ziore's jar. Pink mist spilled from the satchel, became a whirlwind of dancing bright motes and finally shaped itself into a woman, tall, serious and quite lovely despite advanced age.

'Which direction?' she asked. The Zr'gsz pointed a black claw south, past the camp. Ziore looked grave. 'The Ullapag lies that way as well.'

'It's guarding the Heart?' asked Moriana.

'So it seems.'

They made their way down the valley to where the others waited. The four Nevrymin waited with the Fallen Ones. Moriana sat on an outcropping of lava and let Darl explain the situation.

'We can't wait for night?' asked Quickspear, a narrow man whose habitual grin was rendered lopsided by a long knife slash down the left side of his face. He cradled the weapon that gave him his name, fingers nervously dancing along its shaft.

'My people do not function well in the cold.' The Zr'gsz weren't true reptiles. They fell somewhere between mammals and lizards – furred yet scaly, nursing their young though oviparous, warm-blooded but inclined to become sluggish when the sun went down.

112

'We've only two hours of sunlight left us,' said Darl. 'Here's my plan . . .'

Vapors steamed upward from the molten rock that bubbled in a pit cut like a slash across the mountain's flank. On a broad expanse of rock above the fumarole sat a vast creature, as unmoving as the lava beneath it.

A tall man could lie comfortably in the space between the bulging half-lidded eyes. Its hide was warty, green dapples on black mimicking the pattern of the Watchers' cloaks. Its immense body lay among four legs that seemed unable to support its bulk. It had the sloped back of a toad instead of the crooked back of a frog. Obsidian eyes stared out, missing nothing.

Moriana scarcely believed the thing lived. No motion of breathing stirred its bloated sides. But she felt its presence in her mind, alien and imposing.

She studied the natural amphitheatre scooped in the side of Omizantrim. Fifteen yards across and forty deep, its open side faced the Watchers' camp several hundred yards downslope. The fumarole lay at the inside end of the amphitheatre, with the Ullapag's rock raised like a dais above it. At either side of the opening stood a single Watcher. Two more Watchers stood in the rocks above the monster, armed with bows and spears. Though the pit's stinging fumes blew in their faces, they showed no sign of discomfort.

The four Nevrym Forest men were sneaking up on the four sentries. Moriana, Darl and Khirshagk, with several of his men, waited hidden on the northern wall. Though the foresters assured her they could capture the sentries without difficulty, she worried. She balked at killing any of the Watchers, and she didn't trust the Zr'gsz to be scrupulous in avoiding the slaying of their ancient antagonists. The bulk of the party of Hissers waited in concealment around the Watchers' encampment to bottle up any attempts at aiding the Ullapag. But that had to be done, moral niceties or not.

If the sentries were alerted before the foresters reached them, Khirshagk and his men would have to deal with them willy-nilly. Moriana and Darl had to confront the Ullapag, by means mystic or mundane as required.

She still had no clear idea what the Ullapag did. It looked too ungainly to run down the fleet Zr'gsz in rough terrain like this. One thing it did attempt was to detect the nearness of the Hissers by a

113

special sense. Ziore hovered beside Moriana, dulling the Ullapag's mental sensitivity to the presence of a hundred of the very beings it was meant to ward against.

A flicker of movement not far away caught Moriana's eye. It was Brightlaugher, a young blond boy painfully proud of the skimpy golden fuzz on his chin. He moved up on the nearest of the Watchers. He was almost in position for the quick final rush.

'Moriana.' The low voice was so distorted by effort she almost didn't recognize Ziore. 'Moriana, you must help. Can't hold by myself any more.'

'What?' she whispered back. Darl and Khirshagk stared at them.

'The Ullapag. Help me blanket it.'

'But . . . I can't!'

'You can!' Ziore snapped. 'Since I've known you your power has increased steadily. Help me, or all is lost!'

The princess wondered if the nun was right. Then she shut her eyes and concentrated.

She didn't have to grope to find the Ullapag's mind. It loomed bright, short of sentience, but old, old and very watchful. A bright thread of suspicion shimmered in the creature's mind. Moriana felt Ziore's presence and realized that the genie couldn't soothe the sense of wrongness troubling the Ullapag. She stretched out her own mind, soothing without words.

The doubt-thread vanished.

I did it! Moriana thought. The realization exhilarated her. Had her power grown because she'd slept with Khirshagk? He said her ancestor namesake hadn't perceived true magic *herself.* Had she gained something her forebear hadn't?

Hidden within her tunic, the Destiny Stone turned black. A rock loosened, twisting away beneath her foot. She stifled a yelp of alarm but couldn't save herself from falling.

The guard below turned and saw Brightlaugher rising from behind a bush twelve feet away. The Nevrym boy lunged. The spear came down, and the boy gasped as he ran onto its broad point.

The other guards shouted alarm. One standing above the Ullapag nocked an arrow and drew. Sprawled among the biting edges of the larva, Moriana recovered her grip on her own bow, drew, fired.

The Watcher stiffened and pitched forward, falling past the Ullapag's perch to disappear into the boiling lava.

Foresters wrestled with the other two. One of Khirshagk's warriors, overcome by battle-lust, leaped past Moriana and struck down the Watcher as he struggled to free his spear from Brightlaugher's belly.

The Ullapag screamed.

Moriana heard it as a bass thrumming, almost below the level of hearing. The Zr'gsz standing over the sentry jerked as if struck by an arrow. He began to twitch and his head twisted to score his own shoulders with his fangs.

'Unnghh.' Khirshagk's body was bent backward like a bow. His jaw was locked and his eyes rolled wildly. In spite of the agony gripping him, he ground out words between his teeth. 'You must . . . slay it. Or . . . we . . . die!'

She stared at the Ullapag. It had grown until the princess realized it had lifted itself upward enough to allow a huge throat sac to expand beneath it.

'It's producing a vibration,' Ziore shouted. Moriana barely heard her, though the hum of the Ullapag wasn't loud. 'It'll kill the lizard men.'

As if to prove her right, the Zr'gsz who had dashed into the open fell to the ground beside his victim. His eyes stared upward. His mouth shone darkly with his own blood.

Moriana drew another arrow from her quiver and shot, aiming for an eye. The broadhead flew true.

It was four feet from target when a pale tongue leaped from the Ullapag's mouth and snagged it in the air like a fly.

Darl was up and running, broadsword in hand, shouting, 'Victory! Moriana and victory!'

The moist eyes swiveled and fixed him with their baleful gaze. The throat sac expanded further, the humming came louder. The monster's vibrations obviously affected humans, but not as they did the Zr'gsz. The uncontrollable contractions of Khirshagk's muscles were breaking him like a thief on a wheel. His men rolled on the ground at his side, hissing in terminal anguish.

The Ullapag was puzzled. Here was a man running at it with hostile intent. Yet its deathsong to Zr'gsz had no effect. Was it possible a human might attack it?

The Ullapag pounced.

Darl escaped being crushed under the monster's bulk by inches. The Count-Duke rolled and came up running. He charged. Swinging his sword doublehanded he hacked at the bloated, warty flank.

His sword rebounded with the sound of a stick striking a poorly stretched drum. The monster's lipless mouth opened and the tongue shot out. Instantly sword and swordarm were tangled in loops of wet, pallid flesh.

Darl tried to pull away. The tongue held him fast. It began reeling him inexorably inward. He twisted, slashed at the tongue with his dagger. Green blood sprayed his chest.

A mental squeal of agony made Moriana and Ziore wince. The Ullapag raised a foreleg and clumsily clutched Darl, trying to hurry him forward into the pink cavern of its mouth. Darl dug in his heels and locked his knees but lacked the strength to resist for more than seconds.

It earned him life. Moriana needed no more than a heartbeat to fit a new arrow, draw and aim, to let fly.

With the monster's tongue coiled like a serpent around Darl, nothing hindered the arrow's flight. It struck the eye and sank to the fletchings. The Ullapag reared, hauling Darl off his feet. A second arrow followed the first.

The tongue uncoiled, spilling Darl onto the hard lava. Even as he fell he struck at the monster's throat sac. The blade cut through the membrane.

A third arrow sang its shrill song of death. The other eye exploded. Darl rocked to his knees and drove his sword into the moss-green belly.

The Destiny Stone turned white. The dying Ullapag fell to the right, rolled onto its back away from the kneeling warrior. Its legs kicked spastically at the air.

As though dropped by an invisible hand, Khirshagk fell limp among the rocks. His men lay about him, frozen in attitudes of ghastly death. Moriana knelt by his side.

His eyes opened, looked into hers, then he said, 'Thank you.'

She was up and running to Darl's side.

'How could you do it?' raged Ludo, the Chief Warder of Omizantrim. 'For a hundred centuries we've kept our faith with Felarod for all humanity. How could you betray us?'

'Don't talk to the princess in that tone, pig,' snarled Darl. He came forward, face dark with menace. Moriana waved him back.

'No, Darl. He has a right to speak that way.' The words threatened to congeal in her throat. 'Listen carefully, Warder Ludo. I'm not betraying anybody. I must explain.'

Ludo spat at her.

'Calm down, old man,' Quickspear said softly, bouncing his spear suggestively in one hand. 'Brightlaugher was my sister's husband's cousin, and well-loved.'

'He got what he deserved.' The old man's blue eyes were merciless and as fearless as a hawk's. 'He was a traitor to men, embarked on a traitor's errand.'

Quickspear raised his weapon.

'Hold!' shouted Moriana. 'Quickspear, leave us.' The dark-haired forester scowled at her, weighing rebellion. He was no fool. He left.

Moriana slumped on her stool. She massaged her face with long, slender fingers. She suddenly snatched them away, screaming. They were drenched in blood.

But it was only a trick of the candlelight.

'I am Moriana Etuul,' she said, 'rightful Queen of the City in the Sky.'

'Pah! You live with the stink of Vridzish magic. What else can we expect of you, witch?'

At a warning growl, Moriana spoke without turning her head.

'Please, Darl, let me finish.' He subsided. 'Thank you, Darl.' Leaning forward, she told the entire story to the Chief Warder, of her sister's usurpation of the Throne of Winds, of Synalon's dabbling with the blackest of magics and her desire to make a compact with the Lords of Infinite Night.

'So it is to fight the Dark Ones that I march against the City,' she told him earnestly. 'The *Zr'gsz* are no more foes to men. They know their time is past. They aid me to recover ancient treasures they were forced to leave when exiled from the Sky City.' She inhaled deeply. 'When they have those things, they'll return to Thendrun in peace. Khirshagk, Instrumentality of the People, gives me his word on this.'

Ludo fixed her with an eye as frosty as the Southern Waste.

'You're either a liar or the most accomplished fool I've ever encountered.' He jerked his head at Darl. 'You can have your bully-boy kill me now.'

'No one's going to harm you.' She started. Ludo stared past her shoulder, his eyes wide.

She turned. A *Zr'gsz* male stood there, a torch gripped in his talons.

'Khirshagk want you,' he said. 'Come. Now. Pleezzz.'

Moriana and Darl looked at one another. Then they followed the messenger into the cool, starry night.

CHAPTER TEN

Their guide led Moriana and Darl from the camp up the slope to the fumarole over which the Ullapag had stood guard. A forest of torches around a sprawling building that had served the inhabitants as school, temple and assembly hall showed where the Zr'gsz guarded the captive Watchers.

Arrows and slung stones had greeted the Watchers when they tried to come to the aid of their fellows and the Ullapag. The Ullapag had given throat then and the Hissers surrounding the camp had collapsed in agony. Before the Watchers could slay more than a handful of the helpless lizard men, the Ullapag's song had been stilled. Shocked by the Hissers' return to activity, the Watchers had emotionally crumbled when Moriana and Darl called on them to surrender. The fact that their immortal co-guardian was dead, and that humans had aided Zr'gsz in slaying it, shattered their morale. They threw down their weapons and obeyed.

Khirshagk's control over his folk was good. Less than a score of the Watchers were killed or injured. The other encampments would send patrols to investigate when no word came from the main village; Moriana was worried but Darl assured her their small detachment could hold until reinforcements summoned by Khirshagk's sorcery arrived from Thendrun. Moriana was puzzled by this – she had been under the impression that so few Zr'gsz had accompanied them because there *were* so few alive. The great crystal keep had fairly rattled from emptiness, and she had scarcely seen a soul other than the Instrumentality and a few silent servants until they were ready to march. But Khirshagk told her more men were on the way, and she deemed it impolitic to question her ally too closely.

A dozen Zr'gsz stood around the fuming lava pit holding torches.

The sun was down but this didn't keep the People from their chores, whatever they were.

'I greet you,' said Khirshagk from the platform that had been the resting place of the monster. 'You have done a great service for my People this day. It is fitting that you witness this, the culmination of years of waiting, of longing.'

Moriana and Darl looked at one another. Stepping forward as near as they dared to the fumarole, they stopped and waited. Their hands found one another.

Still in loincloth and mace-belt, Khirshagk no longer looked the rude savage he had appeared by day. In the smoky torchlight and lit below by the hellglow of melted stone, he was weird and magnificent, the king-priest of an ancient people, an ancient faith. Moriana wondered what ritual he enacted here. She tensed in anticipation, feeling forces all around her.

Khirshagk raised his arms and threw back his head. A wind rush of syllables blew from his lungs. Moriana couldn't understand the words, not fully. But the clicks and hisses and unvoiced vowels struck strangely half-familiar chords within her mind, tantalizing her with hints of understanding. She stole a look at Darl. He watched with curiosity but with no trace of comprehension.

Moriana forced the name to form in her mind: *Ziore?*

I can make nothing of this speech, child, nor can I read the emotions behind it.

That negative reply caused Moriana's unease to grow. Powers definitely beyond the pale surged in this stony amphitheatre.

Moriana sensed excitement growing in the *Zr'gsz* though their expressions remained unreadable behind masks of torchlight and alien musculature. Khirshagk finished his oration in a cry that was almost a sigh, a breath expelled toward the stars, expressing transcendent passion. The *Zr'gsz* thrust their torches into the face of the night with a wild sibilance.

Moriana's nose wrinkled from the brimstone fumes drifting out of the fumarole. A crust of partially cooled lava rode the turbulent surface of the pool and cracked in a not quite regular pattern like mud dried on a flat. Yellow-orange glare burned along the fracture lines. Bubbles of gas rose from the depths of the mountain popping loudly to vent noxious vapors and spit glowing hot gobbets in all directions. One struck the ground near her boot. The heat stung her even through the thick leather.

Khirshagk stood silent, looking from one *Zr'gsz* to the next. In spite of the undercurrents of emotion about her, Moriana suppressed a yawn. It had been a long day, and her body demanded rest.

Darl squeezed her hand.

'I hope they finish soon with whatever they're doing.' She caught his eye and grinned. Perhaps she wouldn't rest so soon.

'My friends.' Almost guiltily they looked at the Instrumentality who had called to them in manspeech across the seething pit. 'You are about to witness an epic moment in the history of the People: the recovery of their Heart, lost to us these ten thousand years.'

A tall, slimly built *Zr'gsz* cast away his cloak. He walked to the edge of the pit, looked down a few seconds, turned to face his leader. She couldn't be sure, but the princess believed the look on his face to be the pure rapture of a religious experience.

Khirshagk pointed with an arm circled in rings of obsidian and jasper. The youth nodded and waded into the lava.

Darl gasped. Moriana stared. Step by step the young lizard man descended into the fumarole. The tendons on his neck stuck out like columns.

'Gods, is he immune to heat?' Moriana whispered.

Darl didn't reply. He only licked dried lips and continued staring at the sight.

The lizard man raised one leg high to wade over an irregularity in the bottom of the lava pool. The meat hung loose on his bones. The bubbling lava reached his groin, his waist, his sternum. His face never lost its look of transfiguration, not even when the liquid stone reached to his chin, his lips. Steam poured from his nostrils as he cooked inside from the awful heat.

He went deeper.

Moriana looked away as the lava reached his eyes. The stench of burned meat clutched at her stomach like a groping hand.

She forced herself to look back. There was no sign of the youth. No creature could desire to survive after having been cooked alive like that. The other *Zr'gsz* gazed eagerly at the roiling surface, Khirshagk among them. The princess knew she would never let him touch her again, not in exchange for any or all powers, magical or temporal.

A plateful of solidified lava slid to one side. A hand thrust from the lava – or the remnant of a hand. Naked bone gleamed in the torchlight but the skeletal hand clutched a jewel, an immense black diamond that smoked from immersion in the molten stone.

Great Ultimate! Ziore cried in Moriana's mind.

Moriana couldn't respond, either with mind talk or vocalized words. She was too stunned by what happened.

Hand and diamond sank from view. The watchers hissed consternation. At a nod from Khirshagk a second lizard man plunged into the fumarole, eyes fixed on the spot where the gem had disappeared.

He brought the diamond five feet nearer shore before he succumbed. Six more *Zr'gsz* made the horrendous journey into the boiling hell of the fumarole before the last handed the great diamond to the Instrumentality and fell back to sink in a cloud of steam.

Khirshagk cradled the gem in both hands. His mighty arms trembled as if it were too massive to hold. He spoke to it fervently in his own hissing tongue, and then turned to Darl and Moriana to address them in their language.

'Ah, this day shall live as long as night comes to cover the land! The Heart is returned to us!'

The diamond glittered darkly from a hundred facets. Smoke streamed from it. The surviving *Zr'gsz* threw themselves down and writhed in rapture.

Unspeaking, Moriana and Darl backed off and then almost ran down the stony path. The princess felt anguish emanating from Ziore's jug, a mental keening. She pitied the genie. It would be horrible to have been cloistered all one's life and then be subjected to such a spectacle.

She saved some pity for Darl and herself. The sight of the young lizard men wading deeper into the killing heat of the lava would live in their dreams as long as they lived. Tomorrow Moriana would attempt to evaluate this shocking demonstration of the gulf that existed betwen the human owners of the Realm and their inhuman predecessors. Tonight they would cling to one another to maintain their sanity and would seek forgetfulness in the sharing of flesh.

'In High Medurim,' Fost told the faces upturned in the dusty gloom of the warehouse, 'this type of technique is called the push-pull. Originally it involved a mature thief and a juvenile apprentice. The urchin, whose appearance was carefully made as scruffy and dirty as possible, would jostle a noble walking the streets. The noble, and guards if any, would either seize the urchin to chastise him for his effrontery or give chase if he was agile enough to evade them.'

He allowed himself a self-satisfied smirk. 'I was only caught once. The best record for any "pusher" in The Teeming. However it went, both the mark and his or her retinue were sufficiently distracted for the well-dressed adult thief to make the "pull," that is, lift the victim's purse. Though manual dexterity was useful, as a general rule the mark was so set on avenging himself on the presumptuous brat that a blind man could rob him without being noticed.'

He leaned back against the cool wall.

'Now, since I didn't drag you through that discourse simply to show you what a fine apprentice thief I was as a lad, who among you can tell me how a variation of the classic push-pull can be employed against a Monitor armory guarded by a dozen armed men?'

Blank looks met him. He crossed his arms, arranged a knowing and superior smile on his lips and waited. On his last sojourn to the City in the Sky he had fallen in with the Underground who resisted Synalon's rule. He hadn't been notably impressed by their competence. In fact, their ineptitude had almost cost him and Moriana their lives when he rescued her from the Vicar of Istu's lustful clutches during the Rite of Dark Assumption. Now he did his best to help them grow more professional and effective. As Luranni, golden-eyed daughter of High Councillor Uriath, had told him, he had little real choice.

He caught Luranni's eye. She sat on a stockfish barrel at the back of the audience of would-be revolutionaries. She smiled at him. He held back the urge to wink in reply.

His eyes slid to the youths of both sexes seated in the makeshift classroom. Their garb was of far humbler quality than that of the people surrounding Luranni. Patches were much in evidence and here and there a ragged hem of tunic or skirt caught his eye. In spite of their less than splendid appearance, it was from among these young people that Fost expected an answer.

He got it. A girl with black hair cut square across her forehead and a piquant prettiness offset by thick eyebrows raised her hand.

'You set children to taunt the guards. Make'em good'n loud so a crowd gathers. Pretty soon all the Monitors'll be able to think about's the way the brats're making them look foolish. While their cods are shrivelled inside their trousers, your team can slip inside.' Her brow wrinkled. 'To think on it, might be still better to have the kids fling rocks'n garbage at the Monnies. That way they're likely to leave station to give'em chase.'

Fost smiled in appreciation at a correct answer.

'Very good, ah — I'm afraid I don't know your name.'

'Syriana,' she replied. She smiled at his quizzical expression. 'I was named for the Royal Twins, Sir Longstrider.'

'Fost will do, Syriana — and for the rest of you, as well.' He glanced at the high, narrow windows of the warehouse and gauged the slant of the sunlight falling through dusty, musty air. 'It's getting near dark. We'll wrap things up for the day.'

The class gave him a ripple of polite applause and rose to file out. He thought it nice to be appreciated.

Fost Longstrider, revolutionary, had such a nice ring to it. Even if he hadn't volunteered.

As the students split up in ones and twos to slip from the building by different exits to avoid attracting attention, Syriana approached Fost with a shy expression.

'Sir . . . uh, Fost,' she said. 'Is it true you, um, you killed a war eagle? All by yourself?'

A rustle of silk, a waft of cinnamon and Luranni's arm slipped cool into his.

'It is indeed true,' she said. 'He's quite a man, my Fost.' Luranni smiled more widely than necessary.

'I, uh, I see.' Syriana licked her lips, then turned and joined the file of departing students.

Luranni looked up at the courier, a glint in her eyes.

'You weren't thinking of letting that lowborn fluff turn your head?' she asked in a fierce whisper Fost was sure must be audible all the way to the Palace of Winds. 'I'll have to braid another knot in my hair to bind you more closely.'

He smiled reassuringly at her. The smile ran no deeper than his lips. He wondered what would happen if — when — Luranni discovered that he was still devoted to Moriana. Given the perilous nature of his very existence in the Sky City, where discovery meant a lingering death at Rann's hands, there was danger of more than an unpleasant emotional scene if Luranni became jealous of the princess.

He donned a cloak, pulled the hood up to obscure his features and let Luranni lead him out into the narrow streets of the Sky City. Sunset was beginning to tinge the western horizon in outlandish colors. Despite the promise of cooling evening breezes, Fost sweltered inside his cowl. Still, this was better than roasting over a grill lit by Rann.

He had killed one of the gigantic eagles of the City's armed forces in single combat. But he hadn't intended to. He had meant to ride up to the City on his captive bird and slip away into the maze of streets hoping to meet some member of the Underground who could tell him where to find Moriana. Only later did it occur to him that he had let fatigue and horror cloud his judgment. The bird could communicate to its keepers in its own speech that it had been forced to bring a groundling into the Sky City. There was no reason for Rann or his secret police to guess the identity of the intruder, but they'd turn the City inside out looking for him. This of all times, the City's rulers couldn't afford to allow possible spies to roam at large.

After flying over the grisly battle between the poison-taloned ravens and the Estil suicide squad, the eagle had touched down in a sidestreet near the starboard beam of the City. Fost had leaped to the pavement.

'Look out!' Erimenes shouted from his jug.

Fost flung himself face down, not even pausing to ask himself why the genie had warned him again of impending danger. Perhaps the long-dead philosopher thought a fight would be small entertainment if terminated at the first stroke by the great decapitating sweep of the eagle's sharp beak that swooshed inches above his back.

Fost rolled desperately. The bird struck again, scoring his hide and striking the flagstones with a jarring screech. Yellow talons groped. Fost got his legs under him and sprang away.

The bird advanced, its eyes bright with the determination to shed his blood. It was bright enough to know Fost must try to kill it; it had struck the first blow. Fost fell back step by step, weighing his chances. He didn't care for them at all. The bird was almost twice as tall and fast, very fast. If he stood, the beast would shred him with beak and claws. If he ran, it would be on him in an instant like an owl falls on a fleeing mouse. The street was little more than an alley between hostelries and shops shuttered for the battle. He had little room to dodge and no place to seek refuge.

'Go *past* him, you fool!' hissed Erimenes. Unquestioning, the courier obeyed.

Shrieking rage, the bird whirled as Fost dived past its legs. The great white head struck a jutting cornice of gray-green stone. As the bird reeled, stunned, Fost regained his feet and closed to make a quick kill with his broadsword.

Bleeding from wounds he didn't remember receiving, wounds

dating back to those given him by the demon-bird in the Black River, Fost ran. Most of the City's police and military were occupied on the walls, but it still took every bit of streetcraft he'd learned growing up in the poverty of High Medurim's slums to reach the familiar short building with its wood facade. The door inside the triple arched entryway was barred by magical means.

'Allow me,' Erimenes said with sardonic satisfaction, and the door swung open to admit the courier.

Luranni's eyes showed no astonishment when she had later entered her third floor flat to find him lounging among fat cushions she used for furnishings.

'I knew you'd come,' she said, a smile spreading across her face. 'I made magic to bring you to me. See?' She reached and undid a braid of brown hair which had been wound around her head. The intricate plaiting made it hard for Fost's eyes to follow.

'Well?' Luranni asked. 'What are we waiting for?' She let her gown drop to the floor.

With an unusual degree of discretion, Erimenes viewed their love-making from within his bottle without tendering his normal lewd commentary. When Fost and Luranni paused to rest, he introduced himself. Once again Luranni showed no surprise. Naked, she pulled the philosopher's jug from Fost's satchel and examined it.

'I've not met you before, have I?' she asked. 'But you spoke to me when I met Fost and the Princess Moriana and guided them to where their eagle waited.'

'Just so,' replied Erimenes.

'So,' she said, turning coin-colored eyes to Fost, 'this is the property Moriana stole from you.'

'Yes.' Like her well-born comrades in the Underground, she may have lacked a sense of the realities of intrigue and insurrection, but she was a highly intelligent woman who had earned high responsibility in her father's import-export business because of her abilities. It was well for Fost to be reminded in a minor matter. It might mean his life if he didn't consider her in more ways than one.

He had to be circumspect in what he told her. Praying that Erimenes wouldn't see fit to contradict him, he explained that he and Moriana had gone off in search of some unspecified treasure, pursued all the way by Rann's bird riders. In Athalau, deep inside the glacier that called itself Guardian, they had become separated.

Fost had been trying to catch up with the princess ever since.

'I just missed her at Chanobit Creek,' he said, lapsing back into truth. 'We found a survivor of her retinue. He didn't live long, but before he died he told us that Moriana was coming here. And so I came to find her.'

'But she didn't come here,' said Luranni.

Fost groaned. His stomach turned over.

'Wh-where is she? Are you sure?' he demanded when he recovered from the shock.

'Synalon claims she has gone to make a compact with the Fallen Ones in Thendrun,' she said. 'It might be a lie. You know what our beloved queen is like.' Fost knew. 'But my father says she appeared to be speaking the truth when she told the Council of it. She was in a rare fury. Sparks were flaming off her the way they do when she's angry, like hot wax from a taper. Poor Tromym got his sidewhiskers set on fire. A servant had to pour a beaker of wine over his head.'

'How did Synalon come by this information?' Erimenes asked. 'I only enquire to expedite this discussion,' he added with a courtly bow, having insisted on being let out of his jug, 'so that Fost can get back to sampling sundry carnal delights with you as soon as possible.'

Fost winced. Luranni only smiled. The courier noted the broad patches of her areolas and the way her nipples stood erect again.

'She divined it, she said. It was hard to tell what made her more furious, her sister betraying humankind or the Dark Ones betraying her. She seemed to think they allowed the Fallen Ones to ally with Moriana in spite of promising to aid her.'

'Mightn't the Vridzish have decided to take matters into their own hands?'

Luranni shrugged, then said, 'Synalon seemed not to think so.' She went to a pewter bowl on a shelf, took up a long slender fruit and began to peel it. 'She spends most of her time brooding and trying to make contact with the Dark Ones, and occasionally torturing some poor soul to death to take her mind off her problems.'

'Synalon has grown rather exalted in her own esteem,' Erimenes remarked, 'if she thinks she can summon the Lords of Infinite Night like some lower caste djinn.' He stroked her nose with a skinny forefinger. 'But enough talk.'

Luranni took a bite from the fruit she held.

'I agree,' she said, reaching for Fost.

Not only did the Sky City woman not seem to mind Erimenes's appreciative presence, she went out of her way to indulge in erotic variations that left Fost gasping for breath. The philosopher was elated.

To each her own, thought Fost, then settled back to enjoy.

Since then he had found himself a full member of the Underground. He had been less than enthusiastic until Luranni pointed out that Fost wanted to join forces with Moriana again, and that Moriana, one way or another, was bound for the Sky City. He might as well lend a hand in the interim both to further the princess's cause and pay for his keep among the City's resistance.

Behind his normal congeniality Luranni's father had not been over-joyed to see the courier again. Fost took it for granted that if he did nothing to justify his continued existence, the High Councillor was fully capable of having him dropped over the skywall some night when the moons were down. In fact, he suspected Uriath might not be beyond hinting to the Monitors where a prize Rann would value highly could be located, but he kept that suspicion to himself.

Fost soon found himself enjoying his role as revolutionary. The subterranean life was far from unfamiliar to him. He had spent his early years dodging the Emperor's police and the goons of the various guilds until opposition to authority had become a part of him. Wandering through the Grand Library of Medurim under the guidance of Ceratith the pedant, Fost had come upon many works on the theory and practice of revolution. He had read them with the all-consuming eagerness with which he approached all learning in that halcyon stage of his life.

His first suggestion had been resisted vigorously by Uriath and the senior members of the Underground. Fost wanted the resistance to be broadened to include middle and lower classes as well as the noble-born.

'I'm a sorcerer,' Fost told Uriath, 'and I can teach your people the secret of invisibility.' By that, he explained, he meant that the Underground was ignoring the best source of intelligence in the entire City.

'Who pays attention to servants? More than that, who heeds the glaziers who repair broken windows, the workmen who clean and polish the building stones, the maids who dust Queen Synalon's bedchamber?'

Uriath looked skeptical. Grinning, Fost gestured past the High Councillor. Plying a feather duster over the elaborate wooden screens hung on the walls stood a servant in the yellow and blue livery of Uriath's own household. Uriath turned a deeper red and agreed to try Fost's scheme.

It had borne fruit. Through workers in the barracks of the bird riders, the Underground had made contact with malcontents in the City's military, the first such breakthrough in the movement's history. Actual armed insurrection against Synalon became for the first time more than a dream as unreal as any evoked by the Golden Barbarians' drugs.

His spectacular rescue of Princess Moriana from the Vicar of Istu gave Fost a reputation with the Underground. It was enhanced by rumors of his victory over a war eagle, which he saw no need to balance by pointing out that the bird had smacked its own fool head against a building. When in spite of initial sullen resistance to the idea of recruiting members of the service class into the movement Fost's outrageous scheme produced results, he could do no wrong.

He'd made further innovations. The Underground's internal security was little more than wishful thinking. As far as Fost could judge, the only reason it survived was that Rann was too occupied with planning and executing Synalon's grand scheme of conquest to give much mind to the business of spying on Sky Citizens. Additionally, the leaders of the movement were too highly placed and valuable to the running of the City bureaucracy for Synalon to arrest without concrete evidence. So far, all the Undergound members had died before revealing the names of anyone important.

But it was only a matter of time.

In the existing organization, the damage was done; each member knew the identities of too many comrades. For new recruits, including servants and disgruntled soldiers, Fost introduced a cell system. An individual never knew anyone outside his own three-person cell and those whom he or she recruited. Contact with superiors was done through those who had recruited the cell members themselves, and the recruiters kept their own identities secret. In this way the damage would be minimized if a captured rebel lived long enough to spill his figurative guts along with his literal ones.

While Fost played rebel leader, Erimenes consulted with various mages in the Underground about means of short-circuiting Rann's magical surveillance net. By using captive fire elementals, Palace sorcerors spied on any events near the direct glow of fire. It netted a fair number of disaffected citizens overly fond of sitting down before their evening fire and spouting off about the oppressions of the crazy queen.

Since that was unlikely to remain the only trick in the secret police's repertory, the fifteen-hundred-year-old sage was also trying to foresee and forestall new approaches of the opposition and to come up with ideas of his own. Though Erimenes's powers were limited, only coming into full potency when he was near his natal city of Athalau, he possessed what Fost grudgingly had to admit to be an excellent knowledge of the theory and practice of Athalar magic, magic involving the intrinsic powers of one's own brain. The Athalar, and Erimenes, were less knowledgeable about extrinsic magic involving the manipulation of powers external to oneself, such as elementals or demons. But even here Erimenes was a fount of useful lore.

To all appearances Erimenes was enjoying his role as hugely as Fost was his. He didn't even seem to mind that his labors and researches prevented him from watching the carnal antics of Fost and the willing Luranni, which grew increasingly more frantic as time passed and the inevitable but as yet unscheduled confrontation neared. Through the grapevine Fost heard intriguingly lubricous rumors about orgies among the younger mages and apprentices fomented by Erimenes. He didn't ask the spirit if there was truth in them. If there was, Erimenes would tell him in vastly more detail than he cared to hear.

But Fost worried. In the past, the genie's sole allegiance had been to gratifying his own lust for vicarious experience, particularly sex and violence. Back in the days of a more innocent eon, when Fost had been a mere courier delivering a parcel of unknown contents to a sorceror, Erimenes had repeatedly gotten Fost into trouble by calling pursuers down on him when he sought to hide. To hear the philosopher, he saved Fost from a life of cowardice. Fost knew Erimenes merely wanted to enjoy the ensuing bloodshed. When Moriana had stolen the jug from Fost and returned to the City to make her fateful reconnaissance, Erimenes promptly transferred his loyalty to the princess. And when Moriana was captured by Synalon, again Erimenes had switched his perfidious loyalties, seeing in Synalon and Rann the chance to sample their offerings of perversion and sadism.

After the escape from the City he helped Fost and the princess.

But he had aided them because they provided him legs and the chance to gain for himself the life-restoring Amulet of Living Flame. Since then, he had befriended Fost consistently, though he was always ready to provoke a good fight whenever he found things dull. Erimenes seemed to be genuinely on Fost's side. But the courier could not forget Synalon's determination to exhaust the possibilities for perversion nor Rann's dark genius with knife and heated iron – or the attraction their activities had for a shade of Erimenes's tastes.

As long as Erimenes acted helpful, there was nothing Fost could do about him but worry. Which he did.

Like metal in a forge, the days warmed and stretched as summer came on. Fost taught urban guerillas in the day and engaged in sweaty sexual encounters every night. He started losing weight and growing dark circles under his eyes. Sometimes he worried about Jennas, who had helped and loved him, even knowing that she could never truly have him. And he thought of Grutz, his war bear; he had grown fond of the beast. But he told himself worrying was both futile and unnecessary. Jennas could care for herself, as could Grutz.

As time passed, he thought less and less about the hetwoman. But all the time he thought of Moriana.

He was not the only one preoccupied with thoughts of the princess.

'But Uriath!' Tromym's whiskered jowls bobbled mournfully above his goblet. 'The princess is laying plans to march against the City with the thrice-cursed Hissers. She might actually win. And then what becomes of us?'

Uriath sat at apparent ease, fingers steepled, allowing his eyes to rove over the screens adorning the walls of his study. They were quite ancient, depicting the Three and Twenty Wise Ones of Agift: Gormanka with his Wind Wheel, Ust rolling the ball of the sun, lithe Jirre and her lyre whose music was irresistibly aphrodisiac, Ennisat blessing the first human settlers of the Realm with the knowledge of double entry bookkeeping, along with the other nineteen. Uriath used the pictures for both relaxation and as an excuse not to meet Tromym's eyes.

Uriath sighed, thinking what a congenital fool Tromym was. And fools quickly outlived their usefulness.

'She might, Tromym. She might also lose. Our most exalted queen has fought three major battles in as many months. And won each, but every time at a cost. What will remain of her strength after the final confrontation with her sister?' He blew out a long breath. 'And if Moriana wins, how strong will she be? In the disorganization following the invasion of the Sky City, it will be easy enough to eliminate her.' He picked up his own goblet and sipped. 'We might become heroes for doing away with her. She's turned traitor to her kind, after all, by enlisting the help of the Hissers.'

He belched lightly, rose, went to the window. It lay open to admit a breeze heightened with the sweet growing smells of the plains a thousand feet below. The two moons hung above the lower reaches of the Thails, pink and blue, casting the High Councillor's shadow behind him and across the table where Tromym sat.

'Don't forget the gift that subcurator of the Palace library made us. We have magical forces at our disposal now, too, ones our own mages don't even know of. That could give us the needed edge.'

'Do we understand these forces enough to tamper with them?' Tromym gulped his wine so hurriedly he choked.

'I am of the Royal Blood, Tromym, even if removed from the present rulers. Sorcery is in my genes. This book reveals some of the secrets of the earliest Etuul. It was written by the original Moriana's daughter, Kyrun.' He turned from the window with a grand sweep of his arm. 'Someday, I shall become a sorceror to equal any, Tromym. When my daughter sits on the Beryl Throne, then shall I make my true mark in the history of the City.'

Tromym looked away nervously. He reached for the decanter of wine, then saw the trembling of his hand and rang for a servant to refill his goblet for him.

'Who'd have th-thought it,' he said, 'that enlisting the help of the rabble would profit us so.'

Uriath gave him a tight smile.

'That damned barbarian my daughter's taken for a pet has proved useful.'

'Y-you think he might be a fit consort for her? Robust barbarian blood might spice up the line a bit, eh?' He tried to wink at Uriath but wound up opening and shutting both eyelids alternately so that he appeared to be trying to blink a message in code. Uriath's cold blue eyes staring back at him chilled to the bone.

'Do you seriously suggest for an instant that my daughter could conceive of forming an . . . an arrangement with a *groundling*?'

Uriath's biting tone indicated he'd judge Synalon's famous hornbull a more likely choice.

'No-no, Uriath, not at all. Making a joke, that's all. Ha, ha.' He squinted into his wine. 'Damn, this thing's empty again.'

A steward entered at Uriath's summons.

'Bring the Councillor a larger vessel at once. And see that the sluggard who provided him such an inadequate thimble is soundly whipped.' Wordlessly, the servant bowed and withdrew.

'Where were we? Ah, the Northblood messenger boy. He'll have to go, I suppose. He's too likely to have some sentimental notions of loyalty to Moriana — to say nothing of the possibility that he might fancy himself to have some claim on Luranni's affections.' The steward returned bringing a soup tureen for Tromym and refilled his master's cup.

Uriath watched and waited for the steward to leave, his fingers working on his fringe beard.

'If only that young fool Chiresko had done as he was told, we wouldn't have the problem of this Longspider or whatever he's called confronting us now. Or of Moriana, either.'

'Do I hear my name spoken, O good and loyal Uriath? In a favourable context, I trust.'

Wine dyeing his sidewhiskers pink, Tromym raised his face from his bowl to compliment his friend on his uncannily accurate imitation of Moriana's voice. The words congealed in his throat when he saw Uriath's face turn as white as his beard.

Experiencing the same endless falling sensation that had come over him when Synalon's silvered sphere approached him at the victory feast, Uriath gaped at the features of Moriana Etuul, laughing back at him from the surface of his wine.

'Dark Ones,' he muttered, fighting down panic. Had she heard?

'Y-your Highness,' he stammered. I didn't expect —'

'Naturally not. Synalon doesn't expect it either. She believes her magics screen my perception from the City. But I have learned much since I saw her last.' Moriana smiled, her teeth rippling as Uriath's hand trembled and conveyed the motion to the surface of the wine. 'It will be pleasant indeed to show her how much I've learned.'

'We all await that time most fervently.'

'We will take your protestations of devotion for granted, Uriath. Now listen. There is much to be done . . .'

CHAPTER ELEVEN

The Sky City crossed first Brev, then Thailot, while the inhabitants of those cities stared up in apprehension. It was wasted emotion. The City passed in gray, stony silence and was gone. It turned northeast at Thailot toward Wirix.

An army of five thousand *Zr'gsz* camped on the shore of Lake Wir. Their numbers were swelled by a thousand foresters from the Great Nevrym Forest, and roughly the same number of adventurers recruited by Darl on a whirlwind tour of the City States. After the fiasco of Chanobit, it was miraculous that any harkened to Moriana's claw and flower banner. After her alliance with the Fallen Ones became known she would have said it was impossible. But the fear of the Hissers was an ancient one. Fear of Synalon burned hot and immediate. And Darl did work miracles. None who heard him failed to be stirred, and those who had heard him before said he spoke as he never had, as no man had. He spoke like an angel come to deliver a new revelation, and his words drew men's hearts like a magnet.

Moriana did not hear his stirring speeches on her behalf. She busied herself preparing for the prodigious battle with the City in the Sky. A thousand details claimed her attention. Food had to be arranged for her growing army. The skystone mines on the slopes of Omizantrim required constant administration. The imprisoned Watchers proved a nagging dilemma. Groundlings had to be drilled in the use of the Hissers' skyraft.

Then there was diplomacy. The Wirixers weren't happy at the presence of the Vridzish. However, they understood which Quincunx city would next feel the might of Synalon's men and magic. With Bilsinx and Kara-Est occupied, and Brev and Thailot having thrown themselves at the City's mercy, the Sky City could take all the time it needed to build its forces for the conquest of Wirix. The mages of the lake city were mighty, but they doubted their ability to master magics such as Synalon commanded. And if Kara-Est's aerial defenses couldn't preserve her from military defeat, Wirix's strictly landborne defenses meant little more than walls of sand. The Hissers might seem unworthy allies but they and Moriana offered the only hope of survival for Wirix.

Nonetheless, the Wirixers were glad when Khirshagk and his retinue turned down their offer to visit their city on its island in the midst of the great Lake Wir.

The city girded itself for war.

It would be a war unique in the City's long history. For the first time since the Human Conquest, the City itself would be the principal object of attack. In the many small squares and parks dotted about the Sky City, the citizens gathered in little knots and gazed at the northeast horizon until masked Monitors drove them on with curses and cudgels. Though they had grown cautious about speaking their thoughts aloud, most wondered whether the victory of either side in the impending conflict might be a loss for them.

Rann drilled his forces hard. From Terror's back he led the bird riders back and forth across the sky in exercises designed to bring them to perfect fighting pitch. Even his own elite Sky Guards grumbled at the severity with which he drove.

He drove himself harder still. He had had to work out the details of the occupation of Kara-Est mostly on his own. Fortunately, Chief Deputy Tonsho had been taken alive. She dreaded physical pain above all things, which meant Rann himself was the perfect threat to keep her in line. Just thinking what exquisite agony the deputy must be going through, knowing herself at his mercy, brought a smile of pleasure to Prince Rann's thin lips. But such smiles were rare and shortlived. Tonsho was a woman of character as well as ability. Sooner or later she would overcome her cowardice and wreak harm on her city's oppressors. But not soon, he judged, and that was all that counted. For the time, a military governor and a strong garrison sufficed to insure her cooperation.

Such cooperation was vital now. Kara-Est had to start functioning again as a seaport and trade center as soon as possible. Moreover, there were matters that would take all of Tonsho's diplomatic skills to straighten out. Since the City was not yet in a position to go to war with such powers as Tolviroth Acerte, the Empire and Jorea, there were reparations to be made for damage to neutral shipping, and the rights of non-combatant citizens had to be guarded. There were problems such as that posed by the ship's captain, half Jorean and half North Keep Dwarf whose vessel had been deposited intact in the Central Plaza of Kara-Est as a prankish parting gesture of the air elemental Synalon had summoned. The outlandish halfbreed demanded recompense far beyond the value of his vessel. In the meantime something had to be done about the ship sitting in the middle of the city. Rann was pleased to have someone, anyone, tend to such matters for him.

Synalon sulked because she felt the Dark Ones should have prevented the Vridzish from allying with Moriana. Several of the queen's advisors pointed out that the Fallen Ones might have fallen into apostasy toward the Elder Gods since the Dark Ones' patronage hadn't benefited them before. Those advisors were not perspicacious enough to realize the fallibility of the Dark Ones wasn't something Synalon wished to be reminded of just now. She had ordered them all exiled through the Skywell to the earth a thousand feet below.

In the meantime Synalon contributed almost nothing to preparing for the conflict with her sister. In a way, Rann found that a blessing, since she was prone to fantastic whims. But it did leave more of a burden on his slender shoulders. Particularly when it became apparent that organized subversion had increased in the Sky City.

Sometimes, however, the queen herself took an interest in the affairs of her City . . .

Flesh parted to the caress of a blade. The naked young man bucked and screamed.

'There, my love,' said Synalon, patting sweat from his forehead with a moist rag. 'Tell me what I wish to hear. Who are the traitors?' She smiled tenderly and caressed his cheek. 'The pain can stop any time. Then you can love me. Tell me, have you ever seen anyone more beautiful than I?'

The Sky Guard lieutenant looked up at her with the eyes of a snared rabbit. They were lovely eyes, really, she thought, the deep dark blue of a winter sky at sunset. Her captive was a handsome youth, taller than normal among the short, wiry Sky Citizens, leanly muscular under tanned skin, his hair glossy brown with blond highlights from spending time in the wind and sun on an eagle's back. His cheeks and eyes were sunken from the terror of confine- ment following his arrest, but to Synalon's taste that merely accented the aristocratic quality of the facial bone structure.

Her breath came shallow and fast, as if after lusty exertion. The aroma of her own excitement was hot musk in her nostrils. She wore a pearl gray silk smock that came halfway down her sleek, silvery thighs. It was opened midway down the front. Heavy, well-shaped breasts with skin like fresh cream hung mostly in view, crested by burgundy nipples taut as a drum with arousal. The young man showed little inclination to look at them.

From below came mutterings, scraping noises, an occasional high, sharp cry. The vast aeries of the City, honeycombed below the level of the street and the very Palace itself, buzzed around the clock with avian activity. The almost subliminal sound transmitted itself through the stone flooring of the dungeon and Synalon's bare feet to tickle its way up the inside of her thighs. She enjoyed the melange of sensations, the sounds of martial preparation and breathing with the jagged catch of panic in its rhythm, the erratic orange light of torches set at the bases of arches which formed the groined ceiling of the torture chamber, and the smell of sweat and blood and her own hunger.

The captive sucked in his breath as Synalon trailed fingers along the tight skin of his belly to toy with his limp penis.

'There, there, I wouldn't hurt *that*,' she said. He quivered as she bent to kiss it. 'Not until the last – *if* you don't tell me what I want to know . . .'

He looked resolutely toward the far wall. Synalon frowned and slashed. Another scarlet line appeared across his chest. He howled in pain.

She worked on his body with passion and artistry. True to her promise, she left his genitals alone. She would break this young buck, and then she would enjoy him. And she would make him enjoy her, despite his agony.

It was rumored in the open air markets and the bird riders' barracks that Queen Synalon could bring a corpse to orgasm. The rumors were not far wrong.

'Damn Rann,' she hissed. The pink tip of her tongue peeked out of the corner of her mouth as she studiously flayed a strip of skin from the bulge of the lieutenant's left bicep. The young man ground his teeth on the leather strap she'd fastened in his mouth to keep him from biting his tongue. His buttocks slapped convulsively against the stone slab to which he was fastened. The bonds were leather, lined with velvet padding; no chains or manacles for Synalon. They might damage the subject by accident. Synalon regarded randomness the bane of artistry.

Reconsidering, she wondered whether she ought to curse her cousin. All bird riders were tough and well-trained, but the Guard was a fanatical elite, handpicked and then honed and polished like the finest North Keep blades. Synalon knew that only philosophical principle would cause a Guard officer to betray the throne. The young fool had decided Moriana would make a better ruler for the City than she. And what a Guard decided on principle, he would adhere to with all the fortitude Rann was so expert at inculcating.

No, she shouldn't curse Rann. She loved a challenge.

The secret police who had arrested this young man had evidence which led them to believe he knew the identities of the leaders in the conspiracy against her. That was why she chose to interrogate him herself; also, she needed surcease from the screaming frustration of beseeching the Dark Ones to tell her: *why?*

By layers she stripped away resistance. The apparent carelessness of cuts she had first made was belied by the way she played on them to create a pattern of pain, of blood and tanned skin. And finally, sobbing uncontrollably, the captive was ready to tell everything the silvery, seductive voice coaxed him to reveal.

Then the change began.

At first Synalon blinked, thinking it a trick of the light or of sweat dripping in her eyes. It was no illusion. The skin blackened before her eyes.

She drew back with a startled exclamation. Did the young man have some loathsome disease that had just entered a climactic stage? Her fingers traced glowing patterns in the air in front of her. She chanted a spell of protection even as the writhing of the bound body became a writhing of the very contours of that body, a change of mass and outline more profound than any wrought by Synalon's knife. The chest expanded, grew so muscular that it was grotesque. The legs shortened and thickened, swelling with muscle until the straps around thighs and shins parted with explosive cracks. The arms grew thicker, too, lengthening so that the huge muscles of the upper forearm burst asunder the straps that had restrained the captive's wrists. The forehead bulged, the jaw became a slab, the nose twisted into a sardonic beak. Eyes like portals to an infinite pit regarded her with infinite amusement.

It was a black Dwarf which lay on the torture table. But a Dwarf taller than any man she knew. The sturdy stone table groaned beneath its weight.

'Don't you remember me, little sister?' The Dwarf shook his gigantic head. 'And after all the caterwauling you've been pouring into the Void I shouldn't think you'd greet me with those paltry protective canthrips you're muttering beneath your breath.' He smiled showing huge perfect teeth. 'Or has it occurred to you that your behavior toward my Masters, alternately whining at Them and demanding that They offer explanation for what you take to be Their deeds, has been scarcely calculated to win Their approbation? And have you thought, lovely one, that the mildest of such punishments I might mete out for your impertinence would have you offering your kingdom and your soul for the chance to trade places with that unfortunate who occupied this berth before me?'

She fell to her knees. Fear and ecstasy numbed her brain, and her heart raced out of control.

'O Messenger of the Dark Ones, forgive me! I didn't realize it was you.' Her hands caressed the gnarled thighs, working upward to their juncture.

The Dwarf chuckled and swung to a sitting position.

'Much would I enjoy giving way to your inviting blandishments. You definitely have your uses, though you've given little evidence of that lately.'

'What do you mean?' She flinched back. 'Haven't I served the Dark Ones well? The mightiest seaport of the Realm lies an offering at Their feet. And how do They repay me? By allowing Their chosen folk to make compact with my sister to drag me from my throne, the throne I consecrated to the greatness of the Lords of the Dark!'

The Dwarf threw back his head and laughed like the rolling of a great brass bell.

'How quickly your ire makes you forget the humility appropriate to a lowly servant.' Beams of scarlet stabbed from his eyes. Synalon's smock flashed into flame. She shrieked and leaped to her feet, clawing at the fiercely burning garment. Her fingers blistered as the fabric resisted a moment, then gave way. She flung the smock into a heap by the wall. It flared to intolerable actinic brightness and vanished, leaving only scorch marks on the wall. All the time the

138

Dwarf's laughter washed over her like oily surf.

Her belly and breasts showed a fiery pink, as though from long exposure to the sun. Her rump felt as if it had been branded. The rancid smell of burning hair choked her. She beat at her head and the juncture of her thighs until the smouldering stopped.

And then the realization struck her like a mace.

The Messenger read understanding on her face and smiled.

'Yes. You thought you had mastered the fire long ago, and yet in its most primitive form it almost consumed you. Think on that lesson, beautiful child.'

He folded maul-like hands across his bulging belly and leaned back onto his elbows.

'Now. What was it you wished to ask of the Masters?'

She took a moment to conquer the fear and rage seething within. She almost blurted out another accusation. She turned it into an exhalation of breath and started again, to the accompaniment of the Messenger's knowing grin.

'I have done my utmost to serve the Dark Ones,' she said as evenly as possible. 'None could have served Them as faithfully. Now They – rather, now it *appears* that They have chosen to aid my mortal enemy against me. I dem – That is, I most humbly beg to know why They have done this thing. And what . . . what redress I must make to regain Their complete trust.'

The black head swung ponderously from side to side.

'O, ye of little faith,' the Dwarf said. 'Is this truly how you venerate the Eldest? By leaping to the conclusion that They betrayed you?' He clucked. 'It is a sore disappointment to our mutual Masters. They harbored great hope for you.'

'But . . . but the Vridzish are worshippers of the Dark Ones! Aren't the Masters permitting them to come against me?'

'The Fallen Ones worshipped the beautiful principle of Oneness which is the Endless Night – ten millennia ago. Because of their own carelessness they lost their power among nations. They chose to blame the Dark Ones, who so loved them that They gave Their only begotten child to aid the Zr'gsz against the interlopers. So they turned away from Grace.'

Synalon stared.

'The Fallen Ones no longer worship the Masters of the Void?'

'Think how easily your faith was swayed. The Hissers lost a world. One can understand their deviance. Almost.'

She ran her fingers through the stubble remaining of her hair. It was brittle and broke with tiny sounds like the snappings of a thousand minute twigs.

'You're saying the Dark Ones have no influence over the Vridzish?'

'Not necessarily. But like their opposite numbers, the Dark Ones work almost exclusively through those who chose to do Their bidding. Much depends on the vagaries of mortal servants on both sides, and even of those who take no side.'

Her nerve returned and with it a measure of defiance.

'Then let the Dark Ones aid me against my sister. It should be sweet indeed for Them to taste complete vengeance against those who have forsworn Them.'

The demon tipped his head back and studied her down his nose before saying, 'It isn't that simple. You are on probation. Your behavior has caused our Masters doubts . . . grave doubts.' He shook his head. 'Only the worthy may receive the blessings of Darkness. You must prove yourself, my dear.'

'But . . . but Moriana has the magic of the Hissers to draw upon!'

'And haven't the Dark Ones given you many gifts of power and wisdom already?' He sat up and rested his heavy chin in the palm of one hand. Unlike a human, his palm was as ebon-dark as the rest of his body. 'Our Masters chose you because They deemed you the most powerful enchanter alive. Do you believe your sister is stronger?'

'Moriana?' She spat out the name. 'That pale-haired bitch-slut? Never!'

'Then you will have no trouble besting her. And in the process, reaffirming the Dark Ones' faith in you.'

He turned and lay down full length on the table.

'Perhaps the next time the Masters will allow me to accept the tribute you tender so well,' he said, a touch of sadness in his voice. 'But until that hour . . .'

'Wait!'

'Farewell.'

The heaving, undulating transformation didn't reverse itself. Instead, white light exploded from the Dwarf, dazzling Synalon and throwing her back against the wall.

When her eyes opened she was on her knees again. The shape of the captive reclined on the table in a pose of mortal agony.

But not in the flesh. What lay on the dull stone was an obsidian likeness of the traitorous officer, perfect to every feature depicting each incision Synalon's knife had left, even showing bloodspills trailing from the wounds.

As such portentous events are prone to do, it happened quite by accident.

Fost dropped by one of the field headquarters Uriath had set up in a safe house after the courier pointed out that the High Councillor might not want the attention of Monitors drawn to too many comings and goings from his own mansion. Fost enjoyed appearing unannounced. It irritated Uriath, but the High Councillor could scarcely refuse to see someone as important and highly regarded in the movement as Fost.

'Time to clench your teeth and loosen your purse strings again, Uriath,' the courier said as he entered the basement of the chandler's shop which was the current secret command post. 'We've a contact who has blackmail goods on old Anacil's chief assistant chamberlain. Seems he's been diverting funds from Synalon's warchest.'

'Who's that?' a voice asked sharply, apparently from nowhere. Uriath looked up from what appeared to be a large pan of water resting on the table in front of him. The look of annoyance on his face quickly changed to surprise.

Fost's heart bounced into his throat. Frowning, unwilling to believe his ears, he moved forward to stare into the pan.

He found himself face to face with Moriana.

'Uriath, what . . . Great Ultimate!' The image wavered as the princess fought to control herself. 'Whoever you are,' she said in a quavering voice, 'you bear too close a resemblance to someone I once knew.'

Fost grinned.

'I don't know whether you'd call it resemblance so much as identity,' he said.

'Ah, Princess Moriana, we meet again,' said a voice from Fost's hip. 'I've never seen you lovelier. Treachery and murder agree with you, it appears.'

'Erimenes?' She gasped. 'Then it's – oh, Gods, Fost!'

'Guilty.' The word cracked across and the flippancy left his face. He opened his mouth only to shut it again. 'Are you well?' he finally asked, and instantly castigated himself. He'd had months to form a

141

proper greeting and had done no better than a lovesick adolescent.

The princess visibly strained to hold back her tears.

'I didn't think I'd ever be grateful that I didn't strike true,' she stammered, 'but now, oh, Fost, I'm so glad you're alive!'

'Don't chide yourself about your aim, Moriana. There's something I need to tell you. You don't have . . .'

His voice stopped. His lips moved but no sound emerged.

'Fost? There's something wrong with the enchantment. I can't hear you.'

'You don't have anything to worry about, my dear,' he heard his own voice say. 'I'm working with the Underground to pave the way for your glorious return.'

She frowned at his peculiar choice of words.

'I'm pleased to hear it. I'm laying plans with Uriath now so that we may strike coordinated blows to bring Synalon down.' She seemed about to say more, then glanced out of Fost's field vision. 'I . . . I have to go now.'

The breaking of the connection hid a choked sob.

'Erimenes,' hissed Fost, picking his way from shadow to shadow through the streets. 'Why in Ust's name did you take over my voice? And how did you do it? This far from Athalau?'

'Necessity,' the philosopher said haughtily, 'is an excellent aid to my already significant ability. And it was urgently necessary that I prevent you from blurting that Moriana had the Destiny Stone instead of the Amulet of Living Flame.'

'But why? By the Emperor's rouged ass, she has to know!'

'Do you really want Uriath to know?' The courier fell abruptly silent. 'That's better. Someone might hear you — hsst!'

A footfall came to Fost's sensitive ears. He melted back into a doorway and concentrated on imitating shadow. A moment later a pair of Monitors swung around the corner and came right at him.

'And then I said to her, "If you'll just be reasonable, it might not be necessary to take you in, my sweet."'

His companion laughed loudly, an ugly, distorted sound through his mask.

'So wha'd she say? Huh?'

They passed by. The first Monitor elbowed his taller companion in the ribs. Fost's fingers tightened on his swordhilt.

'What do you think, Nalgo? "Oh, you Monitors have always been my ideal, so strong and brave! I'll do simply anything for the service of my Cit –'''

They rounded the next corner, going in the opposite direction from the candle shop Fost had just left by a back door. He let himself breathe again and set off down the street.

'I don't trust Uriath farther than I can throw him,' Erimenes said as if nothing had happened.

'A vaporous entity would be hard pressed to throw a man that portly.'

'My point exactly. I think he suspects Moriana ventured to Athalau in search of a talisman of some sort. Whether or not he knows she was after the Amulet is irrelevant. If he thinks she got something powerful, he might just decide to lay hands on it himself.'

Fost chewed his lips, rolling the problem around in his mind.

'I wouldn't put it past him,' he conceded.

'And if he finds she's got the Destiny Stone – and if he has any idea of its properties – he may just decide to have nothing to do with her. At all.'

'You mean the thing's that potent?'

'Potent beyond imagining.' *Was* it imagining or did Fost sense trepidation in the genie's voice? 'It's vastly stronger than the Amulet ever was. But it was always valued less because its powers were uncontrollable. In my time some theorized it possessed a sentience of its own.'

For once Fost wasn't yawning at one of Erimenes's lectures.

'But we've got to tell her.'

'Agreed,' said the spirit. 'But can you suggest how we might go about it without sharing the information with the great and noble Uriath?'

'I'll think of a way.'

'You hope.'

'Ziore?'

Yes, child.

'I . . . I feel strange.'

She felt rather than heard gentle laughter.

You kill the only man you've ever loved, only to behold him healthy a half year later. Did you not *feel strange, that would be the strangest thing of all.*

'Did I do right, Ziore?'

'Do you think what you did was right?' came the genie's soft voice, both to ears and mind.

'I did then. But now, I don't know.' She sat up in bed. A moon balanced on the edge of the Thails, laying a golden trail across Lake Wir. In the distance a nightbird sang to it. 'But somehow the decision to ally myself with the Fallen Ones came easier because . . . because I killed him.'

'Because you felt you'd already soiled yourself.'

'Yes.' Moriana hooked a thumb around the silver chain she wore always around her neck and fished the Amulet into the moonlight. As usual its surface balanced white against black, revealing nothing. 'Now I hate myself more. Fost's being alive almost makes things harder.'

'I know.' The words came soft, caressing, soothing.,

Moriana kneaded her face with one hand. 'I do love him,' she said softly. 'How can I find myself resenting that he's alive?'

'You're human.'

'It's so easy for you to be so glib, you who've never known human passion!' She stopped, horrified at what she'd said. 'Gods, Ziore, I'm sorry. I didn't mean . . .'

'You did,' Ziore said with a trace of sternness. 'If nothing else, I've learned too much to heed words spoken in anger.' A moment's silence, then, 'But speaking of anger, I confess I was angry when I heard you address Fost's unseen companion as Erimenes. If you hadn't had things of more import to say, I would have told that vile charlatan a thing or two!'

Moriana grinned wryly at Ziore's vehemence, so unusual to the placid spirit. In an oblique way the nun was chastising her. It was the fault of Erimenes's philosophy that Ziore *hadn't* known human passion.

'I'm glad Darl's away,' said Moriana. 'I . . . I couldn't face telling him yet.'

'I understand.'

'Thank you.' The princess let the Amulet fall and lay back down. The pillow was cool and sweet-smelling beneath her head. 'To think I'll see him again!' she whispered. 'Oh, Ziore, I'm not a murderer!'

But a voice in the back of her skull asked: *am I a traitor*?

CHAPTER TWELVE

In increasing desperation, Fost attempted to tell Moriana that the talisman she carried was not the Amulet of Living Flame but the mercurial Destiny Stone. The opportunity eluded him. As the City moved toward Wirix and the waiting army, the press of preparation drove each of them ever faster. Not infrequently Fost was on hand when Uriath and Moriana were in communication. They exchanged a few hurried words, looks which Fost *hoped* meant certain things but couldn't be sure.

But Uriath was always there, somedays bland, sometimes avuncular, always giving the impression of something hooded coiled beside him. Even with Erimenes there to hold his tongue for him, Fost found himself unwilling to speak of the Amulet and the Stone with Uriath near.

As the City crossed the Thail Mountains and began to descend from the height to which it had climbed to clear the peaks, Moriana's army broke camp and moved southwest from Lake Wir to meet it. The Wirixers didn't want the battle fought over their heads and were unwilling to take active part in the action. They had given Moriana's forces the right to stay for a time and had provided her with supplies. More than that they wouldn't do. It mattered little. The battle for the City would be fought in the City's own element: sky.

It was the last day before the two sisters met, doomsday for unspecified numbers on both sides. Fost had gone without sleep for three days trying to accomplish a million things at once, laying out tactics for the joint invasion and insurrection, trying to keep the morale of his untried revolutionaries from disintegrating totally at the prospect of battle, dodging the last-minute push by the Monitors that wiped out a quarter of the Underground's cells overnight. He stumbled like a zombie when he entered Uriath's current catacomb to confer with the resistance chief.

A silent youth guided him down a slippery flight of stairs. Rank and humid smells clogged his nostrils. Why did Uriath pick a mushroom farm for his new command post?

A door streaked with a rainbow array of fungus was pushed open. Fost caught a glimpse of Uriath slamming a book closed and slipping it into a compartment on his desk. The courier was too exhausted to care what the volume was or why the High Councillor acted so furtively.

He nodded to Uriath, spotted a blond wood stool, navigated to it as the door shut behind him with a groan like an arthritic giant. He gave the stool a quick once-over before sitting. The wood was warped and water spotted but showed no signs of mold. He sat and leaned back against the wall with a sigh.

'I think I've got the damage patched up,' he said without preamble. 'Rann, or whoever is handling internal security for Synalon, actually struck too soon. We didn't give out the final assignments until this afternoon, which means no one they netted knows our exact plans or dispositions. As a bonus, it's easier to change assignments and then distribute them instead of changing them abruptly after they've been issued and confusing hell out of everybody.'

'Your idea,' said Uriath, more curtly than usual. Crediting the courier irked him.

'All our reports indicate Synalon's going to be locked up tight in the Palace, working her magics from there. So I've cut the number of people on other squads, the ones attacking the aeries and Monitor stations, to get the full complement for our push at the Palace. What we really need . . .'

A chime shimmered in the air of the room. Hairs rose on the back of Fost's neck though the sound was now familiar to him. He still wasn't used to sudden tones issuing from tubs of water.

Energized again, he stood and went to peer into the tin vessel. Uriath swiveled in his chair, gave Fost an annoyed look, and bowed his head to the water.

The surface turned murky. The cloudiness began to swirl without stirring the liquid. The murk coalesced into Moriana's tired but radiantly beautiful visage.

'Fost,' she said smiling, 'you're upside down. Good evening, Uriath. I trust everything proceeds according to plan.'

146

'We have experienced some difficulties, Princess,' said Uriath with a sigh, 'But we are persevering, even in the face of such great adversity.'

Fost saw that Moriana tried hard not to laugh at his sententious manner.

'It pleases me to hear that, good Uriath. Now, as for our plans tomorrow, we must coordinate . . .'

A door opposite the one through which Fost had entered swung inward on oiled hinges. Councillor Tromym entered unsteadily. His nose glowed the color of Uriath's florid face.

'Uriath, I have to talk with you,' he said with the meticulousness of the truly inebriated, seeming to pick each word out precisely and exactingly with a pair of tweezers. 'It is about this . . . oh. Ah, well, yes. Hello.'

Fost grimaced. Tromym showed every sign of collapsing completely under the strain. In the courier's opinion the best thing the whiskered little man could do was climb into a rumpot and stay put until the shouting was over.

Uriath was visibly unhappy.

'Tromym,' he said sharply. He heaved his substantial bulk from the chair. 'If you'll excuse me – I'm sorry, Your Highness. I'll be but a moment.'

Moriana nodded graciously as the pair left her line of sight. Fost looked at her wondering if she was eager to have him gone so they could speak privately. He held his own passions in check. He had more important things to tell her.

'Listen, I've got to tell you something,' he began.

'No, I have something I must tell you,' she said. 'Oh, Fost, I can't express how it makes me feel to see you. When I stabbed you, I knew I was doing the right thing, though part of me died with you. Or when I thought you died.'

In his befuddled state it took him until now to realize that what he'd taken for a necklace about her neck was the all too familiar pendant, a big-faceted stone in an elaborate silver setting. Half of the stone's surface shone white, half radiated blackness. He had only seen the gem once, briefly, but was unlikely to forget it.

'But . . .'

She raised a hand, cutting off his words.

'No, you need say nothing. Even though you didn't die, I can never atone for what I did, not in my own heart.' A tear welled from

147

one eye and rolled down her cheek. 'I . . . I'll try to make it up to you, Fost. I promise!'

But the courier wasn't listening. He stared in horror as a wave of black slowly washed over the Destiny Stone entirely blotting out the white.

'So,' a voice said from the outer doorway.

Slowly, Fost turned though he knew what he'd see. He would have felt better at meeting Istu himself awakened from a ten-millennium-long nap. Luranni stood there, her gaily colored smock in sharp contrast to the dull gray of her expression. She looked as if she'd just been struck in the belly.

'Fost? Fost, what's wrong?'

He didn't answer Moriana. Luranni's oval face was stricken. She knew. As Fost opened his mouth hoping some inspiration would make the proper words come forth, she turned and ran.

He caught her in the antechamber of Uriath's office, at the foot of the slimy stairs. Rows of mushrooms stood at attention in boxes, rank on rank until they were lost in the gloom. An eerie pallid glow rose from some of them to mingle with the green shine of the tube filled with miniscule luminous beings that lit the room. Other than sunlight and moonlight, the light vessels provided the only form of illumination by which it was safe to conspire in the City.

He seized her wrist as she tried to race up the stairs. Her arm seemed ridiculously skinny against his scarred fist and burly forearm. He thought with a pang how such restraint wouldn't be possible with a woman like Moriana.

'Wait,' he said. 'I can explain.'

Her eyes called him a liar. He felt shame at uttering the faithless lover's age-old plaint.

'You still want her,' she accused. Her voice, normally so musical, rang out in the cellar as husky, broken.

'I do.' He released her slender wrist and moved closer to her rigid body. 'I'm sorry, Luranni. We . . .'

'Don't say anything. I thought you believed in our cause – in me.'

He took a deep breath and let out a sigh.

'I care for you, Luranni. But I came to the City to help Moriana. I chose to help the princess because of . . . the way I feel about her, and because I fear what Synalon intends.'

'But I thought you believed in our revolution! Don't you want to bring popular government to the City?'

He hesitated, unsure how to answer.

'I guess my upbringing warped me. When I look at any government, no matter how popular or benevolent, all I see is the field of spearpoints holding it up.'

'So you did it all for the love of her!' she cried. She was gone before he could deny it.

But then he could never have denied so plain a truth.

The tattoo of her steps faded up the stairs, ended with the bang of a door. He turned back and raced for the office.

'Moriana, you've got to listen to me! The pendant . . .'

'Yes? What about a pendant?' Uriath's eyes glittered.

Fost looked into the tub. Water. He turned and walked out without another word.

Evening settled on the camp of Moriana's army. The clink of the armorer's hammer drifted to the ridge of the human's camp, along with the murmur of talk around the cooking fires, occasional snatches of song. From the dark pavilions of the Zr'gsz nearby came only silence, as ominous and complete as that in which their oblong skyrafts flew. Rarely, she heard a stacatto burst of syllables, and once came a chanting in a voice she recognized as Khirshagk's.

'Come,' she said, taking Darl's hand. She led him down the far side of the rise, toward the stream above where it curved around the bluff to run beside the twin encampments. The cool, moist air danced with the smell of growing things, and the songs of crickets and frogs and tree lizards hummed and reverberated. Once below the lip of the hill, it was impossible to tell or even believe that within half a hundred paces beings of two races prepared for war.

She led him to a fallen log by the river, shaded and covered with moss. They sat together, watching the sun light the nearby Thails with evening colors. Darl looked robust and heroic in tight whipcord breeches and a silken tunic of the palest blue. This evening Moriana dressed feminine and soft in a long beige gown that made her eyes glow like emeralds.

She hadn't worn her swordbelt; at her waist rode a sheathed poignard. No satchel bounced at her hip. Many things had to be resolved, and she would speak of them herself without having Ziore to soothe her.

'There's something I must tell you.' Her thoughts echoed Fost's earlier in the eveing: *I care so much for this man. Why can't I think of anything that's not inane?*

149

'I know,' he said, a tiny smile wrinkling his lips.

She looked at him in surprise.

'You do?'

'Yes. I've known for some time.' He laughed at her stricken look, took her chin in his hand and kissed her. 'A blackness lay upon your soul, Moriana. When I came back from the City States, it had vanished. I don't know how it happened but one thing alone could have lifted that burden from you.'

'He lives.' Her whisper tried to lose itself amid the sighing of the stream.

'I told you before,' he said, his arm encircling her, 'he must be a man indeed to leave so deep a mark upon you.' He smiled lopsidedly. 'I wish that I could meet him.'

'Oh, but you can! Tomorrow, if . . .' She couldn't bring herself to say *if either of you live*.

He shook his head.

'I have but one tomorrow remaining to me.'

'What do you mean?'

He pointed to the evening star twinkling on the saw-toothed edge of the wall of the mountains to the west.

'I shall not see the Crown of Jirre again, Bright Princess. I know this.'

'How can you know?' She wanted to jar him from this prophecy, but a thought jarred her instead. 'You have the Sight.'

'It may be so. I've felt at times I have a Gift. How else could I stir men as I do with simple words any can utter?' He hugged her tight, kissed her forehead. 'But don't grieve for me, Bright Princess. The end comes for us all. And this I know – tomorrow I shall have that which I desire most. No man can ask for more than that. And many receive much less in their lives – and deaths.'

'You're rationalizing,' she said weakly. 'You're trying to spare my feelings.' She tried to convince herself that Darl's belief he wouldn't live out the next day was only morbid imagination. Something within her knew better.

'Will you love me one last time?' she asked, her voice barely audible above the rippling of the stream.

'Princess, I'll love you forever,' he said.

Tenderly he touched her breasts, dipped his head, nuzzled her cheek, touched his lips to hers. Her mouth opened to his. In the last light of day they stripped and made love beside the river, with the bittersweet languor of those who know there will be no other nights for them.

A trumpet skirled from the highest tower of the Palace of Winds as the dawn spilled over the rim of the Central Massif and fell upon the swarm of shapes rising from the hills ahead. A thunderclap broke the City's stillness as four thousand eagles seized the air with eager wings. For a moment, they hovered like a feathered cloud above the buttressed towers of the City in the Sky. One eagle broke to rise above the rest, a huge bird as black as the bedchamber of Itsu but for the scarlet crest blazing on its head. The tiny figure on its back waved a lance. Eight thousand throats, men's and birds' together, answered him with a fearsome cry. Then the aerial legions of the City in the Sky formed and flew to meet the attack of Moriana and the Fallen Ones.

Moriana's heart quailed as she saw the arrowhead flights streaking toward her. She had known all along that her quest must end with this. She faced the eagles of the City in the element they had ruled for eighty centuries. More than anyone else she knew how near that course skirted outright suicide.

But the skyrafts had plied the air for uncounted generations before the first of the giant war eagles were bred by Kyrun Etuul for the armies of Riomar shai-Gallri, first human queen of the City. More than a thousand of the rafts formed Moriana's aerial armada, from small swift two-man flyers to great stone barges mounting powerful war engines and carrying scores of men. Her own raft fell midway. It was thirty feet long and fifteen wide, ringed with a stone bulwark that came waist-high on the princess.

A wooden box atop the bulwark gave added protection. With her rode forty men in the green and brown of the Nevrym foresters. The only Hisser aboard was the pilot, a stunted male in a loincloth who hunkered at the stern, moving his clawed hands over the surface of an obsidian ball. The globe somehow steered the craft. Moriana had felt magic tingling beneath her palms when she had handled one experimentally, but she couldn't attune herself to it.

It was Vridzish magic, like the skyrafts themselves.

Most of the craft were less well protected than hers. Most made do with movable screens of wicker or wood, and some augmented the stone ramparts with sandbags. It wasn't solely to protect the princess that her craft carried so much cover. Along with four other craft similarly equipped and crewed, hers would be running the gauntlet of the defenders in advance of the main force and land in the City to link up with the Underground's rebels. The other rafts would engage the bird riders while Moriana fought her way into the Palace of Winds and the meeting with her twin.

The princess looked to her right. Darl stood resplendent in plate armor, the golden slanting sun turning him into a demigod. He had one booted foot on the bulwark of his raft and his head was thrown back, grinning into the wind with his long brown hair streaming out behind. He saw Moriana, brought hilt to lips and kissed it. She mocked a smile and waved.

To her left rode Khirshagk. Like Darl's, his raft was mostly open and like the Count-Duke's his vessel had a mixed crew. There seemed two classes of Zr'gsz: tall, well-built males who were possibly nobles and resembled their Instrumentality. The other type of lizard men was more numerous and seemed of the same caste as the pilots. They were smaller and armored rarely, if at all. They carried shortbows, slings, javelins; another was assigned to every noble, Darl included, and bore only a large shield.

Here and there on the other rafts Moriana glimpsed the paleness of human skin. There were many more of the green Hissers. She wondered where they had come from, as she had many times since the first columns marched to Omizantrim from the keep at Thendrun in strength greater than she would have believed the Zr'gsz could muster. This was no time to question their presence; the eagles were on wing and she could only be thankful for the numbers of her allies.

A wedge of birds flew straight for the three long rafts in the lead. Moriana appreciated having the three paramount commanders each on a different skyraft – she had insisted on it – but at the moment she wished fervently she had Darl at her side.

Or Fost.

Spears, stones and arrows arced to meet the attacking formation. From the way the bird riders flew, Moriana knew these weren't Sky Guards. She nocked an arrow but kept her attention high. Far overhead an echelon lined out with mathematical precision. The Guard, no doubt led by Rann himself, waited for the common bird riders to draw the attention of the enemy so they could swoop and kill.

'Above!' she called. 'The Sky Guard. Rann!'

Darl turned, then shouted back, 'I see them! Thank you, Bright Princess!'

She had to shout again to attract Khirshagk's attention. The king-priest of the Hissers solemnly bowed but didn't look above. Moriana considered shouting again to be sure he understood, then decided to save her breath.

He would discover soon enough what he faced.

The nearest attackers were three hundred yards away and closing fast. Without thinking, Moriana drew and loosed. The lead bird rider somersaulted over his mount's tail feathers and fell, flailing his arms in a futile attempt at flight. Moriana heard a buzz of admiration from the Nevrymin. A half-dozen of them had shot and none of their shafts had found a mark. They considered themselves fine shots, and so they were − by groundling standards. The princess was a full-fledged Sky Guardswoman and could put fifteen shafts into a palm-sized mark at two hundred yards in a minute's time.

The foresters loosed another volley. This time one eagle fluttered groundward and another shrieked mourning for its fallen rider. Only a few of the Nevrym men could shoot through the firing slits at a time. The others hunkered on the deck and grumbled. But they weren't meant to shoot it out with the bird-borne marksmen. They must be preserved as shock troops for the landing.

'Well shot,' she called to her men. They turned rueful smiles in her direction. She obviously outshot them. They applied themselves to the attack, concentrating in an attempt to better her towering skill with a bow.

Shooting methodically, Moriana emptied four more saddles with five shots. Then the eagles were rushing past in a whirlwind of sound. A bluff blackbearded forester to her right gurgled and sank with an arrow through his neck. Arrows fell like the sleet against the plank protection of her raft.

She darted a glance at Darl's raft. He still stood exposed, his foot on the low wall.

'You fool!' she cried out.

'But a magnificent fool,' said Ziore from her secure spot at Moriana's hip.

The powerful eagle Terror uttered a brief cry to its master.

'I see her, old friend,' Rann said, leaning forward to pat the sleek black neck. It took eagle-keen eyes to make out the princess's slim form through the slits of the covered raft. Rann's tawny eyes were second only to those of the great bird he rode. He smiled, raised a gloved left hand. Then he put Terror into a steep dive

Moriana glanced up, saw the Guards peeling from their echelon formation and streaking down. She widened her stance, nocked a new arrow, waited.

'Damn the bitch!' cursed Rann. 'She sees me.' But to his surprise, the prince found himself laughing in sheer delight. He had personally trained his cousin. He would hate to have her disappoint him. He nocked his own shaft, grinning a taut grin devoid of all humor. This would decide so very much. Him against her, arrow against arrow, teacher against prize pupil.

'Goodbye, Moriana,' he said softly. 'If only I could consummate my love for you at greater length.'

He drew.

Darl's raft bucked upward. Before either cousin could loose an arrow, his craft had swung protectively over the princess's. Rann shrieked a curse and shot at Darl. He'd at least take care of Moriana's damned lover.

He didn't.

Darl watched the arrow, calmly awaiting death. With contemptuous ease, the Zr'gsz at the Count-Duke's side thrust up his shield. The arrow thunked into it. Darl stared at the malformed head gleaming an inch from his breastplate.

'My thanks,' he said dryly.

The lizard man grinned.

Moriana tracked Rann the instant Terror plummeted past Darl's craft.

'Die, you devil!' she screamed, and shot.

The Destiny Stone went black. The glue binding one of the three feathered vanes to her shaft gave way. The arrow slewed wide. Moriana wept with frustration as Rann and Terror were lost to sight beneath her skystone raft.

More bird riders rocketed in. Archers Zr'gsz and human got the feel of aerial shooting and took a grim toll of the attackers. But the Sky City riders took a toll of their own. Men and lizard men fell writhing on the decks. Red blood mingled with green.

A clump of riders bore down on Khirshagk's raft. He stood as defiant as Darl. The Heart of the People smoked in his right claw. Only one rider reached the raft and that one died as he flew overhead. But he cast down the heavy clay vessel he carried.

154

It shattered on the prow of the Instrumentality's raft. The *Zr'gsz* leader turned at the acrid odor of turpentine. Four hundred yards away, three bird riders dropped fire lances, heard the chittering of salamanders, released them.

Moriana gasped as three lines of blinding fire reached for Khirshagk. He revolted her, ally or not, but it was hard to see him die in this diabolical manner.

Khirshagk uttered a laugh that resounded above the clamor of battle. He held the Heart high. Smoke boiled into the sky. The salamanders streaked straight into the core of the huge black diamond and were absorbed without sound.

Deadly quiet filled the sky. Watching from her throne room in the Palace, Synalon choked out an obscenity and raised her arms in invocation. The sleeves of her robe flapped like wings in the wind streaming through the open windows.

'It's time!' Moriana cried to her steersman. He shook his head in *Zr'gsz* affirmation and the raft plunged ahead. She heard a wolf cry from the Nevrymin foresters in the skystone rafts behind as they sped up to keep pace.

'Moriana and victory!' she heard Darl cry.

She raised her bow in salute. There were no words adequate.

Rann's death plunge had carried him far below Moriana's raft. Levelling out at the bottom of his attack, he found himself in the midst of an angry swarm of two-man rafts. Rann's bowstring snapped in a furious exchange of arrows. Terror finished that duel by clutching the stern of an eight-foot raft with his mighty talons and bodily flipping the craft, sending its occupants tumbling to their deaths.

Angrily Rann flung the useless bow away. Not even he could restring a bird rider's bow in flight. He satisfied himself that the rafts were being dealt with successfully – even at the high cost of half his elite flight – and put Terror into a climb, searching the sky above for Moriana's raft.

He found her. A mile in advance of the others he saw the five wooden-clad skyrafts, almost to the ramparts of the City itself. There was little point in pursuing now. Rann allowed himself a sardonic smile. Synalon would soon be learning the extent of the powers she'd accepted from the Dark Ones.

He drew his sword and led the flight steeply toward the armada floating overhead.

*

Eyes as wild as an animal's, Fost glared up and down the street. He had hacked down three Monitors in a storm of blood without being aware that he did so. Erimenes still cheered hysterically.

He tested the heft of the round shield he carried. This was his first real, full-dress battle. He wasn't fool enough to go into it with no more protection than his broadsword and chainmail shirt.

'Back!' cried Erimenes. Fost jumped into a doorway. An arrow splintered the doorpost near his head. A girl with close-cropped red hair popped out of the next doorway and let fly her arrow. The sniper did a high dive from a minaret across the cobblestone street. His scream ended in an ugly thump.

'Excellent shot!' applauded Erimenes from his jug. Fost's lips curled back from his teeth in a wordless snarl. The genie's bloodlust sickened him, but Erimenes still seemed inclined to help – and help he had. He'd just saved Fost's life.

'Where's Luranni?' came the inquiry from the street.

Fost cautiously peered from his niche. Two young men trotted toward him surveying the heights all around. He recognized Prudyn and Chasko, two of the ablest of the lower caste recruits. Short and stocky Chasko carried a javelin and bird rider's target shield. Prudyn loomed over him, holding a bow with professional ease, brown eyes keen beneath the rim of a stolen helmet.

'I don't know,' Fost replied as the two ducked into the niche with him.

'We thought she'd be with you,' said Chasko. Fost shrugged and turned away. He'd futilely sought her at her apartment the night before and wound up sleeping with his assault squad in a warehouse. By the time the unit had to move, the High Councillor's daughter hadn't shown up.

A sea-gray eagle flecked with brown swept over the rooftops. Prudyn whipped up his shortbow and shot. The rider tumbled off and disappeared behind the buildings. Prudyn whooped delight. Chasko and Fost pounded him on the back.

They calmed enough to take stock. The tumult of street fighting raged all around. Smoke sprouted from a dozen fires. To his right, the soaring architecture of the Palace lorded it over lesser buildings. Two hundred yards away, Fost judged. He had an appointment on the steps of that edifice. He prayed fervently to gods he still didn't fully believe in that the other party would arrive unharmed.

The door opened behind them.

They jumped into the street snapping weapons around. A pudgy feminine-looking hand reached out holding a green glass bottle. Prudyn hesitated, accepted it and lifted it to his lips and drank.

'Thank you kindly,' he said. The arm withdrew and the door closed once more.

The three passed around the wine bottle until it was drained. Fost called for the rest of his squad and they moved toward the Palace.

A melee raged among the rafts of the People. Sky City men had birds shot from under them and if luck favored, they managed to drop to the decks of the enemy rafts and continued the fight at close quarters. Others, out of arrows or simply eager to come to grips with the ancient enemies of their kind, landed deliberately to fight side by side with their birds. Riderless eagles plucked Zr'gsz and Nevrymin from the skystone slabs and cast them down.

Both sides fought with fanatical intensity. More than a few of the bird riders passed under the rafts after firing their arrows, only to have the hissing Vridzish fling themselves onto them so both fell, struggling viciously until the hard earth mingled their substance and rendered all issues moot.

Darl's great blade reaped lives like grain. A war eagle knocked his shield-bearer to the deck and disembowelled him with his talons. Darl decapitated the bird with a single cut and spun to split the rider's skull to the teeth as the man closed with a spear.

The deck teemed with battling men and near-men. A green-clad giant loomed over a knot of wiry little bird riders, flailing at them with his bow. So great was his strength that he batted three of the black and purple clad troopers over the edge before the others brought him down.

Darl leaped upon the giant's slayers. They turned as quick as serpents, but their speed and skill meant nothing against the Count-Duke. They died.

Behind him Darl heard a boom of wings, a scrape of talon on stone.

'Very well done, my good Sieur r'Harmis,' came a cultured voice. 'We seem to find ourselves alone. Shall we?'

Darl turned and slowly smiled at Prince Rann Etuul.

In eerie suspended silence, Moriana's raft soared over the rimwall of the City in the Sky. She fancied she floated on the wings of a

157

dream until a ballista thrummed and a barbed iron head punched through the wooden shielding to kill a Nevrymin. She came out of her reverie and shot an artillerist as he bent to the windlass of his engine.

Eagles screamed and circled. Arrows hammered the walls and roof. Moriana cast aside an emptied quiver and stooped to pick up another as a sweating forester drew his dagger across the throat of the howling man with the ballista-bolt in his guts. She said nothing. She understood battlefield mercy all too well.

Quiet and outwardly untroubled by the carnage around him, the Zr'gsz steersman guided the raft between the airy spaces of the City, making for the Circle of the Skywell in the center of town. Moriana peeked through the slit to check on the craft following hers.

She saw only three. Something had happened to the other; its pilot slain perhaps or it might have been knocked down by the catapults. As she watched, the next raft behind hers careened abruptly to the right. She caught a glimpse of its steersman slumping from behind his globe, arrows sprouting from his back.

The raft brushed a thin tower and brought it crashing into the street. The impact caused the raft to straighten.

'Please, survive,' the princess called quietly. She had little hope they would.

It ran headlong into the forward wall of the Lyceum and disintegrated, flinging Nevrymin about like dolls. And then there were only two rafts remaining.

She felt the deck tip beneath her. Her heart missed a beat but a quick glance aft showed her steersman intact and in control. She looked out again.

The Circle wheeled lazily below. The Skywell opened onto a pastoral landscape a thousand feet below. The pilot banked to follow the Skullway to the very portals of the Palace. To the left she saw armed men and women racing for the Palace. Ahead a squad of Monitors fled toward the same destination, heedless that their feet were defiling the skulls of the City's past rulers.

Some sense made her turn and look back toward the battle she'd left behind. With terrible certainty she knew what she'd see.

A thousand yards ahead of the City's prow two figures fought back and forth across the deck of a raft crewed by corpses. Moriana knew the splendid black bird who stood to one side watching the humans; she knew the tall figure in shining armor who swung his

158

broadsword with skill apparent even across the distance; and all too well she knew the smaller black and purple figure darting in and out while his scimitar parlayed with the huge straight blade.

As the princess watched, Rann tripped and fell back toward the bulwark of the raft. Darl rushed. Rann ducked under the blow and swung with his scimitar. Darl's plate was sturdy but Rann's strength belied his size. The curved blade sank into Darl's side.

The Count-Duke spun, snapping the sword from Rann's grip. Rann danced away. Darl's heels came against the bulwark. He raised his broadsword to salute his foe. Then he turned, looked at Moriana and saluted again.

And fell.

'He knew,' came Ziore's anguished words. Moriana returned his salute with her own broadsword. Her eyes stung but she wouldn't cry. Tears would cloud her vision.

And then they were down.

CHAPTER THIRTEEN

Lungs burning, Fost pounded across the pavement towards the Palace. Fifty rebels raced at his side, while a score hung back among the buildings on the perimeter of the grounds to cover the attack with bow and arrow. As he ran Fost kept staring at the spectacle before him. One after another, three large slabs of gray stone flew over the Skywell and turned up the Skullway to approach the Palace.

The leading raft bumped to a halt. The walls fell away as foresters hacked at lashings with sword and axe. Green and brown clad men tumbled out – and one in achingly familiar russet and orange. Even in helmet and hauberk, Fost knew Moriana.

Shouting incoherently, he angled to meet her as she led the foresters up the Skullway. Her last trip along that avenue had been as a captive, jeered by multitudes as a traitoress, regicide, matricide. Now spectators had even better reason to name her traitor – but the only watchers on hand were the rebels swarming across the paved Palace grounds, and a platoon of Palace Guardsmen on the steps.

'Moriana!' shouted Fost. She cried his name in return and they flung themselves violently into each other's arms. Rebels and Nevrymin clasped forearms and pounded backs, instant comrades. The exuberance of the rebels was partly due to the humanness of their new allies. They'd expected green scaly skins.

Fost and Moriana wasted precious seconds in a kiss. They reluctantly broke apart, laughing, weeping, dabbing at the blood streaming from their nostrils. The Destiny Stone swung free outside Moriana's armor. It shone benevolent white.

Fost pointed at it.

'Moriana, that's not . . .'

'Eureka!' screeched Erimenes. 'May this day be blessed forever! I've found a woman of my own kind!'

'Don't "my kind" me, you perverted mountebank!' Ziore screamed back.

Dead silence. Moriana goggled at the satchel by her side. The foresters gaped, too, having come to recognize the princess's familiar as sweet and shy.

The sweet, shy presence proceeded to deride Erimenes with the profane bravura of an Estil fishwife.

When Ziore paused to think up even more insults, Moriana spun quickly to face the Palace Guards, who stood clumped at the portal to the Palace wondering what was going on.

'Surrender at once!' she ordered. 'I, Moriana Etuul, your rightful queen, command it!'

For long seconds nothing happened. Then a Guard pivoted on his heel and split the chest of the man next to him with a stroke of his halberd. The Guardsmen quickly paired off and slew one another. Fost grinned. A little subversion was a wonderful thing.

Moriana raced for the portal. Fost followed, shouting for her to listen, that she didn't have the Amulet, that she carried another talisman instead, that her life depended on getting rid of the Destiny Stone. But Monitors poured into the far side of the Circle and men shouted and moaned and butchered each other on the steps of the Palace, and the mysterious shade Moriana carried still berated Erimenes the Ethical at the top of her nonexistent lungs.

A fleet-footed rebel darted past Moriana as she mounted the steps and heartily kicked open the centermost pair of doors. A flight of arrows buzzed out like angry hornets. Most of them struck the impetuous youth, lifted him from his feet and tossed him lifeless down the narrow steps.

The foresters' bows sang in reply. Screams echoed in the Palace's vestibule. Moriana plunged in, sword in hand. Fost followed. He prudently sidestepped as he passed through the door to prevent being silhouetted. When his eyes adjusted to the relative gloom, he saw a groined chamber radiating out in three directions. From the one ahead came the sound of running boots.

Moriana.

As he followed, from the hallway to the right poured a stream of Palace Guards. One lashed at him with a halberd. Fost took the blow on his shield, grunting as the blade split hide and metal and bit into his arm. He swung the arm violently, letting go of the shield's handgrip. The halberd flew wide as the shield's mass carried

161

it along. Fost lunged and slashed the Guard across the face.

Rebels and foresters were crowding through the doors. Two Guards attacked Fost from opposite directions. Prudyn shot one, then cast his bow aside as another Guard rushed him. Prudyn stayed alive by seizing the haft of the Guard's weapon and battling him up against a wall.

The other Guard intent on Fost lunged, the spiked head of the polearm spearing for Fost's midriff. Fost whipped Erimenes's satchel off his left shoulder and swung it. Erimenes screamed.

The heavy satchel knocked the halberd aside. Fost thrust. The Guardsman sank. Fost ripped his blade from the foeman's chest and ran for the corridor Moriana had taken.

Above the fighting, Synalon waged a battle of her own from the throne room. Even as Moriana's flotilla surged ahead of the other rafts, the air began to dance as the immense air elemental took form.

A tornado howled toward the armada sucking boulders and uprooted trees high into the air. Khirshagk brandished the Heart of the People. A beam of blackness exploded from the center of the jewel and struck to the core of the approaching whirlwind.

A frightened, gusty wail split the sky. The elemental diminished, drawn down the black tube into the diamond. In a heartbeat it vanished. A rain of rocks and trees spattered the countryside below.

Shocked, Synalon stared in wonder and dread. She spoke new words of Summoning. She pointed to the earth. It heaved, a hill appearing where none had been before. She pointed to the sky. The hill shot upward toward the raft carrying the Instrumentality.

Black rays from the Heart stabbed into the soaring hillock. It exploded in all directions sending out a cascade of dirt and stone lasting for long minutes. Synalon screamed. She waved her arms. Sinkholes appeared among the hills below as boulders buried underground winked out of existence . . .

. . . to rematerialize above the vast fleet of skystone rafts.

Now Synalon's magic took full effect. A dozen rafts were stricken and fell, dooming a hundred of the People and scores of humans. A huge boulder dropped straight down for Khirshagk's raft.

The Heart radiated black energy. The boulder slowed, then stopped in midair, defying gravity above Khirshagk's head. He gestured with the Heart. The boulder soared away toward the City to plow a furrow of ruin from the prow halfway to the Palace.

Synalon tore her robes to free her arms for uninhibited gesturing. The fleet drove inexorably onward. She shrieked and the heavens rained fire. Men died screaming in the embrace of flames, some of them her own bird riders; the queen was beyond caring who died as long as she blasted the monsters who dared assail her City. But the Heart emitted a funnel of total blackness into which the flamedrops were drawn. The smoking diamond absorbed the rain of fire and glowed with even greater energy.

As the queen hurled spell after frantic spell against the Instrumentality, the earthly battle raged with undiminished fury. Khirshagk's raft was the nexus of a cloud of eagles, diving and slashing as their riders swept the decks with arrows. Shield-bearers kept their leaders from harm, though they died with the regularity of the Heart's black pulsation.

Still holding the Heart, Khirshagk tossed down his shield and caught up his mace. A bird dropped at him, claws extended. He swung the heavy mace and crushed the eagle's breastbone with a single stroke.

His inhuman laughter rang across the battle-torn skies.

Synalon sent black clouds to confuse the invaders. Beams blacker still stabbed through them. With a hurricane wail the clouds were drawn inward. Fire and steel and plague she sent against the Fallen Ones, and a horde of winged demons from a lesser tenement of Hell. The Heart smote them all. The more power Synalon expended against it, the greater its own force waxed.

Unnoticed by Synalon, Moriana's rafts crossed the boundary of the City itself. Their route had been chosen with cunning. Once in the City, they had roofs to hide them. When they made their run-in along the Skullway the Palace itself hid them from sight. Singlemindedly, Synalon hurled destruction at the *Zr'gsz* only to see her every enchantment turned back upon itself. Many of the Hissers fell before her might. But the Heart kept Khirshagk inviolate and safe.

Rann stood on the lip of the raft, watching Darl's body turn end over end as it fell. Only when Darl struck ground did the prince swing back onto Terror's back.

Khirshagk saw the prince's mount take flight from the deck of his sister ship. He dropped his mace and seized a javelin. Straightening, still holding the Heart in his right claw, the Instrumentality cocked his arm and flung the dart with all his might.

163

Impact jarred Rann's body. Terror coughed. The scars criss-crossing the prince's face tightened like a net as he stared at the spearshaft jutting from his war bird's chest a handspan away from his right knee.

The rhythm of its wingbeats lost, the mighty bird began to sink.

Synalon watched in horror as her cousin's mount spiralled earthward. Channeling her grief and rage and hatred, she called up a storm. Thunderheads gathered, rolled down on the Zr'gsz fleet with avalanche speed. Violet lightnings speared skyrafts from the air.

Energy raved from the Heart and the demon storm was torn apart, wisps of cloud spinning away to disperse in midair.

Synalon clenched her fists until the veins stood out on her forearms. She endured the agony of summoning a salamander of awesome proportions, a fire elemental so powerful that the hangings on the wall burst into flame, then the carpet and the wooden furnishings. The surface of the walls and the Beryl Throne itself began to turn soft and glow from the heat emanating from the sorceress-queen's body before the conjuring was done. Then her Will drove the elemental deep into the earth through crust and mantle in search of live magma. A new Throat of the Dark Ones would speak with an authority the Heart of the People could not refute.

The smouldering door to the throne room opened.

'Greetings, sister,' said Moriana. She stepped inside, frowned.

Synalon felt the salamander she had summoned at such cost wink out of being.

'You've fought long and hard to come here,' she snarled at her golden-haired sister. The charred fragments of her robe fell in a black rain at her feet. 'I'll see you enjoy a death commensurate with your achievement.'

Synalon spoke rapid words. Moriana felt a detonation in her brain and reeled against the wall. It seared her shoulder.

Rage gripped her. She knew the spell – Synalon had used it to subdue her when she had tried to kill Synalon with her bare hands on the eve of her sacrifice to Istu. It would not bring her down again.

She willed the pressure in her mind to go, and it was gone.

'You *have* learned things during your sabbatical,' said Synalon in a voice like milk and honey. 'I should have expected no less. Even you can learn, if given enough time.' She raised a slender hand. 'My demons shall . . .'

164

The words died in her throat. She tried to force them out. She failed. It was as if a hand closed on her neck and bottled the words inside her.

'You shall not call your demons, sister dear,' said Moriana. 'Your Guardsmen are surrendering below or being slaughtered like sheep. I will not suffer you to call for supernatural aid. There's no one to help you. You must fight me, Synalon, with what power you have within you. If you've any of your own, that is.'

Synalon's eyes blazed.

'Don't . . . count yourself the victor yet,' she gasped out.

The real battle for the City in the Sky began.

Fost was breathing hard when he reached the tenth floor of the Palace, and motes of blackness spun in his brain.

'This is the proper level,' Erimenes told him.

'I know,' panted Fost. 'Been here before, remember? When Moriana and I . . . rescued you.'

'Rescued?' Erimenes said, outraged. 'I wouldn't use that term.'

'Neither should I. As I recall, you were busy collaborating with the enemy.'

'That's the true barbarian spirit,' a familiar voice said. 'Holding a colloquy with a ghost while the fate of worlds is decided around you.'

Warily, Fost watched High Councillor Uriath enter the room. The tall, portly man had a massive volume tucked under his arm. He radiated a fey humor Fost hadn't detected in him before.

'I'm not a barbarian,' said Fost.

Uriath laughed. It was the first genuine laugh the courier had ever heard him utter.

'Ah, but you are. A pathetic groundling barbarian. Also a fool.' He giggled. 'And in another moment – dead.'

'Kill him, Fost!' Erimenes bawled. Fost brought up his sword and lunged.

Uriath had flipped open the book. His lips moved quickly. A unlit oil lamp set in a niche along one wall burst into incandescence. Fost yelped and fell back as the flaming oil drew a line between him and the demonically grinning High Councillor. A shape cavorted in the center of the inferno, sinuous and vaguely reptilian.

Uriath pointed at Fost.

'Kill him,' he commanded.

The salamander sprang. Fost flung himself to one side. Stone exploded, spraying him with glowing hot fragments. The fire sprite backed away, hissing, slavering sparks.

Fost crouched, keeping his sword between his body and the fiery thing, even though this was puny defense against the elemental.

'Erimenes? What do I do?'

'You pray to Ust,' the genie said. 'And I'll try Gormanka.'

The elemental darted forward. Fost danced aside. He screamed as the being grazed his side leaving his chainmail glowing in a yellow-white swath along his body. He could barely breathe from the pain. The monster's next rush would end him. The salamander hovered between him and the gloating Uriath. A wild rush at the High Councillor would buy him nothing except a death quicker by milliseconds.

'Father!' Was it his imagination? 'Father, what are you doing?'

'Removing the next to last obstacle between you and the throne,' Uriath said without turning away from his victim.

Past the intolerable glare of the hovering elemental, Fost saw that Luranni stood behind her father, her face a portrait in horror. Her eyes were ringed with dark smudges, and she still wore the same bright smock she had the day before when she'd interrupted Fost and Moriana in their conversation.

'So it's true, Father. You've intended to betray Moriana from the start.' Her voice was firm, flat, low. It didn't sound like the romantic, vaguely mystical Luranni he had come to know.

Uriath laughed.

'Of course! The Etuul have grown decadent. Haven't they wasted the City's substance, threatening its existence — no, the very order of the world! — fighting among themselves?'

'And when Fost went to rescue Moriana from the Vicar of Istu, you ordered your people to hold back.' The words spilled from her in a torrent of accusation. 'And Chiresko and the others — you turned them in!'

Sweat streamed down Uriath's florid features.

'Chiresko had outlived his usefulness,' he explained. 'Just like that fool Tromym. Now stand back, child, and stop bothering me. This beast's fearfully tricky to control.'

'I won't let you murder the man I love, Father.'

'Love?' Uriath turned. 'Him?' His laughter rang out mad.

'I mean it.'

'Too much is at stake for me to indulge your youthful folly. Salamander . . .' he began.

'No!' As her father spoke his words of command Luranni shrieked and drove past him through the dwindling wall of flame. She flung her arms around Fost, kissed him hard. The scent of cinnamon welled around him.

The world exploded in flame and pain and the smell of burned flesh.

The battle of powers was over. The vanquished sprawled senseless on the floor and the victor staggered, trying to keep her feet, trying to control the shaking of her hands and change double vision back to clear focus.

A tall figure appeared in the doorway.

'My heart rejoices to see you, Your Majesty,' said Uriath. Though tears had left shiny trails down his cheeks, he smiled hugely. 'This day's horrors have cost me my daughter, who meant more to me than life itself. But all of it is worthwhile if I can only receive the boon of being the first to hail the rightful Queen of the City in the Sky in her moment of triumph.'

He came forward with a drunkard's step and fell to his knees before the City's monarch by right of mystic combat. Moriana gazed down at him, not quite understanding what he said. Why, she wondered in a daze, did he have a huge, ancient book tucked under his arm?

And why was the stone on her breast glowing black?

Uriath's hand shot out. Silver links snapped as he snatched the Destiny Stone from her neck.

'I have it!' he crowed, leaping up and away from her with an agility amazing in one of his bulk. 'The Amulet of Living Flame! I've won! I'm immortal!'

Moriana sank to her knees beside Synalon's prostrate form. Defeat tasted of ashes on her tongue. So much and all for naught.

She had never even had to use the Amulet. She had overpowered her sister, Synalon the invincible, whose powers of sorcery had always before outmatched her. She had won her birthright.

And lost it.

The book lay open in Uriath's palm. He did a little jig as he began to read. Moriana smelled the magic gathering about the tower.

The room grew warm. A strange cackling, wailing sound drew

167

Moriana's attention to the window. Salamanders danced outside, whirling round and round the tower so rapidly she only saw them as lines of light, red and green and white, weaving a garland of fire about the spire.

She tried to dismiss them. A tiny electric blue spark danced from her fingertips. That was all the magic she could Summon. She lacked the strength.

'Foolish slut!' cried Uriath. 'This is the book of the deepest secrets of Kyrun Etuul! For generations it's mouldered, neglected on the shelves of your Palace library. And now it has passed to my hands – where it belongs!' He stopped his capering and beamed down upon the sisters. Beside Moriana Synalon began to stir.

'Your time is through, Etuul witches. Perhaps the reign of women is done, too. Yes, I think so. It's an abomination that women should rule men.'

'The people will never accept you.'

'No?' He hugged the book to his chest and tittered. 'They accepted Synalon, didn't they? And you believed they'd accepted you, too, you who loosed the Fallen Ones upon the world again.'

She sank back. Synalon rolled onto her side, moaning. Moriana took her hand. It felt cold and lifeless, more like marble than living flesh.

'Enough words,' the High Councillor said. 'Prepare to burn.'

A scuffling sounded from the corridor. Uriath looked up sharply from his tome. An apparition stood in the doorway, manlike in form but as black as Istu save for the bared white teeth. A naked steel blade gleamed in a blackened hand.

'You can't be here. You're dead! Burned up! The salamander took you when it took my poor Luranni.' He began to weep once more.

'You haven't finished me, friend Uriath,' said Fost Longstrider, advancing on the High Councillor. 'I'm still blood and bone under this char. And I'm about to spit you and serve you piece by piece to your own salamanders, you murdering fat bastard!'

'No!' It was the squeal of a child in terror. Uriath's chubby fingers flew as they flipped through the pages of the book. He kept glancing frantically from the pages to the courier advancing on him step by merciless step. 'Ah, here, here!' he cried, and screeched an incantation.

A dome of flame surrounded him. Fost flinched from the killing heat. A moment more and a dancing veil of fire sprang up in the doorway.

'You've come a long way to die, Longstrider,' said Synalon in a cracked voice. 'Still, there are worse companions with whom to receive the Hell Call.'

Fost gazed around the room. Outside raged the firestorm.

'Isn't there anything you can do?'

Wearily Synalon shook her head.

'Isn't it humorous? My sister and I spent all our energies contesting with each other. And for what? So this treacherous blubbergut can roast us to death and claim the Beryl Throne for himself.'

It was getting hotter.

'Erimenes?' The answer was a formless wail. Fost thought he heard a new note to it, a note of real anguish.

Moriana pointed at Uriath, dimly visible through the orange and blue shimmer of his fire shield.

'He's building his control of the salamanders outside. When he has perfected his grip on them, they'll come for us.' She shook her head. The tears flowed freely now. 'Oh Fost, my love, my only love. I'm sorry I brought you to this.'

But the courier's attention fixed on Uriath. He coughed.

'Perhaps it's premature to apologize,' he said in a parched voice. The heat rose around them like a clinging, choking blanket.

'What do you mean?' asked Moriana.

Her eyes followed his. The Destiny Stone was a black so complete it seemed to burn a hole through the fires surrounding the High Councillor. Synalon looked on, curious about all matters mystical even in the face of death.

The heating of the air inside and outside the chamber caused a miniature whirlwind. Burning shreds of cloth swirled up around them. Fost cursed and slapped at one that stung his cheek like an insect.

Uriath's voice rose above the rush of wind and fire, chanting in a long-forgotten tongue. A flake of ash was swept up over his bald domed head. It settled downward bursting into sudden fierce flame as it fell through his fire shield.

It landed in the middle of the page from which he read.

The page flared. Uriath's eyes bulged.

'No,' he cried. 'No, no! This can't be. This is the last page. It's almost there, it isn't fair. I . . .'

Fire roared. Lines of flame converged from the window on the magical dome, merged with it. Uriath dropped the book and stared

169

at fingers burning like candles. Cackling, freed of human control, the salamanders turned on him with all the capriciousness of their kind. The screaming went on and on.

And from the midst of the conflagration while the fire sprites played and Uriath danced his insensate dance of death, the Destiny Stone cast a beacon of intense, pure white light that outshone even the werefire of the elementals.

Fost collapsed at Moriana's side. They clung to each other, watching mute as the fires burned down. Uriath melted like tallow. With his passing the salamanders dwindled. When they winked out, only a blackened spot on the floor remained of High Councillor, elementals or the pendant.

'But he had the Amulet of Living Flame!' exclaimed Moriana, shrill with the nearness of hysteria. 'Why didn't it save him?'

Fost drew her closer.

'He never had the Amulet,' he said. 'No more than you.'

CHAPTER FOURTEEN

'The Destiny Stone,' said Erimenes, obviously enjoying Moriana's expression of horror. 'A different item entirely.' The bright flush the heat had brought to the princess's cheeks drained rapidly as the genie told her of the true nature of the stone she'd carried with her for so long. The shiny, treacherous bauble for which she'd murdered her lover.

'He really died?' she cried, clinging to Fost. 'Then why . . .'

'Why is he alive? Simplicity itself. The other pendant, the plain lump of rock tied on a thong, so rude a thing you both scorned it at once as trash – that was the Amulet of Living Flame. With his dying reflex Fost clutched it as he fell.'

'And does he have it?' Hope brought life flooding back into her features. 'Perhaps some of those who fell today . . .'

Gently Fost shook his head.

'It used up the last of its energies reviving me.'

She buried her face against his breast and wept.

'At the end, Erimenes, why did it glow white?'

The sprite chuckled.

'It was bringing the greatest luck of all its existence.' Fost cocked a singed eyebrow at him. 'It was removing itself from the world, dear boy. What more fortunate a thing could it do?'

'I see your point,' said Fost, smiling.

Motion at the edge of vision caught his eye. Synalon! In the aftermath of the Destiny Stone's passing they had forgotten her.

She stood on the ledge of the outermost window gazing down, the wind stirring the stubble of black hair remaining on her head. Her naked skin appeared almost translucent in the brightness of the day.

'Synalon?' asked Moriana.

171

The dark-haired sister turned her head and smiled wanly.

'You've not yet started to wonder what to do with me.'

Moriana licked her lips. For a moment Fost saw hatred burn in her green eyes. Then it faded.

'There's been destruction enough,' she said. 'You're free to go. But you must leave the City.'

'Oh, I intend to,' said Synalon, smiling crookedly. 'But not as you imagine.'

The two stared at her. She laughed at their blank looks.

'What a marvellous new generation you'll breed! You look precisely like sheep. Your offspring will go about on all fours and crop the grass.' She raised a hand to cut off their angry retorts. 'Save your breath. The City was my life; when I lost it, I lost all. And I prefer not to live as a groundling.'

'Synalon,' Moriana began.

Her sister stepped forward into space.

Moriana screamed. The tears began again, more than before. She clung to Fost and wept great wracking sobs, wept for all those who had died. Her mother, Kralfi the faithful retainer, Sir Ottovus and his brother the grand old hero Rinalvus, young Brightlaugher of Nevrym, poor dear Darl. And even Synalon.

When the grief had exhausted her, Fost helped her off the floor and led her downstairs to greet her subjects.

As the sun passed the zenith and started back down the sky, the crowds began assembling in the Circle of the Skywell. There were plain Sky Citizens, looking timidly about them as if at some alien vista. There were the prisoners, bird riders and Sky Guards and Monitors and Guards from the Palace, watched by vigilant men and women who wore strips of blue and scarlet around their arms to show allegiance to Moriana.

Resistance had long since ceased. When Rann fell from the sky, the heart went out of the bird riders. In a matter of minutes, some quick-thinking rebels had raised Moriana's claw and flower banner from the Palace flagstaff. While the sorcerous battle for the City had continued to rage, the physical battle for the Sky City had ended with this simple action.

Moriana stepped out into the sunlight. In a few seconds, the entire City had taken up the cry.

She gestured. Fost joined her. His hair was black and his gaze a heroic blue, and only those nearest could see the way his eyes shifted nervously. Having just lived through horrible ordeal, Fost Longstrider found himself suffering from stage fright.

Moriana took his hand and led him down the steps to the Skullway.

'Relax, Fost,' she said in a low voice. 'It's over. There's no need to be nervous now.'

'I'm not used to this,' he said, looking out over the crowd assembled to cheer and venerate Moriana – and him.

'They're friends, all of them,' she assured him. And it seemed to be so. He saw Prudyn and Chasko, carrying weatherworn satchels containing Erimenes and Ziore. The muffled sounds of acrimonious dispute rose from within, each making vile and impossible claims about the other's actions. And beyond them Fost sighted Syriana and the red-haired young lady who was sudden death on rooftop snipers, and tanned foresters and bearded Northern men and even a few diffident men in the breastplates of Palace Guards.

As they neared the Circle of the Skywell, however, Fost's unease returned.

'Moriana, where are the Fallen Ones? I don't see a single one of your Zr'gsz anywhere.'

'They're hardly *my* Zr'gsz,' she answered. 'They're in the catacombs inventorying their religious relics. I suppose they'll want to load them on their skyrafts and be gone as soon as possible. After all, it's been millennia since the Zr'gsz had much commerce with humans. All this must upset them greatly.'

'It upsets me,' said Fost, with feeling. But the nagging unease returned. What exactly was it that upset him? Perhaps it was nothing more than the presence of the Vicar of Istu in the Skywell. He peered suspiciously at the basalt statue. It remained immobile.

Then Fost's attentions were diverted to the ceremony. The crowd melted away to give Moriana room. A pimply adolescent knelt with her burden at Moriana's feet. Moriana bade her rise.

'As the youngest of the warriors who took part in the capture of the Palace of Winds,' Moriana declared, 'Ufri Tonamil has earned the privilege to crown the new ruler of the City in the Sky.' The crowd roared agreement. Moriana knelt as the child fumbled with the wrappings on the package. She soon revealed the winged silver crown of the City's rulers.

Ufri Tonamil hoisted the crown high, held it a moment, then stepped forward to place it on Moriana's head.

173

'All hail Moriana!' she cried. 'Queen of the City in the Sky, Scion of the Skyborn, Mistress of the Clouds!'

Moriana rose. The crowd went to its knees as one. Fost watched, then decided he should kneel, also. Immediately Moriana seized his arm and yanked him to his feet.

'No one need kneel before me,' she proclaimed. 'Rise, my people.'

They did. They swept forward and raised their new queen to their shoulders. Fost laughed at her expression, then cried out as he felt hands raising him, too.

Moriana caught his eye. His lips formed the words, 'We won!'

And they had. They'd won not just the Sky City, they'd thwarted the Dark Ones themselves. The Second War of Powers Jennas had direly predicted would never happen. *That* was their true victory.

The boiling crowd turned Fost around. For a brief instant the Vicar of Istu flashed in his sight. His heart missed a beat. Then the crowd was bearing them toward the Palace of Winds, and its jubilation caught him up like the surge of a sea-wave.

And in the depths of the City, a Demon stirred.

BOOK TWO
In the Shadow of Omizantrim

For Joseph Wm. Reichert
A prince of a fellow.

—vwm—

Por mi querida.
Hoy, mañana, siempre.

—*rev*—

CHAPTER ONE

For a woman plummeting a thousand feet to her death, Synalon Etuul was uncommonly relaxed. The rushing air caressed her naked body like a thousand subtle hands. Her black hair, charred and frizzled from her contest of magics with her sister Moriana, fluttered inches above her seared scalp.

Overhead floated the City in the Sky, a vast soundless raft of gray skystone. Around the mandiblelike double docks at the prow of the City swarmed hundreds of rafts of the same substance, from eight-foot flyers to hundred-foot barges, swarming with warriors both human and inhuman. A few of the eagles of the City's war force circled dispiritedly, herded by small two man flyers. For the first time in their long history, the warbirds of the Sky City knew defeat in the element over which they ruled as haughtily as kings: the sky.

The dethroned queen paid attention to neither the birds nor the rounded hills cloaked in green that spun around and around beneath her feet. All her concentration was devoted to a single mental summons. Her eyes closed and the thought formed, surged outward, questing, commanding. In a moment, she heard a distant piercing cry and knew that her call was heard.

Without warning, the arrow shape of a huge war eagle shot by her, wings folded to its glossy black sides, head thrust forward so that its yellow beak sliced the air like the prow of a ship. Synalon smiled and sent the bird encouraging thoughts.

Once beneath her, it unfolded its full thirty-foot wingspan with a thunderous crack. Synalon fell by it again. Still, no concern touched the sorceress's aristocratic features.

The wings furled like sails. The black warbird fell until it flanked Synalon, then spread its wings carefully so that they dropped side by side.

'I'm ready, Nightwind,' she called, no longer requiring the tiring mental communication. The bird let itself drift down until it was directly beneath her. She spread her legs and floated down until she sat astride the bird's back, her legs thrown over its churning shoulders. She let her head slip back and uttered a small cat cry at the pleasure of the bristly feathers brushing between her slender legs. Defeated, exiled, and without so much as a cloak to her name, Synalon still took pleasurable sensation where she found it, and savored it well. The better, perhaps for the novelty of the circumstances.

Slowly, the eagle increased its wingspan and the tempo of its wings' beating, until the full weight of the tall, lean woman was borne upon it. As it pulled into level flight, it curved and began winging along the City's track. Its mistress had prepared well for this eventuality, though her power in the City had been absolute, and her favor in the eyes of the Dark Ones had seemed to render her invulnerable. Its blood had seethed with the need to be out of the confines of the special aerie in the depths of the City, but Nightwind had waited patiently as instructed, for its mistress's mental call. Having rescued her according to plan, it strained powerful muscles to put as much distance as possible between the former queen and her former domain.

A cry of pleasure broke from Synalon's throat and was whipped away by the wind of Nightwind's passage. Stolidly, the bird flew on. Only once did it have to correct its flight as the woman suddenly shifted her weight back and forth. It knew its mistress's foibles well.

Flushed and breathless, Synalon cast a glance upward. The City was several miles distant. Her sister was undoubtedly on her way to having herself crowned Queen of the City in the Sky. Synalon reached forward and stroked the straining bird's neck, feeling the taut muscles beneath her fingers.

'The silly slut,' she said, 'is probably wiping away a tear for her evil twin,' she said to her eagle. Synalon grinned savagely. 'Ah, yes, the evil but great-souled twin who took her own life rather than face the disgrace of being exiled among the groundlings or lifetime captivity.' She laughed, long and loud.

Synalon had feared only one thing as she stepped to the windowsill in her throne room. The heat from the living firestorm of the salamanders summoned by the traitorous Uriath to slay both her and Moriana had abated slightly. But under no circumstance did she fear the fire elementals — or even the Destiny Stone Uriath had stolen and which had destroyed him. The major obstacle to overcome had been Moriana's lover Fost. He might suspect trickery and check to see if she had actually fallen to her death. He may have been a lowborn groundling but he was as cunning as if he had spent his life untangling the threads of intrigue in the Imperial court at High Medurim.

In other circumstances Moriana might have suspected some ploy on her sister's part. But she had been exhausted physically and spiritually by the last duel with Synalon for possession of the Sky City they both coveted. Besides, she had wanted to believe her sister capable of making such a noble choice as suicide over imprisonment or exile.

Wary of pursuit, Nightwind swiveled his head back and forth constantly studying the horizon and the sky to both sides. Looking back the way they'd come, he gave a sudden sharp cry.

Synalon came immediately alert. Her vision wasn't that of an eagle but it was far sharper than an ordinary human's. On a distant knoll almost swallowed by the shadow cast by the City in the noonday sun sat a small figure. Before the figure a great black cruciform object lay on the ground. Synalon's eyebrows arched in surprise. Her thin lips drew back in a smile. With pressure of her knee, she set Nightwind into a long banking curve and headed back.

The procession turned into the alley and stopped. Quiet lay like a blanket on the streets. From the center of the City came wild cries of celebration. Most of the population had massed in the great Circle of the Skywell to acclaim the new queen. Of the rest, some waged a final hopeless fight against the invaders in back streets and ware-houses, or huddled behind shuttered windows fearful of the forces that stalked the City in the Sky that day. The backs of deserted buildings looked down blankly upon the knot of the faithful.

It was an unremarkable wall constructed of seamless gray stone shot through with veins of dull green, worn to a glossy smoothness by the passage of wind and countless ages. Like the older structures in the City, like the bulk of the City itself, it was a gigantic crystal grown in the ages before the coming of man to the Southern Continent. Rooms, passageways and doors had been hollowed out of it by the patient labor of clawed hands.

179

A hand like those of the original builders, dark green, finely scaled, possessed of thumb and three clawed fingers, held aloft a black diamond that smoked as though plucked from a furnace. The huge gem's facets glittered dully, not in the light of a sun masked by a high cloud layer but with an inner luminescence of its own. The worshippers fell silent. The hand pressed the stone against the wall. The jewel smoked furiously and a section of wall vanished soundlessly, leaving no trace.

The jewel bearer stepped through the oblong opening into a passage that had lain hidden for a hundred centuries and more. Heads bowed, twinned hearts pounding with religious rapture, the faithful followed him into the dark — into the Dark. No light penetrated the downward-winding tunnel. The noonday light outside seemed incapable of crossing the threshold of the secret passage. But the giant diamond carried by the leader provided enough dark illumination of its own to guide its bearer and his twelve followers.

Downward, ever downward they trudged. Darkness deepened, became tangible. No fear touched their hearts. The Dark was their element. They drew comfort and strength from it. The expectation of a great gift grew among the faithful.

They came to a door. It was twice as tall as a man, made of oak and bound with brass that showed no tarnish, no sign of the ages that had washed over this door like a flowing stream. All was illusion: the door was not wood and brass. It was wrought of a substance no mortal could work or even alter. The physical aspect given to a binding force of incredible power, it defied any other power in the world.

Any other but one. And the source of that power was only lately rediscovered.

The twelve threw themselves to their knees. The thirteenth raised the smoking jewel above his head and began a reptilian hissing, a triumphant chant.

In the bosom of the Dark a Demon slept, as it had for ten millennia. Hatred and despair washed over one another in an endless ebon swirl. But lately the Demon's dreams were shot through with bright threads of hope. Presences long unfelt had drawn near, uttering soft words, seductive words, promising that which the sleeping Demon desired above all things: freedom.

Or had that been another fragment of dream, the mind of the sleeper taunting itself with a hope it knew must remain unconsummated?

The nebulous awareness of the being existed without volition, could not summon events into focus or bring back recollections. It had no tests of truth or falsity. Still, the memories of newborn promise carried a sharpness, an appealing immediacy, that set them apart from the vagueness of dreaming. Like the memories of soft white flesh, and pain, and pleasure . . .

Something tickled the Sleeper's mind. It stirred within its womb, within the stone that imprisoned its limbs as the old enchantment fettered its mind. For a long moment the Sleeper believed it was just another taunting shard of dream. Or did it hear once more the voices of those who had worshipped it in the days of glory, lost so long ago?

It sensed presences. As the words of the Song of Awakening came to it, a pulsation of power ran through the Sleeper's body and mind. The Demon's consciousness began to swim upward through the clouds that had lain so long on it. Many times in eons past it had attempted this crazy hegira. But now it felt the singing certainty that this time would be different.

'Well met, cousin,' Synalon called cheerfully as she circled Nightwind in to a landing on the rounded hilltop. Prince Rann looked up from contemplating his warbird's corpse. The fallen eagle was a twin to Synalon's save that it bore a blazing scarlet crest. It lay spread out on the hillside before him, the butt of a *Zr'gsz* javelin protruding from beneath one wing.

'Rather absurd of you to say so, isn't it?' he asked, rubbing at the gingery stubble on his chin. He noticed her nakedness then, and looked away, blushing.

She laughed and jumped down from Nightwind's back. The eagle spread its wings above the corpse of its nest brother and uttered a single desolate cry.

'A pity about the bird,' the princess said. 'He was such a noble creature.'

Still looking away from her, Rann nodded.

'I suppose it's reassuring,' he finally said.

'How do you mean?'

'To know that I can feel remorse over the death of a friend.'

181

Laughing easily, Synalon sat beside him. The warmth of her body washed over him. He began to fidget. He was a small, intense man who seemed put together of wire and spring steel. His eyes and swept-back hair were tawny, his face displaying the same haughty, almost ascetically classic sculpting as Synalon's. The perfection of his features was marred by a tiny network of white knife scars stretched over the skin like a mask. The nearness and nudity of his cousin was for him as exquisite a torture as any he might devise for victims of his sadism.

'You're turning soft,' she taunted him. Then, as mercurial as always, she switched from banter to flashing anger. 'Perhaps that's why you lost my City for me. The security of my realm lay in your hands. You let it slip!'

He jumped to his feet, glad of the chance to get away from the smell of her, the feel of her provocatively bare thigh pressing against his purple-clad leg.

'You're a fine one to talk,' he said quietly. He paced away. His scabbard flapped empty at his hip. His scimitar had plummeted to earth sheathed in the body of Darl Rhadaman, Moriana's champion. '*You* fought the real battle. What happened in the air was secondary. I grant you, I failed to stop Moriana's entry into the City. But ultimately, cousin dear, it was up to you to prove your superiority in a test of wills and magic, face to face, alone.' He turned back to regard her sardonically. 'And evidently it was a battle you lost. Or else you wouldn't be in such . . . dishabille.'

She leaped to her feet.

'Don't lecture me, half man! How can a eunuch such as you understand what I have lost this day?'

'What you have thrown away this day!' His face was taut and pale under the lattice of scars. 'With the favor of the Dark Ones, you thought, no price lay beyond your grasp. And now look what you've won. Exile to a lonely hilltop without so much as a cloak to cover your nakedness. A prize fit for a queen – or nothing!'

She smiled at him, savage and evil, raised her arms and stretched so that her heavy breasts rode lazily up her ribcage. His tongue flicked lizardlike over his lips. He turned away again.

'What will you do now, cousin?' Synalon asked silkily. 'Will you leave me on this hilltop fate has set me to rule?'

His head drew down between his shoulders.

'You know I cannot do that.' For the first time in Synalon's long

182

memory, the prince's voice was hoarse and choked with emotion. She laughed musically in delight.

'No, of course you can't abandon me. Because, while you hate me, you love me far more. And vastly more even than that, you desire me, O cousin Prince!'

Abruptly, Synalon flung forth her arm. Blue lightning coruscated from outstretched fingertips and struck Rann full in the back. He uttered a croaking cry and fell forward onto his knees, arms hugging his chest, bobbing and gasping in a paroxysm of agony.

'And because you fear me, my good and loyal Prince,' said Synalon, sneering. 'Because you fear me well.'

Painfully Rann struggled to his feet.

'It would . . . seem that you're the one – oh! – who grows soft,' he said, enunciating each word as if a dagger twisted in his bowels at every syllable. 'Still you fail . . . to exact the final price of my failure.'

'I'd prefer having you available to redeem yourself,' she said in a matter-of-fact tone. 'You are adroit, for all that your recent efforts have not exactly been crowned with success. And you're a tough bastard, Rann. A normal man would at this moment be lying before me unconscious or dead from the bolt I gave you.'

Turning, Rann gradually forced himself to uncurl and stand upright before his cousin. He felt like he was stretched on the rack. He forced his lips to smile.

'A normal man, perhaps, but not a half man, eh?' He shook himself as though throwing off the last of the pain the lightning had left. 'What now, cousin?'

Synalon paused, rubbed her palms together, as if rolling a pill between them.

'We travel to Bilsinx, or Kara-Est perhaps, and marshal our resources. The bitch Moriana found some way to increase her powers. So will I. And whose damned lizard allies of hers – their magics seemed all of a defensive sort. They were potent, but even more so is my hatred. I will find the way to defeat them in spite of that damned smoking jewel of theirs, and then pull Moriana down to a lingering death in the sight of all the City she thought to wrest from me!'

Rann might have pointed out that Moriana had indeed wrested the City away from Synalon. He didn't. He was too preoccupied staring past the pale angle of Synalon's shoulder, past the charred fall of her short hair. She frowned at him. The roundness of his eyes, the relevation of his brows and the slight parting of his lips were equivalent to a shout of horror and disbelief from another man. She followed the stare.

Small objects detached themselves from the rim of the floating City and fell. First a few, then hundreds spilled from all sides of the Sky City like beach sand from a child's palm. The objects rotated as they fell. Synalon's wondering eyes made out the flail of limbs desperately seeking purchase on the air. Screams came to her ears like the cries of distant gulls.

CHAPTER TWO

Fost Longstrider sat slumped in the bishop's stool someone had produced for him and wondered whether or not to get drunk.

All around a crowd cheered itself hoarse. Moriana stood proudly beneath the winged crown of the City in the Sky, her arms outflung as if to embrace her new subjects. For having just fought two desperate battles, one of arms and one of sorcery, and then having come close to flaming death from the stolen magics wielded by High Councillor Uriath, she looked remarkably fresh and radiantly beautiful.

Fost, on the other hand, was slipping from the frenzy of battle into the fog of after-action depression. He was charred all over from his own near incineration by one of Uriath's fire elementals, and was uncomfortably aware that the stench of burned flesh clinging to his sweat-lank black hair had come from Luranni. She had bought his life with hers. Where he wasn't black, he was bloody; where he wasn't scorched, he was scored by swordcuts. His helmet and shield were gone, his breeches blackened and torn beyond recognition and his hauberk reduced to a few rings of steel mail hung around his powerful torso. He still had his broadsword hanging at his hip in a well-smoked hornbull leather scabbard.

He looked more like the vanquished than a conquering hero.

In battle he'd always felt a vivid, singing awareness, had felt alive in a way he didn't at other times. Lately he had started to go into a berserker's fury that grew madder as the battle grew more intense. Afterward, however, he felt depleted, soiled, and not at all proud of his prowess at wreaking destruction on his fellow man.

His only consolation was that the venerable ghost of Erimenes the Ethical wasn't crowing in his usual fashion over the glorious bloodletting he had witnessed that day.

185

Still, Fost thought, his lot wasn't so bad. The woman he loved stood by his side and received the adoration of her City. She had succeeded, as had he. Moriana had regained her precious Sky City; he had been reunited with his lover. An added bonus was that Synalon's madness would never unleash a second War of Powers on the world.

A fatuous smirk crossed his face when he realized he was a hero. Like in all the fairy tales of his youth, he was a hero and had won the privilege of living happily ever after.

He drained his goblet of wine and eyed the swell of Moriana's rump inside her tight breeches. Living happily ever after was a marvelous prospect, he decided. He just wished this state business would be finished soon so they could get down to doing the happy living in earnest.

With harsh shouts and proddings with spears, a mob of prisoners was herded into the circle to stand before their rightful queen. Some cowered on their knees pleading for forgiveness with clasped hands and desperate voices. Others stood aloof, disdaining to beg for their lives. Even they had a certain hunted look to their eyes. Fost guessed that their apparently prideful refusal to prostrate themselves and grovel for mercy sprang from a knowledge that it would do them no good. Moriana was an Etuul, from the same stock as Synalon and Rann.

Most of the troops guarding the prisoners wore the ragged garb and odd bits of armor of the Underground's street fighters, the brown and green of the Nevrym foresters or the bright colors and well-tended armor of Moriana's handful of allies from the City States. A few, though, wore the black and purple of the City's military, and here and there Fost caught a glimpse of the brassards of the elite Sky Guard worn alongside the blue and red ribbons of Moriana's sympathizers. The captives were an equally mixed lot: common bird riders and Sky Guardsmen still haughty and erect despite the numbing shock of their first defeat; Bilsinxt auxiliaries in drab earth tones; gaudy Palace Guards; even a few scattered Monitors bereft of their leather helmets and looking about wildly like beasts being led to the slaughter. So hated were Synalon's Monitors that only those fortunate enough to find outlanders — Nevrym foresters, men from the Empire, even Hissers — to surrender to before the mob caught them had survived this long. Now they faced Moriana's justice. But unlike the other prisoners, to them it made little difference whether she chose to be harsh or lenient. The crowd had seen their faces. Their fates were immutable.

As the crowd backed away as if to set themselves apart from those who had dared oppose the return of the City's rightful queen, Fost wondered again where Moriana's reptilian allies were. He hadn't seen one yet. But he knew Moriana had won their cooperation by promising to give them certain religious relics they had been forced to leave behind when Riomar shai-Gallri and her sorceress adventurers wrested the City from them millennia before.

One of the religious artifacts was in view at this moment, and not as far away as Fost would have liked. Across the Skywell from where he and Moriana stood, squatted the Vicar of Istu, leering at the proceedings with a grotesque basalt face. The statue's form was manlike and exaggeratedly male. Its head bore horns. This was the most disconcerting feature of the great icon, because all of the world's horned creatures wore them decently on snout or forehead and pointing forward. The Vicar of Istu's sprouted unnaturally from the sides of its round heads and curved upward.

A substantial pedestal had been carved from the foundation stone of the City, but the Vicar didn't occupy it. Fost felt cold all over remembering the sight of the statue coming alive and moving from that pedestal to threaten Moriana so long ago. He hoped that the Vridzish were nearly finished rounding up their precious religious treasures. The sooner they got that ghastly mannikin out of his sight the happier Fost Longstrider would be.

'Men of the Sky City!' Moriana's voice rang like a trumpet, stilling the murmurings and occasional catcalls cast in the prisoners' direction. 'You stand before me because you have committed a most grievous deed; resisting by arms the return of your legal and rightful queen to claim her throne.'

Instantly, a dozen men fell to their knees, sobbing and pleading and shaking clasped hands in the air.

'We did no wrong! Your Majesty, there has been some terrible mistake!'

A short, slightly built youth in black and purple pushed his way arrogantly through the crowd to stand before Moriana, his black hair thrown back, his blue eyes blazing defiance. The brassard of the Guard surrounded one wiry bicep.

'We fought in defense of our City and our crowned queen, so acclaimed by the Council of Advisors in accordance with ancient

187

law. Your claim to the Throne of Winds may be just but you chose to come as an invading enemy. If resisting you was a crime, then my comrades and I must plead wholeheartedly guilty!'

A wild babble filled the air. The crowd growled like a hungry beast, and a guard shouted, 'On your knees before the queen, scum!' The captive Monitors and sallow men in the robes of Palace bureaucrats and mages swore that this madman did not speak for *them*. The other Sky Guard captives raised a shout in a different key.

'Well said, Cerestan! We fly and fall with you!'

Moriana raised her hand, commanding silence. The uproar died.

'You are Cerestan, young man?' she asked. Fost watched, judging the man to be a year younger than the new queen – which made him older than the courier.

'I am flight lieutenant of the Guard,' Cerestan said proudly.

'Very well, Lt. Cerestan. You are brave. Since you have thrust yourself forward so bravely, then you shall hear my judgment upon you and upon your comrades, as well.' More piteous outcries broke from the captives. Cerestan paled but set his jaw resolutely.

'You, and those who fought beside you in resisting my entry into the City in the Sky – and your fellows of the Guard particularly – hear now your doom. You are from this moment free men and women, to leave the City or remain in her service, with the thanks of monarch and people, providing only that you are willing to swear fealty to me, your new and rightful queen.'

The crowd uttered a formless, astonished gasp. The prisoners looked stunned. Cerestan blinked rapidly and cocked his head as if uncertain he had heard correctly.

Moriana laughed at his confusion.

'Did you think I was insensible to your dilemma? Being the younger sister I was heir to the throne by City law, but the Council named Synalon rightful queen. Which was right? You chose what you thought was the moral course. You fought for your City as best you knew how, and you fought bravely.'

She paused. A few cries of disbelief floated from the spectators, and she noticed that the men in Sky City uniforms who guarded the captives were beginning to acquire an angry look.

'I am most grateful now and forever to those who chose to side with me, and I shall do you all the honor it is in my power to do. But I will not punish loyalty to my beloved City, nor courageous striving on her behalf. So you who fought against me are no longer prisoners — not pardoned, for you have done nothing to be pardoned for.

'As for the rest of you, you Bilsinxt are likewise pardoned, but you are to be exiled at once from the City.' Some of the Bilsinxt cried out in terror. The usual form of exile from the City was to be given a hearty push into the Skywell to fall the thousand feet to the ground. Moriana raised a placating hand. 'I mean nothing drastic. You'll be allowed to collect your belongings and be given transport to the surface by balloon. Your city is still occupied, but I intend to withdraw the Sky City forces. With Synalon dead, no reason remains to maintain such a force.'

Startled comment rippled through the listeners. Though everyone knew that Synalon was dead, it had not been confirmed in words before. Moriana waited until the commotion was over before going on.

'For the rest of you, for the functionaries who officiated over the reign of terror waged by Synalon and Rann against the people of the City, and the Monitors who were the instruments of that oppression, I remand you to prison, to be tried individually according to your acts, by a tribunal over which I personally will preside. Look to your conscience, gentlemen. On my own behalf I am not vindictive, but on behalf of my people I harbor no mercy!' She gestured imperiously, the graceful but definite handsweep of one born to rule. The wailing mages and officials were hauled to their feet and hurried off to prison, Moriana's men forming a cordon to protect them from the fists and feet of the crowd.

A noise tugged at the fringes of Fost's mind. The mindless oceanic sounds of the crowd blanketed all other sounds, but beneath the roar he felt more than heard a discord, unidentifiable and unsettling. He shook his head to clear it. The aftermath of the battle was getting the better of him. And he knew the precise way to combat it.

He held forth his goblet. A grinning serving youth refilled it with amber wine.

'Here, Chasko, refresh yourself,' he shouted to the bearded man who stood beside him with Erimenes's satchel slung over one shoulder. His friend Prudyn, normally inseparable from him, stood some distance away holding an identical satchel loosely by the strap. The two had moved apart so that Erimenes and Ziore could no longer rant at each other.

189

Fost took Erimenes's satchel and slung the strap over his shoulder. Chasko accepted a fired clay vessel of liqueur and moved off to rejoin his comrade.

'You've made a sorry spectacle of yourself, old smoke,' Fost told the spirit, knowing Erimenes could read the words from his mind if he didn't hear.

'It's all the fault of that brainless witch who claims to be an Athalar. She couldn't be one, or if she is then my city decayed greatly in the years following my death. Imagine the weak-mindedness and credulity to be so taken in by an obviously spurious doctrine as to waste one's whole life on it!'

'That's your own spurious doctrine you're talking about,' Fost reminded him.

'If I've told you once, I've told you twelve thousand times,' Erimenes said loftily, 'I despise your barbaric imprecisions. Neither I nor that foolish cow Zir or Zor or Zoot or whatever she's called could possibly have made a spectacle of ourselves, since we're not visible. Why do you insist on changing the subject?'

'Majesty! Your Majesty!' Standing near Fost, Moriana looked up from a consultation with a group of officials who for reasons of conscience had allied with her.

A girl in her teens pushed her way through the throng almost to the queen's side. She wore breeches and a tattered tunic and a shortsword so thoroughly nicked as to appear sawtoothed. Her face was deathly pale beneath a coating of soot and grime, and one cheek was laid open to bleed freely and disregarded. Ribbons in Moriana's colors circled one arm.

'What is it?' asked Moriana, brow creasing in annoyance. She restrained the men who moved forward to disarm the girl, though the functionaries clucked with disapproval at her raggedness and impudence.

The girl took a deep breath. She swayed. Moriana caught her arm and supported her.

'The Hissers, Your Majesty,' she got out, and then her knees buckled with the onslaught of a coughing fit. She finally controlled herself long enough to blurt out, 'The Vridzish're attacking, Your Majesty! All over the whole damn City they're falling on top of us, armed and unarmed alike. It's t-treachery!' She fell forward so abruptly that Moriana scarcely prevented her from smashing face down on the pavement. It was only then that the queen saw the broken shaft of a black *Zr'gsz* arrow protruding from the girl's shoulder.

At the aft edge of the Circle, screams announced the arrival of the Hissers.

The stink of burning warehouses stung Fost's palate as his mind, fogged by drink and post-battle depression, struggled to come to grips with the girl's jagged-voiced warning. A flickering caught his attention, a quarter turn around the Circle of the Skywell. He looked that way in time to see a black flash and a fountain of scarlet. The Hissers swarmed into the Circle from the broad avenue that ran aft along the City's main axis. They freely wielded obsidian-edged swords.

He turned to Moriana. Her face was the color of a corpse's, and her lips moved without sound.

Then, 'Ziore!' she cried. Without waiting for the genie to answer, Moriana spun away to snap orders at the warriors who stood about staring in horror at this unexpected attack.

Gathering a knot of armed men and women about her, Moriana set off toward where the street mouth disgorged a stream of greenish *Zr'gsz* into the wide Circle. She and her troops made slow progress, bucking the current of humanity fleeing the wrath of its ancient enemies.

Fost felt a pang of surprise and betrayal that Moriana had called upon her Athalar spirit rather than upon him in her anguish. Then he decided that she was far more used to turning to Ziore in recent months than to him. The leaden lethargy that had gripped his limbs evaporated into a bright humming of adrenaline frenzy. He hitched Erimenes's satchel higher on his shoulder and drew his sword with a jerky motion.

A hand gripped his biceps. He whirled, swordarm preparing for the thrust. At his side a Sky Guardsman who bore Moriana's colors turned ashen but didn't flinch.

'Sir Longstrider,' he said, not quite knowing how to address this obviously important groundling. 'The captive soldiers — what shall we do with them?'

Fost glanced after Moriana, who was fighting her way through the panicking crowd like a fish swimming upstream, shouting for her men to come to her aid. It was hopeless trying to call to her over the wails of the multitude. Off toward the end of the City he saw thin trails of smoke twisting into the air.

191

He looked at the captive bird riders and Guardsmen, who stood where they had before, still unable to assimilate that they were free.

'Tread warily, my impetuous friend,' advised Erimenes from his jug. 'If you presume to give orders that Moriana finds objectionable, you may regret it later. The lady has shown a marked propensity to place the dictates of statecraft above those of the heart.'

'Shut up, Erimenes,' snapped Fost. Worry and anger grew. He felt the Guardsman's wondering eyes on him.

'The Hissers are unlikely to distinguish between us and them,' he told the waiting soldier. 'Arm them.'

With Erimenes belaboring him as a fool, Fost dashed off in pursuit of his queen and lover.

Faint and distant, the sounds of conflict seeped through rock and penetrated the awareness of the thirteen who wove mighty magics in front of the ancient door. Khirshagk paused, the harsh incantation rattling to a stop in his throat.

'Our people strike prematurely, Instrumentality,' one of his assistants reported.

He nodded. His long, handsome face was composed, serene. Despite the absolute darkness in the long-sealed and forgotten chamber, his twelve followers discerned every detail of his features, of the feathered ceremonial cloak he'd donned over his scratched green cuirass, and of the immense black diamond held smoking in the clawed hand. A black radiance pulsed from the depths of the stone, its tempo increasing second by second, like the beating of a heart touched with growing arousal.

'It matters little,' he murmured. 'The Children have waited many centuries for this moment. After such patience, the Dark Ones will forgive them their impetuosity. It will not alter the outcome.' And so saying, Khirshagk, Instrumentality of the People, raised his black diamond that was the Heart of the People and resumed the chant to weaken the spells laid long ago by Felarod.

'Come, lads, we've got them on the run!' cried a bearded Northlander, brandishing his broadsword so that the rings of his mailshirt tinkled musically. Up the narrow street a clot of low caste Zr'gsz in loincloths broke and fled under a vicious rain of arrows from Nevrym foresters and grounded bird riders. Knowing something of the Nevrymin and their attitudes toward the Hissers, Fost had been concerned over which side they'd take in this fight. However, the Vridzish had made savagely clear their intention of slaying everything human in the City. The foresters allied with the Sky Citizens by default. Their longbows did much to roll back the advantage of surprise gained by the Zr'gsz.

Seeing Moriana's troops strike the attacking Hissers with spear, sword and a singing cloud of arrows, a group of defenders had veered down a sidestreet to meet a probe by the lizard men. Fost had gone along, and already felt useless. By his own estimation the very worst archer in the world, Fost wished to close and use his sword.

He trotted up the street between the clanking mailed City States man and a rangy Nevrym forester with one eye. They passed the bodies of several of the Zr'gsz quilled like porcupines by the human archers. An obsidian-tipped spear lay by one's outflung talon.

'Ha! What fuss to make over these decadent savages,' Erimenes said scornfully. 'If they craft weapons of stone they cannot be too formidable.'

The one-eyed forester glanced at Fost. Having accompanied Moriana and Ziore in the assault on the City he was accustomed to disembodied voices emerging from satchels.

'You'd soon learn better had you a body, old one,' he told the genie. 'The volcano glass of the Zr'gsz holds –'

A small, light-skinned lizard man popped from the doorway of a shop a few steps ahead and brought his arm whipping forward. An obsidian axe whirled to embed itself with a crunch in the mailed chest of the bearded Northlander. The man coughed astonishment and blood. His legs gave way beneath him. The Nevrymin drew and loosed his arrow as the Hisser dodged back into the doorway.

'– holds an edge far sharper than the finest steel,' he finished. He paused, only slowing the fluid rhythm of his run, and confirmed with a quick glance at the City Stater's unnatural posture and unwinking, glazed stare that he was beyond assistance. 'Course, obsidian'll shatter against steel plate, or even good iron. But it can bust right on through mail.'

Fost gulped. In his imagination, his own mail vest already rent by ill-use took on the consistency of wet paper. His grip tightened on his sword as he loped past the doorway from which the axe-wielding Hisser had emerged. The Nevrymin didn't spare a glance. The Vridzish lay huddled inside the pointed archway with his sharp chin slumped to the shaft of the arrow jutting from his sternum.

Fost's peripheral vision noticed the timeworn frieze graven around the shop's arched door. The architecture and ornamental stonework of the City in the Sky had disturbed him before, though he'd never been able to understand the reason. Now he knew the cause of that uneasiness. The City had originally been constructed by the Zr'gsz. The many additions later wrought by humans had imitated the original style. While these additions lacked the eldritch quality of the older structures, they still jarred the unaccustomed eye. But it was the ornamentation that bothered Fost the most. The figures in the bas relief were wrong in nameless ways, subtly distorted, yet apparently human. But they were not human; they were Zr'gsz or the products of Zr'gsz imagination.

The City turned alien and cold around him.

The two of them continued their curving course and spilled into an intersection. Fost yelped as a streak of yellow lightning crackled past his elbow and blasted the cornice of a building. Glowing gobs of stone spattered in all directions, drawing sharp yips of pain when they struck flesh.

'Fost!' cried Moriana. 'I'm sorry. I didn't know it was you.'

'Think nothing of it,' he said sarcastically. Her deathbolt hadn't singed him, nor had the molten masonry hit him. But he now had a fused patch in the mail beneath his left arm to match the one a salamander had given him that morning. 'I didn't know you could do that.'

She showed her teeth in a grin of wolfish satisfaction.

'Neither did Synalon,' she said. 'I've learned a few things since we parted, my love.'

A shout turned her attention back to the street, where more Zr'gsz had massed. Fost jumped to avoid the javelins and slung stones that glanced off the walls and clattered on the paving.

Several of their followers died from the missiles. The rest dodged back into doorways or around corners to avoid fire. Moriana stood her ground. She held a Highgrass bow in her left hand, but made no effort to pull an arrow from the few remaining in the quiver slung across her back.

She raised her right hand. A short arrow whirred by and dug a furrow in her cheek.

'Damn you, treacherous serpents!' she screamed. 'Die for your faithlessness!'

The hand came down. Blinding white exploded from her fingers.

194

Fost saw bright orange and blue after-images dancing before his eyes, but from the corners he glimpsed *Zr'gsz* bodies flung in all directions by the blast.

'A most impressive display, Queen,' remarked Erimenes. 'However, I wonder if your prowess will suffice against the forces I perceive are about to be —'

'Silence, rogue!' squalled Ziore from her jug. 'Moriana is the most powerful mage in all the world.'

Weaving like a reed in a breeze from the energy spent on the deathbolt, Moriana turned a stunned look toward the leather bag carrying Ziore. Her expression showed she was unused to this facet of the genie's personality.

Moriana staggered. Fost caught her arm and supported her. Her fingers gripped his forearm and squeezed down weakly.

'You've grown more powerful,' he said, 'to be able to toss lightning around like that so soon after your duel with Synalon.'

'I have.' She swept hair from her forehead with a quick thumb movement. 'And my anger gives a greater store of power than I'd have otherwise.'

'You should rest and marshal your power.'

'No! If I stop now I'll collapse.' She shook her head tiredly. 'Even without my magics, we're winning. The human warriors of my army and Synalon's are too many for them.'

She gestured up the street. As far as a distant curve, it was strewn with arrow-skewered *Zr'gsz* corpses. Near at hand several Underground fighters fished a limp green-scaled body from the sunken stone pond of a aeroaquifer. The magic fountain continued to produce water and music alike from thin air. The calm beauty of the sound drove back the warlike clamor from the surrounding streets.

'Now, where's that foul pact-breaking Khirshagk?' demanded Moriana. 'I'll scatter his ashes over the Keep of the Fallen, and the Heart of the People be damned!'

The warriors raised a cheer. Fost started to ask what the Heart of the People was, but a giant hand slammed into his ribs and dumped him on his rump in the street. An instant later, a tidal wave of sound crashed into him and sent him sprawling.

He rolled, recovered, found himself tangled with Moriana. A strange, dead silence descended. Moriana's lips moved but no sound emerged. Fost wondered what had happened to her voice, to the sounds of battle and the soothing song of the aeroaquifer. Then he saw a Sky Guardsman sitting a few yards away. A trickle of blood ran from one ear.

Fost felt his own ears. His fingertips detected no wetness and a quick inspection of Moriana showed her ears weren't bleeding either. The concussion had deafened them but hadn't burst their eardrums.

The Guardsman had gone as rigid as a marble statue. His arm was extended, pointing along the street they'd just cleared of the Hissers. Fost and Moriana exchanged looks and turned their heads that way.

A rolling black cloud rose above the dizzying spires and rooftops of the Sky City, burning a hole in the sky as it climbed. Blackness shone from it like light from the sun. They had to look away, the bright afterimages dancing in their eyes.

Moriana's cry pierced the armor of Fost's numbed ears. He looked back to see the great shape hovering just above the steep roof of the armory directly below the rapidly receding cloud. It was manlike in shape, though many times larger than the largest of men. And the horns that grew from either side of its blunt head were anything but manlike. It was the very image of the Vicar of Istu.

No, you idiot, Erimenes's voice rang in his head. *It's the original.*

The Demon of the Dark Ones shot upward and was gone.

196

CHAPTER THREE

The spells were sung, the aspects properly aligned.

The mystical forces Felarod had forged to contain Istu had been hammered thin like gold beaten on an anvil. Yet still they held the ancient and mighty Demon caged in his stone prison. It would still take unearthly power to break the barrier.

'And now that which we have awaited so long,' cried Khirshagk, '*shall come to pass!*' For a long minute, he held the blackly blazing Heart high above his head. The others turned up their faces in rapture. His own twin hearts close to bursting, the Instrumentality brought his arm down and flung the diamond aganst Felarod's magic.

The giant gem exploded. The ancient door was volatized by a ball of jet flame, as was the living stone for yards in all directions. Khirshagk and his twelve followers had only a split second to scream out their ecstasy before being engulfed and destroyed. Khirshagk and the others had known what fate awaited them and embraced death with the fanaticism of true martyrs. Not just their own lives but ten thousand years of their People's history had built toward this instant.

Khirshagk fulfilled his role as Instrumentality. His hand released the Demon Istu and began the Second War of Powers.

Free!

The Demon's being crackled with unfamiliar energy. Its first reaction had been the reaction of its id: sheer terror. But its awesome mind awakened to the knowledge that centuries-old chains were no more.

Free!

With the fullness of that knowledge, awful and magnificent, Istu soared upward following the path the dark fireball had slashed through the foundation of the Sky City. Nothing dimmed his exaltation. Not even the sunlight, the contact with that hated aberration Light. He shouted defiance at the sun and soared upward to once again touch the Void, the disruption of order that was Dark.

Free!

In a single beat of the massed hearts of the tiny paleskinned ones who infested the City of his children, Istu surged above the atmosphere, filling this being with the essence of the Void and Dark. The sun ball blazed at him, furious and impotent, and the stars looked down with malice. His laugh rang among them, echoing to eternity. In Dark and Void had the Universe begun, and to them it would return. Once again would the Dark Ones rule over placid oblivion, and their child and servant Istu would become One with them, One with Nothingness.

Free!

Great joy surged at being liberated from the walls of stone and magic that had pinioned His mind and body for so long. Greater still would be the joy of revenge.

Free!

The Demon of the Dark Ones turned his attention downward.

Stunned, Fost, Moriana and the rest scarcely had time to pick themselves up from the flagstones before Istu descended again like a flaming black meteor. With a strange, high keening the Demon flashed over their heads to touch down out of sight among the towers of the portside quarter of the Sky City.

'Moriana?' asked Ziore from her jug. 'What happened? I feel the most peculiar presence . . .'

'*Don't!*' screamed the woman. 'Keep your mind away from it. Don't try to read its thoughts or emotions. Don't even *try*!'

'But . . . oh.' Ziore read the knowledge of what had just occurred from Moriana's mind. She knew better than to disregard such advice. If Moriana told her to keep her perceptions clear of the Demon, she must obey. The sorceress-queen had more intimate experience of Istu than did any living entity. Ziore read exactly how intimate that knowledge was and sent ripples of mental horror radiating outward.

Fost wiped tears from his light-blinded eyes. First Moriana's firebolt, then the eruption from the center of the City and now the

Demon's return had all etched their patterns on his retinas.

'It's real, isn't it?' he asked, appalled at the power of the thing he'd witnessed. 'A demon. A real demon.'

'The most powerful of all,' announced Erimenes, managing to sound melodramatic despite the enormity of the moment.

Fost didn't feel his knees give way. He was simply standing one second and sitting the next.

'Itsu. He's real.' He had seen the Demon manifest itself before, had seen the Vicar touched with unholy life, seen the hellglare of the Demon's soul burning yellow through the slits of the statue's eyes. But the Demon, the *Demon*, Istu, child and servant of the Lords of Infinite Night, had never been real to him. The Vicar had been evil and horrifying, but no more than a golem to be outsmarted with a simple cunning twist from an agile mind. Fost had defeated it and rescued Moriana. A mortal had vanquished an animated statue.

But that force animating the Vicar had been the tiniest splinter of an immensely potent and incomprehensibly ancient mind. Before, Fost had faced only Istu's id, childlike and primal, a mass of drives and desires. He had witnessed awesome power — and this was only the smallest fraction of the true force of the Demon.

And this!

Above the highest spires of the portside district Istu reared up from the street, appearing to be a man-shaped hole cut into the overcast sky. His eyes blazed like windows to the surface of the sun. From them darted beams of impenetrable blackness. The tower of the Palace of Winds exploded. Moriana cried out as if her nerves were twined with the tower as it was dashed into a million fragments.

Gazing numbly into the sky, Fost watched a block the size of a hornbull turn end over end and crash through the starboard wing of the Lyceum. Head-sized fragments rained into the intersection about them, knocking smaller chunks from the edifices. One boulderlike fragment struck the magic-powered aeroaquifer, forever stilling its voice and stemming its waters.

The Demon laughed.

His laugh pierced souls, rimed hopes and aspirations with quick-frost like that which Fost saw glazing the shards blasted from the Palace. Warriors whose bravery had gone without questioning a dozen times that day fell to their knees sobbing in dread.

'He's real,' Fost repeated over and over to himself. No one else listened to his dazed litany. 'It's all real. Gods, Dark Ones, the War of Powers and all.'

'Yes, you bemused jack-fool!' Erimenes snapped acerbically. 'Don't you understand? This day has truly seen the opening of a *Second* War of Powers!'

Fost's response was to drop his face into his hands and moan. It did add up. One didn't need to be a bespectacled clerk in a Tolvirot counting house to arrive at the sum.

He felt someone tugging at his shoulder. He shook his head with a peevish motion. All he wanted now was to crawl into his mother's lap — what did she look like? What was her name? — and cry himself to sleep. And maybe if he were very lucky, he'd awaken and find this all a nightmare sent by Majyra Dream Mistress to bedevil him.

An openfisted blow slammed into the side of his head and sent him sprawling. His panic had been stripped from him like a wrapper, to uncover sudden fury.

Moriana stood over him. Her expression was one of stark contempt. She thought him a cowardly groundling seeking the comfort of despair. He snarled and started up.

When he gained his feet he saw the hauteur was gone from her face. Her eyes met his and he understood.

'Let's go,' she said simply.

They raced back toward the center of the City and the broad promenade of the Circle. The Sky Citizens who had not been there to acclaim the new monarch now gravitated there naturally after escaping the Hissers and their demon ally. Moriana rapped orders, brisk and businesslike in the face of calamity, marshalling her armed forces for resistance.

A warning cry sounded. A platoon of *Zr'gsz* broke from a nearby avenue. An arrow storm cut them down. A triumphant shout rose from the crowd.

'They don't know what they've got to contend with yet,' said Erimenes. 'But they will soon. All too soon,' muttered the spirit. Fost didn't bother listening. He stood frozen, his gaze riveted to the spectacle unfolding in the Sky City.

Far down the avenue the Demon appeared, striding on two legs like a man. Edifices of grown or graven stone slumped into ruin as his swinging arms casually brushed them. The Vridzish were massed about him, insignificant insects beside the stories-tall entity.

Arrows winnowed the ranks of the People. Dauntlessly, they

came on, trotting to match the bandy-legged strut of Istu. Unbidden, the Sky Citizens rushed to the attack, black and purple-clad troopers and Underground fighters together, brandishing swords and spears.

Istu stopped. The horned, misshapen head bent down to inspect these presumptuous pale worms. The burning eyes narrowed, reminding Fost of shutters closing on a magical vessel containing a fire elemental. But the glare of a salamander was mere heat and mindless malice. Istu's eyes burned without heat, but the hatred of old, soul-destroying evil that shone forth made Fost shrivel inside.

Istu blew forth a black breath. The miasma billowed downward, impenetrably dark. Some of the advancing Sky Citizens quailed and fled. Others stood their ground. The same fate took all. Like a living fogbank, the black breath rolled over them. As it did, each of the soldiers exploded into a pink cloud of bodily fluids and shards of skin, leaving the skeletons to clatter hollowly to the street. The bones, still joined by sinew, gleamed pale and white.

The black breath cloud enveloped all those who had been so bold as to rush upon the Demon of the Dark Ones. The noise of the explosions reminded Fost of unpierced fruit popping in the oven, a sharp sound with wet undertones. His stomach gave a queasy heave. Onward came the cloud. The crowd realized it would soon overtake them. In terror some of them turned and flung themselves into the Skywell rather than have the Demon's breath on them.

Moriana stepped forward from the line of troops she'd ordered across the avenue. Istu stood impassively, waiting to see what this golden-haired mortal made of its deadly exhalation. Silence seeped up from the very stones of the Sky City as Moriana raised her hands. A golden radiance sprang from her, resolved itself into a spear of light that leaped forward to pierce the cloud of darkness. The cloud exploded as had its victims. A few tatters of blackness danced on the wind, then vanished.

An avalanche of sound rumbled deep in Istu's throat.

'It recognizes Moriana,' suggested Erimenes.

Fost's throat constricted. For the queen's sake he hoped the Demon didn't realize this wasn't his first encounter with the tall, slim, defiant woman.

Moriana flung out her arms. Her fingers reached, grasped, drew back toward her breast. The facade of a tall structure on Istu's left toppled forward onto the Demon.

Istu roared and staggered. His horned head was above the level

201

of the buildings and mere stone couldn't harm him. But the torrent of masonry affected him like a sudden gout of water would affect a human. He was driven back even as the falling stone crushed the Zr'gsz clumped around his feet.

'She's learned a great deal, that girl,' Erimenes remarked approvingly.

The black beams lashed from Istu's eyes. Moriana was prepared. Her hand was already in motion, drawing a curtain of shimmering flame across the air in front of her. The black radiance struck the flame shield; both disappeared.

Breath pumped rapidly in and out of Fost's powerful chest. He felt helpless in the face of such magic. He clutched his sword, wishing for action and knowing this battle far outclassed his abilities.

'Can she defeat him?' he whispered. 'Has she gained power greater than Felarod's?'

Somewhere in the fracas, the lid of Erimenes's jug had come loose. In a whirlwind of blue fog and sparkling light motes, the genie appeared at Fost's elbow. As his long narrow head took form, it was shaking, a look of paternal disappointment on his ascetic features.

'I hardly think so. Nor would you, if you truly thought on it. Consider, my foolish young friend. How alert are you after waking from a long, long sleep? Especially one deepened by wine or drugs. I suspect the after-effects of Felarod's compulsion have a similar effect on the Demon. Yes, they are definitely analogous to those of more mundane soporifics used extensively in the . . .'

'I get the drift,' said Fost, waving a hand to stem the tide of Erimenes's pedagogy.

Istu had shouldered through the rubble. He strode purposefully up the street, and Fost wondered if it was only his imagination that perceived a fiercer light in those yellow eyes.

With a crack like thunder, a vast circular pit yawned before the Demon. Istu dropped instantly from sight in a welter of debris. Buildings to either side, their fronts undermined, slid into the hole. From the rush of air through the Skywell at his back, Fost knew the hole went all the way through the stone slab on which the City rested.

Almost at once a black hand appeared, three fingered and taloned like a Hisser's. Once more Moriana had cast magic of incredible power at the Demon – and had only succeeded in delaying his progress along the avenue. With icy shock, Frost realized the Demon was playing with his mortal opponent. He could simply have flung himself to the Circle of the Skywell with the speed of rushing wind had he so desired.

'Perhaps Istu treats this duel as a warming up exercise,' said Erimenes, reading the courier's thoughts.

A look of alarm gripped Erimenes's features, and he shouted, 'Oh, no, you can't take that upon yourself!' The genie had mind read Fost's intentions.

Unheeding, Fost looked around, then went to the young loyalist officer Cerestan, who stood with bow and arrow in his hands and glared with impotent fury at the Demon.

'We need balloons and birds,' Fost shouted as the lieutenant's head whipped around. 'We have to evacuate the City. *Now!*' he added as the young Sky Guard started to protest.

Still Cerestan objected, 'We cannot abandon our City!'

'This goes beyond the fate of your damned City! Any human who stays here will be dead within the hour. Don't you see? A new War of Powers is upon us. We need live humans to fight back, not dead fools who threw away their lives in useless heroics.'

Fost watched as understanding sank into Cerestan's mind. He nodded, lank black hair falling across his forehead. He turned to obey, then halted with a jerk like a dog reaching the end of its tether. He faced Fost.

'The queen! What of her?'

Fost read the look in those fervent blue eyes and inwardly groaned. He may have battled against Moriana but Cerestan was smitten with her all the same.

'I'll take care of her,' he said, emphasizing the first word more than was necessary.

Cerestan wheeled and raced off, calling to uniformed men and women as he passed. Some wearing Moriana's ribbons hesitated, but only for an instant. What side each had fought on before didn't matter now. They were all the same in the yellow eyes of Istu. And Cerestan was an officer of the Sky Guard, which meant that his orders were worth heeding. Rann promoted no fools to command his elite.

Fost worked his way through the crowd, yelling to warriors and unarmed civilians alike to evacuate. Erimenes floated by his side, pleading with him to stop this folly and see to the security of his own hide. For Erimenes to encourage the courier to flee the scene of imminent violence was tantamount in likelihood to the spirit again adopting his old philosophy of abstinence. Fost realized the situation was grave if Erimenes was willing to forego bloodshed in favor of what he had termed cowardice on many prior occasions.

'Get out, it's hopeless, get out!' was all the genie said. But he repeated it continually, his voice rising to shriller and shriller pitches.

To Fost's astonishment, Cerestan led a tentacle of the frightened crowd aft from the Circle along one of the lesser streets – seemingly into the face of the Hissers. Even though his wits were dulled by fear and fatigue, Fost figured out the ploy. Istu himself was playing cat and mouse games on the main avenue with Moriana and most of the Zr'gsz were with him. The Hissers Cerestan and the rest ran into could be quickly dispatched. Then the Sky citizens would get to work inflating the huge cargo sausages in the aft hangars. Since Istu fought forward through the City, they'd be safer there than those who retreated to the City's prow, at least until Istu and his reptilian allies consolidated their hold on the Sky City.

Then no human would be safe.

'– have you impaled for impertinence, if she doesn't feed you to Istu,' babbled Erimenes as Fost broke from the ranks of soldiers and raced for Moriana. 'Great Ultimate, you know how fanatical she is about her City!'

Moriana had blocked the avenue with a shimmering, rippling curtain of light burning scarlet and blue and gold and white. Buzzings and fat black sparks burst forth as Istu touched it. The Demon fell back with a bellow of pain. Fost saw all this as he sprinted after Moriana.

With a sound like water sizzing on heated iron, a black hand reached through the shimmering curtain. With another anguished, angry roar, Istu hurled himself through the auroral wall. It caused pain but no damage. Pain was enough to infuriate him; he reached a clawed hand for Moriana.

'Duck!' screeched Erimenes. The courier had only a split second to evaluate the situation. Moriana stood poised, her face strangely calm, a blue nimbus of energy scintillant around her form. Her arms slowly rose, as if imploring the gods for aid. Fost dived headlong, not wanting to be caught in whatever defensive magic Moriana was about to unleash.

He felt a tingling close about his middle like a noose. He hung suspended in midair, the pressure around his waist threatening to crush him. Fost gasped, then reached out and gripped a protruding cobblestone with his fingertips. Straining every muscle in his body, he pulled. Like a seed squeezed between thumb and forefinger, he squirted out of the magical grip holding him. He tucked his shoulder and rolled on the hard street.

'What're you doing here?' Moriana's voice sounded odd, flat. Fost sat up and saw that they were encapsulated by a dome of dull silver. 'The force shield will keep him out for a few minutes.' She shook her head tiredly. 'I learned this magic years ago but have never been strong enough to use it before.'

Fost thought about frail mothers who lifted impossibly heavy blocks to free their trapped infants. In those moments of adrenaline fury, they became more than human. The urgency of battle against this cosmic being had elevated Moriana's powers in the same fashion.

'The City is being evacuated,' he told her. 'I came for you.'

'*Evacuated!*' she screamed. Her face twisted in rage. 'On whose craven order?'

'I told you, friend Fost, nothing good would come from that rash action of yours, but you didn't —'

'My order,' Fost said, cutting off Erimenes.

Moriana raised a slender hand. Fost stood firm, though he knew magics capable of fending off Istu for the barest fragment of a second would blast him into a scorched cinder.

'*You!* By what authority?'

'As your acknowledged consort. But mostly common sense.' He cast a quick glimpse upward at the pewter-colored wall of force. It held. The Demon seemed unsure how to deal with it, but Fost didn't doubt that Istu would eventually penetrate the curtain.

'The City's lost. All that remains is for her people to save themselves. And you, too. You most of all.'

'I'm holding Istu!'

'You hold him — barely. He hasn't fully recovered from his enforced ten-thousand-year nap.'

'But I grow stronger with every instant. I feel it!' Her eyes burned like balefires. She had won her City at horrendous cost. The thought of losing it almost in the same instant of seizing it drove forth her sanity like a beast.

'Are you Felarod?' he shouted at her. The dome began to bulge

205

inward like a tent roof filling with rainwater. Istu had decided to push his way through using brute strength. 'Do you control the power of the World Spirit? Can you overcome a demon born among the stars?'

'He's right, Moriana.' The calm voice seemed to come from nowhere. Fost finally realized it emerged from the satchel so much like his own that Moriana carried over her shoulder.

The queen's shoulders slumped. The sight squeezed tears into Fost's eyes. He knew again how much he loved her, and her loss was a shared wound.

'Come,' she said, almost imperceptibly. Serpentlike her hand darted out to catch Fost's wrist. She dragged him toward the wall of the dome. He hung back, recalling what it had felt like going through the barrier as it formed.

The silvery hemisphere burst like a soap bubble. Istu's iron-black claw plunged deep into the pavement where they'd stood only seconds before.

The Circle was almost deserted when they reached it. At the fringes of the great plaza Zr'gsz began filtering in from the side streets. Moriana stopped to gather a full quiver of arrows and kept running, pausing now and then to cast some enchantment at the Demon following them. Fost didn't even look back to see what spells she hurled at Istu. It was too painfully apparent they were little more than annoying inconveniences to Istu.

Forward of the Circle, they ran into a crowd. Off to their left an elongated cargo balloon surged into the sky. Screaming people dangled from its gondola as the sausage rose from the streets to be dragged clear of the City by a laboring eagle. Bird riders helped refugees mount eagles. Each could carry only a single passenger, and Fost saw more than one scimitar fall and come up red as hysterical men and women tried to fling themselves onto already overburdened warbirds.

Moriana's step faltered.

'My poor people!' she cried. 'Only a handful will escape!'

Fost knew beyond doubt she was about to decide that she had to remain until all the Sky Citizens possible had been saved. He prodded her with his broadsword.

'Go on, damn you! We need your magic if we're to have a prayer of winning this!'

Her eyes were green daggers, but she picked up the pace again.

206

Something whined past Fost's cheek. He slapped at it, thinking it an insect. His palm came away red.

He glanced back. The Vridzish had taken the Circle and were slaughtering refugees intent on fleeing forward to the prow decks. The lizard warriors moved with inhuman swiftness, their weapons all but invisible as they struck yielding flesh. Behind them, Istu stood in the Circle of the Skywell, horned head thrown back, raping the sky with his basso profundo laughter.

A pressure on Fost's arm brought him up short. They were at the waist-high wall ringing the City.

'Now what?' he asked.

Moriana's answer was to sling her bow over her shoulder, jerk out her longsword and parry the blow of a mace with one smooth motion. This snarling lizard man riposted with increasing speed. Moriana scarcely weaved out of the arc of the flanged mace before Fost lopped off the gray-green arm and plunged his blade through the Hisser's chest.

Other lizard men ran toward them.

'Can you hold them?' shouted Moriana.

'No!'

Ignoring his response, Moriana turned and leaped as lithely as a cat to the top of the rimwall. She stepped forward into space. Fost cried out in loss. Her despair had driven her to suicide!

'It's you who's about to suicide, dolt! Turn around. Fight!' At Erimenes's urging, Fost moved to slap away a spear jabbing for his midsection. The spear pulled back only to shoot forward again and take him in the belly. He doubled over, gagging. The Hisser's throat swelled in triumph.

Grabbing the haft of the spear, Fost stabbed out with his sword. The Hisser gave a croak of surprise as the blade pierced his throat sac.

Fost rose, ripping his sword free and wrestling the spear from the lizard man's death grip. The Vridzish hadn't struck with enough force to drive the obsidian-pointed spear through Fost's mail, though links had parted under the force of the blow.

Luck had been with him this time.

A high caste Zr'gsz stood before him, breastplate gleaming green. The finely scaled skin of face and hands were so dark as to be almost black. The Vridzish flicked a two-handed mace at Fost. Instinct made Fost turn and block with the spear, which was almost knocked from his grasp. He cut at the Hisser's head. The mace knocked his sword aside, lashed out again. It struck chips from the wall as Fost dodged to one side.

Recovering his balance, he launched a whining multiple attack, one-two-three cuts in rapid succession. The mace met and countered each. He only saved himself from the crushing head by falling forward. The wooden shaft that had saved his life once now slammed into his left shoulder. He gasped in pain as his clavicle snapped.

He hacked at the Vridzish noble's side. His blade met the metal breastplate and was robbed of its force. He heaved, bringing his sword up along the inhuman's armored side to slice into the unprotected armpit. The Hisser dropped the mace between his body and Fost's and shoved the courier back.

Wary of the head with its five ugly flanges, Fost was caught off-guard when the Vridzish shifted his grip and whipped the butt of the weapon into Fost's face. Fost heard the crunch of his nose breaking. Lightning ricocheted inside his skull and nausea turned his flesh to water. He reeled, blinking to clear his eyes, saw the gleaming metal head rise up, up, up, poising to smash in his brains . . .

Shot from pointblank range, the broadheaded arrow stuck the Hisser in the neck with such force it nearly severed the neck. Fost saw the lizard man's look of final surprise as the head lolled to one side. Then the *Zr'gsz* fell flopping and kicking while black blood fountained from its neck to spray the lower caste Hissers behind.

They shrieked mad sibilants and lunged forward with weapons raised.

'Jump, you fool! It's your only chance!' Impossibly, the voice was Moriana's.

His skull pounding, his sight blurred, his left arm swinging at his side like so much dead meat, Fost couldn't hold back the reptilian Hissers for even a heartbeat. Knowing he was going to his death and loath to fall to these villains from a child's fable, he spun and dived over the rimwall into open air.

The ground loomed up at him from a thousand feet below.

CHAPTER FOUR

Fost Longstrider fell only four feet.

He had both arms crossed in front of his face. They took most of the force of his landing on the slate gray stone platform. His broken nose smacked hard against his forearm, sending a white-hot lance of pain into his brain. The wire-wound grip of his broadsword twisted in his hand, giving him a nasty cut on his left forearm. Even worse than the other abuses to his body, the force of his fall caused the stone platform to sink beneath his weight, leaving his stomach inches above his spine.

He felt the platform stir, rise. Fost lay dazed, watching the fireworks in his head and wondered whether or not he was glad he hadn't plunged the other 996 feet to the ground. The stone slab rocked gently like a boat bobbing at a dock. The nausea he felt from his broken nose was made all the worse by the motion. He guessed what had happened and where he was, but he kept his eyes clamped tightly shut. At this stage he didn't want to *know*.

'Is he all right?' he heard a worried feminine voice ask. Since it wasn't Moriana, it had to be Ziore. Her voice came out sounding elderly but strong and resonant and distinctly different from the screeching sounds she'd made at Erimenes.

A thump and a scrabble of claws came only a foot away from his head. The raft rocked under the impact of the added body. He heard the swish of a weapon cleaving air, the thunk of Moriana's longsword intercepting the axe-cut aimed at the back of his head.

The reek of Zr'gsz stung acridly in his nostrils. Anger filled and drove back nausea and pain. If the reptilian bastards weren't going to let him lie in peace, he'd make them sorry for it.

He seized the lizard man's ankles. The skin rippled smooth and dry, its texture differing only slightly from human skin. Before the reptilian Hisser reacted, Fost yanked hard on the ankles and flipped the creature into space between the blunt nose of the slab and the City wall.

He still wanted little more than to lie down and die, but the berserk fury he'd come to know in moments of battle settled on him like a cloak. He rose up and scythed three *Zr'gsz* from where they stood poised to leap from the rimwall.

'Bravo!' cried Erimenes, as the three sundered bodies plunged from view to the ground so far below.

Moriana thrust by him with a spear, not at a Vridzish swarming up onto the sky wall to attack but at the gray stone of the Sky City itself, pushing the skyraft clear. With a speed he didn't know himself capable of, Fost parried the stab of an obsidian-headed spear, then severed with a rapid backlash the claw that gripped it. Surprised, the *Zr'gsz* spearman lost his balance and fell into the rapidly widening gap betwen skyraft and City.

With the raft slowly drifting from the City, Moriana flung the spear at the Hissers, striking one in the shoulder. Panting with the fury of his own bloodlust, freshly roused and scarcely satisfied, Fost chanced a glance at the young queen.

'Faith-breakers!' she screamed. 'I'll pay your folk back as I pay you now!'

Like sheet lightning, a wave of red flame burst from her body. The dozen *Zr'gsz* crowding onto the rimwall screamed, not screams of agony but the screaming of superheated air blasting from their lungs as the flame consumed them. So frightful was the energy blazing from Moriana that when the fire died it left a huge glowing yellow spot etched on the very stone. The few *Zr'gsz* left alive in the vicinity of the rimwall broke and fled toward the Circle of the Well of Winds and the comforting presence of the Demon.

Fost opened his mouth. Before he could speak Moriana's sea green eyes dimmed and closed. She fell heavily. Only reflexes honed to unnatural keenness by the berserker fit enabled him to catch her before she pitched headlong over the nose of the raft.

Squatting, he lowered her to the stone. Strength drained from him like water from a tub with its plug pulled. His legs refused to lift him upright. Instead of trying to stand, he sat beside her, staring back at the City as it slowly receded.

His first thought was of pursuit. Hundreds of rafts nosed against the forward edge of the City as the one they now rode had been, bobbing gently on passing air currents. Had the Zr'gsz wanted to, they could have sent flyers to run down the fugitives in a matter of minutes like hawks bringing down a fleeing dove. Somewhere in the dizzy whirl of that day, Moriana had mentioned to Fost that she didn't know how to operate the Hissers' skyraft. He certainly didn't have the foggiest idea how to maneuver it or to speed it up.

If the Zr'gsz wanted them, they were easy pickings.

But the Vridzish obviously didn't care about the fugitives. The pale green faces of lower caste Hissers watched the raft blankly from the ramparts of the City. Here and there the darker features of a noble turned their way to scrutinize them briefly, only to turn away again. Fost sensed that they knew well that the potent human sorceress whose friendship they'd betrayed, whose vengeful might had actually given the mighty, eons-old Demon of the Dark Ones pause, escaped them on the tiny raft. And they did not care. Their indifference chilled him more than pursuit.

Nowhere did the Zr'gsz show any sign of pursuing the humans as they fled from the City in the Sky. Fost saw shrieking women and children hounded like beasts through the streets, saw the shapes of the Vridzish hunch over the bodies of fallen human warriors, some of which still writhed with life, tearing at the bloody feast with their sharp, inhuman teeth. Only those humans they brought down did they bother with; their main purpose seemed to be to rid the City of the pale, soft-skinned creatures who had stolen that realm from them so long ago.

Like men hunting vermin.

Fost's flesh crawled at the thought.

And the vermin were fleeing the City. The sky above the lofty spires and buttressed wall of the Sky City seethed with eagles winging away in search of refuge, burdened with human cargo. Balloons broke from the confines of the City and floated downwind, humans dropping from their gondolas like ill-shaped raindrops. Too numb to feel horror, Fost wondered distractedly how much of the City's populace had escaped. There had been so little time, though Cerestan and the rest seemed to have wrought miracles in saving those they could. A large number of the sausage kites and round passenger balloons drifted in the City's wake.

But there were too few balloons, too few eagles to hope that any significant number had been rescued. As Fost watched, scores of

211

giant warbirds beat back to the City gathering frantic humans onto their backs or into their strong claws to make a second, or third or fourth trip to the ground. The sheer number of refugees mocked their efforts. Those not fleet enough to outrace the hissing, croaking Vridzish died horribly. Those who outdistanced their pursuers, only to reach the rimwall with no means of transport to the ground, cast a single look over their shoulders at the horror being wrought on their City — and jumped.

In the middle of the Sky City Istu made sport.

He was kicking the haughty Palace of Winds to pieces and flinging giant building blocks for miles in all directions. Great pillars of smoke rose from a dozen locations within the City. A minaret of some noble merchant's mansion collapsed in the street, undermined by unseen claws. Streams of trotting low caste Zr'gsz made their way to the rimwall and back into the tangled streets bearing varied bundles: rolls of cloth from warehouses, tables and chairs, cabinets and crates. Some bundles had human shape and some of these still kicked with frantic life. All to no avail — over the edge they went, along with oddments and artifacts of human existence in the Sky City.

'See what they do, my young friend,' intoned Erimenes. During the battle he had retreated into his jug, leery of getting caught in the nimbus of some stray battle-magic. Now he appeared in the air at Fost's side once again. 'They seek to expunge all trace of the hated interlopers from the City in the Sky. I suspect that even those structures they originally built themselves, but which have been extensively modified by men, shall be razed.' He shook his head. 'It is an awful hate that can bide for eight millennia.'

Fost had no ready retort. His head felt like a ball of lead and his eyelids like leaden shutters. His own exertions overwhelmed him. He had fought two desperate battles, faced dangers mortal and mystic a dozen times, and seen the realization of the fear that had been nurturing since Jennas of the Ust-alayakits had begun hinting to him months ago that a new War of Powers could be in the offing. It was enough action, danger and horror to last a hundred lifetimes. He had no idea how Moriana felt after her ordeal. He was only glad she was unable to see the singleminded ferocity with which her former allies cleansed the City, even to the point of casting her people over the side like so much rubbish.

He heard a vast, many-throated squawk and a cracking of wings

212

like sails snapping to a stiff breeze. His last sight before unconsciousness was of Synalon's ravens billowing upward from the rookeries like a huge evil black cloud.

'Good morning, friend Fost,' a cheery voice said. The words were muffled by layers of fog and pain. 'You know, you actually look quite dashing with your nose mashed down like that. It makes you seem positively rugged. And since it has never lain altogether true, it's no detraction from your personal beauty, such as it is. An improvement on the whole, I'd say.'

'Shut up!' bellowed Fost, heaving himself to a sitting position. His roar set his head ringing like a bell. He groaned and fell back, clutching at his temples.

'Tut, tut, my dear boy.' He heard the philosopher's infuriating tones as if they came from far away. 'You really do need to curb that impetuous nature of yours.'

'Shut up, you querulous old fool,' Ziore's voice snapped. Through the tear glaze covering his eyes, Fost became aware of an unfamiliar outline bending over him. He blinked to clear his vision. He saw an elderly woman clad in a long, flowing robe similar to the one Erimenes 'wore.' Her aged features were smooth, serene, beautiful. Erimenes was blue; this apparition was pink, with long unbound hair so pale as to be almost white. Tiny reddish sparks danced within her substance.

Fost felt peace and comfort suffuse his body. His face, which had felt as if a heated torture mask had been clamped to it, began to relax from agonized contortion. He still felt agony in his head and aching weariness in every limb, but somehow the sensations no longer troubled him.

'Moriana woke briefly and let me out. She's sleeping again. I hope she sleeps a long time, the poor girl. She's suffered many hurts. Only a few of them are of the body.'

Fost moved his head tentatively, gingerly shaking it as if unsure whether or not pieces might break off or fall out. When nothing untoward happened, he straightened and spoke.

'Water,' he said in a voice sounding like it came from another's throat.

A look of concern passed over the slender, aged face.

'I cannot help you. But I perceive you have your magic water flask with you.'

213

In objective terms, it probably would have taken more out of Fost to climb hand over hand from the ground to the Sky City on a rope than to open the satchel in which he carried Erimenes's jug and bring forth the silver-chased black flask. But certainly the chore seemed onerous. With fingers that felt as agile as the City's great sausage-shaped cargo balloons, he unstoppered the flask and held it to his lips.

The tepid water was as sweet as nectar rolling through his cottony mouth and down his parched throat. When he had found the body of Kest-i-Mond the mage murdered in the sorcerer's own study a few thousand years ago – was it only last fall? – it had seemed at first that his only reward for braving the Sky City soldiers to deliver Erimenes's spirit to the enchanter was to be the flask and a silver-covered bowl of similar make. A paltry reward, the flask produced a perpetual flow of lukewarm water and the bowl gave an inexhaustible supply of tasteless thin grey gruel. However, this wasn't the first time Fost had cause to be thankful for those items.

He wiped his lips and tossed back his head, which was a mistake.

When the sledgehammer pounding in his brain had given way to a tackhammer tapping insistently at his temples and forehead and the bridge of his nose, he dared a look around. The raft was an oblong eight feet wide and twelve long. The gleaming black sphere at the stern controlled the raft's movements – under the guiding hand of a Zr'gsz.

Around him the day was overcast. A rumpled ceiling of cloud hung above his head. The clouds thinned to admit rays of watery sunlight of a sour lemon shade more unpleasant than plain shadow. Aft he saw a massive purple bulwark he eventually identified as the Thail Mountains dividing the continent. Oriented, Fost scanned all around, swivelling his head slowly to keep it from falling off his neck. North he saw the green of forests, bordered by the broad brown flood plain of the River Marchant. Beyond that the play of light and shadow on fallow lands and those planted in spring wheat turned the Black March into a giant's game.

Off to starboard lay an irregular metallic splotch with a dark mound in the middle. Its color was that of an Imperial klenor-piece whose silver wash had worn away to reveal base metal. Fost recognized Lake Wir, with Wirix unapproachable at the center. The lake was ringed with an irregular dark line that the courier didn't think was vegetation. After a moment, his eyes moved involuntarily to

Moriana, who lay huddled at his side, her shoulders rising and falling to the tidal motion of her breathing. She had mentioned leaving a force of Hissers camped on the shores of Lake Wir. Now they had become a besieging army, and a sizable one at that.

Fost wondered where they'd come from in such huge numbers.

'Moriana often pondered that question,' said Ziore, causing him to jump. 'When we visited Thendrun, the place appeared deserted. More of the Vridzish were involved in the attack on the Sky City than the princess thought were exiled.' Her face grew thoughtful. 'I suppose I should call her queen now.'

'Princess is probably as accurate as any other term,' sneered Erimenes, 'since she has no domain to rule.' He wagged his head censoriously. 'Her ambitions cost her dearly. Though I daresay others will pay far more before this mess is done.'

'How can you say that!' flared Ziore. Her form became darker and redder, the light flecks within her substance blazing like tiny suns. 'This has been terrible for her! She knows well what she's caused. Indeed, she blames herself far too much since all she did was what she believed to be right.'

'She couldn't possibly blame herself too much. Should she accept an adequate share of guilt for the evils she's wrought, she'd cast herself over the edge.'

Ziore's form turned almost white in rage.

'You dare . . .'

'Shut up!' Fost bellowed. Ignoring the aftershocks in his head, he scowled at the two genies and went on in a low, deadly voice. 'I have endured as much of your squabbling as I intend to. Another word of argument from either of you and I'll cast both your jugs over the edge of the raft.'

Both shades opened their mouths at the same time. Fost's eyes became slits of a gray ice. Both mouths promptly closed.

'That's better.' He lowered himself back on his elbows and continued his cursory survey. Black clouds obscured the country to the south, belaboring the Highgrass Broad and the Quincunx territory around Bilsinx with lightning and heavy rain. 'Where's the City?' he asked.

'Due south of us,' said Erimenes after a moment of sulking, his eyebrows lowered and his thin mouth pouted to let Fost know how miffed he was at such cavalier treatment. 'It's hidden by the clouds.'

215

Fost nodded, very deliberately, as if he had an egg balanced on his head and didn't want it to roll off.

'They can't see us. And I can't see *them*, which makes me just as glad.'

He put a hand up and gingerly explored his face. The contours weren't altogether familiar.

'How long was I out?'

'You've slept since yesterday,' Ziore answered. She didn't seem as angry over Fost's outburst as was Erimenes. She was a forgiving soul, save where Erimenes the Ethical was concerned. 'We do seem to be slowly outdistancing it.'

'Not that it matters now that they can't see us.' Being able to contradict his antagonist brought a pleased smile to Erimenes's lips. 'We floated in plain sight of the City until night came, and they showed no sign of molesting us.'

Fost lifted the flask for another drink. He still felt no hunger; the thought of food made his stomach surge and roll like a boat in a moderate sea.

'Are we just floating at random, then?'

Erimenes shook his head.

'Where are we going?'

The genie inclined his head. Fost followed his gaze and found himself staring at the smoke-wreathed fang of Mt. Omizantrim. His stomach dropped away beneath him.

When he awoke, the first thing Fost saw was black Omizantrim looming over them like a hammer poised to fall, its head dense smoke shot through with lightnings. The steady rumble of the angry mountain beat against his ears. Brimstone clutched at his throat and wrinkled his nose. Even his skin gritted unclean with a sheen of ash and volcanic dust.

The second thing he saw was Moriana, sitting with her knees drawn up and her arms encircling them. Her face was haggard and pale. She turned toward the fury of the volcano as if with longing.

'Moriana,' he said softly. She neither spoke nor stirred. Cautiously, he raised himself. His head didn't start vibrating like a gong. He reached out and took her arm.

She turned to face him. Her eyes were like coals and only vaguely the green he remembered so fondly.

'Erimenes is right.' Her voice fell heavy and black like a burnt ember. 'I should fling myself over the side.'

After an ugly glance at the philosopher who stood by the port edge looking sadly at the thunderhead piled above them, Fost said, 'Nonsense. You should know better than to listen to him.'

She pulled away and looked back toward the mountain.

'I've brought disaster on the world. I wanted to save my City. Instead, I destroyed it. And I murdered you, the man I loved. Oh, you live, thanks to my error in taking the wrong amulet. But the deed was done, is done, and cannot be revoked.

She dropped her face into her hands. Her hair hung in lank strings, its normal glorious gold dimmed to mousy brown.

'Was it power I truly sought all the time I quested and connived and killed to regain my throne? Am I no better than Synalon?' Her body jerked with sobbing, convulsive despair.

Ziore's pink, smoky body fluttered in a slight breeze crossing the raft. She looked in appeal to Fost.

'I've tried to gentle her from this dark mood,' the genie said. 'But she will not be consoled. She loves you. Can you do something for her?'

A quick stab of Fost's eyes spiked the contribution Erimenes was about to make. Dragging himself forward on his arms like a cripple, he took Moriana's shoulders and turned her around.

A bright spark of rebellion blazed and died in her eyes. Knowing by that sign he was right, Fost spoke roughly and to the point.

'Whatever your motives, the deed is done,' he said. 'The Fallen Ones are in control of the City again and Istu is loose, and I doubt the Dark Ones will fail to press their first real advantage in ten millennia.' Her face tightened as he spoke. That was good, too. It was more encouraging than the slackness of depression it replaced.

'You're the most powerful magician in the Sundered Realm, probably in the world,' he went on. 'Back in the City you were potent enough to hold Istu off while some of your people escaped.'

Her eyes dropped. A single tear spattered onto the gray stone.

'Only my fury at the Zr'gsz for their betrayal – and at myself for mine – gave me that power. I doubt it will come again.'

'I don't say you'll ever have power to stop the Demon of the Dark Ones. But you can do more against him than anyone else alive. We need whatever power you've got if we're to have a chance.'

'We?'

He paused.

'Uh, humanity.' It sounded bald and grandiose. But it was the truth.

Realization nerved him to say what must be said.

'You brought this about, Highness, Majesty, whatever I should call you. By the Five Holy Ones, you should stay alive and try to undo the disaster you've wrought!'

He released her. She slumped, her slender shoulders hunched and shaking in reaction.

'Die, if you want,' he said harshly. 'That's the coward's way out.'

Her slap bowled him over onto his back and set loose an avalanche in his head. For an instant, fireflies danced in front of his face. They faded to orange and yellow points and the accompanying pain slowly subsided to a dull aching.

'No one calls me coward!' she screamed. 'Take it back, you groundling worm!'

Despite the agony in his skull, Fost grinned when he pulled himself erect. He got his feet under him and braced his arms on either side of his knees, the roughness of the stone assuringly firm.

'Is that all I must do, Princess dear?' he said. 'Welcome back to the living.'

She was in his arms, her tears hot on his cheek.

CHAPTER FIVE

'It's apparent these rafts return automatically to their place of origin on being abandoned.' Erimenes was in his best pedantic form, not one whit deterred by the unorthodox setting for his lecture. 'I assume the function is intentional, though it may of course be serendipitous. Further, I reason that abandoned skyrafts follow lines of magnetic force back to Omizantrim, which accounts for our circuitous route from the City to . . .'

Thunder drowned him out. Fost ducked reflexively, spilling a spoonful of gruel into his lap.

'I think the mountain's building up to a major eruption,' Moriana announced.

She had resumed her previous station in the bow of the raft, gazing at Omizantrim as the volcano grew ever nearer. Fost gulped a last mouthful of the tasteless gray slop, covered the bowl with its silver lid and replaced it in his satchel, then slowly crawled forward to sit beside her. Cautiously, he stationed himself several inches farther back from the rim.

No one – no human, at least – had ever accused Mt. Omizantrim of being beautiful. It looked threatening and grim from far away, which was the only way Fost had seen it before. Close up, it was a tall cinder cone, dark gray, its flanks slashed with black striations and scarred with fumaroles. The open-wound pits in the mountain exuded thick clouds of dark blue and maroon gas, then lit them from below with a lurid glare. The very crest of the mountain was obscured in a billow of slate-gray smoke spilling away into the northwest. A gaudy necklace of lightnings surrounded the heights, both from the smoke and dust cloud and from the storm clouds above. Sulfur stung eyes, nose and throat; dust clogged them.

Omizantrim was far from beautiful. But Fost failed to discern the reason why Moriana thought it was going to erupt. As far as Fost could tell, the mountain looked little different than it had when it hiccuped to noisome life on the eve of the Battle of Chanobit Creek.

Fost couldn't figure it out. He asked her. Moriana shrugged, still studying the mountain with wrinkled brow.

'The displays seem more violent than at any time when we were camped there. And do you smell the ozone, the prickling in the very air? You should see yourself. It's making the hair stand up at the back of your neck.'

'It wouldn't take dormant lightning in the air to cause that, let me tell you,' said Fost. 'But couldn't it be due to our height alone?'

Moriana glanced down. The gray and black landscape writhed below like a tortured animal. Patches of vegetation clung tenaciously to the jagged, blade-sharp lava, deep green in some places, dusty and faded like old dry moss in others. One-horned and domestic deer moved below, not browsing but running in full flight across the broken land away from the great mountain.

'It's just a feeling,' she confessed. 'See? The animals feel it, too. They're more sensitive to such things than humans. They know the moods of the volcano from long exposure.'

'Our height isn't great enough to make much difference,' Erimenes cut in. 'We've stayed about a thousand feet up since leaving the City. That puts the mountaintop eight or nine thousand feet above us. Even that noxious looking cloud is easily thousands of feet above our heads.'

Fost felt the skin on his back try to creep into a bunch at the nape of his neck. An instant later, a brilliant yellow flash burned itself into his retinas. The light was so intense he wasn't even aware of the wall of sound that struck him. But several minutes later as he blinked away the last of the purple afterglow, his hearing had only just returned.

'Weather magic,' Erimenes said in his usual peevish tone. 'Can't you keep the lightning off us, at least?'

Ziore stared at the blue shade, her expression remarkably reminiscent of the clouds overhead. Mindful of Fost's injunction against further squabbling, she stayed silent.

'Perhaps I could,' Moriana said. 'But the battles I fought in the Sky City drained me so.'

She broke off to look at Fost with peculiar intentness. A wan smile played about her mouth.

'No, since you told some harsh truths to snap me out of my self-pitying fog, you've lapsed back into being too perfect a gentleman to point out the obvious. Yes, I have to start using my powers again sometime, and the longer I wait the more painful it'll be.'

She stood and stretched, oblivious to the emptiness yawning an inch in front of her toes. Fost shuddered. It was easy to forget what an insane disregard for heights the Skyborn had.

'Now's as good a time as any,' she said firmly. 'I've slept for two days and have a stomach full of that delicious provender of yours.' Her sarcasm elicited an uneasy smile from Fost. Though they had both devoured the gruel from the magic bowl so avidly it seemed its supply must be exhausted in spite of the self-replenishment spell, neither was ravenous enough to mistake the stuff for anything but clammy glop.

Moriana folded her long legs beneath her and closed her eyes in concentration. Fost saw her lips flutter, heard the ghost of an incantation above the grumbling of mountain and clouds.

'She needed a brazier and special herbs to make weather magic at Chanobit,' Ziore said in an awed whisper. 'She's learned so much since then.'

Erimenes grumbled, but all ignored him. Seeing that Moriana required total concentration, Fost took an oiled rag from his satchel and drew his sword. He examined it, clucking over its condition. Its blade was dimmed, streaked with blood and grime, and dirt had caked in places. Though the blade itself was fine North Keep steel, its edge was nicked and pitted from heavy use. Fost rummaged in his sack and brought out a whetstone, then began to rub the sword down with the rag.

As he cleaned the weapon, he kept one eye on the mountain. It grew until he scarcely saw where the cone disappeared into the wreath of greasy smoke. The heat of its many mouths washed over him like the uneven breathing of some immense creature. Throat of the Dark Ones, Omizantrim meant. Fost wondered if that was Their sulfurous breath that blew so hot on his face.

Just when he began to worry that the craft would drive head-on into the mountain, Omizantrim swung across the bow and began to slip by to port.

221

'We're circling,' said Erimenes unnecessarily. 'Probably going to the very skystone drift where the raft was mined.'

Lightning barraged the mountain's stony flanks, but none came near.

'Your magic's working,' he told her. She replied with a distracted smile. In fact, he didn't have the slightest idea whether it worked or not, but he wanted to encourage her.

'We're losing altitude.' Reluctantly, Fost glanced down and saw that Erimenes spoke the truth. The crags and folds of the mountain's skirts grew closer as he watched and the landscape took on more detail. Cave-sized openings were soon revealed to be great bubbles that had burst. Drifts of white ash and a gray stone touched with a curious sheen appeared in sharp relief that he guessed was skystone itself. Small animals scurried among the stunted stems of bushes, tails streaming behind as they fled the coming wrath of the mountain.

They passed a cluster of huts. Blocks of the incredibly durable lava had been hewn laboriously by hand and fitted to form walls capped by big slabs of basalt. The buildings, while grim, were suited to withstanding the mountain's caprice. But not even the stout construction of the Watchers could withstand the cosmic disease of change. The massive roofs had been levered from their places, the walls that held them pulled down into jumbles of black stone. Ash had fallen since the destruction, piling like blown snow against the few walls and doorposts that remained standing, filling in the outlines of the ruined huts so that they resembled a collection of haphazard children's sandboxes. Splintered pieces of wood thrust above the dust in some of the buildings, and Fost saw a few drably colored scraps of cloth waving in the breeze.

'They didn't loot,' he said to himself. 'Only destroyed.'

Moriana's face had turned the color of the ash strewn below.

'Wise Ones,' she whispered, 'have they slain the Watchers?' The thought of this new guilt showed on her face like a fresh swordcut.

'This isn't the main camp. It's only an outpost. The Vridzish were gathering the Watchers out of the smaller camps when we were here before. The Watchers are no doubt held captive at their village, as they were before.' Ziore's expression belied her hopeful tone.

'Who do you think works the skystone mines?' came Erimenes's question.

Lightning cracked dangerously close. Fost jumped, almost losing

222

his whetstone and small oil flask over the edge of the raft. The conversation took a turn that was not only distressing to Moriana but distracting as well.

'Where are the Hissers, anyway?' he asked.

'Look beyond you,' said Erimenes.

Despite the heat, Fost's throat had become a column of ice leading from the glacier of his stomach. The spirit wasn't lying. A two-man flyer had just rounded a stony buttress behind them, and three more appeared followed by a much larger barge teeming with green-skinned figures. Fost swallowed hard, thinking that the Zr'gsz flew much sloppier formation than Rann's bird riders. Perversely, he wished Rann could be here now to pit his genius against the lizards.

Moriana looked up as he touched her arm.

'Forget about the lightning. We've got worse things to worry about.'

She glanced back at the pursuing raft. The craft bucked now in updrafts from malevolently glowing mouths gaping below. She picked up her bow and began replacing the string, which had been ruined by a shower sometime while she and Fost slept.

Repacking his cleaning gear, Fost watched the enemy rafts gain on them. Under control of Zr'gsz pilots, the craft moved much faster than the humans' drifting raft. A three-man flyer edged out in front of the others, and a Hisser stood amidships whirling a sling. He loosed. Nervously, Fost watched the stone arch up and then down, apparently headed straight for the bridge of his nose. He watched in hypnotic fascination that didn't lose its grip until the missile dropped harmlessly in the raft's wake.

An angry bee whined past his right ear. The slinger stiffened as two more arrows sped past Fost, aimed with uncanny precision. The slinger pitched over the side of the small raft when the pilot slumped across the skewered corpse of the third Zr'gsz, an eagle-feathered arrow jutting from his eye.

Upon this attack, the loose formation of the skyrafts broke apart. They climbed rapidly out of range. Moriana shot two more arrows and killed the pilot of a second small raft which skidded sideways, spilling its occupant out over a lake of lava that glowed perceptibly brighter orange when the Vridzish struck.

'Damn them,' Moriana said. 'They're sharp. They've put their rafts between themselves and me.'

'They'll have to show themselves to shoot at us,' observed Fost. As he said the words, a head and shoulders appeared at the side of one raft. A javelin rocketed toward them. The dart went wide; so did Moriana's return shot.

The woman cursed reptilian reflexes and nocked another arrow. She drew the shaft to her ear and waited. Another Hisser leaned out to aim a short bow at the humans. Her arrow took him in the throat. The bow dropped from clawed hands, and the body dangled a moment before its fellows released its ankles.

'Your reflexes match theirs,' Fost said admiringly.

The look she gave him was not what he expected. He felt chilled by the flat, almost hostile expression. He was starting to speak when the mountain blew up.

The shockwave bowled him over. Moriana's witch sense gave her a split second's warning of the blast, and the same reflexes he'd just complimented saved his life. Bracing herself, Moriana caught hold of Fost's swordbelt just as he pitched over the brink. She dragged him back, aided by his groping fingers tearing on the gray stone of the raft. Erimenes shrilled terror as his satchel momentarily hung above nothingness.

'Thanks,' shouted Fost over the roar of the eruption.

Moriana bobbed acknowledgement to the thanks she read on his lips. She couldn't hear anything. The mountain was roaring in the voice of a million angry hornbulls. Fost stared in wonder that transcended fear as an orange prominence reached heavenward from the crater. The blast had blown the dust free of the mountaintop, and the heat of the geysering lava dispelled the clouds above like an enchantment gone insane. The top of the flame stream wavered, tipped, arced toward the far side of the volcano in a fountain of molten rock.

Something exploded nearby with a sound loud enough to hear even through shockwave-deadened ears. A fragment grazed his cheek. He blinked at ash and cowered inside his mail shirt.

A bomb, he heard Ziore say inside his mind. *A partially cooled lava shell surrounding hot gases. It must have struck the mountain-side nearby.*

He cursed. Apparently all Athalar waxed pedantic at the damnedest times. Fost glanced back at their pursuers in time to see something streak down and smash the big raft amidships. The stone platform came apart in midair. Fost saw superheated gases strip the living

224

flesh from the Hissers' bones as the blast scattered them away among the debris of their vessel.

That sort of thing happened a lot when I had the Destiny Stone. It was Moriana's voice now inside his head. He guessed Ziore acted as a repeater for the woman, since oral communication was out of the question in the din of eruption.

A spire of black stone flashed by on their left, its pitted face almost near enough to touch. Fost's head snapped back to see where they were heading.

I'll bet things like this did, too, he thought at Ziore. *Look where the damned thing's setting us down!*

Moriana looked where he pointed. A patrol of Vridzish stood gesticulating at a torrent that flowed through a cut in the same glossy gray stone Fost had seen before. A few hammers and prybars lay scattered about, and a knot of unarmed Zr'gsz huddled near the soldiers, staring at what resembled a cascade of extremely muddy water – or watery mud. Fost knew from the mad dance of super-heated air above the stream it had to be lava. Water would hiss instantly to vapor. The Vridzish stood on the side of the lava stream. The raft was making for a point just beyond them – in the midst of a river of melted rock!

The ground raced by beneath. Fost sheathed his sword and clutched the edge of the stone slab, leaning out to judge the distance to the ground. The agonizingly slow progress of the raft had become a mad careening – or so it seemed. Fost hoped this was only illusion. If they were moving too fast when they jumped from the raft, they'd tumble end over end across the cooled lava on the slope. It would be like rolling across a field of razorblades.

'We'll have to jump!' he screamed at Moriana. She nodded assent. Ziore's satchel was already slung over her shoulder. The pink genie hovered by her side, looking concerned. Erimenes had disappeared back into his own jar. Fost heard his whimpering even above the god's bellow of the exploding volcano.

A hundred feet short of the patrol and the lava flow, they jumped. Fost landed with a jolt that seemed to drive his ankles up to his knees and went on over to slash his arms and face on the jagged lava rock. Some good fortune spared his much-abused nose. Wiping at the blood pouring into his eyes from a nasty forehead cut, he looked up in time to see Moriana hit, tuck and roll with perfect form. She continued rolling on down the slope and came to her feet with barely a scratch. He cursed her Sky City training. He'd jumped from a few second-story windows in his time, to spare himself unpleasant scenes with unreasonable husbands bearing swords, but he'd never had occasion to jump from a second-story window that moved.

His plaints inaudible in the uproar, he accepted a hand up from Moriana.

'You heedless barbarian, how could you endanger me with such utter recklessness!' Erimenes screeched. 'My jug could have been smashed to flinders!'

The abandoned raft brushed the feathered headdress of a *Zr'gsz* officer. The Hisser looked up and gaped in astonishment as the raft drove on to plunge into the rushing lava stream. One of the lizard men clutched his face and fell kicking as molten stone splashed him.

The others turned their heads to see pale distorted shapes scrambling across the lava field. No vocal commands were needed. The officer waved his two-handed mace and the patrol raced in pursuit.

'Here they come!' Neither Fost nor Moriana needed Erimenes's warning to know the patrol slowly closed the distance between them. Choking and coughing on the dust clogging the air, the pair ran as fast as they could over the treacherous, broken ground. After what seemed an eternity of struggling in the sulfurous atmosphere, Fost turned to see how near the *Zr'gsz* were. The Hissers had lost interest – or perhaps their lives, since they were nowhere to be seen.

The mountain shuddered under Fost's feet. And the black stone was fever hot, burning him despite his thick bootsoles. With every third step it seemed a loose rock turned under him, twisting his ankle and adding a gash on unsuspecting calf or thigh.

'You incomparable dolt! Watch where you're going!' screamed Erimenes from the relative safety of his satchel.

Tricky as the ground was underfoot, Fost refused to look down. The spectacle of the volcano in full throat riveted his attention. A column of maroon smoke shot through with sheets of fire blasted upward from the crater. A ceiling of black cloud hung over the mountain. A hellwind raged within. Fost glimpsed the glow of incandescent gases swirling in the guts of the cloud.

It was as if battle raged between sky and earth. The Throat of the Dark Ones vomited lava and smoke and boulders and searingly poisonous vapors. The sky retaliated with incessant whip strokes of blue-white lightning. Rain lashed down all around, but no longer fell on the mountain itself. The monstrous upswelling of heat from the Throat cast it back upward again as steam.

A barbed spear struck a humped rock in Fost's path. Erimenes howled incoherently as a hammerblow landed on Fost's left shoulder.

The man bent and spun with the force of the blow. Instinct made him draw steel as he turned, and the training he'd bought from renegade fighting masters in High Medurim made him turn the draw into a savage backhanded cut at the black shape looming on the fringes of his vision. A black-clawed hand released its grip on a mace to make a frantic, futile effort to stuff back in the greasy, green ropes of guts spilling from the lizard man's opened stomach. The intestines tangled the Hisser's feet as it fell.

Fost kept spinning until he faced the way he had before the attack. He lit out running after Moriana. With his left arm numbed by the slung stone, he was at a worse disadvantage than usual against the inhuman reflexes of the Vridzish.

'Stand and fight!' Erimenes yelled at him.

'You're crazy,' he howled back. 'That's what you always say!'

'No, you idiot! *They're almost on top of you!*'

Fost flung himself to one side without even looking. A vicious spear thrust missed him by scant inches. He tumbled onto his rump among the jagged rocks. A screaming Hisser lunged at him. He brought up both feet and kicked the creature in the belly. It fell away. He scrambled to his feet, hacked as he rose. The blade bit flesh. He didn't wait to see where. He just ran.

Perhaps the furor of the eruption was subsiding or perhaps it was his imagination that he heard the lizard men on his heels hissing triumph and baying like a pack of hunting hounds closing for the kill. There was no doubting they were almost on him. Over a long run his superior endurance would have told, but in this short, desperate sprint over jagged ground they were fleeter than he.

Fost dashed up a long slope of relatively smooth lava and found himself flying across a crack that yawned abruptly under his feet. On the far side of the crevice, he turned and lashed with his sword taking a Hisser in the torso as it leaped after him. The lizard man fell back into the six-foot gap.

The crack ran up and down the slope as far as he could see in both directions. It was a natural place to make his stand.

'Run!' he shouted at Moriana as he set his feet and took his sword in both hands to prepare for battle.

Moriana's voice rang in his brain: *No! Don't be a fool. You haven't a chance!*

He took this mental communication as an indication that Ziore still relayed their messages.

'It's the only chance,' he shouted, not sure how to form the thoughts for Ziore to translate. He immediately regretted even opening his mouth. His throat was raw from breathing dust. 'You're the one who matters. Now run.' He saw Moriana start to protest. He shouted her down. 'Do you think I like being a hero?'

He had no chance then to see if she obeyed. A second *Zr'gsz* scrambled up the lava ramp and launched itself at him, only to meet the same fate as its comrade. The tall, feathered helmet of the officer appeared, bobbing purposefully toward Fost.

Movement made him glance upslope. A stream of thin, fast moving lava slopped over a lip of rock and splashed down onto a ledge a hundred yards above. Fost swallowed, though it felt as if a metallic rasp worked on his throat.

The lava rushed straight for him.

'Moriana, don't go! Save me from this lunkhead's folly!' For the first time in Fost's recollection, Erimenes pleaded to be taken from a promising fight. He obviously didn't like the notion of spending the rest of eternity entombed in a lava flow. The courier had little time to savor the spirit's abject fear because the big, dark-scaled officer was closing fast.

Had he been smart, the Vridzish would have waited for his men to come up and had them finish Fost with darts and slung stones. But either he lusted for personal revenge or was simply headstrong. He gripped his mace in both hands and swung at Fost.

Fost knew how fortunate he was that the officer had immediately attacked, but his heart dropped just the same. He recalled his last duel with a mace-wielding Vridzish noble.

Even the mace's long haft had a hard time reaching across the crack. Fost avoided the first swing simply by leaning back. He couldn't retreat from the brink, however, without allowing the lizard man to jump across. With the Vridzish's advantage in reach, Fost doubted his own ability to win should the lizard man succeed in crossing the gap.

The *Zr'gsz* swung again, leaning dangerously far out. Fost staggered as the volcanic glass head of the mace brushed across his belly. He cut recklessly at the Vridzish. The lizard man jerked away. The rest of the patrol had come up to join their leader. Only a half dozen could stand with the officer on the narrow lava ramp. The others milled behind, one of the javelin men hopping impatiently from foot to foot hoping for a clear cast.

Savagely, man and *Zr'gsz* duelled over the abyss. Fost held out longer than he thought possible and even managed to chop a feather from his opponent's green metal helmet. But the lizard man was quicker and stronger and could commit himself further due to taloned feet gripping the rock. They traded blows, wood cracking on steel with impacts that jarred Fost's arm. Then the inevitable happened. Fost extended his blade too far; the Vridzish swung with awful force and knocked the broadsword to the side, almost tearing it from Fost's grip.

Time flowed like the molten rock as the heavy mace swung back at Fost's unprotected body. He didn't have time to even duck. He took a breath and braced himself for the impact, the stabbing of shattered ribs through lungs and heart, oblivion.

A lava tide washed over the officer and swept him and his death-giving mace away like a twig in a millrace. Fost heard awful croaking cries as the molten stone engulfed the other Vridzish. He stumbled back, tears welling in his eyes from the awful heat.

He saw Moriana rise from the shelter of a boulder. She smiled.

'Did you bring down the lava?' he asked.

'No. The mountain did that.' The smile widened. 'But I diverted it where I wanted it to go.'

She took his hand and led him off across the badlands. The lava river gurgled at their backs.

CHAPTER SIX

Morning found the volcano quiet, at least in comparison to the prior day's cacophony. But its tip still smoked like a North Keep forge. The greasy smoke trailed off toward Lake Lolu in the north, but it was unadorned black smoke without lightning or glowing clouds or hurtling bombs. A constant peevish grumbling rolled from the depths of the mountain, as if it suffered indigestion. Erimenes, who claimed knowledge of volcanoes, said that the rumblings would subside over the next few days until the mountain lay quiet again. Unless, of course, it decided to once again erupt. Neither Fost nor Moriana found the tidings particularly cheering.

They had reconnoitered cautiously, Moriana alert with her bow, Fost ready to snatch out his sword at the first hint of danger. As expected, Erimenes derided him for not going forth with naked blade in hand like a proper hero. Fost decided it would be unheroic for a rock to turn under his foot and cause him to fall on his sword, as was likely to happen in such treacherous landscape.

They had worked their way well south of the smouldering mountain, both in the hopes that any fresh lava flows wouldn't extend so far and to come on the Watchers' village from above rather than from below. Otherwise, they'd have had to pass near the ledge where the Ullapag had kept watch over the skystone mines and the steaming fumarole into which Felarod had cast the Heart of the People. Moriana had a total horror of the place. Since yesterday they had exchanged snippets of their respective stories when they stopped to rest or eat, and Fost had learned enough of what had happened at that spot to understand why Moriana dreaded it so.

The sun had barely struggled above the humped flows to the east when they came upon the first new stream of lava. They guessed it to be the one which had swallowed the Hissers the day before. The surface had already hardened into a crust that showed rusty black in places through its coating over the ubiquitous gray ash. It looked solid enough.

Fost and Moriana exchanged looks, then Fost said, 'There's only one way to make sure it's really hard enough to support us.' He took a deep breath, then boldly stepped out, only to find the thin crust cracking beneath him at the same instant the stench of burning leather rose. He jackrabbited back to solid ground, scalding his feet thoroughly in the process.

'Look at him dance. Have you ever seen such a fine tarantella, even in the courts of High Medurim?' Erimenes howled in laughter which infuriated Fost even more.

'Fost,' said Moriana over the genie's ridicule, 'we must get across. The *Zr'gsz* will be after us. And I . . . I am uneasy in this place.'

He agreed with her. He sat beside the solidified but still hot river of rock and thought. Eventually, he hit on the plan of lashing bits of loose lava to their feet and walking across using them as insulation.

'Yes,' she cried, 'it'll work. It has to! If the pieces of lava we use are wide enough, it will be like snowshoeing. The larger the stone, the better our weight will be distributed.'

'And we won't break the crust,' Fost finished. 'Do you think the insulation from the rock will be enough?'

'Certainly,' said Erimenes in his best professorial tones. 'The thermal gradient in such a portion of the stone will be sufficient to prevent a repetition of your hotfoot.' The genie began snickering again.

With her archer's skills, Moriana deftly wove strong cord from the tough bunchgrass that grew among the dogthorn bushes. Then the two tied the chunks to their boots using projections to anchor the cords so they wouldn't come in contact with the hot crust more than necessary. Before they set off, Moriana insisted that each cut two stout staves of ofilos wood to use for balance. Reluctantly, Fost agreed. They spent an hour hunting for relatively straight limbs. Fost's allergy to the ofilos caused his hands to break out in a rash but this discomfort was offset by his enhanced ability to balance. With the ofilos poles to prop him, he made it to the other side with a minimum of flailing, cursing and heartstopping attempts to go facefirst onto the hot stone crust.

In less than an hour they came to another flow, the one into

231

which their raft had dived. Fost was amazed at the distance between the two flows. Either they had diverged considerably in their course down the mountainside or the fleeing pair had made record time crossing the saw-toothed terrain.

'The same trick should work,' stated Fost, gently prodding the tip of his ofilos pole into the semi-solid rock beneath the hardened surface. He pulled out the shaft when it began smoking. He beat out a tiny blaze, then began tying new lava rock to his boots.

Halfway across, the lashings on Fost's right foot burned through. He stood with one leg upraised like a nesting stork. His mind raced, trying to decide what to do next. Fate decided the issue for him. The other set of cords burned through, leaving him stranded twenty yards from cool, safe gound.

'Fost!' yelled Moriana. She had safely reached the far side of the frozen stream.

'Dark Ones take Fost,' shrieked Erimenes. 'Save *me*! I'll be marooned in this rock for all eternity. And gods, it is hot!'

'Of course it's hot,' cried Fost. 'It's molten stone. I thought you knew all about vulcanism.'

'Don't drop my jug,' pleaded the genie. 'I don't want to roast for a thousand years!'

The crust began bending inward beneath Fost's feet despite the weight-distributing lava rock. In seconds he would be ankle deep in the fiery river, in minutes only his charred skeleton would remain. He forced himself not to panic. That meant instant death.

'Moriana!' he shouted. 'Use some magic to get me out of here!'

'I can't, Fost. I . . . I'm too drained.' Even as she spoke, she worked at weaving new cords. Fost watched uncertainly. He didn't think much of tying new lashings to his chunks of rock; the balancing act that would require seemed beyond his ability. He settled by perceptible degrees into the lava. He could only trust her.

Instead of bringing the new cords out to him, though, she sat down and tied them to her own feet, reinforcing the charred lashings that had already carried her across the flow. Then she trudged out to him.

'Climb on,' she ordered, bending down and bracing herself on the balancing poles.

'You're joking.'

'No, she's not,' screeched Erimenes. 'Believe her. Fost, damn you, do as she says! Don't let us die out here!'

'Hurry, Fost,' said Moriana. 'For once, Erimenes is right. Unless you like it out here, climb on!'

Despite the dryness of his throat, Fost swallowed. Casting aside his own poles, he gingerly climbed onto the woman's back. She sank alarmingly beneath him, then rose again, seeming to support his weight with ease. Though her own stone shoes made deep impressions in the elastic crust, they didn't break through. After a few heartpounding minutes, they gained solid ground.

'She's quite a woman,' Erimenes said now in a natural tone.

Fost agreed.

Crows crossed the disk of the setting sun, black cruciform motes on an angry eye, an eye whose upper lid was a layer of dark, heavy cloud and whose lower was the tortured lunar landscape of the lava drifts south of Omizantrim. A bloodshot, angry eye.

Had Fost believed in portents he would have been catatonic with fright.

It had been a night and a day since the hazardous landing on the slopes of the exploding mountain. After Moriana's sorcery had changed the course of the lava stream to kill the Zr'gsz patrol, they had headed south away from the erupting cone and had laid up for the night in a wild land of knife-edged ridges and razor-cut draws. Their only company was the mournful howling of the hot wind down the slope of Omizantrim and the stunted vegetation that somehow thrived. The gnarled ofilos possessed a beauty of sorts. Early summer was their blooming season and the trees exploded with yellow-rimmed fragrant white blossoms that defied the gray dust all around. Such delicate beauty against the backdrop of stark desolation reaffirmed their faith in life itself.

After running, Fost decided it was time to be more aggressive. They had picked up spoor from the reptilian Hissers all day and had avoided it. Now he crawled on belly over what felt like broken glass, but the discomfort proved worthwhile. Fifty feet away he spied a Zr'gsz sentry. He waited, watched. The lizard man's partner approached and the two exchanged words, then resumed walking their posts.

Fost cursed the ofilos and its beguiling blossoms. He was violently allergic to the frail five-petalled flowers. His nose streamed the way Omizantrim had leaked lava the day before; his eyes watered and his nose felt as if it had been broken again. Worst of all, he didn't know how long he could contain the sneeze caused by the pollen.

If a sneeze escaped . . .

'It is only a histamine reaction,' came Erimenes's soft explanation. 'The body attempts to reject the formation of . . .'

Fost stiffened. Why in the name of hell had he brought Erimenes along with him on this furtive mission? The same spirit who, when Sky City troops pursued Fost, had repeatedly called out to attract their attention to Fost's hiding spot and provoke a rousing fight?

'Ust,' he moaned. He stifled a powerful sneeze and felt the pressure almost explode his eardrums.

'Bless you,' Erimenes said softly. 'And you need have no fear that I'll betray you, friend Fost.' The shade was bottled up in his jar, but Fost felt the weary, wounded headshake. 'To think you put so little trust in me.'

He huddled, trying to make himself appear part of a dogthorn bush. Its two-inch spikes stung like fire ants as they pierced his flesh. The only consolation for the man was in the bush's cycle; it didn't bloom until fall.

Cautiously, he raised his head. The Vridzish sentries went on down the arroyo and disappeared around the southwest corner of a compound wall. He cursed to himself. The wall was impressive, built to more than man-height with blocks of dressed lava looted from demolished buildings and topped with dried branches of dogthorn in much the same way a rich man of High Medurim might top his wall with broken glass. But there was a difference. The wealthy Medurimite did it to keep out intruders; this barrier kept the occupants inside. As Fost spied, he came to the conclusion this was the prison for the Watchers.

Moriana had been astonished and horrified to see what had sprung up on the former site of the Watchers' village. What had cut deepest of all was the realization that in spite of her orders that the captives be well treated, her erstwhile allies had enslaved the Watchers the instant she left. The Zr'gsz must have worked dozens to death to build this compound so quickly.

The discovery had almost thrown her into another spell of depression. Ziore had said or done something to pull her out of it. Fost didn't know what since their communication hadn't been oral. Even lying on his belly being perforated by thorns, he felt jealousy at the intimacy Moriana and Ziore shared, an intimacy no amount of love would ever make it possible for him to share.

The guards came around again and this time Fost successfully timed their patrol, counting monotonous seconds with a childhood chant: *one fat courtesan . . . two fat courtesans . . . three fat courtesans . . .*

When he reached three hundred and four the pair passed by his hiding place again. Five minutes.

He mentally directed the information at Erimenes and hoped the spirit passed it on. It had taken an hour's arguing, cajoling and threatening to get the two genies to form a communications link between Fost and Moriana. They weren't far apart – Moriana lay a hundred yards downslope hidden in a cave – but the mental noise from the captive Watchers inside the black thorn-topped wall made it impossible for Ziore to make out Fost's thoughts at that distance. Fost guessed that they passed most of the long, hot afternoon in psychic squabbling, which was fine with him. He couldn't hear it.

Erimenes beamed Moriana's acknowledgement. The sun had sunk so that only a dazzling silver remained in view. As Fost watched, it sank beneath the skirts of Omizantrim.

From the south came shouts and the tramp-tramp-tramp of trudging feet. Craning his neck and getting his left ear pierced by a thorn, Fost saw some of what was happening. A file of people, men, women and children, in drab clothing rendered drabber still by sun and dust and toil, dragged themselves up to the wooden gates of the compound. The Vridzish guards hurried them along with strokes of lizard hide whips and switches made from thornbush, chivvying them in wheezy pidgin manspeech. The lizard men were eager to get their captives penned up before the cool evening rendered them torpid. The Vridzish could function after dark, but their reflexes slowed.

When the last straggling child was whipped through the gates, they thumped closed and Fost heard a bar rumbling into place across the outside. New guards replaced the old; a mental signal from Moriana confirmed that the setup was the same as before, two on the gate, two patrolling the perimeter.

Night settled in to stay. Crickets tuned up off in the scrub, their chirping joined by the warbling of night lizards distending purple throat sacs to sing plaintively. The ofilos closed their lovely, treacherous blooms and some night blooming succulents released sticky sweet perfumes. Though Fost found their odor cloying, he wasn't allergic to them.

Some of the buildings in the Watchers' main camp had been left standing by the new occupiers, and Moriana reported that most of the soldiers who had escorted the prisoners went into them for the night. There were fewer of the lizard men than she'd expected. From the patrol activity of the day before — and today, as well, when they had dodged skyrafts floating around the mountain — Moriana reckoned there must be several times as many camped around Omizantrim as were bivouacked in the Watchers' village. Probably the rest were posted around the flows to keep out intruders, and concentrated around the mines themselves.

Fost was glad of that. It'd be no easy task to sneak even a few of the Watcher captives out from under the noses of two hundred sleeping Hissers.

Knowing something of Zr'gsz military routine, Moriana waited until midway through the new watch, giving the evening cool sufficient time to weigh down the limbs of the patrolling Hissers and render them drowsy. Then she beamed her readiness to Fost.

He listened until the lizard men's sandalled feet crunched through the dust and gravel of the arroyo running along the western wall of the compound. When they passed, he started counting again. He counted two-twenty-five. The Hissers would be midway along the northern wall unless something had disrupted their routine. He'd heard no disturbance and Moriana informed him that the lizard men needed to relieve themselves less frequently than humans.

Now! he thought.

From her bubble cave, Moriana put a compulsion on the two armed guards at the gate. When she'd outlined that part of her plan, Fost expressed his surprise. He thought the mental compulsion worked only on her fellow Sky Citizens, who were steeped in the magics of their City and thus susceptible to them.

'The magics of the City,' she'd replied, 'are closely allied to those of the Zr'gsz.' The peculiar light in her green eyes had discouraged further questioning, not that he cared. Fost knew as little of magic as he did of hydraulic engineering. Now he hoped fervently she was right.

He wished she could have compelled the lizard folk on the gate to slay their fellow guards. But she lacked the ability to impose so drastic an act as the murder of a comrade. She could turn them into living statues for as long as it took Fost to eliminate the patrolling pair and get to the gate, but that was all.

His heart thumped in his throat as the two appeared around the corner, two lumps of black against fainter darkness. He heard the crisp sounds of their steps, fancied he heard their breathing over the animal sounds of the prisoners on the far side of the wall. On the count of one-fifty he eased his sword from its scabbard. He shifted his hand to make certain of his grip on the wire-wound handle. Fear danced in his veins and pounded in his temples. He knew all too well the horrible speed with which the *Zr'gsz* reacted. He had to pit his merely human reflexes against two of them.

Part of him expected Erimenes to sing out a challenge at any moment. But the genie stayed silent as the footfalls drew nearer. Gleams of reflected starlight danced by in time to the footsteps. Fost sucked in a huge breath and sprang.

He landed with feet widespread and sword swinging, held two-handed in a madman's grip. He struck left and right with hysterical speed and power, crazed with fear that the lizard men's preternatural reflexes would cut him down before he could act. But even *Zr'gsz* reflexes take time to react; these Hissers were slowed by the soporific caresses of the chill night. When the pale creature materialized between them with his star-gleaming blade blazing a deadly trail through the darkness, they had no time to react.

The sword thunked home in the neck of the second sentry by the time Fost's nerves recorded the impact with the first. The leading Hisser fell, his head lolling from the half-severed neck that spewed dark blood onto the volcanic sand. The second's head simply sprang from its shoulders, launched by a powerful jet of blood.

Fost was so astonished that he just stood there staring for several heartbeats, his sword seeming to pulse like a living thing in his hands. Stinking black blood dried quickly on clothes and hair and skin.

'I'm alive,' he whispered. 'I'm *alive!*'

'Shrewdly struck,' observed Erimenes. It was true. Fost had read about mighty warriors, generally great-thewed barbarians from the equatorial forests of the Northern Continent, who decapitated foes with a single swordstroke. Once he'd started learning swordcraft he'd dismissed the tales as mythic. A horizontal headcut was too chancy to be useful – a shoulder or upraised arm was too likely to get in the way. And it was *hard* to cut through a human neck, even with a well-honed steel blade.

In his panic, Fost had been unable to do anything but lash out

237

horizontally and hope the sentries kept their arms by their sides. They had, and he'd chopped one of their damned heads off.

Maybe he *was* a hero.

'Don't get carried away.' Erimenes advised him sourly, picking up the thought from his brain.

Grinning, Fost jogged down the arroyo. He felt a laugh rising in his throat and pushed it back down sternly. He hadn't honestly expected to survive the ambush. Reaction to finding them dead while he still lived made him giddy.

He reached the end of the wall where the arroyo wall was only a few feet high, scrambled up and peered around cautiously. The buildings beyond were black and silent like so many crypts; the garrison had finished its meal and gone to bed, wrapped in heavy cloaks against the cold. Two more sentries stood as rigid as statues exactly where Moriana had predicted.

But the *Zr'gsz* could stand motionless far longer than a human. Were these under Moriana's compulsion or just standing their usual watch? Fost knew only one way to be certain.

He dropped from the wall and slowly walked around the corner. Nothing. The sentries might have been carved from basalt. He repressed a lunatic urge to whistle as he glanced around. Far away a pink glow stained the eastern horizon. The lesser moon was poised to fling itself into the nighttime sky. Fost picked up his pace.

Affecting a boldness he didn't feel, he walked directly between the sentries to the gate. Neither Hisser stirred. He reached for the wooden beam securing the gate.

'Kill them, idiot,' hissed Erimenes.

Fost paused to consider. Neither sentry showed any more life than the blocks of lava in the wall, but there wasn't any guarantee Moriana could hold them much longer. Fost had considerable cause to fear and loathe the lizard men, but he didn't like killing helpless beings.

But he saw no alternative — and time passed. He made two swift jabs with his dagger and turned back to moving the massive wooden bar.

The creak it made coming free of the brackets could be heard all the way to Port Zorn. But as soon as Fost had freed Moriana of her need to hold the sentries under compulsion, she'd shifted her attention to the buildings where the Hissers slept. She relayed via Ziore and Erimenes that no movement occurred at his slip. With a grunt of satisfaction, Fost heaved the bar away and opened the gate.

If the Zr'gsz hadn't heard him removing the bar, the captives had. A knot of men and women in ragged smocks clustered about the gate. Their reaction surprised him. A gasp of fear raced through the small group. Then it passed and he saw furtive expressions of hope dawn on their haggard faces.

Their gauntness appalled him. Obviously, the Zr'gsz fed their slaves only enough to enable them to drag their bodies down to the skystone mines every morning and toil the day away. That their slaves' numbers diminished every sundown made no difference to the reptiles.

A man pushed his way through the crowd. Not a tall man, he walked erect despite the air of deprivation, exhaustion and despair that swirled about him like a cloak. He'd once been a stocky man, Fost judged from the folds of loose skin on the scarecrow frame. But his eyes blazed clean, firm.

'I am Ludo, Chief Warden of the Watchers of Omizantrim. Who are you and what is the meaning of this?'

'I'm Fost. This means you and your folks are escaping. But they have to *move*.'

'The Hissers —'

'Are taken care of. We can have a nice chat later. But get your people moving and do it now unless you love such lush accommodations.' He waved his hand at the rude makeshift huts, little more than slumping piles of rock or tens made from tattered clothing.

Ludo took a deep breath and came to his decision.

The Watchers moved silently and efficiently, even the children. While Fost hovered by the gate watching the barracks nervously for sign of movement, they filed out through the gates and dispersed into the night. Leery of the apparent ease of their rescue, Fost advised them to scatter so that pursuers would have the hardest time possible rounding them up. In a few minutes all but a few lean men and women Fost took for the leaders had slipped out of the gates and blended into the darkness.

'I can't believe it's gone this easily,' Fost said.

'It won't be,' came Ludo's calm voice. 'They'll have their hounds on us as soon as they realize something's amiss. I only hope enough of us get free to wage effective war against the evil ones.'

Moriana hadn't mentioned hounds, but she couldn't know everything about the Zr'gsz.

239

'My partner's hiding that way in a bubble cave,' Fost said, pointing toward Moriana's command post.

'We know of it,' said Ludo.

'I'll meet you there.' The Watchers made for Moriana's cave. Fost admired their skill. They didn't beeline for the cave and risk being spotted on the open ground. Instead they bent over and scuttled to the jumble of rocks and bushes on the far bank of the arroyo and worked their way down from there, all but invisible in the light of the pink moon.

Before he followed them, Fost had work to do. Hurrying, he shut the gate and dropped the bar back into place. Then he picked up the guards one by one and propped them back in place, their spears serving to support their slack bodies. One he couldn't get into more than a slumping squat, but he thought it would fool anyone casually glancing down from the buildings. A close inspection would give the whole game away. But the deception might buy precious minutes, and time was more precious than gold.

Grabbing his scabbard so it wouldn't flap against his legs, Fost followed the Watchers into darkness.

'You!' Ludo's face turned to a mask of blood-dark fury in the light from twin moons. 'You witch! Traitor to all mankind! What are you doing here?'

Moriana faced his anger squarely, hands on hips and head held high as she replied, 'I'm setting you free.'

'And who caused our imprisonment?' the Chief Warden hissed. Fost respected the man's self-control. Despite the consuming rage, he kept his voice low. Fost and Moriana and the band of fugitives had travelled a good ways from the prison compound across terrain that gripped at them with knife-edged fingers before stopping and revealing to the Watchers the identity of their second benefactor.

'You speak only the truth, Ludo,' said Moriana. 'But I didn't know the Hissers would do this to you. Indeed, I had instructed that you only be detained so that you didn't impede the . . . the Vridzish mining operations.

Ludo spat into the sand between her feet.

Her lips pulled back in a snarl, then relaxed. She was better able to accept impertinence from this lowborn groundling than any other of her kindred, but it was by no means easy. Still, she had to empathize with the man.

'I was wrong.' A note of desperation pushed its way into her voice. 'I thought allying myself with the Fallen Ones was the only way to prevent my sister from seizing control of the Realm for the Dark Ones.' Her eyes dropped from his. 'Now it seems I and not my sister was the tool of the Lords of Endless Night. But I did not know!'

Fost's gaze made a nervous circuit of their surroundings. He saw nothing but the blank black walls of the draw and the hunchbacked shapes of trees along the banks. The pink moon had ridden past the zenith and the blue one just began its mount of the eastern sky. This took too long. And Moriana revealed too much before the hostile Watchers.

'It doesn't matter.' No scion of the Sky City could have bettered Ludo's haughty disdain. 'You served the interests of mankind's enemies. You are a traitor; your life is forfeit. Were it not for the dilemma posed by the fact that we now owe you our freedom, we'd take your life.'

Fost cleared his throat and loosened his sword in its scabbard. Moriana laid a hand on his forearm.

'Yes, kill the witch!' a woman's voice hissed from the darkness, sounding almost like one of the Hissers.

'Idiots.' Glowing softly, Erimenes hung in the air by Fost's right shoulder. 'The past is gone. You must deal with what pertains now – and the simple fact is that only Moriana's sorcery gives humanity any chance of defeating the Fallen Ones.'

Ludo looked at the spirit, his face still bleak with anger.

'The princess knows she did wrong,' continued the genie. 'She said as much, and if you don't know the effort that took, you know little of the Skyborn. Now she's set you free. The Vridzish are militarily naive. The ease with which we released you proves that. Instead of wasting the night with recriminations you should be laying out a guerrilla campaign to deny the Hissers access to their skystone.'

The Watchers murmured among themselves. Finally a man whose chin was fringed with a silvery beard spoke.

'This is true, Ludo. Killing the princess won't bring back the Ullapag or pen the damned lizards in Thendrun once more. If she'll help us we can't say no. Or so it seems to me.'

Scowling with fierce brows that were still as black as the surrounding lava, Ludo turned on his followers.

'The witch has brought ruin on us all, on all of humanity,' he exclaimed. 'Justice must be done!'

'We failed in our charge,' a woman's voice cried. 'That's what's rankling you, isn't it, Warden? Moriana helped the Hissers overcome us – but we were charged to guard the mines and we failed. Don't we share the guilt?'

Ludo's broad shoulders slumped. He turned back to Fost and Moriana, as if his limbs had transmuted to lead. Fost almost hated to hear the acquiescence of this proud, strong man.

'Charuu is right,' he said slowly. 'So be it. On behalf of the Watchers of Omizantrim I hereby . . .'

He broke off to stare past Fost's shoulder. Fost felt a soft breeze tug at his sleeve, heard a quick, soft moan. Ludo jerked. He raised his hands to his chest, spread them against the dark stain spreading across his smock from the arrow embedded in his chest.

Fost spun, sword ready. Brilliant light blinded him.

'Don't do anything foolish, my friend,' came the command. A soft chuckle accentuated the order.

And it was a voice as human as his own.

CHAPTER SEVEN

'And what of my sister?' Synalon leaned forward, her eyes narrowing into slits. 'What became of my sister?'

She hissed the words like an angry serpent. The young Sky Guard lieutenant flinched but held his ground.

'Your Majesty, I did not see —'

'I am not my Majesty until I know whether or not my sister lives!' she snapped. The young officer's gaze slid around nervously, looking for something other than the blazing pits of his queen's eyes. The walls of the makeshift tent around them were made of the collapsed skin of a silk hot air balloon. Giant ruby red, blind, legless spiders who ate the Sky City's organic refuse produced the light, virtually unbreakable threads. Saplings cut from a nearby stand of tai had been lashed together to provide a dome framework. The covering silk was rolled some feet off the ground to provide shade without cutting off the sultry breeze.

Prince Rann, despite the rents and stains disfiguring his black and purple uniform, managed to look as neat and collected as if he'd just turned out for a morning inspection. He appeared to be un-interested in the byplay between officer and queen; this made Lt. Cerestan even more uneasy. He forced himself to look directly at Synalon. She leaned forward even farther, waiting for his answer with the predatory intensity of a falcon watching its prey.

'You must have seen it!' persisted Synalon. Her words snapped like a banner in a brisk wind.

He flushed. Cerestan felt even more uncomfortable for what he had to report.

'Y-Your Highness, I was commanded to organize the evacuation of the City.'

Synalon's eyebrows shot up. Her right breast popped out of the robe she wore loosely wrapped about her lush body.

'What? My sister ordered the City in the Sky *abandoned*?' Sparks popped and ozone edged the air. 'That weak-kneed, cowardly slut! How *could* she!' She brought her hands up to angrily tear her garment. It resisted her wiry strength. Fat blue sparks travelled the length of her frizzled strands of hair and exploded in the air.

Cerestan made himself watch the princess's head shed sparks as a duck's wing sheds water. It kept his eyes off the naked breast which bobbed about in tempo with her efforts to rip her robe. The skin was the translucent white of snow the upper crust of which has melted in sunlight and then frozen again to a fine glossing. The nipple was a dainty blossom pink . . .

'She thought it necessary to save as many of our people as possible.' He forced himself to hold his head high. But it put a severe strain on his nerve to face Synalon this way, a fact that only peripherally had to do with her spiritual and temporal power. 'She herself battled the Demon Istu and bought time for as many to escape as possible.'

Rann had been watching the officer sidelong, his tawny eyes distant. Now they fastened on Cerestan.

'You did well. You saved several thousand of our subjects.'

Hardened as he was, Cerestan shuddered. Several thousand people – perhaps a quarter of the City's population. And the rest . . .

He looked out under the rolled tent wall. In all directions vultures crowded the sky and dotted the landscape in grave clumps, strutting stiff-legged with hooded heads drawn between their shoulders, bending down to partake of the unprecedented feast. The voracious birds extended in a line hundreds of yards across and a mile long, following the route of the Sky City. Though the hills were bright with fragrant wildflowers, the smell riding the wind was a ghastly charnel stink.

'So?' Synalon slumped back on her stool. 'Well, she defeated me and that made her the most potent wizard alive.' She propped her chin on one hand. Sparks stopped dripping like raindrops from her hair. 'How did she fare?'

'I couldn't see – not more than quick glimpses – Your, uh, Highness. But she must have survived because she kept the Demon at bay for a long time.'

Synalon slapped her knee. Her other breast bounced into view. Cerestan swallowed hard.

'That's my sister! I knew she could achieve real power if only she'd quit dabbling with her pathetic healing spells.'

Glancing toward Rann in his growing discomfiture, Cerestan noticed that the prince, too, was looking pointedly away from his cousin. The scarred cheeks showed pink like sunburn, though no bird rider of Rann's experience could possibly sunburn. For a fleeting instant, Cerestan almost shared a human bond with his commander.

'Very well.' Synalon settled back on the stool as if it were a throne. 'Now tell me,' she said, purring the words, 'tell me, good Cerestan, which of your brother and sister officers did you happen to observe wearing the armband of my sister's faction?'

Cerestan squared his shoulders and took a deep breath. Conflicting loyalties pulled in opposite directions like dogs, worrying a corpse, but one loyalty overrode all.

'I saw none, Highness.' Then realizing how bald the lie sounded, he quickly added, 'None so well I'd recognize them, at least.'

A blue glow started to play around the roots of Synalon's hair. Cerestan prepared himself for death. She would either fry him with a lightning bolt or summon other soldiers to exact a painful penalty for his defiance. He cast a quick look out over the plain covered with feasting vultures. With luck, that was the least of all possible fates awaiting him at Synalon's hand.

'I'm sure you didn't, Lieutenant,' Rann murmured. Cerestan stared at him, trying not to show his surprise at having such an unlikely ally. 'In the press of prisoners you probably got no clear look at your captors. And later during the evacuation you had no chance to see which of your comrades might be wearing Moriana's colors. Isn't that so?'

The prince ended in a tone well-known to his men, one that clearly stated anyone contradicting him would shortly wish he had died in his sleep the night before.

'Y-yes, milord.'

Rann nodded. Frowning, Synalon glanced from Cerestan to her cousin. It seemed to her that the young lieutenant should have recognized some of the traitors at least. By the Dark Ones, yes! But Rann was expert in internal security and he must have reasons for this action. She pouted slightly in frustration. It was bad enough that her own loss of the City was compounded by her fumblewitted sister

245

losing the damned place the very same day. She had counted on at least a dozen agonizing executions of rebels this very night to take away the sting of her disappointments.

'Very well. You've done the Guard proud, Cerestan. Dismissed.' Rann turned and bent his head toward Synalon. Cerestan stood as if his feet had put down roots. It couldn't be this simple.

Rann's head swiveled.

'I said, *dismissed*. Are you waiting for your mother's beak, Lieutenant?' It was a bird rider taunt referring to a weak fledgling that must be physically shoved from the nest. Cerestan saluted and fled.

Once more Rann bowed his head to speak to Synalon. A slim, raised finger cut him off.

'Cousin dear, what was that young man's name again?'

'Cerestan, Your Highness. Flight Lieutenant of the Guard. A good man.'

She smiled wickedly.

'I judged as much.' He was a well-proportioned youth, tall for a Sky Citizen, wide-shouldered, with black hair and blue eyes and a look of innocence hidden behind the veneer of veteran hardness that marked so many of Rann's officers. And Synalon hadn't missed the bulge between his legs and the way he oh-so carefully looked anywhere but at his monarch's naked breasts. 'But tonight, I think, I shall find out for myself what kind of man he is. We should always strive to know the more promising underlings. Well, Rann, isn't that so?'

Rann licked his lips and his cheeks flamed scarlet.

'Yes, Your Highness.'

Blinking into the sudden glare, Fost was momentarily transported back to his childhood. Night was the favorite time for street urchins of High Medurim to play their games. Usually there was some reward. Always there was penalty for losing. Adding spice to the game was the possibility of being caught by the watch for violating curfew. What happened next depended entirely on the whim of the arresting officer. A low caste, impoverished out-Guild youth pulled in after sunset could be let off with a lecture, whipped . . . or enslaved.

It was all in the luck of the game.

The yellow beam shining directly into his eyes came from a bull's-eye lantern exactly like those the Medurim city guard used.

246

Fost felt the familiar, clammy thrill: *caught*!

An almost pleasant voice brought him back to reality.

'Ho, my friend, don't do anything foolish now. It would be a shame for you to end up like that dolt on the ground.'

He tore his gaze from the lantern's shine. Ludo lay on his back, kicking spastically at the black sand, his motions becoming more and more feeble. Moriana knelt by his side, but the man was clearly beyond the reach of her healing magics.

Dark shapes detached themselves from the misshapen trees along the bank. The men appearing held flexed bows on the huddled people in the arroyo.

'Why was it necessary to shoot the Warden, Fairspeaker?' a voice from the darkness asked.

''Twas necessary so that these rabble shouldn't attempt futile resistance, great Sternbow,' replied the first disembodied voice in tones both oily and smooth and suasive. 'It brought their helplessness home to them. So now it proves unnecessary to slaughter them. Such forebearance does us all credit.'

The lantern was uncovered and flooded the draw with sallow light. Tall men jumped down from the banks with swords drawn and herded the recaptured Watchers together. They wore tunics and trousers that reflected black and gray in the torchlight. In sunlight they would have been forest green and brown.

Beside the lantern at the head of the draw stood a tall, stately forester, his arms folded across his chest, his sword sheathed. His blond hair and beard were sprinkled with gray. His brow creased and the frown-lines deepened as he studied Fost.

'Longstrider,' he stated quietly.

The courier folded his arms across his breast.

'Sternbow.'

'What? You fail to recognize me? I'd thought your memory more tenacious, good Fost.' The unctuous voice belonged to the lantern-bearer who stood at Sternbow's side. He was young and slender, with a chestnut fringe of beard adorning his jaw and brown eyes that laughed at some private jest.

'I know you, Fairspeaker,' Fost said quietly.

Slowly and ponderously, Moriana rose from the side of the fallen Warden.

'He's dead,' she said. 'What's the meaning of this senseless murder?'

A look of pain crossed Sternbow's angular face.

'No murder,' Fairspeaker put in quickly, 'to shoot a fleeing felon.'

'Felon?' Moriana's eyes blazed. 'How can you call him that? He was a victim held as a slave by the *Zr'gsz*.'

One of the Watchers moved to touch her arm.

'Save your breath, Lady. These are the very hounds of the Hissers set to hunt us down even as Ludo foretold.'

'But they're *men*,' she said, stunned. The Watcher's chuckle was as dry and bitter as an old root left in the searing desert sun.

'On behalf of our ally the Instrumentality of the People I hereby place you under arrest for aiding and abetting the flight of prisoners of war,' Sternbow said formally.

'Am I not your ally, as well?' demanded Moriana.

'The wise Sternbow takes cognizance of the fact that you have been an ally of the foresters,' said Fairspeaker. 'Yet he is also well aware that relations between Thendrun and the Tree go back to a time long before the name of the Princess Moriana was ever heard in the Great Nevrym.'

'Don't you understand? The Hissers turned on me — turned on us. They helped me capture the City, then they wrested it from me. They mean to drive all humans from the Realm. They've freed the Demon Istu to help them do it!'

Shaking his head, smiling sorrowfully over human duplicity, Fairspeaker looked to Sternbow.

'Honored sir, is it not clear that she has had some falling out with our friends the People and means to turn us against them with these fanciful tales?'

Sternbow's already thin lips disappeared in a pensive line. Moriana's pulse raced. She had touched him with doubt. She could tell.

'Father.' A stocky young man, face wreathed in golden ringlets, pushed his way into the draw to stand beside Sternbow. 'She's telling the truth, can't you see? I've told you repeatedly we can't trust those lizards.'

Fairspeaker laid a hand on Sternbow's shoulder, squeezed reassuringly.

'A sad burden it must be to you,' he said softly, 'that your son Snowbuck has not learned the meaning of faith among friends.'

Sternbow shook himself free of the hand.

'We waste time here,' he grated. 'Brookrunner, Stagsnarer, disarm the princess and Longstrider.' Fost and Moriana stood in stony silence as the Nevrymin relieved them of their weapons.

More torches were lit. The Nevrymin, a score of bow and swords-men, ranged themselves around their captives and began to drive them back down Omizantrim's rocky slope. Above them the mountain rumbled to itself, and a brimstone smell stung their nostrils.

'Do those boorish forest dwellers all have doubled names?' Erimenes demanded from his jug. 'Frogbaiter. Leafeater. Shitkicker.' He produced a decidedly unphilosophical snort. 'Absurd.'

'They seem to know you, Fost,' Ziore said hesitantly.

'Indeed they do.' In spite of their predicament, a lopsided grin appeared on the courier's face. 'In fact, they gave me the name Longstrider.'

With neither gentleness nor excessive force, the foresters guided them around a seething fumarole.

'Ah, well, of course, there is a certain bucolic charm to the custom of bestowing two-part descriptive names,' said Erimenes loudly, his wavering form peering down into the fumarole. 'In fact, I once composed a monograph on . . .'

A loose rock turned under Fost's foot. Moriana caught his arm, steadying him.

'How did that come to pass?' she asked, cutting off the philosopher's nervous word flow.

'Lawless men plotted together to assassinate our king,' said a forester walking nearby. 'The outwood courier learned of the scheme and went to warn Grimpeace. Though he couldn't match the woodscraft of the rebels, he was able to outpace them and reach our king in time.' He spoke without looking at the captives and he continued to hold his bow relaxed but ready. 'In reward for the feat, the King in Nevrym bestowed upon him the forester's name Longstrider.'

'It is indeed a pity that one who so nobly served the interests of our king should now place himself in opposition to noble Grimpeace.' Fairspeaker had materialized out of the night. The forester clamped his bearded jaw tight and kept trudging through the lava flows.

The former village of the Watchers was awash in torchlight. Armed Zr'gsz, torpid with the chill, milled about the compound without apparent aim. An officer in feather helmet emerged from what had been the Watchers' assembly hall and held a vigorous discussion with Sternbow. The Hisser spoke in sibilant, garbled human speech augmented by violent gestures. Fost and the others were too far away to make out what was being said, but as far as the courier could tell the reptile was determined the escapees and those who had helped them should be put to death immediately. His only point of uncertainty was whether they should be speared where they stood or flung into the lava pits, thereby saving wear on obsidian spear tips. Fost did think Fairspeaker added his voice to Sternbow's in arguing they be speared. He found it cold comfort, somehow.

At last, Fairspeaker lowered his voice and, shaking his head with the lugubrious regret of an inquisitor ordering his assistants to crank the rack a few more turns, said something that caused the Vridzish officer to turn moss green and immediately begin issuing orders with even more histrionic gestures.

Sternbow strode to where the captives stood. He had to make his way through a mob of lower caste Zr'gsz surrounding the prisoners in unmoving, silent ranks. Somehow their silence, their apparent lack of emotion, seemed more threatening than a display of hostility. Fost saw little approval on the Nevrym leader's face as he pushed aside the scaled bodies.

'The Vridzish officer was adamant that you pay full price for your crimes.' Though he stopped a foot behind Sternbow, Fairspeaker quickly thrust his presence to the fore. Sternbow showed no sign of irritation at being pre-empted. 'But Sternbow, whom all know as a merciful and just man, prevailed upon him to let you live.' Fairspeaker shrugged slightly. 'For a time, at least. The People are much outraged by your treacherous defection, Princess.'

'*My* defection?' She held her anger back with visible effort.

Sternbow locked his gaze on Fost's.

'You were a loyal friend to the Forest,' he said. 'I hope this breach can be healed.'

'So do I.'

The compound gates swung open. The Hissers made quick, menacing jabs with their spears. The prisoners were marched into the lava rock walled pen.

'Wait!' cried Erimenes as the gates started to swing shut.

Fairspeaker appeared in the gap between the gates.

'Why should we wait, friend spirit? I judge you are another bottle-bound shade, such as the one known to accompany the Princess Moriana.'

'Yes. I mean no! I'm not like that vacuous creature at all. I'm much, much wiser. And I know many things that might interest you.

250

Things your masters would give a great deal to learn.'

An eyebrow arched.

'My masters, eh?' Fairspeaker pursed his lips, nodding to himself as he meditated. Then he bobbed his chin. 'Well, there's no harm in listening to you if you wish to speak.'

He gestured. A pair of Hissers approached Fost with the curious sporadic movement of their kind, their spears at the ready. Fost plunged a hand into his satchel. The Vridzish stopped, pointing the spearheads at his heart. He ripped Erimenes's jug from the pouch and flung the red clay vessel onto the hard-packed earth at their feet.

Unfortunately, it bounced.

'Really, Fost, such petulance ill-becomes you,' Erimenes sniffed. 'I could never abide such a poor loser. Come then, Fairspeaker, let us converse.'

'Let us, indeed.' The young man accepted the jug from a clawed hand.

'I must confess the smell in that sty was quite revolting,' Erimenes said as Fairspeaker walked out cradling the jug in one arm. 'Say, you're a strapping young fellow. Are there any lively wenches in the vici –'

The gates slammed shut.

CHAPTER EIGHT

The air in the prison compound lay like a thing dead, hot and still and decaying. Upslope toward the rear slit, latrines festered like wounds under buzzing clouds of flies. The tents and huts Fost had seen the night before were gone, torn down and trampled by the enraged Hissers. Crude makeshifts though they had been, they were sorely missed.

Fost had awakened with a pounding in his head and the sun pouring like hot wax on his eyelids. He lay near the gate, where exhaustion had claimed him when the curdled gray of false dawn started to seep into the eastern sky. Moriana sat nearby, her hair tied back from her face, her head bent in earnest conversation with Ziore. She and the spirit seemed to take turns reassuring each other.

Fost pulled himself upright. For a moment, he expected the longwinded complaint that was his usual morning greeting from Erimenes. Then he remembered. He spoke a heartfelt curse and dug his magic water flask from the satchel.

Moriana and Ziore noticed he was awake and greeted him in subdued voices. He handed the flask to Moriana and looked around the compound. The lava pen was almost empty. Two score Watchers stood in sullen knots. He spat to clear his throat.

'Most of the Watchers got away, I see,' he finally said.

'But for how long?' Moriana answered, reluctantly pulling the flask from her parched lips. She pointed skyward. It was busy up there. No clouds were visible, and if Omizantrim breathed this morning its exhalation streamed away northward and out of their sight. But the skyrafts of the Zr'gsz teemed in the air like flies around the latrines.

'You'd know that better than I,' Fost pointed out.

'I think they've got a chance,' she said slowly. 'If they have sense to lie up in the bubble caves during the day, the Zr'gsz will never find them.'

With his usual touch of the inappropriate, Fost marvelled at the ease with which she pronounced the Vridzish's name for themselves. It wasn't intended for human tongue, yet she grated out the hissing and gutturals as if she'd hatched from an egg in the emerald depths of Thendrun. Fost took out his bowl and traded it to Moriana for the water flask.

As they ate, they talked about their adventures since parting in Athalau, the city in the glacier, the fabulous lost city of sorcerers and savants in which Ziore and the treacherous Erimenes had been born centuries before.

Fost's account was straightforward. He looked away from the hardness that came into Moriana's eyes when he spoke of having been discovered outside the glacier by Jennas, the hetwoman of the Bear Clan. Moriana had known that even before their precipitous separation in Athalau he and Jennas were more than mere friends. Fost recounted his journey north to find Moriana and tell her that the magic bauble she possessed wasn't the one she thought. Jennas had travelled with him, partly out of love, but mostly because her bear god Ust had revealed to her that a new War of Powers loomed, and that she must discover what that implied for her folk. Fost had nervously discounted Jennas's claims of visions and divine revelation. The farther they travelled, the less he was inclined to do so. They found powers afoot in the Realm beyond simple shades and sprites and hedge demons.

Most of the rest Moriana knew, including how he had gotten in touch with the Underground opposing Synalon in the Sky City.

He watched the skyrafts drift overhead as he spoke, since this part of his journey held painful memories of Luranni and how the woman had given her life to save him from her traitorous father's fire sprite.

Fost fell silent. Moriana's slender fingers made patterns in the gray ash in front of her, then erased them. After a while she related her travails to Fost.

Moriana glossed over her stay in Thendrun, and not simply because thought of the place raised gooseflesh all over her body. Despite herself, she gave awed account of the Keep of the Fallen Ones, of the fortress hewn from giant emerald crystals grown eons ago in the heart of the Mystic Mountains by Zr'gsz magic. She talked about the witchfire that lived in the walls, and the emptiness of the castle that had made her think she treated with a dying and helpless race — she talked about everything but what actually went on within those walls of green crystal.

Fost studied her intently, sensing evasion, but did not speak of it. Instead they discussed the question of the numbers of *Zr'gsz* Moriana had seen since departing Thendrun. It had worried her all along and now was of vital importance. How many foes did mankind face? Fost could offer no insight. Their fellow captives might have but they remained aloof, refusing even to talk with Moriana, whom they blamed for their present troubles — and with good reason. Though their jailers hadn't brought the breakfast allotment of brackish water and rancid slop, all refused to acknowledge Fost's offer to share his inexhaustible stores of food and water.

As the morning wore on, it became apparent that the slaves weren't to be driven forth to work in the mines. The Hisser garrison had its work cut out hunting other fugitives across the inhospitable flanks of Omizantrim. Fost and Moriana moved into the shade of the eastern wall and continued to talk.

Without Erimenes on hand to incite her, Ziore turned out to be a warm and soothing presence, full of concern for her mortal friends. She made Fost feel as if she had known him her whole long life and cared for him dearly. He was even flattered when she told him he was fully the man Moriana had described in such loving terms.

In the course of Moriana's narrative, Fost had picked up the spirit's history and something of her attributes. Now he asked, 'But I thought you had the power to influence men's emotions. Couldn't you influence Sternbow to let us go?'

'I tried,' said Ziore, looking stricken. 'Such was his natural inclination, too. Yet Fairspeaker's influence proved greater than mine.'

'Is he a mage?'

'No. He holds Sternbow in bonds of love and fear and duty. I don't fully understand their relationship.'

'Perhaps I do. Fairspeaker is Sternbow's youngest sister's son. She died of fever not long after Fairspeaker's birth. Her husband fell in battle not long after. Custom provides that Sternbow should take Fairspeaker into his own house and raise him as a foster son. But Sternbow's wife wouldn't hear of it, claiming the boy was born under an evil sign.

'Fairspeaker was raised by a succession of foster parents. Even

254

when he was young, he earned quite a reputation for his skill with sword, spear and bow. And far more for his prowess with words.' Fost shook his head. 'It's strange, too. His talent is akin to magic, if not identical with it. What he says sounds empty and often ridiculous – as long as he is saying it to someone else. When he turns his attention on you, it's damned hard not to agree with everything he says. It's as if other folk are puppets, and he knows just the strings to pull.'

'An appeal that went beyond charisma,' sighed Moriana. 'Darl Rhadaman possessed a similar talent.'

'It may be that I was wrong about Fairspeaker's not being a mage,' Ziore said musingly. 'This ability you speak of may be a talent of the mind, like Athalar magic, though it is of a kind unfamiliar to me.'

'Or perhaps too familiar,' said Moriana. 'It strikes me as similar to your talent for emotional manipulation, Ziore, but not as well controlled.'

The genie looked first rebellious, then sheepish.

'You may be right,' she admitted.

'In any event, he had grown to manhood when Sternbow's wife died. Fairspeaker returned from a campaign in which he had distinguished himself in battle against bandits from the Lolu country. He demanded the patronage Sternbow had withheld so long. Guilt wouldn't permit the older man to refuse.'

He drew idle designs in the dust at his feet. The growing heat made him sweat. Fost wondered what it had been like for the Watchers in the skystone mines. Hell, no doubt. And the man he spoke of contributed heavily to a renewal of that living torture.

'When I was in Nevrym,' he continued, 'Fairspeaker was already something of a force to be reckoned with. He was little different from the way he is now. No one quite trusts him, unless you happen to be the subject of his immediate attention. Yet when he's around no man quite trusts his comrades, either. No one can tell who is under Fairspeaker's influence. And no one knows who Fairspeaker backs.' Fost rubbed his chin. A wiry black stubble rasped under his hand. He'd lost his razor in the City, and the dagger he shaved with now had been confiscated by the foresters. 'He keeps his own balance and keeps all others off theirs. He is dangerous,' he finished.

'But why is he helping the Zr'gsz?' demanded Moriana. 'He must know they're enemies of all humanity.'

Fost shrugged.

'I don't know. One thing no one's ever accused Fairspeaker of lacking is a keen perception of where his own best interests lie.'

A creak and a thump announced that the bolt on the gate was being withdrawn. Fost was on his feet instantly, Moriana beside him poised to take advantage of the slightest opportunity to escape. Deep down he knew escape was but a forlorn hope. The inhuman speed of the *Zr'gsz* and the keen eyes and ready bows of their human allies were too formidable a combination for them to overcome unarmed. Even if Moriana summoned up a fearful battle spell from inside her, all that would accomplish would be to take some Hissers and foresters down to Hell Call with them. That might be the only sensible thing to do, but despair hadn't progressed that far. Yet.

'My ears burn, gentle friends,' said Fairspeaker, stepping through the gate with a brace of *Zr'gsz* spearmen at his heels. A leather pouch with a suspiciously familiar bulge swung familiarly at his hip. 'Could it be you did me the honor of discussing me?'

Fost favored him with a long, dour look and folded himself back down to the ground.

'We've more pleasant topics to discuss, Fairspeaker. The state of the latrine, for example.'

Fairspeaker threw back his head and roared with laughter, as if this were the choicest joke he'd ever heard.

'Ah, good Longstrider, you were ever the droll rogue. You are sorely missed in the Great Nevrym. The dullards and dotards who infest the Tree haven't among them the wit to fill a thimble.'

Fost found himself listening intently, even thinking Fairspeaker wasn't such a bad fellow. After all, he did appreciate Fost's finer qualities.

Fairspeaker looked from the courier to Moriana who stood with legs braced and arms folded beneath her breasts, glaring defiantly at him. He met her eyes, shrugged at the message he read in them and turned his attention back to Fost.

'You'd be a valuable ally for the Dark Ones,' he said. 'Why throw away your life for this Sky scum?'

Why, indeed? It was all so lucid Fost wondered why he hadn't thought of it before.

'Are all Nevrymin allies of the Dark?' demanded Moriana.

'No, Lady,' he said, laughing at her. 'But soon they will be. As soon as those of us with the vision to see what's best for the Forest have assumed the mantle of power and cleared away a certain amount of the deadwood.'

Moriana's answering laugh was as jarring as steel on stone.

'I, too, thought the Hissers my allies,' she said, 'and I gather my sister thought the same of the Lords of Infinite Night. You can see how wisely we chose those to trust.'

A shadow crossed his pale face, then was gone, as fleeting as a bat crossing a disk of the lesser moon.

'I have my assurances from parties of great power – or Power, if you get my emphasis. Synalon was weighed and found wanting; you merely sought to exploit the People for your own base ends and found your wickedness turned against you. I, and those of like mind, deal with the Dark from a position of strength and good faith. We will be honored well when the final victory is achieved.'

His brown eyes found Fost's gray ones. Fairspeaker smiled and Fost felt himself stirring to the gaze.

'Well, Longstrider? May I have your hand upon it . . . comrade?'

As if of its own accord, Fost's scarred right hand rose to touch Fairspeaker's slimmer, softer one.

Idiot! A voice cracked from the back of his skull. *He's playing you like a lute!*

He struck the proferred hand away.

'Go drown yourself in a bucket of shit!' he snarled, deliberately using the crudity to dispel the last of Fairspeaker's verbal spell.

Fairspeaker only laughed, and waved the fingers of his raised right hand languidly in the air as if to cool them.

'Well, that's your decision. All I can say is that I am deeply regretful.' He turned to Moriana. 'Perhaps you have a clearer perception of your own interest, Princess. I can tell you that a high official of the People arrives on the morrow from Thendrun to interrogate you. You can save yourself much anguish – by which I mean earn yourself a quick and painless death – if you simply tell me now of your plans.'

'Plans?' Moriana's laugh turned bitter. 'I have none. Except to escape this stinking pen.'

'Don't lie, Princess.' The liquid eyes showed hurt. Fairspeaker patted Erimenes's new pouch. 'Your former accomplice has revealed to me many of the salient features of your scheme to turn the skystone mines to your own purposes. But the servants of the Dark need details. For example, which traitor revealed to you the workings of the skyraft controls? We know you flew here on a craft stolen from the Sky City. I tell you this so you'll understand that we know enough to tell if you try lying to us.'

Only instinct prevented Fost from dropping his jaw in amazement. It took iron self-control to keep from turning to see if Moriana was as dumbstruck. Where in the wide Realm had Fairspeaker gotten such an extravagant notion?

'Confess all, Fost.' Erimenes's voice lacked nothing of the unctuous tones Fairspeaker carried off so well. 'You've not been a bad companion, though you are uncouth and rather less valorous than I might have wished. I'd hate to see you suffer needlessly on account of your murdering wolf bitch.'

Fost turned an ugly grin on Fairspeaker.

'I might even reconsider your offer to join you, my friend,' he said in a deadly quiet voice, 'if you could promise me one reward. Return Erimenes to a living, feeling body so that I could give him the fill of sensation he so craves. My vaporous friend, I think I've picked up some useful pointers from your old friend, the late, lamented Prince Rann.' Fairspeaker guffawed.

'You'd jest on the gibbet, friend Fost.'

'Who's jesting?'

'Mark my words, Fost! You'll regret this.'

Fairspeaker looked at the sky. A few fat, fleecy clouds gamboled in the southern sky. He let his gaze drift meaningfully at the traffic of skycraft streaming in from the northeast.

'You'll have until tomorrow morning to think over your refusal.' Fairspeaker's eyes filled with concern. 'You must understand, my friends, that once Lord Nchssk arrives, affairs will pass from my hands and I will be unable to win you any mercy.'

They ignored him. He shrugged elaborately and walked out. The Zr'gsz guards waited until he had left the compound before backing out. The gates boomed shut and the lock fell with a sound like a headsman's axe.

Fost and Moriana exchanged looks. The tale Erimenes had fed the Nevrymin was a combination of truth and utter fabrication. Had the genie thought to insinuate himself into the good graces of the Dark Ones by inventing an imaginary menace, banking on the near certainty that the more fervently Moriana and Fost denied the existence of such a danger the more fervently the questioners would disbelieve them?

Or had the ages-old spirit simply gone insane?

Fost slept through the heat of the afternoon. With a sentence of death looming over him as tangibly as the bulk of Omizantrim, it might have seemed strange he could sleep at all. But sleep shielded him from having to think of his fate.

He woke to find Moriana bending over a younger Watcher woman seated on a flat rock. Moriana worked on the woman's arm, which was twisted unnaturally. The woman's face was drained of color and feeling; it showed no pain.

Moriana finally stood up, wiped sweat from her forehead and regarded the job of splinting and bandaging.

'It'd be best if you wore that sling for several weeks, Beiil. Right now the thing to do is sleep.' The woman nodded dully and rose, walking to the nearest group of Watchers who were busily not watching what the princess had done. One spoke to the woman in hushed tones and looked disbelievingly at her quiet answer.

'Damn the Hissers,' Moriana swore fervently. 'And thrice damn the Nevrymin for aiding them now that they've shown their true shade! That girl's arm was broken in the capture of the village. They locked her in a storeroom with others wounded and dying. The others were too weak to help her; she bound her own arm, but set the bone wrong. By the time the Hissers let her out to join the others, it was too late to reset. I had to break it over again.'

'She was certainly quiet.'

Moriana mopped at her forehead with the hem of her tunic. Fost looked at the bare skin of her trim midriff with a pang of longing. It had been so long for them, and now they'd never have the chance to complete their reunion.

'Ziore helped. She suppressed sensation in the girl's mind while I worked. She even left a residual block that will keep the pain from becoming too severe.'

'I keep being surprised at the way your powers have grown,' Fost said. 'Tell me. You'd rather heal with magic, wouldn't you?'

Her eyes answered for her.

When the sun dipped low enough in the sky to become entangled with the black tentacles of the Omizantrim flows, Fost broke out his bowl and flask. He and Moriana ate a little, then offered the vessels once more to the Watchers. Wan and shaky, Beiil rose from her pallet and came over. Fost helped her and Fost fed her with her own spoon. When she finished, most of the other Watchers lined up wordlessly to partake of the food and drink.

As the other prisoners ate, Fost lay back with his head in his hands watching the sky set in layers of color, slate-gray and blue and orange. His mind wandered. First, he thought about Moriana's account of her trip to Thendrun. There was something missing from her story. He didn't perceive the lack as he would, say, the hollow left by a missing tooth. Rather, it was like detecting wine watered by a dishonest innkeeper. Moriana had diluted the truth.

Why?'

He'd never find out. In a short time it would no longer matter. But it hurt him to think she'd keep anything from him.

His thoughts drifted to Erimenes. He had travelled so long in the company of the garrulous and horny spirit that he'd come to like him. Certainly there were scores – hundreds! – of times when he had felt like abandoning the sage. Yet he had come to regard Erimenes as something of a comrade in arms despite the genie's superciliousness and insatiable appetite for vicarious stimulation.

And Erimenes had repaid that loyalty with treachery. Fost had no one to blame but himself for his credulity. Erimenes had shown his true essence before, when as a messenger, Fost had been charged with delivering the genie in the jug to its original owner. It had seemed to Fost that the genie was gradually changing over the many months, though, was actively trying to aid Fost rather than goad him into impossible and potentially entertaining situations.

Aye, *seemed.*

The Watchers finished eating and drinking and, still wordless, returned the utensils to Fost. He sat unspeaking with his arms around Moriana while the light went out of the world. Then they lay down side by side and slept.

They awoke to light.

Instinctively, Fost groped for his sword. He found a handful of soft flesh. Moriana automatically brushed his hand from her breast and sat up beside him.

They blinked into the yellow eye of a hooded lantern. Fost's blood chilled. Had the *Zr'gsz* inquisitor arrived ahead of schedule? The light winked out. Fost's eyes adjusted to the darkness again, and he made out a stocky form in a narrow gap between the gates.

'Sir Longstrider? Princess Moriana?'

'What do you want?' Moriana asked cautiously.

'Save the hackneyed dialog for later,' a familiar, testy voice snapped. 'Right now, time is of the essence.'

'Go play your vicious tricks elsewhere, you treacherous bottled fart,' said Fost hotly.

'Yes! You're a disgrace to noble Athalau!' exclaimed Ziore.

'Gentles . . .' the husky young man said, raising his hands in a placating gesture.

'The just must suffer,' Erimenes said. 'May the Three and Twenty Wise Ones of Agift witness what dullards I am saddled with as friends!'

'You've small right to call upon the Wise,' hissed Moriana.

'Gentles, now . . .'

'Must I bear such abuse heaped upon my noble head? After all I've done? Oh, it is a bitter lot dealing with such as you.'

'*Silence!*' The command snapped like a whip. Fost peered most closely at the youth. Whoever he was, he had the habit of command. 'Gentles, you may not know me, for you only saw me briefly. I am Snowbuck, Sternbow's son. I've come to rescue you.'

'Then why are you signing your death warrant by carrying that jar around with you?' Fost got to his feet.

Erimenes called upon the gods to witness his sorry fate.

'But gentles,' Snowbuck said, 'It was the good Erimenes who talked these men into helping free you. I couldn't convince them by myself.'

A tall shadow appeared at his side.

'It may do us little credit but it's no light thing to cross that devil Fairspeaker.' Fost recognized the voice of the bowman who had told his naming story to Moriana the night before. 'But when Erimenes told us what had happened in the Sky City, we could no longer doubt that the People are enemies of all our kind.'

'As if it wasn't before all our faces long ago!' Snowbuck said passionately.

'Ah, Snowbuck, you've won now. Don't chop a tree that's fallen.'

The rebuff was offered in a friendly tone and Snowbuck took it gracefully.

261

'You have the right, Firesbane.' He gestured and men spilled into the compound. 'Help these others out.' He didn't have to tell them to be quick and quiet; they were Nevrym foresters.

As the Nevrymin began to usher out the Watchers into the night for the second time in two days, Snowbuck pulled Erimenes's fat clay jar from its pouch and handed it almost reverently to Fost. Fost accepted it with both hands. For a second, he considered drop-kicking it over the wall, then thought better of it. That would have been too noisy. He stuffed it back into the satchel.

'At least, you're not totally lost to feelings of gratitude,' Erimenes said waspishly.

'Erimenes, what are you up to?' Fost demanded. He stood in front of the gate so that the escaping Watchers had to part and pass to both sides of him like a stream around a jutting rock.

'A scheme worthy of my high intelligence' the spirit replied smugly. 'It was almost a pity to waste such ingenuity on so paltry a project as saving you from certain death. But it offends my sense of esthetics to contemplate a beauty such as Moriana's passing from this world.'

'I'm flattered,' the princess said, 'but what was all that bizarre claptrap about our plotting to field our own fleet of skyrafts?'

'I had to tell that rogue Fairspeaker something that would convince him I was truly on their side — and, incidentally, would keep him from bowing to the insistence of the Zr'gsz commandant and allowing you to be killed.'

'"Allowing" us — what power has he?' Fost demanded.

'The Hissers realize it is Fairspeaker who keeps their Nevrymin allies allied. And he does have the favor of the Dark Ones. He wasn't lying about that.'

In the starlight it seemed that patches of color had come to Snowbuck's broad cheeks.

'You owe Erimenes a debt, Sir Longstrider, and you, too, Princess,' he said. 'And . . . and I, as well. For he's made it possible for me to save my father's honor!'

His voice almost cracked the armor of his whispering. He collected himself and clapped the two on the arms.

'We must hurry.'

'Lead the way,' said Fost.

CHAPTER NINE

Sure-footed in the dark, Snowbuck led Fost and Moriana up the arroyo that ran along the western wall of the prison compound. He then threaded his way eastward over the brushy slope of Omizantrim between the fumarole where the Ullapag had kept its vigil and the village itself. The mountain was moody tonight. Its mutterings crescendoed from time to time to a roaring like blood in the ears. Purple lightning played around the summit. Explosions crashed in the crater playing lurid light on the underside of the wide cloud that issued from the mountain's guts.

Fost sensed movement on both sides. He didn't waste energy casting about to see who or what was nearby. He trusted Snowbuck's sense better than his own. It would have been foolish to fall down a hole simply to keep track of unseen friends.

Like Moriana, he ran with sword in hand. Nevrymin had returned their weapons as they emerged from the compound. As dark as the night was, the princess had decided not to string her bow and wore it slung over her back next to a fresh quiver of arrows.

They passed through narrow draws, struggled up slopes where the lava threatened to crumble underfoot at any instant and fling them facedown on the sharp rock, and once hopped across a recent flow that burned the soles of their feet. Luckily, the crust didn't give way beneath them the way the half-hardened lava had when they first made their way to the Watchers' village.

At one point, Fost almost went headlong into the yawning pit of a skystone quarry. He drew a sharp rebuke from Erimenes for his clumsiness. The major drifts and mines lay downslope, which meant the Zr'gsz garrisons and patrols of Nevrymin still loyal to the lizard folk would be concentrated in that direction.

As he scrambled from the pit something flew into his face. He struck at it, thinking it a bat or nocturnal insect. To his amazement it flashed by and continued soundlessly upward, losing itself in blackness.

He heard Snowbuck chuckle softly.

'Skystone,' the youth explained, then pushed on, using the dark brush that grew upslope to pull himself along.

'How in hell's name does the stuff ever get deposited?' Fost grumbled.

'I believe,' answered Erimenes, 'that it is a component of the magma extruded through the crater to become lava. As it flows down the mountain it rises to the top of the flow. Yet it adheres to the heavier stuff of common lava, which holds it down until it cools.'

'Is that true?'

'How should I know?'

The moons poked up into the eastern sky. Both were past full. The light made it easier for any pursuers to see them but also made the going quicker. As they put what Fost's experience told him were miles between them and the Watchers' former village, the courier began to believe they might actually escape.

Then a figure detached itself from a tall, dead tree at the top of a razorback of lava and stood looking down into their surprised faces.

'So,' said Sternbow, 'my own son.' He shook his head. 'I hardly believe it.'

Snowbuck scrambled the rest of the way up the slope to stand beside his father. More figures rose out of the wasteland, drawn bows in hand. Fost groaned. He was already thoroughly sick of this routine.

'I must speak with you, Father,' Snowbuck said. 'As man to man.'

Sternbow looked around. Fost wondered where his faithful shadow was. Sternbow's words told him.

'Fairspeaker became separated from the party as we made our way to wait for you,' he mumbled. 'He should hear this.'

'No!' Snowbuck's voice rang loud and clear above the volcano's growl. 'He should *not* hear! Or are you no longer capable of listening for yourself, Father?'

Sternbow raised his hand to strike his son. Snowbuck held his ground. The tall forester chieftain let his hand fall to his side and seemed to shrink an inch.

'It may be that I cannot.' His words were barely audible. 'But it is high time I learned once more. Speak.'

'Father, the . . .' he began but was interrupted by a cry from behind.

'Snowbuck!'

At the sound of Fairspeaker's voice, Snowbuck spun, hand dropping to sword hilt. He was half around when an arrow struck him in the left temple. Snowbuck jerked, then dropped to one knee.

'F-father,' he said. His eyes rolled up into his head and he fell, lifeless.

Sternbow uttered a warning cry of rage and grief and desolation. For a moment, the mountain fell silent as if to mark the enormity of his loss. He raised his eyes to Fairspeaker on a hill fifty feet away, a bow held loosely in his hand.

'I came just in time, great Sternbow.' The young man sounded out of breath. 'Another instant and the faithless young pup would've . . .'

Sternbow tore forth his broadsword and flung it at Fairspeaker.

Paralyzed with disbelief, Fairspeaker stood and watched as the blade spun toward him. The whine of split air was loud in the awful silence.

At the last possible instant, Fairspeaker flung himself to the side. He was too late to save himself completely. The sword tip raked his cheek, opening it to the bone. He screamed shrilly and fell from view. As he did, a line of flame crackled from Moriana's fingertips. A bush burst into orange flame where he had stood.

Across the black nightland Nevrymin faced one another across drawn swords and levelled spears. A few Watchers stood with hands high, dazed by the course of events. One by one each turned until all faced Sternbow.

The tall man knelt on the unyielding stone, cradling his son's head in his lap. A thin trickle of blood, black in the moonlight, ran from the wound and stained his breeches. Slowly, he raised his head. He had aged ten years in one tragic minute.

'After him!' he cried. 'Hunt down the traitor Fairspeaker!'

With a roar, the Nevrymin turned from confronting one another and raced off into the night. That was an order most of them had longed to hear for some time.

Sternbow rose to face Fost and Moriana.

'Apologies will not suffice for what I've done, so I will not offer them,' he said. He composed himself visibly. 'You are free to go. I wish I could call you friends, but I will not presume. O Snowbuck, you saw far more clearly than I!' His head slumped to his chest and tears flowed down his bearded cheeks, bright silver rivulets in the moonlight.

'What of you?' asked Moriana, reaching out to touch the man's quaking shoulder.

He raised his head with effort.

'Fairspeaker was — is — not alone in feeling that our interests and those of the Hissers lie along the same path. But I think the men of my band will be with me. We'll organize the surviving Watchers, wage hit-and-run war against the mines. It's a kind of war my men understand. The Watchers should learn quickly enough.'

He looked down at his son's body. Snowbuck lay partially on his side with one arm crossed over his breast and the fingers of his right hand still grasping the hilt of his half-drawn sword.

'Now I will hunt the murderer of my only son. Or one of them — the real guilt rests on these shoulders!'

There was nothing more to say. Fost and Moriana started away. They hadn't picked a dozen cautious steps across the razorback when Sternbow's voice halted them. He walked to them, moving effortlessly over the uneven ground.

'I have something to give you, and something to ask.'

'Very well,' said Moriana.

'First, I beg you travel to the Tree and tell the King in Nevrym what has befallen Snowbuck. The Forest Maiden alone knows what schemes the People and their sympathizers have set in motion against Grimpeace, for he is known as a foe of the Dark Ones. That was why he agreed to ally with you, Princess, because you offered the best chance of thwarting your sister's aim to return the Realm to the Night Lords. Friendship with the People was not the way of Grimpeace, though I allowed Fairspeaker to convince me otherwise, to my eternal grief.'

'It shall be done, Lord Sternbow,' Moriana promised. 'But I fear we will be a long time reaching the Tree afoot.'

Sternbow almost smiled.

'Perhaps not. Don't forget the famed Longstrider accompanies you.' His eyes turned somber once more. 'But what I have to give you may solve that difficulty.' He reached to the broad leather belt circling his waist and removed a heavy bag of sewn doe hide. 'Uncut gems. My share of the pay from the Hissers. They should buy you adequate mounts.'

Moriana's eyes widened. By the pouch's heft, the stone would buy adequate mounts for a squadron of cavalry.

'But we can't take it all!'

266

'You must.' He slashed his hand through air in a peremptory gesture. 'I couldn't touch those stones again, no matter how precious they are. Accept them or I shall drop them into Omizantrim's mouth.'

'You are gracious, milord.'

He bowed tautly.

'Farewell, milady, Longstrider. We shall not meet again.'

A few days north of the frozen flows sprouting like tentacles from the ancient mountain, they came upon a breeding kennel. The land here in the Marchant Highlands ran to slow rises and wide dales like a gentle ocean swell made solid. The land was green and gravid and exploding with summer. They passed bawling herds of horncattle, lowing sheep and goats and flocks of tame striped antelope that fled at the strangers' approach. The country folk were close-mouthed and grim. The shadow of Omizantrim lay long across their land. And many was the morning in which the beauty of a clear blue sky was marred by silent black flights of rafts, flying south in formations like migratory birds. At first, Fost and Moriana took cover whenever Zr'gsz skyrafts appeared overhead. They soon gave it up as unnecessary. None they had seen showed the slightest interest in what went on below. They did keep alert for any sign of rafts from Omizantrim, or any that searched rather than simply travelled from one place to another.

'What's your pleasure?' The kennel master was a long, lean sort with a face consisting mostly of wrinkles. Faded carroty hair had been trimmed to an alarming scalplock cresting his sunburned pate. A small white clay pipe hung from one lip as if glued there, emitting occasional wisps of blue smoke.

He didn't seem overly suspicious of the trailworn and heavily armoured strangers who had trudged up the side road from the highway. But to read any expression on the face was beyond Fost's ability.

'We seek mounts,' said Moriana.

The man stiffened. Her travels outside the City, often as a hunted fugitive, had rendered her broadminded in her dealings with both commoners and groundlings; the man she loved was both. But sometimes she slipped into the royal hauteur to which she had been raised. Fost saw it had an adverse effect this time. The face remained unreadable, but the man's posture spoke eloquently.

'Freeman, we grow tired of faring afoot. We asked directions of a yeoman driving a wagon down on the highroad. He told us you raised strong steeds.' Foist hoped the fat, squint-eyed peasant had been telling the truth. He knew about all there was to know about sled dogs but had little knowledge of riding dogs.

The breeder relaxed.

'This way,' he said. He paused to scoop a small pouch from the nail where it hung by a red porch post, then stepped down onto the turf and led them around back of the house.

A wild clamor greeted them. Dogs of all descriptions and colors, stocky war mounts and whippet-lean racers, black and white and roan and brindle and spotted all penned in wooden kennels, flung themselves against the fence and barked madly. The breeder whistled. A tow-headed urchin of indeterminate sex appeared from a shack at the end of the long aisle between the cages, wiping his hands on a dun smock.

'Master?'

Fost pretended to study the caged beasts. His eyes left the animals and scanned the surrounding countryside. The fields, like the road, were well tended and dotted with the bulks of grazing horncows ambling over flower-decked pasture. He saw no sign of humans other than the kennel master and the urchin. That was strange; it took a goodly number of workers to keep a dog farm operational. The best maintained their own herds of cattle to feed the dogs, both to keep down prices and to control precisely the type and quality of feed the animals received. That took hands – and there were only two in view.

'It's hard times since the mountain upchucked this spring,' the kennel master drawled. 'Then them lizards came through here bound down for Wirix, or so 'twas said. ''Taint natural, those lizards. Didn't do nary a bit of lootin' and rapin'. Not a bit of it.' He dug a handful of green herb from the pouch and stuffed it into the bowl of his pipe. 'Then them flyin' thingies started floatin' overhead all the time. The hands got spooked. I don't mind admittin' I did, too.'

He smoothed his scalplock with a gnarly hand. The urchin stood by, tugging at the hem of its smock. Her smock, Fost judged, by the small peaks in the front of the dilapidated garment.

The breeder looked around at the cages of yammering dogs. Shiny beads of moisture appeared at the outer corners of his eyes.

'You folks come by at the right time. I'm sellin' out.' He made a gesture encompassing the whole establishment, dogs, dwellings, fields, cattle and urchin. 'Choose what you want and name a price. I'm movin' cross the river into the Empire. Cain't take more'n some good bitches and dogs for breedin' stock. Dogs is damn trickish to move overland.'

Fost stared in open amazement. The generosity of Realm dog breeders was legendary, along with that of Tolvirot bankers, Medurimin tax collectors and clerics from Kolnith. If a successful kennel master — and there was little doubt this wrinkled man was successful, judging by the size of his spread and the way it was kept – was selling out at a loss, then the threat of the *Zr'gsz* was already making itself felt.

They'd made their journey to this point as idyllic as possible, a long holiday of riding through beautiful summer lands by day and making love all night with passion and skill, as if each time was the last. Both knew that the inevitable last time might arrive soon, too soon. Though they scarcely slept, each morning they rose refreshed and filled with energy. To Fost this was little short of miraculous. In emergencies he could go from sound sleep to alertness in a single heartbeat. But without danger to goad him, he generally took long minutes to come even half awake. The fact made it curious he had chosen the life of a courier, which called for agonizingly early rising. Every morning of his life on the road, Fost complained bitterly of the necessity of arising before noon to his companions or dogs, depending on who would listen.

They picked their way down from the Central Massif and curved northeast around the Mystic Mountains. No longer did they see *Zr'gsz* skyrafts. All traffic flowed south from Thendrun. With the skyrafts went their last barrier to enjoyment.

Or almost the last. With the leisure of hours on the road and lazy hours in camp after dinner and before lovemaking, the two spirits resumed their feuding. Only threats to tie them to long ropes and drag them behind the riding dogs ever shut them up, and that only for a while.

The kennel master hadn't lied about the prices he asked for his stock. For forty klenor he provided them with two mounts of their choice and complete tack. He even skirted the subject of selling the urchin, too, but Fost evinced complete disinterest, to what seemed the girl's disappointment. By a miracle, Erimenes said not one lewd word. In fact, both genies sensed the uneasiness of the breeder and the girl and kept silent to avoid panicking them.

Fost and Moriana didn't actually benefit from the bargain. The smallest stone Sternbow had given them was worth easily ten times the price the breeder quoted. The two had between them only a few rusty sipans in the bottom of Erimenes's satchel. Finally, Moriana chose a rock at random and tossed it to the kennel master as payment. The man's amazement was so great his pipe dropped from his lips and threatened to kindle the sawdust between the rows of cages. The pair had mounted and quickly departed before he could press the urchin on them.

Moriana had picked a stocky red dog with a short, smooth fur and heavy tail for Fost. The animal wasn't quite a war mount but had the breadth of jaw to fight and looked durable enough to bear Fost's weight over a long haul. Also, it was an intelligent beast able to compensate for its rider's lack of experience. In travelling with Jennas, Fost had grown expert in riding the immense war bears of the Ust-alayakits, but riding a bear and riding a dog differed as much as flying a Sky City eagle and piloting a *Zr'gsz* skyraft.

For herself, Moriana chose a gray courser, huge of chest and narrow of skull, that could run down an antelope in a sprint. The beast was utterly neurotic, fearful of anything that lived except when it grew hungry enough to hunt, at which times it used its two-inch fangs to good effect. Moriana seemed able to gentle the creature, though it was prone to emit a shrill, unnerving keening for no apparent reason.

The mounts proved sound and the travellers made good time. Though time did not matter for them on this journey.

At least, they pretended it didn't.

Erimenes.

By unspoken agreement, Fost and Moriana had neither past nor future for the duration of their ride. But Fost privately broke the pact. There was a question that nagged him day and night and refused to go away.

The night they camped in sight of the dark line of the Great Nevrym Forest, Fost lay awake after Moriana drifted to sleep, sweetly exhausted from a bout of passionate lovemaking. For a time he watched the constellations perform their slow, circular dance overhead. Then he slipped into the forest. The scattered shunnak trees loomed above the mighty black anhak comprising most of the forest. There were few of the giants; had they grown close together they'd have prevented any light from reaching the thickly clustered trees below.

'Erimenes?' he called softly.

'Are you fishing for compliments, my boy? Your performance was adequate, I'd say. What it lacked in finesse, it certainly made up for in vigor.'

Fost sighed. Moriana slept a dozen paces away and was unlikely to be awakened. What he wanted from the garrulous genie might take a long time to extract – if it could be done at all.

'Why?'

'Why what? Why was the Universe created? Why does evil exist in the world? Why did –'

'No,' Fost said sharply, cutting off the spirit's diatribe before it gained too much momentum. 'Why did you help us when the Hissers held us captive? Or any other time, for that matter. Of late, you've been assisting more and more and hardly ever pulling your stunt of trying to get me killed in some grisly fashion.'

'It is out of the goodness of my soul. I would say heart, but alas! that noble organ has been defunct these fourteen centuries. Besides, I'm often moved to pity by the bumbling way in which you approach life. I wish to help you as a child wishes to help a sadly uncoordinated pup learn to walk without falling over.'

Fost made a rude sound.

'You and Istu are equally noted for philanthropy,' he said. 'And I've caught you at last! You've been dead thirteen hundred and ninety-nine years, *not* fourteen hundred. Ha!'

Erimenes uttered a weary sigh.

'I have, since coming to know you, celebrated yet another anniversary of my tragic demise. Thus I came round to the fourteen hundredth year of my death. I wish I could remain thirteen hundred ninety-nine – or properly, fifteen hundred and seven – indefinitely.'

Fost ground his teeth together. Trying to pin down the shade when he wanted to be contrary was like trying to grab an eel. The more so now when he couldn't yell at the spirit without waking Moriana.

'Answer the question, you old dotard,' Ziore said from Moriana's pack laying nearby.

Erimenes sniffed and said haughtily, 'I did.'

Moving quietly and carefully, Fost picked up Erimenes's jug.

271

'Erimenes, I want a straight answer from you. And I want it now.'

'Or what?'

'I want an answer, Erimenes.' Something in his tone convinced the spirit that the time had passed for light banter.

'Very well. I'm helping you because I want you to win. That should be obvious to even you.'

Fost began bouncing the jug up and down in his palm. Erimenes made choking sounds.

'Stop it! That horrid motion nauseates me.'

'Tell the truth.'

'I am, you fool!' Erimenes's voice lost its normal nasal overtones. Fost had never heard him speak this way before. 'Damn it, can't you see why I'm helping you? Before, it was all a game to me. No matter what happened, *I* couldn't get hurt. And I was the only one who mattered.' Silence. 'Are you surprised?'

'Hardly.' He set down the satchel and braced himself against a sturdy tree trunk.

'But that was before. Before I started to detect the black hand – or claw – of the Dark Ones in events surrounding you. By the time we left the Ramparts, I was starting to fear that what we faced imperiled not only humanity but *me*.

'And when Itsu was released, there was no longer any doubt. The Dark Ones are mighty, and their malice is as infinite and ineffable as they are mysterious and unknowable. They could snuff me as you'd snuff out a candle flame. Or . . . or make me wish throughout endless ages for true death.

'No, my young friend, I cannot remain neutral in this War of Powers.'

'Why don't you join the other side?'

'Really, I thought you held me in higher esteem.' Fost's brows shot up. The spirit sounded genuinely hurt. 'I am human, or was once. And unlike Fairspeaker and his ilk, I don't delude myself as to what the Dark Ones intend for humanity.'

Fost shuddered thinking about all he'd seen, all that was promised.

'To purge the Realm as they did the Sky City.'

'No.' Fost stared at the satchel in surprise at the contradiction. 'That is an aim, but far from paramount. They would purge human-kind from the *world*, Fost. From the Universe, from every plane of being, if the theories espoused in my day of the multiplicity of planes of existence hold any truth. They intend no less than to return the

272

Universe — Universes — to the primal Dark from which they sprang.'

'I see,' Fost said after a while. His voice almost squeaked through his constricted throat.

'So. Now that we've dealt with theology and cosmology, why don't you prod that lusty wench over there feigning sleep with your finger and rouse her so that you can prod her with a much more gratifying implement?'

Fost shook his head. In some ways, Erimenes hadn't changed. He had to admit being glad. To himself, at least.

Then Moriana rolled over, groping for him. He quickly slipped next to her and followed the sage's advice. After what Erimenes had said about the Dark Ones, this seemed more important than ever.

They rode boldly into the forest of Great Nevrym. The foresters were suspicious of unwanted guests, but Fost was known as a friend and there was little to gain trying to enter by stealth. Their mission was sad and aboveboard.

They were two days in when the foresters showed themselves. Riding through the forest was like moving along the nave of an enormous cathedral with the shunnak rising a hundred stories above their heads. Birds sang, squirrels chased one another along cool green avenues and at night scarlet tree toads a yard long crawled from their holes in the boles of the black anhak to trill timeless songs.

Fost had been aware of being followed, which told him no more than that the foresters didn't care if he sensed their presence. If they didn't want travellers to suspect they were near, it would take Ziore's perceptions to discover them.

They followed a broad avenue between the tall anhak. It seemed no different from any that ran through the wood, but by various subtle signs Fost knew this for the road to the Tree.

A young man rose from a bush and stepped into their path. He smiled, which relieved Fost.

'Good day,' he said. 'Seldom are these ways travelled by those who use feet other than their own.'

'Good day, Darkwood. I apologize for the princess and myself for riding mounts in these woods. But we have a message too urgent to bear on foot.'

'You, the Longstrider, say that? Oho, that's rich, indeed.' He wiped his eyes from laughter. 'But you must know, Longstrider who sees fit to clutter his good and proper name with the graceless noise *Fost*, that you'd be ever welcome to go upon these ways in any manner you choose.'

'Thank you, Darkwood.'

Moriana's gray was tossing its narrow head and whimpering. Feeling that she had to assert her part in these slow proceedings, Moriana shook back her hair and said, 'You may carry along the tidings that Moriana Etuul, Queen in exile of the City in the Sky, has arrived on a visit of state to the King of Nevrym.'

'Oh, indeed. Is that the way it is now?' Green eyes twinkled. He had seemed a young man at first but reading the fine wrinkles in his face convinced Moriana he was past forty. 'But that's something of a problem, Your Majesty. The man you seek does not exist.'

'But I . . .' She stopped in confusion, then organized her thoughts. 'I don't understand.'

The forest echoed with Darkwood's laughter. Fost grinned but kept an eye on her in case she decided to try to chastise this presumptuous groundling for laughing at her.

'Ah, forgive me,' Darkwood said. This time he pulled a scarf from a hidden pocket to dab tears from his eyes. 'But you see, Majesty, there is no King of Nevrym — unless you refer to the Tree, Paramount, Lord of All Trees. But the idea that a *man* could rule a forest, ah, you outwoods folk are droll. The man you seek is Grimpeace, ferocious to foe and fair to friend — and king *in* Nevrym, never *of* it.'

Moriana smiled with visible effort.

'Please be so good as to guide us, Sir Darkwood.'

'So I shall. For none is allowed to travel the ways of the wood unescorted.' He smiled approvingly when she didn't try to claim they had done just that in the last few days.

They rode for several more hours. Still smarting from her humiliation over the matter of who was king of what, Moriana kept her twitchy greyhound at a long-limbed trot for the first several miles until it became apparent that the ever-smiling Darkwood kept up the rapid pace without breaking into a sweat.

'Great Ultimate, Fost, how did you ever manage to outrun a party of these folk?' she asked as she reined in the gray dog to a walk.

'I was young and in good shape,' he said, slowing to match her pace. 'Also I was scared cross-eyed.'

By design, the road took an abrupt turn around a dense stand of anhak so that the clearing in which the Tree stood appeared suddenly to view. Moriana gasped at the sight of it. Though he'd seen it before, Fost felt his heart clutch convulsively in wonder at the sight.

This was obviously the Tree. Next to it everything else was shrubbery.

It rose over a thousand feet in the clear forest air, a giant conifer with dark green needles and a red trunk. Their master of all trees was more than the symbol and pride of the Nevrymin, it was the seat of their government as well. For hundreds of feet its bole was honeycombed with entrances, passageways, small apartments and halls as grand as the Audience Hall of the Palace of Winds. The many tiers were a history of the foresters carved in wood. The Tree still grew and every generation a new level had to be hollowed out. Stairways and catwalks spiraled around the massive trunk. When Moriana realized that the antlike figures moving along them were people, wonder flooded back anew.

'Well, my friends,' said Grimpeace around a mouthful of good venison. 'Where do you go now?'

Fost and Moriana traded glances. It was a good question. Oddly, they hadn't discussed it on the way from Omizantrim. They had barely thought of it.

Each sensed that the life they'd known before had perished. The world had become a strange and awful place, a battleground for forces beyond their comprehension. Even if both survived, which seemed increasingly unlikely, they little knew what kind of world they'd be living in when this new War of Powers came to a resolution.

If it ever did.

The message delivered, Fost and Moriana sat looking at one another on their side of a well-laden banquet table. It was a board fit for the Tree, forty feet long and eight across. No knife scars defaced it, as was customary at feasting tables, and spilled wine was hastily mopped up by attendants. In return, the wood, shining with a luminous luster, surpassed in beauty any piece of furniture Moriana had seen. Like the capital of the foresters, it was carved from the living wood of the Tree and kept alive by special magics known only to the Nevrymin.

'Where are we going?' Fost asked. Now that the news of the Hissers' defection was delivered, he didn't know the answer.

Moriana did.

'High Medurim,' she answered.

CHAPTER TEN

'Whoa!' cried Fost, motioning for a halt. Moriana's greyhound squealed in terror as she reined in harshly. In a single fluid movement, she dropped her bow from shoulder to hand and pulled an arrow from her quiver. By the side of the track, Darkwood stood looking on with his habitual smile. He didn't unsling his bow.

Heart racing, Moriana followed Fost's gesture. She expected enemies. What she saw made her heart leap, but not from fear.

A unicorn stag stood on a knoll to the left of the path. The trees grew sparsely there. The great beast stood between two of the black, gnarled anhaks and gazed down at the travellers, one forefoot raised.

Something in the animal's attitude told Moriana the posture was not that of a creature poised for flight. It regarded them with disdain, its eyes huge and amber, set in the capacious skull on either side of the single straight horn. Its hide was a glossy chestnut and its throat and wide chest glowed silvery. A long tail ending in a tuft of auburn was held curled over the animal's back like a manticore's sting.

'Will you shoot, Lady?' Darkwood's smile had taken on the tilt they had come to associate with some private jest. 'Their flesh is a delicacy beyond compare.'

Moriana looked at Fost. His mouth was compressed in a curious fashion as if he tried to suppress a grin. Erimenes swayed at his side.

'Shoot!' the genie urged, his eyes gleaming with spectral bloodlust.

'No,' begged Ziore, floating beside Moriana. 'He's too magnificent!'

Moriana lowered her bow, relaxed the string and slid the arrow back into its sheath.

'She's right. I could only slay such a beast if I starved. Never for sport.'

As if it heard her words, the stag dipped its horn once and vanished as abruptly as it had appeared.

'You chose wisely, Highness,' said Darkwood. 'You'd never have hit him.'

Moriana's mouth tightened. This groundling made jokes at her expense, and she didn't care for it.

'You forget I'm Skyborn,' she informed him haughtily.

'Oh, I know that, Lady, and I know well you could put three arrows out of three through my chest with that monster bow of yours. But skill counts for more in hunting the Nevrym unicorn than cleverness of hand and eye. You'd have missed him, this I know.' His grin widened. 'Even as I'd know you'd next have seen him charging from that clump of blackleaf.' He pointed at a clump of shrubbery twenty yards distant. 'With his head down and blood in his eye. And I know a unicorn's fighting horn will pierce a quarter inch of the finest North Keep plate as if it were parchment.'

Moriana started to protest. Thinking she'd suffered enough, Fost put in, 'They're intelligent. And very cunning.'

'Intelligent? Nonsense. They're mere beasts.' Erimenes sniffed his contempt for such a notion.

'And are the war eagles of the Sky City mere birds?' Darkwood shook his head. 'No, my friend. You've now met the third part of the triumvirate that rules Nevrym.'

'The third?' asked Moriana, intrigued despite her anger.

'We're another.' Darkwood doffed his triangular cap and bowed. 'The last is the trees, of course.'

'The *trees*?' Moriana scoffed.

'He's telling the truth. Do you think you could find your way to the Tree again unaided?'

'Of course.' She glared at Fost. She was a veteran warrior. Once she'd passed over terrain she knew it by heart.

'Of course,' agreed Darkwood, in an infuriating imitation of the woman's voice, 'provided your intentions were peaceful toward the forest and its various inhabitants. Were they otherwise, your party might wander lost until you died of starvation.' He smoothed straw-colored hair back from his forehead. 'Only foresters can find their way unimpeded by the trees' magic. And where our allies of wood don't want us, we generally don't go.'

'But your people are well armed and prepared for invasion.' Moriana was genuinely puzzled. The many-tiered keep carved into

277

the heart of the Tree was meant to serve as a fortress, its outer walls dotted with arrow slits and its interior honeycombed by well-stocked caches of emergency stores. Most of the humbler dwellings of the foresters were built like birds' nests high up and secure in the embrace of anhak limbs, reachable only by ladders.

'It's not unknown for Nevrymin to settle their little differences by force of arms. We are individualists at heart and not prone to taking commands of others.' Reminded of this, Moriana recalled that most battles the Nevrymin fought were internecine. That was the key to the seeming puzzle of a jovial king in Nevrym named Grimpeace.

It had been Fost who explained this to her.

'He's a friendly man, but he's friendly because we come as friends. He earned his name by the way he imposed order in Nevrym when he acceded to the Tree twenty-three years ago. The Nevrymin all respect the Tree, but they're divided into factions as antagonistic and rivalry-ridden as tenement blocks in The Teeming. North Nevrymin, Central Nevrymin, Eastcreekers, Coastrunners, a score in all. Few of the factions were inclined to pay much heed to the authority of a boy who'd scarcely started to sprout his first growth of beard. They learned what the young king offered was a grim peace, indeed. Since then, banditry and sectional strife in Nevrym have been at an all-time low.

'Then, too,' said Darkwood, all trace of mirth vanished from his blue eyes, 'it isn't unknown for Nevrymin to guide outwoods foes along these ways in defiance of tradition and the trees.'

'What kind of man would do that?' asked Ziore in wonder. Her empathy gave her an appreciation keener even than Fost's of the sacred nature of the compact between men and beasts and trees.

'You've met one, I fancy.' Darkwood's voice turned winter cold. 'Fairspeaker by name.'

But not even the thought of Nevrymin breaking faith with their forest was enough to keep the summer in Darkwood's nature suppressed for long. He warmed and the skin around his eyes and mouth settled into well-worn smile lines.

'But the day's too lovely for talk of that, and we've leagues yet to travel before reaching the North Cape range.' He set the cap on his head at a suitably jaunty angle and started off along the leaf-carpeted path.

'One question, my good man.' Darkwood stopped and regarded Erimenes with his hands on hips. His grin hadn't been dented by the spirit's supercilious tone. 'How do you know the flesh of the unicorn stag is succulent if your folk lack the gumption to hurt them?'

The forester's cheer was the equal of even Erimenes at his most infuriating.

'My good ghost, from the height of your exalted years you must realize that any forest exists in a delicate balance,' he said in the tone of one explaining a simple lesson to a dull student. 'No single population can be allowed to grow unchecked. So we hunt the unicorn stag, and a most demanding sport it is.' His smile showed prominent eyeteeth. 'And they, of course, hunt us. We give them rare sport, too, or so I'm led to believe.'

Their reception at North Keep was less than cordial.

In response to five minutes' pounding on the twenty-foot-tall iron gates, first with Fost's fist and then with the pommel of his sword, a small peephole set four feet off the stone roadbed scraped open. A single bloodshot eye peered forth without any hint of friendliness.

'Go away,' came the growl from within.

'We've come a long ways up the coast road,' said Fost. 'We're in need of food, baths, a good night's sleep. We're prepared to pay.'

The latter phrase usually unlocked the domain of the dwarves. The dark maroon eye blinked once.

'We want nothing to do with your filthy money. The gate's shut for the night. Go away.'

Fost's dog growled. Astride her sidestepping dog a few yards behind, Moriana tightened the grip on her reins. She didn't like the dwarf guard's tone any more than the dogs did.

'My good man, I suggest you open this gate immediately if you desire that your head should keep company with your shoulders. I am a guest of state and your rulers will be little pleased by your insolence to me.'

'Who're you?' came the rude question, the eye swivelling to bear on her.

'I am Moriana Etuul, Queen in exile of the City in the Sky, and if you don't admit us at once . . .'

The eye withdrew but only to permit heavily bearded lips to appear and spit through the grill.

'*That* for you,' said the eye, appearing again, 'and for all decadent lordlings who oppress the people! And for their running dog lackeys, as well,' he added for Fost's benefit. The peephole slammed shut.

279

As the clang reverberated down the valley, Fost thought Moriana's hair was about to start smouldering at the roots as Synalon's had done when she was angry.

'Why, that horrid upstart, that, that groundling! How *dare* he take that tone with me!'

'He's got three inches of iron and a foot of anhak between you and him,' pointed out Fost. 'That's how he dares.'

'Small good that protection will do him when I loose my wrath upon him.' She let reins fall and raised her hands.

'No, no, don't start flinging salamanders or deathspells or anything like that,' Fost said quickly, waving his arms in hope of breaking her concentration.

'And why not?' she demanded.

He pointed upward. Forty feet above the poorly kept road two grotesque figures squatted in alcoves set on either side of the gates. Spindly limbed with squinty eyes and oddly spurred elbows and knees, they regarded the travellers over ludicrously attenuated noses and mouths thrust out to form lipless tubes.

'And what might they be?' She eyed them with distaste.

'Old dwarven caricatures of true men,' he said. 'The mouths go to funnels in a room dug out of the rock. The dwarves keep a pot of lead bubbling by each in case applicants rejected for entry react the way you were about to.'

Moriana dropped her hands to her sides.

'We'll have to find lodgings in the Outer Town. It's only a few miles away on the other side of the mountain.'

'But it's getting dark!'

'All the more reason to start now.'

When they got to the Outer Town they got some insight into the nature of the recent developments in the Realm. The moons hung high in the sky when they came around the tip of Northernmost, the mountain cradling the dwarvish citadel of North Keep. Built on a slate beach butting up against the western face of the mountain, the Outer Town was an odd conglomeration of black dwarf masonry, scattered cosmopolitan edifices of Imperial dome and column marble, prim Jorean geometry, pastel stuccoed Estil, and shanty-town. The streets were paved with rubble and indifferently repaired. Though the dwarves ruled the Outer Town, it was primarily a place for the gangly Other Folk to stay while doing business. The dwarves weren't noted for their hospitality, though Fost had hoped they would invite Moriana to stay in their keep because of her royal status. For the most part, the Others entered North Keep solely to strike bargains and were ushered forth with varying degrees of politeness when the deals were done.

A smell of fish and less identifiable refuse hung in the pitted street in front of the inn Fost chose. A faded clapboard sign portrayed a flatfish grinning with drunken goggle-eyed delight.

'*The Happy Flounder*,' Erimenes read as the pair dismounted and tied reins to a sagging hitchrail. 'I believe they take fancifulness too far in naming these establishments.'

The innkeeper was a young dwarf with a thready beard and a premature bald spot on the top of his head. He was skinny for a dwarf but had the usual protruding eyes. He examined his prospective guests with suspicion.

'What do you want?' he rapped. His prominent nose wrinkled.

'Lodgings for the night, possibly longer,' Fost said hurriedly. Moriana was getting a dangerous glint in her eye. 'But who knows? We may spend some time sightseeing in this quaint and hospitable town of yours.'

Sarcasm was lost on the innkeeper, as it was on most dwarves.

'Vouchers?' he demanded, in a tone of bored antagonism.

Fost had no idea what the dwarf asked for and told him so.

'Well,' the little man said, folding his arms across his chest and tilting his fringe beard disapprovingly upward. 'I must accommodate you even if you can't pay, unless I want a drubbing from the damned militia, may their barracks roof fall on their pointed heads.' He drummed blunt fingers on the counter and turned to peer through a door leading to a muddy yard in back. 'I suppose there's room for you in the kennels.'

'We haven't any vouchers, whatever they are,' said Moriana, 'but will you accept this as payment for room and meals?' She held up an emerald from the pouch Sternbow had given her.

The innkeeper goggled more than usual. He snatched it away with deft fingers, held it to the dismal light of the guttering taper, scratched it along the table, and finally bit it.

'By the tunnels of Agift,' he murmured. 'I do believe it's real.'

He pulled in a breath that swelled his barrel chest until Fost thought the jerkin would burst. He looked from the emerald to Moriana, and an avid light danced in his immense dwarf eyes. Then the glint faded and he expelled a heartfelt sigh.

'I cannot but tell you that a stone such as this would pay for my finest accommodations for a fortnight — possibly longer, depending on the water of the stone.'

Moriana shrugged it off. The Zr'gsz had been generous paymasters. There were many more where this one came from.

'For however long, then. I doubt we'll stay more than a couple nights at most.'

'I cannot change this with any currency you'd want to have.' Sweat stood out on his high, broad forehead. It cost him great anguish to tell them this.

'Don't bother.'

He came out from behind the counter, waddled to the door, stuck his head out into the noisome, muggy night. Nothing stirred in the streets except a fat yellow-striped tomcat roving in search of ship's rats on shore leave.

'You're strangers to North Keep,' he accused.

'Not altogether,' said Fost. His fingers played with his sword hilt. The publican's nervousness made him uneasy.

'But you don't know how things have stood in the dwarflands since the revolution, that much is clear.'

'Revolution?'

'Of the proletariat. Since the Worker's Party seized power a year ago, the use of money and barter are outlawed. Outlanders are compelled by law to convert their negotiables into credit vouchers before dealing with dwarves.'

'Who's head of state now?'

'Maanda Samilchut is the Party Chairman.'

Fost frowned but said nothing.

'Normally I'd have to report your presence to the Militia headquarters on Exchange Square — er, pardon me, it's Liberation Plaza now. But, by your leave, I think I might overlook this procedure.' Moriana nodded assent. The innkeeper sighed with relief and mopped his brow with a gray linen kerchief. 'I take it you'd prefer accommodations above ground, gentles?'

When the thick wood door of their second-floor room shut behind the now overly solicitous innkeeper, Fost dropped onto the low bed and broke out laughing.

'What's so funny?' asked Moriana, lowering herself more cautiously onto a bandy-legged stool.

'"Maanda Samilchut is Party Chairman,"' he quoted. 'Up till a year ago, North Keep was a republic; the President for Life was Maanda Samilchut. Before that it was a parliamentary democracy, and the Premier was Maanda Samilchut. And just before that, the dwarves had a constitutional monarchy, with, as self-crowned queen, Maanda Samilchut.' He fell back across the bed and rubbed his eyes. 'Need I go on? Dwarves have devilishly long life-spans.'

Sitting as much at ease as he could on a chair built for someone with legs a quarter the length of his, Fost batted idly at the fly circling his head and studied the bust of Chairman Samilchut in its alcove on the wall.

'How much longer will they keep us waiting?' Moriana stopped pacing a groove in the worn stone floor long enough to ask.

'A while longer, I suspect. The folk we're dealing with are bureaucrats as well as dwarves, and both groups tend to have cosmic sense of time.'

Over by the wall the two satchels had been laid side by side so that Erimenes and Ziore could carry on their perpetual squabble in relatively soft voices. Though every now and then a voice rose in a crescendo of indignation, for the most part their quarreling blended in with the incessant murmur of North Keep.

The North Cape Mountains lacked the size of the Mystics or the Ramparts, but they were second to none in ruggedness. Taking the coast road along the western face of North Cape had spared Fost and Moriana from struggling through the sawtoothed range until the road forked inland to the southern gate of North Keep. Northernmost was the tallest mountain in the North Capes, home to that peculiar, industrious, delving, grasping race, the dwarves.

The dwarves were the miners and smiths of the Sundered Realm. Their metalwork, especially blades and armor, were renowned throughout the world. The Thailot were more skilful artificers, the Estil unsurpassed in civil engineering, but in matters involving stone or stone worked with the principle of fire to become metal, the dwarves were unexcelled.

No one knew where they came from. Some said they had lived in their mountains, which like them were short and craggy and inhospitable, when humans first arrived on the Southern Continent twenty-two thousand years before. Others claimed they predated the Hissers; still others maintained they were descended from a troupe of freaks imported to entertain a Northern Barbarian lord in the sixteenth century before the Human Era. So the stories went.

Their patron was Ungrid An, the dwarvish goddess, one of the few members of the Three and Twenty to belong to a particular race. She was a harsh, dour goddess personifying fortitude, determination and sheer hard labor. She was also goddess of political upheaval representing both repression and rebellion, which helped account for the odd political climate in North Keep.

Keep and mountain were actually inseparable. Like the Nevrymin, the dwarves made their capital inside the dominant physical feature of their domain, but unlike them they didn't work upward from ground level only. Over uncounted millennia the dwarves had burrowed deep into the roots of the mountains, some said for thousands of feet below the surface.

Fost started to rise to offer Moriana his stool. She motioned him back and went around the paper-strewn miniature desk and sat in the absent functionary's chair. Fost grinned, partly in acknowledgement of her small defiance and partly because she looked silly with her piquant face framed by her knees.

He turned to study the bust again. It had been carved recently. He could tell because Samilchut wore a severely cut tunic with a high buttoned collar. Last year at this time, her representations had been draped in a graceful toga that left one massive deltoid bare, in imitation of Jorean state garb.

Moriana started tapping her fingers on the desk. Fost allowed himself to focus on the spirits' debate.

'— obvious to anyone with the least knowledge of etiology that this couldn't possibly —'

'— piffle! That doctrine was decisively refuted by —'

He sighed and let the faraway sounds of thousands of dwarves at work in the bowels of the mountain, that strangely rhythmic pulse of North Keep, drown them out again. Their argument grew more and more abstruse with each passing day. If they followed their usual pattern, in a short while they'd degenerate to name calling and, with luck, fall into silent sulking for a blessed interval until one or the other said something and started the argument afresh.

'Ahem.'

Fost jumped, blinking away the drowsiness that had been coming on him. The obvious target of the guttural throat clearing sat behind the desk holding steepled fingers to her lips.

284

'You certainly took your time,' Moriana said to the stumpy woman in the shapeless black gown who stood glowering at her from the office doorway. 'You have a favorable reply for us, I trust?'

A smile shoved up the tips of the official's thin, dark moustache. Inwardly Fost groaned. All too well he recognized the unpleasant triumph of a bureaucrat presented with the opportunity to put the dagger to a member of the public displaying inadequate respect for the nobility of the petty functionary's calling. If Moriana read the same message she showed no sign. Given her background, Fost doubted she did.

'No.' She had a fine baritone, Fost noted. 'Worker Samilchut has no time to spend on discarded royalty – or self-proclaimed royalty – who try to disturb the peace of North Keep with bizarre tales and schemes.'

'She won't even talk with us?' Moriana stared in disbelief.

'Not at all.' The official consulted the sheaf of papers in her hand. 'Further, I must advise you that even if all you claim is true, you can still expect no help from the dwarves. For we sympathize with the so-called Dark Ones, as we do with all those who rise up to cast off the yoke of feudal oppression.'

She snapped her fingers to summon guards to escort the visitors out. Moriana was too stunned for words, which was probably fortunate. Fost took her by the arm, helped her from the chair and led her past the smirking official into the corridor.

Both had to bend down almost double to follow their escorts, militiamen in brown corslets topped by flat-bottomed iron hats resembling inverted pie plates. Each guard carried a lead-tipped cudgel in one hand and a lantern in the other, with short-hafted throwing hammers at their belts. Dwarves hurrying in the opposite direction either flattened against the walls or backpedalled until they came to a cross corridor they could pop into.

Fost and Moriana stood blinking in brilliant sunlight as the massive iron western gate slammed shut behind them. Fost yawned, gazing out over the Outer Town and the oily gray heaving of the North Cape harbor. With the hooked tip of the Cape itself shielding the bay to north and east, and the added protection of a long stone breakwater projecting south from the rocky, gull-decked headland, the harbor should have provided decent anchorage. It didn't. The breakwater was too short and too low, disappearing completely just before high tide each day. After a southwesterly gale, the dwarves made handy sums dragging ships off the stone docks and refurbishing staved-in hulls. Fost suspected the arrangement wasn't exactly co-incidental.

At the moment, a dozen craft chanced the unseasonal southeast-erly blow. Largest was a lethal and lean war-dromon flying the red and black flag of the Tolviroth Maritime Guaranty company.

'If,' Moriana said, speaking with the slow deliberation of anger, 'if and when I am restored to my throne and powers, I will come back to this North Keep and repay the dwarves for their friendliness and hospitality. By pulling their damn mountain down around their hairy ears!'

'No, you won't,' Fost said louder than he intended.

'What did you say?' she snapped.

With that look in her eyes, his only defense was the truth.

'I said you'll do no such thing. Even if you – and humankind – loses this new War of Powers, life in North Keep will go on pretty much as always. Forever, if the Vridzish have any sense. Northern-most is a fortress no amount of mining, bombarding or ramming will bring down. The dwarves can and will fight for every inch of every tunnel with the ferocity of a cornered weasel. In the days of the Barbarian Dynasty, somebody estimated that there were more miles of passageway in their Keep than there were miles of Realm roads on the entire continent. They go down for *miles*.

'And I'd think even the Hissers' pet Demon would think twice about going down too far in the shafts of Northernmost Mountain. There are things lurking in the roots of these mountains that are only a little younger than the planet. Some of the things living there the dwarves made peace with; others they keep at bay with sheer ferocity and arts not even you can guess at. If they get loose aboveground, not even the Hissers are going to want the Realm.

'Other than that, I'd imagine you can just stroll in and take over anytime you please.'

'Quite impressive,' complimented Erimenes. 'You display hitherto unsuspected depths of erudition.'

Fost had the uncomfortable feeling Moriana was trying to decide whether to cinder him or merely turn him into a newt. A gull wheeled overhead, crying down mockery on both man and dwarf. Abruptly, Moriana laughed.

'Come along,' she said, grabbing Fost's arm. 'Let's get back to the inn before dark. I'm tired of watching the proletarian regime in action.'

The gradually opening door brought Fost awake with all senses wire-taut. A greenish dawnlight spilled across the floor from the partially shuttered window. Outside, a handcart creaked and thumped over the potholes in the street.

A hesitant footfall sounded; another. Fost lay still, forcing himself to breathe with the metronomic regularity of a sleeper, while he mentally estimated distances. In a leap he came to his feet, broadsword snatched from the scabbard hung at the bed's head post.

'Eek!' The innkeeper cringed back against the doorpost, eyes popping, trying to pull his head into the collar of his jerkin. He looked like a frightened turtle. 'P-please, gentles. I meant no harm!'

Fost became acutely aware that he stood naked in the middle of the floor menacing a three-foot dwarf with a sword nearly as long as the dwarf. Moriana stirred on the bed, wondering drowsily why her nude body was so precipitately uncovered.

'Fost, what's – oh!'

His initial fear dissolved into embarrassment. He resorted to the old masculine position: blustering rage.

'What do you mean by this, sneaking into our rooms? Come to murder us in our beds, no doubt!'

If the dwarf shook any harder, pieces of his body would come rattling to the floor.

'No, no!' he moaned.

'Aha! You voyeuristic scoundrel! Come to peep at the Princess Moriana in her nakedness, then, are you?'

'But the princess is so skinny and malproportioned, gentle sir. Why would I do that?'

Moriana cleared her throat. The conversation was clearly out of control.

'Just what is it you want, innkeeper?' she asked, sitting and making no effort to cover herself.

The dwarf glanced at Fost, who was still standing with sword menacingly pointed, then made the effort to calm himself.

'It's the militia. They're searching all over town. You must flee at once.'

'But why? What do they want from us?'

'Because of the news,' the dwarf choked out. *'The Sky City has stopped!'*

287

CHAPTER ELEVEN

The ship sang. The lyre sang harmony.

Soprano sang the rigging, squeaking on the blocks, sighing in the warm west wind. Bass sang the hull, moaning and cracking as seams opened and closed to the play of the sea. High sang the lyre, as silver and fleeting and lonely as the cries of seabirds. And low sang the lyre in bell-shaped tones. Standing by the starboard rail with Moriana at his side, Fost thought he'd never heard a sweeter sound or one sadder.

The song dwindled and became one with the past. Fost and Moriana looked up at the ship's captain, who had folded his unlikely body between two crenellations of the stout forecastle looming over the deck. He smiled and inclined his head.

'It was Jirre herself who taught me to play,' he said.

Moriana turned questioningly to Fost. He answered with a silent shrug. That the captain of the ship *Wyvern* was mad was indisputable. But knowing him as he did, Fost couldn't be wholly convinced he wasn't telling the truth.

Five days ago Fost's brain had reeled in incredulity at the innkeeper's tidings: the Sky City had stopped. *Impossible*! was his first reaction. The City had not simply kept immutably to following the Great Quincunx for all Fost's relatively short life, it had done so since before even humans had seized the City from its rightful owners eight thousand years ago. It had done so for two thousand years of the Hissers' tenure, since the end of the War of Powers when Felarod had confined the once free-floating City to its pattern above the center of the continent . . .

Since the War of Powers not even the Hissers had been able to alter the City's course. Since the binding of Istu.

But Istu was no longer bound.

The word had come first to the Outer Town courtesy of a Wirixer factor who lived in a sprawling marble pile built during the occupation by the Northern Barbarians. The Wirixers had a sorcerous communications network, as did the Sky Citizens, though the Sky City had had no direct representative in North Keep for several years. The news that the City had come to a halt in the air after passing over Wirix soon spread to the Keep itself. The reaction was immediate.

The grapevine hummed with news that Chairman Samilchut was drafting an offer of alliance to be transmitted to the Zr'gsz, though how it was to be sent was still uncertain. The Wirixer wasn't going to do it, not while his home city was besieged by an army of the Fallen Ones. While it was true, as Fost said, that even with Istu on their side the Hissers would take years to reduce North Keep, Samilchut deemed it wise to try to get on the good side of a power that could stop the ten-thousand-year progress of the City in the Sky. The fact that she would be a long time losing didn't encourage the dictator to seek war.

It took no great deductive powers to realize that the former ruler of the Sky City, onetime ally of the Fallen Ones, might make a nice gift for North Keep's chairman to send the People as a token of her friendship. Fost and Moriana had found themselves shivering in the wet dawn wind on the swaybacked docks of the Outer Town, wondering how they were going to reach the ships anchored out in the harbor.

Teeth chattering, Fost eyed the ships. Apparently no one left small boats moored at the dock overnight and whatever boatmen plied the harbor were still in bed on this bleak morning. He wondered if they could swim out with their dogs to one of the vessels. He and Jennas had escaped Tolviroth Acerte in similar fashion a few months ago plowing right into the bay on the backs of their bears. This time, they couldn't be sure of the reception awaiting them once they clambered over a strange ship's gunwales and asked for asylum.

His gaze kept coming back to one ship in particular. It was the largest, anchored next to the Tolvirot warcraft. Fost knew little of ships but could tell there was something peculiar about this one. Its proportions were wrong, as if its designers had set out to make it one thing and midway decided to change it into another. And it had a familiar aura to it as well, a combination of sloppiness and a shipshapeness that reminded him of a man he knew to be dead.

'Down there,' Moriana said, tugging at his sleeve. 'There's a boat.' Bumping its nose against the seawall like an amorous dolphin bobbed a square-prowed dinghy. They walked the hundred yards to the boat. Three men stood on the deck near it. One leaning against a pile of cordage was obviously the crewman who had rowed the boat to shore. Another, a tall storklike man in a flapping black cloak whose sleeves fluttered in the wind as he gestured gave the impression he was trying to become airborne. He had to be a local merchant.

And the third . . .

Fost stared hard. He was well above average height for a dwarf, but there was no mistaking the shortness of limb and the sturdiness of body. His kinky hair was a golden cloud floating around his head – no pure-blooded dwarf had any but straight hair. As the disbelieving courier grew closer, the aristocratic fineness of the man's profile became apparent, another blatantly un-dwarven characteristic.

'What a strange man,' Moriana whispered. 'I've never seen the likes of him before.'

Fost said nothing. His eyes remained on the man. He was certain there couldn't be two such men in the world – and the one Fost knew was dead.

The golden dwarf turned in irritation at the intrusion. Immediately, his face transformed into a mask of sheer joy. Ortil Onsulomulo smiled and bobbed his outsized head. Luck had finally smiled on Fost and had continued during the past five days aboard the *Wyvern*.

'Yes, a goddess taught me the arts of the lyre. Do you doubt it?' He struck a chord and the listeners felt their eyes fill with tears. He strummed another chord and mirth bubbled up inside. A third and Fost and Moriana felt that some ultimate truth hovered just beyond their fingertips waiting for the tiniest exertion before they could grasp it.

'No, Captain Onsulomulo,' Moriana said, shaking her head. 'I don't doubt it.'

'I'm sure the captain speaks metaphorically,' put in Erimenes.

Onsulomulo shook his head stubbornly. His jaw set and the expression on his cheerful face hardened.

'I speak unvarnished truth, blue ghost who thinks too much about screwing.' He bounced to his feet and tucked the instrument under one arm. 'The Wise Ones love me. Because Fate has cursed me, the goddesses and gods pity me.'

'I can almost believe it,' muttered Fost. He had last seen Onsulomulo peering over the rail of the dwarf's ship Miscreate, which was being drawn up in a waterspout formed by an air elemental Synalon had called to devastate Kara-Est harbor. It was impossible that Ortil Onsulomulo lived. Yet it obviously took more than a howling elemental to stop him.

The courier still had the eerie feeling that the Three and Twenty kept their eye on him, too, just as Jennas maintained. Not only was the half-dwarf captain overjoyed to see him, he insisted on providing Fost, Moriana and the ghosts and dogs immediate transport to High Medurim – free. And more than mere transportation, Onsulomulo also offered the pair the protection of his escort, the TMG dromon Tiger.

'You, my friend,' Onsulomulo had said, hugging Fost to his barrel chest, 'you are the source of all my good fortune!'

It was hard to deny. Instead of smashing him and his ship to splinters, the air sprite had deposited Onsulomulo and the Miscreate in the Central Plaza of Kara-Est with loving care. It had presented the city's conquerors with a knotty problem. No matter what their eventual plans of conquest, the City in the Sky couldn't afford to alienate either the dwarves or the Joreans. The fact that since siring his bizarre bastard Ortil's father Jama Onsulomulo had become Minister of Education for the western Jorean province of Sundown made it difficult to adopt the expedient solution of bashing in Ortil's head and claiming the elemental had killed him in combat. Ortil Onsulomulo was just not the kind of neutral one could kill with impunity, in the heat of battle or otherwise.

At the advice of Pavel Tonsho, former Chief Deputy of Kara-Est now the governor of the conquered city, the Sky Citizens had given Onsulomulo a ship, crew and a fat indemnity and sent him on his way.

The Wyvern seemed designed especially for Ortil Onsulomulo. Like him it was a freak, a crossbreed. Laid down in the Estil shipyards as a gigantic round-sterned cargo ship, its construction had been halted midway when the backing company had gone bankrupt. The receivers couldn't afford to complete a vessel of this size, but neither did they wish a half-constructed ship to go to waste. So the hull was cut down. The Wyvern was transformed into a cog. And it was ugly.

It had just slid − or waddled − down the ways into Kara-Est harbor when the Sky City appeared overhead. No one knew or cared if it was seaworthy; the crew sent aboard after the battle got horribly seasick on a bay as smooth as a mirror, which wasn't a good sign. But no one said the Sky City had to offer Onsulomulo guarantees. Just a ship.

He took it.

Perhaps no other mariner could have sailed the *Wyvern*. Probably none other skilled enough would have stayed aboard longer than three minutes. Onsulomulo fell in love with the ship at once.

He did more than sail her. He took her up the Karhon Channel to Tolviroth Acerte, a journey which made the refugee Estil seamen wonder if they wouldn't have been better off taking their chances with Prince Rann. At the City of Bankers, he took on a cargo so valuable that he hired a Shark class dromon from TMG to squire him to High Medurim, the port of delivery.

As the *Wyvern*'s boats had warped her around the end of the breakwater, the fugitives had speculated among themselves as to the nature of the cargo. Moriana thought *Wyvern* carried strategic materials vital to Imperial security; Ziore, priceless art objects; Erimenes staunchly held out for aphrodisiacs. Knowing High Medurim and its Emperor Teom the Decadent, Fost tended to agree with Erimenes.

As it happened, he'd been as wrong as the others.

He felt the deck quiver under his feet.

'Good morrow, Magister Banshau!' called Onsulomulo, launching himself into space off a battered crossbeam. Fost shut his eyes as the dwarf dropped ten feet from where he had been inspecting the mast and landed jarringly on the deck. None the worse for the experience, the captain strolled past Fost to greet the newcomer who had emerged blinking and puffing into the daylight. 'I trust the morning finds you well?'

'I am *not*!' roared the corpulent man blocking the hatch. 'I couldn't *possibly* be well, forced to ride in this wallowing monstrosity. How you could think for one instant that I might be, completely eludes me.'

'I thought you Wirixers were used to boats and such,' said Erimenes. 'You live in the middle of a lake, after all.'

The man glared at Erimenes with beady black eyes almost lost in a face like a full moon. He reached chubby, ring-encrusted hands to straighten the square green felt hat, then smoothed the golden silk cord fastening his purple robe about his vast equator. He shuffled bright orange toe slippers into a wider stance, as if bracing to attack the spirit, and blew out through his moustache like an angry walrus.

'Of all the nerve, you ghastly blue violation of the laws of nature!' he bellowed. 'You insult my vast intelligence! Wir is a lake, and *this*, as even the ghost of a discredited philosopher ought to be able to see, is an *ocean*.'

'A discredited philosopher, am I?' bristled Erimenes. 'You bilious cretin!'

'Justly are Wirixer sorcerers renowned for their wisdom,' Ziore declared in fervor.

In unison, Fost and Moriana sighed. This was the cargo Onsulo- mulo carried to High Medurim, the cargo that rated escort by the *Tiger*. A Magister of the Academy of the Arcane Arts in Wirix was a rare commodity, but not rare enough to justify the enormous expense of TMG protection. There had to be more to Zloscher Banshau than met the eye.

A three-way screaming match ensued among the two Athalar genies and Banshau. Captain Onsulomulo stood to one side smiling slyly. The mage's elephantine rage had been deflected from him. Truly, he was beloved of the gods.

With common accord, Moriana and Fost unslung their satchel straps. They looped them over a belaying pin and went below. The music had gone out of the day.

Moriana yelped as a wave clawed at her feet before falling back to lose itself in the chaos of the sea. A few more quick heaves on the line by grinning Tolvirot sailors and she was swaying above the decks of the *Tiger*, dripping legs dangling from the boatswain's chain.

She was too high up for Fost to reach her. *Tiger's* first officer stepped up beside him, reached, plucked the tall blonde woman from the chair and handed her down as if she were a child. Tirn Devistri was the tallest human Fost had ever seen. He had the mahogany skin of a Jorean tanned the black of Nevrym anhak by the sun. It was all but unheard of to find a Jorean serving as a mercenary of any kind, not that the TMG sailors thought of them- selves as mercenaries.

'Why so skittish?' asked Fost. 'I thought you were used to being up in the air.'

'Over land,' the princess told him. 'That doesn't come right up and grab you.'

Ignoring a lewd comment from a female Tolvirot sailor, Fost said, 'You know, you've turned the most amazing gray-green. Almost as if you had Vridzish blood.'

She turned deathly pale. He let go, stepped back and watched killing rage in her eyes change into shocked hurt.

'Forgive me, I didn't know. That is, I was thoughtless . . .'

'No,' she said, shaking her head sadly, 'I'm the one who is sorry. I don't know why I reacted like that.' She gave him a wan smile and squeezed his arm.

He watched her turn, wondering what had happened to her in Thendrun. It couldn't have been pleasant, he decided.

Captain Nariv Shend took them for a tour of her ship. She was a stocky woman of middle height and years. Incredibly broad shoulders and back showed she still took her turn pulling an oar, as did many TMG captains. There were no slave rowers on a TMG ship, only skilled and highly paid professionals.

At the moment, those professionals lounged about the narrow deck, the men barechested, the women in scant black halters. Others slept in the crowded hammocks slung between the benches below while the *Tiger* beat southwest under sail.

Bareheaded so that her short-cropped black hair was ruffled by the breeze, the captain herself led them on a tour of the ship.

'A Tolvirot dromon's the epitome of the naval architect's art,' she informed them in a voice gone husky from bawling orders over the years. '*Tiger*'s the latest design. She lives up to her name, too. You'll not find a tiger shark sleeker or deadlier. We're only fifteen feet shorter than the tub *Wyvern* –' She gestured with contempt at the larger ship, which even in the mild sea wallowed worse than the slender warcraft. '– but we're less than half as broad beamed and don't displace a fifth of what she does. And look at this.' She bent over the starboard rail and pointed down at the hull. When the ship surged up as it came off the crests, they saw shiny yellow streaked with green. 'Copper sheath. Cuts through water like a knife. And our spur up at the prow can punch through an enemy's hull like a spear.' If Erimenes were here, Fost reflected, he'd make some comment about the captain's propensity for metaphor. Which was only one of the reasons the genie wasn't here.

She straightened and looked at them. Her eyes were pale blue and almost hidden in wrinkles etched by squinting against the harsh sunlight blazing down and glancing off the broken surface of the sea.

'That's with rowers, of course. Peaceful times, when there's any kind of wind, we sail and let the rowers off.'

Fost thumped a boot heel on the stout anhak deck that covered the ship from rail to rail.

'I thought most rowed vessels were open.'

'*Tiger*'s fully armored. The deck gives us a good fighting platform in a boarding action. And you see our gunwales are pretty high, and we've these stout mantlets for added protection from archers.'

She led them around her ship while they looked on and tried to ask informed questions. The Tolvirot sailors watched with amusement but no contempt.

'And up here in the forecastle, we've got the pump for our flame projector.' She nodded to her first officer, who stood by the forward mast directing a sail drill in a voice like a thunderstorm. He acknowledged and went back to the drill. Like this captain and everyone else aboard, he wore a short blue kilt with a dagger at his belt. But he didn't wear a short-sleeved blue tunic like Shend. His titanic chest was bare. Fost eyed him, hoping that no turn of events pitted them against one another. And in the same thought, he hoped Moriana wasn't eyeing the enormous sailor too closely, either.

'Now the flamethrower's a tricky proposition,' Shend said as she opened a hatch in the square forecastle. 'It's a very effective weapon, but you can't get more'n one or two good shots out of it. Can't carry fuel for more. Now here –' A blunt hand indicated a squat, dully gleaming brass assembly. '– here's the pump, and that's . . .'

A cry from above brought her head sharply up. Fost saw she almost quivered like a hunting hound on the scent. Her hand dropped to the short axe at her belt. Tolviroth Maritime Guaranty were notorious for avoiding fights that were none of their concern, but that was only because a finely honed instrument of destruction shouldn't be blunted needlessly. But when the time came, the TMG sailors took an unholy joy in battle.

A sailor, dark and sexless against a piling of clouds, sat in a bucket at the top of the forward mast. The lookout pointed toward the low green shoreline. They crossed delta country where several rivers drained from Lake Lolu into the sea. From the concealed mouth of one of those rivers pirates often sallied forth to attack shipping.

295

And that was what Fost presumed the three low, black shapes crawling like insects across the rumpled green blanket of sea had in mind.

'An outrage!' The immense Wirixer mage quivered with rage as he twisted a mottled silk handkerchief in his hamhock hands. 'That my personage should be subjected to treacherous assault! Oh, woe, woe!'

'Be silent, you bulbous bag of wind,' sneered Erimenes. 'Be a man! You should look forward with keen anticipation to the virile shedding of blood, as I do.'

'You only do that because you've no blood to shed,' Fost said dourly, trying to fit a conical helmet on his head so that the noseguard didn't scrape his skin.

The spirit ignored him.

'Besides, these vagabonds doubtless aren't attacking us to get at you. That's merely a paranoid delusion of grandeur on your part. Likely they're just run of the mill pirates. Murderers, rapists, robbers, that sort of thing.'

'Be silent, you old fool!' Ziore's voice throbbed with exasperation and worry. 'They come to attack Moriana. I know they do!'

Teetering on a rail, resplendent in gilded and shaped breastplate and greaves that would have pleased the Emperor Teom, Ortil Onsulomulo laughed gaily.

'Whatever their motives, their intentions are clear.' He waved a stumpy arm at the approaching ships.

'So are ours,' said Moriana, holding her bow between her knees as she adjusted the buckle of her own helmet borrowed from the ship's armory.

The pirate craft had become distinct shapes with discernible details. Two were low with single banks of oars, which Onsulomulo sneeringly called pentekonters. The third was more ominous, a big bireme with staring eyes painted on the prow.

'Laid down in the Kolnith Shipyards, by her lines,' the captain observed.

'You think Kolnith is backing this?' Fost asked.

'Some City State could be, but I doubt it's Kolnith. Not even the Archduke's fishheaded enough to send his lackeys a-pirating in a ship traceable to him.' Onsulomulo pointed his shortsword at the pirate ships. 'You'll notice their decks are fairly black with men, not to imply they are crewed by my Jorean cousins.' He interrupted the lecture with a short laugh. 'Each is carrying two or perhaps three times its usual crew. They've just put out from land a few hours past and don't need to worry about provisions.' He sighed and shook his large, golden head. 'We are sadly outnumbered, I fear.'

'Woe!' lamented Magister Banshau.

Though according to the half-dwarf captain the bireme would be quicker, the smaller pentekonters coursed ahead, their rowers working frantically to drive them through the incoming rollers.

'It seems they've a basic sense of tactics,' Onsulomulo said dryly.

'How do you mean?' Moriana asked.

'The two little cubs are off to worry our sheepdog while the wolf makes straight for the fold.'

The cry went up, 'There she goes!' from the *Wyvern*'s rail, and *Tiger* slid under her bows, hitting the crests with loud bangs as she pulled for the attackers.

'They haven't a chance,' said Fost.

The low, black shark-ship shot between the two oared galleys, spitting arrows in both directions. In passing, the ballista mounted amidships thumped and sent a two-yard-long iron dart smashing among the crew tightly packed between the gunwale of the pirate on her starboard. Fost heard the screams.

The bireme had already turned her bow into the west and made to pass to port of her fellows to intercept *Wyvern*. Onsulomulo shouted for his ship to come about, leading away from the distant green shore. It seemed wasted breath to Fost. They were beating into the wind as they had for ten days and could never hope to out-maneuver the big bireme.

The *Tiger* swung to port trying to turn about and come to grips with her attackers again. Shend had plotted well. The other pirate galley, inflamed with the lust for loot, kept coming arrow straight for *Wyvern*'s fat flank.

Even at the distance of several hundred yards, Fost heard Shend's voice, 'Star'rd oars, full back! Port oars, full for'ard!'

'A turnabout.' Onsulomulo's eyes gleamed.

It was incredible. The long black hull simply swiveled in the water, as deft as a waterstrider. When her spurred prow pointed the way she had come, Shend roared, 'All for'ard full!' and the ship leaped ahead as if shot from a catapult.

The men packed on the decks of the galley screamed as they saw death bearing down on them. The little galley was broadside to the swell and lost way as the rowers lost rhythm. The slave rowers were trying to tear loose from their chains and flee the path of that deadly spur.

Tiger took her broadside with a rending screech that made Fost's neck hairs rise. For a second, it looked as if the pentekonter would ride out of the blow. Then the deadly iron spur tore free with a harsh squealing of sundered wood and the irresistible pressure of seventy-two strongly pulled and perfectly coordinated oars simply rolled the smaller vessel over. The watchers in the *Wyvern* clearly heard her keel breaking as the *Tiger* ran her down.

Erimenes shrieked in bloodlust ecstasy, Moriana shouted and Fost found his throat raw now. Even Banshau had quit blubbering and gazed on intently.

Tiger lunged away from the foundering body of her prey. Still apparently fresh, her rowers pulled her past the surviving pentekonter in a quick shooting pass. Again her arrows and engines worked execution on the thronging pirates while the return missile hail had no visible effect against the Tolvirot's well-shielded complement.

A hundred yards ahead of the pirate, almost in bowshot of the *Wyvern*, the dromon spun in another breathtaking turnabout and went head to head with the pentekonter.

'Is she going to ram?' Moriana asked.

'Do you jest, Lady? No TMG captain would ram bows-on except as an uttermost final resort. No, Highness, you'll see. Captain Shend has more daggers than one in her fine bodice.'

The pirate oarsmen slacked off, apparently asking the same question Moriana had. Fost heard whips cracking as the rowing master frantically sought to build up headway again. If the Tolvirot really did have a suicidal attack in mind, it wouldn't do to be caught dead in the water.

Tiger veered to port to pass wide of the pirate. He almost felt the sigh of a relief go up from the enemy ship.

'Fecklessness!' Erimenes cried disdainfully.

At the last possible instant, the *Tiger* swung back at her foe.

'Star'rd oars, *trail*!' Shend howled. As one, thirty-six oars snapped back alongside the ship, resting inside the line of her iron sheathing.

The pirate never had a chance. *Tiger*'s prow ran over her oars. Damned wails and screams burst from the pentekonter as her starboard oarsmen were crushed between oars and benches. When at last the horrid grinding was over and the *Tiger* swung around her foe's high stern, the pirate galley lay motionless in the water.

Then with a thump and a scrape, the bireme came alongside. Fost forgot the *Tiger*.

Moriana had kept her eye on the approaching bireme and sent some shrewdly aimed arrows in its direction. Now she laid her bow aside and took up sword and shield. She had provided herself with a light leather jerkin for body protection and her Grasslander boots were rolled up to protect her thighs. Fost hoped it was enough. He hoped he had enough, too, with shield and helmet augmenting his tattered mail vest.

Screeching like angry ravens, the pirates swarmed up over the side. The bireme only lacked a foot of *Wyvern*'s freeboard, so there was only Onsulomulo's crew to fend them off. *Wyvern* held a hundred and twenty men; the bireme easily three times that many. The fight was hopeless from the outset.

'Magic!' Erimenes cried as Moriana and Fost engaged yelling pirates in a skirl of blades. 'Use your magic!'

'Can't!' she cried, taking the thrust of a boarding pike on her shield. 'Too many!'

'A fireball'd cool their ardor,' said the genie, mixing metaphors wildly. 'Shrewdly struck, friend Fost.'

'It'd set the ship ablaze, you dunce!' Fost shouted back, as the partner of the man he'd just killed swung an axe at his head.

The battle came to him in surrealistic flashes. Bearded faces distorted with rage or pain as his blade bit home; Moriana's slim sword flickered like a tongue of flame, its tip tracing lines of blood in the air as it struck and darted away; Onsulomulo danced through the crush of sweating, bloody bodies and fought using two short swords, hamstringing, stabbing kidneys, capturing swung cutlasses between his blades and spinning them away with a scissors twist; Magister Banshau, prodded in the belly by a blond-bearded pirate, raised a shrill keening of fury, swept a large tar barrel up above his head and sent it bowling down the decks like a runaway boulder crushing half a dozen pirates to bloody gruel. They all fought well. Erimenes crowed encouragement and Ziore, wincing with pain at what she must do, clouded the minds and slowed the reactions of pirates as they closed with Moriana. But it was all in vain, as Fost knew when he thrust his sword into an angry face and counted the

299

eighth he'd killed with no slackening in the tide of enemies. The day was lost. Sheer value wouldn't offset the crushing weight of numbers.

Then with a bang! the *Tiger* drove its spur through the bireme's stern and her corvus thumped against the stern to allow Tirn Devistri to lead the Tolvirot crew, rowers and all, up and over and in among the pirates.

The battle was as good as ended.

Later, Fost and Moriana lay exhausted in their stateroom. The sweat of battle had been washed from their limbs in a cold stream of water pumped by bloody, bandaged, grinning seamen. Now their limbs were clad in the sweat of lovemaking of a fervor unusual even for them. The nearness of death had made the sensations all the sharper.

Moriana lay at Fost's side running fingers through the hair on his chest. He yelped as they explored a sticking plaster the ship's surgeon had slapped over a shallow puncture where a lucky pike thrust had popped a few more rings of his hapless chain mail shirt.

'I never would have thought the Tolvirot could fight like that,' she mused. 'They're mercenaries, after all. They fight for money, not conviction.'

'They've convictions. They're protecting freedom of trade, and that's powerful medicine to a Tolvirot. And does a highly paid artisan do lesser work merely for being higher paid?'

'I suppose not.' The ship creaked and sighed about them, a note of smugness in the sounds, as if the ship, too, were happily surprised to find itself still alive and free.

'Most of all, I guess, they fight for pride. A sense of honor.' He shrugged. 'Most soldiers fight for that, in spite of claims for creed or country.'

'You may be right.' She turned to nibble on his ear.

He squirmed. He resisted, only for the sheer pleasure of prolonging the sensation. She reached down and grabbed none too gently.

'Oh, well,' he said as he turned eagerly toward her. 'At least we're safe. Nothing can get past the *Tiger*.'

CHAPTER TWELVE

The whole populace of High Medurim had turned out to greet the *Wyvern*, complete with a skirling and banging military band, colored streamers and a troupe of naked dancing girls and boys, without which no public occasion was complete.

'At last,' Erimenes had said, puffing up like a courting frog, 'we receive attention commensurate with our status.'

Burly stevedores had swung *Wyvern's* fat stern up to the pier. The joyous tumult climaxed as the long wooden ramp was let down and the weary, shaken, but nonetheless gratified travellers set foot on the ancient stone of High Medurim. Singing traditional songs of welcome, the crowd swept forward . . .

. . . and engulfed Zolscher Banshau, hauling his vast bulk up onto its collective shoulders, bearing him forward in triumph to a state carriage waiting at the waterfront. An assembly of great and learned men, if their phenomenal beards and dizzingly tall hats were any indication, welcomed him aboard, while gorgeous maidens wearing diaphanous robes and foil haloes placed a wreath on his head and smothered his moustache with kisses. Magister Banshau, lying at ease on a sumptuous divan, beamed from the depths of gaudy floral wreaths as if he'd been named the Twenty-fourth Wise One of Agift. Shouting with joy, the crowd pelted along the sidewalks on either side of the carriage. The band fell in behind while nude brightly painted dancers scattered flowers and hard candies.

'Welcome to High Medurim,' Ortil Onsulomulo called down sarcastically to Fost and Moriana from the sterncastle.

Not even Erimenes had anything to say to that.

They were still standing at the foot of the ramp when a carriage appeared. A fraction the size of the one bearing away the Wirixer mage, it was impressive enough, black enamelled and polished so obsessively that a courtier could use it as a mirror. The muffled, hooded driver brought the landau to a noisy halt in front of Fost and Moriana. A curtained door swung open and a clean-shaven man wearing a gleaming black uniform stepped out.

'I am General Falaris, Imperial Intelligence Service,' he announced. 'You are the Princess Moriana?' Startled, Moriana nodded. He bowed perfunctorily. 'Please come with me, Your Highness.' He shot hurried looks in both directions. 'Get in quickly before anyone sees.'

Fost felt nostalgic tears sting his eyes. 'Imperial Intelligence' was a contradiction in terms. Any Medurimin above the age of three knew who the shiny black landaus belonged to. They could as effectively keep secrets by hiring criers to proclaim that mysterious visitors had arrived by ship to confer with the Emperor.

The general's invitation had not included Fost. Moriana solved that problem by grabbing his arm and dragging him into the box after her. General Falaris looked doubtful at this turn of events but said nothing.

Fost went to Emperor Teom the Decadent's palace in a daze. The familiar sights and sounds of his birth city overwhelmed him. The richness, the poverty, the places of learning, the pits of dismal ignorance. He peered out from behind the golden curtains in the landau and saw urchins begging in the streets, old men, toothless and blind, directing pickpockets and cuffing the younglings incapable of stealing enough. He had been there – once.

Now he was on his way to the palace of the Emperor.

'Welcome to High Medurim,' Emperor Teom said languidly. Draped over the arm of his throne, his wife and sister Temalla smiled and nodded in greeting, as well.

Moriana and Ziore bowed. Fost stood upright until a none too gentle elbow in his ribs from Moriana made him bend forward at the waist. It wasn't that he meant to defy the Emperor. He was simply struck numb by meeting the man who had once possessed so much power over him as a youth.

'The blue ghost does not bow.' hissed the small man at Teom's left. 'He does not pay proper reverence to Your Ineffability.'

Teom waved a hand. The fingers were slightly doughy and devoid of rings.

'Peace, Gyras. Were I fourteen centuries old I'd not be reverent

302

to a mere emperor either.' His voice rang in mellifluous low tones. Though he sprawled bonelessly across his gilded throne, he seemed to be a tall, well-proportioned man.

Flushing turquoise in pleasure, Erimenes performed a deep bow. His domed forehead sank alarmingly into the marble floor before he straightened.

'Your Radiance is too kind,' he murmured. 'Far be it from me to contradict you, however, but I must point out I am fifteen centuries old, and a shade over, rather than fourteen.'

A growl emerged from Gyras's throat. Teom silenced him with a wave. The dwarven advisor drew his balding head down angrily, accentuating the hump on his back.

'I've never seen an Athalar spirit before, though I've heard of them,' Teom said.

'We are alike,' said Erimenes, fawning and again bowing so his head vanished through the floor clear to his brows, 'for I have never before seen an emperor.'

With superhuman effort, Fost bit back his reply. Fortunately, Temalla interrupted Erimenes's sally into diplomacy by fixing Fost with big dark eyes made bigger by a liberal application of kohl and saying, 'Oh, but you must have had a *long, hard* journey.' Her husky voice accentuated the adjectives with undue emphasis. The Empress's voice had a curious quality about it that sent shivers up Fost's spine.

'Yes,' Teom said. A light came into his brown eyes. Reading his mood, his sister leaned forward and slipped a hand into a fold of his robe. She was of medium height, plump and with tightly curled brown hair hanging to her shoulders. Though she had not withstood the onslaught of middle years as well as her husband-brother, she was far from unattractive. The breasts hanging above the high waist of her blue gown were ample without being ostentatious, and the gown's gauzy fabric was drawn taut by her position poised on the throne arm, revealing a pleasing curve of hip and thigh. Her left hand toyed with the ringlets framing Teom's face, while her shoulder rose and fell in a gentle motion.

Fost held his breath when he realized what she did to her brother. Teom's eyes were shut and he sighed in pleasure. Fost felt Temalla's eyes burning into his. Moriana tensed at his side.

'You are welcome to High Medurim,' the Emperor repeated breathlessly, 'though I'm afraid it was a bit unorthodox.'

It had been that, Fost thought, looking everywhere but at Teom's lap, his sister's smiling face, Gyras's hot glare and the narrowing of Moriana's eyes. He wound up gazing down at his feet. The sight of his boots among the mad geometric patterns of the carpet intensified his unease.

Teom stiffened, then sighed. Temalla's smile broadened. Unspeaking, she promised Fost unspeakable delights. Sweat poured down the inside of Fost's tunic. He was very glad its hem came down below crotch level. Teom's eyes opened.

'I apologize for the furtive way you were brought to the Palace,' he said, as if nothing had happened. 'Given the sensitive nature of your mission – Magister Banshau gave us a somewhat garbled account by means of that mystical communication Wirixer mages use – we thought it best your arrival be kept secret for the moment.'

'We are most grateful that Your Effulgence chose to receive us as promptly as you did,' said Moriana. 'Now, if we could get down to the matters I've come to discuss.'

'No, dear Princess!' Teom cried, holding up his hand. 'We have ordered an extraordinary session of the Assembly for the day after tomorrow to hear your proposals. Time enough then for me to hear what you've come to say.'

'So much for secrecy,' muttered Fost. Gyras looked as if he'd just found a family of dung lizards nesting in his beard.

'Time enough to send these beggars packing, Your Magnificence,' Gyras said in a voice like two stones grinding together.

'Gyras,' chided Temalla, 'where's your hospitality?' She jumped to her feet and stretched with a litheness belying her years. 'Personally, I'm looking forward to entertaining our visitors.' She looked directly at Fost. 'Will you excuse me? I'm late for my riding lesson.' She glided out, licking her fingers.

'Good Gyras,' said Teom, rising, 'we thank you for your attendance on our person.' At this formal dismissal, Gyras folded his hands across the front of his frayed gray robe, looked plague and poison at Fost and Moriana, then followed the Empress out. 'Now, my friends,' Teom said. The words trembled with barely suppressed excitement. 'I should like to show you my great Project. It was to complete this Project that I imported Magister Banshau to High Medurim. And once you behold with your own eyes what the Magister's science has made possible, I believe you shall understand the extravagant reception we gave him!'

*

'And here on the right,' the Emperor waved his hand so that the fingertips protruded ever so briefly outside the shade cast by the parasol, 'we have spider monkeys from the Northern Continent. Careful, there, good Erimenes! If you regard them too obviously they tend to become excited. And they fling handfuls of dung with fearful accuracy.' He chuckled indulgently at the quaint proclivities of his pets.

Erimenes recoiled.

'Why do you care if they pelt you with offal?' demanded Ziore. 'They couldn't possibly hit you.'

'It is beneath the dignity of an Athalar scholar to be bombarded with excrement by members of inferior species. Besides, what if one of the little monsters drops a ringer in my jar?' He shuddered and turned his aquiline profile away from the monkeys' wizened, curious black faces.

'On the left are more exotic specimens. Lizard monkeys from the Isles of the Sun.' Fost peered at them with interest. Though shaped like the mammalian monkeys across the gravel walkway, the lizard monkeys were obviously reptilian. Their skins were scaly green, their eyes flittering black beads, and tiny hands and feet three-clawed. Their bellies were yellow, as were the ruffs of skin around the necks of the males. They had prehensile tails, several hanging upside down regarding the humans with sprightly curiosity.

Moriana shuddered and turned away. No doubt they reminded her of the Zr'gsz. Fost thought they were cute, but as he reflected on it, they began to make him uneasy. In the Library of High Medurim he had once read that many savants, including Wirixer genetic magicians, believed humanity had evolved from monkeys not dissimilar to those penned on the right side of the walkway.

Might not the Zr'gsz . . .?

He hurried to catch up with Moriana and Teom. The Emperor was as proud as a small boy showing off his famous menagerie. It was indeed impressive. Pens on either side contained small bits of alien environment for the comfort of the imprisoned fauna. He sauntered past tall tanks of some durable crystal filled with water, through which clouds of fishes small and not so small swirled and flashed brilliantly in the evening sunlight.

'Where are the naked dancing girls?' demanded Erimenes in a petulant whisper. 'The orgies in the street, the extravagant displays of wealth? I am sorely disappointed in this High Medurim of yours, Fost.'

305

Fost winced. It wasn't his fault. Still, he had been raised on tales of the opulence of life in the Imperial court. It had been something of a shock when they were ushered into Teom's presence in the private audience chamber and found it so austere. Likewise, Fost wondered at finding Teom attended only by his sister-wife and the dwarf advisor. Where were the coveys of courtiers said to follow him everywhere, panting with eagerness to obey his every whim?

He admitted his puzzlement to Erimenes.

'But you did see nude dancing girls, Erimenes,' he pointed out. 'This morning on the pier. They came out to greet Magister Banshau along with the cherubs and savants and that tinny marching band, remember?'

'But they were too far away to *see* anything.'

As they came back within earshot, Teom was pointing with pride at a shaggy mountain with a tail at both ends and two huge yellow tusks curving from the vicinity of the thicker tail.

'A Jorean mammoth, from Amsi Province in the south. They tame the beasts as dray-animals, I'm told, as we do hornbulls.' He indicated a block of ice melting in the corner behind the listless, hairy giant. 'It's fortunate we have an adequate ice house in the Palace. Otherwise, the poor beast would swelter to death in this frightful heat.'

He turned to nod at Fost, his smile mocking.

'Perhaps I had motives beyond secrecy in receiving you so surreptitiously and informally, friend Longstrider. Perhaps I felt a yearning to meet with people who had been to strange places and done wonderful things, and talk with them as *people* – not as mannikins decked with plumes and ribbons and walled off from all true contact by layer after layer of protocol. And without a flock of gaudy, useless songbirds fluttering about cooing in awe at my every utterance. Their songs are pretty, I confess, but they are also empty.' He reached out and touched Fost fleetingly on the shoulder with his long, soft, pallid fingers. 'Perhaps one day I should like to sit down and hear you tell me about life in my city's streets.' His tone was serious and his eyes were touched with bleakness. Fost almost missed his next words. 'That might be the most alien environment of all, to me.'

Then he laughed and turned away, his robe swirling about his legs.

'And perhaps a man as well-travelled as you should consider how keen must be the hearing of an Emperor to survive Palace intrigues long enough to keep the throne.'

Fost hardly thought of himself as a citizen of Medurim any more. But still . . . the Emperor had touched him and named him friend. In a way, that was as strange and wonderful as anything befalling him.

They came to the end of the rows of enclosure.

'Here's a sentimental favorite of mine,' Teom said. It was a seashore enclosure, a rocky beach and a pool dark with seaweed. Resting with half its bulk in the water was a mottled brown sea toad as big as Magister Banshau and covered with warts. 'It's three hundred years old,' Teom said. 'It sings with a beautiful, high soprano when the moons are full. But mostly I keep it because it reminds me of my dear, departed mother, the Dowager Empress.' He snuffled and wiped his eye. Fost stared. The thing *did* look like the late Dowager.

'What do you think of my menagerie?' Teom asked. He made a slight hand gesture and a balding servant appeared from nowhere bearing iced goblets and a flask of wine. Erimenes nodded. This was more like it, although the servitor didn't fit his conception of what a servitor should be. Too old, too male.

Fost sipped the cool wine. It was sweetened to the verge of cloying, but refreshing nonetheless.

'It's beautiful, Your Supremacy,' Moriana said. 'But am I correct in assuming it's not the Project you spoke of?'

'Indeed you are, Princess.' Teom had taken no wine himself. 'When you've refreshed yourselves, I will show you the great work whose culmination Magister Banshau has brought about.' He closed the parasol and handed it to the servant.

Moriana set her empty goblet back on the tray held by the immobile servant, saying, 'I'm ready.'

Teom led them through a door in the northwest corner of the Palace. Inside was cool and dim. They passed down a narrow corridor toward a shine of lamplight and a low murmur of conversation.

A stentorian whoop of joy echoed around a large chamber as they entered. Magister Banshau stood before them, his garish garments mercifully hidden under a white smock, holding his hands above his head and performing a dancing bear two-step of glee. He saw them and uttered another joyous bellow.

'Your Imperiousness! I have suceeded! I, the Magister Zolscher Banshau, now assume my undoubted rightful place among the

307

greatest of Wirixer mages!' And he seized Teom by the arm and waltzed him around the room.

A few old men in robes who sat crosslegged in a semi-circle on the floor looked up reprovingly at the commotion, then went back to reading in droning monotones. Fost spared them barely a glance; even the bizarre spectacle of the Emperor of High Medurim practically swept off his feet by a balloon-shaped wizard couldn't compete for his attention with the beast occupying the center of the room.

It was huge, the size of the Jorean mammoth and more, sporting a featureless hump, corpse-white and touched with blue-gray near its base. It lay in a pool of horribly bubbling brown, viscous liquids. The wrinkled, robed men were arranged around the pit, and they appeared to be reading to it.

'It looks,' Erimenes said, tapping his nose judiciously, 'like an enormous mushroom cap.'

'You're right, my excellent Athalar friend!' Banshau released the Emperor and started to grab the genie. He only succeeded in dispersing Erimenes's thin substance. As Erimenes coalesced in a blue whirlwind, the mage grabbed Fost and kissed him wetly on both cheeks. His moustache was redolent of wine and salt fish. 'It is a fungus. But a fungus such as the world has never seen!'

How a new breed of fungus merited such excitement escaped Fost.

'Where is — where is it?' Teom almost danced with excitement.

'There.' Banshau pointed to a door opposite the one through which they'd entered. In a single bound Teom was pulling it open and tumbling inside like a child opening his Equinox presents. Fost followed, careful not to jostle the imperial personage while craning his neck from side to side to see.

The cubicle was bare of furnishings. A small, round man sat crosslegged on the stone floor. His skin was very pale. At the sound of the door, he raised his head. His cheeks swelled in an infectious smile. Colorless eyes surrounded by laugh-lines glowed.

'Your Radiance,' he said, bowing.

'O Oracle!' cried Teom. He fell to his knees. 'This is the greatest moment of my life! My name shall live forever for this!'

'And mine,' added Banshau.

'Oracle?' Erimenes's brow creased. 'I remember the Magister saying something about an Oracle aboard the ship. Who is this Oracle, anyway?'

'I am, honored sir,' said the pale, round man. A pudgy hand pointed past the kneeling Emperor and Fost to the swollen fungus mound. 'And that is the Oracle, as well.' His merry laughter peeled like a bell.

'Many years ago,' the Emperor said around a mouthful of food, 'a certain Wirixer mage was on an expedition to the Isles of the Sun. He gathered specimens himself, since several of his assistants had been killed and eaten as a result of some slight unpleasantness with the Golden Barbarians.' He paused to wet his throat from a goblet of iced water. 'He was wading in a tidepool, whistling to himself. He lost his footing and stopped whistling while he caught his balance – only to hear the last few bars of his tune whistled back at him from nearby.

'On investigating, he found the sound had come from a fist-sized growth at the edge of the pool. A small amphibious predator lived nearby; the fungus imitated the cries of various seabirds and lured them into the creature's reach. In turn, its droppings and the remnants of its meals nourished the fungus. Remarkable symbiotic development.' Temalla made a face at the mention of droppings. She picked a leg of roast fowl from the silver platter and began to tear at it with small, neat teeth, gazing at Fost as if she'd decided to have him for the next course.

'The mage brought the fungus and its partner home. He waited until it produced spores, then went to work. The work was long and exacting, but over generations the Wirixers altered the nature of the fungus. It was found to have a rudimentary consciousness. By selective breeding and the most cogent and subtle genetic enchantments they expanded it until it equalled a man's. And then exceeded it.

'Their aim was to produce a variety of the mimic fungus that could store information, sort of within its own, well, *mind*, and not only produce facts but actually make deductions of its own.'

'But why bother, Your Sublimity?' asked Erimenes. 'You've the Library. It's the greatest in the world. Or was, when I lived.'

'It's the greatest still, though recently it has fallen into neglect. At times, it seems I am the only Medurimin with any interest in abstract knowledge.' He took a bite of the seaweed pod marinated in brandy. 'Be that as it may, the Library possesses over ten million volumes. It contains within its walls virtually the sum total of human knowledge, of history, of nature, of the workings of politics and the Universe. And ninety-nine parts of a hundred is as good as lost. No human intellect can absorb a fraction of it.'

He leaned forward. His dark eyes glowed with passion.

'But Oracle's intellect can. For the first time in human history, man can actually make use of the immeasurable trove of facts.'

Fost felt his own pulse race. He remembered his frustrations as a boy under the tutelage of the pedant Ceratith, when he had completed learning how to read and in part appreciated the sheer size of the Library. He had been frustrated to tears when the truth first struck him. To his small-boy mind it had been like being confronted with all the sweets in the world and knowing if he lived to be a thousand he could sample only a paltry few.

'How does Magister Banshau come into this?' asked Moriana. 'I gather he wasn't involved in development of the Oracle himself.' She leaned to the side to let a serving maid refill her goblet. Dusky breasts threatened to pop from the maid's tight, skimpy bodice. At long last beauteous serving girls had made an appearance, to Erimenes's vocal delight.

'You gather correctly, Princess. What Banshau did, and what has earned him all the bounty I can bestow, is discover a new kind of nutrient. It enhances the Oracle's mental energy level so that it is capable of telepathy and projections and similar feats. Mental feats such as flourished in lost Athalau.'

The jolly, white-skinned little man who had been in the room adjoining the fungus solemnly entered and sat quietly beside Moriana. Teom smiled broadly and gestured to the man, saying, 'Tell them about this wonderous accomplishment, Oracle.'

The man nodded, then spoke.

'This is similar to the mental magic that flourished in Athalau, what is now termed intrinsic magic as opposed to extrinsic, which involves manipulation of elementals and demons and other forces external to the magician.'

Fost looked at Moriana. She returned a small smile. Then she stiffened a little. Teom laughed.

'Ah, you perceive my little jest.'

'I don't,' said Fost. 'What's wrong?'

'Nothing is wrong, Fost,' said Teom. 'This being you see beside the princess is nothing more than a mental projection created by the fungus.'

'A Wirixer spell,' the little man said. 'I can teach it to you, Highness, since your mind is both powerful and agile.' He laughed at Moriana's thunderstruck expression. 'The Wirixers have been at the game of magic almost as long as your folk, Princess. Do not begrudge them their little abilities.'

While this interchange took place, Erimenes was growing livid, turning gray-blue with the veins standing out at his temples. If he'd been corporeal, Fost would have feared him to be on the brink of apoplexy. Erimenes was far from resigned to the existence of a second Athalar spirit. Oracle's projection struck him as a cheap imitation of himself. It was too much to bear. He was on the point of fulminating when Oracle turned to him, eyes widening.

'Oh! It comes to me now. Your pardon, sir, I have only recently attained consciousness. But you are the spirit of Erimenes? The mighty Athalar philosopher known as "the Ethical"?'

Guardedly, Erimenes admitted he was.

'This is marvelous! You are a great man, sir. Your life and works are a part of history. Ah, to think I meet in person a man of such legendary erudition and wisdom.' He clapped his hands together – through one another. Oracle blinked rapidly and said, 'Please forgive me. I haven't learned all the possibilities of projection yet.'

'Pardon me, Your Magnificence,' Fost cut in. 'It's astonishing that Oracle can project his image like that. But I don't see the importance.'

Teom waved his fingers airily.

'The projection is a mere trick, a side effect, if you will. You saw the old men sitting around the nutrient pool reading?' Fost nodded. 'Well, now Oracle can absorb knowledge directly from men's brains. Not only can it pick up the accumulated knowledge of a learned man's whole life, but it can read new material as fast as a man's eyes can scan a page. Can you imagine the lifetimes that will save teaching it?'

Having stripped the drumstick to bare bone, Temalla flung it over her shoulder and slumped back in her chair.

'You've grown so tedious, Teom,' she complained. 'All you can talk about is that horrid giant toadstool.'

Teom's fist slammed onto the table, setting goblets dancing. His own crystal goblet jumped off the table to shatter on the floor.

'It is *not* a giant toadstool. Oracle is the greatest achievement in

311

High Medurim in a thousand years. It is my Oracle who will bring about a renaissance of knowledge and wisdom and make Medurim mighty again.'

Sneering, she yawned ostentatiously and raised her arms above her head, squeezing her shoulderblades together so that her heavy breasts jutted straight at Fost. Areolas like targets showed clearly through the gown's flimsy fabric.

'You spend all your time with that unnatural thing!' Inch-long lashes batted at Fost; he almost felt the wind. 'I'm sure Sir Fost would never neglect me so.'

He felt as if someone had poured molten wax into his stomach. Damn the woman! Why didn't she leave him alone?

And why did she have this effect on him?

'Unnatural?' Teom's voice rose to a shrill scream of outrage. 'Unnatural, you witch? How can you say that about my creation?'

'Because it is. And it's not your creation.'

'I sponsored it. Without my patronage it would never have been completed!'

'But what's it good for?' the Empress shouted. 'Will it fill the Imperial coffers? Can you eat it, drink it, make love to it?' Her lip curled and her voice lowered. 'But knowing you, dear brother, you probably could. And enjoy it!'

'It would make a livelier bedmate than you.'

In the thick of silence, Fost and Moriana rose and murmured excuses which went unheard amid the gathering storm. Scooping up the genies' satchels, they pushed through a group of serving maids that had crowded around to watch. As they began walking rapidly toward their suite, they heard the explosion of a shrewdly hurled crystal decanter against a wall.

No sooner had they entered their chambers and chased out the dewy-eyed blond youth and girl they found already in their bed, than Moriana went to Fost and ripped his shirt open from collar to navel.

Swaying, he put a hand on the wall to steady himself. They were both more drunk than sober.

'What'd you do that for?'

Her hands slid cool and smooth along his ribs. She undulated against him, her breath warm and sweet in his ear.

'The way that slut Temalla's been making eyes at you,' she purred, 'I thought it best to give you something else to think about tonight.'

Moriana kept him occupied until dawn, when they both slipped into an exhausted sleep.

The next morning, they took advantage of their leisure to tour the fabled Imperial Palace. They wandered to and fro along the marble corridors, gazing at paintings hung on the walls and statues standing in silent alcoves. The place had been decorated in early plunder. Whatever hadn't been nailed down or too heavy to move, the Imperial Army had taken from its country of origin. There was no scheme to the collected art. Much of it was dross, much incomparably fine. What impressed Fost was that the collection spanned two continents and almost a hundred centuries.

The sun was high when they drifted into the western courtyard. It was a garden replete with tinkling fountains and divided into nooks and crannies by an ornamental hedge. Fost suggested it had been designed as a trysting ground. That gave Erimenes much satisfaction imagining past activities.

He waved a vaporous arm at a marble statue in a niche as they passed along the grassy path.

'That's what I call art,' he announced. 'Consider the interplay of line and form, consider the dynamics of the poses, the subtle imbalance inherent in the juxtaposition of human form and delphine. And such mastery of expression. Behold the girl's face. Was ever a transport of ecstasy made more concrete? And see how the dolphin smiles at it . . .'

'Dolphins always look like that,' said Ziore. 'Can you find no pleasure in art that isn't lascivious?'

A puzzled frown creased his face.

'Why, no. Why should I?' Then he brightened and said, 'During my own lifetime it was definitely established that male dolphins were altogether willing to mate with human females. Keeping in mind that this is High Medurim, Moriana, you really ought to consider . . .'

Fost would have liked to hear Moriana's retort. He never had the chance. Just at that moment they rounded a corner to see Gyras sitting on a bench, huddled head to head with another. As arresting as the dwarf's appearance was, it was the other who brought a gasp from Moriana's lips and made her hand crop to where her sword hung.

Gyras spoke to a Zr'gsz.

The Hisser saw them before Gyras. He came to his feet in a fluid motion, a dazzling white smile splitting his dark green face.

'What have we here?' His voice was a well-modulated baritone, quite human in pronunciation and inflection. 'You must be the Princess Moriana, and you, sir, you'd be Fost Longstrider.' He clasped clawed hands at his breasts and bowed. 'I am honored to meet you.'

He was as tall as Fost, clad in a single garment of shimmering gray cloth that reached down to his sandalled feet. His shoulders were broad, his waist lean. Gyras hurriedly pushed himself off the bench, landing with a thud.

'May I present Zak'zar, Speaker of the People.' Shrewd eyes studied Moriana. 'I take it you've not met?'

Moriana's lips moved but no words emerged.

'No, we haven't,' Fost supplied. The words ripped at his throat.

'But he's an enemy!' Erimenes shrieked. 'How can you welcome this viper into your nest?'

Zak'zar bowed again.

'And you would be Erimenes the Ethical. It is a pleasure to meet you, too, sir.'

'I assure you, fellow, the pleasure is entirely yours! Lord Gyras, what does this mean?'

Gyras feigned astonishment.

'Surely, you do not think we would convene a debate and hear only one side, especially one as important as this?' Malevolent glee shone in his huge eyes. He raised one eyebrow before saying, 'The revered Speaker arrived the day before you did, my friends. I'm surprised your good friend His Radiance the Emperor neglected to inform you.'

CHAPTER THIRTEEN

The languid young officer leaning back in the uncomfortable chair on Fost's left stifled a yawn with the back of his hand. The President of the Assembly was hammering for order to quell a minor riot taking place on the floor.

Ensign Palein Cheidro said to Fost, 'The Guilds oppose going to war with the Hissers. It'd disturb their precious status quo.' He examined the lace at the cuffs of his blue velvet doublet.

The President recognized a nervous cricket of a man from Jav Nihen. Fost didn't even bother listening to a speech he'd heard a dozen times before, reworded but essentially the same in content.

'Why do the Guilds oppose war? They were quick enough to back the Northern Adventure when I was a boy.'

'That was a war conducted safely on foreign soil,' explained the ensign. He smiled a lazy half-lidded smile. 'Until a suicide commando raid landed and burnt a dozen warehouses, that is. *Then* the Guilds cried to bring home the troops. If you offered them a really safe war against some foe too primitive to strike back at Medurim, they'd jump at it right enough. Think of the fat government contracts.'

'But that large gentleman denounced expansionists,' Ziore said. 'Do you say the Guilds really want a foreign war in spite of that?'

'My dear lady, do you mean to say you actually believe what politicians say in speechs? Oh, my.'

In Fost's youth, the Imperial Life Guards had been a fighting organization of renown. Ensign Cheidro made him wonder if the Life Guards had been devalued along with the money. Painfully thin, cat-elegant, dressed always in outfits that cost a common trooper a year's pay, Ensign Cheidro didn't fit Fost's image of a member of an elite unit.

Whether by coincidence or otherwise, no more invitations to dine

315

in the Emperor's apartments were forthcoming after Fost's chance meeting of the *Zr'gsz*. On the morning after, the ensign had appeared stating he was to be their guide. That he was also their keeper was left unsaid.

The debate over Moriana's petition to the Empire to declare war on the Fallen Ones had now dragged into its second day. During the long-winded disputes, Fost had come to a grudging liking for the officer, highborn fop or not. Cheidro had wit and used it utterly without regard for place or prestige of each speaker.

'Why do they go on so?' Fost heard Moriana complain. 'I thought they were discussing whether or not to hear that damned lizard.'

As if on cue, a small man with impressively broad shoulders bounded to his feet and shouted, 'We won't listen to the snake! We border folk have had enough words. It's time our swords spoke for us!' The men around him rushed to their feet, waving their fists in the air and shouting.

'Assemblymen from the Marches,' Cheidro said in bored tones. 'Excitable fellows.'

'Order!' cried the President, using his gavel freely.

'Up yours, Squilla!' the small Marcher shouted back.

The turmoil grew until a figure rose in the center and climbed from the floor toward the spectator's gallery. Silence fell as the commanding figure leaned forward, hands on the railing.

'Foedan speaks rarely, and never without effect,' said Cheidro. 'This could bode ill if he favors hearing Zak'zar.'

'Assemblymen,' began Foedan in a voice like a bass drum striking up a slow march. 'The question is not whether the Speaker or the princess is right or wrong, it is whether we should hear what Lord Zak'zar has to say in answer to Moriana's request that we make war upon his people. There can be but one answer. In fairness, we must hear him before making so grave a decision.'

Squilla pounded down the tumult greeting the words and called for a voice vote. No roll call was needed. Overwhelmingly, the Assembly voted to permit Zak'zar, Speaker of the People, to plead his case.

Moriana sat staring at Foedan as the vote was called, twisting the hem of her tunic as if it were the Kolnith Assemblyman's neck.

Zak'zar walked out on the floor of the Assembly Hall in silence. The usually rowdy delegates seemed hypnotized by the Hisser. He held all their attention in one clawed hand — and he knew how to wield it.

'I will be brief,' he said. He let the small ripples of comment die before continuing. 'You are asked to go to war with my People.

What have we done to you? We menace no Imperial holding. No resident of any City State has suffered at our hand. What wrong have we done that you would raise hand against us?'

'The Princess Moriana Etuul's written petition claims it is your duty as humans to resist Zr'gsz aggression. What aggression? And if it be the duty of your people to fight mine to the death, why did she come of her own accord to Thendrun seeking our aid in reclaiming her throne?'

A babble of voices washed about the podium. He raised his hand, stilling them.

'The Princess Moriana tells you we treacherously seized the City in the Sky from her, our ally. Examine the record. Who first built that fabled City – and who seized it by treachery from its rightful owners? We assisted her in unseating Synalon – but for our own ends. Is this wrong? Who among you would not resort to subterfuge to avenge the murder of your kinfolk and reclaim from thieves the house you built? We only took back what was ours.

'I come before you in the name of my People, bearing the willow-wand of peace. For your own sakes as well as ours, I ask you not to grasp instead the firebrand of war!'

He bent forward, voice dropping to a sonorous whisper that penetrated to the farthest reaches of the room.

'Weigh well your decision, men of the Empire. Much hangs in the balance.' He straightened and strode from the podium amid a barrage of cries.

Moriana vaulted over the rail and scattered Assemblymen in all directions as she moved forward. Head back, eyes ablaze, she walked down the aisle to the podium Zak'zar had just vacated. Squilla faced her, gavel raised as if to repel her attack on orderly procedure. Their eyes met; he fled before her.

She needed no gavel to bring the hall to silence, any more than Zr'gsz had. With hair streaming about her head like liquid fire, she launched into an impassioned speech.

The door to the Assembly Hall crashed open. Moriana paused, one fist raised in emphasis of a point. An old man stalked into the room. He walked ramrod straight in spite of the burden of years. Gray hair hung lank about his haggard face. The lips Moriana remembered so well were now twisted from emotions too great to be expressed. He was clad in scarlet and his eyes shone with fanatical light.

317

'Sir Tharvus!' she exclaimed.

The only survivor of the three Notable Knights who had ridden her banner at Chanobit Creek stopped and flung out his arm to point at her.

'Do not heed this witch!' he shouted. 'Her wiles lured my brothers and thousands of our countrymen to their deaths.

'On peril of your souls, don't listen to her!'

'So what happens now?' Fost asked.

A smile pushed up the ends of Cheidro's moustache.

'Why, what always happens when there's an impasse in a matter close to His Effulgence's heart.'

'What's that?'

'He throws a party.'

'This is more like it!' crowed Erimenes. Fost stirred from his fog.

'What is?'

A tall, lithe girl, nude except for diagonal stripes of blue and gold, walked by on the arm of an officer in a purple plumed helmet.

'This is!' A sweep of Erimenes's vaporous arm indicated everything.

At long last the travellers were face to face with the seamy, steamy decadence of High Medurim. The Golden Dome was every bit the voluptuary's vision of heaven popular repute made it out to be. Niches lined the wall, dark and inviting. Already Fost dimly made out writhing tangles of pale limbs in alcoves across the circular chamber. In the center, a round pit was filled with lustrous furs in careless profusion. Tables bowed under the weight of delicacies. Serving maids circulated everywhere to keep the wine and high spirits flowing. Many wore no more than kohl and inviting smiles.

In the middle of the pit reared a dais. On it lay a throne and on the throne sat the Emperor. He wore a ludicrous tentlike garment patterned in white and black diamonds.

Here and there Fost saw forms or faces he recognized. Magister Banshau sat with his chubby legs dangling over the edge of the pit, his garb standing out even in this profusion of color. He held a wine jug in one hand and the shapely thigh of a young noblewoman in the other. He looked mightily pleased with the world. Over by the far wall stood the dignified Foedan of Kolnith. His doublet was askew, his hair rumpled and he gazed on the crowd with bleary-eyed gravity while a short, plump redhead poured brandy into a snifter the size of his head.

At the center of an eddy of gay costumes rode Zak'zar, laughing like a rakehell at something the two young women he had his arms about said, a striking, chilling figure in a robe of woven midnight.

'Great Ultimate!' Erimenes shouted in Fost's ear. 'Look at *that*, will you?'

Moving through the crush with lithe grace was a strange and beautiful figure. Her body was that of a voluptuous woman but it was clad in soft, short, creamy fur. A long, sensitive tail swung behind her. Her face combined the best characteristics of human and feline. Her ears were pointed and set high on her head, poking out from the midst of a lustrous cascade of blue-black hair. And at her back was folded a pair of wings.

'I'll be damned,' said Fost with feeling.

'So you like Ch'rri?' A slender blonde woman in a short tunic, her hair cut boyishly short, dropped onto the bench at Fost's side. 'She's quite a sight, isn't she? If you have a taste for the exotic.'

'Uh, Ch-chu-chri?' Fost couldn't manage the throaty purr.

'Ch'rri,' the blonde woman repeated, laughing at Fost's doleful look. 'She's the only one of her kind, poor thing. Another Wirixer experiment. Or work of art, perhaps. One of their genetic wizards wanted to see what a winged cat woman looked like, and she was the result.' She frowned. 'She's a terribly lonely thing. But she does know some interesting ways to make up for it.'

'What are you waiting for?' demanded Erimenes. 'Introduce yourself! You're the hero of the hour, Fost. You'll sweep her off her feet'

'I think that sums it up well, spirit,' boomed a voice. Fost turned to look at the group approaching. 'Wild tales of your exploits are flying all over the city. We'd be honored to hear the truth from your own lips.'

The speaker was a rangy man in a flame-colored robe. His head was shaved and a gold earring swung from one earlobe. A tawny-haired woman, taller than Fost and with a patch over one eye, walked to one side. On the other was a shy, towheaded youth.

'I'm Sirsirai. This is Osni, and Jerru.' He nodded to each of his companions in turn.

Something in the way they moved clicked in Fost's brain.

'You're fighting masters,' he said, almost accusingly.

The one-eyed woman bobbed her head in agreement.

Erimenes cleared his throat, then said, 'What you've heard about Fost is true. All of it – and none of his marvelous adventures would have happened without me . . .'

Across the room, Moriana smiled and nodded mechanically and fended off still another smiling face. She was a celebrity. That she had balked at wearing frilly, fleecy finery in favor of her russet and beige tunic and trousers seemed to draw rather than repel the revellers.

'Why don't you relax?' said Ziore. 'Enjoy yourself.'

'You're as bad as Erimenes,' she accused, then softened her tone. 'I'm sorry. That was unfair. But I've no appetite for this sort of thing.'

'That might be a pity,' Ziore said, her voice holding a tone of longing.

On his dais, Teom sat fondling his chin and regarding various gorgeously painted and costumed courtiers, male and female, who had arranged themselves in front of his throne to vie for his attention. Deciding, he flicked his little finger. A slender woman in a feathered skullcap and sky blue tights widened her eyes in happy anticipation and scampered to the dais in response to his summons. His knees spread. She knelt between them, took hold of the tentlike robe and hiked it up about his Imperial waist. Beneath it Teom wore trunks and a codpiece of epic proportions that laced up the front. Licking her lips, the woman undid the laces . . .

And fell back as something sprang at her.

All sound ceased as every head turned to see a giant wooden phallus crowned with a painted jester's head bobbing at the end of the spring which had launched it from Teom's crotch.

It was the signal for the orgy to begin in earnest. Flinging his pink-trimmed orange blouse off, Magister Banshau teetered with his splayed toes gripping the edge of the pit. Then with a happy mating-walrus bellow, he launched himself into the sea of naked bodies below. A crowd stood watching as Zak'zar took advantage of a physiological peculiarity of his race to pleasure simultaneously two naked and ecstasy-flushed young women who lay back to back on a buffet table.

Tapers were touched to cones of incense. Thick musky smoke rolled into the air, scents and sandalwood and amasinj mingled with the tangy sweet aroma of a Golden Barbarian narcotic herb. Ch'rri the cat woman grabbed a passing serving boy, shoved him down on a stool and climbed astride him, folding her wings protectively about them so that no one quite saw what happened. Ortil Onsulo-mulo, his golden body naked except for a woman's green scarf wrapped around his neck, dancing in a jig while a clutch of noble-women of middle years giggled and grabbed at a certain portion of his anatomy. Erimenes pointed out to Osni that Onsulomulo either disproved a certain racial canard pertaining to dwarves or proved the one about Joreans.

'And so there I was,' explained Fost, warming to his audience, 'in the dark, and that little bastard Rann came at me with his scimitar.' He broke off when he saw the expressions of his listeners. 'What's wrong?'

'You crossed blades with Rann?' asked Jerru.

'Twice. Once in the foothills of the Ramparts and again in Athalau.'

Osni's one eye went round as she asked, 'And you lived?'

'As far as I know.' Fost started feeling defensive.

'It seems the rumors don't do you justice, friend,' declared Sirsirai.

'What do you mean?'

'Prince Rann Etuul,' said Osni, 'is without question one of the top blademasters alive today. To think you faced him twice, and lived . . .'

The room started to spin around Fost. He spilled his goblet of wine, then realized he had been steadily draining it, only to have it automatically refilled. He had no idea how much he'd drunk.

'Excuse me,' he said thickly. 'I've got to get some fresh air.'

He put Erimenes's satchel on the bench before stumbling away.

'Never mind him,' said Erimenes. 'He tends to be long-winded, like any hero.' The genie smiled slyly. 'Why don't you take off your clothes and forget all this idle chatter?'

Fost made his way out into the gardens. He breathed deeply and tried to quell the revolt in his stomach.

A finger was laid across his lips. He started, turned, saw it was Empress Temalla. She was nude. She took his hand and led him off through the shrubbery maze.

He followed numbly, fascinated by the way her buttocks moved when she walked. She pulled him into a secluded cubicle and pushed him down into the cool grass. The broad leaves of the shrubbery rustled inches away. Her body shone softly silver in the moonlight as she swung herself astride him and shuffled forward on her knees. The smells of crushed grass and her musk were heady in his nostrils. He took a deep breath and a double handful of her behind and lost himself in the pleasures she offered so freely.

Moriana sat on the floor with her knees drawn up and her back to a wall. Not even Ziore could pierce the armor of her loneliness. She felt drained, defeated. Sir Tharvus's appearance in the Assembly Hall the day before had destroyed her hopes of fielding an Imperial army against the Hissers. The Empire would react only when the lizard men came swarming across the River Marchant. Then it would be too late.

She sensed someone over her and looked up into the liquid brown eyes of Emperor Teom. He extended a hand to her. After a slight hesitation, she took it and let him lift her to her feet and lead her out of the Golden Dome. They passed within arm's length of Ensign Cheidro, engaged passionately with an auburn-haired youth. He never looked up.

As the evening wore on and various participants wore themselves out, some mischance brought Erimenes and Ziore face to face with their jars laying side by side on a table.

'What are you staring at, you vapid bitch?' Erimenes asked with that special tact he reserved for his fellow Athalar.

'The man who blighted my life! Whose obscene philosophy deluded me into denying myself all worldly pleasure in favor of a life of serene meditation.' Her face twisted in anguish. 'Meditation! I'd trade a lifetime of it for one hour of passion!'

'What do you know of passion? Ice water would run in your veins, had you veins!'

'Bastard!'

'Bitch!'

'Asshole!'

Heads began to turn. Grinning a cat's grin, Ch'rri appeared carrying a bronze waterpipe in a ringed stand. Her tail was held upright, its tip twitching mischievously. She set down her burden next to the two jugs.

'What game do you play now, darling Ch'rri?' a male voice asked.

She held up a vial filled with yellow crystals. Delighted gasps rose from the onlookers.

'Tusoweo,' a man breathed. 'Enough to make a statue of Felarod jump off its pedestal and start buggering tom-cats!'

The short-haired blonde who had sat by Fost earlier ran up with a clear glass bottle containing aromatic oils. Ch'rri pulled the cork, emptied the bottle and smiled wickedly.

Ch'rri shook a pinch of the yellow crystalline tusoweo into the waterpipe's bowl. Holding a smouldering incense cone to it, she puffed it alight. A thick yellow cloud welled up. Her slit pupils dilated.

'— your mother!' Erimenes was saying with malicious precision. '*And* your father. Wha —?' Ch'rri picked up his jug and popped home the basalt plug. He disappeared with a dismal squawk of rage. She pulled out the plug again and poured the spirit into the oil bottle.

'Now, you just wait a minute,' he protested as he spilled like smoke into the new bottle.' Just because this is an orgy doesn't mean you can take indecent liberties with my person! What are you doing? Great Ultimate, you can't pour that hag in here with me!'

Having plugged and reopened Ziore's jar, the blonde was doing just that. Hissing and spitting like cats, the two genies whirled in a dizzying vortex inside the glass jar, each trying to keep his or her substance discrete from the other's.

Ch'rri drew in a deep lungful of the yellow aphrodisiac smoke. Leaning forward, she puffed it into the bottle and hurriedly corked it.

Coughing sounds emerged. For a moment, the spirits were obscured by the thick vapor. Then it was absorbed, and the pink shade and the blue glowed with a new intensity.

'I say, woman, don't jostle me like that,' said Erimenes. 'I . . . my word, I felt it. I *felt* it!'

'And do you feel this?' Ziore asked in an unspeakably lewd slur.

His response was a wordless wail of ineffable lust.

The bottled genies began to spin again. This time they quickly blended into a purple vortex.

'Ohh!' cried one and 'Ahh!' moaned the other.

The mutant cat woman's experiment, combining the most powerful aphrodisiac known to sorcery with two highly telepathic spirits, produced spectacular results. A lust so pure and fierce it was almost tangible pulsed from the jar and expanded like the wavefront of an exploding star. Every being it touched went into immediate sexual frenzy. The occupants of the dome yowled as one and went for each other. Out in the streets of High Medurim, pandemonium reigned. Dogs madly humped cats, cats screwed rats. Married couples who hadn't touched each other in years broke bedsteads all over the city. Lonely night watchmen pounding their beats were seized with unaccountable yearnings to pound something else.

Time passed, to the accompaniment of groans and moans and glad cries.

*

323

In darkness, a traitor's hand opened a hidden door. Masked and muffled figures slipped into the Palace. Steel glinted.

The door of Emperor Teom's bedchamber burst open. Three men lunged into the room. Stark naked, sitting astride the Emperor and gasping in the throes of passion, Moriana still reacted to the danger. She threw herself clear of Teom, rolling toward the sword-carrying trio, seizing the furs on the bed as she hit the floor. Continuing her roll, she came to her feet and threw the fur pelt into the assassins' faces. It caught two of them by surprise, and they flailed at it as if it were a living attacker. The third sidestepped and lunged at her.

She grabbed at a tall wrought-iron lampstand and swung. Bones crunched. The man dropped. Oil spilled over him, then the ghastly odor of burning flesh filled the air.

A second assassin struggled free of the fur and ran at her, sword high. She tossed the lampstand in his face, then wrested the sword from his hand. She disembowelled him with his own weapon. The third would-be murderer still struggled on his knees. A single blow split his skull.

Through the handful of seconds of the savage, silent battle, Teom had sat huddled in his bed, watching, quivering, his face waxy. He silently rose and beat out the flames devouring the first assassin while Moriana shouted for help.

Fost lay face to face with Temalla while she sleepily twined fingers in his hair. Through a mellow fog of intoxication, satiation and exhaustion, Fost heard a flurry of cries coming from the north wing of the Palace.

'Istu take it, where're the others?' he heard someone nearby whisper. A soft drumming of feet came and a masked swordsman ran by their little alcove in the shrubs.

Without thinking, Fost launched himself in a flying tackle. Over they went, the assassin's hooded head crashing into a bush. Desperately, Fost tried to pin the man's sword hand while driving a fist repeatedly into his assailant's body. The man grunted and kicked. His knee caught Fost in the groin. It was a light blow but still set off bright explosions of pain.

It also sobered him. He groped at the man's belt, found the dagger, used it. The assassin squealed through his mask, then lay still.

The dead man's sword in his hand. Fost ran to the Golden Dome knowing he couldn't find his way out of this labyrinth in any other direction. He burst through an open archway and sagged against the door frame as a wave of lust hit him like a blow. His flaccid organ stirred and thrust out straight ahead of him like the bow of a ship.

Ch'rri was on hands and knees in front of him, wings poised above her back, purring like a bass fiddle as a man in black took her from behind. The man's head was covered by a hood. Though the initial irresistible psychic impulse the spirits had sent out had long passed, the sexual energy still crackled in the air.

Fost wrenched himself away, unlike the assassins in the Dome who had been intent on murdering the celebrants. As Fost ran for the north wing, a suspicion formed in his mind. He had seen the two jugs laying side by side and apparently empty on the table and beside them a squat glass bottle in which a purple whirlwind spun and motes of light danced intolerably bright.

He reached the north wing. Off to his left he heard shouts and the clash of arms and then the unmistakable booming of Magister Banshau's wrath.

'Oracle!' he cried to himself, then set off at a run.

The corridor widened into an antechamber just before the door that led into the laboratory. A hasty barricade of furniture blocked the hallway, a group of hooded killers and Zr'gsz defending it against a squad of Household Guard. The door into the laboratory had been broken down but the Wirixer mage, totally naked and clumsily wielding a paddle used to stir Oracle's nutrient slop, prevented their entry. A low caste Hisser, back broken by a blow from the paddle, lay kicking at his feet like a dog run down by a carriage.

Even as Fost watched, a Vridzish spearman sank his weapon deep into Banshau's vast belly. The killers swarmed into the laboratory.

A lithe, naked figure vaulted the barricade, steel flashing in both hands. A Hisser swung on Ensign Cheidro with a mace. With a speed scarcely less than a Zr'gsz's, Cheidro whipped his blades into a defensive cross, caught the mace and sent it spinning away with a deft twist. His rapier licked out and killed the Vridzish. Fost hurtled the barricade, joined the effeminate Life Guard, helping him clear the enemies remaining in the antechamber.

'You're well named, Longstrider,' Cheidro said in an unruffled nasal drawl. 'That was quite a leap.'

Fost smiled. Some of the Household Guards, encumbered by heavy armor, had finally struggled over the barrier. They charged into the laboratory.

The unarmed and untrained sages tending Oracle had died under the *Zr'gsz* onslaught, but none before impeding the headlong rush for a few brief instants. Their deaths allowed Fost, Cheidro and the Household Guards to burst among the intruders like a bomb.

Fost sighted Zak'zar and made for him. A black steel sword in hand, the Speaker of the People had engaged one of the Household Guard when three more rushed him, shortswords poised for the kill. He pursed his lips and blew. Black vapor issued forth. The inky cloud swept over the three. They screamed as the flesh festered and fell from their faces in black gangrenous lumps. They collapsed as their bodies rotted inside their armor. The Guardsman Zak'zar duelled gaped in horror. The Speaker hacked him down.

'Beware the cloud!' cried Fost to the men behind him. Zak'zar turned to Oracle. With a feeling of fatalism, Fost hurled himself at the handsome Vridzish.

Spitting a curse in his own tongue, Zak'zar swung back to meet the attack.

'So you've chosen this way to die, Longstrider?' He grinned.

Zak'zar dodged with impressive speed as Cheidro hacked at him. 'Perhaps you'll do the dying, friend,' said the young ensign.

By unspoken consent, Fost and Cheidro separated to attack the Vridzish from two sides. Zak'zar took a cautious step backward. The spur on his left foot found only empty air.

'You gentlemen have the tactical advantage. Make of it what you may!'

Fost and Cheidro attacked. In a prolonged contest, a human had the advantage over a *Zr'gsz*; the lizard men were quicker but lacked staying power. Zak'zar was obviously exceptional in more than his command of man-speech. Fost felt his reactions slowing, though the fury of the Vridzish's defense did not flag. A sudden slash opened a long gash down the left side of his chest, and Fost knew that the fatigue lag in his reflexes and Cheidro's would hand the *Zr'gsz* both their lives. The Hisser's grin showed he knew too.

The door to the north side of the room caved inward, riding a yellow fireball. Masked men ran to bar the way, only to fall like grain before a scythe as Foedan of Kolnith hewed his way through using a huge sword.

Zak'zar's blade slowed to visibility as he glanced toward the flash and thunderclap. Cheidro's rapier pinioned his right shoulder. Tearing the blade free in a welter of blood and a horrid sound of snapping sinew, the *Zr'gsz* wheeled and sheared through the young ensign's face.

Reversing the longsword in his claws, he raised his arms into the unprotected swell of Oracle's flank. The hilt of the sword abruptly turned incandescent. Fost heard the sizzle and smelled the stench of frying flesh. With an explosive hiss, Zak'zar dropped the weapon and jumped back. He blew his black breath. Moriana dismissed it with a wave of her hand.

She made a quick sweep of her fingers and a semicircle of blue flame crackled and roared to the height of a tall man's head. The *Zr'gsz* was trapped.

'Have you anything to say before you fry, serpent man?' she called.

His hair smouldering from the nearness of flames, his right shoulder a torn and gaping ruin, Zak'zar showed sharp teeth in a smile.

'This round goes to you, Lady. But we shall meet again quite soon, and I believe I can promise a different outcome!'

'Meet again?' Her fine features showed disbelief. 'Not unless they've integrated Hell!'

'I'm not due there for quite a while, yet. It may be that you will precede me, unless your pitiful friends manage to defeat the army of the People that even now prepares to cross the River Marchant!'

The listeners gasped. Fost's face stung with the infernal heat of the flame. He marvelled that Zak'zar endured them so calmly.

'An army! Where would you get the men?' Moriana asked.

'Haven't you divined that? It is an army of the Children of Expectation. Since our exile from the City in the Sky, entire generations have grown to adulthood and then entered hibernation in vast crypts beneath Thendrun, waiting for the day we'd meet you in battle. I number myself among them, Your Highness. I have waited six thousand years for the day of final victory.'

'You won't live to see it!' screamed Moriana. She flung forth her hands. The flames devoured the wall.

Before the hungry blue tongues reached Zak'zar, the Speaker disappeared. There was a sharp crack! as air rushed to the space he had vacated. Then the only sounds were the disappointed clucking of the flames, and the moans of wounded men.

CHAPTER FOURTEEN

'It seems we've been through this before,' Ziore remarked, looking down at the armies spread out at the foot of the bluff. Moriana had to agree. In many ways, the impending battle shaped up like the conflict at Chanobit Creek.

Vigorous interrogation of the assassins captured in the Palace revealed a plot laid by Zak'zar in collusion with the Guilds of the High Medurim – and Gyras, late advisor to Emperor Teom. The hunchback had been intercepted riding along the coast road that led to North Keep. After undergoing suitably painful torments, the dwarf was impaled as an object lesson for others.

Had Teom been with a Medurimin woman trained from birth in helplessness instead of Moriana, or had the dozen assailants infiltrating the Golden Dome not succumbed to the libidinous emanations from Erimenes's and Ziore's coupling, High Medurim would now be dominated by the Fallen Ones. Ten days after that night of lust and slaughter, Fost still had nightmares. One image in particular haunted him. Exhausted and bloodied, he had been helped back into the Golden Dome. He saw Ch'rri the winged cat woman kneeling above the body of her erstwhile lover licking the blood from her whiskers and paws. In good feline fashion, she had taken her pleasure from the lust-crazed assassin, then ripped him to pieces.

Badly shaken, Teom had named Fost a Marshal of the Emperor and given orders to march for the River Marchant. In two days, the Imperial Army issued forth from the high walls of Medurim, winding in a mile-long serpentine of trudging foot soldiers, baggage wagons and proud war dogs stepping out beneath armored riders. Temalla was left behind to cope with the administrative tangle ensuing from

328

the attempted coup. Not the least of her problems was cleaning up after rioting had broken out the night of the attack when the Watch had attempted to arrest over seven thousand Medurimin for fornicating in the streets in violation of the traffic code.

As rapid as Imperial response had been, it had not come quickly enough to prevent the Vridzish from pouring across the Marchant and laying waste to half the Black March. Like locusts the Zr'gsz devoured everything edible in their path, including human inhabitants who didn't flee in time. Unlike locusts, what they couldn't consume they put to the torch.

A hundred spires of smoke reared up into the blue sky beyond the black ant-mass of the Zr'gsz armies. For the hundredth time since the sun came up, Fost tried to estimate how many there were. For the hundredth time, he gave up when the numbers became too hopelessly huge.

'Why did Zak'zar tell us about the Children of Expectation?' Fost asked, pulling up a clump of black-tipped grass and thumping the sod around its base listlessly against his thigh.

'To seize psychological advantage,' said the short, round, bald man in the white robe. Oracle tuned himself to Moriana's mind and succeeded in projecting his image several hundred miles from High Medurim as a result. 'We already know the Hissers had greater numbers than expected. By letting us know where they came from, Zak'zar also gave us reason to fear there'd be so many we couldn't possibly win.'

Fost plucked out a blade of grass and chewed on it.

'Yes, if they've been stashing away the rising generation for thousands of years . . .' He let the sentence trail off. It was too depressing to finish.

'Well, Fost my boy,' Erimenes said avuncularly, 'see how you've come up in the world under my tutelage? You're now a bonafide hero, and Marshal of the Empire as well, with a fine suit of armor and a strapping black and white war dog.'

'Marshal of the Empire, indeed.' He spat out the grass. 'Being Marshal doesn't mean those highborn fools listen to me, much less take my orders.'

'But Foedan of Kolnith and the Border Guards heed your counsel,' Ziore said. She favored Erimenes with a wink of surprising lewdness.

'That's all well and good,' replied Fost. 'The high and mighty chivalry of High Medurim and the knights of the other City States all think

Foedan's a traitor to his class. And the Border Guards and militias of the various Marches — never mind their experience — are considered nothing more than low born dabblers in the fine art of war.'

He pointed with an armored arm.

'Behold the main strength of the Medurimin army. Fifteen thousand spearmen, every one of whom is a conscript wanting nothing more than to be somewhere else. Then there are eight thousand regulars of the Imperial Army, who look sharp in drill and who have never seen blood shed outside a barroom brawl. Then the infantry. On both wings are men who will win the day for humanity, if you care to listen to their boasts. Six thousand knights from Medurim and the City States, all of whom can be relied on to do the worst thing possible in any given circumstance. Sandwiched between are the only troops likely to do a damned bit of good, longbowmen from Samazant and Thrishnor, and there're only a scant four thousand of them.—

'But what of the Borderers and the militiamen you think so highly of?' asked Ziore.

In disgust, Fost waved at men drawn up well to the rear of the front ranks.

'Back there where they can't get in the way of the precious cavalry.'

Oracle rubbed his plump chin with fingertips. It was a mannerism he'd picked up from Fost, which unnerved the courier every time he saw it.

'Is not the reserve a good place for them?' the projection asked. Fost swallowed hard. The sunlight contrived to shine through Oracle's body.

'It may turn out that way,' Fost answered, 'if the battle isn't lost before they can come to grips with the Hissers.'

Moriana walked over and laid tender hands on his shoulders. He couldn't actually feel her hands, since his body was encased in a lobster carapace of metal, but he still appreciated the gesture. He reached up and clasped her hand to his.

'At least you're near me, love,' she said quietly.

Fost's joy at hearing those words was short-lived. The two genies had heard the words, too, and triggered off a now-common response.

'Yes, my own true love,' Erimenes said in a disgustingly honeyed voice. 'And I shall be here, not far from your side!'

Ziore batted nonexistent lashes and said, 'Never leave me again! Oh, swear you won't, my blue darling.'

'Never, so long as we both shall live, sweetums.'

'Sweetums?' Fost and Moriana cried in unison. They shared a groan. It had been like this ever since the night in the Golden Dome. Neither ghost was a stranger to lust, but with the discovery that they could at long last *do* something about that particular passion, they had fallen in love – sticky, sweet, gooey love – and had become hopelessly mired in emotion. They lapsed now entirely into unintelligible baby talk.

'Do you know,' Fost declared, 'I liked you both better when you fought all the time?'

'How could you take that seriously, Fost?' Erimenes shook his head in pity for his friend's ignorance. 'That was but gentle teasing. From the first sweet moment we met, we both knew that it was love.'

'Isn't he poetic?' Ziore sighed to no one in particular.

'No.' Fost rose and pulled on his gauntlets.

Moriana pointed to a dark form high above.

'Ch'rri's signalling,' she said. 'The *Zr'gsz* skyrafts have taken to the air.

Fost shuddered, remembering Ch'rri and her lover, her dead, dismembered lover.

'At least the damned City's not with them. Nor the Demon.' Where City and Demon were, they didn't know. Moriana was blocked from directly scrying her lost Sky City, but her perceptions did tell her that it and its resident demon floated somewhere to the southeast. It was little enough that they wouldn't have to match strength with Istu.

Yet.

'I'd best mount up,' Fost said, eyeing his war dog. He was not happy about riding into battle on the back of a dog. He managed to stay aboard one – and that was about all. But the fact remained no one in the Imperial Army took orders from any unmounted commander. Even the border men were peculiar that way.

After banging his head against the wall of noble obduracy and class pride, Fost had resigned himself from any direct role in the conduct of the battle. He knew he lacked the experience to be a field officer commanding vast armies of men, yet his choice still nagged him because few of the Imperial nobles and swaggering regular army officers had more experience than he. Fost had settled for command over Moriana's own guard, a unit of volunteers. To Moriana's surprise, the men from the Marches had joined her personal unit in large numbers, some of the veterans from the fiasco at Chanobit Creek. And even a hundred lancers from Harmis, domain of her lost lover and champion Darl Rhadaman, had joined the unit.

Moriana's unit had a vital role to play. They were to ensure that Moriana could work her magics in safety during battle. They were to keep out of the thick of fighting off on the left flank. That was fine with Fost. He had little taste for battle. Personal combat, yes, man to man, face to face. He savored that, sometimes. But not the wholesale butchery promised this day. That sickened and scared him.

A line of skyrafts appeared above the Zr'gsz army and floated silently forward. Fost swung into his saddle and waited.

Responding listlessly to the insistent notes of their officers' whistles and the lead-tipped cudgels of their sergeants, the conscript spearmen shuffled forward. The Zr'gsz moved toward them in a wedge, black massed ranks of low caste spearmen and slingers in the center. Higher caste Hissers rode giant lurching lizards on the trailing flanks. The wind shifted and brought a rank reptilian smell wafting across the Imperial lines. Dogs began an excited barking.

The first wave of skyrafts swooped toward the Medurimin ranks. Arrows sleeted down. Screams of agony and shocked surprise rose, spectrally thin at this distance. Moriana bit her lip. Her biggest concern was choosing the precise moment to use her magic. She had only so much strength and she had to marshal it against the moment of crisis, of greatest tactical need. She looked left and right along the bluffs, checking the preparations she'd made. All seemed in order, but the time for magic wasn't yet.

'It's hard to let those men die,' said Ziore quietly.

'My only consolation is knowing they trade their lives so future generations of humanity will be free of the Hissers. And Istu.'

Trying to psych his mount into believing he was both calm and in command, Fost looked to Oracle and asked, 'How're you doing?'

'Well, I think. Magister Banshau himself is overseeing the balance of nutrients in my pool.' There was a spot of light against the darkness — or Dark, as Fost thought with a thrill of horror. Despite the Hisser spear in his belly, Banshau lived and would recover. There are worse armors than several inches of flab.

The skyrafts rained down a continuous storm of arrows on the Imperial foot soldiers. Already, the ill-dressed lines began to waver, though the Medurimin had not yet come to grips with the foe.

'Poor bastards,' Fost said with feeling.

Moriana's fingers itched with the need to hurl spells, to smash the Hissers who fought from the smug safety of their skystone rafts. But she knew she had to conserve her strength.

The borderland archers had opened on the flitting rafts. The Zr'gsz craft were slower and less maneuverable than Sky City eagles. Many shafts found their marks. Small, twisting shapes began to fall among the ranks of spearmen.

Deep thrums punctuated by tocking sounds announced that the Imperial catapults had joined battle. A big skyraft suddenly slewed in air, spilling dozens of occupants to their deaths. The shot had probably been loosed by one of the crews of refugee Estil artillerists Fost had bribed away from Ortil Onsulomulo. They were superlative with their missile engines, though the Imperial crews were far from poor.

The lines of foot soldiers met. A clash of arms and clamor of voices went up. Fost thought it impressive, but Moriana found it almost anticlimactic. It was wholly unlike the rending clash with which her knights and Grassland allies had met at Chanobit.

Almost at once, the Imperial infantry began to be pushed back. Moriana's muscles started winding themselves into knots.

'Commit your cavalry, damn you!' she shouted at the enemy commander.

But the Zr'gsz general, whoever he was – Zak'zar? – was much too canny. He knew that to approach the Imperial cavalry too closely with his own mounted troops would trigger a charge. Haughtily disdainful of their border reserves, the knights would never think of charging in support of their own infantry. So the Vridzish held his mounted men back as long as possible, his infantry chopping up the footsoldiers unmolested by the knights.

'I see it,' Oracle murmured. 'If the Zr'gsz cavalry were not closing on the flanks, the knights would charge the foot soldiers. The lizard riders are bait of a sort, aren't they?'

'Of a negative sort, yes,' Fost said sourly. 'Shrewd of you to see it.' His mouth twisted. 'Shrewd of that damned serpent to think of it.'

It began as a tiny ripple along the line of conscript spearmen.

Men in the front rank turned in fear from the flashing stone-edged weapons of the Hissers. Poorly armored, they still had the advantage over the Zr'gsz, who wore none at all. But it would take men much better motivated to face the inhuman speed and ferocity of the Zr'gsz. The first rank turned and shoved back in panic on the men behind, who resisted and then sought flight themselves. In moments, the whole formation was beginning to erode like a dirt clod dropped into a fast-running stream.

A squadron of Imperial cavalry surged forward on the far right flank. Fost saw a black chalice on a white pennon at the fore and smiled grimly. Foedan led his Kolnith knights into Zr'gsz lines, knowing his fellows would have to cover him against a counter-charge of Hisser cavalry. No sooner had the Kolnithin driven deep into the body of the Vridzish foot soldiers than the Imperial knights and the Zr'gsz lizard riders charged one another.

Moriana had seen the giant lizards the Hissers rode before, sprawling green monsters with a crest of long yellow spines running down their backs. Not even she had seen them in full charge. Awesome as the full charge of the Northern heavy cavalry was, the lizards' charge was even more awesome. The whip-tailed monsters raised their bloated bodies off the ground and sprinted with legs at full extension. Six thousand dog riders met fewer than half as many Zr'gsz, but the Hissers' lizard mounts gave them the edge in height and speed. At first contact, the Imperial squadrons on the right flank reeled and fell in confusion, while on the left the Hissers were brought to a halt. As the resounding surf-boom of the collision died, the battle degenerated into swirling melee, Zr'gsz and humans hacking one another with axe, mace and sword. Triangular lizard heads darted to snap knights from their mounts and crush them in sawtoothed jaws; dogs grabbed wattled throats of the dragons and clung, tearing out huge gobbets of flesh.

'Strike!' Moriana commanded, raising her arm. For hundreds of yards along the buffs, pageboys struck padded hammers against brass gongs. The Imperial treasurer winced at the expense of gongs and ridiculed them as an extravagance. But Moriana had got her way; the gongs were the most lethal weapon.

The reverberation of hundreds of gongs filled the air, dampening even the mad tumult of battle. Moriana closed her eyes and concentrated all her energy, her being, her very soul, on modulating the booming waves of sound.

With Ziore to help draw the memory from the depths of her mind, and Oracle to analyze the memories, Moriana had been able to determine the exact pitch which the undying toad creature Ullapag had used to induce torpor and death in Zr'gsz venturing too close to the skystone mines of Omizantrim. Now she altered the voice of the gongs until they cried out in the inaudible voice of the Ullapag.

Skyrafts began skidding crazily all over the sky, scattering their passengers like a farmer scatters handfuls of seeds. The relentless advance of the Vridzish foot soldiers in the center and the lizard riders on the right stopped as if it had run into a wall. The riding dragons uttered hissing squeals of fear and fled, their senseless riders dropping from the saddles.

The rout of the Imperial center was stemmed. Even the ranks of the regulars were being disrupted by the panicking conscripts.

With the upper hand already, the left wing cavalry squadrons ran the stunned lizard riders off the field. Fost was shouting and pounding in his saddle.

'You've done it, Moriana! You've won the battle for us!'

Oracle noticed the black cloud forming above the battlefield.

'I beg your pardon, Your Highness,' he said to Moriana. Her eyes opened and glared at him. She needed every ounce of her concentration.

He pointed to the cloud. Her eyes went wide.

'Get down!' she screamed.

Fost flung himself face down on the sod. His dog bolted and smashed into a silver dome that hadn't been there seconds before. As he lay blinking, he realized the jagged purple lines of afterimage were caused by lightning. The pewter dome above flickered and went out of existence. He looked at Moriana. Her face was drawn and pale.

'I don't know if I can do that again,' she said, her voice weak.

He scanned the line of gongs – or where the line had been. Charred corpses remained behind where humans had once stood. He swallowed hard. Had it not been for Oracle's alertness and the quickness of Moriana's reactions, they would have shared the fate of those feckless pageboys.

'Why is the cloud going away?' demanded Erimenes. 'It could blast our whole army to rubble.'

'The Zr'gsz sorcerer – or sorcerers – must spend their life energies to cast spells, just as I must. They couldn't maintain the lightning cloud.' She smoothed hair back from her forehead. 'Its work was done, anyway,' she added bitterly.

The left wing's pursuit of enemy cavalry ended abruptly in disaster when the deadly vibrations ceased. The Hissers turned back on their pursuers while a living sea of footmen swamped the knights from the side. The dogs began to mill in confusion. Having lost momentum, the heavy riders were doomed. They could work destruction on their foes, but it was only a question of time before the last was dragged from his saddle and slain.

The center gave way to total flight. The Imperial ranks behind began to fall apart as the supposedly invincible regulars joined in the disorderly retreat. Behind them, the men of the border states waited, grim and firm.

When Moriana's force dome winked out, Fost's war dog had run down the face of the bluff where it was intercepted by the picket of Black March bowmen guarding the foot of the hill.

'I'll be back,' Fost promised, and began picking his way down.

Summoning her resources, Moriana began to fling forth spell after spell. None worked as well as the vibrations; that had been their best chance and she knew it. The Zr'gsz magic met her every spell and cancelled it. She felt the deadly frustration her sister must have felt during the battle for the Sky City, when the Heart of the People harmlessly absorbed her most potent magics. But one thing encouraged her. The Zr'gsz magic was all defensive. No lethal conjurations were loosed against the Imperial armies.

On the other hand, the Zr'gsz were winning without them.

'Here, Marshal,' a grinning boy said, handing Fost the reins of his dog. Fost nodded, trying to look gruff and martial.

'Thanks, son.' He hoised himself into the saddle. The skitterish beast danced and growled.

The Zr'gsz foot soldiers advanced again, harrying the routed Imperial forces. The Marchers waited tensely, weapons ready, but the Hissers didn't come their way. The green tide swept past their knoll in pursuit of fleeing foes. Fost looked that way and tried not to wince. It seemed the end of the battle wasn't far off.

His dog turned and caught sight of the enemy. Fost's dog was a finer charger, a mount fit and trained to be ridden by a knight. And like the Imperial knights, it was bred to be headstrong, ferociously brave, and as dumb as a stump.

The dog charged.

On the hill Moriana sank down sobbing as her legs gave way.

'It's no use,' she moaned. 'I can't go on!'

'Don't give up,' Ziore gently urged.

'Don't you understand? Every spell I try they counter before it's completed. It's over. I'm sorry I brought you into this.'

Hesitantly, Oracle touched her shoulder. She didn't feel it. He couldn't project a tactile illusion this far. He cleared his throat.

'If I might suggest something . . .'

'I'm telling you, I don't have any power left!' she shrieked.

'Highness,' Oracle said softly, 'that might be so, but you might be able to make them *think* you still have power. Or rather that another does.'

Moriana looked up at Oracle, the idea germinating in her brain. She slowly smiled and rose. The damned Hissers would never forget this day after she — and another — finished with them.

Fost tried valiantly to stop the animal but his lack of skill in riding betrayed him. His arms flailed wildly and it appeared that he urged on his troops. None heard his cries: 'No, you forsaken son of a bitch! No! Stop! Halt! Oh, shiiit!'

Shieldless, unhelmeted, Fost rode through the surging masses of *Zr'gsz*. He struck out in truly heroic fashion, left and right in great looping arcs, so fast his blade blurred like a hummingbird's wings. His usual berserker madness failed to take him. What gave Fost such superhuman strength was stark terror.

He swept among the reptile men. His blade lopped limbs, crushed skulls, stove in chests, and Fost did not tire. He didn't dare.

The low caste *Zr'gsz* were much less intelligent than the darker skinned nobility. They could cope well enough with normal battle situations: Find enemy, kill enemy. Nothing in their limited experience prepared them for anything like this.

The Hissers' front ranks ran up against the lines of Borderland spearmen — and recoiled. The Border Guards and militiamen from the Marches had already stood firm in the face of their own fleeing comrades. Now they met the full force of the *Zr'gsz* charge and did not yield. But off to their right the surviving wing of cavalry was being pushed back slowly. It wouldn't be long before the lizard riders overwhelmed the knights. Then they would fall on the border men like an ocean wave falling on a sand castle.

A tall noble in whipping black robe and shiny green armor turned

337

the wedge-shaped head of his riding dragon toward Fost and kicked it into a run. Still hewing frantically, Fost saw the lance drop to the horizontal. He had no shield and in the crush of reptilian bodies surrounding his dog he couldn't dodge.

He was a dead man.

He stopped the wild flailing of his arms. Immediately, fatigue turned them leaden. He gripped his sword two-handed, trying to make himself believe he had a chance to knock the lancehead aside before it skewered him. He saw the Zr'gsz grin above the rim of the shield, saw the triangular lancehead streaking toward his chest . . .

With a scream of demonic fury, the nobleman was plucked from his saddle by sudden claws seizing his head from above. His plumed helm fell away. Black blood fountained from his punctured eyes. With a drumming of wings, Ch'rri bore the Vridzish up and away. Fost swatted the riderless dragon across its scaly snout with the flat of his blade. It turned tail and ran.

From five hundred feet in the air, the body of the Zr'gsz warrior plummeted down to smash into the ground not ten feet from Fost. The Vridzish bounced once, limbs waving like a rag doll's. Then it lay still.

The low caste Hissers scattered in all directions. Fost raised his eyes to the terrible apparition hovering above his head. He saluted Ch'rri with his bloody sword. It seemed an appropriate tribute.

But Ch'rri paid him no heed. Her blue slit-pupilled eyes stared toward the north where men of the Empire made their final stand. Fost followed the gaze. He couldn't believe the sight.

Jirre had come.

Tall as the sky she strode across the hills. Her hair blazed golden and her eyes were emeralds. Her flowing robes shone green and gold. In one hand she held a lyre, in the other a sword. Beholding her, men forgot their mortal peril to drop to their knees and worship.

Jirre had come.

Jirre, named by some priests the foremost of the Three and Twenty Wise Ones of Agift, Jirre, of all the gods one of the bitterest foes of the Dark Ones.

Vridzish hissed in dread. 'The devil-goddess! She comes again!' The lower caste foot soldiers knew Jirre and hated her, as they hated all gods of Light.

Half mad with fear, the nobles and officers tried to bring their troops into a semblance of order. Clouds of arrows were loosed at the apparition. She did not deign to notice. Skyrafts drove at her, *through* her. All to no effect.

Jirre struck her lyre. A pure, sweet tone throbbed in the air. The *Zr'gsz* skyrafts crumbled to dust beneath their crew's clawed feet. She swung her sword, and the Hissers fell. They fell without mark of violence on their bodies, but fall they did up to the very feet of the hard-pressed border men.

On the hilltop, Moriana raised herself on tiptoe and held her arms high above her head. Ecstatic, she felt the power pulsing through her. She blessed Oracle for his inspiration, for the idea of the illusion of one whom the Fallen Ones dreaded above all others.

'It's working!' she cried as the *Zr'gsz* armies disintegrated below her.

Fost flung his sword down so hard it buried itself to the hilt in the soft, blood-drenched turf. He jumped off the dog's back, letting it run off to drag down any fleeing Hisser it could catch.

He stood shaking on the now stilled battlefield. The *Zr'gsz* that still lived were in full flight back toward the River Marchant. Many wouldn't stop running until both their hearts burst from exertion. The armies of the North stared into the sky at their deliverer. Teom came to the door of his great pavilion and dropped to knees before the Goddess.

'Well done, Moriana! Well *done*, girl!' Erimenes cried.

'You've beaten them,' sang Ziore.

And the apparition turned to face Moriana. The princess turned white.

'*Daughter,*' boomed Jirre. '*We love you well but never again can any of the Wise aid you in this manner. Only because you opened a pathway was I able to come. I cannot come again. But know that we will do what we can, that Night shall not claim this world again.*

'*Farewell, most-favored daughter. Know that I love you above all.*'

And Jirre was gone.

'That's what I call verisimilitude,' said Erimenes with a knowing wink. Moriana couldn't control the shaking of her hands or the cold knot in her stomach as she continued to stare into the space recently occupied by Jirre.

339

EPILOGUE

The hills and meadows of the Black March shivered with joyous celebration. The night air rang with boasts and jubilation. Many brave men had fallen but others still lived. Foedan of Kolnith was there, his huge domed head swathed in bandages. And Sir Tharvus, one of the pitiful handful surviving the catastrophic pursuit of the routed *Zr'gsz* by the cavalry on the left, sat as far from Moriana as possible, giving her poisoned glances over the rim of his goblet.

But seated at the great table of honor inside Teom's pavilion, Fost and Moriana picked at the sumptuous banquet spread before them with neither joy nor appetite.

Emperor Teom had knighted Fost where he stood in the middle of the battlefield, and the battle-weary survivors had hoisted him on their shoulders, bearing him directly to the pavilion.

Moriana arrived in much the same way. Their eyes met. An infinity of meaning flowed between them.

'Now tell me, Your Highness,' said the knight sitting at Moriana's right, 'how did you get the Lady Jirre to answer your call?'

She slammed her fist down on the table. Heads turned toward her.

'I did *not*! It was an illusion,' she said.

Disbelieving, the heads turned away and returned to light conversation or serious consumption of food and wine. Fost laid his hand on Moriana's leg and gave it a reassuring squeeze. She nodded acknowledgement without looking at him.

'Erimenes,' he heard Ziore whisper. 'You were magnificent!'

'Of course.'

Fost shut his eyes and shook his head.

At the head of the table, Teom pounded for silence with the golden pommel of a sword never drawn in anger.

340

'Silence! Let us have silence! I propose a toast!'

The noise died. He rose, resplendent in a gilded breastplate sculpted in the likeness of a muscular torso, with a robe of yellow lacebird silk thrown over his shoulders, the jewelled rings on his fingers shining with inner lights of their own. He raised his goblet.

'To the Princess Moriana,' he cried. 'Mightiest sorceress of the Realm, favored by the Lady Jirre, and . . . and . . .' His Adam's apple rode slowly up and down. Even the rouge and paint on his face failed to give him color. Tense silence gripped the revellers as all eyes followed his to the uppermost part of the pavilion.

'Greetings,' said Zak'zar, Speaker of the People. 'I foretold we would meet again, dear cousin Moriana. And so it has come to pass.' A corner of his mouth twisted. 'Not precisely as I predicted, I grant you, but this is after all no victory you've won. A petty respite, at best.'

He floated at the top of the tentpole, his body radiating a cold black light. Sputtering on a mouthful of wine, the captain of the Guard bellowed for archers.

'It will do no good. I am not here. Only my likeness. A trick your Oracle knows well.' He inclined his head toward the pale, round man beside Fost.

Fost found his voice and said, 'You're bluffing, Zak'zar. We whipped you from the March like dogs.'

Zak'zar's laugh chilled him to the bone.

'See then, friends, what *we* were doing while you were whipping dogs.'

He stretched forth his hand. A globe of intense blackness formed. A point of light danced in the middle, expanded to become a picture. The City in the Sky floated over the slate roofs and boxy pastel structures of Kara-Est.

Fost wondered why he was showing them the conquest of the seaport by the floating City; this was old news. Then he realized no eagles winged over the City and saw the strange blackness that filled the Well of Winds in the center of the City.

A black vortex extended downward from the Skywell. Where it touched, stones, people, entire buildings were uprooted and drawn upward into the blackness where they . . . disappeared.

'Istu!' The name ran through the tent.

'Istu,' Zak'zar agreed. 'Do you see what the great victory you won today signifies, Pale Ones? Do you, my cousin?'

Moriana wouldn't look at him. Her eyes were fixed on her plate, her face hidden by her golden hair.

'Why do you name her "cousin," you wretched creature?' Ziore shrieked at him.

Counterfeit surprise crossed Zak'zar's face.

'Why shouldn't I call her that, good Ziore? Surely, you cannot object if I call my blood kin by their right name?'

'You lie!' Fost screamed as he came to his feet.

'Ah, poor Fost,' Zak'zar said, a sad chuckle escaping his throat. 'Do you truly think you can change the truth by denying it?' He raised his head to address them all. 'Know you the truth: nine thousand years ago an Athalar-trained adept came to Thendrun to receive the secret of true magic, not the petty mental tricks which the Athalar knew how to play.'

Erimenes sputtered in outrage.

'Azrak-Tchan, Second Instrumentality of the People, gave her the secret of true magic, which is the providence of the Dark. He also gave her a child.' Heads swung toward Moriana.

'This Moriana, surnamed Etuul, received great powers. But it was her daughter Kyrun, half human and half Zr'gsz, who possessed them in full measure. She aided Riomar shai-Gallri, accursed traitress, in casting my folk from the Sky City. So the blood of the People entered the Etuul line. And it has been passed down from that day to this. And renewed, perhaps, by the late Instrumentality Khirshagk, blessed be his name.'

'He's dead?' demanded Moriana, looking up sharply.

'He is. He delivered Istu from bondage and fulfilled the role for which every Instrumentality had trained.'

'You're lying, you filthy scum, lying!' Fost screamed, shaking his fists at the Hisser.

'Am I?' Zak'zar asked softly. 'Moriana does not deny it.

'I hope you will find some measure of happiness, all of you, in the time you have left before we come for you with He Who Will Not be Denied. Farewell to you all. And to you, cousin.' He folded taloned hands across his breast and faded.

Moriana sat in a silence and isolation unlike any she had ever known.

BOOK THREE
Demon of the Dark Ones

CHAPTER ONE

The man was a sadist, a killer, a eunuch. He was also a genius. But now Prince Rann Etuul gave little indication of those traits. He wore a plain robe that covered him from neck to ankles and made him appear to be little more than a hermit. The only outward signs that this man was different lay in the coldness of his tawny eyes and the network of fine scars glowing on his face where the light from the dying sun touched him.

He leaned forward, hands on a dilapidated table covered with maps, and stared out to the west. His mind worked methodically, savoring the sunset and the coolness and varied scents blowing in from the Gulf of Veluz. The songs of cinnamon birds and the evening lark mingled and vied for his attention over the cries of vendors in the city streets eastward and below his vantage point in the Hills of Cholon. He watched the western sky with little appreciation for the beauty of a vivid sunset. His mind was focused on a demon.

The Demon of the Dark Ones.

Rann tensed at the sight of a mote floating among clouds touched with the colors of gods. At first a spark less bright than the evening star, it grew and became cruciform. Growing still more, underwings burning with the reflected glory of the now hidden sun, it took on detail.

Thunder sounded. With a loud scrabbling of claws, the war eagle found a perch on the sill jutting from Rann's window. The window, like the others in the former Ducal Palace of Kara-Est, had been built in such a fashion that the opening was too small to admit the war bird, twice as tall as a man. Even the rider, small and lithe like most Skyborn, had to duck to pass through the opening before dropping to the stone floor. The eagle's rider dismissed the mount, leaving it to find supper and a roost in the aerie the fugitives of the City in the Sky had constructed in a lesser tower of the Palace.

The rider turned to face Rann. Her hair hung lank about a face high of cheekbone and narrow of chin. Under the grime and exhaustion masking her slightly foxlike features, she might have been attractive. Her hair was a lusterless tangled brown giving only hints of its possible beauty when cleaned. She carried a bow and quiver, and circling her left biceps was the gold brassard of the elite Sky Guard.

'Sublieutenant Tanith,' Rann greeted her. His voice rang out like the pealing of a silver bell. When he desired, his tone increased the terror he inspired. He gestured toward a wrought-iron stand holding a large ceramic bottle and a goblet similar to the one he held. 'Drink, if you like.'

'I'm on duty, sir,' the Guardswoman said instinctively, her voice hoarse with dryness. Rann merely looked at her. He was not above tricking the members of the Guard into infractions of discipline. But in a moment of reflection, the sublieutenant realized such behavior belonged elsewhere, in the City in the Sky now lost to the Demon. Too few of the Skyborn had survived in the Demon's onslaught or the reptilian Hissers' vengeance for Rann to further reduce their numbers over petty crimes againt corps discipline.

'Thank you, lord,' she said, pouring the wine.

He permitted her to refill his cup. She drained hers at a single swallow, then quickly filled her cup again. Rann watched without comment. The mellow ale was not that heady, and her farings would have given her a great thirst.

'What have you learned?' he asked when she had lubricated her throat sufficiently to speak in a natural voice free of dry croakings.

'The City approaches, milord, even as you said it would.'

'How far is it?'

'It should come into view sometime before dawn of the day after tomorrow. We could launch an eagle strike against it tomorrow.' Her voice rose in hope that Rann would order such an attack. The Sky Guard had been shamed by the loss of their City. Tanith was like the other survivors who wanted nothing more than to redeem themselves and feel as if they were *doing* something to recoup their intolerable loss.

'And what did you see in the Sky City?' he asked, choosing to overlook her eager recommendation.

'The Hissers are at work, lord. They've completed the destruction they began the day . . . the day they cast us out. They build now. Defensive works, missile engines, and some construction that seems of no military purpose.'

Gripping his left wrist with his right hand, Rann nodded above the rim of his goblet. He understood, or thought he did. No sooner had they turned on their human ally Moriana and the forces of her sister Synalon that earlier had been their common foe, than the *Zr'gsz* had set about erasing any hint of the nine-thousand-year occupancy of the humans who had supplanted them, the original builders of the City in the Sky. That done, it was obviously important to set their mark anew upon their recaptured prize to prepare to defend it.

Or to prepare to reassert their dominion over a continent. And eventually an entire world.

'The Demon,' Rann almost hissed, leaning forward, his eyes gleaming in the last glow of twilight. 'Did you see Istu?'

'My lord, I . . . I do not know.' Tanith averted her eyes and bit her lower lip in consternation. For a heartstopping instant, she thought he would reach across the table and seize her by the throat, shaking her the way a terrier killed a rat.

'What do you mean you don't know?' Rann's voice was calm, level, deadly. Tanith now feared it more than if he had shouted.

'I saw Istu the day he was released, milord, as you did. A black shape towering in the sky like a doorway into darkness, his body like a man's but with horns set on either side of his skull. His eyes were slits of yellow fire.' She shuddered at the memory. Better to face a hundred swordsmen than to even think about the Demon. 'Like the Vicar of Istu, lord.'

'That statue is his likeness. Now, I ask you again, did you *see* him?'

'Perhaps I did,' she said, and met his polar stare. She managed to suppress another shudder. 'But if so, he did not wear the same shape.'

Breaking the bond of their locked gaze, Rann wheeled.

'Explain!' he snapped.

'I saw no such towering dark being as walked through the streets of the City . . . that day. But the Skywell is filled with a blackness, lord, a rounded blackness that gleams like a giant black lens. I've not seen anything like it before. I thought it might be some

347

manifestation of the Demon.'

'The Black Lens.' A look of stark pain flitted across Rann's ruined features. 'One of the last tricks Istu concocted before Felarod bound him. And we must face it at the outset of this War of Powers.'

He turned to her. Her eyes were wide above dark fatigue hollows. Rumors had flown among the ragged refugees streaming to Kara-Est and Bilsinx from the Sky City and the fury of its returned builders that a second War of Powers lay at hand. She had tended to dismiss such saying as idle gossip.

The scarred lips of Prince Rann confirmed those rumors of truth.

'And skyrafts, Sublieutenant. Did you see any?'

'Few, lord. Ten or a dozen flew around or beside the City, but no more than that. We were observed, I think, but none pursued us.' Her teeth showed bright in the twilight dimness of the room. 'They've learned that lesson, at least!'

Rann waved his hand. The dearth of skyrafts mystified him, but it was only a minor mystery. The reptiles holding the City might have dispatched their fleets elsewhere for some arcane mission. A few sharp skirmishes since the day the City was conquered had demonstrated that, without magical aid, the skystone craft the Hissers rode couldn't survive long in the sky against the eagles of the bird riders. It was a trivial fact. The real enemy was the Demon of the Dark Ones. Against him the might and speed of the war eagles were little more than a sparrow smashing senseless into a stone wall.

Rann chose not to tell the officer of the insignificance of the superiority to which she had alluded with such feral delight. He did not play his torment games with his own soldiers. Not now, not when so few remained. As spurious as it was, he would let her revel in the superiority of eagle over skyraft. All humans needed what comfort they could find now.

He sipped the ale. His cheek muscles contracted to give him a slight squint.

'The others remain to shadow the City?' he asked.

'Yes, lord. Four of us alternate resting on the ground and following the City. We've had luck in the form of clouds to hide in.' She shrank again from her own cup. 'But still, I think they know they're being watched.'

Rann nodded. That was one of the disadvantages of aerial observation. As a general rule, if you can see your foe, he could also see you. But this, too, meant little. Such was the strength of the reptilian Vridzish that they didn't care if they were spied upon or not. They now held the City – and had freed it from its once-set course over the center of the Sundered Realm. Using this immense aerial rock raft as their base, they could now travel at will and lay siege to even the most heavily defended cities.

'Well done, Sublieutenant Tanith. Go below and get some food and rest. You've earned them.'

She paused beneath the doorway arch and asked, 'Do we strike them tomorrow, lord? Or wait till they come to us?' In the dusk, her eyes shone with their own inner light.

'I shall take your suggestions under advisement, Sublieutenant. I assure you I'll undertake no weighty strategic decision without first consulting you.' Feeling the lash of his irony, the officer turned and fled.

He listened to her heels tackhammering down the stairs. He had been harsh with her. That struck him as an ill omen. He usually controlled himself with far more precision. His skill in inflicting hurt led naturally to his knowing how not to inflict it, and when not to. This had been one of those occasions.

He shook his head and poured more ale. He was losing his grip in obvious ways. It was a new problem for him, more alien than the ways of the reptilian *Zr'gsz*. Though he knew how to manipulate that problem to maximize the despair and suffering of others, he didn't know how to cope when it came to haunt him.

Prince Rann knew fear. Great fear, overwhelming fear, for the first time in his life.

Her fear almost as tangible as the perfume of the two burly youths standing behind her, Governor Parel Tonsho fumbled at the door of her apartments, the brass key clicking against the lockplate as her fingers jumped and jittered. To cover fear and clumsiness alike, she cursed the smoky yellow glare of the oil lamps set in alcoves along the hall. If either of the youths realized that her difficulty had any cause but the dimness of the corridor, neither spoke the thought aloud. One did not maintain a much sought after position in the Governor's harem by being quick to find fault.

The key finally slid home with a thin screeching. Tumblers clicked and the door opened. She cast a quick look up and down the hallway before pushing into the darkened chamber beyond. Her pretty-boys were skilled with swords, but if the doom she'd feared so long had decided to overtake her now on the eve of battle, neither these two nor an army like them would help her in the lèast.

Then she was in the foyer, her heart hammering, as though she'd escaped a stalking, half-seen menace. A lamp flared in the room. With an odd relief she saw the small, neat figure sitting at ease in a fur-draped chair, hand raised to turn up the lamp even more. The long-awaited doom had come and, in coming, removed all fear of the waiting.

The door closed softly behind her. She sensed that neither of her kept youths had entered.

'I suppose,' she said bitterly, 'it would do me little good to call for help.' ·

Prince Rann smiled the lazy smile of a cat that has awakened to find a mouse creeping across an expanse of open floor.

'Does it surprise you that your playmates are in my employ?'

'No.' Her lumpy body sagged against a cool, plastered wall. Her pitbull eyes closed to weary slits. 'Not really.'

'Come in and sit down, milady Governor. Join me in a glass of this excellent Jorean Chablis. I find it vastly more palatable than that turpentine you Estil squeeze for yourselves.' He gestured at a square bottle cut from blue glass bearing the wax seal of a renowned Jorean vintner.

Knowing the hopelessness of her situation, she saw nothing else to do but comply. The soul of graciousness, Rann poured full the crystal cup he had set out on the stand at his elbow, rose, handed her the glass, then eased back into the chair.

The thick furs strewn across the floor clutched at her feet as she walked to the divan opposite Rann. Cushions sighed protest as she dropped listlessly, spilling drops of white wine down the front of her purple silk tunic.

Reflexively, she took the glass in both hands and gulped the wine, needing the warmth and reassurance of its alcohol more than the sweetish taste.

'You've done well for yourself under the aegis of the City in the Sky, Governor.' Rann's eyes, cat-yellow in the light, appraised her over the sparkling arc of his glass. 'You've already accumulated a Tolvirot banker's ransom worth of new furs and silken cushions to replace those spoiled during the late, uh, unpleasantness. And by the diligent scrubbings of your servants and application of incense, you've almost managed to eliminate the smell of the blood that was spattered so liberally throughout these quarters.'

At his words she twisted at her necklace of tiny seashells so violently that the strong silk thread snapped. The shells clattered to the floor in a pink and yellow rain.

'We have even provided you with a new seraglio to replace the one Colonel Enn found necessary to have shot down in this very room. And you still possess one of the finest cellars in all the Sundered Realm.' He hoisted his glass in salute, drained it, swirled the wine across his palate for a long moment before swallowing. 'No, all in all, the yoke of the City has lain lightly on your shoulders, Governor Tonsho. This you must admit. And in my turn, I admit that none other could have done as splendid a job administering the recovery of your city. You have amply earned both the rewards we your conquerors have lavished on you, and –' He leaned forward, eyes hardening, brightening. '– and the confidence we put in you.'

Knowing the hopelessness of her position, she dashed her glass into fragments on the marble floor at his feet.

'Enough of this fencing. You know what I've done, damn you. Isn't that why you're here?' Her puffy face twisted in a sneer. 'Since we're both admitting so much tonight, let's get it all out into plain sight.'

He laughed.

'Ah, my good Governor. Of course I knew who employed those assassins in Bilsinx. Trying to assassinate me before we attacked Kara-Est was a clever move. Had I been in your position, I'd have done much the same myself.' He sipped wine. 'By the way, you'll be pleased to know that the young mage who saved me recovered not only from the trauma he suffered when the magical communications geode to which he was tuned shattered over the killer's head, but that he also escaped the massacre in the City.'

As he spoke, a spark appeared in Tonsho's almost colorless eyes. She ran her hand repeatedly through her frizzy, graying hair. Rann smiled. She was allowing herself to hope.

'Or do you refer to the team of assassins you sent off for to Tolviroth Acerte, when you'd learned I'd be coming to Kara-Est after we were forced from the City? I'm afraid they won't be carrying out their mission. We intercepted them at the dock.' He dropped a hand to his sword belt and toyed with something thrust between leather and tunic. 'You were better advised to go with Medurimin fighting masters, as you did the first time. The Brethren of Assassins are much overrated, I fear.'

Parel Tonsho hadn't risen to Chief of the Chamber of Deputies and de facto ruler of the richest seaport in the Realm by being slow witted. But it still took several seconds for the portent of Rann's statement to penetrate her numbed mind. She uttered a strangled sob and covered her face with chubby hands. He had learned all.

He sat quietly drinking as she wept. Soon, the ragged rhythm of her sobs faltered, broke. She raised a tear-wet face to his, jaw quivering with the effort it took to defy him.

'Did you bring that for me?' she asked, gesturing at the object he toyed with. 'Do you plan to tranquilize me, to make it easier to carry me to your torture chambers? Or does the tip carry some terrible poison that will give me a lingering, painful death?'

He raised an eyebrow.

'This?' He took his hand away from the object. Briefly, Tonsho wondered that she hadn't remarked on it before. It was a hand dart used by the savage tribesfolk of the Thail Mountains, a bit over a handspan in length, carved from yellow wood, fletched at one end with yellow bird feathers. The tip was weighted with a ring of stone strapped to the shaft by strips of cured human skin. From the tip jutted a stiff black spine. It was incongruous for Rann to carry such an artifact; one similar had been used on him by the Thailant savages to drug and capture him. Before a band of his bird riders could rescue him, the prince's genitals had been burned away by the tribal leman.

'No,' said Rann softly, shaking his head. 'It's not for you. It's for an experiment.'

She forced her upper lip to curl into a sneer.

'Whatever you'll do to me, you'd best start now. You'll need most of tonight to make final preparations to oppose the new inhabitants of the Sky City.'

'You surprise me, Tonsho, you really do. I know how you dread the very thought of pain. And for that very reason I have come to personify all you fear most. It was, I grant, a factor in choosing you as Governor of Kara-Est. I judged that your fear would keep you in line. Yet you dared hire assassins a second time, knowing they would fail.' He touched the glass to his lips. 'That took spirit, Tonsho. I always judged you had great moral strength, but I didn't judge it could overcome your physical cowardice.'

'I had to do something.' She almost spat the words. 'You hold my people in bondage.'

'And how, as well,' he said quietly. She shrank back, seeking shelter among the velvet cushions. Her flesh crawled as she considered the way she had just spoken to Rann, whose pleasure was the pain of others, whose face was her most familiar nightmare, whose elegant hand held her fate like a palmful of sand. He had her in a horror as excruciating as any physical torment; and he took no notice.

'As for preparing for the city's defense,' he went on in a soft voice, 'there is to be none.'

She stared blankly.

'That's what I came to tell you. Get out. There won't be a Sky Citizen inside the walls of Kara-Est by the time the sun rises over Dyla. Kara-Est is doomed. For us to defend your city against Istu is to lose precious men. We can ill afford more losses.'

'But Synalon! She's a mighty sorceress! I've not forgotten how she summoned the greatest air elemental seen to smash our ships and how, against all nature, she brought forth a salamander and forced it to cast itself into the waterspout. Can't she use those magics against the City and the Demon?'

Rann threw back his head and laughed. To one who knew him better than Tonsho — who knew him only as a nightmare figure — it was a strident, rare sound. She merely winced. To her, Rann's laughter was a thing to fear.

'Synalon *is* a mighty sorceress,' he said when he had recovered himself, 'but her sister defeated her in a duel of magics. And that same day Istu cast Moriana from the City like a man puts out a tomcat at night.'

Her eyes narrowed until only wet yellow gleams of reflected lamplight showed beween the lids.

'Why do you tell me this?'

He leaned forward. Had this been anyone but the devil Rann, Tonsho would have said he had a look of . . . desperation.

'You are able. You took a crushed, conquered city and made it a functioning seaport again in a matter of weeks. You've a rare gift. In the days to come, humanity will need all such gifts it can muster, if we're to have the slightest chance of survival.'

To her amazement, she laughed in his face.

'What do you care for humankind?'

'More than you might think, milady Governor.' His smile thinned. 'More than for the damned *Zr'gsz*, at any rate.'

'No, no, I can't believe this,' she moaned, grasping her temples with both hands and rocking back and forth. 'It's a trick.' She raised her pallid face, fear and uncertainty etched in the flesh. 'That's it! You trick me into abandoning my post so you'll have an excuse to put me to death.'

'If I wished to put you to death, do you think I'd need an excuse?' He was becoming exasperated. Only rarely did he argue. 'Or if I desired you removed from office, that I'd go to such lengths to manufacture one? Tonsho, all I'd need to do is spread the word that you had been negotiating with the Wildermen of Dyla to deliver your city to them. You'd soon be writhing at the post out in the Plaza, with the sorry collection of marionettes we've set to playing Deputies standing by bobbing their heads and applauding my wisdom and justice.'

He saw that he fought futilely against her adamantine fears. Such sorry stuff as reason would not dispel her image of him any more than Synalon's magic could turn the wrath of Istu away from Kara-Est. He stood, smoothing wrinkles in his midnight blue trousers.

'Good evening, Governor Tonsho,' he said.

'Highness.' He stopped. 'Now that you've failed to work your trickery on me, where do you go?' She all but giggled the words, giddy at her escape from pain and her imagined triumph over the wily prince.

'I've an appointment with Her Majesty to discuss tomorrow's events. I plan to tell her exactly what I told you. Perhaps she'll find it less amusing.' He bowed. 'I do hope your wit serves you equally well with Istu. Goodbye.'

'Do you jest, Rann?' Synalon spun from the window and faced him squarely. 'Evacuate?' She laughed, the sound evilly clinging to the very stone of the walls.

Standing by the door, Rann absently eyed the alabaster curve of her throat. Tonight the princess had arranged her hair in two raven wings standing upward and out from the sides of her head. On a woman with less beauty or presence — or less power held in dubious check — it would have looked ridiculous. On Synalon it stirred both lust and dread. Her slender body was wrapped in a gown of some gauzy stuff, more diaphanous than translucent, that showed the pink points of her nipples and the trim dark thatch between her thighs. Rann's tawny eyes, drifting downward now and again against his will, could almost pick out the fine tracery of blue veins on the flawless, milky skin, of breasts, belly, well-shaped legs. He knew she had dressed in this manner solely for him. Such was the game they played.

The black-haired enchantress stopped laughing and gave him a cool, appraising look.

'Come, Prince. Tell me what you really intend. How shall we face this menace?'

He grimaced, as if she had made to strike him.

'I wasn't joking, Your Majesty.' On arriving in Kara-Est after the flight across the Quincunx lands, Synalon had resumed the title of queen, though of what she had failed to specify. From his unique position, Rann generally disdained to give her that title and addressed her as Highness. But now much rode on her good favor. If he could get it by feeding her vanity, he would do so.

'We are prepared for defense,' she said tolerantly. 'We have walls against ground attack, and our eagles fighting beside the Estil gasbags and rooftop engines will make short work of the skyrafts used by the stinking Hissers.'

'Very well. The Vridzish we may defeat. But not Istu.'

'No?' A frown clouded her fine features. 'I have meditated much since we were driven from my City. I have some new tricks, half-man.'

Ignoring the jibe, he shook his head and replied, 'Moriana defeated you, and she couldn't best Istu. Moreover, Istu had just awakened when she faced him. He had yet to come to his full power.' He slapped his gloves across the palm of his left hand. 'No, Your Majesty. If your sister could not defeat Istu, neither can you. We have no chance of defeating the Fallen Ones.'

'But my own powers . . .'

'How much of the powers you've come by of late have been through the dispensation of the Dark Ones? I doubt they will allow you to muster strengths which they have lent you against their sole begotten son.'

She folded her arms. Mad blue sparks danced in her eyes and crackled in the roots of her dark hair.

'Would you have us skulk away in the night then, cousin? Come, I thought you were a man in spirit, if not in flesh.'

The scars at eyes and mouth turned white with strain.

'We would only throw our lives away.'

'What of it?' she demanded, head held high. Blue flames raced along the wings of her hair. 'If it's our lot to go down to defeat before these inhuman scum, then we shall die fighting, as befits the Skyborn! Let the groundlings flee, if they wish.'

'While we live there's always a chance of finding some way to win,' Rann said doggedly. 'Felarod did, after all.'

'Damn Felarod!' she spat. 'That creature!' As a devotee of the Dark, Synalon had always despised the man who had undone the Lords of Infinite Night before.

'His enemies are now our own, cousin,' Rann pointed out. 'But if you hold him in such contempt, why not seek a way to do him one better?'

She smiled and turned away, the gown swirling like mist around her long, sleek legs. Below her spread the glimmers of the seaport city, red torches, yellow lamps, green lanterns bobbing at the corners of ships out in the harbor. Somewhere in the distance a dog barked. The wind had veered to come up from the fens with the thick, moist breath of corruption riding on it. She drew it in like a fine perfume.

'Maybe I will. Moriana was a weakling at heart. She let me live when I lay naked and powerless against her. I am steel at the center, not mush. If Istu would pit his will against my own, it may be the Demon who is surprised.' Her words glowed with hatred. The Demon's progenitors had used her for their devious ends and cast her aside. Her pride still smarted over the injustice. Had a human injured her pride, death would have been painful and long. So fierce was her rage that she would forge from it a weapon fit to wound even the Lords of the Void.

Rann sighed. Like Tonsho, Synalon was a genius in her own way. He had to grant both women that. But he had long ago learned the sad lesson that not all of genius were stable.

'Is that your answer?' he asked, his voice as soft as wind among swamp reeds.

'Yes.' She spoke without turning. 'We fight.'

The corners of his mouth drew up in an expression that wasn't a smile. His left hand dropped to his left boot-top, withdrew the yellow dart which Tonsho thought he'd brought for her. His hand whipped up.

The dart blurred across the room. Wary as a unicorn stag stalking a hunter, Synalon had half spun when the missile thunked home in soft, white flesh between her ribs. Red blossomed like an insane flower against her skin's pallor.

Both Rann and the Thailint poison were quick acting, but neither was fast enough. Rann's face twisted in agony as blue-white lightning lashed from Synalon's fingers and bathed his right side in flame. They fell together.

The doors burst open. Young Cerestan of the Guard stood there, eyes wild and hair awry, curved blade in his hand. He saw the royal cousins sprawled on the floor a few paces apart and gasped. The Guards crowding in at his back stopped and looked in horror.

But both forms refused to remain still. Synalon lay on her back, arms outflung, closed eyes turned to the vaulted ceiling, her entire body spasming. Rann, his jacket and tunic smouldering, painfully hoisted himself from the limestone floor.

'It is done.' The words fell from Rann's lips in jagged fragments. 'Cerestan, see that the evacuation continues. We must be away from here before . . .'

Strength left him. He fell face-down on the cold stone.

CHAPTER TWO

'I know little of practical magic but have read much of the theory in books,' the small, round man said. 'But from what I do know, yes, it could have been an illusion and nothing more.'

Fost Longstrider leaned back in his chair, fingering his chin thoughtfully. The appearance of the goddess Jirre at such an opportune time at the Battle of the Black March troubled him. Moriana Etuul was a great sorceress, yes, but she had been physically and emotionally drained by the *Zr'gsz* magic and was hardly able to fling a small lightning bolt, much less maintain a greater than life-sized illusion. The battle had been ill-conceived due to the bickering between the various factions comprising the army, and Fost was still more than a little surprised at the victory against the superior army of reptiles. His eyes narrowed. He didn't have to ask Oracle the question. The being – the projected image – read it from his mind.

'It seems to me,' the image of the little man went on, 'that an illusion properly cast, especially by one who'd never performed such a spell – and the Princess Moriana had not – might befuddle the caster as well as its intended objects. So, assuming that the apparition of the goddess Jirre was no more than it seemed, it still might have served to uncover untapped reserves of power within Moriana. Focusing that power might account for the destruction of the *Zr'gsz* skyrafts when the apparition struck its lyre. The way the Hissers died when she swept through them can be attributed to suggestion. But as you pointed out, it stretches credibility beyond the breaking point to speculate that the rafts themselves possessed some consciousness for the illusion to play upon. I,' said Oracle firmly, 'therefore conjecture Moriana has unsuspected powers that caused the craft to disintegrate.'

Oracle possessed much of the knowledge stored in the great Library of High Medurim and shared it willingly with Fost. The real body of the entity called Oracle lay in the next room. It was nothing more than a gleaming blue-white mound of fungus the size of a peasant's hut. The nutrient vat in which it rested bubbled and reeked like garlic, but this didn't stop the legion of savants whose droning penetrated the wall in a beehive buzz as they read aloud from ancient volumes. The more they read, the more Oracle absorbed into its consciousness, and the more information it could integrate, evaluate and pass along to Fost.

The living, thinking, reasoning fungus was a triumph of genetic magics commissioned by the Emperor Teom.

In spite of Oracle's logic, something nudged at the former Realm-road courier's mind. Oracle had learned much in its short existence. Perhaps too much from Emperor Teom and his sister-wife Temalla when it came to subterfuge and intrigue. Fost felt that Oracle held something back, but the illusion of a pudgy, self-content man sitting cross-legged beside him was unreadable.

'You're being less than candid,' Fost accused. 'That body of yours is no more than an illusion, yet you are able to cast it all the way to the Black March to view the battle. I'd say that shows more than theoretical acquaintance with magic.'

The pale eyes slid from his gray ones.

'There's magic and magic, my young friend, and —'

'Young?' Fost snorted. 'With all due respect, I'm not as young as you, who were first cultured in the vat a scant three years ago. And as for magic, I'm one who truly knows little of it, but I do know the kinds. There's extrinsic magic, the ability to manipulate powers like elementals and lesser demons, which was passed to the Etuul bloodline by the Hissers back in the days before the reptiles were driven from the Sky City. And there's intrinsic magic – Athalar art – springing from the powers of the magician's own mind. Moriana's hardships on the slopes of Mt. Omizantrim honed her intrinsic powers to the point where she was able to best Synalon's largely extrinsic magic. Befuddling minds so only illusion is perceived is clearly intrinsic magic – and happens to be exactly what you're doing to me, you charlatan.'

Oracle spread his hands and smiled.

'No evading the question,' Fost pressed. 'Was the apparition of the goddess Jirre simply illusion – or something more?'

359

The cheerful mask dropped from Oracle's face. He hesitated, and his eyes seemed to probe Fost's very soul.

'Are you sure you want the answer to that, my friend?' he asked in a soft voice.

'Uh, no, maybe I don't.' Fost licked dry lips. He had thought he needed the answer. Now he wasn't so sure of himself. Moriana had learned much during her stay in the Hisser's city of Thendrun. Some of her own new-found knowledge struck him as truly alien, a thing better suited to the reptilian than the human. And if she had somehow accomplished the impossible feat of actually summoning a goddess to do her bidding, she ranked as the most powerful mage in all of history.

'You fear the gods, don't you?' Oracle asked after a long silence.

'I fear the fact of their existence. No, not even that. I dread living in a world that's a battleground for forces beyond it. If the Dark Ones exist, and the Three and Twenty Wise Ones of Agift, too, fine. That's no concern of mine. But if they choose to settle their differences on this little mudball wrapped in a blanket of air where I live . . .' He shuddered at the magnitude of it all. Sometimes it was difficult enough dealing with human royalty. This transcended petty, bickering humanity and opened the Universe to unknowable dealings. 'I don't know if I can bear the thought of being no more than a pawn in a cosmic chess game.'

Oracle's face mirrored the pain Fost felt.

'You must bear it, my friend,' he said quietly. 'Istu is loose again, and a Second War of Powers is already being fought. Whether you like it or not, you are one of the principles.'

In moody silence, Fost sat and remembered. The Battle of the Black March had been swung from defeat to victory for humanity by the startling, unexpected apparition hundreds of feet tall that may or may not have been the goddess Jirre herself. After Fost had talked himself into believing it only an illusion, the image of Zak'zar, the Speaker of the People, had appeared at the victory feast in Emperor Teom's pavilion.

The *Zr'gsz* leader had destroyed the triumphant mood with twin revelations. Humankind had won a feeble victory; the Sky City carrying the Demon of the Dark Ones easily conquered the great city of Kara-Est. Even more unsettling for Fost was the shattering indictment of his lover, Moriana Etuul. Zak'zar revealed that Moriana had lain with one of the Hissers to seal her alliance with the

People, and that she, and all of the Etuul bloodline, were descended from another human-reptile union nine thousand years earlier.

Fost's walls of self-assurance had slumped into ruin. He had endured so much, and now he was forced to withstand even more. It wasn't enough that Moriana had once killed him, driving her dagger deep into his back. Athalau, the city buried in the glacier beyond the Rampart Mountains, held many objects of magical lore; one of them, the Amulet of Living Flame, had restored his life. And Fost had followed Moriana, not for revenge but for love. Her act had been one of patriotism and idealism directed toward saving her precious Sky City from Synalon's demented rule. Fost could even admire Moriana for her devotion to her subjects, though his hand unconsciously went to the spot where the dagger had been driven into his body. He had endured all that and more until this moment.

Now he hardly knew what to believe.

With a sardonic bow, Zak'zar's image had winked out, leaving Moriana alone in a sea of silence. Fost had wanted to go to her, to comfort her, yet found himself stunned and immobile. She had left the tent and gone into the night. Fost had been sure he would never see her again. But the next day just after dawn, Moriana had returned to the encampment of the Imperial armies, obviously distraught but forcing herself into composure. She bore up well under the hostile gazes and proved herself truly regal by her demeanor.

Seeing her again had washed away some of the misgivings Fost had. He loved her; what matter that she was not altogether human. As Erimenes the Ethical, an Athalau ghost bottled for fourteen hundred years, had pointed out, the Zr'gsz blood was diluted by several hundred generations. The philosopher's spirit, usually acerbic and argumentive, had mellowed considerably since Fost had first come upon him. No longer did Erimenes seek out the vicarious thrill of bloodshed and voyeuristic sex. His contact with another Athalar spirit, the nun Ziore, had caused Erimenes to temper his behavior greatly. For that Fost was thankful. Dealing with the emotion-twisting knowledge of Moriana's heritage was problem enough for him at the moment.

About her liaison with the Hisser to complete their military aid pact, Fost discovered it meant little to him. He knew she had had other lovers when they were apart. He himself had stayed far from celibate while tracking her across the continent; what was one more

361

lover between them? If one of Moriana's lovers wasn't human, he was more nearly so than the hornbulls Moriana's sister had imported for her own wayward pleasures, on the advice of the ever-helpful Erimenes.

'Tell me of the gods, Oracle,' Fost asked abruptly.

The small man smiled.

'You wish a discourse on theology?'

'No, but I think I'd better have one just the same.'

Oracle sat for a moment, rocking back and forth. Outside, the afternoon sun had sent the residents of High Medurim scurrying to shelter to escape the glare of heat. Here in the marble precincts of the Palace it was cool, and a stick of incense smouldered in a corner of the cubicle taking the sting from the smell of Oracle's nutrient pool next door. Fost's eyelids turned heavy in spite of the coolness. He and Moriana had arrived only the day before, a long and dusty ride on the heels of arduous battle. Emperor Teom had reckoned the menace on the frontier serious enough for his personal attention, but with that settled and the Zr'gsz massacred, he had felt the precarious civil unrest in his capital called for a prompt return. This resulted in little time for rest for any of them.

The humming of the savants next door had a soporific effect, too. Fost found himself trying to follow their sing-song reading, their education of Oracle.

'To theology,' said Oracle. 'Best begin with the Dark Ones, since everything does begin with them. No, don't shudder.' He shut his eyes and spoke in a low, rhythmic voice like an incantation. 'In the beginning was the Dark, single and undivided, holy. And the Masters dwelt within darkness and nothingness and all was at peace, for all was One, and this was the blessed rule of Law.

'Then Perfect Dark was disturbed by Light, and the Oneness became Two. And the Masters of the Void set to destroy this defilement. But a mistake occurred, even then indicating Perfection had been lost. The Light was not destroyed; it was dispersed. Bits of Light were scattered across the face of the Dark. And some cooled and became Matter, and some of these specks of filth began to quiver with Life, the ultimate perversion. And so was Chaos born.

'And it came to pass that Gods rose up in opposition to the Dark, Gods favoring Light and Matter. First one, then two, then many; and so the efforts of the Masters to return all things to Unity were thwarted by the accursed, the Lords of Light and Chaos. Many were

362

their numbers, and their names were legion.

'But the Masters of the Void, who do not suffer their names or numbers to be known, gave their only begotten son to the Universe, that it might one day be returned to the rule of Law and Darkness, and the great struggle was commenced.'

Oracle paused, took a deep breath he hardly required, then opened his eyes.

'This was taken from the preamble to *Gospels of Darkness*. The Library has translations going back to the First Migration. It is one of the most ancient of texts. I take it you've not seen or heard this before?'

Despite the coolness, drops of sweat stood out on Fost's forehead.

'No, I've never come across that.'

'It's peculiar, given your lust for knowledge, that you've shied away from the subject of religion,' said Oracle. 'Also revealing.'

'I suppose. What about the Three and Twenty?'

The little man rubbed his chin. It gave Fost an eerie feeling since it was among many gestures Oracle had copied from him in trying to perfect the humanity of his simulacrum. It was like shaving in a mirror and seeing a hand hold a razor to a stranger's face.

'The first thing to understand,' said Oracle, 'is that the Twenty-three are ladies and lords of Chaos, and few generalities can be made about them. It is written in old, old tomes that once humanity's gods each had a single attribute: war, birth, lust, fire, water. Worship in such a fashion is rare today, although you find traces of it among the Thailint and Dyla savages, and the more debased cultures of the Northern Continent. On the other hand, each of the Three and Twenty represents several principles and has several attributes. With a few exceptions, of course, since these are first and foremost Chaotic deities. This disparity betwen old religion and new tends, I believe, to support a thesis I formulated before you came to High Medurim.' Oracle cocked his head to one side to see if Fost still listened.

He did and asked, 'And what's this theory of yours, Oracle?'

'I do not believe humanity is native to our world.'

Fost's eyebrows rose. Though Oracle smiled indulgently at his attempted interruptions, he held relentlessly to his subject of the confusing and confused array of gods and goddesses.

'I'll discuss my theories of how humankind came to this world with you later. But bear with me for a short while longer.

'Chief of the Three and Twenty is generally held to be Jirre. Jirre's the goddess of both Creation and Destruction, a typically Chaotic contradiction. But this contradiction may be only apparent. Her devotees argue that Creation and Destruction are two sides of the same coin, hence only one goddess is required. Another way of viewing it is the Dualist philosophy, which holds that Twoness, not Oneness, is the natural order of things. That accounts for the creation of Light in the first place. Of course, the doctrine raises unanswered questions of its own since Light and Dark are but two faces of the same coin.

'But I see your eyelids drooping. I fear I bore you like that discursive old fart, Erimenes.' Oracle spoke faster to hold Fost's attention. 'You're already familiar with Ust, the Red Bear; Gormanka of wind and wayfarers, your patron of couriers; Somdag Squid-face. There are others, of course, less commonly known.'

'Wait, wait, wait.' Fost held up both his hands in despair. 'This is going too fast for me. I'm not sure I can work through the contradictions in all you're telling me.'

'I told you that these are lords and ladies of Chaos. In a nutshell, Justice, alone of the attributes of Chaos, is immutable but takes many forms. Law always takes a similar form but its nature changes according to what best serves the ends of the Elder Dark. I admit it doesn't make much sense, even to me. But it is often said that expedience is an attribute of Law and Darkness, and Justice cannot be expedient.'

Fost stretched, yawned.

'You're the one doing the talking, but my throat's as dry as dust,' he said. 'Thanks for the lesson.'

Oracle arched a pale eyebrow.

'The lesson's far from complete,' he said,. 'but I perceive the chamberlain, the one you always think of as "the slug," approaches along the corridor. He doubtless means to drag you to another rehearsal or lesson in protocol. As always, it was a pleasure speaking with you. I look forward to our next session together.'

'I'd look forward to it more,' said Fost, rising, 'if we could talk about something less unnerving and more coherent.' But the image of the little, fat man was gone, leaving Fost alone with the smell of incense, the sound of mumbling savants, and the petulant pit-pat of the chamberlain's sandals coming down the hall.

CHAPTER THREE

The thick stone walls of the temple muffled the bustling sounds from without as they muffled the oppressive heat. Fost and his companions wandered along the cool flagstone-paved aisles, glimpsing here and there priests robed in the color of the deity they served, or worshippers laden with small offerings to plead their petty cases, seeking the mending hearts or the winning of good luck for themselves and bad luck for their enemies.

'What I want to know,' said Erimenes the Ethical, laying a long, vaporous blue finger beside his beaky nose, 'is why the Temple of All Gods, by rights the fairest in all the Sundered Realm, should be so prodigiously ugly.'

Fost laughed, winning him a dirty look from a pinch-faced priest in a white and yellow robe. The pillared hall swallowed the sound without a trace, however, so that only those nearby heard. It might have been that among the deities whose likenesses were housed here were those who did not disapprove of voices raised in laughter.

'You can thank the Northblood Barbarians for that,' he said. Ziore tilted her head, partly in respect for the sundry deities and mostly to hear his words, which were spoken now with decorously lowered voice. He saw Moriana looking on with apparent interest, and his heart lifted. There were times since the battle when she seemed to be drifting into another world, a world divorced from this one. Anything that captured her interest and took her away from her own problems merited his approval. That Ziore likewise appeared interested also heartened him. The nun's ghost and Moriana had become closely linked in a way that he could not truly fathom. Their emotions merged into something beyond telepathy. If Ziore smiled, that communicated directly to Moriana's mind.

He nodded polite acknowledgement to a statue of Ust the Red

Bear as they passed. The god was one of Fost's patrons, entrusted with guarding the Realm Roads, and he felt an obligation to pay slight obeisance since he had called upon Ust so many times in the past. In spite of his reflexive invocations of the bear god, he wondered if it did any good. He had no proof one way or the other, yet the hetwoman of the Ust-alayakits, Jennas, believed in the god. The time he had spent with Jennas getting through the Rampart Mountains and crossing the length of the Sundered Realm had instilled in him a healthy respect for – if not belief in – Ust. Jennas had predicted this War of Powers long before he had seen the signs forming. Whether her knowledge came from shrewd insight into the ways of man or true revelation by Ust, Fost couldn't say. Either way, Jennas was a superior woman of rare courage and even rarer abilities.

'The barbarians knew only a few of the Wise Ones when they invaded nearly five thousand years ago. Like most barbarians who pride themselves on virile vigor and their superiority to effete civilized folk, the first thing they did on conquering Medurim was to settle down to emulating the Medurimin citizen in earnest. They somehow decided that gods prefer ostentation. So, they rebuilt the Temple of All Gods according to their own ideas of splendor fitting for a house of deities.' Fost waved a scarred hand. 'These are the results of that wild, misguided fit of building.'

They looked about. Some of the statues stood free on pedestals, while others were sheltered in alcoves, the gods' and goddesses' preferences determined by their devotees. But the statues mostly predated the barbarian dynasty and were not what captured the eye.

In his youth, the unschooled and half-wild street urchin named Fost thought that the Temple was ugly. From the outside, its hewn granite blocks were set in massy tiers appearing to form crude steps in the ultimate shape of a pyramid. Now that Fost was grown and had seen other architectures offered by cities in the Realm, he *knew* the place was an eyesore.

Inside was no better. High up, where the tiers jutted together, crossed and criss-crossed a spiderweb of struts and supports of wood and iron. The Temple's original plan called for the stepping-in to continue until the ranks of stone met. Planning exceeded expertise in construction. The huge blocks were poorly balanced and would fall if the building had continued upward as intended. The Emperor Gotrag II had ordered his artificers to roof over the partially finished upper structure. The lofty courses were dangerously unstable, as a result, and the latticework of joists and struts grew more complex with every passing year. Should one single succeeding Emperor fail to add bracing, the Temple roof would certainly collapse.

'But whoever heard of square columns?' demanded Erimenes on a rising note of outrage. The genie whirled about in a tight vortex of blue mist as he pointed out the offending supports. Ziore wavered nearby, her substance lightly mingling with his and giving the philosopher silent approbation. 'And who saw fit,' he continued, 'to build them of alternate blocks of rose granite and whatever that ghastly chartreuse stone is?'

'It's a type of limestone,' explained Fost. 'And in answer to both the other questions – the Northern Barbarians.'

Ziore looked puzzled and slightly pained.

'Forgive my asking, Fost, but I thought the Northern Barbarians founded High Medurim, and that the residents were descended from them.' She bit at her non-existent lip, fearful of giving offense.

Fost laughed.

'They did; I'm descended from them, just as you and Erimenes and Moriana are mostly descended from the Golden Barbarians. The Golden Barbarians have achieved a static society while the Northern ones have locked themselves into a cycle of renaissance and regression; every few centuries they work themselves up to the level of barbarism, then they fall to fighting and knock themselves back to savagery. They call it progress.'

They stopped in front of an alcove containing still another of the seemingly endless statues of a goddess. It was a conventional enough rendering of a lovely, slender woman bearing sword and lyre. Fost was struck by the resemblance between the chiselled stone features and those of the illusion Moriana had brought forth in the Black March. The exiled Sky City princess had duplicated well, never having set foot in this Temple before.

If she had duplicated, Fost found himself thinking.

Wordlessly, Moriana slipped the strap of the satchel containing Ziore's jug from her shoulder and handed it to Fost. She stepped forward and fell to her knees in front of the statue, placed a sprig of blue wildflowers at the statue's feet and bent her head in prayer. Fost held his breath, half-expecting and half-dreading some sign. But the statue remained stone.

Moriana finally uttered a small sigh and rose.

'The goddess thanks you, milady,' came a voice behind Fost.

367

Fost turned to see a stout, short man dressed in green and gold, with a fringe of gray hair hanging lank from the base of his bald head. Around his neck rode a gold chain supporting a medallion struck with the signs of sword and lyre. His eyes shone surprisingly green and youthful from a leathery, seamed face.

'It's I who have come to thank her,' Moriana said.

The priest's brow knit, then his face underwent a remarkable migration of lines and wrinkles that eventually sorted out into a broad beam of joy.

'But you, Princess Moriana, are the one who called her down to succor our folk at the Black March!' He dropped to his knees and reached an arthritic hand out to catch the hem of her gown and raise it to his lips. He fumbled a moment, uncertain when he found no skirt, then took the hem of her suede tunic and kissed it instead.

'This is the happiest day of my life! All my devotions are rewarded. I come at last into the presence of one truly touched by blessed Jirre!' Great tears of happiness rolled down his round cheeks. Even Fost, skeptical of priests and politicians, was moved by the intensity of the emotion displayed.

Tears gleamed at the corners of Moriana's eyes as she reached down and helped the little priest to his feet.

'You need not kneel to me,' she said. Fost thought she was going to tell him it hadn't been Jirre at all but rather an illusion she had summoned to confound the *Zr'gsz*. But her eyes caught Fost's, a corner of her mouth quirked upward, and she said nothing.

'They cried at the portal that you were within,' the priest babbled in rapture. 'But I did not dare hope. Joy, joy!'

'Wait a minute,' Fost said. 'Who was crying at the portal that Moriana was within?'

'The mob.'

Fost swallowed. He exchanged bleak looks with Moriana. There was no need to ask which mob it was. News of the way Moriana had brought the battle to a conclusion had preceded the returning army by a full day. Coming between that news and the first tired riders had been the tidings borne by Zak'zar of Kara-Est's destruction and Moriana's lineage. When Moriana had entered High Medurim, she had been beset by two masses of people, one throwing flower petals and naming her holy and the other naming her witch and traitor to her kind. It was even rumored old Sir Tharvus wandered the streets dressed in a mendicant's rags and egged on the violent faction. He had lost brothers in battle and blamed Moriana. If a mob truly gathered at the Temple door crying Moriana's name, she and her companions were in danger.

As the priest hopped from one foot to the other pleading to be told what troubled the holy lady, Fost corralled a worried-looking woman in white and red. He found that, as he had dreaded, half those thronging the Temple screamed for Moriana and the other half screamed for Moriana's blood.

'But won't the ones who call you savior protect you from the others?' asked Ziore.

'More likely the two factions will pull her apart in a tug of war,' Fost answered grimly. 'It's happened before.' He had lost his own parents to a riot many years ago when the mob rose up in rage at learning the dole was to be cut to cover the expenses of celebrating Teom's ascension to the Sapphire Throne.

'If I must face them, then I shall,' she said, tossing back her hair. 'Where's my sword?' Moriana walked toward the front of the hall.

Fost seized her arm. Her eyes blazed as she spun on him, but she neither broke his grip nor fried him with a lightning bolt.

'You won't defeat the Dark Ones by getting yourself torn to pieces on the Temple steps,' he pointed out.

'What would you do? Do you want me to cower among the statues until the mob rushes the gates and drags me out? If I must die, I'll do it on my own two feet, with my head held high.'

Fost knew it wasn't bravado speaking. She had gone to what seemed certain doom in the Sky City and the Circle of the Skywell to face the Demon Istu himself. She had succeeded in slowing the Demon's pace long enough for many of her subjects in the City to escape; not once had she wavered in front of that black, soul-sucking being.

'No need,' he said. 'Where are the Wardens of the Temple?'

Grasping the peril of the situation, the portly priest gathered up his skirts and hustled off in search of one of the brown-robed custodians of the Temple. Two figures soon returned, both tall, both with brown hoods drawn well up and closed to cover their faces. They carried faded leather satchels containing ceramic jars slung over their shoulders. They paused for a moment listening to the battle raging on the other side of the vast structure, and then hurried off through the puddles and refuse that desecrated the interior of the Temple. They slipped through a side door and made their way through the city's alleys.

They dined as they generally had since coming to High Medurim, alone in their apartments except for the two genies. After they had finished, the chamberlain arrived all atwitter to go over the protocols they would be called on to observe on the morrow when Teom invested them both as nobles of the Empire. When the man left at last, pale hands fluttering like a mother bird drawing attention away from her nest, they both felt as tired as if they'd been forced to run around the entire city of Medurim – twice. A sultry, sticky sea breeze blew in through the windows, laden with the smell of dead fish.

Moriana had a stack of scrolls and books piled in the corner, grimoires that a servant had brought over from the Library. But she claimed to be too tired to make sense of them. For his part, Fost toyed with the notion of paying a visit to Oracle.

He just as quickly discarded the idea. Since the night of the orgy celebrating their initial arrival to the city, Empress Temalla had taken to popping out at him as he walked the corridors, particularly at night. He knew all too well what would happen if he angered her, and he was running out of tactful refusals to her sexual overtures. The last time had been the most embarrassing. He had admitted – lied – that he had contracted an uncomfortable fungus infection from riding so long in a wet saddle. At that, the Empress had laughed uproariously and told him she was too old to believe in a child's fable and that he must have gotten the blight by becoming more familiar with his war dog than was conventional, even by High Medurim's permissive standards. He had been blushing quite authentically when they parted.

Fost and Moriana finally retired for the night, to separate pallets. Though she had not rejected his company since the battle, she hadn't encouraged intimacy, either. He had considered asking for separate quarters, yet hoped that their nearness would again spark the feelings for one another they'd lost. He undressed quickly and lay down, turning his face to the wall and trying to ignore the rustlings and shiftings Moriana made as she disrobed.

The two Athalar spirits had been cooing and making calf-eyes at one another constantly while the humans ate. Before going to her own bed, Moriana poured them together in a bronze vessel Teom had provided for just that purpose. There were many times Fost wished Erimenes and Ziore had remained as hostile to one another as when they'd first met. He had thought their incessant squabbling wearisome, but it was nothing compared to this. Thanks to Ch'rri, the Wirix-magic spawned cat woman and a healthy dose of aphrodisiac vapors, the two genies had discovered the art of incorporeal love-making. They may not have had bodies but they carried on like pigs in rut. In spite of the squeals, moans and titters, sleep soon found Fost.

Walls of light, flowing curtains of blue and scarlet and white shifting relentlessly, colors blending seamlessly one into another circled Fost. He reached out an arm turned curiously insubstantial. Warmth met his fingertips. He pushed into the colored fog and the wall vanished, revealing a long corridor.

Unafraid, Fost walked forward. His feet met only softness, as if he marched on the very stuff of which clouds were made. The particolored walls remained just beyond his reach as he walked and walked and walked, for what seemed an eternity. Suddenly, he realized he had acquired a companion.

'Erimenes!' he cried out in surprise. 'You have feet!'

'Of course I do, dear boy. Did you suspect tentacles — or perhaps another head?' The spirit appeared as tenuous as ever, but now Fost joined him in this ghostly state.

Ziore reached out and caressed Fost's cheek. Surprised, yet curiously calm at all happening to him, he caught up her wrist. His fingers momentarily felt substance, then his fingers flowed through her forearm. He couldn't tell if it were she or himself lacking a real dimension.

'Ahead,' came Moriana's voice. 'How lovely it is!'

Fost felt ineffable calm. His friends had joined him in this dream world, this dream. He looked in the direction Moriana pointed. Unbidden, the name 'Agift' came to mind. This was the home of the gods and goddesses. His mind flitted around the idea this was more than simple dream, then hastily moved from such conjecture. He was too caught up in the swirling nothingness at the end of the corridor. Even as Fost watched, the mists solidified into a subtly hued chamber filled with light that cast no shadow.

He blinked, then noticed a table at the far end of the room, the figures grouped around it strangely familiar to him.

Radiant in her gown of green and gold, Jirre rose as the four approached.

'Daughter,' the goddess said to Moriana. 'It is good to see you again. I had not planned on it. You may thank Majyra for this meeting.' She nodded to a young woman at the head of the table, stately in a lavender gown that left milkwhite shoulders bare. Deep red hair was piled atop her head. Her eyes shone out as black as night.

'Sit and be welcome. You can stay only a short while.' As she spoke, her gown's color changed to icy blue.

Fost hadn't noticed the four chairs before. He and the others took seats and faced the Three and Twenty Wise Ones, their gods and goddesses.

'We are not all here,' said the older woman to Majyra's left. 'Tothyr and Avalys won't come because they find Majyra too frivolous, and several of the others are missing for whatever reason. Who can say with us?' She drew deeply on a leaf-rolled cigarette, then blew the smoke out. The smoke danced and formed fleeting caricatures of those missing from the table. Fost blushed when he recognized the acts being performed by those smoky figures.

'I thank you for your hospitality, Lady Majyra,' said Moriana, gathering her wits more rapidly than Fost. Of them all she took this with the most aplomb. Even Erimenes remained uncharacteristically silent in the presence of the deities.

'And to you, Jirre,' continued Moriana, 'I offer my thanks and eternal devotion for the aid rendered at the Black March.'

'You are welcome,' said Jirre, a smile curling her lips. 'I truly wish I could do more. But as I told you, I cannot.'

'What of the others? My world is your domain. The Dark Ones threaten it. Can't you take an active part in defending it?'

Several of the deities stirred impatiently. Fost felt the shape of the chamber altering, as if the emotions rising somehow changed the very physical dimensions of the room. He sensed that few of the Three and Twenty assembled were favorably disposed toward him — or Moriana.

'Let me explain,' Jirre said, looking down the table and silencing the grumbles. 'We summoned you here to tell you that we cannot aid you. Or if aid might be possible, then it must be given indirectly.'

'But why?' asked Ziore.

'The ways of gods are not the ways of men,' pontificated Erimenes. The spirit fell silent when Jirre scowled in his direction.

'We have grown apart from your world. Even brief visits to it are tiring for us. There is also the fact that we tried our might against the Demon of the Dark Ones before. We failed. And we were stronger then.' Jirre spread her hands in a gesture of helplessness. 'There are other reasons, but those are the primary ones.'

'Well, we're grateful for the help you've given us this far,' said Fost, wondering at himself for speaking so familiarly to the Wise Ones. 'Lord Ust,' he said turning to a huge bear sitting a few feet away down the table, 'you especially have my thanks for aiding me.'

Ust frowned and rubbed his cheek with a claw.

'You've been a dutiful son,' he rumbled, 'though like all of them you think of me most often when in distress. But I cannot recall intervening on your behalf. You seem well enough equipped to sort out your own problems.'

'But,' Fost sputtered, confused, 'but that time the Ust-alayakits rescued me from Rann and his killers and spared my life because I called on you . . . and those other times when Jennas told me you had aided me. You didn't?' He felt hot tears of frustration stinging his eyes. He had come to have faith in Jennas and her forecasts. He felt cheated she'd failed him in this way.

'Jennas is my chosen,' the bear god said in his rolling bass. 'Her I do watch over, for she leads my people. But you – if someone's been helping you, it hasn't been me.' He scowled, his eyes turning red. 'An impostor, is it? Just let me find out who –'

'Ust, control yourself,' chided Jirre. 'Your muzzle is growing.'

'I won't sit next to a *bear*,' declared Majyra. 'They smell!'

Reddish hair retreated from the bear god's face, and his face and brow took on a more human appearance. But he huddled himself down and growled as if hating the shape change.

'Best I return you to your bodies,' said Jirre. 'I am truly sorry. Our hopes and best thoughts go with you, for what they're worth.'

Fost felt the chair dissolving under him. He stood rather than be dropped to the floor. Beside him were Moriana, Erimenes and Ziore. They bowed. There was nothing to say, although Fost's mind churned with unanswered questions. Jirre had dismissed them. When a goddess bids a mere mortal leave, it was best to depart.

As they walked back the way they had come along the auroral hall, the shifting hues of the walls faded from view and were replaced by swirling fog. Gradually the others drew ahead of Fost. Though he picked his own way through the foggy terrain as quickly as he could, they moved inexorably away, hardly seeming aware that they did so. Fost felt panic grip his throat when they vanished into the misty distance.

'Be calm,' a voice said beside him. 'I wanted a word with you in private.'

Fost turned and saw one of the Wise Ones. The goddess seemed tantalizingly familiar, yet he could place no name to her. She had remained silent in the hall while Jirre spoke.

As if reading his mind, she reached out and plucked a tiny rose from behind his ear, saying, 'Now do you know me, Fost? I am Perryn.' A dulcet laugh filled his ears, yet had a peculiarly flat quality to it. 'Perryn Prankster, some call me.'

The goddess of laughter and anarchy handed him the miniature rose.

'I will tell you something, my friend,' Perryn said, laughing at Fost's discomfort. 'It might be that the Wise Ones, aligned together, could defeat the Dark Ones and cast Istu back into spaces between the stars. It just might be,' he said, grinning savagely. 'And it might be that you should thank me for helping prevent it.'

'Thank you?' cried Fost. 'But you've thrown us to the Dark Ones, left us defenseless!'

'Not defenseless. Felarod defeated Istu before without our aid.'

'But the World Spirit . . .'

'Is a thing apart, closer to you than to us. It is not of Agift but rather of a more basic origin. In many ways, it and Istu are so similar.' She shook her head. 'Because you're ignorant in matters of the gods, I will state the obvious and not think less of you for it. We are us and you are you.'

Fost looked blank.

'Our interests are not yours,' said Perryn, eyes boring into Fost's gray ones. 'If we fight for your world and conquer it, it will be ours. No longer yours, except by our sufferance.'

'That is all . . . hard to accept.' Fost licked dry lips.

'It'd be harder for one raised a pious believer. We are good allies but poor masters.'

She clapped Fost on the shoulder and said, 'You'd best get along now. Remember not to count on assistance from us.' Perryn smiled wickedly, adding, 'Well, perhaps a little. I do like you, mortal. You're cute.' The goddess laughed and this time the waves of mirth smashed into Fost's brain like ocean waves against a beach. His head rang as he felt himself spinning away.

He cried out, 'Perryn! Who was it who helped me before, if not my patron Ust?'

Ghostly laughter brought Fost awake. He sat upright, drenched in cold sweat, his heart triphammering wildly in his breast. He took several deep draughts of the fish-smell laden air and calmed down.

'What a dream,' he said to himself, reaching up to brush away the perspiration on his forehead. A single tiny rose was clutched in his right hand.

CHAPTER FOUR

'Wasn't that the most lovely aurora last night?' chirped Zunhilix the chamberlain as he flitted about the apartment. 'I'm sure it was a most auspicious sign for your investiture.'

Fost and Moriana looked at each other.

'We didn't see it,' the princess said.

'Oh, but I'm sure you had better things to do than watch the sky, didn't you?' He tittered, hiding his petal-shaped mouth behind a delicate white hand.

Fost felt exasperation and a tightening of the muscles in his belly. It had been some time since he and Moriana had lain together, and the strain he experienced now was as much emotional as physical. But paramount in his mind was the question of what had happened the night before. Aurora? His eyes darted to where one of the servants made up his bed. Nothing but a withered stalk of the miniature rose remained on the bedside table. Yet he had clutched that delicate, living flower in his very own hand the night before. A sense of being little more than a leaf caught in a millrace seized him.

'Most certainly my companions had something better to do than watch the sky,' Erimenes piped up. 'But unfortunately, all they did was sleep. I'm beginning to despair of those two, chamberlain.'

As two plump stewards, painted even more gaudily than their master, laced Fost into a molded gilt breastplate, the courier rolled eyes up in his head in mock horror at the genie's words. It seemed nothing kept Erimenes's libido at bay.

'Now, Erimenes,' chided Ziore. 'I thought I kept you too busy to care what *they* did.' The nun's spirit produced a throaty and quite unvirginal chuckle.

'Of course you did, my love. I simply find myself grieving that our young mortal friends are so profligate of the little time they have in life as to waste the nocturnal hours on a pastime as unrewarding as sleep. They actually went to bed to sleep! Great Ultimate, what a waste! It is solely concern for their well-being that motivates my interest in this matter, nothing more.'

Ziore made a skeptical noise. She may have been besotted with the lecherous old ghost but she wasn't *that* besotted.

Ignoring this byplay, Zunhilix busied himself attending to Moriana's coiffure. It was her one concession to Medurimin mores. She would wear a sculpted breastplate and back, a kilt of gold-plated strips of hornbull leather and glittery gold greaves, just like Fost. Zunhilix had pleaded with her to wear one of the stunning selection of ceremonial women's ensembles he had at his disposal, from weblike concoctions of Golden Isle shimmereen that left breasts and pubes bare to a chaste, long-trained robe of green lacebird silk. Sternly she had shaken her head. She was not eager to be invested as a noble of the Empire, no more than Fost, but both had deemed it impolitic to refuse the great honor Teom had offered them. Not only did they need the help of the Empire in battling the Fallen Ones and the lizard folk's Demon ally, the situation in city and Palace was such that they needed his goodwill to continue living. The mobs demanding Moriana's head grew increasingly bold. But if Moriana had to add some insignificant Imperial title to that which was her birthright as lawful heir to the Sky City's Beryl Throne, she was going to do it as a warrior, not as one of the simpering damsels of the north.

To mollify Zunhilix, who had fallen to weeping and tugging at his pointed beard on learning how adamant Moriana was, the princess had agreed to allow the chamberlain and his staff to do as they liked with her hair. The warrior's investiture garb included a helmet of dubious value in real battle due to its impractical design. To their mutual relief the helmets needed only to be carried beneath one arm during the ceremony. This gave Zunhilix free rein with her hair.

Eyeing her sidelong now as the stewards laced up her cuirass at the sides, Fost had to admit the chamberlain and his elfin crew had performed admirably. Moriana's hair had been washed in aromatic herbs, then brushed by giggling stewards until it shone like spun gold. Then it was swirled atop her head and held in place with golden pins, then hung about with fine gold chains bedecked with glittering emeralds that set off her seagreen eyes.

In her gleaming breastplate, with long, slim legs carelessly sprawled beside the stool on which she sat, her finely-coiffed head held high with great hoops of gold wire dangling from either ear, the princess made a fantastic spectacle, splendid and exotic and enticing. Fost felt himself hardening futilely against the steel cup of his codpiece. He squirmed on his own seat, eliciting further laughter from his own attendants who immediately noticed his predicament.

A cool breeze gusted through their suite, tinted with subtle fragrances of the Imperial garden and tainted with tar and rotting fish from the harbor. The Imperial Palace, unlike the Temple of All Gods, was no product of barbarians obsessed with mass and size. Justly famous Imperial architects at the height of their craft had wrought their superb best in the design. Everywhere were cool white marble and clean lines. And meticulous care had been paid to the circulation of air so that even the northern wing of the Palace where guests resided remained comfortable throughout the sultry summer days.

Fost rose and examined himself in a full-length mirror.

'Not bad,' he said, more to himself than to the others. He was a tall, powerfully built man, raven-haired, with startling pale gray eyes looking forth from a tanned and considerably battered face. The Medurimin ceremonial armor was silly, but the frivolity of the outfit somehow made the man within seem more rugged. Secretly, Fost was delighted. He had been uncomfortable being dressed by others. However, he had to concede that the half hour perched on the stool trying not to fidget or growl when a steward squeezed him under the pretext of sizing him had proven worthwhile.

'Magnificent,' applauded Erimenes. 'I have never before truly appreciated how well-matched a couple you are. Tall, lithe. Moriana as radiant as the sun, Fost dark and brooding. In that gear even your habitual expression of surliness is not unbecoming, friend Fost.'

Fost winced.

'Oh, Erimenes,' said Ziore. 'I think they both look marvelous.'

'Yes, yes.' Zunhilix bobbed his head, basking in the reflected glory of his creations.

Cradling his sharp chin in one palm, Erimenes studied first Fost and then Moriana, and nodded judiciously.

'The design of those kilts is quite propitious,' he said, 'in that

378

merely by elevating a few of those strips fore and aft the two of you can easily clear for action. The good ship Fost can ram Moriana in the stern, or perhaps seat himself on a chair and ready his pike to accept boarders!' He smirked with delight at his own risqué metaphors.

'Erimenes,' Fost said sharply. Moriana turned away, color burning high on her cheeks. Ziore reached with an insubstantial pink hand and tweaked one of the philosopher's ears.

'Ouch!' he exclaimed. 'How could you do that, woman?'

She leered.

'The same way I can do this,' she replied, and reached for the front of his loincloth.

'You don't have to go,' Moriana said quietly.

'Huh?' was Fost's confused reply. His mind churned, as he tried to figure out what she meant.

Her shoulders rose and fell in a sigh.

'You don't have to come with me. I'm the one who loosed the Fallen Ones on the world. I must deal with them or fail in the attempt. That's my destiny. This is no fight of yours.'

Fost turned a foreboding thunderhead of a look upon Zunhilix. A query died in the chamberlain's throat and he hurriedly gathered up the skirts of his robe and his covey and underlings and fled. When the doors had shut behind them, Fost turned to Moriana.

'It's my fight, too,' he said, low-voiced.

She shook her head, and her eyes were jewel-bright with unshed tears.

'I've lost too much already by letting those I care for follow me into peril.'

His heart thrummed like a bowstring, and though he knew he should not, he blurted, 'Is that why you've been so cold to me? Because you're afraid of drawing me into danger?'

She nodded and turned away.

'First I feared you would reject me because of my . . . my heritage. Then it came to me that I was a bane to all I've loved, or who have loved me. Darl died on my behalf, along with so many fine men and women. Brightlaugher the Nevrym boy, and poor old Sir Rinalvus, and before that Ayoka my faithful war bird, and Kralfi and Catannia whom Rann tortured to death to torment me . . . and you, whom I loved most of all!'

'And me,' Fost said, nodding. 'Alone of all those, I died by your hand, and for my death alone you bear responsibility. And yet here I am.' He raised his brawny arms to shoulder height and made a deep, courtly bow. His eyes remained fixed on Moriana's slender frame. He saw a delicate shiver of dread pass through her and the silent word 'why?' form on her lips.

He straightened and laughed softly at his own tangled, often confused motives. A question Erimenes asked beside a campfire in the days before Chanobit and the treacherous battle there – a question he had since asked himself a hundred times in a hundred different ways with no better answer than the one he had given the sage.

'I could be romantic and say that I would rather die at your side than live without your love. And –' With a surprised twitch at the corner of his mouth, he finished, '– and that would be true, oddly enough.' He looked quickly away. Such words embarrassed him. 'But let's be practical. If you fail, neither I nor any other human of the Realm will long survive you, save for ones like Fairspeaker and others who play traitor for the Dark. And even they wouldn't last for long, not if they depended on the sufferance of the Dark Ones. Let me put it this way. I'd rather be with you than away from you, and I'd be in no more danger at your side than anywhere else.' He smiled, regaining some of his composure. 'And perhaps I can even be of service to you, milady.'

She stretched out a hand to him.

'Never call me that. To you I am Moriana – or, if you will, love.' She smiled through tears running down her cheeks and spoiling Zunhilix's carefully applied makeup. 'And you have done much to help me already.'

He went to her, mouth pressing to hers, tongue questing. He felt her cool fingers moving urgently against his thigh. He drew his face back from hers.

'Much as I hate to gratify Erimenes by following his advice . . .'

Her mouth muffled his words.

With a brave shout and a clash of spears on bronze round shields, the Twenty-third Light Imperial Infantry marched in review past the wooden bleachers that had been erected in Piety Plaza. Squinting against the glare of the afternoon sun, Fost was able to conceal his reflexive grimace of distaste. They made a brave show with their brightly feathered round helms and their shield devices of a fist gripping a barbed spear, and their hobnailed boots rang in perfect unison on the broad blocks of blue-veined marble. But at the Battle of Black March they had bolted like frightened lizards, tails high and elbows pumping. They were typical Imperials: parade ground beauties.

The four-story structure vibrated in sympathy to the measured tread of the regiment. Instinctively, Fost clutched at the bench beneath him.

'I hope this damn thing doesn't collapse,' he said sidelong to Moriana. She cocked a brow at him. 'It's happened before,' he said defensively.

She shrugged slightly and turned her attention back to the parade, but not before giving him a smile that caused a comfortable warmth to grow in his groin. When they had permitted Zunhilix and his attendants back into their apartments, the chamberlain's emaciated features had crawled with horror and his hands fluttered like agitated white birds when he saw the dishevelled condition his charges were in. He had only a half hour before the investiture ceremony to patch up the damage. Nonetheless, he had rapped out brisk orders to his underlings, and by the time the brightly-plumed officers of the Life Guards had arrived to escort them to the Plaza, they both looked as good as new. Zunhilix might have been effeminate and prone to twitter, Fost reflected, but he got things done. All things considered, he might do a better job commanding the Imperial armies than the officers now in charge.

Fost glanced to his left, where Teom and Temalla sat side by side, a particolored parasol shading the stinging sun from their pasty white skins. The Emperor and his sister-wife smiled and waved at the marching troops from the midst of a flock of courtiers and dignitaries, all as brightly hued as so many tropical birds, and chattering as loudly. Temalla noticed Fost and favored him with a lewd wink, at the same time dipping one pale shoulder slightly so that her milky gown exposed an ample, burgundy-tipped breast to his view. He swallowed and looked across the square, over the heads of the marching troops.

A detachment of the Watch tramped by beneath. These were special riot troops, as well-trained as the regulars and vastly more experienced, given the Medurimins' penchant for rioting. They sported burnished blue plate armor, short swords at their hips, small spiked target shields on left forearms and over each right shoulder lay a halberd with an eight-foot ironshod haft.

'Weren't these the men who killed your parents, dear Fost?' came Ziore's tentative, curious, soft words.

He glanced at the satchel resting on the bench by Moriana's hip. All had agreed, Erimenes with the worst possible humor, that it would be best for the genies to remain out of sight today. The city was feverish with talk of magic; to have a ghost hovering in the bleachers would do nothing to calm the dangerous passions of the anti-Moriana faction and might even incite to violence those favorably disposed toward her.

Fost shrugged.

'I don't really know,' he said in a voice equally soft, but laden with emotion. 'I was only eight when it happened. I never got a clear account of how they died. It was during festivities like this, only grander. Teom was being crowned. The mob caught the rumor that their dole would be reduced to pay for the celebration and rioted. But who killed my parents? The guard, the mob, what difference?'

Lacking telepathic skills, Fost was unable to read any unstated response on Ziore's part, and she made no attempt to broadcast it. He guessed the cloistered genie was shocked at his apparent callousness. But the death of his parents had been history for twenty years, and he had cried all the tears he had for them long since.

'One thing the death of my father and mother taught me,' he replied to the still silent nun, 'later, when I had the chance and maturity to think it over. The fact that a group is oppressed doesn't mean it's any better at core than its oppressors. If the rioters killed my parents, they did so no less heedlessly than the guardsmen would have done.' He flicked sweat from his forehead where it threatened to bead and roll into his eyes. 'This transition from guttersnipe to noble of the Empire makes little impression on me.'

He looked around at the panoply of fabulous costumes, a profusion of gilt so extreme it transcended bad taste and achieved silliness. He thought of melting down any five hangers-on and getting enough gold to keep the entire Imperial Navy afloat for a whole year. He smiled mirthlessly. He knew how things were done in High Medurim. The state of their army showed that all too clearly. All things considered, the gold was probably better off where it was. At least, it wasn't going to finance further bloodthirsty follies on the Northern Continent.

Off to the south, slate-blue clouds hung over the foothills of

Harmis. Flashes of yellow heat lightning played among them with a dull rumble. Fost thought he caught the scent of ozone mixed with the aromas of the day. Nearby vendors fried sausage and sold it wrapped in paper with hot mustard and sweet seaweed. The men and women around him were drenched in the rarest perfumes, some sweet, some tart, only a few exotic and elusive, wordless. Intermixed with these heady odors came the rank smell of war dog droppings, the heavy smell of farmed land south of the city, the pressing intrusive odor of unwashed bodies. They kept Fost's memory turning ever backward to his childhood, for smell is the most reminiscent sense of all.

A heavy gonging rattle like giant coins shaken in a sack drew him back. Sensing a shift in the crowd noise, a note of subdued hostility like the warning hum of a beehive when an intruder nears, he looked down at the street. A strange, outlandish sight greeted his eyes. A full troop of Highgrass Broad dog riders rode by at a trot, colored streamers flying from the spires of their helms, their scale armor ringing to the tempo of their war dogs' gait.

'I've heard of these,' Fost murmured to Moriana, seeing her puzzled frown at the presence of the Highgrass mercenaries. 'They just got back from serving out a contract in the Sword Kingdoms, battling the southern Northern Barbarians.' The Sword Kingdoms lay above the equator, in the northern half of the Northern Continent. 'Teom heard about them when their ship landed here in Medurim and hired them for the city's defense. Wise move, too.'

Moriana looked skeptical.

'They do have an impressive collection of trophies,' Erimenes said. Fost's companion had been unable to stay in his jug like Ziore, but in the babble of the crowd no one was likely to notice either words or a partially exposed blue head peering from the satchel.

The genie was correct. Every other dog rider held lance couched in a stirrup with one hand and a captured banner or insignia proudly aloft in the other. There were bicolored, slender pennons of rival Highgrass units, flags worked with the devices of a score of small cities and minor nobles, and the beaten-brass plaques the Northern Barbarians used in place of banners.

'There,' gasped Moriana, pointing. 'See that white, spiralled staff hung with human skulls? It's the tusk of a thunderflash. That was the sacred war totem of the Golden Barbarian horde we fought in the savannas west of Thailot six years ago.' She shifted her hand, now pointing to other units. 'Red and black streamers – that would be Captain Mayft's troop.'

'The Gryphons,' Fost added. 'It's easy to see why they call themselves that.' It was indeed. Like their riders, the big, thick-legged Grassland war dogs were all encased in scale armor. Each beast's head was covered with a steel mask worked in the shape of a beaked, sharp-eared face which gave the animals the appearance of wingless gryphons. Most of the riders had mask visors as well, but rode with them raised to reveal the typical broad, sun- and wind-tanned Grasslander features.

'They're a free company, aren't they?' asked Moriana, with a trace of distaste. At Fost's affirmative, she shook her head. 'I don't see how one can hope for discipline from such as those.'

There were dozens of bands of Grasslander mercenaries, from small squads up to regimental size. They were formed to a dizzying array of models. Some were based on clan affiliations, others on village of birth, still others on religious creed. Some were wholly communal, sharing rations and booty and bodies, as well, in great orgies. Others were stern and abstemious. Captain Mayft's Gryphons were one of the least interesting varieties, a purely volunteer company raised at its commander's own expense.

'Obviously one can,' Fost replied dryly, 'since here they are, still together six years after you first encountered them. And they've done pretty well for themselves. I doubt they paid klenors for those trophies.'

'Bought with blood and life,' cackled Erimenes from his satchel. 'Obviously. Oh, what battles they must have fought!'

Moriana turned away. The dog riders clattered on past, lance heads winking in the sun, heavy unstrung bows riding in dogskin cases beneath the skirt of each saddle, to take their place in ordered ranks among the other troops assembled at the far end of the broad avenue. The native soldiers drew away from them; the foreign mercenaries were little loved by their ostensible comrades in arms.

Fost smiled grimly. With the exception of a few truly tempered units such as the Imperial Life Guards, the Grasslanders were unquestionably the finest troops on hand. For precisely that reason they were hated. He would not have ridden in Captain Mayft's saddle for anything, and not only because he was a poor dog rider.

Diplomacy had failed, so Fost had finally come out and flatly refused Teom's offer to become Grand Marshal of the Imperial

Armies. Moriana would have made a better commander; she was trained to war and well seasoned in battle strategies both physical and magical. In High Medurim, women fighting masters were accepted out of necessity, since many masters of the first quality hailed from locales in which women were not raised as docilely as they were within the Empire. For that small concession, the City States reckoned Medurim decadent. Certainly, they would accept no woman as general over them.

As for Fost, he had no desire to commit suicide. He had been resented enough when Teom had named him mere marshal, and that was a position without power or influence. The lords of Imperial arms would sooner have a foreign barbarian from the North or a hairy, uncouth wild man from the Isles of the Sun placed over them than a commoner bred in the gutters of their own city.

Finally, the parade was over. The great gates – gilded, of course – of the temple across the Plaza swung open. Out marched the bull-necked, heavily bearded Patriarch, Spiritual Protector of the Empire, clad in vestments of cloth of gold. On his head he wore the tiara, a three foot, gem-encrusted golden cylinder, surrounded by flying buttresses and less functional protrusions of silver. After him in bright array came the lesser prelates. Last of all came the Sexton, more profoundly bearded than the Patriarch, his whiskers as white as sea foam and stuffed into his girdle to keep him from stumbling over them.

He was a full one hundred thirty-eight years old, emaciated, and somewhat befuddled by all the hoopla around him this day. He had an uncanonical pushbroom propped over one skinny shoulder, not knowing what all these people were doing tracking up his pristine Plaza but sure that a broom would be needed before the ceremony was over. An alert acolyte relieved him of the implement after only a brief scuffle, and the ceremony resumed.

Ignoring the byplay, the Patriarch launched into his benediction in a voice remarkably shrill and thin for one so stoutly built. His voice reminded Fost of a mosquito's whining as he went through the liturgy. Fost was thankful for the annoying voice; it was all that kept him from falling asleep. A half-dozen spearmen had collapsed in ranks from heat and ennui before the Patriarch, with a final flourish of his golden staff, announced his blessings on High Medurim and the proceedings.

Temalla's sharp elbow nudged Teom awake. He blinked and

shook his head, confused as to his surroundings, causing Fost to reflect that truly rank hath its privileges. The Emperor stood, cleared his throat, then fumbled for his notes stashed away in the front of his immaculate gold-trimmed robe.

'Thank you, Holy One.' He clapped his hands. At once, a stream of nearly naked dancing boys and girls poured into the streets from beneath the bleachers, strewing flowers and marring the mood of chaste piety, though by the way the Patriarch's black eyes glittered beneath beetling black brows it was clear he didn't take the interruption amiss.

Teom paced down the tiers of bleachers with a servant trotting at his heels keeping the parasol between sun and Emperor. Though the Imperial party sat at the midpoint of the bleachers, Teom didn't have to fight his way through a horde of notables. A broad, clear swath ran down the center of the stands, with the nobles seated on either wing. He had made it down only one flight of steps when it became apparent to all that the Emperor had been taking counsel with a bottle, and the Imperial tread, while grand, was none too steady.

In the center of the wide wheel of the Plaza, a small kiosk had been assembled hurriedly after the troops passed in review. An avenue crossed the Plaza left to right, running between high, stately, marble edifices. The troops were drawn up in armed array to either side. The hewn granite walks flanking the street were thronged with thousands of Medurimins, jostling, shouting, haggling with vendors. Young boys and girls dressed in identical white robes circulated throughout the mob, their skirts hiked high to reveal plump, rouged buttocks. As Teom wove through the bleachers, a cry rose from the crowd. The Emperor acknowledged it with a fond nod and a wave of his pale hand. But something in the sound caused Fost to tense.

'My word, this is tedious,' grumbled Erimenes. 'When do we get to the good part?'

Teom mounted the dais where he was being embraced and kissed on both cheeks by the bristly bearded Patriarch.

'This is as good as it gets, I'm afraid,' Ziore answered peevishly.

'Perhaps there'll be a riot,' Erimenes said hopefully. 'Medurim is famous for the fine quality of its riots, I understand. Sometimes they rage for weeks, with considerable looting, burning and raping. Now *that* would be a sight to see, especially after this.'

Fost shivered despite the heat that sent rivulets of sweat steaming down the back of his armored shell.

'Don't say that,' he muttered.

Preliminaries over, Teom began to announce the names of those who should step forth to be recognized. Though this ceremony had been decreed expressly to honor those who had distinguished themselves in battle, Fost didn't know most of the names called out by the red-faced herald at the Emperor's side. Not even their faces were familiar. He did recognize Foedan, a tall, knobby man with high-domed forehead and deeply sunken brown eyes. And Ch'rri, the mutant cat woman, who at the call of her name shook out her broad wings with a thundercrack and glided down to stand before the dais, her long hair streaming behind. A rumble rose from the crowd. Whether in approval for her voluptuous nudity or out of superstitious dread of her strangeness, Fost couldn't tell.

Fost ran a finger around the inside of his linen collar beneath the cuirass. The armor sweltered fearsomely.

'I know more of those who aren't here,' he said in an aside to Moriana, who nodded, busily mopping her own brow with a cloth from a bowl of scented water brought by a page.

Harek was absent, the small argumentative Assemblyman from Duth; he had fallen under the blades of the Zr'gsz. The immense bulk of Magister Banshau of the Wirix Institute of Magic was conspicuously absent, fortunate in the light of the bleachers' continuing threat to collapse. He still lay recovering from wounds received during the abortive coup. Nor was the Dwarven Jorean Ortil Onsulomulo on hand. The half-breed captain was on board his ship making preparations to sail with a cargo of Medurimin patricians who were less than optimistic about the outcome of the new War of Powers and thought this a propitious time to relocate to Jorea or the Sword Kingdoms.

Also missing was the gaunt old knight, Sir Tharvus, last of the three Brother Knights of the Black March. He had disappeared after the victory in his home country. Dark, dire rumors were whispered about his current doings.

The first to the platform were duly honored. Ch'rri accepted the rank of marquessa by seizing Teom's head with both hands and kissing him deeply, so that he flushed red from lack of air. Lascivious hoots rose from the crowd. This being High Medurim, such doings were not wholly alien even to the elaborate Imperial punctilio, so proceedings were not delayed, though it looked as if Teom wished they could be to pursue Ch'rri's further gratitude.

The herald cleared his throat. His eyes darted over the bleachers and signalled to Fost an instant before the call went out.

'Fost, called the Long-Treader, Marshal of High Medurim, arise and come forward,' he intoned in a voice several sizes too large for him. Fost managed to grimace only slightly at the mangling of his name, got to his feet, crossed his arms and waited.

The herald blinked myopically. This was irregular, but Fost was not going to walk down in front of all those people alone. It had been arranged in advance that he and Moriana should go forward together. Obviously, arrangements had been mislaid.

The waiting game stretched on for long seconds. Fost began to regret the whole thing, particularly since he roasted inside his armor. At last, the herald blinked, cleared his throat again, and boomed, 'The Princess Moriana, Pretender to the Throne of the City in the Sky, step forward and be recognized.'

Moriana rose and the two went down hand-in-hand, she tight-lipped at being called second. They were halfway down when Fost became aware of the weight bumping at his right hip.

'Damn,' he swore.

Moriana squeezed his hand.

'It's all right. I forgot to leave Ziore behind, too.'

'Just as well we brought them, I suppose. Erimenes would probably heckle me from the stands.'

'Very perceptive, friend Fost,' the genie tittered.

'Quiet!'

They approached the kiosk and, after a slight hesitation, fell to one knee before it.

'Fost Long-Treader,' the herald said again.

'Long*strider*, you dunce!' hissed Erimenes.

Paling at being corrected out of thin air, the herald cleared his throat again.

'Fost Longstrider, rise and approach the Presence.'

His hand itching to clout the spirit's jug, Fost rose, stepped forward the requisite three paces and went to one knee again, thanking Zunhilix silently for providing padded greaves.

'For Honors Won and Services Rendered on the Field of Battle,' the herald began, his words ringing with pomposity, 'it pleases his Sublime and Imperial Majesty, Lord of All Creation, Conqueror of the Barbarians, Caster-down of the presumptuous Fallen Ones —' Erimenes snickered. Fost squeezed his eyes shut and prayed to be struck by lightning. '– to invest you Archduke and Knight of the Empire.'

Fost started up but the herald droned on relentlessly.

'As such you are elevated to the highest ranks of Imperial patrician. Know that from this day forth you shall receive all perquisites appurtenant to your exalted rank: the right to stand between Sub-Archdukes and Grand Archdukes in the bedchamber of Their Imperial Majesties –'

'Is that good?' whispered Erimenes.

'It means I outrank the boy who empties the chamberpots.'

'I thought the Palace had waterclosets?'

'The Guilds won't let them abolish the job. Now shut up!' Fost felt a million eyes on him. He was sure that the herald heard the byplay but the man plowed ahead with his recitation.

'– and of *droit de seigneur* –'

'*That's* promising,' said Erimenes, this time not even bothering to whisper.

'Hush!'

'– and to administer the High Justice, and the Low Justice –'

'What's that?'

'It means,' said Fost, exasperated, 'I can hang thieves and collect taxes. Or maybe hang tax collectors. Same thing.'

'– and to be immune to seizure of person and all real property without direct order of His Celestial Majesty, wherever the Writ Imperial shall run.'

'Ought to be safe as long as you don't wander off the Palace grounds,' Erimenes said. Fost shook the satchel. Erimenes's words were cut off by his sputtering attempts to avoid the buffeting.

The herald's words droned to an end. Fost felt the heavy jeweled scepter Teom held thump him on first the left shoulder, and then the right. The clanging seemed to fill the entire Plaza as his armor quivered under the onslaught.

'Arise, Sir Fost, O well-beloved subject and servant of the Sapphire Throne.'

None too thrilled at having attained the exalted rank of servant, Fost pushed himself upright. His left knee emitted a splitting crack. He wobbled to be caught and kissed full on the mouth by the Emperor. Released, Fost staggered backwards to Moriana's side. The Emperor's aphrodisiac perfume made him unsteady and decidedly aroused, even though this was hardly the time or the place for such

389

things. Backing up a half pace, he stumbled again. Moriana's strong arm circled his waist and held him upright until he cleared the cloying perfumed vapors from his head and regained his balance.

'Well done, Your Grace,' Erimenes told him sarcastically.

'Moriana Etuul,' the herald roared, pointedly ignoring the extra voice chirping in from time to time, 'Princess and Pretender to the Beryl Throne, Mistress of the Clouds, beloved cousin of our Emperor Teom the Magnificent, arise and approach the Presence.'

Moriana did as she was bid, but before she could step forward, a loud rumble like an avalanche in progress rolled from left to right across the Plaza.

'Thunder?' asked Fost.

'We should be so lucky,' shot back Erimenes. 'Look to your left.'

His heart nearly jumped free of his chest.

'Death!' shouted the mob as it crashed like surf against a line of blue-plated Watchmen, who stood their ground with halberds levelled. *'Death to the foreign sorceress!'*

A sergeant rapped an order. The gleaming blue line of the Watchmen took a step back and prepared for the crowd.

Across the cordon of armored Watchmen a figure arthritically mounted the steps of the Ministry of Sanitation. A tall figure, thin almost to the point of emaciation, clad in torn and faded tunic and trousers that had once been as red as freshly shed blood threw up his frail matchstick arms and emitted a wordless screech of pure hatred. The crowd surged, rallying to him.

'Seize the witch, the traitress!' shrieked Sir Tharvus of Black March, flinging out an accusing arm and pointing straight at Moriana. 'Slay her, slay the betrayers of humankind who shelter her in their bosoms! They are traitors and deserve to die with her!'

Roaring like a rabid animal, the crowd surged forward.

CHAPTER FIVE

The halberds flailed, blades rising to flash white-hot in the sunlight, rising again to the company of screams to gleam the dull red of blood. The mob faltered. It momentarily lacked a leader, someone to urge them forward into the face of death. The faint-hearted in the crowd began to edge away from the soldiers. But the crowd didn't disperse. In the back rallied tight knots of angry citizens. Parties of stout men in dusty aprons finally pushed forward, hauling great chunks of pale-veined white stone. The others in the mob heartened and began to chant cadence as their newfound heroes cast the hundredweight blocks. Unwieldy in their carapaces, a half-dozen Watchmen went down beneath the crushing chunks of marble.

It was enough. The crowd rushed forward again while Sir Tharvus's voice whipped it, crying out for blood. The remaining Watchmen fought, then vanished from sight as if they were sailors drowning in the vast Joreal Ocean. Teom stared, his eyes wide with terror at what befell his troops. Fost gripped the hilt of ceremonial sword and swore. Moriana had her own straight blade, but Fost's broadsword had been judged too unorthordox for the investiture. That left him armed with a weapon hardly fit for swatting flies.

The soldiers assembled down the avenue held ranks, though whether by design or confusion of their officers there was no knowing. Across the hundred yards of cleared space in the Plaza raced the crowd, waving sticks and bats and other makeshift weapons. Above their shrill cries came the shriller chants of Sir Tharvus. Madness had seized him and lent his frail frame power beyond reckoning. And that power transmitted to the crowd and fed their pentup hostilities. There was carnage.

'You hoped things would get better,' Fost told Erimenes, pulling the satchel flap back from over the jug inside. If he and Moriana were about to be murdered by the mob, Erimenes might as well get an unobstructed view.

'Stop!' The voice rolled like a great bell, drowning even the strident cries of Sir Tharvus.

Quiet descended over the crowd scattered across the marble flagstones of the Plaza. Down from the bleachers strode Foedan, tall and unafraid, holding his arms wide as if smoothing the jagged emotions of the crowd. The crowd faltered, lost impetus. He walked toward the bloodstained leaders. Fost and Moriana clearly heard the padding of his soft suede boots on the marble.

'Cease this display,' he said. The mob stared at him, weapons hanging limp in a hundred hands. 'This woman has saved you from destruction. You should fall on your knees with gratitude, not attack her like so many jackals.'

'But . . . but she's a witch!' a voice faltered from the middle ranks of the crowd.

'She is a sorceress. Were she not, the Fallen Ones would have arrived in these streets by now, bringing with them flame and thirsty blades. You and all your families would be dead, the death meted out by the damned reptiles!'

'Don't listen to him!' Tharvus shrieked. 'Slay her! She sold out humanity to regain her throne. Slay her!'

Still the mob remained poised on the knife edge of indecision.

'No,' Foedan said, not loudly but distinctly.

'He'll never hold them,' said Ziore. 'Moriana, do something.'

Fost's stomach twisted to a sudden premonition.

'No!' he shouted. But it was too late.

Moriana raised a hand, swept fingers in an intricate gesture. A globe of pure white light appeared over Foedan's head, competing with the sun in intensity. A moan of fear and awe swept through the crowd. The knight gazed at the mob, not seeming to notice the luminous display above his head.

'See? He's sold out, too!' Tharvus cried. His eyes blazed with a mad light as bright as the mystic sphere hanging over Foedan. 'Behold, the witch has set her mark upon him!'

The crowd gave throat to an animal cry of rage. They fell upon the lone, unarmed knight with club and cleaver and bare fists. He stood unmoving until the seething bodies hid him from view.

Teom yelped like a scalded cat and raced to the steps of the Temple crying, 'Sanctuary! Give me sanctuary!'

The platoon of Life Guards that had attended him on the bleachers went clattering by the kiosk and up the wide steps after their master. They ran as much to protect him as to save their own hides. No amount of training prepared their officers to face sure suicide by standing and fighting off this mob.

'What ho!' Erimenes sang out. 'A battle!'

'I'm glad the prospect pleases you.' Fost drew his blade and held it in front of him without conviction.

One of the members of the masons guild who had helped strike down the Watchmen raced at Moriana, swinging a long pry-bar he had used to lever up chunks of the paving marble. She snapped out of her fog of horror at what her attempt at help had won Sir Foedan and backed with a ringing clang of steel on iron. She fought to retain her grip on the sword as the stonemason attacked again and again. A laborer swung a hammer at Fost, and he had no time to worry about Moriana.

Fost's blade crossed the haft of the hammer with an odd sound. The workman reeled back, mewling like a lost soul.

'Shrewdly struck,' congratulated Erimenes.

Fost stared. The man's right hand hung from a rag of skin, yet Fost's parry hadn't come anywhere near it. Then Fost saw that his sword had bent itself into an L shape around the hardwood shaft nearly severing his assailant's hand at the wrist.

'Come on!' he shouted to Moriana. She thrust into the twisted face of an attacker and spun, following him back to the bleachers with the mob hot after them. The flimsy wooden structure thundered and vibrated beneath frantic feet as the assembled notables fled the wrath of the populace. The mob was pouring into the Plaza from both directions now. As hazardous as the bleachers were, they offered the only ground on which to make a stand. As Fost and Moriana went booming up the stands, a hairy-armed man made a grab at Erimenes's wavering form.

'Unhand me, you rogue!' shrilled the genie.

'Oh, my darling, are you hurt?' cried Ziore. Fost moaned. The man snatched again and seized one of the straps flapping wildly on Fost's kilt. His sword useless, Fost swung Erimenes's satchel and caught the man squarely on the side of the head. The man fell backward and went cartwheeling down the tiers of benches. One of the benches at the bottom gave way under the added weight with a loud snapping noise. The man's back was obviously broken.

They made the top of the bleachers and turned, momentarily ahead of the pursuit. Here the angry crowd could only come at them with difficulty, and some of the most vocal members of the mob sheered off short of the steps, wary of the bleachers' penchant for falling. The would-be killers came in ones and twos. Moriana was able to send them reeling down again, gashed and bloody, while Fost propped his sword tip against the bench and tried to kick it straight again.

He slipped, slashing his right calf, cursed, looked accidentally over the edge. The hard marble of the Plaza was a good forty feet below. There was no escape that way.

'Where the hell are the soldiers?' he shouted, swinging his almost-straight sword against a long-haired man hacking at him with a billhook. The blade struck edge-on and didn't bend. Fost put a sandaled foot in the man's belly and sent him staggering into the sweat-streaming faces of a dozen fellows.

'Don't expect help from them,' Moriana panted through a lull in the attacks. She pointed her chin up the street.

'It appears your elevation is resented more than anyone antici-pated,' Erimenes said dryly. 'Or perhaps the Twenty-third is paying off some long-standing grudges against the City Watch.'

The lightly armed but more numerous infantrymen had thrown themselves against the massively armored Watch, preventing them from coming to the aid of the Imperial party. In the other direction, Imperial troops fought each other, too. Fost shook his head and spat blood. A blow had caught him in the mouth, and he hadn't noticed it until now.

'Their commanders won't even stand trial for this,' he said bitterly. 'Look. Teom's out of it.'

Moriana glanced across the sea of bobbing heads that flooded the Plaza. Teom and the innumerable clerics had disappeared. The great gilt valves of the Temple were shut and guarded by a line of Life Guards with raised shields and lowered spears. A fresh wave of attackers flowed against Fost and Moriana leaving no time for talk.

An apprentice stonemason dressed in a leather jerkin thrust at Fost with a shortsword taken from a dead Watchman. Fost disen-gaged and ran the man through. Screaming, the apprentice toppled off the verge of the bleachers, but not before the courier had wrenched the sword from his grasp.

Fost turned back and found a big man almost on top of him,

394

swinging a makeshift club at his head. He caught the thick wrist in his free hand and aimed a disembowelling stroke at the giant belly squashed against his hips.

'Ellu!' he gasped into a face he knew well from the streets of his childhood. He faltered.

He recalled in a flash the foundling kitten they'd found and nursed together with scraps of food purloined to ease the complaining of their own bellies. No such memories stayed Ellu's now-fat hand.

'Traitor!' he snarled through spit and a cloud of reeking breath. He twisted his burly arm free of Fost's grip and cracked him across the face with his cudgel. Fost saw blackness and dancing sparks, fought to keep his balance with heels dangling over emptiness.

Ellu raised the club to finish him off. His arm stopped in midstroke, as if caught and held by an invisible hand. A look of consternation gripped the man's florid features. Then Moriana seized his shoulder, spun him from her lover and struck him down, crying her thanks to Ziore for staying the man's hand with her emotion-confusing powers.

Dizzy and nauseated, Fost dropped to his knees.

'It's lost,' he croaked. 'We can't stand them all off. The War of Powers is lost here and now.' A blackness beyond physical oblivion clutched at him.

He felt Moriana's hand on his shoulder, looked up through red mists of agony. He heard barks, snarls, screams, saw the crowd streaming away to the right, eastward toward The Teeming in which he'd been born. No one had reckoned with Captain Mayft and the outland cavalry. Now they came with lances couched and war dogs snapping left and right and made reckoning of their own with the mob.

Slow and lazy the stained wooden deck rocked beneath Fost's bare feet. He smoothed wet hair from his face, drank in the salt air rich with the tar and cordage smells of the big ship and felt more relaxed than he had in days.

He stood near an opening in the rail. A rope ladder had been let down from the gap to hang just above the dancing green surface of the sea. As he watched, a slim hand reached out of the waves, catching the bottom rung. In a few seconds, Moriana was lithely scaling the side of the ship, shimmering with wetness.

Like him, she wore a minimum of clothing. To a simple loincloth like the one knotted around his waist she had added a brief halter bound about her chest.

'I must say the princess makes an impressive sea sprite,' remarked Erimenes. His jug had been lashed to the railing so that he could watch Fost and Moriana swim without fear of being tossed into the sea by the sway of the ship.

'A good thing this is a Tolvirot craft with a mixed crew,' said Fost. 'If Moriana appeared dressed like that on deck of an Imperial vessel with an all male crew . . .' He shook his head.

For all that, he found himself appreciating the suppleness of her body and her great beauty. He approved, heartily.

'Have fun with the sharks?' he asked as Moriana stepped on deck.

She nodded, doing a brief dance as her feet accustomed themselves to the heated deck. Fost glanced over the side to where lean, silver shapes knifed through the water. A wedge of fin broke water hard beside the ship. A blunt snout thrust above the surface and a dead-gray eye regarded the deck with inhuman detachment. Fost shivered, but Moriana called out to the creature and waved. It slipped soundlessly into green water and vanished, all thirty feet of it.

'You shouldn't have left the water when they arrived, Fost,' chided Moriana, wringing out her long hair. 'They're very friendly. It's fantastic to ride on one. They're so fast, they move so cleanly, with such strength – it's like being on the back of an eagle, almost.' Her voice dropped and her eyes were troubled. He slipped an arm around her shoulders and hugged her reassuringly, savoring the feel and smell of her tanned flesh.

'Friendly?' He shook his head, grinning. 'I could swim down the throat of that monster without getting scraped on his teeth along the way. And I'm not even sure he would consider me as more than an appetizer served before the main course. I prefer not to take my chances with a beast like that.'

'Perhaps we need such powerful friends.' Her tone was not wholly joking.

'I wonder if it's true what Oracle said,' asked Ziore, hovering at Erimenes's side with her fingers vaporously mingled in his. 'That in the old days the world belonged to the *Zr'gsz* and the giant lizards and the great furred beasts, the hornbulls and mammoths, that humanity came here from somewhere else and brought certain animals with them, dogs and pigs and sharks and those darling little animals Teom showed us just before we left, the new ones imported from the Far Archipelago. What did he call them? Horses?'

Erimenes sneered.

'That's right,' answered Fost, ignoring him. Teom had taken them into the menagerie he kept outside the north wall of the Palace, on the very bluff overlooking the harbor. The Emperor had chattered volubly as if a second attempt on his life and throne had not been crushed in a bloody street battle only two days before. The new acquisitions to his enormous zoo filled him with delight, for they were rare beasts with intriguing legends surrounding them. Indeed, Fost thought they were rather cute. Tiny elfin things, the largest male no more than eighteen inches high at the shoulder. They were built like hornless deer, but their small hooves were continuous, not cloven. They had long silky brush tails and similar manes of hair growing down their necks. Their dished faces held eyes liquid brown and large.

In their last interview with Oracle a little later, Fost had mentioned the beasts. Oracle's eyes lit up.

'I have heard of such,' he said eagerly. 'Do you know the most intriguing legend of all concerning them?' The four had shaken their heads, Erimenes with a crabbed look. He hated being lectured to by someone more knowledgeable.

'It is written in old, old documents that once these creatures called horses grew larger than the biggest war dog, as large as Nevrym unicorn stags, and that they were tamed as dogs are now, to be ridden in travel, the hunt, war.'

'But they're so tiny,' objected Ziore.

'The ones surviving today are. They were a special breed, nurtured by the scholar-priests of the Far Archipelago as objects of amusement and wonder. What happened to the others?' He shrugged imaginary white shoulders. 'What happened to the cattle of olden days, short-coated like riding dogs, with horns set on either side of their heads? The only beast in the world today who wears his horns like that is Istu himself – oh! Your pardon, Princess,' he said to Moriana, who had suddenly colored and dropped her eyes. The mention of the Demon had triggered a train of memories in her that were anything but pleasant.

'I suppose you think all this supports your ridiculous theory that humanity came to the world from another plane of existence,' said Erimenes, elevating his nose to a contemptuous angle.

'I do, in fact. The legends aren't conclusive, but they point strongly to the possibility that we – or you, I suppose – originated elsewhere.'

'It also points strongly to the certainty that our kind is given to flights of imagination,' Fost pointed out, loath to rank himself with Erimenes in debate with Oracle. 'The Archipelagan Reduction states as a matter of principle that the simplest theory to account for a phenomenon is the most likely to be true.'

Erimenes turned his sneer on him.

'I'm ashamed to learn you've been taken in by the naive and simpleminded doctrine of Reductionism. We sages of Athalau had more wisdom than that.'

'Did the Athalar sages ever disprove the Reductionist axiom?' Oracle asked with interest.

'Ah, no, not exactly. But there are contentions too patently absurd to require that wise men waste their precious time deigning to disprove them.'

The discussion had gotten tangled in sticky strands of epistemology. Only Moriana remained aloof, lacking the others' interest in abstract knowledge for its own sake. The question of humanity's origin on this world or elsewhere was never solved, unsurprisingly.

Moriana took her place at the ship's rail by Fost's side, pressing her hip against his. He smiled lopsidedly. He didn't dare turn from the rail now, not without revealing the state of his scanty loincloth and displaying to the entire crew of the ship *Endeavor* the extent of his interest in the nearly naked woman. She sensed his discomfiture – or maybe read it from the surface of his mind. Since recovering Ziore's jug from the glacier-swallowed city of Athalau, Moriana's mental abilities had been increasing. She began to rub her hip slowly back and forth against his, teasing him until he felt as if he would explode.

'You shouldn't start something you don't mean to finish,' he said.

'Why not finish it? You seem to have a good start. A very good one, from what I can see from this angle.' She leaned forward and peered down meaningfully.

His mind tumbled and roiled like a storm-wracked ocean. For no reason, he remembered the conclusion of the final talk with Oracle. The others had gone ahead after offering their farewells. The projection of the 'man' had requested Fost to stay behind.

'Will you win?' Oracle had asked.

'I'd hoped you could tell me,' Fost answered.

'I have insufficient knowledge.'

'I don't know,' Fost said, sighing deeply. 'Moriana is as powerful a sorceress as lives, perhaps the strongest in centuries. But is she Felarod?'

'Even Felarod needed Athalau and the aid of the World Spirit.'

'Athalau lies buried in a living glacier, an intelligent being named Guardian. He – it – was created by the first War of Powers and is entrusted with . . . guarding Athalau from intruders.'

'Yet you penetrated it once before.'

Fost ran fingers through his hair.

'We've had this out, Moriana and I. I think she knows we'll have to return to Athalau to seek the means to overthrow Istu – if it can be done again. But now she's concerned mainly with getting to the City of Bankers with this draft Teom has given us so she can raise troops and supplies to try to check the Hissers in the Quincunx.' He shook his head. 'I have to admit the menace of Istu and the Dark Ones is great enough that it's easy to forget the purely physical peril the Fallen Ones pose. If their armies defeat us in battle, the relative strengths of the Powers is moot. But I think Moriana fears – or maybe resists – the idea of confronting the Powers with which Felarod trafficked so long ago.'

'But it must be done. I know enough to tell you that.'

They sat in silence for a time, flesh and blood man and a figment of an alien mentality.

'If you win,' Oracle finally said, 'will you come back here? You are my friend. And you look upon me as a friend rather than a challenging project in scientific sorcery or a surrogate offspring of a man who fears both he and his era will be without issue.'

'I'm touched,' Fost said truthfully. 'I'll come back.' He mentally added, If I can, if I live, if there's anything to come back to.

'I can tell you one thing, friend Fost,' Oracle said diffidently. 'Though I don't know if I should.'

'Go ahead.'

'You have been troubled by the profound question of why you continue with the mad adventure. At first you thought it was because you were in love. Erimenes claimed you continued because you feared being alone. Now you have the added motive of wishing to do all possible to preserve humanity and throw back the ultimate orderliness offered by the Dark. There's truth in all these, I think. But I perceive a further, even more fundamental truth.'

'What's that?' He tapped fingers tensely on one thigh.

'Why,' said Oracle, a broad grin splitting his moon face, 'you go

399

along because you want to see what happens next. You have a great curiosity.' The grin widened even more. 'And that's as good a motive as any.'

A seabird's cry passed Fost on its way downwind, breaking his reverie. He let his fingers trail down Moriana's back until he found the wet, warm curve of her rump. She jumped when he pinched her and jammed an elbow into his ribs. Laughing, they came into one another's arms for a long kiss. Breaking apart, they headed below to the portside cabin they shared. Though most of his thoughts were for happy lechery and enjoying Erimenes's pitiful, futile pleas to be brought along to watch, he still had time to tell himself Oracle was right.

His curiosity about what would happen next drove him onward.

Considering the difficulties they'd encountered on their way to North Keep, the twice-longer journey around the northeast shoulder of the Realm passed with almost ridiculous ease. A huge Imperial Navy ship had escorted them to the delta of the River Lo marking the easternmost extent of the Imperial dominion. Teom's parting gestures to them were of a truly Imperial magnitude, as well they should be. Not only did he owe his continued life and throne to them, specifically to Moriana, the king actually felt a certain kinship with her and her companions. Alone of all those surrounding him, these stalwarts were objects of Teom's real affection. Getting them out of the Empire safely was the most gracious thing he could do. Two serious attempts to overthrow him in a matter of weeks, interspersed with a desperate battle with the reptilian invaders, constituted an ominous record even by High Medurim standards. The intervention of mercenary Captain Mayft and her heavy dog riders on the day of the investiture had broken up the mob and foiled the plot hatched by the commanders of several Imperial Army regiments in concert with the mad Sir Tharvus to overthrow Teom and Temalla and murder Fost and Moriana. It had also caused such a violent reaction on the part of the populace that the mercenaries had to be released from their contract and sent trotting home with a huge bonus. Tharvus was still on the loose crying for Teom's downfall and Moriana's death, and it seemed that more Medurimin citizens heeded his call each day. So Teom was only too glad to see the last of his controversial guests and did all in his power to speed them on their way.

One last bit of ill-tidings had arrived before they could quit the Imperial city, however. The day before the *Endeavor* was to sail there was a great commotion at the gates of the Palace ground. After hurried consultation with Teom's surviving advisors, the gates were opened to admit a ragged, desperate, footsore band of refugees.

Grimpeace, King in Nevrym, and a scarred and battered retinue sought asylum.

'That damned Fairspeaker came back,' Grimpeace told Fost as they had gripped forearms in greeting. 'With fifty skyrafts laden with Hissers. They dropped down on Paramount just as dawn turned its upper branches gold. They drove us — drove me — out of the Palace like ferrets starting rabbits from their hole.'

Fost and Moriana had nodded with grim understanding. Someone, Fairspeaker or the canny Zak'zar of the People, had a shrewd grasp of tactics. Had they attacked the Lord of Trees from the base, as many others had tried and failed at, they would have found themselves battling upward level by level against a foe who couldn't run but must fight and sell themselves as dearly as possible. Attempts had been made to force Paramount before; none had succeeded.

But with skyrafts dropping in from above, the startled defenders would be driven downward, level by level along a path to safety their foes had thoughtfully left open. A quick strike by the Hissers and their turncoat allies and the defenders found themselves in the foyer of their own keep, with the enemy holding the rest against them. A simple plan, and a deadly one.

Moreover, an assault borne on skyrafts avoided the problems of passage among the eldritch trees of Nevrym. Fairspeaker and his ilk were foresters and could never be seduced from the trail by the sleights of the trees. But as intruders had often found in the past, those who walked the ways of Nevrym unbidden met with a multitude of fates, none pleasant. The Hissers had flown above; the trees were impotent to stop them.

'What are you doing here?' Fost asked his friend in puzzlement. Nevrym had seceded from the Empire during the Barbarian Interregnum and had kept its king and sovereignty when the rightful native dynasty was restored. There was little love between High Medurim and the Tree. Lifestyles and modes of government were too different.

Grimpeace's brown eyes had slipped from Fost's, and the courier knew the answer before the man spoke it.

'I've come to make submission to the Emperor and beg his help,' the exile said softly.

Fost's first impulse was to shout, 'You can't!' but he schooled himself against it. Grimpeace bore a heavy burden of responsibility, weightier than Fost could readily imagine. Also, Fost himself had bent his knee to Teom just a few days past with no good result. He pointed that out to Grimpeace.

'Teom can barely cling to the Sapphire Throne with both hands and all his toes,' he said. 'If you must sell the free birthright of the forest, can't you at least get a better deal?'

Grimpeace shook his great head, bone-weary and bitter at all that had happened.

'Where else can I go?'

'Back to the forest. Fight a guerrilla war against the intruders. Make a treaty with the trees and unicorns. They can't desire Hisser masters.'

Still the king shook his head.

'Too many of my people chose to go in with Fairspeaker. The Hissers control too much.'

'They can't be everywhere,' pointed out Moriana.

'No, Princess, not everywhere. Not yet. You have stymied them at the Marchant — for now. And the Watchers of Omizantrim have all but closed the skystone mines.'

'See!' cried Fost, eagerness seizing him. 'It can be done. You can do it, too! Go back and fight them on your own ground, where all the advantages are yours.'

'The advantages are those of Fairspeaker and the other traitors,' Grimpeace said bitterly. He sat heavily in a creaking chair. 'Besides, the heart's not in me for such a war. I must face reality. Mayhap all I'll find here is my own death fighting to defend these stinking crowded streets from the Fallen Ones. But better that than to skulk like a thief through Nevrym-wood, *my* wood, while the monsters at Thendrun sit like kings within the Tree.'

There'd been little more to say. Grimpeace parted from Fost with a few uncomfortable words, bowed courteously to Moriana, and was gone. The encounter had left Fost deep in black depression. It wasn't just the misfortune of his friend that possessed him or the triumph of the evil Fairspeaker. The tradition of almost fifty centuries, the tradition of Nevrymin freedom, lay in ruins at the clawed feet of the Vridzish. Kara-Est was a raw wound in the soil at the head of the Gulf of Veluz; Wirix had not been heard from, even via magical means, for weeks. The Empire was tearing itself apart from within, while the Hissers squatted in their fortifications across the Marchant and watched with chalcedony eyes, waiting until the stone thunderhead of the Sky City darkened the sky above the homeland of their enemies.

He had the awful sense that the People were victorious everywhere, that such pinpricks as the defeat in the Black March and the interruption of the Omizantrim mining operations were sad, silly, futile against the might and cleverness of the lizard folk and their patrons. Istu had scarcely shown his strength and yet the dominion of humanity fractured like rotten stone.

Fost was impotent with Moriana that night. Not even Erimenes found voice to complain. And Moriana hardly seemed to notice, her thoughts distant and her body tense. They clung to each other, unsleeping, unspeaking, needing the reassurance of closeness rather than the release of desire.

Oared galleys had warped *Endeavor* out of the harbor the next day, accompanied by her escort. No cheering crowds lined the waterfront to see them go. Teom's advisors had insisted on keeping the time and manner of the departure secret. Teom and Temalla took leave of them at the Palace with tears and presents and lingering kisses, but did not go with them to the dock. Only painted Zunhilix, his normal ebullience subdued, and a detachment of Guards had accompanied them to the docks.

They did not leave unnoticed, however. The tugs pulled *Endeavor* within a hundred yards of Onsulomulo's ship the *Wyvern*, already riding low in the scummy water with her hold swollen with the goods of refugee patricians. And there was Ortil Onsulomulo clad only in Jorean kilt and dawn light, golden on the rail of his vessel, dancing and playing a mournful hornpipe. He was a strange one, this half-breed, but he had in his way been a friend and they were sad to see the last of him. Somehow, though, Fost couldn't find it in him to worry about Onsulomulo. The half-breed claimed the gods and goddesses watched over him, and the evidence bore this out.

The wind came from the port quarter, fair for passage west to the turning of the land, fairer still for Tolviroth. They made good time to the place where the outflow of the Lo stained green seawater brown. Their escort made a slow turn, dipped flag in salute and began to pull back for High Medurim, a proud and lonely remnant of lost Imperial might and grandeur.

Despite Fost's apprehensions, there was not real trouble. A flotilla of galleys with drab sails set had come out of North Cape Harbor when the *Endeavor* passed in sight of the Northernmost Peak to try to claim this rich prize for the Dwarves' revolutionary government and its new allies, the Zr'gsz. Big as she was, *Endeavor* was a smart sailor with a good Tolvirot hull, and she put them easily in her frothy wake.

Down came the sails, out went the oars, and the Dwarven ships began a waterstrider crawl in pursuit. *Endeavor*'s master, a native Tolvirot only a few years Fost's senior, medium built with the broad shoulders and dancing tread of a fencing master, casually ordered an onager unwrapped from its oiled cloth coverings. The *Endeavor* had been laid for deepwater and open sea storms. She was much more strongly built than any oared war craft, and could carry heavy engines, true shipkillers, whose workings would damage the lighter hull of a war ship. Captain Arindin stood with one hand in the voluminous pocket of the embroidered green coat he was never without, calmly munching a fruit held in the other, while his crew unshipped the onager and set it bucking, hurling great rocks against the pursuing galleys. The fourth shot sent a hundredweight stone smashing through the bottom of the leading vessel, breaking her back and foundering her in the rollers heaving in from the line of squalls hanging far to the north. Abruptly less avid for the chase, her companion ships crowded around to assist in rescue operations. One was so intent on breaking off the chase and aiding the damaged ship that the would-be rescuer rammed another just aft of the bow and holed her. The last sight the *Endeavor* had before twilight drew a dark curtain over the scene was a confusion of uncontrolled ships and angry heads bobbing in the swells.

'If the wind'd died we might have had hot work,' was Captain Arindin's only comment.

An eeriness, a foreboding, attended the rest of the voyage, or so it seemed to Fost. Dark clouds hung like a line of distant cliffs in an unbroken wall across the northern horizon, sometimes sending down dark mutterings of thunder, flaring by night with maroon lightnings like no other Fost had seen. Sometimes it seemed that huge shapes stalked among the clouds, and sometimes there were splashings and tumults in the sea, too far for *Endeavor*'s lanterns to reach even with their cunning lenses of Tolvirot manufacture. The loudness became all the more unsettling for that. Alarum was cried shortly after midnight and Fost and Moriana came tumbling onto deck, she in a cloak, he naked except for his woebegotten mail vest.

No attacker threatened.

A huge wheel of light, eight-spoked and hundreds of feet across, rose from the depths to make the surface bubble and glow a yellow-green a thousand yards ahead of the *Endeavor*. As the astonished passengers and crew watched, the monstrous colored wheel sank a score of feet, then, still clearly visible, moved toward them, spinning faster and faster as it came. It cleared the keel of *Endeavor* and passed beneath them without sound or heat, though the heavy ship rocked at its passage. It crawled along under the long wake of the ship and was soon gone from sight. Arindin ordered wine broken out and, fortified with drink, the vessel's folk went back to duty or bed.

Erimenes and Ziore chattered brightly about what the apparition might have been and where it might have come from. The Tolvirot mariners, hardheaded as they were, seemed disconcerted and exchanged muttered speculations of their own as they clambered into the rigging to dress the furled sails. Fost and Moriana said nothing about it between themselves. Privately Fost thought the wheel was a sign, a proof, that the reality he had grown up to accept was unraveling all around him.

The Powers intruded more and more into his daily life.

No further disturbance occurred until *Endeavor* rounded the coast, headed south for the Karhon Channel and Tolviroth. Fost was on deck drinking wine, enjoying the double moons, the stars, the velvet sky, the warm rich smells of the land breeze and the comfortable speculation as to what awaited him when he joined Moriana in their cabin in a few minutes. His reverie was broken by a footfall behind him. He turned to see Moriana, her face strained and pale. At first he thought the cunning light playing down on them from the twin moons caused the effect. Then he knew it was no illusion. Tears glowed brightly in the corners of her eyes.

'Come,' she said urgently, gripping his sleeve.

'What's wrong?'

'Come on!' she hissed at him. He went.

A lantern shed mellow light in their cozy cabin. Fost looked around, saw nothing unusual, said so.

405

'On the bed,' Moriana said tonelessly.

For the first time, he noticed the flower lying across the pillow they shared.

'A gift from the crew? Is that what's bothering you?' He laughed reassuringly and slipped his arm around her waist. 'It seems more thoughtful to me than anything else. Besides, I thought your emblem was a rose.'

'Look at the color.'

He frowned, took his arm away and went to the bed, bending down to more closely examine the flower.

'Don't touch it,' she said. He shrugged. To humor her, he didn't reach out for the flower.

He went cold all over. The flower was black. Not just the bloom itself, but the stem and long, long thorns, as well. He recoiled, fear clutching at his stomach.

'What . . .?'

'It means the Dark Ones wish us to know they've not forgotten us,' she said.

CHAPTER SIX

Wholly at ease and hoarding the sensation like a marooned man hoards crumbs of a rapidly dwindling food supply, Fost ate small, tart berries from an iced bowl and admired the scuff marks his boot heels made on the marble table in front of him. The bankers of Tolviroth Acerte had given the city its name. But the other residents of Tolviroth did not have to *like* the bankers, and his birthplace notwithstanding, Fost had come over the years to consider himself as much a Tolvirot as anything. So he ignored the scandalized looks from the reed-thin clerk behind the reception desk and propped his feet on the marble table while he relaxed in a soft chair and plied himself with iced fruit.

'Do you have to do that?' Moriana demanded, striding to and fro nervously. 'We've come here to ask for money.'

'We've come here to demand money, against the Emperor's note,' Fost corrected. He popped another grayish berry into his mouth, sucked cool juice down his throat, chewed the skin and swallowed. 'Besides, you're doing more damage to the place than I am. You're wearing a hole in the carpet.'

The clerk, sexless in a long brown toga, gave Fost another venomous look and went back to scratching entries in a leather-bound ledger spread across the desktop.

'You musn't worry, Moriana,' said Ziore, 'Certainly there will be no trouble with the bank honoring Teom's draft.'

Fost looked thoughtful but said nothing.

'Remember the good fortune I had the last time I dealt with the bankers of Tolviroth?' Moriana said, her words edged in irony.

'But you didn't visit this particular institution on your last trip.'

'That's why I chose it this time. I'm leery of dealing with people who turned me down once before.'

407

A squarely built woman of medium height appeared in the painted stucco archway. Her eyes roved over the room, hardly stopping on any of the people there, as if she considered all beneath her notice. She turned, as if to leave, then hesitated. Her gaze stopped on Moriana. No hint of emotion tainted her calm face.

'Princess Moriana?' she inquired in a courteous but cool voice.

'Yes,' said Moriana. 'Freewoman Pergann?' Fost smiled in approval at her remembering Tolvirot protocol by choosing the proper form of address. The bankers were touchy about such matters. Protocol meant as much to them as did the proper pomp and ceremony to the chamberlains tending the patricians in High Medurim.

The woman showed even teeth and her manner chilled even more, if possible.

'A Freewoman Pergann. I'm one of the Daughters of Pergann.' She swept the small group again with a gaze that revealed nothing. Fost vowed never to get into a game of cards with her. He had the feeling Pergann knew everything about him after a single glance while he could never begin to fathom her depths. 'If you would be so kind as to step into my office.'

Fost lifted his feet from the table, trying not to call attention to himself. The woman wore a severely cut ice-blue tunic with balloon trousers tucked into the tops of low, soft boots. This wasn't the garb he'd come to expect from bankers, nor was her attitude. She lacked the usual supercilious manner of other Tolvirot bankers and even approached glacial coldness toward them. Since he had not been excluded from the invitation, he picked up Erimenes's jug and followed the woman and Moriana, who had scooped Ziore's jar into her arms.

Freewoman Pergann seemed no more nonplussed to have the odd assembly of mortals and ghosts facing her across her own desk than she had been to discover them in her anteroom. The desk itself was plain, dark anhak wood, of more modest dimensions than the androgyne secretary's in the waiting room. With his usual tact, Erimenes pointed this out before anyone else had a chance to speak.

'Ostentation,' answered Pergann, with a thin smile, 'is fine out front to impress the customers, or so Mother believes. The company is still hers. I work here and see no need for extravagant display.' She pinned Fost with her cool eyes. He felt like a bug being placed in an exhibit, but without the passion normally the domain of avid collectors. 'Usually folk are somewhat impressed by the lavishness of the waiting room's decor, if not its attention to dictates of taste. But then, most of our clientele falls between the extremes of those too wealthy and those too barbaric to possess taste.'

Fost flushed at the implied insult and studied the wooden carvings on the wall that were the cubicle's sole decoration. They were Jorean, portraying the equinoctial devotions to the goddess Jirre. They were old, stained by time and Tolviroth's humid climate. Fost glanced down at Erimenes's jug, hoping the genie hadn't noticed the subject matter of those carvings. For a staid banking office, they were quite risqué. But the spirit gave no attention to mere bric-a-brac.

'About the Emperor's draft, Freewoman,' urged Moriana.

The woman's mouth set into a thin line. At first glimpse, Fost took it for intransigence, but soon realized that the woman was reluctant to say what was on her mind.

'I can see no profit in being circumspect in this matter, Your Highness,' she said finally, 'though it gives me no great pleasure to tell you this. The cheque is worthless. There's no money in the Imperial account to cover it.'

'None?' Moriana blinked rapidly. 'But that's impossible!'

'With all due respect, Your Highness, it does not speak well of your knowledge of Imperial fiscal policy that you find the penury of Emperor Teom's account so startling. A nation that will cast clay slugs, fire them in a kiln, cover them with pewter wash and call that *coinage* is capable of anything from a financial viewpoint, anything save responsibility.' She spoke of the Imperial Treasury's latest seigniorage scheme in the same tone one might use to speak of someone who enjoyed eating dog excrement for breakfast.

Realizing she might have been harsher on Moriana than intended, she softened her tone and said, 'Let me explain about money. Economics has few laws. One is that devalued money will soon replace more valuable coin. No one continues to use a one klenor piece of silver when the Imperial pewter klenor buys the same amount of goods.' Pergann leaned back and said, smiling, 'It does speak well of your own fiscal attitudes that you find the Empire's doings so hard to grasp.'

'I . . . I still find it hard to believe there's no money in the Imperial accounts. You're sure? There's nothing?'

Pergann's eyes and face hardened slightly.

409

'I would not be a responsible banker if I made inaccurate reports to my clients,' she said primly. 'Your friend there with the big boots is smiling. You're from Medurim, sir? Or know about it?'

'I was born there,' admitted Fost.

'I might have guessed.'

He wasn't sure how to take that. He reached out and gripped Moriana's hand firmly in his.

'Don't be upset,' he told her. 'We're not penniless – at least you're not. You're Queen of the Sky City. That withered old goat Omsgib will have to open the Sky City accounts to you.' Realizing the unflattering description of one of Pergann's fellow bankers, he added, 'Uh, sorry, Freewoman.'

'No pardon needed,' she said gravely. 'I see that for all your roughness of manner and need to elevate your feet, you are an astute judge of character.'

Moriana rose, saying, 'We won't take up any more of your time, Freewoman. Thank you for seeing us.'

'You're quite welcome. I hope we can have dealings in the future, dealings of a more mutually productive nature.'

Fost stood, too, paused uncertainly, stuck out his hand to the banker. She shook it with strong, dry fingers. Then she came around the desk to hold open the door for him and Moriana.

'Great Ultimate!' Erimenes yelped as Fost passed through. 'Have you seen what they're doing on that hanging?'

Ostentation at the House of Omsgib-Bir went more than skin deep. Tulmen Omsgib faced his motley visitors across several acres of desk, nodded judiciously, and popped a jellied sweet into his mouth. His thin beard, long face, high-bridged nose and big, sad eyes made him look like a goat, an effect accentuated by the unconscious nodding of his head up and down as he chewed.

'It is a pleasure to see you again so soon, Your Highness,' he said in a voice so oily it might have been poured from a bottle.

'Let's not mince words, Omsgib,' snapped Moriana. 'You never expected to see me again when you sent me penniless from your door. You were so smugly sure my sister would win. And did you think she might reward you for failing to release the City's funds to me, the rightful ruler?' She laughed, a harsh, strident sound. 'I'm sure Synalon would have rewarded you amply. But in a coin other than you expected.'

His goat eyes took on a look of abject pain. Fost, who knew the banker by sight and reputation but had never seen him up close, halfway expected to see a goat's bar-shaped pupils peering forth.

'I'm sorry Your Highness fails to appreciate my discretion. Mine is a fiduciary trust; the welfare of my accounts is in my hands.' He held up brown claws dabbed with cornstarch powder to hide the age spots covering them. 'When you have acquired more of the mellowing and maturity that aging brings, you will understand that my caution was motivated by sincere concern for your best interests. I not only look after my client's account, I attempt wholeheartedly to take the welfare of that client into account, too.' He smiled at his small play on words.

Moriana looked as if she were about to spit on the deeply woven purple carpet. Dolefully, the banker ate another sweet. Fost shifted on the uncomfortable velvet upholstered stool a servitor had brought, and wished it had been Omsgib's table he'd rested his boots on. However, no sooner had they entered the elaborately graven portals of the House of Omsgib-Bir than they were ushered in to see the master himself, after first being courteously but firmly relieved of their weapons. Evidently, news of Moriana's victory in the Sky City, no matter how shortlived, had reached Omsgib's ears. Or maybe the goatlike gleam that came into his eyes whenever they fell on the swell of her breasts accounted for the solicitousness with which he'd greeted her.

'I don't see any need for further discussion,' Moriana said stonily, marking the direction of the banker's gaze. 'I am the Queen of the City in the Sky. I want the funds held in the City's accounts released to me. And I want them *now*. Any excuse for not releasing them I suggest you save for a court of arbitration.'

He looked aggrieved and tossed three more candies into his mouth, one after the other.

'I do wish you'd not take that attitude, Highness.'

'So you are going to try to weasel out!' She half-rose. Fost expected to see smoke rising from the roots of her hair, as had happened with Synalon when she was murderously angry.

Omsgib flung up his hands, as if to protect himself.

'No, no!' he bleated. 'I mean – well, that is . . .'

'Yes,' Moriana finished for him. She permitted Fost to take her arm and draw her back into her chair.

'I believe . . .' started Omsgib, then his voice cracked. He ran a thick, pale worm of a tongue over bloodless lips. He sipped hurriedly from a silver goblet of wine at his elbow and cleared his throat. Seeing that he was in no real physical danger, his composure settled over him once again like a thick, greasy blanket. A small smile curled the corners of his mouth and his eyes regained their luster.

'I believe, Your Highness,' the banker started again, 'that on your last visit I pointed out that, from my standpoint as administrator of the Sky City's accounts, actual possession of the City accounted for more than legal niceties. A cruel fact, but a fact nonetheless, and as a responsible banker I must deal solely in facts.

'And the fact is, you are an exile, and therefore not properly Queen of the City in the Sky, any more now than before.'

Her eyes glowed wrathfully beneath scowling brows. Her fingers tensed into fists, then uncurled again. The princess forced herself to take several deep breaths before speaking.

'That's as it may be. But there's no denying I'm the sole surviving heir of the royal family of the Sky City. On that basis you cannot deny me access to the funds.'

He placed his palms together like a mendicant goat. His expression told that he was beginning to enjoy this exchange of verbal sword thrusts and thought he had the winning blade.

'I could not deny you access to the funds,' he agreed sanctimoniously, 'were that the case.'

'Were that the case?' demanded Moriana, her face darkening with an inrush of angry blood.

'That you were the sole surviving heir.'

She lunged to her feet with such speed that her chair fell over and its back cracked on the floor. Her hands tightened into hard fists and she leaned forward onto the desk. Omsgib cowered back, even though she was a full desk's width distant.

'What nonsense is this?' she cried.

Fost had to admire the way the banker recovered to face the raging princess.

'What I mean,' Omsgib said, satisfaction in his oily voice, 'is that you are the second party in two days to come forward claiming to be sole and rightful heir to the City.'

'Who's the damned impostor?' Had her arms been long enough, Fost thought she would have reached across the desk to choke an answer from the banker.

'No impostor at all, or so I believe. She's a quite striking young lady, who goes to no pains to conceal her considerable personal beauty.' He looked meaningfully at Moriana's businesslike garb of tunic and trousers and boots. 'She's tall, like yourself, and as inclined to be overbearing. Her hair is as black as the soul of Darkness, if I may wax poetic. Her name . . .' He drummed thin fingers on the desktop while he studied the ceiling with one eye, the other closed. Moriana quivered with need to hear the name.

'Ah! I have it now,' said Omsgib, donning a crudely counterfeited expression of recollection. 'Her name is Synalon Etuul.'

Squinting in the bright sunlight cascading in through the translucent skylight, Fost peered into faces he had only expected to see again in a nightmare.

'You're looking well, Long-*strider*,' said Prince Rann Etuul, giving the peculiar Sky City inflection to Fost's Nevrym-given surname. 'You should thank whoever broke your nose like that. It gives you an impressively rakish air.'

'It was one of your damned lizard friends.'

'Indeed?' Rann replied, one slim eyebrow arching. '*I* had no "lizard friends." If by chance you refer to one of the *Zr'gsz*, I might remind you it was your comrade Moriana who enlisted the Fallen Ones as friends.' He smiled, showing a hint of fine, white tooth. 'If that's the case, I sympathize. I narrowly escaped death from one of the reptile folk myself.'

Fost looked down at the tabletop, cursing himself for letting fear-spawned anger speak for him. Even in the most secure room of the most prestigious negotiation and intermediary firm in Tolviroth Acerte, with the company's armed guards standing by in case one of the parties attacked the other, Rann jockeyed for advantage. And letting emotion run away with him, Fost knew, gave Rann considerable advantage.

'We both made our pacts with the Dark Ones, sister dear,' said Synalon from where she lazily sprawled at Rann's side. 'And they both proved worthless. Let's leave the past and see what the future provides, shall we?'

For the first time since the Safesure Intermediary Company guards had escorted her into the room, color came to Moriana's face.

'I made no pact with the Dark Ones!' she flared.

'You bargained with Their chosen,' the darkhaired woman pointed out. 'Surely, you didn't think that the Fallen Ones would

413

do anything contrary to the interests of their masters?' It was Moriana's turn to avert her eyes and berate herself for giving advantage to a foe. She had thought exactly that, and she did not need the studied irony in Synalon's voice to tell her how foolish that thought had been.

Fost took a drink from the cup of wine at his elbow. One of the attendants, swaddled in white scale armor, looked to his sergeant, who nodded, and then stepped forth to refill the cup. The cup was of thin beaten silver, not for purpose of decoration but because a heavier one might be used as a bludgeon. Even one of ceramic might be broken to provide a sharp-edged, makeshift knife. Silver was too soft to hold an edge, and the flimsy cup would simply collapse if used to strike someone. The wine itself was scientifically diluted and its serving carefully overseen to produce a calming effect. Safesure took its responsibilities seriously, which was why Captain Arindin had recommended them so highly for this ticklish reunion. It was fortunate that the rival royal parties had encountered each other in Tolviroth Acerte, where secure neutral meeting ground could be had for a suitable price. Armed guards remained in the room with them; Wirixer mages were stationed outside, in case magic was called for. Fost tried to imagine dealing with Synalon and Rann in the common room of some country inn and found it too unsettling to ponder long.

Even in spite of the precautions, the safety of all concerned was beyond the company's ability to guarantee. Even though the Wirixer mages had been assembled, Fost knew all too well that if the sisters began tossing occult lethality about there was no way anyone in the world could stop it.

The silence in the room grew dry and scratchy with age. Fost cleared his throat.

'Excuse me for asking such a silly question,' he said, quailing inwardly at the quick blue light of anger blazing in Synalon's eyes, 'but why aren't you dead?'

She laughed. Her breasts shook vigorously to the full-throated merriment, threatening to break free of the inadequate restraint of her lacebird silk bodice.

'Ah, you poor, trusting fools. Moriana, you actually thought I'd step to my death in a fit of pique over a little setback?'

'As far as I could tell, you did,' said Moriana with an evenness of tone that amazed Fost.

'Yes, beloved sibling, I did. And before even I stepped from the window, I sent a mental call out for my dear eagle Nightwind. I hardly had the chance to enjoy the feel of falling free when he was between my legs and carrying me safely away.'

'And you, Rann?' piped up Erimenes, fidgeting at being excluded from the conversation. His and Ziore's jugs had posed a problem for the guards. Since there was nothing visible in either jar, and since the two most potent sorceresses were to be in the same room together anyway, it was decided a couple of genies made little difference. 'How do you come to be sitting here, looking so hale and hardy? I thought Khirshagk's spear brought you down.'

'It brought my eagle down, may he who cast that damned spear writhe in hellfire!'

Erimenes paled before the force of the prince's passion. The fury passed from Rann's tawny eyes and he relaxed.

'But Terror was the greatest of a great breed. The war eagles of the City are trained to preserve their rider's life at all costs. And though his every wingbeat added to his agony, Terror controlled our descent until he could set me safely on a hilltop. Then he died.'

'My dear Rann, I do believe I detect sentiment in your voice.' Some of Erimenes's cockiness had returned.

'No one cares what you believe, demon!' snapped Rann. His scars glowed like white-hot wires.

'If there's hellfire, Khirshagk's writhing in it,' Fost cut in quickly. 'He used that peculiar black smoking gem the Hissers took from the fumarole on Mt. Omizantrim and freed Istu with it. However the breaking of bonds Felarod created worked, it killed Khirshagk in the process.'

'Lucky all in the City weren't killed,' murmured Synalon. 'I've tested the magic that bound Istu, and know its potency.' She tapped her daintily pointed chin. 'No, come to think of it, from my viewpoint it wasn't lucky at all, for if all within the City had been slain, I might have returned at once.'

Moriana wasn't listening.

'There's hellfire,' she said softly, staring unfocused at the center of the table. Silence crowded in again. Everyone knew why Synalon had tested the bonds pinioning Istu in the City's foundations, and it wasn't with a view toward strengthening them. Likewise, no one had to question how Moriana knew the reality of hellfire. She had seen it glowing through the slits that were the eyes of the Vicar of

415

Istu, and it had touched her, left its mark on her.

'Perhaps if you'll explain how you came to be here,' suggested Rann. Moriana scowled, not wishing to follow any path the prince pointed out. Hurriedly, Fost began talking, telling what had happened in the City after Synalon's apparent suicide. Soon, Moriana joined in the telling, and the two spirits as well.

As she listened, Synalon's fingers idly stroked at her exposed breastbone. When the tale came to the night of the Golden Dome, they slipped into the top of her gown, at which Rann cleared his throat and looked away. Fost imagined that the Safesure attendants were grateful just then that their helmets hid their expressions. They would certainly earn their fees this day.

When the bloody aftermath of Teom's orgy was told, Rann's eyes glowed and he massaged one fist, cracking the knuckles and nodding appreciation of Fost and Moriana's exploits. Then came the story of the Battle of the Black March, and he pounded his fist excitedly into his palm. He obviously wished he could have been there, commanding, fighting, taking in the ebb and flow of the battle. It was for such things the man lived — and it was in such things that Rann was a true genius.

Fost wondered whether Moriana, who had the narrative at this point, would tell of Zak'zar's apparition that had soured the victory celebration following the battle. She looked at him and stopped short.

'We had a visit from the Speaker of the People that night,' he said, hearing her breath catch. 'He showed us the fate that had befallen Kara-Est that day. How did you come to escape it?'

The rest was Moriana's to keep or give.

Synalon's fingers curled into fists.

'We would have fought the Hissers at Kara-Est,' she growled, 'but for the treachery of this worm beside me.'

All stared at this, even the faceless attendants lining the whitewashed walls, for Rann's devotion to his princess was as legendary as his prowess in war and torture. The hair on Synalon's head began to untwine itself from its elaborate coiffure, and blue sparks crackled through it. Looking stricken, the guard sergeant started to draw his sword, knowing that it might be the last thing he ever did. Moriana raised a slim hand.

'Stay,' she said to the guard. 'She does that when she's angry. It means nothing.'

Synalon was known throughout the Realm for her behavior when angry. The sergeant did not look encouraged, but if Synalon uncorked anything horrible Moriana would catch the brunt of it, and it was Moriana who bid him not be concerned. He only hoped she wasn't going to commit suicide on *his* shift.

Rann had dropped his head until his sharp chin rested on the embroidered yoke of his dark brown tunic.

'I did what I thought best served the interests of my queen,' he said quietly.

While Synalon sat looking disdainful and dripping the occasional fat blue spark to sizzle and die and leave small charred circles on the floor, Rann told how he had determined that resistance to the might of Istu was futile.

'I read the old accounts of the War of Powers,' he said.

'The First War of Powers,' Fost corrected dully.

Rann studied him for a moment.

'I suppose you're right in making the distinction. At any rate, I had some idea of the nature of the Black Lens, the form in which our scouts reported that Istu manifested himself. In that aspect the Demon can draw matter and energy irresistibly into himself, and only the mightiest of magics can forestall him.'

'I would have fought!' shrieked Synalon. A blue nimbus flamed about her head.

'You would have died,' answered Rann. Synalon whirled on him, raising her hand. Fost knew the gesture. Time slowed to a crawl before his eyes. The guardsmen sensed the intent but hesitated, not having expected the princess to turn on her own ally. Moriana made no motion, so it was up to Fost to act. He snatched up the goblet by his elbow and flung the contents onto the enraged princess.

A loud hiss and a cloud of steam filled the chamber. From outside came a dull thump. The Wirixer mages had detected the magics being mustered in the room; one had fainted upon realizing how potent they were. Synalon turned to Fost with eyes like lances of blue fire. For the courier, time seemed to flow like molasses. No matter how fast he reacted, it would be far too slow to stay his death. He remembered the searing caress of a salamander and wondered if a lightning bolt would feel the same.

Synalon tipped back her head and laughed.

'You're a brave fool, courier. You must still hear Hell Call ringing in your ears. Death was that close.'

417

'I live,' he said doggedly.

The laughter died.

'So you do. As does the renegade Rann. Perhaps you're not so much a fool, after all.'

'I could have told you Your Highness as much,' Rann said dryly.

'There's more to you than is immediately apparent, Longstrider, though it's not displeasing, either. It may please me one day to take you from my sister; I doubt she fully appreciates you.' Before either party named could respond, the sorceress turned to Ziore. 'And you, nun, I warn you. Don't try your emotion play on me a second time, unless you want to learn what true death is.'

Again a long silence fell as all sat back and composed themselves, for the next round in this battle of wills.

'What precisely happened in Kara-Est, if it's not too much trouble to tell us?' demanded Erimenes, in a pet because the promised mayhem had failed to materialize.

The sergeant of the guard had dispatched one of the attendants to fetch a bowl of water and a towel to clean the wine from Synalon and the table. He entered without noticeable enthusiasm and began mopping up the sticky red mess. Synalon undulated beneath the caress of the cloth, making the man so nervous he dropped it three times. The last time one end fell down between Synalon's breasts. His hand shot reflexively in pursuit. Synalon raised an eyebrow at him, smiled. He threw up his hands, uttered a thin scream and fled the room.

'Now that the comic relief is over, we can get down to business,' said Rann, rapping his knuckles on the table. 'To answer your question, demon, I made preparations to evacuate Kara-Est, without advising Synalon. Then, the night before the City was to arrive overhead, I went to her to tell her the only logical thing we could do was get out.' His eyes avoided his sovereign's.

'And she refused,' said Moriana.

'Just so. As I had anticipated.'

'So what happened?' Fost asked.

'I struck her with a Thailint drug dart. The chemical acts almost instantaneously. Not altogether so, unfortunately.' He raised his right arm and drew up the tunic sleeve. The underside of his wiry arm showed angry red, as if recently scalded. 'I'll bear the marks of her anger a long time.'

'You deserved worse,' Synalon said, but without heat.

'I did what I thought best,' Rann repeated. 'We had no hope of winning. And as far as I knew, Synalon was the strongest magician alive, and the only one with a faint hope of ever commanding the power to defeat Istu. But then and there, she had no hope at all.'

'So what do you intend now?' asked Ziore.

'Isn't that obvious? We join forces against Istu and the Vridzish.'

Moriana and Synalon jumped to their feet screaming denial; the Safesure attendants stood by the walls fairly quaking in their armor. They were well-tempered men and women, normally fearless, but this was like dancing with an unconstrained fire elemental. In the commotion, Fost's gaze met Rann's and perfect understanding flowed between them. The sensation made Fost's skin crawl, but he knew that he and the prince alike knew what must be done. Sharing a thought with the likes of Rann was not something Fost found comfortable.

For all their mutual hate, for all the many ways they were opposites, both royal sisters possessed intellects on the same order as their egos – enormous. And between them they knew almost all of the magic learned by humanity over the ages. Slowly, reluctantly, they calmed and resumed their places.

'He's right,' Moriana said grudgingly. 'Alone, neither of us has a chance against the Demon. Together . . .'

'Together, you've scarcely more of a chance,' said Rann.

'Have you learned so much magic,' Synalon said, looking at him narrowly, 'that you can predict the future?'

'No. But I know history. Felarod and his Hundred – a hundred Athalar savants of the heyday of that city's skill in magic – couldn't contain the Demon of the Dark Ones. They had to invoke the World Spirit, and in that act almost died.' He looked from one cousin to the other. 'Recall that not even Felarod long survived his triumph.'

'I don't fear dying to defeat the Demon!' shouted Moriana. She of all those assembled had the deepest hatred of the spawn of the Void.

Rann faced her coolly.

'What about dying uselessly? I don't know magic as you do, but this I know. Even if you and Synalon act in perfect harmony, you have no more chance of overcoming Istu than I have of hiking to the Pink Moon.'

'It sounds as if you're refuting your own argument,' Fost said, arguing against himself as much as Rann. 'If our joining forces won't bring Istu's fall, why should we take the risk? Either of us?'

'I'll tell you something, Longstrider,' said Rann. 'When we were antagonists I found myself wishing that we could work together, you and I. You continue to show yourself perceptive, and to prove the soundness of my judgment of you as a shrewd man, rough-edged and not well schooled in subtlety, but able. I hope we can yet work together, Northblood.'

Fost moistened his lips from his cup to hide what he assumed correctly to be the expression of unwonted pleasure. The prince was flattering him. And he seemed to mean it.

'But to your question. I still feel that the means of bringing down Istu can be found. Just because a weapon doesn't lie conveniently at hand doesn't mean it doesn't exist.'

'Istu was overcome before.' Instantly, Fost cursed himself for speaking. He was actually trying to elicit the prince's approval and had wound up mouthing the obvious.

Rann seemed not to notice.

'Just so. We can find the means.' He smiled cheerlessly. 'But there's the problem of staying alive until we do.'

Moriana leaned forward across the table. She held her anger back with obvious effort, yet what her cousin said had merit.

'You've thought on the situation,' she said with only the faintest hint of begrudging it to Rann. 'Outline it for us, if you will.'

Fost nodded to himself. Subconsciously at least, Moriana had accepted the necessity of joining with those who had been her deadliest foes. Now she spoke to Rann much as she must have when the two of them fought the Golden Barbarians together, years before.

'First,' Rann started, 'the strengths and weaknesses of our enemies. They have Istu, of course. But even the Demon of the Dark Ones has his limitations. According to the lore – and it's unanimous on this subject – Istu is in some way linked to the City itself. He's a creature of the Void, of the nothingness between suns. This world's as much a hostile environment to him as the bottom of the sea would be to us. The historical evidence indicates that he is most powerful when he is physically present in the City. Apparently, that was one reason Felarod bound him there; so strong are the forces binding him and the Sky City together that they might have drawn him forth from another prison, no matter what spells Felarod devised to hold him.

'The City itself provides severe limitations, at least to his movement. It is no longer constrained to follow the Quincunx. However, neither in the past nor in the days since Istu was freed has it ever been observed to go faster than the mile-an-hour pace it has maintained throughout the centuries. It *may* be able to go faster. It's safe to assume that speeding it up would tax even Istu's powers.'

He steepled his fingers in front of his lips. Even Synalon listened now, with only a trace of contempt lingering on her face.

'Now, as to the People. Their population is limited, and even given that they put whole generations into hibernation to await this moment, they still must number vastly fewer than us. They do not work well at night. As Fost's friend Oracle discovered in old writings, the caste differences among the Hissers are more than social; it takes more gestation time and special nourishment for a mother to produce a noble Zr'gsz. Thus the lower caste ones are more numerous and are physically and mentally inferior to the higher orders. You can thank that fact for your present survival, Longstrider. The common Hissers at the March just didn't know how to deal with your one-man charge.'

'I know,' Fost said glumly.

'Thanks to the Watchers, the skystone mines are in disorder, and the Hissers' military might depends on their air power as heavily as did ours. Also, the Hissers have a severe disadvantage in terms of experience. Even among the Children of Expectation there can be few seasoned officers. They simply haven't fought any wars since Riomar shai-Gallri cast them from the Sky City, and really none since the War of Powers. So, though some of them like this Zak'zar may be shrewd, we still have a considerable edge in skill.'

'You make it sound as if they were at the point of being whipped all the way back to Thendrun,' Erimenes complained.

'Not at all, demon. Our forces, such as they are, are scattered throughout the lower half of the Realm. We have concentrations in Brev and Bilsinx, but let the Sky City appear over them and they fall just as Kara-Est did. Wirix is perhaps fallen; none has heard from them, either by messenger or magical communication, in over two weeks. We must assume the worst in this instance. The Dwarves of North Keep and the Nevrym foresters have made an open alliance with the Zr'gsz; and the Empire has rotted like a melon, from the inside out. Only at its peak long ago would the Imperial Army have counted for more than a moment's annoyance to the Hissers. It's victory at the Black March was almost totally illusory. No, friend

421

Erimenes, even if the Fallen Ones lacked the aid of Istu we would still be like the drunk who fell in a cesspit. We'd be forced to stand on tiptoe to keep our noses out of the shit.'

A nervous look passed among the listeners. Rann seldom used such earthy expression.

'What good does all this talk of military matters do?' demanded Synalon. 'They have Istu; we have myself. And my sister, of course. What more needs to be discussed?'

'We are faced with two problems, cousin. The magical one posed by Istu, and whatever wizards the Hissers have. And the military threat of the Vridzish armies. We ignore either at our peril. I grant, if we undo Istu we win. But to do that we'll have to buy time. For that we'll need armies to keep their soldiers off our necks.'

'Very well,' said Moriana. 'But our efforts need direction. Where do we seek the means of defeating Istu?'

'Athalau,' Fost said, and was immediately sorry. Both sisters turned to stare at him. 'That's our one and only lead. It was Athalar magic that broke Istu before. My knowledge of these things is limited, but nothing I've seen so much as hints at an answer elsewhere.'

The others all began speaking at once, arguing, expostulating, objecting.

'Enough!' shouted Synalon after a few minutes. 'The groundling's right. It turns my stomach to walk a path trod by Felarod, but the Dark Ones have proven no true friends. If nothing else we know where the means of defeating Istu once lay. Isn't that the best place to search now?'

Erimenes muttered something about Reductionism.

'Aren't you forgetting something?' Rann asked. All looked at him. 'Felarod didn't defeat Istu alone. He needed a hundred Athalar savants. They weren't just trained but were specially bred to their talents. Where can we find their like today?'

And Fost put back his head and laughed the roaring wild laughter of the mad. Where, indeed?

CHAPTER SEVEN

Everyone looked at Fost. He teetered on the brink of hysteria, caught himself and drew back from it.

'I'm all right,' he said. 'I'm not crazy — not yet, anyway.'

'Will you share this rare jest with us?' Synalon asked disdainfully.

'I know where the survivors of Felarod's Hundred went, and where to find their descendants. Yes, you do, too, you treacherous blue wisp, so don't try to look innocent.'

Moriana looked from Fost to Erimenes, who was twiddling his thumbs and gazing at the skylight overhead.

'I know, too,' she said quietly. 'The Ethereals.'

Erimenes made a face.

'You mean the folk who live by the Great Crater Lake north of the Ramparts?' asked Ziore.

'What's everyone talking about?' Synalon asked pettishly. 'I'm sure I have no idea.'

'Yes, you do, cousin dear,' Rann said. 'I paid a visit to the Ethereals while pursuing your sister and Longstrider after they escaped from the Sky City. A group of ascetics who live in the mists surrounding the lake. Totally divorced from reality.' He spoke in a bantering tone, but with a small hint of respect.

'Do you think I pay attention to such trivial details?'

'Had you paid more mind to them, you might not be sitting here.'

Synalon's lip curled in a snarl. The tang of ozone filled the room.

'But what do the Ethereals have to do with Felarod's Hundred?' asked Ziore, easing some of the mounting tension with her question.

'The quality of education,' Erimenes said, shaking his head sadly, 'must have declined in the years following my death.' He tugged thoughtfully at his chin. 'But then, it's only to be expected. After me, Athalau's intellectual progress could only take a downward turn.'

'It all happened ten thousand years ago, Erimenes,' Fost pointed out. 'It wasn't considered a necessary part of the curriculum where Ziore spent her life. Your teachings never addressed the War of Powers, as I recall.' Erimenes turned his attention back to the skylight. The fact that Ziore had spent her physical life in a convent devoted to the abstemious tenets laid down by Erimenes the Ethical before his own death still produced friction between the genies.

'In answer to your question, Ziore,' continued Fost, 'I assume you do know the broad outlines of the legend, how Felarod needed the help of a hundred specially trained savants to summon the World Spirit and defeat Istu and the Hissers. You've probably also heard that ninety of the Hundred died from contact with such sheer power. And that the ten survivors were so horrified at the cosmic destruction they had helped wreak that they left Athalau, vowing to keep themselves isolated from humankind and magic.'

'Yes,' Ziore answered, frowning. 'I heard versions of the story as a child, even in the convent.'

'But did you hear where the survivors of the Hundred went after Felarod's victory?'

'No.'

All eyes were on Fost now.

'They went to the Great Crater Lake,' he said, 'where their descendants now style themselves the Ethereals.'

'Those cattle?' Synalon blurted, evidently remembering more of Rann's report than she'd admitted.

'Yes,' Erimenes said, in leaden tones. 'It's all true.'

'And there's more to the tale,' Fost said, grinning, 'to account for Erimenes's mournful expression. For years of their self-imposed exile, the Ethereals were without any kind of philosophical base. Schools of thought came and went, but each seemed tainted by the magic they had come to fear and despise.

'Then fourteen centuries ago, an itinerant sage of Athalau stumbled across their village. He brought with him tidings of a new philosophy sweeping through Athalau like a rising spring wind. It preached total denial of the physical world. Pleasures of the flesh, monetary concerns – and yes, magic. All these matters were shunned. It was a doctrine tailor-made for the Ethereals.'

He gestured grandly.

'And the tailor who made it was none other than Erimenes, called in those days the Ethical.'

'Hold me up to derision, if you will,' Erimenes said, scowling. 'Have you never made a mistake?'

'But do you think they'll help us, Fost?' asked Moriana.

'We can only ask.'

'I'd best not be among those who negotiate with them,' Rann observed wryly. He had tortured the villagers while seeking information and wouldn't be forgotten soon.

'But they've no concern with what goes on in the world,' persisted Moriana.

'They'll see Istu's release as making it their concern,' said Fost.

'It's been so long since damned Felarod's triumph,' said Synalon. 'What if they've lost what powers they had?'

'Don't damn Felarod too lightly, Highness,' said Rann, 'since we find ourselves on his side now. I see no other course than to try the Ethereals and Athalau.'

Synalon curtly ordered more wine, and the six of them, four mortal, two spectral, began laying plans.

The sun was low and its light the color of wine when the discussion was done. Rann nodded in satisfaction at the campaign they had outlined. Seeing this, the others sat back in their seats and relaxed a trifle. If Rann approved their planning, it meant that it was the best that could be done under the circumstances.

Whether the best was enough remained to be seen.

'Where are you staying, cousin?' Rann spoke, his eyes half-lidded.

'The Twisthorn Inn,' Fost answered for Moriana, seeing her tense. He met her stare with steady eyes. 'We have to trust them. I know the odds are that they'll betray us, but we'll have to chance that.'

'I've had a bellyful of betrayal,' Moriana said tautly.

'Perhaps if they gave their word?' suggested Ziore.

Erimenes emitted a strangled squawk. Ziore was his beloved, but it took all his self-control to swallow the scorn he had for her naivete.

'Would it be believed?' asked Rann.

'The word of the Queen of the City in the Sky is not to be doubted,' said Synalon loftily.

'By what right now do you name yourself queen?' Moriana demanded, half rising and placing her hand on her empty scabbard.

Fost gripped her arm.

'She held the title longer than you did,' he pointed out, 'and

425

you're both fugitives now. When the Vridzish butcher you for their victory banquet, will you squabble over who'll be swallowed first?'

Fost felt the electric tension mounting. These were extraordinarily powerful sorceresses. The alliance, still fragile, threatened to come apart over this. He cleared his throat and raised his voice.

'By the Great Ultimate, I swear to take no action against anyone gathered here, save to defend myself or another of this party against treachery, until this War of Powers shall be settled.' He paused, then, 'For good or ill.'

'Well spoken, if not concisely,' Erimenes said. 'You're sure your father wasn't a lawyer? Or a confidence man?'

'Swear,' Fost said grimly, his eyes moving around the small circle. One by one they took the vow until Fost came to Synalon. Fost refused to break the gaze and, such was the intensity of his feeling, it was Synalon who turned away.

'If you insist,' she said, making an irritable gesture with one hand, 'I'll swear your silly little oath, as well.'

'Then let's drink to it,' Rann proposed. The toast was drunk. And Fost wondered what he was getting into.

In her official capacity before Synalon had driven her into exile, Moriana had dealt with many of the financial matters of the Sky City. Haggling for provisions and material proved second nature. And, after Rann had visited the House of Omsgib-Bir, money began to flow from the official coffers of the City. Fost was never sure what Rann had threatened, but the goatlike banker now fell over himself to supply ample amounts of money, presumably drawn against Sky City accounts. But such was Rann's effect on people that Fost didn't discount the possibility that Omsgib gave them money from his own pocket – out of fear.

While Moriana purchased supplies, Fost and Rann went to the waterfront district to find mercenaries seeking employment. Rann promptly sought out the biggest braggart of the lot, a big red-bearded man who wore his hair plaited into pigtails. Physically he was imposing enough, but it was obvious to Fost that the man knew even less of military arts than of discretion.

'You're the man I'm looking for,' Rann told the giant.

'What's that, little man?' the giant bellowed. He obviously wanted to have some sport with the diminutive Rann. Fost waited to see the color of the fool's blood, but instead of a blade, Rann brought forth a well-filled purse and swung it slowly before the big man's bloodshot eyes.

'I hear you,' the giant said, and followed Rann and a thoroughly bemused Fost to a booth in the shadows at the rear of the inn.

'What I'm about to tell you,' Rann said conspiratorially, 'must be kept in the strictest confidence. I am empowered by certain parties who cannot be named to raise a company of stalwart warriors to march to the relief of the Empire. As a man as well-informed as yourself is doubtless aware, the Empire is beset by inhuman foes camped along the River Marchant. We – those I represent – intend to mount an expedition to take the Hissers in the rear.'

The big man nodded slowly and thoughtfully, though Fost doubted he understood a word in ten.

'And you want me to join this expedition.'

Rann's eyebrows shot up in surprise.

'Why no, my good man! I want you to *lead* the expedition! You will, discreetly of course, raise a company and march north. Yours will be one of several secretly travelling to a rendezvous. However,' he said quickly, as the man began to frown, 'I don't doubt that with your obvious talents you'll find yourself in a position of authority. Perhaps even overall command.' And to Fost's further astonishment, Rann simpered in a fashion that went well with the dandefied accent he had adopted.

'How much?' the big man finally said, after his mind had slowly worked over the ramifications.

Rann swept his arm across the table, sowing circles that rang with deep, true tones. Coins of Tolvirot gold, not Imperial clay and tin, sprouted. The giant's eyes grew as big and round as the klenors winking seductively at him from amid the pools of spilled drink.

'Elhard Lanisol's your man,' he said with ponderous sincerity.

The deal was quickly done. Half the princely sum scattered on the table went directly into the big man's pocket. The rest was to be used to begin recruiting. Rann said he would return to meet Lanisol in a few days. Before Lanisol found out the name of his employer, Rann and Fost were pushing through the door and out into the street.

'You look as thick witted as our friend inside,' laughed Rann.

Fost set his jaw. He wasn't going to ask for an explanation. Rann smiled and answered, as if he had.

'The Nevrymin and the Dwarves are openly ranked with the

427

Vridzish,' the prince explained. 'It's safe to assume that other human allies of the Dark exist who keep their sympathies concealed. And I suspect there are such here in Tolviroth Acerte. And it is no assumption at all that they'll have heard about the small, scarred man and the expedition he's mounting to save the Empire.'

'I don't follow you,' Fost said reluctantly.

'The hypothetical minions of the Dark are going to learn that Moriana and Synalon have joined forces, and that they are spreading their coin liberally about Tolviroth Acerte. That much we cannot hide.' He flicked a speck of soot from his shirt collar. 'They'll wonder, of course, where we intend to go – and lo! the worthy Master Lanisol will tell them, as he's no doubt done to all in earshot by now.'

'But you wouldn't tell him who you were. How will the spies know who's recruiting?'

Rann looked at him sidelong. Fost instantly regretted the question.

'How many men have you encountered matching my description, Longstrider? If it got back to someone with wit, this Zak'zar, say, that the renowned Prince Rann was accosting drunks under his own name to raise an army, what would that someone think? He'd feel the trap as sharply as if its jaws were closed about his ankle.'

Fost still looked doubtful.

'Of course,' Rann went on, 'I'll have to hire a few legitimate mercenaries to march north to lend some credence to the tale. But mostly I seek out ones like Lanisol.'

'Likely, he'll keep the money himself,' said Fost, confused by the prince's devious mind.

'What of it? His ego won't let him keep quiet about the important secret mission that brought him such a weight of gold. That the story reaches the proper ears is all that matters.' They rounded a corner and Rann lightly touched him on the sleeve. 'Let's go in here, and see if the Blow On Inn is as ghastly as its name.'

CHAPTER EIGHT

'So, friend Fost,' asked Erimenes, expansive after a night spent cavorting with Ziore, 'what do you think of our travelling companions? They're not such monsters, eh?'

Mostly occupied with trying not to think about the way his piebald riding dog's trot traumatized his kidneys, Fost didn't answer immediately. He let his gaze sweep the horizon, front to rear. The ground sank slowly behind into the green woods and metallic luster of the River Wirix, which could be glimpsed in its windings far away. To the right – north – the land became a sea of grass rippling on the frozen waves of hills. There in this season the grass grew taller than a man on dog-back; from this it had gotten the name Highgrass Broad. In front rose a barrier that had grown day by day, dark when the sun hung in the west, but a dry yellow light when the sun still mounted the cloud-piled eastern sky. It was the rim of the central massif, a great slab of land that tilted upward from the foothills of the Thails to a line meandering south of Mount Omizantrim. Now the cliffs were near, sheer and forbidding, looking as if they'd been scooped out by a great trowel. They were over a thousand feet high, though numerous and perilous trails ascended the many faces. They planned on reaching the foot of one such trail, which Fost and Moriana both knew from their travels, by early afternoon, completing the climb to the top before night made the way too dangerous.

'Did you say something?' Fost asked, belatedly aware that the spirit had.

'That's what I like about you, Fost. Always on the alert.'

'Ziore would never forgive me if I accidentally dropped your satchel halfway up the face of the rim.'

'I've told you before, you have exceedingly dubious tastes in humor.' Erimenes shook his head, tiny trails of vapor drifting from his forehead as he moved. 'As I was saying, I believe you've learned that our new companions aren't the fiends you'd thought. Of course, I realized long ago that Rann and Synalon were not wholly lacking . in merit. But then I had more intimate contact with them . . .'

'Collaboration is the word, Erimenes.'

The genie heaved a melodramatic sigh and drew himself up even straighter.

'For all your experience in the wide world, and for all my tutelage over this past year — think of it, Fost. We've spent almost a year in one another's company.' Ignoring Fost's groan, he carried on brightly. 'At any rate, though I've no doubt been a maturing influence on you, I find to my deepest regret that you are still callow, unable to appreciate the subtler motivations of your elders.'

'*Your* motivations aren't subtle. They come down to only one thing. Hedonism.'

'Fost, you must curb this tendency to stray from the subject.' Erimenes wagged a finger at him. 'Now, about Prince Rann and the exquisite Princess Synalon . . .?'

Fost considered. Again his eyes made a quick circuit of his surroundings. The little party was strung in a winding line picking its way around clumps of scrub and outcroppings of rock. Moriana rode lead on her dog, heavy Highgrass war bow strung across the rounded pommel of her saddle. Next rode Fost, then Synalon and Rann at the rear on a shaggy red animal, his own, smaller Sky City bow likewise resting across his saddlebow. This was caravan season, and bandit country.

'I don't know,' he confessed. 'I think Synalon's insane, but all the same there's something I can't quite name about her . . . something magnificent, I think, though evil. And Rann . . .' He shook his head. 'I've heard enough of his handiwork to keep me well-stocked in nightmares the rest of my life. But it's also said he's a genius. And I believe that, too. I can't forget that day in the City when I rescued Moriana and found myself singlehandedly facing both Istu and the whole damned army. I had no choice in that and ran like hell as soon as Moriana was freed. But down dropped Rann from the safety of his eagle to put himself between the monster and Synalon, though he knew his blade couldn't even scratch the thing. That's the bravest thing I've ever seen.'

'It bothers you to find that your former foes aren't wholly the black villains you'd like to think them?'

Irritation darted through Fost. He smiled unevenly.

'You know, Erimenes, it's when you're at your most perceptive that you tend to be the most annoying.' He let the reins lie across the dog's neck while he raised his broad-brimmed felt hat and smoothed lank black hair from his eyes. 'It does gripe me, though, to concede any goodness in a creature like Rann.'

'And Synalon, ah, but I perceive the lady herself comes to join our small soiree.'

Fost looked around too sharply and almost lost his balance. Synalon had indeed nudged her mount into a gallop and drew up on the courier's left side.

'Greetings, milord Duke,' she called gaily.

Fost felt himself blushing. He tried to stop and only caused a deeper reddening of his features.

'Are you unaccustomed to folk employing your proper title?' she asked, her voice as clear and sweet as a mountain spring, and seemingly as guileless.

'I —' The words stuck in his throat. He desperately needed a drink, though he'd last sipped from the canteen bouncing by his knee not ten minutes earlier. He cleared his throat and started over.

'Your Highness, I confess I don't really think of myself as a duke. Nor a knight, if it comes to that.'

'But you had those titles granted you from the hand of the Emperor himself. What more could you want? For one of those tiresome Wise Ones to come down from Agift and personally hand you a ducal coronet?'

'No. In all truth, Highness, I never wished to be a knight, or a duke, either. I wanted only to be a free man, and to lead my life in peace.'

He didn't need her laughter to tell him how silly his words sounded.

'Besides,' he said quickly to cover his embarrassment, 'Imperial titles don't mean much. The Emperor tosses them around the way dancing boys and girls strew sweets at every public function.'

'So the honor was too common for you.' She nodded sagely. 'You are a proud man, Longstrider.'

Damn the woman! She was watching him out of eyes the deep, strange blue of turquoise, laughing and yet not laughing.

'I will make you duke,' she said softly. 'But there is that which you must do.'

He faced ahead in stony silence. Thirty yards in front of him rode Moriana, now looking neither left nor right, and by the set of her shoulders he realized she knew that Synalon spoke with him, and feared both to interfere and not to.

'I will not help you work treachery against Moriana,' he said stiffly.

Her laughter bounced off the rock face and echoed downward.

'Ah, Sir Knight, you see fit to jest with me! But I assure you, sir, the ceremony of investiture would be much less traumatic than those of High Medurim you told us of – and considerably more *intimate*.' Laughing still, she spurred her mount ahead to go alongside her sister.

Fost felt as if the heat in his ears would make his hat burst into flame. Synalon could fling lightning bolts with words as well as magical gestures.

'Are you truly as ponderous of wit as that byplay made you appear?' Erimenes demanded indignantly.

'But she was . . . she was . . .'

'Of course she was,' said Erimenes. 'And is that such an unpleasant prospect? She is lovely, as lovely as your Moriana. Lovely in the manner of a cataract or a catamount, trickish and even lethal. But lovelier for all that.'

'What would you know about it?' snarled Fost. Erimenes only smiled an offensively superior smile. Fost cursed himself for letting the spirit know just how deep his barb had sunk.

Not altogether willingly, he studied the dark-haired princess as she rode knee-to-knee with Moriana. They were in deep discussion now, seeming as casual as any two sisters out for a late summer ride. It was difficult to believe they had been – still were – the deadliest of enemies and bitterest of rivals. But not even Moriana could long maintain a bowstring tautness of wariness and suspicion indefinitely; with time had come relaxation and a certain fatalism. If Synalon betrayed her, no amount of worrying would stay her. As for Synalon, she had, once past her early tempest of objection, taken the arrangement with a calm that bordered on insouciance. Fost didn't know if this was more madness or confidence.

From behind she looked younger than her sister, though Moriana was younger by minutes. Not having addressed herself to war and physical exertion – of the martial sort – the black-haired sorceress was slimmer, almost girlish, though there was little girlish about the flare of her hips and the roundness of her buttocks so clearly visible through the thin cloth of her trousers.

Erimenes chuckled, and Fost shook his head as if that would clear it of such thoughts. He made himself concentrate on Synalon's garment, pretending that had been his intent all along. It was all of the sheerest silk, a blouse low-cut in front, trousers that fit like a second skin at the top. It was vastly impractical for travelling, but everyone knew better than to make an issue of it. Synalon was proud, strongminded.

Fost remembered the unfortunate scene with the dogseller back in the coastal village before they started their trek southward toward Athalau. The merchant had suggested to Synalon that she select something other than a stud dog, that if they encountered a bitch in heat he would bring them trouble. Fresh from High Medurim though Fost was, her answer had shocked him both with its content and its explicitness, and he was surprised to see Rann color and look away. It had taken even Erimenes several seconds to fully comprehend the possibilities she'd outlined.

But now Moriana was pointing ahead and Synalon wheeling her mount and riding back to him.

'Get to the ground,' she shouted. 'Find a hole and slip inside!' She flashed him a sunbright smile as she passed and then called her warning to Rann.

As he drew sword, he marveled at the way in which the woman infected even emergency with salacious innuendo. Up ahead he saw that Moriana had now nocked an arrow from the quiver at her back. Ziore was also pointing, her arm misty pink and hardly visible in the sunlight.

At first, he thought he saw a cloud, oblong and dark, floating into view above the hard yellow line of the Rim far off in the north. Then he saw the white, fleecy clouds rolling as if to meet it, and he knew what it was.

At a stately, ominous pace, the City in the Sky floated east.

Moriana sat erect in the saddle's stirrups, her dog prancing and sidestepping, tasting urgency in the air and the sweat smell of its rider. Her eyes were wild, wide and faraway. Her face had gone stark with a terrible rage and fear and grief and longing and a winter bleakness of soul. He looked behind and saw Synalon, too, rigidly upright and staring, and he knew then that they were truly sisters, twins.

Rann loped by, his bow slung across his shoulders in easy acknowledgement of the futility of battle.

'The Hissers are none too sharp of sight,' he called, as happy as if he were on the hunt and were the hunter rather than the prey. 'But they may be looking with more than earthly eyes. Time we went to ground.'

Sheathing his sword, Fost did just that. He hoped Synalon and Moriana weren't too caught up in the tidal surge of their emotions to heed the prince's warning. He dismounted and got the burly creature to lie down in the lee of a large oilbush, dropped into loose soil beside it and began to burrow – and also to sneeze. The oilbush exuded a slippery, fragrant sap that aggravated Fost's allergies.

A thumping of paws, a scattering of small stones, and Rann was at his side, hauling his own dog down expertly and flopping belly-down at Fost's side. He grinned. To all appearances, he enjoyed this hugely.

Fost wasn't. His stomach tied itself in knots and his heart tried to beat its way to freedom. He felt blackness swim behind his eyes. Even if Istu had stood atop the highest tower of the Sky City, Fost could not have seen him from where he lay itching and sniffling next to a man who, until very recently, had been bending every effort to arrange a painful, messy death for him. But it was as if he could see the Demon of the Dark Ones, horned and great and invulnerable, and he was laughing, laughing . . .

'Where's it going?' asked Erimenes. Eagerness almost masked the other tremor in his voice. Here was something Fost could find comfort in. Erimenes had at last found something to fear.

'Tolviroth Acerte, I'd judge.' Rann shifted to a more comfortable position, cupped his hands around his eyes to cut the glare. 'Damn! It's too far to make out anything. But still, I think we quit the City of Bankers just in time.'

Fost felt a leaden weight condense in his stomach. He was a Realm-road courier and called no place home – and every place. But Tolviroth Acerte came close. And he had friends there . . .

A swirling breeze tossed dirt into their faces. Rann blinked and spat, and Fost was glad to see him with even this small a human frailty.

'I don't like the timing,' Rann murmured. 'Unless the City lingered long conquering Wirix.'

'What do you make of it, cousin?' asked Synalon's call.

'Shh!' Erimenes hissed, turning skyblue in dread.

Rann laughed at the genie.

'If they can hear us at this distance, we're done for. Rest easy, jugged spirit.' Fost noted that the prince didn't call Erimenes *demon*. It would have been incongruous with a real demon's presence so ominously close.

'No good,' Rann answered with raised voice. 'I fear High Medurim has seen the shadow of the City.'

High Medurim. Fost saw crowded filthy childhood streets, wharves piled with bundles for distant ports, markets with bright colors and intriguing spices; he saw Oracle and Teom and yes, pale, hungering Temalla. His eyes turned wet and stung. He clutched handfuls of sand in futile anger. They spilled through his fingers and, he thought, so goes the world, so goes all I've known or loved.

He did not feel the time slip by and only noted it had passed when Rann touched him on the shoulder. He came back to himself to find the sun hidden by the cliffs and the City low in the darkening eastern sky, merging with the thunderheads of a distant storm.

CHAPTER NINE

Brev bustled as it had not in years. It was the least of the Quincunx cities. It owed what little prosperity it had to the geographic fact that it lay at one corner of the Quincunx and could serve as a center for trade. Before the binding of the City in the Sky to the Great Quincunx, Brev had been an anonymous spot on the map. Even in the ten millennia since that event, it had failed to distinguish itself. Thailot boasted skill in artificing and glassworking, particularly the grinding of lenses; Wirix had its sorcerers with their genetic manipulations; Kara-Est was Kara-Est, grandest seaport of the Realm and a high city of the world; Bilsinx, central of the five cities, was the strategic and economic center of the Sundered Realm.

Brev was a dispirited huddle of drab stone buildings with the Broken Lands to the west and the Steppe to the south — and occasionally the Sky City overhead. That was all.

Now envious Brev could hold her head up, for she was queen of the Quincunx. Kara-Est was destroyed, perhaps Wirix as well; the island city was taken and sacked, at the very least. Thailot huddled behind its hedge of mountains. The onion domes of Bilsinx watched over empty streets, her citizens following the Sky Citizens fleeing south to avoid the wrath of the City's new owners. For now, all roads led to Brev. The merchants rejoiced in the influx of bright gold, and her leaders spoke of the dawn of a new era.

The travellers had desired to keep word of their arrival quiet. It was too much to ask. They were greeted by shouts of acclaim, with speeches by members of the ruling hereditary council, and rum punch and floral wreaths in the Triangle where the paths of the City converged. Fost and Moriana and the rest looked on with tired eyes, even the genies subdued and weary from the desperate pace they'd maintained since sighting the City.

Not even Rann had the heart to tell the crowds that their dawn would prove a false one.

The Palace was an appropriate setting for the grim meeting of the sisters and their loyal, if somewhat confused, subjects. It was drafty, cold and damp and dark, and lacking in adequate fireplaces. The halls had a few cracked windows that admitted breezes but little sunlight. What light there was inside came from lanterns with panes no one had cleaned in recent memory. Dusk rose out of the east when a steward ushered them into the council chamber. Blue and purple shadows lay like curtains across the windows. The rafters were all but invisible above, not so much from height as murk. Fost decided this was a perfect place to discuss the end of the world.

'Your Highnesses,' greeted Colonel Ashentani, lately governor of Bilsinx. 'It gives us all great pleasure to be reunited with you once again.'

'We thank you,' said Moriana, leaving them to wonder whether she meant both sisters or simply employed the royal we. 'But let's have an end to ceremony. We've serious business to discuss.'

The two were seated side-by-side at the head of the table. Rann sat to the left, nearest Synalon. Fost tucked Erimenes's jug under one arm and took his place at the foot of the table, hoping he would have no part in the proceedings so he could find a place to sleep.

Ashentani he recognized. Most of the others he didn't. Moriana did and Ziore picked the information from the surface of the princess's brain and relayed it to Fost. Mostly they were Sky City officers. For their part, Ziore told him, they were frightened by the events of the past few months, afraid of the Demon and the Fallen Ones, scared that they might make a slip that would put them out of favor with one or the other sister.

Toward one, however, Moriana felt cold hostility, which Ziore reported was returned in kind. Destirin Luhacs had succeeded Count Ultur V'Duuyek as commander of a Grassland mercenary regiment at Chanobit Creek. Moriana disliked the woman for the part her troops had played in smashing the army she and Darl Rhadaman had raised. Luhacs, a square-faced woman with eyes like blue ice, blamed Moriana for the death of the count, who had been her lover as well as her commander.

Further down the table sat Cerestan, the young lieutenant of the Sky Guard. He'd aged considerably since the first time Fost saw him. Since escaping the City and Istu's wrath, he had waged a quiet

437

battle against the dangers besetting the refugees – hunger, thirst, exposure – as they fled first to Bilsinx and then to Brev. His eyes were sunk into pits and a hint of gray sprinkled his temples.

A servant came with mugs of steaming broth. Fost drained his in three swallows, almost revelling in the way it scalded his tongue. Though he barely tasted it, the warmth spread through his body and revitalized him. He felt closer to life than death for the first time in days.

'So that's our story,' finished Synalon. 'What of the Empire? Wirix?'

Colonel Ashentani squirmed uncomfortably in her chair.

'Well?' demanded Moriana. 'We must know. Killing messengers bringing bad news is something I've never done.' Moriana darted a quick look at her sister, who sat back in her chair and tented fingers in front of her slightly smiling lips.

'There are few facts,' said Ashentani, 'but they are grim enough. After Bilsinx fell and Brev collapsed, Wirix recalled its citizens from those cities. But there was a small colony of Wirixers in Samadum and it is from them we received news of Wirix's fall. The Fallen Ones launched an attack with small boats on the lake and their skycrafts above. When the City floated overhead, Istu appeared. He cast down lightnings, but the strength of the Institute was arrayed against him and the force of his bolts tempered. The Wirixer mages conjured an air elemental and set a waterspout against their invaders.' Ashentani paused, noting she had the rapt attention of not only Moriana and Synalon but Rann, also. The small man sat with eyes half closed, evaluating her every word. She went on. 'Istu bellowed in rage and disappeared.'

'And then the Black Lens appeared in the Skywell,' put in Rann.

'Yes,' said Colonel Ashentani in a choked voice. 'Istu absorbed the air sprite by drawing it into the blackness. Then the City crossed over Wirix.'

'Tell me exactly what happened,' said Rann, leaning forward now, his arms resting on the table, hands clenched.

'A black vortex descended from the Lens. It drove into the center of the city, digging to bedrock, coring Wirix like an apple. The government buildings were torn from their foundations but the Institute and most of the city proper were intact. The defenders, magicians and soldiers alike, were demoralized by the Demon's power. The purely physical storm that began when the vortex vanished destroyed what the Black Lens hadn't.'

'And High Medurim?' Fost heard himself asking.

'Only rumors,' answered the colonel. 'Again the Demon used the Black Lens. The Hissers were dug in along the Marchant. The Lens blazed a black trail of death and devastation across the farmlands of the City States like a spear pointing straight at Medurim's heart.'

'Enough poetry, damn you!' flared Fost. 'What of the city?'

She shrugged, her face a mask showing the deprivation and horror she had lived with. Fost regretted his sharpness with her.

'The Imperial capital has fallen, whether captured like Wirix or eradicated like Kara-Est, I haven't been able to discover.'

'Thank you, Colonel,' Fost said softly. He turned his empty cup in his hands, staring into the depths as if to read some augury there. It was true. Medurim was no more, and likewise the friends he had known in both slums and palace.

After supper, Fost heard Cerestan's shrill voice asking the question he dreaded to hear.

'Why must we turn tail and run? Can't we *fight* the damned lizards?'

Fost feared that Synalon would renew her own objections to the plan and break the fragile coalition. Glancing up, he saw Rann twisting a linen napkin between his fingers with quiet vehemence and knew he wasn't the only one fearing for the alliance.

'Are you a master of magics?' snapped Synalon. The young officer recoiled at the fury flaming in her eyes. 'Or do you presume to judge the decisions of your betters . . . and find them wanting?'

'No, Your Highness,' he whispered, his face deathly white.

'Very well,' said Synalon. 'Now, caravans are bound from Tolviroth Acerte, some here, some for the Gate of the Mountains. A small cargo fleet should be standing off the Southern Waste near Athalau awaiting our word, if they met with no misfortune rounding Cape Storm. These carry supplies for our people. This is your task, Cerestan: remove the Sky Citizens and our allies to Athalau.'

Gasps met the announcement. 'But the barbarians of the Steppes —' '—impossible—' 'But Athalau's buried in a living glacier—' ' —impossible!'

'Impossible?' The hair began to rise on Synalon's head. She tossed back her spark-crackling hair and sneered. 'If you find it impossible then I must depend on others not so easily daunted. You don't find this impossible, do you, Master Cerestan?' Her eyes fixed on the hapless young officer who had not joined in the chorus of protest at the announced exodus. 'You've acquitted yourself ably. In honor of that, and in view of your increased responsibilities, I hereby appoint you Constable of the City in the Sky and charge you with seeing that the resettlement proceeds expeditiously.'

As thunderstruck silence settled, Synalon turned to her sister and added, 'With Moriana's approval, of course.'

The anger that had been growing in Moriana's eyes faded.

'I approve,' she said, clearly less than happy with her sister usurping power in this fashion. Moriana leaned forward and used the opportunity to regain her position of authority.

'As for the rest of you,' Moriana said, sweeping the group with her gaze, 'you know that Fost Longstrider and I penetrated the glacier which covers Athalau, as did Prince Rann.' She looked at Rann who stared back with perfect calmness. 'The way through this sentient glacier, who calls itself Guardian, has been opened before. We must convince it to trust us and open wide enough to accommodate all.'

'It shall be done,' said Colonel Ashentani, glaring at Cerestan.

'You all know the task ahead of us. Let's get to it, because we have no idea how much time the Fallen Ones will give us.' All rose when Moriana did and silently left. She turned to Fost and stretched out a hand, saying, 'I'm bone-tired. I'm going to bed.' He took her hand and she squeezed his fingers as if they were her last grip on sanity.

A steward led them to their chambers. Glancing back, Fost saw the leaders clumped in excited knots, Rann sitting calmly with boots propped on the Count of Brev's table and ignoring the commotion. Cerestan stood gazing after Moriana; Fost saw Synalon regarding the young officer with thoughtful intensity.

A tug on his hand drew him away and down the hall.

As it had every day of the week since leaving Brev, the wind blew icy in Fost's face. He shivered, gathered his cloak more closely about him and rode on. In a few more hours the sun would be high and beat on the travellers like hammers. But now, in the gray, early morn, the frigid breath of the Southern Waste scoured the barren land. He shifted his weight in the saddle, no more comfortable now for all the time he'd spent in it, and thought of Moriana.

It had been hard leaving her, but there hadn't been any other choice. They had to split, with one group going to the Great Crater Lake and the Ethereals, the other heading for the Gate of the Mountains and glacier containing Athalau. Alliance or no, oaths or no, it would have been sheer foolishness for Rann and Synalon to go one way and Fost and Moriana the other. Each princess had to be sure her interests were represented by both groups. To do so didn't guarantee safety, but to do otherwise was to invite betrayal.

Moriana had gone with Rann to Athalau and Fost guided Synalon to the Ethereals' village. Likewise, the genies had to split up. Erimenes, who had helped gain entrance to Athalau before, went with Moriana. Ziore rode with Synalon and Fost in hopes her ability to sway emotion would help convince the Ethereals to forsake their ancient isolation and join the battle against the Dark.

Orange and swollen, the sun peeked above a blanket of clouds stretched across the eastern horizon. Fost scanned the sky. Twice they had glimpsed skyrafts in the distance, and once they had scarcely managed to find shelter in a steep-walled arroyo when a twenty foot slab of stone passed soundlessly overhead. Rann's ruse must have failed; it was rare for the Vridzish to commit their aircraft this far south.

A few times they had glimpsed other riders. To Fost's surprise, the jet-haired princess made no objection to evading them. But as she pointed out, there was no honor – and damned little diversion – to be gained in battling brigands.

Beyond these incidents, little transpired. Several times Ziore detected the nearness of some hunting animal but was always able to deflect the creatures before they came near enough to attack. Unlike Moriana and Rann, neither Fost nor Synalon was a competent archer so they had taken plentiful provisions, and the necessity of hunting didn't slow them. Having reassured himself the sky was clear of foes, Fost's main concern was to keep an eye out for the fierce barbarians of the Steppe. Eventually some agreement would have to be reached with them to allow the passage of unprecedented numbers of northerners across their territory. It wouldn't help if Synalon reduced a score of them to cinders before Fost had a chance to open negotiations.

Synalon rode behind, wrapped in her cloak and her own thoughts.

'What are you thinking?' Ziore's voice asked from the satchel bumping at Fost's hip.

He started. He wasn't yet accustomed to the gentle feminine voice that now accompanied him or the equally gentle presence that went with it.

'I'm sorry,' he mumbled, and quickly twisted off the lid of the nun's jar. 'I forgot you were there. Erimenes would have made his presence known long before this.'

A surprisingly girlish giggle emerged along with a streamer of pink smoke that swirled in a familiar fashion and became the form of Ziore.

'Erimenes can be trying sometimes. But still, he's awfully cute.'

Fost couldn't think of anything to say to that and so rode in silence. The land here was almost flat, tan dotted with the green of occasional bushes as far as the eye could see. The very uniformity of the land was treacherous for it made the terrain seem flatter than it was. The Steppe boasted hills, ridges and deep gullies which could hide large bodies of foes until one was almost on top of them. The sameness of the land lulled one into thinking none could approach without being seen far off.

'I wish I knew what to make of our friend back there,' he said.

'I, as well. Can we trust her? Moriana is afraid that she'll betray us.'

'We don't have much choice. And she's got as much reason to hate the Dark Ones as Moriana. More, in fact.'

'But she's not always rational.' In spite of himself, Fost laughed at this. It was a marvel of understatement. 'Perhaps her hatred of Moriana will overrule her bitterness toward the Lords of Infinite Night.'

He took his black water flask from the satchel and drank. The taste of gruel was still in his mouth, and the tepid water the vessel provided did little to wash away the taste. He took a mouthful, swirled it around in his mouth, spat at a clump of amasinj bush.

'Have you had any luck at reading her?' he asked.

'She sensed it at once when I tried probing her at that first meeting, and since then I've been careful. Her emotions are so strong she can't altogether hide them. Her passions surge with the power of ocean waves, Fost. They practically swamp me.'

Fost was grateful he didn't possess Ziore's sensitivity.

'I can't get past them to her thoughts. But some of the passions are clear. Pride. Ambition. Rage. Longing. So great they'd tear apart a lesser psyche.'

'And Rann?' he asked. 'Have you tried reading Rann?'

'He's got some manner of protection, or perhaps he is just good at shielding his thoughts.'

'But no emotions? I imagine he's as cold as fresh caught cod.'

Ziore's vaporous eyebrows rose and turned pinker.

'Not at all. He's almost as passionate as she. But I cannot define his passions as well as hers. Pride, great pride. Longing and rage, I think. And . . .' She paused as if afraid he'd ridicule her for saying the next. 'And fear, I think.'

His impulse was to laugh, and he held it down. A frown formed on his face as he rode. The nun was most likely wrong. She admitted that Rann's warped passions were harder for her to make out than his cousin's.

But what if she weren't wrong? What would it take to frighten a man like Rann?

Fost spent the rest of the day trying to push that thought from his mind.

The sun had passed its zenith when Synalon picked out the low dome of fog that squatted endlessly above the Great Crater Lake. When they made camp that evening, Fost judged they would reach the Ethereals' settlement early the next morning.

The three of them shared conversation over the small campfire. The first day Fost and Ziore had kept to themselves, wary of speaking to Synalon and frankly unsure of the reception they'd get if they tried. Slowly the ice had thawed and the two began to talk guardedly about the sorceress-queen. They still feared her, and Fost was a long way from liking her, but there was something about the empty immensity of the Steppes that made humans seek each other's company. Their differences all became trivial in the face of the lonely spaces and distant skies that dwarfed and mocked human fears and aspirations alike. Even Ziore, who was to all intents immortal, confessed to being made to feel ephemeral by the changeless waste.

Fost did most of the talking. To his surprise he had found Synalon a good listener. She sat across the crackling fire, her cloak casually open as if to let the moonlight shine on breasts barely contained by her low, silken blouse. Her eyes were big and seemingly self-luminous, and always on him.

He spoke of his childhood in High Medurim, as he had to Moriana a year before when they journeyed to Athalau. Synalon encouraged

443

him with questions, with attitudes of head and body implying receptive interest. She had a lively mind, he reflected, to have learned as much as she had of the difficult magical lore. His experiences as a slum child in Medurim must be as alien to the highborn sorceress as any work of demonomancy.

At times like this, with both moons high and waxing in the sky, Ziore was mostly silent, too. Fost almost lost awareness of his audience; he talked to the moon, himself, the restless wind, the insects that sang beneath the canopy of stars. He even found himself speaking of what he and Moriana had undergone together, after their flight from the very woman who sat watching him with such rapt intentness. He told of the journey south, the encounter with the Ethereals, the attack by Rann and his men at the foot of the Ramparts and what befell him and Moriana after they were separated. He told of Athalau, lost and splendid, and what he had found within. He told of how he had died and been revived and gone looking for the woman who had slain him. And he told of what he had gone through to find her. All this to the person who, for the past year, had personified evil in his thoughts. And she nodded in appreciation of the things he told her, even when what he spoke of was how he and the woman he loved had smashed the plans of this other.

It was lonely on the Steppe. The sound of his own voice was comforting.

After the need for speaking had burned itself out, he sat with his knees drawn up before him and his arms around them, staring into the slowly dying campfire. In a detached way, he was aware of Synalon scrutinizing him. Perhaps it was to the wind and stars he had spoken and not to her.

With a rustle of grass and fine cloth, she rose and stepped to his side. Her touch was both cool and hot upon his cheek.

'You're quite a man, Sir Longstrider.'

He sat dead still. He had dreaded this moment — and yet he felt ambivalent. He had seen the looks she gave him as they rode from Tolviroth Acerte. If nothing else, he had piqued her interest by thwarting her consistently across a year; and she was beautiful, heart-stoppingly beautiful. The double moonlight fell as soft as a caress on her skin. He tensed, fearing her, fearing that within him which longed to respond to her.

But her fingers were soon withdrawn — too soon? — and she walked grand and serene back to her side of the fire. Trying not to betray the confusion he felt, he said a quick goodnight and stretched out on the ground, with his saddle beneath his head and Ziore at his side. He glanced from the silver and black of Synalon's form into the blank darkness of the Steppe where hunting beasts cried down the moons. In time he felt Ziore's touch upon his mind, soothing, lulling. He slept.

A timeless interval. Sleep departed. He was awake at once, sword in hand. A touch on his arm aroused him. His senses strained.

'Who is it?' he asked softly.

I, Fost. Ziore's feathery thoughts brushed across his mind. *Something's amiss.*

Aware of the strange stillness, he twisted about, studying the Steppes. The pink moon Astrith was gone and blue Raychan prepared to dip into the Golden Sea. Dark shapes huddled off across the flatness and movement flirted at the corners of his vision. He was wise to the wild and knew his brain created the motion. Whatever was going on, it wasn't happening in that direction.

Keeping his breath as regular as if he still slept, he shifted and murmured to himself, preparing to roll onto his other side. Ziore sent him no further thoughts. The Athalar spirits never needed sleep, and he had been content to fall asleep himself without caring whether Synalon stayed awake or not. Ziore was a better sentry than either of them, and could be trusted. It would have been like Erimenes, before his apparent change of heart, to let some toothy horror out of the Ramparts creep up almost within distance to make its final savage leap before rousing Fost.

He made another sleepy sound and rolled. At the same time, he moved up one arm as if to pillow his head. He used the motion to lessen the chance of firelight glinting off an eyeball and betraying his wakefulness.

The fire had been tended since he'd dropped off to sleep. It flickered low but not as low as he'd last seen. Synalon sat beyond it so that the yellow tendrils of light barely reached her. Her head was nodding, one slim hand tracing elegant figures in the air in front of her. With a shock, Fost realized she was not alone.

Her companion sat farther from the fire than she. With the black mountains at its back, Fost couldn't limn it by the stars it blocked. But by the faint glimmer from above he saw — or thought he saw — a Dwarf.

445

That's odd, he thought to Ziore. The creature had a Dwarf's outsized head and stumpy limbs yet it appeared taller than Synalon.

I'm frightened. He felt a contact on his arm and twitched, barely stifling a yelp of surprise. *I need to touch something — somebody.*

He knew of Ziore's illusory touch from Moriana; Oracle had known the same trick though he'd never used it to hold hands as the genie was doing.

It's all right, he thought back. *But what is that thing?*

Synalon glanced his way. He quickly shut his eyes.

I don't know. But it scares me. It broadcasts no emotions that I can detect. Fost, I . . . I fear to probe it.

He squeezed her hand.

Then don't. I don't think it'd be wise to fool with that thing, whatever it is.

Are we betrayed?

He felt his muscles winding tighter. The question lay like a lump of lead in his mind.

We can't assume anything. Wait and see.

He opened his eyes. Synalon sat alone. Her chin was sunk to her breastbone. Asleep or not, she showed no sign of movement.

Fost rolled over again. Even with Ziore's help, he was a long time finding sleep. And when he did, it was filled with dreams of Dwarves and twisted faces and roses as black as death.

CHAPTER TEN

Tendrils of fog reached for Fost's face, making him think he rode through cotton. He could scarcely see the alert, upright ears of his dog a few feet in front of his face. The padding of his dog's footfalls came as though from far away. Behind, Synalon's dog existed only as rhythmic sounds even more remote.

Now and again the whiteness parted briefly, eddying around a clump of rock or a sick looking shrub. But for these occasional sights, and the jogging of his mount's steps, Fost would have thought he was standing still, lost in the mist.

For the tenth time in the last five minutes he fought down the urge to ask Ziore if she was sure she knew where they were going. Erimenes had reluctantly led him and Moriana to the Ethereals' village, the only alternative being freezing to death in a blizzard. He had sensed the nearness of humans and steered his companions toward them. Ziore had the same senses and used them. But with Fost's visual world constricted to a sphere the radius of his arm, it was hard for him to believe that Ziore knew her way.

Abruptly the mist parted. Before him rose a random clump of huts rudely made from chunks of slag cast up when a meteorite had struck the Steppe during the contest between Felarod and the World Spirit on one side and Istu on the other. A few pale folk, as wispy as the mists through which he rode, drifted without purpose among the buildings. The smell of drying seaweed and an open latrine assailed his nostrils.

'See,' Ziore said smugly. 'I told you I steered us truly.'

He felt an impact behind his right leg. His dog jumped, doubling back with a snarl. He swatted it briskly on the head before it snapped at Synalon's mount which had blundered into it. He cursed under his breath. This collision was his fault. He'd been so surprised at seeing the Ethereals' village that he hadn't given the agreed upon two tugs on the rope tied between Synalon's saddle and his own. He looked back to see the princess rearranging her garments and got the impression she had drawn her black silk tunic open wide to let the damp mist play across her breasts and belly. He saw color on her cheeks. She smiled; he quickly looked away.

'We're here,' he said unnecessarily, feeling the need to be saying something to cover the awkwardness he felt.

Synalon gestured imperiously to him to lead the way. They wound their way around sad, slumping huts to the large round building in the center of the settlement. Fost recognized this as the temple where the Ethereals gathered to meditate. As the two reined in before the irregular door, a man emerged, stooping to pass beneath the sagging lintel. Fost recognized him as well.

'Greetings, strangers,' the Ethereal said in a high, sweet voice. 'I know not what brings you, but you are welcome to rest. And who knows? You may come to share the wisdom of our ways and give up the distress and discord of the material world, which is the world of illusion.'

'It's plain to see we received the more difficult task,' Synalon remarked sardonically.

'Greetings yourself,' said Fost, swinging off his dog. '*I'm* no stranger. The woman with me is. Meet Her Royal Highness, Synalon Etuul, Princess of the City in the Sky, currently in exile. Your Highness, this is Itenyim, of the Ethereals. He's an exile, too. From reality.'

'That's not very diplomatic,' Ziore chided softly. Fost shrugged it off. He hadn't realized how bitter he was toward the Ethereals.

'We employ no titles here,' said the Ethereal, ignoring Fost's jibe. 'But you are welcome.'

Synalon stayed on her dog, regarding the Ethereal. She had taken him for a woman at first, because of the slim, frail form and the effeminate features. But the bone structure of the face and the protuberant Adam's apple were clearly masculine, as was the body clad in a simple, dirty green robe that hung to the knees.

'I see the temple wall's finally caved in,' remarked Fost, gesturing to a gap in the melted rock wall. 'They put me to work there when Moriana and I stayed here before. I wasn't at it long enough to do much good, it appears. Where's Selamyl?'

A shadow crossed the flawless features.

'Selamyl met with misfortune after you and the woman departed.'

'A misfortune named Rann?' The Ethereal didn't answer. Not looking at Synalon, Fost said, 'Well, round up your people as best you can. We need to talk to them at once.'

'They are about their dances and duties and meditations.'

'Those dances and duties and meditations are about to be permanently interrupted,' said Fost briskly. 'Tell them that unless they listen to the princess and me they are going to have visitors who make Rann look as saintly as Erimenes himself.'

Itenyim's face, already alabaster, turned a shade lighter. He turned and walked off, almost hurrying. A strap was broken on his sandal, giving him a limp.

'Saintly?' asked Synalon, arching a brow.

'They think he is,' said Fost. 'I told you they were divorced from reality.'

'Return to Athalau?' The Ethereal woman's face was a marble mask of incomprehension. 'That's impossible.'

'It had better not be impossible,' Fost said, 'or you and I and the princess and every other human being in the Realm are going to be dead before this winter's snow is melted.'

'Life is illusion,' answered the woman.

Fost bared his teeth. He had the urge to grab her and shake loose her complacency. But that wouldn't only be wrong, it'd be futile. If these people had resisted Rann's special brand of persuasiveness as long as they had, mere shaking wouldn't do any good.

'Are the Dark Ones an illusion?' he asked, voice ragged with exasperation. 'They're what we face.'

A ripple passed through the small crowd assembled in the temple. At least, mention of the Dark Ones got some response.

'What have these matters to do with us?' asked another.

Fost glanced at Synalon, at ease beside him on a three-legged stool that gave every indication of collapsing beneath her. Her lips were curled, and it wasn't just at the odor of stale clothing and indifferently washed bodies that permeated the low-roofed building. Even the air current blowing between the door and the hole in the wall failed to freshen the atmosphere.

'Do you know what's happened?' he asked.

It was a foolish question. He didn't need the sheep-like faces turned to his, some already showing unmistakable traces of boredom, to tell him so.

'We do not trouble ourselves with the gross affairs of the world beyond our village,' said Itenyim loftily.

'The world outside your village is about to trouble *you*, however,' Fost said, 'and what it will do to you is more than a little gross. The Fallen Ones are back in control of the Sky City, my friends, and Istu rides it like a raft.'

His listeners shrank away.

'The Demon is loose?' another woman asked. Fost nodded.

The Ethereals turned to one another and spoke in subdued, quavering tones. Their ancestors had turned their backs on their own past, but fear of the *Zr'gsz* and of the Demon of the Dark Ones lay deep in human bones.

'Istu knows who you are,' Fost said, which was quite possible. 'He hates you for what your forebears helped do to him.'

'But have we not made amends?' Itenyim gasped. 'Our fathers and mothers forsook Athalau and came to this spot in the wilderness out of remorse for what they had wrought. Is this not enough?'

The air exploded from Synalon's lungs in a surprised snort. Fost scarcely believed what he heard. The Ethereals were hoping Istu would forgive them for their ancestors helping to cast him down!

'Nothing you could do would be enough,' said Synalon. 'The Demon of the Dark Ones knows as little of forgiveness as he knows of mercy. What he *does* know would shrivel your souls if you heard.' The effect her words produced on the Ethereals hardly seemed great. By normal standards they were still impassive.

'What is it you want of us?' asked a more or less male voice from the rear of the temple.

Fost felt like cheering. They'd gotten through to at least one of the Ethereals.

'What we're asking is grave, I won't deny. We need some of you – as many as we can get – to come with us to Athalau. There we must find the Nexus and use it to get in touch with the World Spirit, as Felarod and your ancestors did ten thousand years ago.'

'But it was for shame at what they'd helped Felarod do that our ancestors came here,' someone cried.

'They helped save the world,' Fost shouted back.

'The material world.' Itenyim practically sneered. 'Had the world been destroyed, think of the generations that would have been spared from suffering its illusions.'

Be calm, Fost, Ziore urged him from her jug. Given the Ethereals'

450

historic dislike for Athalar magic, she had agreed it was best she not show herself to them.

'Suffering?' Fost spat the word. 'For all that the world is illusion, Master Itenyim, you acknowledge suffering as real. And I tell you the suffering the Hissers and their ally have inflicted, and will continue to inflict unless stopped, is a thousand times greater than anything humanity has suffered from the illusions of the material world.'

'But the sufferings of the body are nothing,' the first woman intoned, as if reciting a litany. 'Serenity of the spirit is all.'

'Faugh!' Synalon shook her hair back angrily and glared at the several score Ethereals crowded into the temple.

'I've always thought myself selfish, but it seems these dung eaters have some things to teach me. Do you think, you vapid bitch, that the sufferings Istu inflicts are of the flesh alone?' She laughed savagely. 'Perhaps I should give your soul a touch of hellfire, a small taste of what Istu can do. That might teach you a measure of compassion, unless it turns you mad – or kills you outright.' She fixed the Ethereal woman with her eyes. A tiny whimper escaped the woman's throat. She began to writhe as if held in place by invisible bonds. The muscles on her neck stood out in stark relief, but she could not look away from the suns that were Synalon's eyes.

Fost roughly grabbed Synalon's arms. Instantly, she turned the full force of her hell gaze on him. He reeled as agony exploded at the center of his being. It was as if all the loss, despair, and agony of a thousand lifetimes were made into a stake impaling his soul. He spent an eternity shrieking into mocking emptiness.

Then the horror was gone, leaving his mind staggering and weak. He felt Synalon's feverishly hot hand grip his.

'I couldn't stop the spell in time to spare you.'

Dazed as he was, Fost still knew that this woman, who could slay with a single glance of her cobalt eyes, was apologizing to him. He nodded weakly, unable to speak. Dimly, he heard the sobbing of the Ethereal woman.

None of the Ethereals moved to help her. All eyes were on Synalon, who stared back at them with fierce contempt.

What do we do now? Fost asked Ziore. *It looks like the diplomatic approach isn't working.*

I don't know, she responded despairingly. *I'm trying to sway them. But I can't change even one's emotion!*

451

'I'm sorry for what my companion did,' Fost said, expecting a deathbolt at every syllable. 'But the world is under a death sentence. It will be carried out unless you help us.'

'We've spent ten millennia trying to expiate the guilt of our forebears,' said an Ethereal in the front row. 'Now you're asking that we shoulder that burden anew.'

Fost sagged. He could find no words to answer.

'Guilt, Cuivris?' a voice asked from the open doorway. 'I will show you guilt.'

Every head turned. Fost blinked and stared as Selamyl, the Ethereal who had tried by guile and argument to restrain him and Moriana from leaving before, made his way painfully into the hall.

'I thought you said he was dead,' Fost said to Itenyim.

'I said nothing of the sort.'

Nor had he, Fost recalled. It had only been said that Selamyl was one of Rann's victims.

He had obviously been a victim. Once he had stood even taller than Fost. Now he was hunched in on himself and shrunken so that the bones of his cheeks poked out through parchment skin. His grace had been almost painful to watch for one less fluid; now he hobbled in a broken walk, supporting himself with a cane fashioned from the haft of some tool.

'I live, friend Fost. And you truly are my friend. I owe you much.'

'It was his fault you were injured!' Itenyim said heatedly.

'If fault lies anywhere, it lies with he who struck the blow. You would like to believe the fault was mine, though, wouldn't you, Itenyim? That I brought this on myself when I tried to stop you from telling Rann where our guests had gone?' Itenyim dropped his eyes. 'No, I was not slain. But I came close enough to death to make me think. Since then I have spent much time away from the others, contemplating what you and the golden-haired princess told me. It is we who live an illusion.'

Itenyim looked at Fost, his eyes swimming with tears.

'He's mad. His wound deranged him. Don't believe what he says.'

Selamyl laughed. The others drew back, leaving him in a circle of loneliness.

'The outsider knows truth when he hears it,' he said. 'And speaking of truth, didn't I hear you say something of guilt when I came to the door, Cuivris? Well, here's a truth. Whether we like it or not, we

452

are wardens of the Nexus and its secrets. If we do not act, those secrets and the Powers they command, will fall into the hands of the servants of the Dark. Is this why we came here ten thousand years ago? So that we could help undo all the sacrifice and devastation the War of Powers brought to pass?

'Istu is freed. A new War of Powers is at hand. If we do not act, it is lost. And the responsibility is ours. *Ours!*'

The Ethereals looked from Itenyim to Selamyl, who loomed above them like the idol of a pagan god. Slowly and subtly, they edged from Itenyim and drew closer to the crippled man.

'Do we murder the world?' Selamyl asked. For the first time in ten thousand years, the voice of an Ethereal rang as harsh as the blow of a hammer onto an anvil. 'Do we let our dread of working evil cause a greater evil still? Or do we turn our faces from illusion, leave behind our toys and scents and contemplation of the emptiness behind our eyes to do this thing which must be done, that only we in all the world can accomplish?'

One by one the Ethereals rose to their feet and came to stand by Selamyl. Soon, only Itenyim remained seated.

A small sound woke Fost. Habit brought him up with blade in hand, even though the strange, deadly creatures of the Ramparts – the legacy of the first War of Powers – never ventured into the Ethereals' village.

Synalon stood in the doorway holding a small lamp. She wore a nightdress of pale flannel that covered her from neck to ankles and hid the curvings of her body. Fost wondered how she'd managed to pack the bulky garment. He swallowed. Somehow, the effect made him hunger for her more than nakedness would have.

'May I come in?' she asked. Taking his silence for assent, she glided in and put the lamp on a jut of black slag in the wall. She pressed her palms together on the flat of his sword. 'You were so masterful today.'

Gingerly, he freed the blade from her grip and slid the weapon back into its sheath.

'I?' he said. 'Being masterful with these people is futile.'

'You swayed Selamyl.' She sat with her hip touching him. Her flesh burned like a brand through thick flannel and thin blanket. 'No, my lord. You give yourself too little credit.'

She reached out to stroke his cheek. He turned away.

'I can't take credit for what another's done. And I'm no lord.'

'Ah, I forgot. The Emperor's ennobling you wasn't sufficient for your pride.' She leaned close. 'I will make you a noble. Then none can question your right to a title — not even yourself.'

'I guess I can't gracefully refuse, can I?'

'No. You cannot.' Her mouth descended to his. Her lips were cool, the contact light. Her tongue swept lightly in a circuit of his mouth. He shivered. His hands wanted to grab her, but he held them rigid at his sides. He couldn't bring himself to cooperate.

'You are reluctant?' she asked, raising her head and smiling down at him. 'Do I displease you?'

'No,' he croaked. 'Never.'

The smile widened. Her nails traced tingling lines down his cheek, his jaw, throat, chest. Her eyes did not leave his. He felt his muscles tightening, felt his groin tingle in pleasurable anticipation.

Moriana! he thought.

Synalon was not without sensitivity. She caught his thought, his emotion.

'Do nothing for now, milord. Nothing.'

The blanket passed his hips. She worked her magic caress down until his organ stood stiff and bucking and his buttocks left the pallet in a spasm of pleasure.

'You don't find me displeasing at all.' Her eyes released his. Her hair fell in a black cascade over his belly, cool and fragrant, dancing with highlights of golden flame. Her lips closed like a noose of fire and ice. He gasped at the first suction, gripped her shoulders with increasing desire. Shudders wracked his body, increased in intensity. He tried to speak but his tongue turned thick and his jaw trembled.

The wet friction was excruciating as she moved up and down. Fost's every sense heightened, expanded. He felt the flannel, the firmness of her flesh, the heavy breasts swinging rhythmically so that finger-hard nipples brushed his thighs through the fabric. He grew drunk on the smell of her hair and the oil lamp and the moss used to seal the walls, on the scent of the night and the musk of her excitement. Up and down she moved, her tongue never resting.

Then came the explosion from within.

His fingers clamped on her shoulders with bruising force. Her mouth was avid and hungry and infinitely delightful.

She raised her head. She licked her lips and brushed back her hair.

'Now the edge is off, milord. The ceremony can truly begin.'

She sat up straddling him and pulled the gown off over her head. Her pale, blue-veined, carnelian-tipped breasts rode up with it, then dropped to swing free. She pulled her hair from the garment's folds, shook it back, looked down on Fost as if from a great height.

Though he was spent, the sight of her beauty electrified him. He felt himself stiffening again, an obelisk lifted in honor of the triangle of black fur below her smooth stomach.

She raised herself on her knees and shuffled upward along him. He grunted as pleasure stabbed into him when she brushed the tip of his manhood. Then she was poised above his face, mysterious and gilded in lamplight. She lowered herself. He had a last thought of Ziore in her satchel beside the bed before his lips touched coarse, dewy hair. His tongue emerged and swept through the tangle to slick, succulent flesh. Synalon shivered delicately, cupped her breasts with her hands, then thrust her pelvis forward so that his tongue probed deep inside her.

Small, insistent animal sounds rolled from her throat. His tongue swirled within her, savoring both taste and texture. She was maddening and beautiful and he was drunk on her. His tongue withdrew, sought, found; it pressed in.

Her cries filled up the small chamber. Her fingers knotted painfully in his hair but he was lost in his pleasurable task. His tongue flirted, teased, bored in.

She screamed.

Walls of pliant flesh clamped on his head. All he heard was the hollow drumbeat of her pulse, racing, outpacing his. He felt her perfect body tremble, felt her leaving, raised his hands and seized her. At last she tore herself away, her body shining with sweat.

'It is as I thought,' she said, her voice husky. 'You are truly fit for a Queen of the Sky City.'

His mind slipped out of gear and coursed back to the night before and the Dwarflike shape by the campfire. What was it? What had it offered? Some connection between that and Synalon's current passion was almost made, then slipped away from him.

She flowed down like water, her breasts falling heavy upon his firmly muscled chest, her mouth seeking his. Fost's fingers trembled on her buttocks as she lowered her hips and took him in. And then the ancient, insistent motion possessed them both. He forgot all but the heat and pressure and pleasure.

455

CHAPTER ELEVEN

'If you're going to kill me,' said Moriana, 'this is a good place to do it.' Her words were almost lost in the wind moaning through the Gate of the Mountains.

Impassively, Rann studied her across the fire. His yellow eyes cast back the light like a cat's. At the third point of a triangle around the small fire wavered Erimenes's blue, misty pillar. The genie looked from one to another.

Moriana prodded the fire with a stick. Blue flames crackled toward the slit of cloudy sky visible high above.

'You say nothing, Prince.'

'I didn't realize comment was called for, Princess,' replied Rann.

'I see no need to fence with words. I don't trust you.' She angrily threw the stick away.

The prince sat within his cloak. Moriana stared at him across the flames as if she could penetrate that narrow skull and lay bare the thoughts within. But Rann was protected against her probing. He remained unreachable, unreadable.

Their journey from Brev had passed in festering silence. Fost and Synalon had been enemies but had no cherished tradition of enmity. But there was bad blood between Erimenes and Moriana and between the spirit and the scarfaced prince.

It had not been a pleasant trip.

But the journey neared its end. Less than a day south lay the fringes of the glacier. Moriana must face the challenge of convincing Guardian to open a way into Athalau, not just for her and Rann, but for the vast mob of soldiers and civilians making its way south from the devastated Realm. And beyond that was the problem of defending the city and the people against the wrath of Istu.

Tension twisted within her, a slowly fraying cord near to breaking. She sought release in anger and the dangerous pastime of baiting her cousin.

'You want me to believe you're on our side. Why should I believe that?'

Erimenes's eyes widened in anticipation. Moriana lashed at Rann with bitter words, practically taunting him. Rann was not known to suffer such jibes in silence.

'What you believe means little to me,' Rann said after a time, 'except if it affects our chances for success. But I perceive you mean to have this out now, whether or not this is the right time for such disputes. Listen well, cousin. I would see the Fallen Ones cast out of our City in the Sky, and the Demon of the Dark Ones imprisoned once more – or better, destroyed.'

'Why should you care?' She remembered the ruined face of old Kralfi who carried the marks of Rann's handiwork to the grave.

'You may not be pleased to be reminded of this, but I'm as human as you are.' He raised a finger to quell her objection. 'Oh, I've done things you find repellent. I don't apologize for them. I merely wish to point out that my deeds notwithstanding, I am a man, not a Zr'gsz. If the Hissers bring down the blade, it falls on my neck, as well. So I am "on" your side, like it or not.'

'Why not join with the Dark Ones? You've done so before.'

'I've never done so. Synalon served the Dark Ones for a time. I served her.' He tipped back his hands and thrust his forefingers against the bridge of his nose. 'I might ask why you do not choose to throw in *your* lot with the Fallen Ones – as you've done before.'

'Because they betrayed me!'

'And didn't the Dark Ones betray Synalon? Think a moment, cousin dear. Her hatred for you springs from mere rivalry. The Dark Ones misled her. You've theatened her ambitions; they've wounded her pride. Which hatred do you think will prove more implacable?'

'Don't listen to him,' said Erimenes. 'He's too glib. He means you no good, him or that damned Synalon.'

'And how much good have you done the princess, demon?' snapped Rann. 'I remember when you were all aquiver to see Moriana tortured.'

'I, uh, that is . . .' Erimenes looked at the rocky ground and fell silent.

'You disclaim all loyalty to the Dark?' Moriana flung the words at Rann like a gauntlet. 'Why do you choose to serve Synalon, who would be the handmaiden of the Lords of Infinite Night?'

'Would *you* have had me?' he asked, almost too quietly to hear above the wind's lament. 'You who turned her face in revulsion when the bird riders brought me back from the Thails? You always spurned me when we were both young because I couldn't learn magic while you seemed to absorb it through your fingertips. What the savages did to me only confirmed what you'd secretly thought: I was less than a man.'

'That's not true!' she screamed. 'I offered sympathy. You wouldn't have it!'

'Not so, cousin. Pity, perhaps. Pity without understanding. You never attempted to understand me. I who loved you hopelessly, from the time we were both children.' She turned red, her cheeks burning. He laughed. 'Yes, my attentions made you uncomfortable when we were both young. I always imagined it was a relief to you, what the Thailint did to me.'

'No, never that!' She squeezed shut her eyes.

'Synalon understood. We understand each other perfectly. She was neither gentle nor kind, but she understood.'

Moriana sobbed brokenly, huddled in on herself, shaking. Erimenes looked from her to the prince.

'A sad tale. Is this your justification for the evil you've wrought? Do I understand that you must torture innocent victims to death because you're not appreciated?'

'You understand nothing, demon!' Rann shouted at him. He turned away in a swirl of his dark cloak and stared up the pass.

There were voices in the dark, and they were laughing, laughing.

Frantic in its fear and pain, the soul raced around the Skywell. It darted inward as if to cast itself through the Well. Istu reached, tweaked with a taloned thumb and forefinger. Its hues blazed up in yellow pain. It collapsed quivering on the pavement.

Istu chuckled.

'See here,' he said to the one standing silently, watching the Demon at his play. He prodded the prostrate soul with one black fingertip. 'The colors of a soul, stripped of obscuring flesh, reveal its nature. Here on the outside is the yellow of pretense. This green layer beneath is lust. Below that the pink of sloth, the turquoise of indecision, and so on.' The taloned finger sank into the midsection of the soul, which still twitched uncontrollably. 'And at the core, we find a pure white light. Interesting. And odd, considering who this was in life. So many of the souls we took at that place were hollow at the core.

The night was chill with the promise of early autumn and lay heavy upon the People. Nothing stirred on the streets radiating from the Well of Winds. The Demon, his captive soul, and Zak'zar, Speaker of the People, seemed alone in the City.

'Is it necessary to torment that soul so?' Zak'zar asked. 'You'll reap more in the weeks to come.'

Istu prodded the soul again. It thrashed spastically, then lay still when the finger was withdrawn.

'Why should you care?'

'I knew this one in life.'

Istu squatted on his haunches in unthinking imitation of the black basalt statue of him across the Well.

'You seem fascinated by the pale, pink ones. Would you have me leave a few alive for you as pets?!'

'I was chosen of all the generations of the People to become Speaker when the Instrumentality at last fulfilled his function and freed you to bring us vengeance and victory. I was chosen because I could deal with the pale ones and understand their ways.' He spread his hands in front of him, palms down. 'With understanding comes a certain sympathy. It troubles me that our victory means the eradication of the enemy ones.'

'You are soft,' Istu sneered.

'I merely appreciate that those soft-skinned folk have virtues of their own. The interest of the People is mine to safeguard; I deplore that we and the Soft Ones cannot coexist. We could learn from them.'

'Is this why you insisted we accept the ludicrous entreaties of the Dwarves and those traitors from the Nevrym Forest, to ally ourselves with them? As if their pathetic efforts contributed anything of worth.' The great horned head shook, obliterating stars. 'And why couldn't I contemplate the destruction of those last three cities, as I did with Kara-Est? I was born to extinguish suns, mortal. I dislike staying my hand.'

'We still have to complete the reduction of this continent,' said Zak'zar softly. 'And the world beyond that. Our victory is far from assured.'

Istu swelled with rage, but Zak'zar carried on.

'I requested that you spare the cities we took because many things have transpired in the world since you and my kind were forced from it. We may find knowledge that will ease our way to triumph. Or we may learn of a deadly threat in time to avert it.

'As for accepting the Dwarves and Nevrymin as allies, why not? If they do our work for us, we will be victorious all the quicker. I fear that time presses.'

'Why should that be? I am Istu, spawn of the Dark Ones. Doubt your own strength, if you will. Doubt not mine. The Pale Ones cannot stop me.'

'And yet some of them are bound for Athalau,' said Zak'zar, 'and it was in Athalau that you found your downfall last time.'

A bellow of rage rebounded from the starred dome of the sky. Istu grew to a black pillar of wrath, raising mountain-smashing fists high as he glared down at the small, small figure of Zak'zar.

'No one slights the power of Istu!'

'Pardon if I gave offense, Lord Istu. I only pointed out the truth. My abilities in this was another factor in the Dark Ones selecting me as Speaker.' At this reminder of Zak'zar's mandate from Powers greater even than his, the Demon subsided a little. 'I would remind you, great Istu, that the Dark Ones themselves agreed to the wisdom of my proposal to expedite the conquest of the Realm by making alliances with those foolish enough to think our victory might profit them. And likewise, They share my concern over efforts to reach Athalau. As you well know, They even take steps of Their own to counter the menace posed by the Nexus and the World Spirit.'

'I wonder at that,' the Demon said sullenly. 'The Dark Ones have already broken Their faith with that woman once. Do They think They can dupe her again?'

'In my study of the Pale Ones,' said Zak'zar, crossing his arms and nodding in concentration, 'I've found that humans are cursed with a thing called *hope*.'

'When I was bound in the depths of the City, sometimes my thoughts turned to the prospect that once again I would know my world-destroying freedom. In a word, I hoped.' Istu shook his horned head. 'Well do you name it a curse.'

'After all,' said Zak'zar, 'why do Fairspeaker and Mauna aid us so eagerly? Their minds should tell them the best they can win is a stay of execution. But hope tells them otherwise, and it's hope they listen to.'

Istu's eyes flared bright yellow in the blackness of his face.

'Verily does the black-haired witch hope in vain,' he thundered. 'I have not forgotten how she lured me forth to pain and humiliation. I shall cherish her soul within mine. And this I will give her: often, very often I will give her clothing of flesh to wear so that she may know my vengeance again. And the same for her fair-haired sister. I had but a taste of her and will have more.'

'I thought you kept all your captive souls in the spirit jars in the warehouse.'

'Most. Those are the subjects of my passing interest, like the ones I collected in High Medurim, like this miserable baggage here.' He nudged the soul with his foot. It huddled in on itself and shook. 'But there are those I would add to my permanent collection. Those two are among them.'

'Even so,' Zak'zar bowed. 'I would ask a boon.'

'Ask,' said Istu, waving a magnanimous claw. 'You are the Chosen of my progenitors.'

'Release this soul and the one you keep next to it. I care little for the souls of the soft-skinned strangers, but these I knew. They deserve better.'

'I will not,' said Istu, hunching his shoulders. 'They were the only ones of their kind. They are special items. I won't part with them. Not until they begin to bore me.'

'As you will.' Zak'zar bowed again and glided away. Istu glowered after him. When the Speaker was gone, Istu gave the cringing soul another petulant kick, picked it up by the scruff and rammed it into its red clay jar. He placed the jug carefully in its spot among the others and went off to find his own repose.

In the morning, he returned to gloat once more over his collection. What he saw made him shake his enormous head in disbelief. Anger flared nova-bright within him.

Two jars that rested side by side containing the souls of Emperor Teom and his sister-wife Temalla had been smashed. The souls were flown to oblivion, unreclaimable. In his fury, Istu danced on the other jars, stamping them into powder beneath clawed feet. Invisible in the sunlight, the freed souls swirled about his columnar legs and were gone.

When the last jar was crushed and its spirit departed, the fit left Istu. He contemplated what he had done. He had a shrewd notion of the culprit responsible. He might have gone then and sought out the knave. Certainly, Istu could punish him in such a way that would make up for the diversion lost in the forms of bottled souls.

Instead, Istu began to laugh. At the sound of his laughter, birds fell dead for miles around.

'It is a grave thing you ask of me.' Each word came slow and heavy like the fall of mountains. 'I must think on it a while.'

'Marvelous!' cried Erimenes. 'What's "a while," you immense fugitive from an icehouse? Until the sun goes out? Or merely next year?'

'Tsk tsk,' said the glacier named Guardian. The boom of its voice hammered the sheer walls of the Gate of the Mountains bringing a fall of boulders thudding into the pass a few hundred yards behind the travellers. 'Were you not of the blessed kindred of Athalau, good Anemones, I should almost think you precipitous.'

Erimenes emitted a squeal of rage and began tearing at the fringe of blue hair surrounding the base of his long, narrow head. The sentient glacier's inability – or refusal – to pronounce his name properly enraged him more than the living ice mountain's geological deliberations.

Gloom filled the pass deepened by mist spilling down from the Guardian that formed a grayish layer thirty feet off the canyon floor. Light and warmth seldom penetrated here yet the cliff base was dotted with clumps of small blue flowers that seemed little daunted by the darkness and chill.

The Rampart Mountains had a heart of cold stone; the rocks of the canyon were those Guardian had swept up into himself on his slow advance from the Southern Waste. They had been ground smooth within the glacier's body and eventually tumbled from the face as it rolled ever onward. In time, Guardian would swallow them anew to begin the cycle anew unless climatic conditions did not permit him to continue his involuntary progress along the narrow canyon.

On one of those polished rocks sat Rann, apparently at ease. Watching him as she paced in front of the glacier, Moriana wondered at his outward calm. He didn't take frustration and delay philosophically; none of the Etuul blood ever had. Under normal conditions he should have been pacing even more vigorously than she. Instead he sat quiet and self-possessed.

Moriana wondered what had gotten into her cousin. His demeanor made her doubt he intended treachery. But still, he was *too* calm.

'Come and rest yourself, cousin,' he said, smiling. 'The glacier will take its own time answering. No amount of stalking to and fro will hurry it.'

She paused, glaring at him more from reflex than anything else. She finally shrugged and seated herself on a rock not too near Rann's.

'I cannot rightfully deny entry to you, Princess, nor to you Irimunas, for you are rightfully Athalar.' The words boomed out, making Moriana jump in surprise. Rann regarded her with calm indulgence. 'But to let so many folk in as you propose? I do not know.'

As before when talking to Guardian, Moriana found herself straining as if this would hurry the words. But that trick of colossal energies released when the World Spirit was summoned by Felarod that had given the glacier life had not otherwise altered its nature. Guardian thought and spoke glacier-fashion. If anything, this speech was a breakneck babble by its standards.

'I have been tricked before,' rumbled Guardian. 'A human named Rann told me he followed to aid you, when in fact he meant you harm and that pleasant, near-sighted fellow with you – Fost, by name.'

'Why can't he remember *my* name?' grumbled Erimenes.

'Yes, it was a mistake to let Rann into Athalau. His friends burned a hole through my back with a horrid fire sprite.' The ice face shuddered. A sheet of ice split from the glacier with a resounding crack and fell, showering Moriana and Rann with sharp fragments. 'It was worse than the ice worms who gnaw at me from within.'

Rann yawned, stretched, stood.

'Prince Rann is a very bad man,' he said. 'You should not judge the rest of us by what he did.'

Another pause. Rann stood with arms crossed while Moriana paced.

'You are right, human,' came back the answer in time, when the sun had begun to bulge from the top of the eastern cliff and burn away the mist. 'But still, so many. Would that not endanger Athalau?'

'As I understand it,' Rann said, placing hands on hips, 'your task was to preserve the city from agents of the Dark Ones. The princess has told you the *Zr'gsz* have freed Istu and once more ravage the continent. Presently, they will turn their attentions this way.'

'All the more reason to guard my city with zeal.'

'*My* city, indeed,' grumbled Erimenes.

'Not even one as vast and mighty as you can hope to resist Istu, Guardian,' said Rann. 'But you hold within you the means of defeating him. You hold the Nexus by which Felarod drew up the wrath of the World Spirit. We must reach the Nexus. The World Spirit is the only power great enough to help us.'

The glacier sat in silence, save for the creakings and groanings from deep within as the sun heated the miles-wide expanse of its body. Eventually Rann sat back down. Moriana joined him. The cool cloud had ceased to stream down Guardian's face. It was fast becoming warm. Moriana dozed.

'Very well.'

She jumped at the words. Rann still sat on his rock, as collected as ever. He put aside his scimitar which he had been burnishing to a mirror sheen and stood, awaiting the glacier's verdict.

'My responsibility is clear. I must open a path large enough to permit many people to enter Athalau, that they might use the Nexus to bring down the Demon once more.'

Moriana sighed in relief.

'Now, my friends, you must move back. This will not be easy for me and could endanger you if you're too close.'

Moriana and Rann retreated and heard Guardian say, 'So many people. Surely they can put an end to those cursed ice worms.'

Out of sight around the winding of the Gate, Moriana found a chunk of dark quartz that had tumbled from above and sat. Her need for action thwarted by the nature of Guardian, she now found herself drawn irresistibly toward sleep. She heard Erimenes and Rann conversing in low, neutral tones, and let consciousness slip away.

An earsplitting crack awakened her. Others followed in rapid succession, louder and louder, mounting toward a crescendo of noise that dwarfed even the roar of Omizantrim in full eruption. She stared up the canyon, saw clouds of mist and glittering ice crystals billow forth like smoke.

She saw movement from the corner of her eye. Before she could react, Rann was upon her, wrapping steel-cable arms around her and forcing her back against the cliff.

Treachery! she thought, unable to fight her cousin off.

Erimenes's satchel swung from Rann's arm, and she wondered if the genie had entered into intrigue with the prince.

Then twenty tons of stone hurtled down, noiseless against the awful tumult, and buried the rock on which she had been sitting.

In time, hearing returned. In the ringing stillness Rann and Moriana picked themselves up from the tangle in which they'd lain at the foot of the cliff. They picked their way through the rubble strewn along the floor of the pass.

'Great Ultimate,' Moriana whispered as they rounded the bend. Rann's fingers tightened on her arm.

It was as if a great maw had yawned wide in the glacier's face. Thirty feet tall, three times that in width, a passageway had been opened into the glacier's guts. Was it Moriana's imagination or could she truly see, far within, a glimmer of that subtle, lovely radiance given off by Athalau?

Erimenes was weeping.

'To think that my city might live again,' he sobbed.

'You won't forget the ice worms, will you?' echoed Guardian's voice from the great, dark archway.

CHAPTER TWELVE

The Steppe was carpeted with wildflowers, the white blooms covering the land like early snowfall but rippling like the surface of a lake changing to the whims of the wind. Sitting atop a knoll whose bare skeleton of rock protruded like a lizard's spine, Fost surveyed the straggling line of men and women wading knee-deep through the flowers and tried to sort his feelings.

One hundred thirty-eight Ethereals had followed the crippled Selamyl from their village to take the arduous path to Athalau, leaving behind a handful of the aged and the reluctant. Ten of the travellers had died already. Fost wondered how many more would follow.

There were dark things in the Ramparts, not natural life but one of the grimmer legacies of the first War of Powers. A score of times they had come forth to beset the travellers, occasionally in the daytime and often at night. In the darkness all Fost had been able to make out of the attackers were glowing eyes and gaping maws filled with teeth that glinted wetly in the moonlight. Sometimes the attackers were many and small, but savage. Other times it would be a great, lone beast like the creatures that had come on them during the day. Those had been similar, huge armored things with spiked tails and burning demon eyes. Fost was almost grateful that most of the attacks occurred at night.

Synalon had plied her battle magic, accounting for most of the creatures when they came. She and Fost had complete charge of the caravan's safety. The Ethereals had no concept of self-defense, nor any will to do so. They would stand looking vacant, even wistful, as a swarm of creatures like stinking scaled rats tore them to shreds. It was tribute to Synalon's sorcery more than Fost's bladecraft that so few had fallen.

'Yet they keep on,' he marvelled aloud. He had feared the Ethereals would lose heart and turn back as soon as misfortune fell. But they took the dangers and the deaths the same way they took the trudging hardship of the trek itself, with a stolid lack of concern. Fost began to see, as Rann had before him, that beneath their veneer of fecklessness and fragility these Ethereals had a strength of their own.

'We've made good time,' said Synalon from behind him. 'Three hundred miles in two weeks, afoot. We shall soon be at the Gate of the Mountains.'

Fost nodded, looking back down at the long file of Ethereals. Many straggled to one side or the other of the winding trail foraging for berries and edible roots. It was something the Ethereals were good at, and supplies had not yet become a problem.

Nor did the straggling bother Fost. As long as none drifted out of sight, it mattered little whether the Ethereals marched in line or not. With only two of them to guard so large a flock, it was luck alone that had kept the varied wolves from taking more.

'Why so downcast?' Synalon chided him. She flung out her arms and drew in a deep breath, causing her breasts to lift dramatically in the thin shirt. The nipples stood out in bold relief against the taut fabric, and he saw their ruddy color. 'It's a lovely day. The sun is high and hot and feels good on the skin, and the wind from the Ramparts still bears the chill of the Waste at its back to take the sting from the heat. And the flowers raise their heads all about, and their perfume fills the air. Aren't these pleasing to you, my Fost?'

'I never thought I'd hear such sentiments from you.'

The music of her laugh filled the air.

'You've spent too much time with my dour sister. She's always striving after tomorrow. I am content to live with today, taking the sensations it gives me and enjoying them as best I can.' She looked at Ziore. 'Don't go all sour on me, little nun. I do lay plans against the future – aye, and hopes as well. But there are days when I immerse myself in the moment and revel in the million flavors of life.'

'Then why did you ally yourself with the Dark Ones?' Fost asked before good sense could stop the words. 'They are the foes of life.'

A shadow passed over her finely sculpted face like a cloud crossing the sun.

'I thought they could give me power, and that power would open

467

gates to new sensations. What must it be like to stride among the stars as Istu did? To know at once the chill and heat of the Void, to shout into airlessness and race the light of suns?' She sighed deeply. 'But you shall now hear something I seldom say. I was wrong. The Dark knows no bitterer foe than I now.'

Does it? Fost wondered, remembering the dying firelight and the great black Dwarf beyond. But the perverse imp of defiance that made him blurt his question about Synalon's earlier pact with the Elder Lords had retreated, and he said nothing. Synalon loved him with a fiercely hot passion, physically at least, and he both feared and hoped that love extended to other dimensions. But she remained the mad, mercurial creature who had ruled the Sky City with a whim of steel and flame, and it wasn't safe to presume too far upon her good feelings.

'Your philosophy is similar to what Erimenes now believes,' Ziore commented.

'Ah, but I'm wiser than your Athalar sage, little sister,' Synalon cried, 'for I have long since learned that lesson and did not have to wait until I was dead.' Her hand shot out with a speed that reminded Fost of the Zr'gsz blood in her veins. She caught him by the wrist. She drew his scarred hand to her lips and kissed it gently. 'And now, my dear Fost, you shall learn why my way is wisest, to wring each moment dry of sensation without thought to the next.'

'What?'

'Look to the northern horizon, dear one.'

He did. His heart dropped into the bottom of his belly.

Like a fleet of ships upon the waves, they rode the air in a bobbing black line across the sky. Still too distant to be clearly seen, shimmering slightly in the waves of heat rising from the Steppe, the skyrafts grew even as Fost watched. Form and detail sharpened. His sword slid into his hand with a fluid motion.

Synalon sent her mount stiff-legged down the face of the knoll, sliding and staggering amid a slippage of small, loose stones. Fost followed, hoping his dog wouldn't break a leg.

Synalon called for the Ethereals to close up into a group.

'No!' Fost shouted, and quailed as she turned a furious look on him. 'Have them scatter and hide the best they can. The Hissèrs are missile troops when they ride their rafts. If the Ethereals clump together, Zr'gsz darts will go through them like a sickle through ripe wheat.'

468

Her dog reached the foot of the ridge and galloped toward where Selamyl still dragged himself inexorably forward with his cane. Fost's beast pounded after.

She let him do the talking. He hurriedly outlined the danger to the Ethereals' leader, and what must be done. Selamyl smiled benignly.

'Holding perfectly still is a thing my folk are good at,' he said. He turned and began speaking, gesturing into the scrub around them.

One by one the Ethereals disappeared. Fost's eyes widened at the completeness with which they vanished. The Ethereals lacked wilderness craft but they could divorce their minds utterly from their bodies and drift among their dreams, immune to physical discomfort. Their bodies bent into unlikely shapes to take advantage of the sparse cover – and then they froze. In a matter of minutes, Fost saw only Selamyl. Then he, too, disappeared.

'Impressive,' said Synalon. 'But remember the Zr'gsz are airborne. They'll hunt the Ethereals from a different perspective.'

'But Oracle told me their eyesight is poor. Their eyes are attuned to movement rather than detail. If the Ethereals stay immobile, we have a chance.'

'I think I can help,' Ziore said urgently. 'This close to Athalau my powers are greater, like Erimenes's. I cannot turn the Hissers away, but I can slow small numbers of them.'

Anything that helped counteract the blindingly swift reflexes of the Vridzish would be of immeasurable aid.

Synalon's eyes glowed beneath half-lowered lids. Her lips moved as she spoke to herself. Ziore shuddered and drew away from the sorceress. Fost felt a thrill as though his nerve ends were tightly brushed by powers beyond his ken.

The rafts drew near, a score, two dozen. Fost's eyes unfocused. He blinked, realizing that there was a blurring of the line of dark stone rafts. A Hisser, highborn from his size and green cuirass, pointed and shouted a sibilant command. The formation split to avoid the disturbance, some going around, others up and over.

The air darkened, swirled, coalesced. A winged shape hung in air, a tiger's head swiveling at the end of a long snake's neck. At least six legs dangled from the bloated body. Fost couldn't be sure because the thing swam in and out of focus.

As the leading raft passed overhead, the thing half rolled, drumming the air with its wings. A claw shot up, up to and *through* the underside of the raft. The pilot hunched over the globe at the rear suddenly gave a ringing shriek. The claw drew down pulling the Hisser's smoking guts with it through the skystone.

'Great Ultimate,' Fost whispered.

'I think you've seen this magic before. Back in the tower of Kest-i-Mond.'

He recalled the striped ape monster, blinded by a deathbolt that failed to save the enchanter who cast it, and the nightmare chase it had given him through the corridors of the sorcerer's keep. Fost's blade had passed harmlessly through it, and it flowed through solid walls and doorways as though they were air. Only by luring it into an open fumarole Kest-i-Mond had built his castle over had Fost avoided death. Synalon's magic now was identical with that he'd faced – and barely triumphed over.

Slung stones and javelins sleeted down at the winged creature. They passed through it like smoke. Clawed limbs lashed out again and again. The monster delighted in eviscerating Zr'gsz and tearing out hearts to fling them in the faces of its foes.

'They'll never get past that horror,' said Fost. Relief almost overwhelmed his dread of the monster.

Synalon frowned. A spot of darkness appeared in the air beside the winged beast, grew. The tiger-headed thing saw it, struck at it with a claw. The beast's arm disappeared. The black hole caught the arm and drew the monster in. It uttered a wail that raked down Fost's spine. Then it was gone. The hole winked out of existence.

Synalon's hair crackled with sparks.

'Damn! They've a mage with them who draws on Istu's power.'

As she spoke, a beam of black light lanced down at her. She gestured contemptuously. It bent abruptly to dig a smoking rent in the ground.

'Even with the Demon's help he has no touch for offensive magic,' Synalon sneered. 'But I fear he can negate any spells I attack with.'

'Is Istu near?' asked Fost, peering all around.

'No, but his power can augment that of any he favors. I myself sought to tap the power of his sleeping mind – as you may recall.'

He had a fleeting urge to strike her. He remembered too well. She had planned to sacrifice Moriana to the sleeping Demon as a bribe for his assistance. Fost had barely rescued the golden-haired princess.

Synalon's hands moved, weaving a new spell. A crack opened in the earth below the skyfleet. A billion black hornets billowed forth

470

to surround the rafts. Stoic as they were, the Hissers began to scream and fling themselves over the edges of their vessels to escape the maddening stings.

Fost couldn't see the enemy sorceror. But he must have acted because the swarm became a cloud of tiny sparks burning unbearably bright, falling to the Steppe in an incandescent rain.

The rafts were almost overhead. Arrows began to pelt the landscape, javelins and stones striking with thumps like hail. Synalon's lips drew back taut.

'They know what we're doing. They're trying to slay the Ethereals.'

'They're shooting blind,' Fost said. Evidently the Vridzish had spotted the Ethereals at a distance and knew they were near, but couldn't pinpoint them. With their eerie self-control, many of the Ethereals died without a sound, without stirring.

The rafts came close enough to speed missiles at the mounted pair. Fost steeled himself. He had no shield and his mail vest would provide little protection against hard-driven arrows.

Synalon waved her hand. The barrage of missiles dropped, arrows and javelins aflame, the stones molten lumps.

'Had they enough archers they could swamp me,' she said. 'But they don't.'

The skyrafts veered off, milling aimlessly in the sky. Fost awaited a new spell from Synalon. None came.

'I do what their mage does,' she explained. 'I conserve strength.'

The rafts spread out, formed a circle around the two and touched down. The craft each held six to eight Vridzish. Six to eight too many for Fost's liking.

The Hissers rushed forth, the nobles splendid in their cloaks and armor, the paler scaled lowborn warriors clad in loincloths and carrying obsidian spears and axes. Some of the latter carried shortswords of plain steel looted from a human armory. Oracle had predicted this would happen. Obsidian held a keener edge than steel but it was brittle. As Vridzish weapons were broken or lost, they had to be replaced. Picking up fallen human weapons proved easier than chipping new ones from glass.

It was small comfort. Two of the shortsword-armed Hissers stopped and hauled an Ethereal woman to her feet. Her face never lost its dreamy look as they plunged their swords repeatedly into her body.

Synalon pointed three times with her finger. Three lines of blue lightning stabbed forth. The two slayers and an officer nearby charred and fell. Synalon laughed delightedly at her handiwork.

'The whoreson can't guard against that!'

The Vridzish commander shouted and waved his sword. The Hissers advanced on Fost and Synalon at a trot. Both dismounted, preparing for battle.

Lightning flared in such rapid succession that Fost was momentarily deafened and blinded. But if the *Zr'gsz* mage couldn't fend off her deadly short range lightning, neither had Synalon speed or strength to cinder all their enemies before they reached the embattled pair.

Instinct made him lash out even before his vision cleared. Fost felt his blade slash through something brittle; then came the unmistakable sensation of steel cleaving flesh. A Hisser gasped and fell, the broken halves of a mace dropping to the Steppe.

A score of the reptiles surrounded the pair. Fost's dog snarled and leaped, taking a deep gash down one side but bearing two of them to the ground. A trio of lowborn Hissers closed on Fost. His eyes searched rapidly and found a small stone lying near his foot. He kicked it between two of the Vridzish.

They were stupid. Their eyes followed the rock and then not even their inhuman speed saved them from Fost's whining blade. He swung left, right, left again and black blood gushed over him.

A noble loomed up ahead swinging an obsidian-edged sword. Fost hurled himself backward. The black stone blade moaned past. Fost felt nothing but as he backpedalled he saw that his tunic was parted in a line running across his chest and blood welled through a sleeve.

Synalon glided forward, her rapier twitching before her like a giant insect's antenna. She attacked the officer, and he retreated a step. Steel rang on stone, and then the tip of the slender sword whipped around a parry to score a heavily muscled forearm.

The *Zr'gsz* whistled in rage and struck, battling Synalon's blade out of the way. She danced back. He smiled then, teeth bright in his dark face, and advanced.

As quickly as he had advanced, he stopped. His eyes rolled up in his head showing greenish white balls. He stiffened. Every muscle swelled into relief on his powerful body, and he began vibrating in the grip of an awful spasm. A keening sounded only to be drowned in a froth of blood. He fell, kicking grooves in the soil. He finally lay still.

'My sword skill's too paltry to put all my faith in it,' Synalon said from behind Fost. 'Come on then, bastards. My venom's good for many more!'

And they did come on, barely giving Fost time to clamber to his feet. He and Synalon fought back to back as the Vridzish rushed. It seemed that each new attack must be the last; Fost didn't know how he parried the blinding strokes of mace and axe and sword. The *Zr'gsz* crowded in on all sides, jostling each other, making it difficult to attack. Fost buried his sword over and over until he was black with their blood. Synalon's poisonous sting littered the ground with convulsing victims. But there were too many Hissers, and beyond the circle of hard, dark faces Fost saw several score others still hunting down the Ethereals.

His face and arms stung from myriad shallow cuts. He dared not even glance over his shoulder at Synalon, but from her constant low-voiced cursing he guessed she was in no better shape.

He refused to have it end like this. The thought of dying filled him with rage.

'O, Ust!' he bellowed. 'Give me the strength to slay these sons of darkness!' Madness came on him, and he waded in among the Vridzish.

He scattered a dozen of the lower caste warriors. Another officer faced him. His speed outmatched Fost's berserker fury. Each stroke of his mace drove Fost's blade perilously near the man's own flesh. Sweat blinded Fost.

Then the noble's head departed its shoulders atop a column of blood.

'Again I greet you, O Chosen of Ust,' said Jennas, hetwoman of the bear clan, as she flicked black blood from the six-foot blade on her greatsword. 'This is getting to be a habit,' she added in a quieter voice.

The timely arrival of the Ust-alayakits threw the *Zr'gsz* into confusion. Jennas wheeled her bear Chubchuk away and launched herself against their common foe. The long hair and body fat of the bears provided excellent armor; the beasts absorbed savage blows without harm. Fost saw the plumed *Zr'gsz* captain fell a male bear rider only to have another rider roll down on him like an avalanche. The rider was a grossly fat woman with a steel cap strapped atop wiry red curls. The Hisser threw up his shining green blade. A giant axe swept down with all the force of that huge body. The green sword snapped. The axehead hurled on. Through gorgeous plume, through green helmet, through skull and body until it sank into the cold ground of the Steppe. The *Zr'gsz* was sheared in two, the halves quivering over dead legs for a second before falling in separate directions.

The Hissers ran for their rafts. The fat woman laughed and threw her giant axe into the air. It cartwheeled up until it was outlined against the swollen disk of the setting sun. Then it returned, a huge hand snared it and the battle was done.

Flames danced high against the nighttime sky. Drunken and boisterous, the bear riders staggered in a victory dance around the bonfire.

Fost sat with Jennas and the monstrous redheaded woman, Vancha Broad-Ax. Her great axe, Little Sister, was laid carefully on the ground by her huge rump where she patted it from time to time and crooned appreciatively to it. The Bear folk still talked about the way she'd struck down the *Zr'gsz* noble that afternoon. Fost had never seen anything like it, and to judge from the talk of the Ust-alayakits, neither had they.

'I had the proper motivation,' Vancha boomed in a voice as big as she was. 'Ust has kept little Jennas appraised of what goes on in the world north of our Steppe, by means of visions.' She laid a companionly slab of arm across 'little Jennas's' shoulders, who was every bit as tall as Fost and just as powerful. The hetwoman smiled, but her amber eyes were troubled.

'It's good to see you again, Fost,' the hetwoman said as Vancha poured herself a fresh mug of rakshak, the liquid fire that these nomads drank. 'It is as Ust foretold.' She looked away quickly.

Fost felt a tingling and glanced over his shoulder. Synalon sat away from the fire on a saddle taken from the corpse of Fost's dog. Her arms were folded beneath her breasts, and she regarded the courier with sullen, smouldering eyes. He bit his lip and turned away.

When the Vridzish had fled, Synalon had seized him and hugged him tight. Her lips had sought his; the slaying had aroused passions in her that wouldn't be put off. Yet he had shrugged her off to share a tearful embrace with Jennas. Only when he had literally felt Synalon's gaze laid across his back like a whip had he turned from Jennas to see the anger and hurt glowing in Synalon's eyes.

Though Synalon drank nothing, she had grown more sullen since the sun fell from the sky. When a young bravo had swaggered up and tried to put his arm around her, she had given him a glare charged with more than anger. He cried out in a high-pitched voice and fled, stumbling and falling into the fire and being badly singed before his fellows dragged him out. The bear riders were of a rough humor and thought this a capital joke. Fost read darker implications in it.

'So you're herding these two-legged sheep to Athalau,' Vancha said, her immense paw settling on his arm. She nodded toward the Ethereals, who sat like so many pallid statues. Silently Fost counted the unmoving figures. They didn't number one hundred. There was only one way of learning if they would be enough for the dangerous task ahead of them.

'Well, we're glad to strike a blow against the foul lizards. We'll gladly escort you to the Gate of the Mountains, won't we, Jennas?'

'What say?' Jennas asked, shaking herself. 'Oh, yes, we must do anything we can to help. Ust wills it.'

Vancha's pig eyes, as green and hard as emeralds, narrowed into slits amid fat.

'Something's eating you, girl.' The eyes flicked to Fost. 'I think I know what it is, too.'

'Thank you, Vancha, but you do not know.'

Fost studied the hetwoman. He had thought her handsome at first, but in the months they had spent together chasing Moriana all over the Sundered Realm, he had come to know the beauty in her strongly sculpted features, her high, proud cheekbones and close-cropped shock of reddish hair. And in ways he loved her, though he told himself Moriana took preeminence.

He hated himself for hurting her, but she knew from the start that he loved Moriana and would go to her if possible. It hadn't stopped them from becoming lovers.

It would be harder for Jennas to understand why they couldn't resume their relationship. He set down his mug, stretched, managed a good imitation of a yawn that turned into the real thing.

'It has been one hell of a day,' he said. 'I'm going to bed.'

Vancha rose and gave him a fond, spine-crushing squeeze. Across the campfire Ziore told dirty jokes to the younger warriors. She knew a surprising number for a nun. The trip to Medurim had given her more than any of the warriors.

He nodded to Jennas, not able to meet her eyes. He turned and walked off into the darkness, away from them, away from Synalon, too. It had all become too much for him. He wanted only to be alone.

He heard the crunch of a step behind him. His spine turned icy with premonition.

'Fost.' It was Jennas, soft-voiced, diffident. 'There's something I must tell you.' She took him by the shoulders.

Her hands were slapped away.

'Get away from him!' screamed Synalon. 'I'll share him with my sister, but he's not going to be soiled by any filthy barbarian bitch!'

Jennas turned to face the sorceress. Her face was calm in the orange firelight. Around the fire voices were raised, asking what was amiss. Torches were lifted and the bear riders came at a run, sensing something deadly wrong.

'You thought to sneak off with him and seduce him,' hissed Synalon. 'Perhaps you got away with this before. But he's too good for the likes of you!'

'He can make his own choices,' Jennas said in a level voice.

'He'll not choose you!' Synalon lunged forward. Fost caught the flash of steel and gasped.

The bear riders growled and closed in.

'No! Get back!' cried Jennas as she sidestepped, dodging the gleaming arc of Synalon's dagger. 'It's between me and her! Leave us be!'

Reluctantly, the bear riders stopped where they stood.

'That's enough,' Jennas told Synalon. 'I've no quarrel with you.'

'I challenge you!' spat Synalon. Her face was an icy mask of fury. 'I'll not even use magic. But still I'll have your heart, you slut!'

She lunged forward, her right arm a blur. Jennas jumped back, not quite fast enough. The slim dagger opened a long gash in her arm. Her face hardened. A heavy-bladed knife appeared in her right hand. She crouched, holding the weapon low for a disembowelling stroke, while Synalon circled her like a stalking panther.

'Fost, Fost, what's going on?' cried Ziore. 'Can't you stop them?' He started forward.

'No!' Jennas cried without turning. 'You can do nothing. This was meant to be.'

Synalon moved in. Jennas's blade met hers with a skirring sound. Grimacing, the princess struck again and again. She could not

476

penetrate the steel ring of Jennas's defenses. With a catlike scream of rage, Synalon launched herself at Jennas. Though the bear rider was heavier, Synalon bore her to the ground. But only for a moment. Jennas's brawny arm caught Synalon by one pale shoulder and flung her away.

In an instant Jennas was astride the prostrate princess, eyes wide, dagger poised for the deathstroke. Then the killing light went out of her eyes. She lowered her arm.

Synalon thrust upward. The needle-slim blade bit through mail and leather, punctured skin, slipped between ribs to pierce the woman's heart. Jennas jerked, reeled backward and fell heavily. The sorceress jumped to her feet waving the bloody dagger.

'Kill her! Kill the bitch!' somebody cried as the bear riders rushed to their chieftain's aid.

'No!' Jennas's voice was strong but ragged with pain. 'It – ah! – it was a fair fight. She challenged and I accepted.'

'She struck when you stayed your hand,' growled a bear rider.

'The fight was fair.' Jennas's body shook. She clamped her jaw against the pain. Blood welled around her teeth. 'You must not harm her. She must yet play her part or all . . . oh . . . all is lost.'

She looked around wildly.

'Vancha! Promise me. You will aid the outlanders as we promised. Do it for our people, or they shall . . . pass.'

The redhead thrust herself forward, shouldering aside the warriors as if they were children.

'I will,' she said through the tears streaming down her cheeks.

Jennas's back arched. When the spasm passed, she said weakly, 'Fost.'

'I'm here.' He knelt by her side and took her head, cradling it in his lap. His own face shone with tears.

'I know,' she said in an almost normal voice. 'Do not blame yourself. This was all . . . foretold.' She seized his arm in an iron grip. 'Keep well, Longstrider. For the sake of your people and mine . . . and your golden-haired princess. And, ah . . . remember Jennas, who loved you.'

Her head rolled back on lifeless muscles.

The Ust-alayakits surged toward Synalon, raising blades and torches. A huge figure stepped between them and her. An axe head glittered against the stars, came howling down to split a stone in a shower of sparks.

'*No!*' roared Vancha Broad-Ax. 'You'll obey our hetwoman's command or I swear I'll butcher the lot of you!' Her face dissolved in tears, her huge body shaking. But the fat-ringed hands that gripped the black haft were as steady as rock. All knew that what Vancha Broad-Ax promised, she performed. The Ust-alayakits drew back.

Heedless, Fost let Jennas fall and lunged for Synalon, ripping his sword from his scabbard.

'You murdering bitch!' he shouted, cocking his arm to run her through.

'Will it be you to break the oath, then?' she asked, a smile playing at the corners of her mouth.

'What do you mean?'

'The oath we swore in Tolviroth Acerte. Was it just words to you?'

'But you've broken it, you murderous . . . *thing*. You killed Jennas.'

'Oh? Perhaps my memory fails me,' she said, tilting her head as if listening to a distant voice. 'When we swore that oath together, I do not recall Jennas being there.'

The strength went out of Fost. His sword tip drooped to the ground. His knees gave way beneath him.

He sensed a nearness, looked up to see Vancha against the stars.

'What Jennas commanded shall be done, outlander,' she said. 'We shall aid you in reaching the Gate of the Mountains, and you and your witch-woman will come to no harm. But I beg you, stay out of my sight from this moment on. I would not betray my hetwoman's last wish!'

With a sob, she turned and fled. One by one, the Ust-alayakits turned and walked away until he was alone with Synalon and Ziore and a grief as boundless as the uncaring skies above.

CHAPTER THIRTEEN

Fost stared in amazement. When the bird rider patrol had spotted them at the head of the pass and winged low enough to shout down that the way into Athalau lay open, Fost assumed that Guardian had opened a narrow passage as he had done previously. Or Moriana had found an ice worm tunnel and convinced the glacier to let the humans use it. Instead, a great arched tunnel yawned ahead. Synalon's dog trotted around the bend and stopped beside the bear Fost rode.

'My sister's done well.'

Fost only grunted. He could still scarcely bear to speak to Synalon. Though last night, only a night after Jennas's murder, when she had come to him – that had required no talking.

Wings cracking like sails in a stiff wind, a flight of bird riders passed low overhead and disappeared through the entrance. Fost heard the scraping of a cane, and Selamyl came into view. He stopped. His face lit with awe and wonder, and then he dragged himself on.

Vancha Broad-Ax appeared at the head of the file of Ethereals. Seeing the entry opened in the living ice, she stopped and stared for a long moment. She turned then to Fost, looked through him, wheeled her huge mount and went back the way she had come. Shouts echoing down the canyon told Fost the bear riders were going home. Jennas's last command had been fulfilled.

Another shout brought Fost's head around. His heart jumped in spite of grief and bone-deep weariness, and he kicked the bear into a lumbering run toward the tunnel and the woman and the blue figure stepping from it.

*

In all his fevered adolescent fantasies, Fost had never even remotely imagined that he might pass a night in fabled Athalau, lying abed on silken sheets with a beautiful princess. Of course, if he had dreamed of the horrors and travails that went along with the fulfillment of the never-entertained fantasy, he probably would have slit his wrists.

The six of them had exchanged terse greetings over dinner in a dormitory in the center of Athalau, next to the Palace of Esoteric Wisdom. On convincing Guardian to open the pathway, Rann had sent back a message via Moriana for a squadron of bird riders to come ahead and provide defensive strength. Their meat that evening was an antelope the flyers had shot in the foothills, quartered and flown in.

After dinner, Fost and Moriana bid good night to Synalon and Rann. Fost had dreaded this moment but Synalon did not explode with temper, did nothing but smile and nod in a specially meaningful way before going off with her eunuch cousin. Moriana watched them go.

'They're up to something,' she said quietly. 'I mistrust them.'

They ensconced Ziore and Erimenes in a room on the bottom floor of the dormitory where the sounds of their reunion wouldn't keep the others awake all night. Then Fost and Moriana climbed the stairs to their chamber on the second floor for a more intimate welcoming of their own.

Half-drowsing afterward, Fost lay on his side, running his fingers through Moriana's hair. It was fine and soft – like Synalon's. He shook himself. He didn't want to take that pathway.

'What's the matter?' Moriana asked sleepily.

'I was just wondering about this room. The bed smells fresh and these sheets certainly don't seem two hundred years old.'

'We had Rann's bird riders fly in the bedding this afternoon,' she said. 'As for the sheets, they're of Athalar make and meant to last.'

'It's just as well,' he said, glancing down at the rumpled bedding. She smiled lazily.

'Let's test them again,' she said, reaching for him.

Finishing, they drowsed for a time, woke, made love again. Privately Fost marvelled at his own response. Synalon had been wringing him dry every night since the first time in the Ethereals' village. But he wanted to lose himself in the taste and scent and feel of Moriana, the textures and tempos of her body, and it was as if he hadn't been with a woman in weeks.

When they were done, he rose and poured them both wine from a crystal decanter.

'It's hard to believe this hasn't gone to vinegar,' he said, carrying the cups to the bed.

'The Athalar magics were versatile.' She sipped the wine. 'I hope their knowledge can be recovered.'

They had made a good start that day, and a vital one. As they had walked the long road leading from the Gate of the Mountains down into the softly glowing city, Fost had remarked that he hoped they would be able to find the Nexus in time. It'd be brutal irony to make it all the way here and then not find that which they sought.

'I don't know where it lies,' Erimenes said. 'But I think it will be no problem. The Ethereals have Athalau in their blood. Being present in the city works on me, makes my powers grow. They will know where they are to go, mark my words.'

And it was true. Selamyl had no sooner set foot on the rim of the depression in which the city lay than he stopped and went as rigid as a hunting dog catching a scent. Fost thought it simple wonder at first. There was reason enough for that. One didn't have to be of Athalar descent to marvel at the beauty of the place, its soaring spires and well-ordered colonnades, a symphony of form and shape and color. A smooth, seamless substance paved the road that sloped gently before them into the heart of the city. Over all shone the sourceless, shifting, polychromatic and restful light of Athalau.

Here and there blocks of stalactites of ice had fallen and damaged buildings. Fost, Moriana and Rann, who had all been there before, kept hands on sword hilts and a watchful eye for ice worms. These creatures, some big enough to swallow a man whole, infested the glacier to Guardian's annoyance, and had over the years filtered down to lair in the city.

But neither the unconscious vandalism of falling ice nor the invasion of the deadly worms detracted from Athalau's beauty. Yet it was not the beauty that gripped Selamyl or the others as they came up behind him to stand transfixed.

'I . . . I remember,' Selamyl said in a distant voice. 'This was meant to be.' As the quiet syllables echoed through the vast dome

481

of ice, he set off at a vigorous walk down the road, neglecting now to use his cane.

No one had seen an Ethereal hurry before, let alone a crippled one, but one by one the rest came out of their trance and followed, some trotting to catch up. As if he had walked these boulevards every day of his life, Selamyl led them to a wide plaza at the center of the city, which was dominated by the most striking building in Athalau, a tower carved from a single giant ruby whose top was lost in the ice above. He turned down the street flanking the plaza and walked quickly to a building whose front was mostly blocked by a great chunk of ice fallen from above, crushing the marble portico.

He looked in dismay at the obstruction, and then down at the sinister rusty stains on the pavement under his feet.

'What has happened here? We must get in.'

Rann stepped forward, a curious half-smile on his hips. He scuffed at one stain with the toe of his boot.

'Blood,' he explained. 'Mine.'

Fost and Moriana looked at each other. They knew this place, and what had happened to it. It was the Palace of Esoteric Wisdom, once holding the Amulet of Living Flame and the treacherous Destiny Stone. The ice had not fallen by random chance. Erimenes had called it down to crush Rann and his bird riders, who had tracked Fost and others here to seize the Amulet for Synalon.

But the way into the Palace was not entirely blocked. Fost scrambled up with Rann close behind. Together they helped Selamyl over the rubble. He led them through the nave without a glance at the altar which had held the two talismans. To a stairway, down; deep below, beyond a door Erimenes swore had not been opened since before his time, to where the Nexus lay.

It didn't look like much. It was only a pattern traced on the floor in some dull metal, a square mandala with various nodes, widening in the metallic track in a distribution that said chance but whispered some hidden design. It stretched thirty feet on a side with ten feet of floor surrounding it, a domed ceiling rising twenty feet overhead. Fost looked at Moriana, who shrugged. He could tell by the disappointment in her eyes that she felt nothing of power here.

But Selamyl walked in with eyes aglow to the center of the Nexus and fell to his knees in rapture. And one by one, the Ethereals followed him in, trancelike in their movements, and each moved to a spot on the design and dropped in turn to a kneeling posture, as if by prearrangement.

Now Fost sat on the edge of the bed gazing down at the princess.

'Tell me what happened after you left Brev,' she asked, and he did so. She caught her breath when he mentioned waking in the middle of the night to see Synalon in conversation with the black Dwarf, though he admitted it might have been some trick of the light. Moriana said nothing to this, but her expression was eloquently skeptical.

She squeezed his hand during the account of the battle with the skyrafts. When he came to what happened next he broke down and sobbed and, holding him, Moriana cried, too. She had been jealous of Jennas once, but had come to honor and even love the brave, wise woman who had done so much to aid Fost.

'I don't know why Synalon did it,' Fost said over and over, shaking his head. 'It was insane. She had no way of knowing the bear riders wouldn't tear her apart.'

'She is insane,' agreed Moriana. 'Rann has spoken of difficulties he had with her, trying to build a strategy on the shifting sands of her whim.' She sat up, gathering the sheets around her, drew up her knees and rested her chin on them, frowning. 'But perhaps it was no mere freak of her temper that made her act so. Perhaps it was planned, to impede our bringing the Ethereals here.'

Fost looked away. A cold lump settled in the pit of his stomach.

'There was more to it than that,' he said reluctantly. And he told her the story of his seduction by Synalon.

When he finished he heard nothing but her measured breathing at his back. He thought he'd hurt her too badly for forgiveness and waited to be ordered from the room.

What came weren't harsh words but a gentle touch on his shoulder.

'Fost, dear Fost.' She raised herself, leaning against him. 'I should have warned you. I saw she admired you.' She took his chin and swung his face to hers. 'I know my sister's ways. She is beautiful and knows how to wield her beauty like a paintbrush or a sword. I think I would not have things otherwise. The man who could resist her attentions once would be more than human.' Her mouth twisted. 'Or less than a man, like Rann.' She kissed him.

A while later he said, 'But what of us? Do you think she'll make trouble because it's you I want?'

483

'Didn't she say something about sharing you with me? I think she accepts our relationship — for now.' He felt her draw away. 'Do you want that, too? To parcel yourself out to both her and me?'

He took her in his arms and let his body answer.

The city came to life again for the first time in almost two hundred years. The caravans Moriana had dispatched from Tolviroth Acerte weeks before arrived bringing sorely needed supplies. The merchant fleet lay at anchor in Dawngold Bay thirty miles east of Athalau, and Guardian obligingly opened a new passageway to permit the supplies to be portaged overland and into the city. He did so eagerly because it was always a source of deep sadness for the glacier that he had watched over the death of the city. Now he could take part in Athalau's rebirth. Sometimes he chuckled to himself, the sounds of his pleasure booming through the tunnels and streets.

No one felt mirth at the word the fleet brought with them. The party Moriana sent out to meet the ships was astonished to find twice as many ships riding anchor in the mouth of the Gulf of Veluz. The extra vessels were refugees fleeing the wrath of Istu, which had descended on Tolviroth Acerte not long after Moriana and the rest departed. The survivors were shocked and scarcely coherent but reported that the city had been captured, not utterly obliterated as Kara-Est had been. It was small comfort.

Under the surprisingly steady guidance of the youthful Cerestan, refugees began to stream into Athalau from Brev. And not only from Brev and Bilsinx but from as far north as the Black March. Word had spread that mankind would make its last stand in the icebound citadel of the south. Perhaps, as Rann speculated, Zak'zar had spread the rumors himself in the hope of straining Athalau's tenuous supply lines to breaking. There were other cities that had yet to suffer the attentions of the Sky City: Port Zorn in the east, Duth and Kolinth and those of the other City States that had not lain in the City's path from the Black March to Medurim, Thailot and Deepwater and the Sjeddland cities west of the Thails. But it was also true that Athalau offered the best hope for humanity's survival — the only hope.

If it was the Vridzish's wish to weaken the defenders of Athalau with hunger, that tactic was in vain. The supplies Moriana had ordered to the lost city were plentiful and great stores of travellers' fare lay in the vaults beneath Athalau. This was magically preserved dried food meant to sustain life over long journeys. It was scarcely palatable, but it did what it was intended to do. Moreover, game teemed in the Ramparts this season; hunting was good, if risky. Eventually the food stocks would run low, but Rann doubted the Fallen Ones would feel they had the leisure to wait. Every day the humans explored Athalau increased their chances of being able to successfully summon the World Spirit. It soon became apparent that the Zr'gsz would not wait. Bird riders reported that the Sky City passed first Bilsinx and then Brev, and Istu smashed each city flat. But they were abandoned by then. He reaped few souls for his collecton.

The Zr'gsz reacted violently when the survivors of the fight with the Palace of Esoteric Wisdom reported back, launching savage attacks against the long columns of refugees and airlifting in an army of foot soldiers from the north, risking the increasingly rare skyrafts in the face of the fierce storms that blew in from the Joreal Ocean in this season.

And there was another danger they faced.

Prince Rann was in the field again, at the head of the reunited forces of the Sky City. No longer were the lizard men and their stone rafts a frightening novelty as they had been when Moriana led the aerial fleet against the City in the Sky; no longer were the Sky Citizens fighting halfheartedly to defend the throne of a queen many thought an usurper and worse. The soldiers of the City and their allies fought with all the skill and courage for which they were renowned – and with a cornered animal savagery, too. When Rann's eagles spread their wings above the rafts of the People, the slaughter they worked was fearful.

Despite all anyone could do, the slaughter the Vridzish worked on the refugees was frightful, too. It was impossible to protect the mile-long columns of trudging, desperate folk. But Cerestan did well, luring an army three times the size of his into an envelopment and massacring it to a man, with a force of Bilsinxt and Sky City cavalry. After that, the attacks on the refugees slacked off.

Encouraging as the humans' successes in the field were, they were insubstantial. It was a bitter war; if the humans lost, they were doomed, but all they could win was a respite, the chance to follow one breath with another until the City and the Demon arrived.

Moriana desperately prepared herself for the coming duel with Istu. The Ethereals had moved into the Palace of Esoteric Wisdom as if it had been built for them and began a strict regimen of meditation and study. Moriana studied, too, in the vast and varied Athalau libraries. Her knowledge grew, but not her confidence.

There was no way to test the Nexus or try calling upon the World Spirit until the actual time came to face Istu. The summoning of the World Spirit had been too much for Felarod and nine-tenths of his Hundred; already Moriana had fewer Ethereals to work with. She dared not risk them prematurely.

She bore the burden well. Sometimes she awakened Fost at night with weeping, but when he held her in his arms all she could speak of was her fear that the best wasn't good enough, that the evil she had loosed upon the world would consume it and humankind.

When she returned to fitful drowsing, Fost brooded over the near certainty that even victory would cost him Moriana. He never let her know of his concern. But sometimes when she slept, he shed tears, too.

During the hectic days he occupied himself with a task as necessary as Rann's. He began the eradication of the ice worms, first in the city and then in the glacier. Guardian was a good and true ally and the humans owed him much.

'Is this a fitting occupation for an itinerant hero?' Erimenes demanded one day as Fost trudged from an ice worm tunnel at the head of a weary, battered squad. 'You should be off soldiering, covering yourself with glory like Rann and Cerestan.'

'I'd sooner be covered in shit,' Fost growled. 'I'll never make a soldier. I admit, sometimes I take joy in fighting and bringing an enemy down, though I'm none too sure that's worthy. Man to man's a challenge. Mass to mass is butchery and chance.'

The genies mostly spent time together, and even Fost admitted – to himself – that he was touched by the joy Erimenes took in sharing the rebirth of his city with Ziore. However, the philosopher did go into sulks for several days when Rann flatly refused to permit him to accompany a raiding party.

Synalon kept her distance, studying in libraries as Moriana did, or in her chambers in the dormitory next to the Palace with the door closed. Moriana muttered dark suspicions of what her sister did, but had no time to act on them.

Until one night a month after they arrived in Athalau . . .

Fost tramped down the arched corridor of the dormitory feeling as if his boots were cast of lead and his joints made of jelly. It had

486

been a grim, brutal day hunting the worms. Two men of his ten hadn't returned. Fost was glad Erimenes had been at a museum sneering to Ziore about how art had deteriorated since his day instead of being with Fost. Erimenes had by and large lost the habit of cheering when his own side took casualties, but Fost wouldn't have liked to tempt him. There were many deep holes within the glacier where a spirit jar could be cast down.

The floor rumbled to a cheer beneath his feet. Prince Rann was being toasted in the refectory. He had another victory to his credit. The *Zr'gsz* had sent a hundred rafts probing into the Gate of the Mountains itself. Anticipating such a move, Rann had long since laid plans with the nomads of the Steppes, who reluctantly cooperated. Only the Ust-alayakit tribe stayed aloof.

When the Hisser rafts were well into the narrow ravine, a storm of boulders, arrows and javelins came crashing down on them from above. As the surviving rafts climbed clear to meet their attackers, Rann and the Sky Guard swept out of the sun like a firestorm from Omizantrim. The humans took a handful of casualties, none among the bird riders. Not one of the rafts escaped.

Fost had to admit the strange, compact man with the devastated face had earned the cheers. Especially since he seemed to work miracles against the *Zr'gsz*. He was a monster, of that there was no doubt. Fost had seen his handiwork. And yet, and yet . . . without the scarred prince the humans would have already lost.

On top of such a day, this was too much to think about so Fost went into the suite he shared with Moriana and fell asleep.

It seemed he had just drifted into blackness when a scream aroused him. He jumped to his feet, yanked his sword from the scabbard and ran into a footstool. Cursing and clutching his shin, Fost found a cloak, wrapped it around himself and went hopping into the hall.

Down the corridor stood Rann. The naked arc of a scimitar gleamed blue in the prince's hand. Fost's blood chilled. Then he realized Rann also sought the source of the cry.

'Upstairs,' he said. He turned and dashed for the stairway. He heard Rann following.

He came out on the third floor. Moriana stood in an open door from which a strange blue light spilled. It was the door to Synalon's room. Moriana looked in with horror that metamorphosed slowly to anger as Fost watched.

He ran to her as she raised a trembling finger and pointed it like a weapon at her sister.

'You –' Fury choked her. 'You *traitor!*'

He came to the door and looked in. Synalon sat on the bed wearing some confection like azure mist that clearly showed the lush outlines of her body even in the dimness. Witchlights danced in clay saucers on the floor.

Across from the black-haired princess sat a gigantic black Dwarf.

CHAPTER FOURTEEN

The Messenger of the Dark Ones rose. He smiled, his teeth startlingly white against the midnight of his face.

'I see our discussion is at an end, daughter,' he said to Synalon. 'To you others, farewell. I regret not having the chance to speak with you before since I shall not see you again – alive.' He faded and vanished, leaving only his taunting laughter hanging in the air.

Moriana's eyes blazed.

'You –'

'No,' Fost shouted, moving as fast as he ever had. He thrust past Moriana and stood, arms outspread, between the furious princess and her sister. 'Hear her out.'

'Get out of my way.'

Fost saw Rann standing just behind Moriana in the door. The scars on his face glowed whitely. Fost knew with certainty that this was betrayal and that the prince was about to drive his curved blade into Moriana's oblivious back.

Then Rann pushed past, taking his place at Fost's side, raising a hand to Synalon who rose from her bed with death in her eye.

'This is fair, I think. Neither of you casts a deathbolt without slaying the both of us. Now, Highness, will you talk?'

Fost felt his neck hairs rise. The air crackled with potent magics barely held in restraint. He waited to die and wondered what the Hell Call would be like.

It didn't happen. Moriana was first to drop her threatening hand, but Synalon followed reluctantly.

'I see nothing to talk about.' She gazed past Fost without warmth.

'What were you doing, Synalon? Do you deny that creature is a sending of the Dark Ones?'

489

'I do not.' Haughtily, she tossed back her head. 'It was the Messenger of the Lords of Elder Dark himself. I have spoken with him before.'

'What did you discuss?' Rann asked in a casual tone, as if mentioning how nice the weather had been that day.

'We discussed my sabotaging your plans to raise the World Spirit against Istu.'

Moriana's hand shot forth. Fost grabbed it.

'Wait, dammit!' He swiveled his head and said in desperation, 'Explain and explain quickly or we're all dead.'

Synalon started to bristle.

'I'd be pleased to hear an explanation, as well,' Rann drawled.

She shook back her hair and straightened her shoulders, as if preparing herself for a wearisome task.

'Very well. Shortly after we left Brev the Messenger appeared to me, after Fost had gone to sleep. He proposed that I rejoin the Dark Ones. He said I had proven wanting before but that if I acted rapidly and well I could earn back my lost grace – and more.'

Moriana dropped her arm. She shook her head in dejection.

'How could you? How could even you?'

'I could not!' Synalon laughed. 'What kind of fool do you take me for, sister mine? Think me a traitor if you will. But I would be a stupid groundling if I trusted anything the Dark Ones said to me.'

'Then why did you tell him you'd go along?' Fost demanded.

'I thought better of you, Longstrider. Is it not obvious? The Dark Ones fear what we do here. They are not certain Istu can prevail so they sought to ensure their success from within. It takes great energy for the Lords to intervene on this plane, even through the agency of their Messenger. So I let them think I was mooncalf enough to heed them, and they wasted their efforts on me. I may have saved us, sister. Small thanks I'll get.'

'I don't believe it,' Moriana stated flatly.

'But what of you?' Synalon flung at her. 'Can we trust *you*? You've treated with the servitors of the Dark before – *daughter of Thendrun*!'

Moriana sagged. She caught the doorframe to support herself. Fost longed to go to her and hold her but sensed it wasn't safe to move.

'He told you,' Moriana said in a weak voice.

'Yes.' Synalon raised her head triumphantly. 'Is it so strange that we are drawn to Darkness, dear sister, with the heritage we share?'

'I . . . I couldn't bring myself to tell you,' whispered Moriana. She turned away. 'Best we die here and let others carry on the fight. We are tainted, touched by the Void and the Night. We do not deserve to return to the City in the Sky.'

'Are you so weak?' Synalon screamed at her. 'Go then. Open your veins and spill your blood upon the floor, if you despise it so! I care not what I do or do not deserve, nor whether I am sprung from Zr'gsz or even if one was my father! I will wreak my revenge upon those who betrayed and used me, and all who stand with them.' She strode forward, pushing Fost and Rann aside as easily as if they were children and seized Moriana's shoulders, spinning her roughly around. 'Perhaps *you* do not deserve to stand in the streets of our City again, sister. Then don't! But *I* shall! The City is all I've ever loved. I shall possess it again – and only death can stop me!'

In the stunned silence following her outburst they all heard the frantic footsteps in the corridor beyond. Synalon shoved her sister from her as a small boy in the tabard of a Bilsinxt drummer looked nervously around the door.

'Your Highnesses.' he said in a shrill voice. 'Th-they sent me from below to fetch you. The Sky City has just entered the Gate of the Mountains!'

Their footsteps rang loudly in Fost's ears as he and the others crowded into the chamber where the Nexus lay. Light appeared from everywhere; no torches were needed in Athalau. The Ethereals had been stirring on their pallets in the nave of the Palace of Esoteric Wisdom when Moriana and the rest raced by. Now they filed into the chamber as they had on that first day.

This time they did not take up kneeling positions on the dull steel pattern. Instead they lined themselves along the walls.

'The time is come, mistress?' Selamyl asked Moriana.

She hesitated, then said, 'The time is come.'

Selamyl strode forward and took his position in the middle of the line and faced the far wall. Soundlessly the others glided forward and knelt, each upon one of the nodes that seemed strewn at random throughout the mandala. With a sinking feeling, Fost saw how few there truly were. Many of the nodes were unoccupied and the silvery patch in the center looked like a gap left by a missing tooth.

He didn't see how they could ever succeed.

'What would Felarod do, were he here now?' Moriana asked aloud.

'You must find your own way,' said Selamyl. His eyes were closed, his voice seemed to come from all around. 'Flow with the universe. The World Spirit will guide you.'

'Can you — can you reach the Spirit?' she asked.

'Yes.'

'Then do so.'

Silence. Fost felt it gnawing inside him like an animal demanding release, felt the tension begin to build and set his limbs trembling. He wanted to scream at the inactivity.

Moriana shifted to stand beside him, and her hand sought his. He willed his hand not to quaver and knew he failed. He looked around. Synalon stood nearby with lifted chin, feigning disinterest. Rann stood with folded arms, his head thrust forward, his yellow eyes wide beneath thin brows.

A greenish glow bathed Rann's face. Fost stared at him for a second, then turned back to the center of the room.

The metallic tracery on the floor had come to life. The green glow flowed from it suffusing the room. The kneeling Ethereals had become translucent. Each slender body shone like a lamp but without heat.

He became aware of a faint pulsation of the light. Shouts rebounded down the stairway from above, and it seemed there was an outcry in the streets.

'Behold the Nexus,' came Selamyl's voice. 'It is Athalau itself. This is the center.'

'And the World Spirit?' Moriana could barely force out the words.

'It comes.'

A chill wind tore at Zak'zar's face and felt as if it would strip away the skin. His cloak cracked behind him like a whip. It was agony to be abroad in this cold night with the icy breath of the Waste upon him. The others of the People lay abed wrapped against the chill. But his place was upon the rampart of the floating City.

Istu stood beside him, set apart from the night only by the absolute blackness of his being unmarred by stars. His yellow eyes watched the rugged terrain below unfold. The City followed his will, its course matching the winding of the black slash that wandered through the mountains.

He stiffened, raised his head as if testing the wind for some scent, some sound.

'What is it?' Zak'zar asked, shouting to be heard above the keening wind.

Istu raised a taloned hand to still him. Then he crumpled his hands into fists and shook them in the face of the south.

'My curse upon you! I lay my curse on Athalau and all within!'

'What's happening?'

Istu's eyes swept down. Zak'zar thought the Demon would slay him in his unreasoning fury. But the mad glare subsided. Istu spoke.

'In Athalau. I feel it, I hear it, it wounds my ears! The Pale Ones have summoned the World Spirit.'

Zak'zar felt strength ebbing.

'Have we lost, then?'

'No!' Great shards of rock detached themselves from the walls below and slid into the Gate of the Mountains as the Demon's voice beat down upon them. 'Never! They lack Felarod, and knowledge, and I am strong! Never again shall I be bound. *Never!*'

Zak'zar gripped the stone guardwall and stared ahead. In the distance he saw a pool of paleness lying against the blackness of the mountains. A glacier. Within it lay his fate.

The wind tore at his eyes.

Hours passed like days, like years.

'Vast is the World Spirit,' Selamyl said when Moriana asked him if the summoning was done, if the Spirit had risen to smite its starborn foe. 'It is slow to anger but its wrath is great.'

Fost sat with his back against the wall of the Nexus chamber. He drifted in and out of sleep. When his body realized that no amount of adrenaline was going to make things happen any quicker, it surrendered to the exertions of the day before. But still an urgency nagged at him causing him to half-rise from sleep and dream images.

At some point a servant brought the spirit jars. Fost roused to listen briefly to Erimenes describing how the whole city now pulsed with the same green light that came from the Nexus. Fost thought the pattern's glow brighter than before, but thinking took too great an effort and he slept again.

He came awake abruptly, sensing something vital was about to happen.

The first thing he saw was the City in the Sky. He shook his head, shut his eyes and opened them again. Still it hung in the midst of his vision, above sharp peaks turned molten gold by the rising sun.

'Disconcerting, isn't it?' Erimenes chuckled dryly at his elbow. 'My humble contribution.'

'You *caused* that?' Somehow, a vision of what was happening miles away had been conjured forth, inside the room.

'Well . . . no. But it was I who remembered the old stories and told the princess how to call it up.'

Moriana stood where she had before, staring at the picture which occupied one whole wall of the chamber.

'And the Spirit?' he asked. 'Has it come yet?'

'No,' said Ziore from his other side. Her face was stark with worry. 'And soon it will be too late. Poor Moriana.'

'It is come.'

The chamber reverberated to the words. The voice was Selamyl's and yet was not. It was deeper, transformed, as vital and surging as the boom of surf on sand.

Moriana raised her eyes to the scene of the Sky City. It jumped forward. Fost gasped. Then he realized that it was the picture that moved with such speed, not the City itself. He saw the black, horned shape on the parapet and felt a cold greater than that of the Waste seize his bones.

'I call upon the World Spirit to destroy the Demon Istu!' Her words rang out like trumpets.

Fost caught his breath.

Nothing happened.

'World Spirit! Strike! Raise up your power against the dark destroyer as you did ten thousand years ago!'

Fost felt it now. The energy folded him, restoring strength to his limbs, clearing his weary, scratchy eyes. Each breath was wine. But still nothing happened, no energies leapt forward to oppose the black Demon.

'World Spirit!' screamed Moriana. *'What's wrong?'*

'Will,' said that voice which had once belonged to Selamyl. 'It needs a will to guide it.'

'But what of you, you Ethereals?'

A pause. Fost thought of the awesome deliberation of Guardian. The world was much bigger than the glacier. Would the Spirit be commensurately slower?

'We . . .' For the first time that transcendent voice faltered. 'We lack the will. We have forgotten how to strike out in anger and lack the time to learn.'

Synalon rose, stretched catlike and sensuous.

'One thing I've plenty of is will. Sister, shall I?'

Moriana stared into the green fire of the Nexus. This was what she'd feared, that she must enter rapport with the World Spirit and risk the dissolution of that small spark that was her soul, her inner being, her self. The time had come for her to match the dedication already shown by the Ethereals.

'No,' Moriana said and stepped forward.

Fost leaped to his feet, lunged forward and caught her wrist, crying, 'You can't!'

'I must.' Her voice was calm.

'You'll die!'

'And what of that?' She reached out and stroked his cheek with the backs of her fingers. They rasped on stubble. 'I must do this. Only then can I expiate the wrong I created when I helped the Fallen Ones capture the City.'

She dropped her hand.

'I love you,' she said. 'Live long and take what happiness you find.' And she stepped into the middle of the Nexus.

Green fire enveloped her. Fost cried out again and started to follow. A steel claw caught his arm. He struggled, then turned back in fury. Ziore held his wrist. There was nothing wispy or insubstantial about her now.

'Do you think she wants you to throw your life away?' the genie asked.

'But . . .'

'You cannot help her now. You can only distract her.'

He stepped back. And the power came up through the floor and shook him and his mind reeled toward blackness.

At the molten core of the planet burned anger.

But it was rage without form, without direction. That vast organism which was the World possessed a thousand senses and each one cried out that something was deathly wrong. A pathogen had invaded its system, a black presence, both alien and destructive. It knew that something must be done but it didn't know what or how.

A feeling tickled the edge of its tiny being, tiny but insistent. Slowly the feeling penetrated it. Slowly it responded.

495

It sensed other presences, miniscule, separate from and at the same time part of it. It flowed toward them. Somehow it knew that here was the means to channel its anger, to bring its mighty wrath to bear on the wrongness.

It touched the lesser entities and became one with them. It stopped. There was nothing, no direction, no guidance, nothing to purge the irritant.

Then a new presence touched it. Will burned within, a hot, white light. Like a plant questing toward the sun, the World Spirit moved to merge itself with this thing of Will.

At the core of Moriana's being burned anger.

Her City was held captive by an enemy who had betrayed her to possess it. She felt it hanging almost overhead now, and her being ached with the longing for it. But more even than Zr'gsz, she hated their Demon ally. He had defiled her, laid surrogate hands of stone on her and ravished her body while his hell-glowing eyes raped her soul. For that her rage would tear the skies asunder, to visit vengeance upon Istu.

Your enemy is near! she thought. *Now reach!*

The mountain called the Throat of the Dark Ones exploded.

It blasted itself skyward, a mountain launched as a missile into the dawn, riding a column of incandescent gas and ash and the dust of pulverized rock. The Zr'gsz skystone mines disappeared, and those who worked them and those who fought to slow the work. So violent was the blast that huge hunks of the shattered mountain entered orbit around the world to spiral down slowly until the tenuous arms of the atmosphere tangled them and drew them to flaming end.

Such was Moriana's wrath united with the wrath of the World.

Though the wavefront of the blast and the titan sound that rode upon it would not reach the Ramparts for over an hour, Istu felt Mount Omizantrim die. He clawed at the heavens and bellowed his rage. His ancient enemy was come. The fight would be to the death this time.

He turned and strode to the center of the City. His bowed legs straddled the Well of Winds. He spread forth the blackness of his arms. He reached outward, began to flow downward, his form subsiding and swelling to fill the Well. The Black Lens appeared where he had been, glistening, pregnant with power.

A thirty-foot wall of water washed over the island of Wirix and scoured it clean, driven by the blast that slew Omizantrim.

But the Wrath had only begun.

With the senses she now shared with another, Moriana knew that her first stroke had missed. She struck again –

– and a range of mountains thrust themselves above the sea on the far side of the world, dark and humped and water-glistening like the back of an aquatic monster.

And again –

– and storm clouds gathered above the Ramparts, a thousand times faster than the normal gathering of clouds. They piled higher, black on black, shot through with lightning. In the streets of the Sky City the Fallen Ones cried out in fear and wonder.

And again –

– and part of the Northern Continent split off and sank into the sea with a crack and a roar and a rushing of water.

Fury raged in silence upon the wall of the Nexus chamber. Fost's back was to the wall and his eyes were wide. He had control of his limbs again, but the power still surged like a drug in his veins.

'Moriana! What's happening?' cried Ziore.

'I . . . I cannot control it.' Her voice penetrated the bones of those in the chamber, transmuted as Selamyl's had been.

The room shook then. Synalon lurched into Rann; Fost fell, cracking his knee painfully on the stone. Imaged on the wall, the western Ramparts tumbled like eightpins to the throes of an earthquake. The Ethereals and Moriana sat statue-still, unmoved by the spasm beneath the earth.

The gathering clouds had grown to a black anvil thunderhead, a mountain above mountains. The watchers saw a sheet of lightning flash from the thunderhead and shear off a slice of the City's starboard rim in a coruscating spray of molten stone. Synalon shrieked as if it were her own flesh being sundered.

Maddened, the Demon retaliated. A black funnel grew from the underside of the Lens and stabbed down. It bit into the ice over Athalau and began tearing chunks from the glacier's body. A moan

497

rolled through Athalau, pitched almost below hearing, so that it rang deep in the bones of the humans within.

'The Demon's killing Guardian,' shouted Fost. 'Can't you do something?'

'Yes,' said Moriana. That much she could do. She folded power around herself, around Guardian, strapping the glacier in a cocoon of forces that held him steady against the pull of the vortex.

Istu squealed with rage as his funnel ceased to bite. He lashed downward repeatedly. But he could no longer gouge the ice that armored Athalau.

'What now?' asked Zak'zar from the edge of the Skywell.

'Wait,' said Istu, 'and you shall see.'

Moriana kept trying to wield the power of the World Spirit, to smite Istu with all the force at her command. The watchers in the chamber beneath the Palace saw earthquake and waterspout and eruption devastate the land. The World Spirit flailed about like a blind beast only landing near its foe by accident.

'Moriana, you've got to stop,' screamed Ziore as they watched Paramount, Lord of Trees, hurled down to smash a hundred lesser trees beneath it. 'You'll destroy the Realm without harming Istu!'

'What can I do? I cannot aim the power. If only I had some way to focus on the City, on Istu!'

Synalon shook back her long black hair and turned from the Nexus.

'I knew I'd find a part to play in this farce,' she said. 'Rann, summon me a bird tender. I wish my eagle made ready at once.'

He gaped at her.

'Because I will be the focus my sister needs.'

'Highness! Why?'

CHAPTER FIFTEEN

'Madness,' declared Rann.

'Not so, cousin. Moriana and I are twins. There is a link between us, though we've spent our lives denying it.' She looked back at her sister, who sat like some green idol in the center of the Nexus. 'And my hatred is great. Give me your power, sister. I shall wield it with a fine rage.'

Moriana did not move. Perhaps she could not; perhaps she was frozen forever in that position with her legs folded under her, her hands resting on her thighs. So complete was her lack of response that Fost feared she had died or utterly lost her identity in the immensity of the World Spirit.

Then, 'Yes,' filled the chamber.

Rann raised a hand to halt Synalon as she went to the door.

'You'll need an escort, cousin. Someone to make sure you have time to achieve rapport with Moriana.'

'You propose I take an army? Where do we get the time for that?'

'A small escort will have a chance to approach the City unseen.' He hitched up his sword belt. 'With your permission, Highness.'

'I'm coming, too,' blurted Fost.

A shadow crossed Synalon's face.

'No!' said Moriana firmly, though her expression didn't change.

'Let me congratulate you on your courage, Fost!' cried Erimenes. 'This is the ultimate adventure of a lifetime.'

He whirled to face the genie.

'It's not courage. I'm doing this because I'm afraid, dammit. I've thought I'd carried on with this mad venture for love or loneliness or from sheer curiosity. But there's another reason. I'm afraid to live in a world that gods and devils use as their playground. We're just pawns to them, all of us. I can't take that, do you understand?'

'Go then,' said Moriana with resignation. Still she remained immobile, apparently lifeless.

Rann clasped forearms with Fost and left the chamber at a run. Fost paused, then picked up Ziore's jug and carried it into the Nexus, jumping across the burning lines and avoiding the nodes. His head swam to tidal surges of power, but he made it, depositing the jug at Moriana's side. He stooped and kissed her forehead; it was icy. Then he turned and ran for the door, slowing only to scoop up Erimenes's jar.

'Farewell, my love!' sang Erimenes. 'I'm off to the wars!'

'Dear Erimenes,' sighed Ziore, wavering at Moriana's side. She waved, sparks flying from her fingertips as they crossed a node.

'Goodbye,' said Moriana.

Fost felt emotion choke him. The word echoed in his brain with grim finality.

'Their counterattack has failed,' said Zak'zar.

Istu's laugh rumbled from the Well.

'They've realized that without a mind the scope of Felarod's they cannot wield their power with any precision. They were doing themselves more damage than I inflicted.'

'Surely, they haven't given up.'

'Your faith in the Pale Ones is touching, Speaker. But it matters not. They've shown they cannot harm me. While I . . .' He chuckled like a poisoned spring. 'Watch, and you shall see.'

From the surface of the orange-red sun a wisp of starstuff was pared like skin from a fruit. An invisible force bent it into a flaming hoop, a strand, and drew it across space toward a green world waiting eighty million miles away . . .

The roar of eagles' wings filled the corridor Guardian had opened to the east. Four war birds flew in a line, their wingtips brushing the frigid walls. Fost hunched close to the neck of his mount and tried to decide whether he preferred the claustrophobic feeling the shining walls rushing by gave him or the dread of falling from the bird.

'Thank you for bringing me along, Fost,' said Erimenes at his side. 'I always knew you were a considerate soul.'

'Don't thank me yet, Erimenes. You yourself said Istu could destroy you.'

'And so he can. But he can destroy me as easily if I'm cowering in the belly of this garrulous glacier. I'd rather be where the battle rages and the blood flows.'

'I'm glad you enjoy the prospect,' said Fost grimly. He shifted the buckler strapped to his left arm so its bronze-bound rim wouldn't gouge his hip. 'As for me, I'm ready to swallow the bravado speech I made back in the Palace, syllable by syllable.'

'Nonsense, Fost. You, too, feel the thrill of approaching battle. And this isn't just any fight, you know. Your feats this day will live in ballads forever, as long as there are men to sing them.'

'There may not be, after today.'

They broke into the light. Fost squinted and let his eagle have its head. It was huge, almost as large as the midnight-black Nightwind Synalon rode, brown with white head and a white bib on its chest, and it knew what to do far better than Fost.

Rann's eagle, as gray as a cloudy sky, moved into the lead. The fourth bird was pure white. Its rider raised a gloved hand in salute to Fost as they took station on opposite sides of Nightwind. Fost waved back. Cerestan was a fool for coming along, but Fost was in no position to be critical.

Rann banked. Fost felt his bird tilt to follow the leftward turn, surging upward toward the City hanging above them, black against muttering storm clouds. He tried not to panic, tried not to think about losing his seat and tumbling end over end to the hard rocks below. He was strapped into the saddle and had both hands clinging to the harness. He looked up, up . . .

The sun reached down and drove its fist into the middle of the glacier.

As the solar prominence Istu had torn from the face of the sun bathed the glacier in flame, great clouds of steam billowed upward with a serpent's hiss magnified a millionfold. A groaning scream rang through Athalau, shaking loose great spires of ice, toppling ancient buildings. Men, women and children fled through the streets, covering their ears as they ran.

Zak'zar reeled back from the rimwall, shielding his eyes against the hellish brilliance. The Sky City began to rock with the force of the superheated steam boiling from below.

When the Speaker's eyes worked again, he beheld Istu standing braced on the rimwall, laughing and laughing as he raised his arms to bring down more sunfire.

Hot water washed down the nave of the Palace of Esoteric Wisdom and cascaded over the steps. The Ethereals did not stir as the tide came surging around them. They were one with the World Spirit and beyond feeling; some had turned dark, no longer touched with the green glow. These would never again feel physical agony.

'Princess.' The word was ground from a giant mill of agony. 'Princess, I . . . I melt! I cannot shield you much longer.' The words came scarcely less quickly than a human would have spoken, so great was Guardian's pain.

'Moriana, do something!' cried Ziore.

'I can stop the waters from flooding the city,' Moriana said, and this was done, the near-scalding tide receding until only an inch of cooling water swirled on the floor. 'But I cannot stop the burning.'

'If Synalon doesn't reach the City soon, we all shall die with Guardian.'

'Great merciful heavens,' cried Erimenes. 'What's going on?'

'They don't seem merciful to me. And I don't know,' snapped Fost, more intent on remaining on top of his eagle than on examining their plight.

There had come a blinding streak of light. It had been obscured at once by an explosion of steam. Only because the bird riders had flown to the eastern edge of Guardian were they saved from being scalded to death. Fost managed to blink back the green line of afterimage that split his sight, and he occasionally saw flashes of the fire streaming down from above through rents in the cloud as though a curtain were being drawn aside to give him a view of Hell.

He glimpsed motion to his right and looked that way. The gray eagle flapped alongside. Rann held up a gauntleted fist, then drove it upward and forward. The gray climbed away.

'What's that mean?' Erimenes asked.

'It means we go on.'

The steam-laden winds buffeted them like the fetid breath of Hell. The clouds proved a blessing; they were shielded from observation from above. But Fost wondered if they veered into that fall of sunfire.

*

Guardian struggled to retain life.

'Princess, the pain. I . . . I am almost pierced through.'

'I'm sorry. I can do nothing until my sister reaches the Sky City.' Moriana had the awful thought, *if she does. If the sunflame didn't take her. Her and Fost.* The thoughts were strong enough to stand out against the inchoate backgound of the World Spirit.

'I must die soon. I cannot be helped. But . . . save Athalau. I have done . . . done my best . . . to . . . guard . . . her.'

'I shall, good and faithful Guardian.' The words, 'If I can,' went unspoken.

Rann shot an arrow through the face that appeared, peering over a rimwall that loomed ghostly in the fog. Fost's eagle burst from the mist wing to wing with Nightwind. The giant black bird slashed a Hisser's head from his shoulders with a vicious stroke of his beak and shrieked triumph as he settled his claws once more on the gray-green stone of his home.

Rann's bird dropped toward a group of Vridzish racing to the wall. Rann shot another, cast aside his bow and leaped from the saddle as his bird came down like fury among the foe. Then Fost's own bird thumped to a landing. Fost forgot about the prince as he struggled to free himself from the safety strap before the half-dozen charging Zr'gsz reached him.

He had a powerful ally in the bird. Screaming in rage, it struck out with beak and talon, disembowelling and dismembering. But the wild movements threw Fost around in the saddle so furiously he couldn't free himself.

Then the bird stood alone amid black-bloodied corpses. Fost tore free the strap and jumped to the ground. His sword sang from its sheath. He felt power and control merge harmoniously within and knew he would fight well this day.

'Sister, I am ready!' he heard Synalon cry at his back. Cerestan engaged a knot of Hissers off to the left. More came at Fost, and he sprang to meet them with a roar of hatred.

His first blow tore apart one's face. His second took a clawed arm off at the shoulder. His third sent greasy ropes of intestines spilling about a Hisser's knees.

A whistling scream sounded and he saw his war bird reel back, blood fountaining from the stump of its neck. A huge Zr'gsz noble had taken the head off with a single stroke of an obsidian-edged sword. Fost ducked under the cut meant to remove his head; his sword slashed at the dark, bulging neck. He ripped his sword free and turned to face the lizard men streaming toward him with weapons in their claws.

'There's no way out for me now,' he cried. 'So come ahead and we'll do this right!'

The Vridzish advanced.

The agonized screams of the glacier cut off as though severed by a knife.

'He's dead,' Ziore said, and began sobbing.

Though she felt the glacier's passing, Moriana never heard the nun. Her whole being strained to hold together under the terrific pressure of rapport with the World Spirit. It was like being twisted and pulled and compressed all at the same time, a million vectors tearing at her soul. She probed for her sister's mind and prayed she could hang on until contact was made.

As Erimenes predicted, Fost earned himself a place in the ballads that day. The spirit cheered hysterically from the jug while the tall man slew and slew like a figure out of legend. He used every trick of swordplay he knew, both fair and foul, and threw in alley fighting from boyhood days in Medurim. He hacked and stabbed and slashed, then smashed faces with his buckler. When an axe-blow split the shield, he hurled it in someone's face, picked up an abandoned shortsword and fought on tirelessly.

But Fost saw through the haze of blood and sweat in his eyes that Rann was the true hero. Fost fought with preternatural strength and fury, but Rann . . . Rann fought as no man ever had, nor would again. With scimitar in his left hand and his knife in the right, Rann walked among the Hissers like death incarnate. He disdained to parry, but no blade touched him. His weapons were in constant, blurring motion, the dagger picking at eyes and throats and exposed bellies; the scimitar slashed left and right and curved around the guard of an unsuspecting enemy to bring bloody death.

The tide of Hissers slackened. Fost staggered back against the wall. To his surprise he saw Cerestan still fought on. Synalon stood with arms upraised, straining to make contact with Moriana. Fost wondered how much longer any of them would be alive.

A figure strode down the narrow street, a green cloak flapping from its shoulders, a sword in hand. It stopped before the prince.

'You are Prince Rann,' said the newcomer. His skin was almost black, and he towered above the diminutive prince.

'And you are Zak'zar.' The scimitar whipped forward. With blinding speed, the sword snapped to guard. But the prince's stroke was never meant to connect. Instead, black blood from the scimitar's last victim spattered Zak'zar's eyes. He blinked and fell back a step. Rann lunged.

Zak'zar's reflexes were still those of *Zr'gsz*. His blade flashed. Rann's dagger whipped up — not fast enough. Fost saw the green blade cave in the right side of Rann's face, saw the tawny eye spilt in blood.

Synalon screamed.

'Get away from her, Fost!' Erimenes shout sent him running to the right, heedless of whether he was attacked or not. He stepped on a javelin dropped by a skewered Hisser, went down, rolled and came up staring toward the wall.

Synalon!

He couldn't look at her directly. Energy pulsed from her, fierce and white hot. The bird rider's garb she had worn burned away in an instant leaving her naked and splendid and terrible. Forces ebbed and flowed around her like the aurora, ghosts of color barely hinting at the potent energy fields of which they were the only visible part.

He got to his feet, looked back in time to see Rann spinning and ducking under the sweep of Zak'zar's sword. Rann whirled in a complete circle, getting inside the *Zr'gsz's* guard. His scimitar struck under the armpit, bit through the metal and Fost thought he heard the grating crunch when it hit the spine. Zak'zar dropped his sword with a clang. His hands spasmodically opened and closed twice, he vomited green-black blood, and died.

Rann stood over his foe's body for several heartbeats, then collapsed across the inert form.

More Hissers appeared. Several ran at Synalon. She gestured, and they turned to pillars of ash, slumping and beginning to flow, becoming incandescent piles of heated sand.

'You must flee,' Synalon said in a voice as vast as the sky. 'No one will pursue.'

She started walking forward. Cerestan lurched after, limping on one leg, determined not to leave the side of his queen. She sensed him, half-turned.

'No.'

505

It was too late. He entered the deadly embrace of the energies surrounding her and, with a last startled cry, turned to ash himself.

'Go, Fost!' Erimenes shouted. 'Great Ultimate, you've done it! You're free! There's two eagles left. Take one and go!'

Fost turned and ran – straight for Rann.

'What are you doing, fool?' shrieked the genie. 'Leave him. You fool, save your own skin!'

Fost stooped and grabbed Rann's wrist. He checked for pulse.

'He's dead, Fost. By the Five Holy Ones, flee *now*!'

He felt the faint flutter of a pulse and rose, swinging the prince across his shoulders. He marvelled at how light he was, then noticed the sunfire had died out and the steam was beginning to dissipate.

'He wouldn't have done the same for you. You fool, you incredible fool!'

Synalon approached. She saw him and smiled. A ripple of sensation passed through him, desire and revulsion and hate and admiration all at once. She was no longer merely human. She came straight on. He dodged to the side of the street, teetering to balance Rann on his back. Synalon swept past. He felt the tingle of the energies. She was growing taller, and at the far end of the street Istu waded through buildings to meet her.

Fost turned to the rimwall and ran like hell.

It was birth and orgasm and death. Moriana's soul expanded in all directions, contracted to a point, and a blazing line surged between her and Synalon. Energy sluiced through her. For a moment the two points came together, merged. Synalon screamed. But Moriana was already fading, and it did not jolt her to look into her sister and see herself.

They broke apart. Moriana was a spark, and she was dimming. Her task was done. Synalon had been right; her malice was the perfect focus for the vengeful energies of the World Spirit. Now Moriana could relax, quit fighting to maintain identity, be absorbed into the World Spirit and know peace. She plummeted down . . .

And was caught by a gentle, unyielding grip.

I have you now, my child, came Ziore's thought. *I won't let go.*

Moriana began to swim back upward through the layers of the World Spirit's mind, back toward herself.

*

Istu lashed at Synalon with his talons. She skipped aside and the swipe brought down a spindly tower. She felt the power in her hand. She struck. Istu felt fire in his bowels and screamed. Her laughter eclipsed his cry of anguish.

The eagle dropped in a dizzying spiral groundward. Somehow, Fost hung on. He heard a tumult at his back as if the sky was breaking open. He dared not look back, nor did he know how the war eagle Nightwind fared, with a half-dead Prince Rann strapped to its back.

An immense round pit yawned beneath. He realized that the flare had burned through Guardian and into Athalau; he saw where the tops of lofty spires were melted and vitrified from the awful heat. He shut his eyes, squeezing out tears.

'Goodbye, Guardian,' he said. There seemed little else to say.

'He's dead?' asked Erimenes. Fost only nodded. 'Oh, no, no, no!' The spirit chanted a liturgy of negation, and Fost was amazed at the real pain in his voice.

The ground wheeled wildly below. The white war bird that had been Cerestan's braked with her wings and landed roughly in the scorched plaza near a silent, dry fountain. She staggered and collapsed under Fost's weight. The courier rolled free. The bird raised her head and stucked in great, ragged gulps of air.

Fost struggled to his feet and started toward the Palace of Esoteric Wisdom at a lurching run. His thoughts were of Moriana.

'Wait,' said Erimenes. 'Look. Above.'

The Sky City careened across a sky gone mad. Black clouds whirled crazily and the storm beat at the City with fists of wind and rain and lightning. Rocks exploded from the Ramparts to smash among the buildings of the floating City. The earth shifted violently beneath Fost's feet and flung him to the ground.

The tremor went on and on. Fost spread his arms and clung to the pavement. Erimenes shouted something that was swallowed in the din of crashing buildings.

The shaking subsided. Fost looked up again.

Some trick of the forces allowed Fost to see only Istu and Synalon facing each other on the parapet. They battled with forces he neither saw nor comprehended.

Though she must have grown several times her natural size, Synalon was still dwarfed by Istu's midnight bulk. She flickered like a flame, dodging the Demon's increasing clumsy charges. The

World Spirit's energies flowed through her to tear at the minion of the Dark Ones.

Suddenly, she darted in, closing with the Demon. He threw back his head and bellowed. To Fost it seemed the slim white arms reached *inside* the blackness of Istu's body.

A gasp burst from the watchers below. Synalon planted her feet and raised the gigantic form of the Demon of the Dark Ones above her head as if he were a child. For a moment, she held him there. He writhed and kicked with clawed feet, roaring with a shrill and frightened voice. She laughed, the sound vibrating in all their skulls.

Then she cast the Demon over the edge.

Over and over Istu tumbled. He changed shape as he fell, became a bird, a block, a blob, a fluttering leaf, crumbling, becoming dust, becoming . . .

Nothing.

Fost felt a tightness in his throat and a stinging in his eyes. Istu had been the very soul of evil, but Istu had been old, had immeasurably endured – and died alone. In this way alone could he claim kinship with the mortals he had oppressed. Like them he died, toy of uncaring gods.

Synalon stood poised on the brink, arms outflung in triumph, infinitely desirable and infinitely frightening. Her hair streamed out like a banner as she rode the Sky City like a raft, wild across the seething sky, faster than ever it had gone before.

And then the City in the Sky struck a mountain peak. It exploded into a million fragments, and Synalon Etuul was joined forever with the City she loved.

EPILOGUE

Erimenes wept for the damage done to Athalau. Limping across the plaza, trying not to put too much weight on a sprained ankle, Fost thought that the devastation didn't look too bad. The city had been staunchly built and most of the buildings had survived.

He stood for a time gazing at the front of the Palace of Esoteric Wisdom without fully realizing where he was. He had lost a lot of blood from wounds he never remembered receiving. He swayed a little and tried to summon the courage to descend into the basement of the Palace and confront what awaited him in the chamber of the Nexus.

Then someone emerged from the Palace onto the portico. She came unsteadily, supported by a young man and a woman in the Sky Guard uniforms.

But she came.

When she saw Fost, Moriana broke away from her helpers and ran down the steps. They met halfway across the street, threw arms around each other, sank weeping as their knees gave way.

They kissed. At length Fost pulled back. He could only look at her, unbelieving.

When he trusted himself to speak, he asked softly, 'The Ethereals?'

Her eyes fell. A tear traced a trail down one cheek. He shut his own eyes and lowered his forehead to touch hers. The sweat on her hair stung a cut; he didn't pull away.

'And the ones who went with you?'

'Cerestan got too close to Synalon after the power began flowing through her. Rann fought Zak'zar and killed him. He was badly hurt, though. I carried him to the rimwall and strapped him to Nightwind's back.'

'Where is he now?'

'I lost sight of him when I got on Cerestan's eagle.' He bared his teeth and shook his head. 'I hate to say it but I hope he got away. You should have seen him fight, Moriana. I've never seen anything like it.'

She paused, then said, 'I hope he made it, too.' He barely heard her words they came so softly.

He glanced around to see Erimenes staring at the Palace and fingering his chin. The genie's face was drawn with worry.

'Your Highness,' Erimenes said, his voice quaking with emotion. 'I don't mean to interrupt, but . . . that is . . .' And while he groped for words to express his fears and hopes, a voice hailed them from the cracked steps of the Palace.

'Highness! You forgot your satchel!'

The trooper brought the battered leather satchel down and laid it reverently next to Erimenes's. He and Ziore drove into each other's arms. Their forms blended into a wavering purple column.

'She was the one who saved me,' Moriana said. 'When I was slipping away, losing myself in the World Spirit, she stopped me, helped me find my way back.'

'She's got my gratitude,' Fost said, hugging Moriana to him. 'What was it like?'

A tremor passed through her.

'Do we have to talk about it now?'

'Never, if you prefer.'

'I may.'

He raised his head, asking, 'What're they pointing at down there?'

She looked up at a group who stood at the foot of the Ruby Tower which had miraculously survived the battle.

'I don't – wait! The sun! It's . . . it's in the west now. It should be well north this time of year.'

'Then . . .'

'It's true!' cried Erimenes. 'The world's tipped back on its axis. Athalau is free from the ice forever!' He wept again, tears of joy, and the others joined him.

Moriana's tears turned sorrowful again, and she clung to Fost.

'Oh, Fost, think of what we've lost! All the people who died. And Guardian. And my City!' She pressed her face into his shoulder. 'And my sister. I only knew her for an instant. One instant out of all our lives.' Her tears poured bitter and free on his mailed shoulder.

'But think of what we've won,' he told her. 'Our lives. The lives of every human who still survives in the Realm — in the whole world. And,' he said, his face hardening, 'a respite from the gods. And you've *got* a city, Athalau.'

He took her face in his hands and lifted it to his. He paused an instant, uncomfortable, then said, 'And we've got each other.'

She grinned and kissed him on the nose.

'That didn't hurt,' she said, and he knew she read his thoughts.

Then he took her by the arm and they rose. Toward them came the folk of their city, of the reborn Athalau, and all were singing.